Praise for *Nevernight*

"Murder, magic, sex, and humor—the first installment in Kristoff's new fantasy series is off to a rollicking start . . . Kristoff has created a rich, vibrant world for readers, borrowing heavily from historical Italian political structures, which provide a base of stability and familiarity to the new creations. Footnotes accompany the story . . . embellishing and further developing the world, and providing a welcome and often biting wit. Dense and measured, this will appeal to fans of traditional and political fantasies."   —*Booklist*

"Assassins, magic, [and] strange creatures are all pluses for me. But my favorite thing about this book is the voice. . . . I adore well-done omniscient narrators with snark and a slight bit of disdain for either the reader or the main character."
—*Book Riot*

"The world-building is delightfully detailed, its baroque flourishes supplied by sarcastic footnotes, but we are drawn through the narrative by Mia's triple quest: to rescue her family members, to avenge her father's death, and to survive her education at the church, where the ultimate test is to avoid being killed by the training."   —*Daily Mail* (UK)

"The first in a new series, this violent, nonstop science fiction/horror story is an intense read from start to finish. . . . Fans of speculative fiction will appreciate this addictive title."   —*School Library Journal*

"Harry Potter meets *The Lies of Locke Lamora*."   —*USA Today*

"A sensuous, shades-of-moral-gray world; a compelling, passionate heroine; a high-stakes quest for revenge—this is a fantasy fans won't be able to put down."
—*Kirkus Reviews*

"This book is brilliant. . . . This gritty, brutally honest, and gruesome story is one that will stick with you for as long as Mister Kindly hangs on to Mia's shadow. The promise of darker shadows and murderous plots for the next book definitely have me eager already."   —YABooksCentral.com

NEVERNIGHT

JAY KRISTOFF

THOMAS DUNNE BOOKS   ST. MARTIN'S GRIFFIN   NEW YORK

THOMAS DUNNE BOOKS.
An imprint of St. Martin's Press.

NEVERNIGHT. Copyright © 2016 by Neverafter PTY LTD. All rights reserved. Printed in the United States of America. For information, address St. Martin's Press, 175 Fifth Avenue, New York, N.Y. 10010.

www.thomasdunnebooks.com
www.stmartins.com

The Library of Congress has cataloged the hardcover edition as follows:

Names: Kristoff, Jay, author.
Title: Nevernight / Jay Kristoff.
Description: First edition. | New York : Thomas Dunne Books, 2016.
Identifiers: LCCN 2016003323 | ISBN 978-1-250-07302-0 (hardcover) |
    ISBN 978-1-4668-8503-5 (e-book)
Subjects: LCSH: Revenge—Fiction. | BISAC: FICTION / Fantasy / Epic. |
    FICTION / Fantasy / Historical. | GSAFD: Fantasy fiction.
Classification: LCC PR9619.4.K74 N48 2016 | DDC 823/.92—dc23
LC record available at http://lccn.loc.gov/2016003323

ISBN 978-1-250-13213-0 (trade paperback)

Our books may be purchased in bulk for promotional, educational, or business use. Please contact your local bookseller or the Macmillan Corporate and Premium Sales Department at 1-800-221-7945, extension 5442, or by e-mail at MacmillanSpecial Markets@macmillan.com.

First St. Martin's Griffin Edition: June 2017

10   9

for my sisters
light and dark and all that is beautiful between

THE SWORD ARM

THE SPINE

THE HEART

THE SEA OF SILENCE

GODSGRAVE
CATHEDRAL

MERCURIO'S
CURIOS

LIISIAN MARKET

THE BAY OF
BUTCHERS

WESTERN NETHERS

THE BRIDGE OF FOLLIES

No shadow without light,
Ever day follows night,
Between black and white,
There is gray.

—ANCIENT ASHKAHI PROVERB

NEVERNIGHT

CAVEAT EMPTOR

People often shit themselves when they die.

Their muscles slack and their souls flutter free and everything else just . . . slips out. For all their audience's love of death, the playwrights seldom mention it. When our hero breathes his last in his heroine's arms, they call no attention to the stain leaking across his tights, or how the stink makes her eyes water as she leans in for her farewell kiss.

I mention this by way of warning, O, my gentlefriends, that your narrator shares no such restraint. And if the unpleasant realities of bloodshed turn your insides to water, be advised now that the pages in your hands speak of a girl who was to murder as maestros are to music. Who did to happy ever afters what a sawblade does to skin.

She's dead herself, now—words both the wicked and the just would give an eyeteeth smile to hear. A republic in ashes behind her. A city of bridges and bones laid at the bottom of the sea by her hand. And yet I'm sure she'd still find a way to kill me if she knew I put these words to paper. Open me up and leave me for the hungry Dark. But I think someone should at least try to separate her from the lies told about her. Through her. By her.

Someone who knew her true.

A girl some called Pale Daughter. Or Kingmaker. Or Crow. But most often, nothing at all. A killer of killers, whose tally of endings only the goddess and I truly know. And was she famous or infamous for it at the end? All this death? I confess I could never see the difference. But then, I've never seen things the way you have.

Never truly lived in the world you call your own.

Nor did she, really.

I think that's why I loved her.

Book 1

WHEN ALL IS BLOOD

CHAPTER 1

FIRSTS

The boy was beautiful.

Caramel-smooth skin, honeydew-sweet smile. Black curls on the right side of unruly. Strong hands and hard muscle and his eyes, O, Daughters, his eyes. Five thousand fathoms deep. Pulling you in to laugh even as he drowned you.

His lips brushed hers, warm and curling soft. They'd stood entwined on the Bridge of Whispers, a purple blush pressing against the curves of the sky. His hands had roamed her back, current tingling on her skin. The feather-light brush of his tongue against hers set her shivering, heart racing, insides aching with want.

They'd drifted apart like dancers before the music stopped, vibration still thrumming along their strings. She'd opened her eyes, found him staring back in the smoky light. A canal murmured beneath them, its sluggish flow bleeding out into the ocean. Just as she wished to. Just as she must. Praying she wouldn't drown.

Her last nevernight in this city. A part of her didn't want to say goodbye. But before she left, she'd wanted to know. She owed herself that, at least.

"Are you sure?" he asked.

She'd looked up into his eyes, then.

Took him by the hand.

"I'm sure," she whispered.

The man was repugnant.

Sclerosis skin, a shallow chin lost in folds of stubbled fat. A sheen of spittle at his mouth, whiskey's kiss scrawled across cheeks and nose, and his eyes, O, Daughters, his eyes. Blue as the sunsburned sky. Glittering like stars in the still of truedark.

His lips were on the tankard, draining the dregs as the music and laughter swelled about him. He swayed in the taverna's heart a moment longer, then tossed a coin on the ironwood bar and stumbled into the sunslight. His eyes roamed the cobbles ahead, bleary with drink. The streets were growing crowded, and he forced his way through the crush, intent only on home and a dreamless sleep. He didn't look up. Didn't spy the figure crouched atop a stone gargoyle on a roof opposite, clothed in plaster white and mortar gray.

The girl watched him limp away across the Bridge of Brothers. Lifting her harlequin's mask to drag on her cigarillo, clove-scented smoke trailing through the air. The sight of his carrion smile and rope-raw hands set her shivering, heart racing, insides aching with want.

Her last nevernight in this city. A part of her still didn't want to say goodbye. But before she left, she'd wanted him to know. She owed him that, at least.

A shadow wearing the shape of a cat sat on the roof beside her. It was paper-flat and semitranslucent, black as death. Its tail curled around her ankle, almost possessively. Cool waters seeped out through the city's veins and into the ocean. Just as she wished to. Just as she must. Still praying she wouldn't drown.

"*. . . are you sure . . . ?*" the cat who was shadows asked.

The girl watched her mark slink toward his bed.

Nodded slow.

"I'm sure," she whispered.

T*he room had been small, sparse, all she could afford. But she'd set out rosejoy candles and a bouquet of water lilies on clean white sheets, corners turned down as if to invite him in, and the boy had smiled at the sugar-floss sweetness of it all.*

Walking to the window, she'd stared at the grand old city of Godsgrave. At white marble and ochre brick and graceful spires kissing the sunburned sky. To the north, the Ribs rose hundreds of feet into the ruddy heavens, tiny windows staring out from apartments carved within the ancient bone. Canals ran out from the hollow Spine, their patterns crisscrossing the city's skin like the webs of mad spiders. Long shadows draped the crowded pavements as the light of the second sun dimmed—the first sun long since vanished—leaving their third, sullen red sibling to stand watch through the perils of nevernight.

O, if only it had been truedark.

If it were, he wouldn't see her.

She wasn't sure she wanted him to see her through this.

The boy padded up behind her, wreathed in fresh sweat and tobacco. Slipping

his hands about her waist, fingers running like ice and flame along the divots at
her hips. She breathed heavier, tingling somewhere deep and old. Lashes fluttered
like butterfly wings against her cheeks as his hands traced the cusp of her navel,
dancing across her ribs, up, up to cup her breasts. Goosebumps prickled on her skin
as he breathed into her hair. Arching her spine, pressing back against the hardness
at his crotch, one hand snagged in his unruly locks. She couldn't breathe. She couldn't
speak. She didn't want this to begin or to end.

Turning, sighing as their lips met again, she fumbled with the cufflinks in his
ruffled sleeves, all thumbs and sweat and shakes. Pulling their shirts off, she crushed
her lips to his, sinking down onto the bed. Just she and he, now. Skin to skin. Her
moans or his, she could no longer tell.

The ache was unbearable, soaking her through, hands shaking as they explored
the wax-smooth swells of his chest, the hard V-shaped line of flesh leading down
into his britches. She slipped her fingers inside and brushed pulsing heat, heavy as
iron. Terrifying. Dizzying. He groaned, quivering like a newborn colt as she stroked
him, sighing around his tongue.

She'd never been so afraid.

Never once in all her sixteen years.

"Fuck me . . . ," she'd breathed.

The room was plush, the kind only the wealthiest might afford. Yet there were empty bottles on the bureau and dead flowers on the nightstand, wilted in the stale smell of misery. The girl took solace in seeing this man she hated so well-to-do and so totally alone. She watched him through the window as he hung up his frock coat, propped a battered tricorn on a dry carafe. Trying to convince herself she could do this. That she was hard and sharp as steel.

Perched on the rooftop opposite, she looked down on the city of Godsgrave; on bloodstained cobbles and hidden tunnels and towering cathedrals of gleaming bone. The Ribs stabbing the sky above her, twisted canals flowing out from the crooked Spine. Long shadows draping the crowded pavements as the second sun grew dimmer still—the first sun long since vanished—leaving their third, sullen red sibling to stand watch through the perils of nevernight.

O, if only it were truedark.

If it were, he wouldn't see her.

She wasn't sure she wanted him to see her in this.

Reaching out with clever fingers, she pulled the shadows to her. Weaving and twisting the black gossamer threads until they flowed across her shoulders like a cloak. She faded from the world's view, became almost translucent, like a smudge on a portrait of the city's skyline. Leaping across the void to his window-sill, she hauled herself up onto the ledge. And swiftly unlocking the glass, she slipped through to the room beyond, soundless as the cat made of shadows follow-ing behind. Sliding a stiletto from her belt, she breathed heavier, tingling some-where deep and old. Crouched unseen in a corner, lashes fluttering like butterfly wings against her cheeks, she watched him filling a cup with quavering hands.

She was breathing too loudly, her lessons all a-tumble in her head. But he was too numbed to notice—lost somewhere in the remembered creaks of a thou-sand stretched necks, a thousand pairs of feet dancing to the nooseman's tune. Her knuckles turned white on the dagger's hilt as she watched from the gloom. She couldn't breathe. She couldn't speak. She didn't want this to begin or to end.

He sighed as he drank from the cup, fumbling with cufflinks on ruffled sleeves, all thumbs and sweat and shakes. Pulling his shirt off, he limped across the boards and sank down onto the bed. Just she and he now, breath for breath. Her end or his, she could no longer tell.

The pause was unbearable, sweat soaking her through as the darkness shiv-ered. Remembering who she was, what this man had taken, all that would un-ravel if she failed. And steeling herself, she threw off her cloak of shadows and stepped out to meet him.

He gasped, starting like a newborn colt as she walked into the red suns-light, a harlequin's smile in place of her own.

She'd never seen anyone so afraid.

Not once in all her sixteen years.

"Fuck me . . . ," he breathed.

H*e'd climbed atop her, britches around his ankles. His lips on her neck and her heart in her throat. An age passed, somewhere between wanting and fearing and loving and hating, and then she'd felt him, hot and so astonishingly hard, pressing against the softness between her legs. She drew breath, perhaps to speak (but what would she say?) and then there was pain, pain, O, Daughters, it* hurt. *He was inside her—it was inside her—so hard and real she couldn't help but cry out, biting her lip to muffle the flood.*

He'd been heedless, careless, weight pressed down on her as he thrust again and again. Nothing like the sweet imaginings she'd filled this moment with. Her legs splayed and her stomach knotted, kicking against the mattress and wanting him to stop. To wait.

Was this the way it should feel?

Was this the way it should be?

If all went awry later, this would be her last nevernight in this world. And she'd known the first was usually the worst. She'd thought herself ready; soft enough, wet enough, wanting enough. That everything the other street girls had said between the giggles and the knowing glances wouldn't be true for her.

"Close your eyes," they'd counseled. "It'll be over soon enough."

But he was so heavy, and she was trying not to cry, and she wished this wasn't the way it had to be. She'd dreamed of this, hoped it some kind of special. But now she was here, she thought it a stumbling, clumsy affair. No magik or fireworks or bliss by the handful. Just the press of him on her chest, the ache of him thrusting away, her eyes closed as she gasped and winced and waited for him to be done.

He pressed his lips to hers, fingers cupping her cheek. And in that moment there was a flicker of it—a sweetness to set her tingling again, despite the awkwardness and breathlessness and hurtingness of it all. She kissed him back and there was heat inside her, flooding and filling as his every muscle went taut. And he pressed his face into her hair and shuddered through his little death, finally collapsing atop her, soft and damp and boneless.

Lying there, she breathed deep. Licked his sweat from her lips. Sighed.

He rolled away, crumpled on the sheets beside her. Reaching between her legs, she found wetness, aching. Smeared on fingertips and thighs. On clean white linen with the corners turned down as if to invite him in.

Blood.

"Why didn't you tell me this was your first?" he asked.

She said nothing. Staring at the red gleaming at her fingertips.

"I'm sorry," he whispered.

She looked at him, then.

Looked away just as quickly.

"You've nothing to be sorry for."

She was atop him, knees pinning him down. His hand on her wrist and her stiletto at his throat. An age passed, somewhere between struggling and hissing and biting and begging, and finally the blade sank home, sharp and so astonishingly hard, sinking through his neck and scraping his spine. He drew sucking breath, perhaps to speak (but what could he say?) and she could see it in his eyes—pain, pain, O, Daughters, it *hurt*. It was inside him—*she* was inside him— stabbing hard as he tried to cry out, her hand over his mouth to muffle the flood.

He was panicked, desperate, scrabbling at her mask as she twisted the blade.

Nothing like the dreadful imaginings she'd filled this moment with. His legs splayed and his neck gushing, kicking against the mattress and wanting her to stop. To wait.

Is this the way it should feel?

Is this the way it should be?

If all had gone awry, this would have been her last nevernight in this world. And she knew the first was usually the worst. She'd thought she wasn't ready; not strong enough, not cold enough, that Old Mercurio's reassurances wouldn't be true for her.

"Remember to breathe," he'd counseled. "It'll be over soon enough."

He was thrashing, and she was holding him still, and everything about her wondered if this was the way it would always be. She'd imagined this moment might feel like some kind of evil. A tithe to be paid, not a moment to be savored. But now she was here, she thought it a beautiful, balletic affair. His spine arching beneath her. The fear in his eyes as he tore her mask aside. The gleam of the blade she'd thrust home, hand over his mouth as she nodded and shushed with a mother's voice, waiting for him to be done.

He clawed her cheek, the vile reek of his breath and shit filling the room. And in that moment there was a flicker of it—a horror giving birth to mercy, despite the fact that he deserved this ending and a hundred more. Drawing back her blade, she buried it in his chest, and there was heat on her hands, flooding and sluicing as his every muscle went taut. And he grasped her knuckles and sighed through his death, deflating beneath her, soft and damp and boneless.

Sitting atop him, she breathed deep. Tasted salt and scarlet. Sighed.

She rolled away, crumpled sheets around her. Touching her face, she found wetness, warmth. Smeared on her hands and lips.

Blood.

"*Hear me, Niah,*" she whispered. "*Hear me, Mother. This flesh your feast. This blood your wine. This life, this end, my gift to you. Hold him close.*"

The cat who was shadows watched from its perch on the bedhead. Watched her the way only the eyeless can. It said not a word.

It didn't need to.

*M*uted sunlight on her skin. Raven hair, damp with sweat and hanging in her eyes. She pulled up leather britches, tossed a mortar-gray shirt over her head, tugging on wolfskin boots. Sore. Stained. But glad in it, somehow. Somewhere near content.

"*The room is paid up for the nevernight,*" she'd said. "*If you want it.*"

The sweetboy had watched from the other side of the bed, head on his elbow.

"And my coin?"

She motioned to a purse beside the looking glass.

"You're younger than my usuals," he'd said. "I don't get many firsts."

She looked at herself in the mirror then—pale skin and dark eyes. Younger than her years. And though evidence to the contrary lay drying on her skin, for a moment, she still found it hard to think of herself as anything more than a girl. Something weak and shivering, something sixteen years in this city had never managed to temper.

She'd pushed her shirt back into her britches. Checked the harlequin mask in her cloak. The stiletto at her belt. Gleaming and sharp.

The hangman would be leaving the taverna soon.

"I have to go," she'd said.

"May I ask you something, Mi Dona?"

". . . Ask then."

"Why me? Why now?"

"Why not?"

"That's no kind of answer."

"You think I should have saved myself, is that it? That I'm some gift to be given? Now forever spoiled?"

The boy said nothing, watching her with those fathom-deep eyes. Pretty as a picture. The girl drew a cigarillo from a silver case. Lit it on one of the candles. Breathing deep.

"I just wanted to know what it was like," she finally said. "In case I die."

She shrugged, exhaled gray.

"Now I know."

And into the shadows, she walked.

Muted sunlight on her skin. Mortar-gray cloak flowing down her shoulders, rendering her a shadow in the sullen light. She stood beneath a marble arch in the Beggar King's Piazza, the third sun hanging faceless in the sky. Memories of the hangman's end drying in the bloodstains on her hands. Memories of the sweetboy's lips drying with the stains on her britches. Sore. Sighing. But still glad in it, somehow. Still somewhere near content.

"Didn't die, I see."

Old Mercurio watched her from the other side of the arch, tricorn pulled low, cigarillo at his lips. He seemed smaller somehow. Thinner. Older.

"Not for lack of trying," the girl replied.

She looked at him then—stained hands and fading eyes. Old beyond his years. And though evidence to the contrary was crusting on her skin, for a moment, she found it hard to think of herself as anything more than a girl. Something weak and shivering, something six years in his tutelage had never managed to temper.

"I won't see you for a long time, will I?" she asked. "I might never see you again."

"You knew this," he said. "You chose this."

"I'm not sure there was ever a choice," she said.

She opened her fist, a sheepskin purse in her palm. The old man took the offering, counting the contents with one ink-stained finger. Clinking. Bloodstained. Twenty-seven teeth.

"Seems the hangman lost a few before I got to him," she explained.

"They'll understand." Mercurio tossed the teeth back to the girl. "Be at the seventeenth pier by six bells. A Dweymeri brigantine called *Trelene's Beau*. She's a freeship, not flying under Itreyan colors. She'll bear you hence."

"Nowhere you can follow."

"I've trained you well. This is for you alone. Cross the Red Church threshold before the first turn of Septimus, or you'll never cross it at all."

". . . I understand."

Affection gleamed in rheumy eyes. "You're the greatest pupil I've ever sent into the Mother's service. You'll spread your wings in that place and fly. And you *will* see me again."

She drew the stiletto from her belt. Proffered it on her forearm, head bowed. The blade was crafted of gravebone, gleaming white and hard as steel, its hilt carved like a crow in flight. Red amber eyes gleamed in the scarlet sunlight.

"Keep it." The old man sniffed. "It's yours again. You earned it. At last."

She looked the knife over, this way and that.

"Should I give it a name?"

"You could, I suppose. But what's the point?"

"It's this bit." She touched the blade's tip. "The part you stick them with."

"O, bravo. Mind you don't cut yourself on a wit that sharp."

"All great blades have names. It's just how it's done."

"Bollocks." Mercurio took back the dagger, held it up between them. "Naming your blade is the sort of faff reserved for heroes, girl. Men who have songs sung about them, histories spun for them, brats named after them. It's the shadow road for you and me. And you dance it right, no one will ever know *your* name, let alone the pig-sticker in your belt.

"You'll be a rumor. A whisper. The thought that wakes the bastards of this world sweating in the nevernight. The last thing you will *ever* be in this world, girl, is someone's hero."

Mercurio handed back the blade.

"But you *will* be a girl heroes fear."

She smiled. Suddenly and terribly sad. She hovered a moment. Leaned in close. Gifted sandpaper cheeks with a gentle kiss.

"I'll miss you," she said.

And into the shadows, she walked.

MUSIC

The sky was crying.

Or so it had seemed to her. The little girl knew the water tumbling from the charcoal-colored smudge above was called rain—she'd been barely ten years old, but she was old enough to know that. Yet she'd still fancied tears falling from that gray sugar-floss face. So cold compared to her own. No salt or sting inside them. But yes, the sky was certainly crying.

What else could it have done at a moment like this?

She'd stood on the Spine above the forum, gleaming gravebone at her feet, cold wind in her hair. People were gathered in the piazza below, all open mouths and closed fists. They'd seethed against the scaffold in the forum's heart, and the girl wondered if they pushed it over, would the prisoners standing atop it be allowed to go home again?

O, wouldn't that be wonderful?

She'd never seen so many people. Men and women of different shapes and sizes, children not much older than she. They wore ugly clothes and their howls had made her frightened, and she'd reached up and took her mother's hand, squeezing tight.

Her mother didn't seem to notice. Her eyes had been fixed on the scaffold, just like the rest. But Mother didn't spit at the men standing before the nooses, didn't throw rotten food or hiss "traitor" through clenched teeth. The Dona Corvere had simply stood, black gown sodden with the sky's tears, like a statue above a tomb not yet filled.

Not yet. But soon.

The girl had wanted to ask why her mother didn't weep. She didn't know what "traitor" meant, and wanted to ask that, too. And yet, somehow she knew this was a place where words had no place. And so she'd stood in silence.

Watching instead.

Six men stood on the scaffold below. One in a hangman's hood, black as truedark. Another in a priest's gown, white as a dove's feathers. The four others wore ropes at their wrists and rebellion in their eyes. But as the hooded man had slipped a noose around each neck, the girl saw the defiance draining from their cheeks along with the blood. In years to follow, she'd be told time and again how brave her father was. But looking down on him then, at the end of the row of four, she knew he was afraid.

Only a child of ten, and already she knew the color of fear.

The priest had stepped forward, beating his staff on the boards. He had a beard like a hedgerow and shoulders like an ox, looking more like a brigand who'd murdered a holy man and stolen his clothes than a holy man himself. The three suns hanging on a chain about his throat tried to gleam, but the clouds in the crying sky told them no.

His voice was thick as toffee, sweet and dark. But it spoke of crimes against the Itreyan Republic. Of treachery and treason. The holy brigand called upon the Light to bear witness (she wondered if It had a choice), naming each man in time.

"Senator Claudius Valente."

"Senator Marconius Albari."

"General Gaius Maxinius Antonius."

"Justicus Darius Corvere."

Her father's name, like the last note in the saddest song she'd ever heard. Tears welled in her eyes, blurring the world shapeless. How small and pale he'd looked down there in that howling sea. How alone. She remembered him as he'd been, not so long ago; tall and proud and O, so very strong. His gravebone armor white as wintersdeep, his cloak spilling like crimson rivers over his shoulders. His eyes, blue and bright, creased at the corners when he smiled.

Armor and cloak were gone now, replaced by rags of dirty hessian and bruises like fat, purpling berries all over his face. His right eye was swollen shut, his other fixed at his feet. She'd wanted him to look at her so badly. She wanted him to come home.

"Traitor!" the mob called. "Make him dance!"

The girl didn't know what they'd meant. She could hear no music.*

The holy brigand had looked to the battlements, to the marrowborn and po-

---

* *She didn't know how to listen yet. You people seldom do.*

liticos gathered above. The entire Senate seemed to have turned out for the show, near a hundred men gathered in their purple-trimmed robes, staring down at the scaffold with pitiless eyes.

To the Senate's right stood a cluster of men in white armor. Blood-red cloaks. Swords wreathed in rippling flame unsheathed in their hands. Luminatii, they were called, the girl knew that well. They'd been her father's brothers-in-arms before the traitoring—such was, she'd presumed, what traitors did.

It'd all been so noisy.

In the midst of the senators stood a beautiful dark-haired man, with eyes of piercing black. He wore fine robes dyed with deepest purple—consul's garb. And the girl who knew O, so little knew at least here was a man of station. Far above priests or soldiers or the mob bellowing for dancing when there was no tune. If he were to speak it, the crowd would let her father go. If he were to speak it, the Spine would shatter and the Ribs shiver into dust, and Aa, the God of Light himself, would close his three eyes and bring blessed dark to this awful parade.

The consul had stepped forward. The mob below fell silent. And as the beautiful man spoke, the girl squeezed her mother's hand with the kind of hope only children know.

"Here in the city of Godsgrave, in the Light of Aa the Everseeing and by unanimous word of the Itreyan Senate, I, Consul Julius Scaeva, proclaim these accused guilty of insurrection against our glorious Republic. There can be but one sentence for those who betray the citizenry of Itreya. One sentence for those who would once more shackle this great nation beneath the yoke of kings."

Her breath had stilled.

Heart fluttered.

". . . Death."

A roar. Washing over the girl like the rain. And she'd looked wide-eyed from the beautiful consul to the holy brigand to her mother—dearest Mother, make them stop—but Mother's eyes were affixed on the man below. Only the tremor in her bottom lip betraying her agony. And the little girl could stand no more, and the scream roared up inside her and spilled over her lips

nonono

and the shadows all across the forum shivered at her fury. The black at every man's feet, every maid and every child, the darkness cast by the light of the hidden suns, pale and thin though it was—make no mistake, O, gentlefriend. Those shadows trembled.

*But not one person noticed. Not one person cared.**

---

*Something noticed. Something cared.

The Dona Corvere's eyes didn't leave her husband as she took hold of the little girl, hugged her close. One arm across her breast. One hand at her neck. So tight the girl couldn't move. Couldn't turn. Couldn't breathe.

You picture her now; a mother with her daughter's face pressed to her skirts. The she-wolf with hackles raised, shielding her cub from the murder unfolding below. You'd be forgiven for imagining it so. Forgiven and mistaken. Because the dona held her daughter pinned looking outward. Outward so she could taste it all. Every morsel of this bitter meal. Every crumb.

The girl had watched as the hangman tested each noose, one by one by one. He'd limped to a lever at the scaffold's edge and lifted his hood to spit. The girl glimpsed his face—yellow teeth gray stubble harelip gone. Something inside her screamed Don't look, don't look, *and she'd closed her eyes. And her mother's grip had tightened, her whisper sharp as razors.*

"Never flinch," she breathed. "Never fear."

The girl felt the words in her chest. In the deepest, darkest place, where the hope children breathe and adults mourn withered and fell away, floating like ashes on the wind.

And she'd opened her eyes.

He'd looked up then. Her father. Just a glance through the rain. She'd often wonder what he was thinking at that moment, in nevernights to come. But there were no words to cross that hissing veil. Only tears. Only the crying sky. And the hangman pulled his lever, and the floor fell away. And to her horror, she finally understood. Finally heard it.

Music.

The dirge of the jeering crowd. The whip-crack of taut rope. The guh-guh-guh of throttled men cut through with the applause of the holy brigand and the beautiful consul and the world gone wrong and rotten. And to the swell of that horrid tune, legs kicking, face purpling, her father had begun dancing.

Daddy . . .

"Never flinch." A cold whisper in her ear. "Never fear. And never, ever forget."

The girl nodded slow.

Exhaled the hope inside.

And she'd watched her father die.

She stood on the deck of *Trelene's Beau*, watching the city of Godsgrave growing smaller and smaller still. The capital's bridges and cathedrals faded until only the Ribs remained; sixteen bone arches jutting hundreds of feet into the air. But as she watched, minutes melting into hours, even those titanic spires sank below the horizon's lip and vanished in the haze.*

Her hands were pressed to salt-bleached railing, dry blood crusted under her nails. A gravebone stiletto at her belt, a hangman's teeth in her purse. Dark eyes reflecting the moody red sun overhead, the echo of its smaller, bluer sibling still rippling in western skies.

The cat who was shadows was there with her. Puddled in the dark at her feet while it wasn't needed. Cooler there, you see. A clever fellow might've noticed the girl's shadow was a touch darker than others. A clever fellow might've noticed it was dark enough for two.

Fortunately, clever fellows were in short supply aboard the *Beau*.

She wasn't a pretty thing. O, the tales you've heard about the assassin who destroyed the Itreyan Republic no doubt described her beauty as otherworldly; all milk-white skin and slender curves and bow-shaped lips. And she was possessed of these qualities, true, but the composition seemed . . . a little off. "Milk-white" is just pretty talk for "pasty," after all. "Slender" is a poet's way of saying "starved."

Her skin was pale and her cheeks hollow, lending her a hungry, wasted look. Crow-black hair reached to her ribs, save for a self-inflicted and crooked fringe. Her lips and the flesh beneath her eyes seemed perpetually bruised, and her nose had been broken at least once.

If her face were a puzzle, most would put it back in the box, unfinished.

Moreover, she was short. Stick-thin. Barely enough arse for her britches to cling to. Not a beauty that lovers would die for, armies would march for, heroes might slay a god or daemon for. All in contrast to what you've been told by your poets, I'm sure. But she wasn't without her charm, gentlefriends. And all your poets are full of shit.

Trelene's Beau was a two-mast brigantine crewed by mariners from the isles of Dweym, their throats adorned with draketooth necklaces in homage to

---

* The Ribs are perhaps the most spectacular feature of Itreya's capital; sixteen great ossified towers gleaming at the heart of the City of Bridges and Bones. The Ribs are said to have belonged to the last titan, overthrown by the Light God Aa in the war for dominion of Itreya's heaven. Aa commanded his faithful to build a temple at the place where the titan fell to earth, commemorating his victory. Thus, the seeds of the great city were planted in the grave of the Light's last foe.

A strange thing, gentlefriend, that in no holy scripture or book will you find mention of this titan's name . . .

their goddess, Trelene.* Conquered by the Itreyan Republic a century previous, the Dweymeri were dark of skin, most standing head and shoulders above the average Itreyan. Legend had it they were descended from the daughters of giants who lay with silver-tongued men, but the logistics of this legend fail under any real scrutiny.† Simply said, as a people, they were big as bulls and hard as coffin nails, and tendencies to adorn their faces with leviathan-ink tattoos didn't help with first impressions.

Fearsome appearances aside, Dweymeri treat their passengers less as guests and more as sacred charges. And so, despite the presence of a sixteen-year-old girl aboard—traveling alone and armed with only a sliver of sharpened gravebone—making trouble for her couldn't have been further from most of the sailors' minds. Sadly, there were several recruits aboard the *Beau* not born of Dweym. And to one among them, this lonely girl seemed worthy of sport.

It's truth to say in all save solitude—and in some sad cases, even then—you can always count on the company of fools.

He was a rakish sort. A smooth-chested Itreyan buck with a smile handsome enough to earn a few bedpost notches, his felt cap adorned with a peacock's quill. It'd be seven weeks before the *Beau* set ashore in Ashkah, and for some, seven weeks is a long wait with only a hand for company. And so he leaned against the railing beside her and offered a feather-down smile.

"You're a pretty thing," he said.‡

She glanced long enough to measure, then turned those coal-black eyes back to the sea.

"I've no business with you, sir."

"O, come now, don't be like that, pretty. I'm only being friendly."

"I've friends enough, thank you, sir. Please leave me be."

"You look friendless enough to me, lass."

He reached out one too-gentle hand, brushed a hair from her cheek. She turned, stepped closer with the smile that, in truth, was her prettiest part. And

---

* Lady of Oceans, Thirdborn of the Light and the Maw, She Who Will Drink the World.

† How drunk would a man have to be to consider romancing a giantess a sensible option, for example? Furthermore, in such a state of inebriation, how could a fellow be expected to safely operate his own equipment, let alone the requisite stepladder?

‡ A poet this one, and no mistake.

as she spoke, she drew her stiletto and pressed it against the source of most men's woes, her smile widening along with his eyes.

"Lay hand upon me again, sir, and I'll feed your jewels to the fucking drakes."

The peacock squeaked as she pressed harder at the heart of his problems—no doubt a smaller problem than it'd been a moment before. Paling, he stepped back before any of his fellows witnessed his indiscretion. And giving his very best bow, he slunk off to convince himself his hand might be better company after all.

The girl turned back to the sea. Slipped the dagger back into her belt.

Not without her charms, as I said.

Seeking no more attention, she kept herself mostly to herself, emerging only at mealtimes or to take some air in the still of nevernight. Hammock-bound in her cabin, studying the tomes Old Mercurio had given her, she was content enough. Her eyes strained with the Ashkahi script, but the cat who was shadows helped her with the most difficult passages—curled within the folds of her hair and watching over her shoulder as she studied Hypaciah's *Arkemical Truths* and a dust-dry copy of Plienes's *Theories of the Maw*.*

She was bent over *Theories* now, smooth brow marred by a scowl.

"*. . . try again . . . ,*" the cat whispered.

The girl rubbed her temples, wincing. "It's giving me a headache."

"*. . . o poor girl, shall i kiss it better . . .*"

"This is children's lore. Any knee-high tadpole gets taught this."

"*. . . it was not written with itreyan audiences in mind . . .*"

The girl turned back to the spidery script. Clearing her throat, she read aloud:

---

*One of only six remaining in existence. Plienes and all known copies of his work were put to the torch in 27PR, in a conflagration briefly known as "the Brightest Light."

Organized by Grand Cardinal Crassus Alvaro, the pyre destroyed over four thousand "incendiary" works and was considered a resounding success by the Itreyan clergy—until it was pointed out by Crassus's *son*, Cardinal Leo Alvaro, that there was no light in all creation brighter than that of the God of Light himself, and that naming any man-made bonfire to the contrary was, in fact, heresy.

After the grand cardinal's crucifixion, Grand Cardinal Alvaro II decreed the pyre should be referred to as "the Bright Light" in texts thereafter.

"The skies above the Itreyan Republic are illuminated by three suns—commonly believed to be the eyes of Aa, the God of Light. It is no coincidence Aa is often referred to as *the Everseeing* by the unwashed."

She raised an eyebrow, glanced at the shadowcat. "I wash plenty."

"*. . . plienes was an elitist . . .*"

"You mean a tosser."

"*. . . continue . . .*"

A sigh. "The largest of the three suns is a furious red globe called Saan. *The Seer.* Shuffling across the heavens like a brigand with nothing better to do, Saan hangs in the skies for near one hundred weeks at a time. The second sun is named Saai. *The Knower.* A smallish blue-faced fellow, rising and setting quicker than its brother—"

"*. . . sibling . . . ,*" the cat corrected. "*. . . old ashkahi does not gender nouns . . .*"

". . . quicker than its *sibling*, it visits for perhaps fourteen weeks at a stretch, near twice that spent beyond the horizon. The third sun is Shiih. *The Watcher.* A dim yellow giant, Shiih takes almost as long as Saan in its wanderings across the sky."

"*. . . very good . . .*"

"Between the three suns' plodding travels, Itreyan citizens know actual nighttime—which they call *truedark*—for only a brief spell every two and a half years. For all other eves—all the eves Itreyan citizens long for a moment of darkness in which to drink with their comrades, make love to their sweethearts . . ."

The girl paused.

"What does *oshk* mean? Mercurio never taught me that word."

"*. . . unsurprising . . .*"

"It's something to do with sex, then."

The cat shifted across to her other shoulder without disturbing a single lock of hair.

"*. . . it means 'to make love where there is no love' . . .*"

"Right." The girl nodded. ". . . make love to their sweethearts, *fuck* their whores, or any other combination thereof—they must endure the constant light of so-called nevernight, lit by one or more of Aa's eyes in the heavens.

"Almost three years at a stretch, sometimes, without a drop of real darkness."

The girl closed the book with a thump.

"*. . . excellent . . .*"

"My head is splitting."

"*. . . ashkahi script was not meant for weaker minds . . .*"

"Well, thank you very much."

"*. . . that is not what i meant . . .*"

"No doubt." She stood and stretched, rubbed her eyes. "Let's take some air."

"*. . . you know i do not breathe . . .*"

"I'll breathe. You watch."

"*. . . as it please you . . .*"

The pair stole up onto the deck. Her footsteps were less than whispers, and the cat's, nothing at all. The roaring winds that marked the turn to nevernight waited above—Saai's blue memory fading slowly on the horizon, leaving only Saan to cast its sullen red glow.

The *Beau*'s deck was almost empty. A huge, crook-faced helmsman stood at the wheel, two lookouts in the crow's nests, a cabin boy (still almost a foot taller than she) snoozing on his mop handle and dreaming of his maid's arms. The ship was fifteen turnings into the Sea of Swords, the snaggletooth coastline of Liis to the south. The girl could see another ship in the distance, blurred in Saan's light. A heavy dreadnought, flying the triple suns of the Itreyan navy, cutting the waves like a gravebone dagger through an old nooseman's throat.

The bloody ending she'd gifted the hangman hung heavy in her chest. Heavier than the memory of the sweetboy's smooth hardness, the sweat he'd left drying on her skin. Though this sapling would bloom into a killer whom other killers rightly feared, right now she was a maid fresh-plucked, and memories of the hangman's expression as she cut his throat left her . . . conflicted. It's quite a thing, to watch a person slip from the potential of life into the finality of death. It's another thing entirely to be the one who *pushed*. And for all Mercurio's teachings, she was still a sixteen-year-old girl who'd just committed her first act of murder.

Her first premeditated act, at any rate.

"Hello, pretty."

The voice pulled her from her reverie, and she cursed herself for a novice. What had Mercurio taught her? *Never leave your back to the room.* And though she might've protested her recent bloodlettings constituted worthy distraction, or that a ship's deck wasn't even a *room*, she could almost hear the willow switch the old assassin would have raised in answer.

"*Twice up the stairs!*" he'd have barked. "*There and back again!*"

She turned and saw the young sailor with his peacock-feather cap and his bed-notch smile. Beside him stood another man, broad as bridges, muscles stretching his shirtsleeves like walnuts stuffed into poorly tailored bags. An

Itreyan also by the look, tanned and blue-eyed, the dull gleam of Godsgrave streets etched in his gaze.

"I was hoping I'd see you again," Peacock said.

"The ship isn't large enough for me to hope otherwise, sir."

"Sir, is it? Last we spoke, you voiced threat of removing parts most treasured and feeding them to the fish."

She was looking at the boy. Watching the stuffed walnut bag from beneath her lashes.

"No threat, sir."

"Just boasting, then? Thin talk for which apology is owed, I'd wager."

"And you'd accept apology, sir?"

"Belowdecks, doubtless."

Her shadow rippled, like millpond water as rain kissed the surface. But the peacock was intent on his indignity, and the walnut thug on the lovely hurtings he might bestow if given a few minutes with her in a cabin without windows.

"I only need to scream, you realize," she said.

"And how much scream could you give voice," Peacock smiled, "before we tossed your scrawny arse over the side?"

She glanced to the pilot's deck. To the crow's nests. A tumble into the ocean would be a death sentence—even if the *Beau* came about, she could swim only a trifle better than its anchor, and the Sea of Swords teemed with drakes like a dockside sweetboy crawled with crabs.

"Not much of a scream at all," she agreed.

"*. . . pardon me, gentlefriends . . .*"

The thugs started at the voice—they'd heard nobody approach. Both turned, Peacock puffing up and scowling to hide his sudden fright. And there on the deck behind them, they saw the cat made of shadows, licking at its paw.

It was thin as old vellum. A shape cut from a ribbon of darkness, not quite solid enough that they couldn't see the deck behind it. Its voice was the murmur of satin sheets on cold skin.

"*. . . i fear you picked the wrong girl to dance with . . . ,*" it said.

A chill stole over them, whisper-light and shivering. Movement drew Peacock's eyes to the deck, and he realized with growing horror that the girl's shadow was much larger than it should, or indeed *could* have been. And worse, it was *moving*.

Peacock's mouth opened as she introduced her boot to his partner's groin, kicking him hard enough to cripple his unborn children. She seized the walnut thug's arm as he doubled up, flipping him over the railing and into the sea. Peacock cursed as she moved behind him, but he found he couldn't shift footing to match her—as if his boots were glued in the girl's shadow on the deck. She kicked him hard in his backside and he toppled face-first into the rails, spreading his nose across his cheeks like bloodberry jam. The girl spun him, knife to throat, pushing him against the railing with his spine cruelly bent.

"I beg pardon, miss," he gasped. "Aa's truth, I meant no offense."

"What is your name, sir?"

"Maxinius," he whispered. "Maxinius, if it please you."

"Do you know what I am, Maxinius-If-It-Please-You?"

". . . D-da . . ."

His voice trembled. His gaze flickering to shadows shifting at her feet. "Darkin."

In his next breath, Peacock saw his little life stacked before his eyes. All the wrongs and the rights. All the failures and triumphs and in-betweens. The girl felt a familiar shape at her shoulder—a flicker of sadness. The cat who was not a cat, perched now on her clavicle, just as it had perched on the hangman's bed-head as she delivered him to the Maw. And though it had no eyes, she could tell it watched the lifetime in Peacock's pupils, enraptured like a child before a puppet show.

Now understand; she could have spared this boy. And your narrator could just as easily lie to you at this juncture—some charlatan's ruse to cast our girl in a sympathetic light.* But the truth is, gentlefriends, she didn't spare him. Yet, perhaps you'll take solace in the fact that at least she paused. Not to gloat. Not to savor.

To pray.

"*Hear me, Niah,*" she whispered. "*Hear me, Mother. This flesh your feast. This blood your wine. This life, this end, my gift to you. Hold him close.*"

A gentle shove, sending him over into the gnashing swell. As the peacock's feather sank beneath the water, she began shouting over the roaring winds, loud as devils in the Maw. *Man overboard!* she screamed, *man overboard!* and soon the bells were all a-ringing. But by the time the *Beau* turned about, no sign of Peacock or the walnut bag could be found among the waves.

And as simple as that, our girl's tally of endings had multiplied threefold.

Pebbles to avalanches.

The *Beau*'s captain was a Dweymeri named Wolfeater, seven feet tall with dark locks knotted by salt. The good captain was understandably put out by

---

* "She may have been the most feared killer in Itreya, murderess of legions, Lady of Blades, destroyer of the Republic, but *look*, she had *good* in her also. Mercy, even for rapists and brutes. O, cue the swelling violiiiiiiins!"

his crewmen's early disembarkation, and keen on hows and whys. But when questioned in his cabin, the small, pale girl who sounded the alarm only mumbled of a struggle between the Itreyans, ending in a tumble of knuckles and curses sending both overboard to sailor's graves. The odds that two seadogs— even Itreyan fools—had tussled themselves into the drink were slim. But thinner still were the chances this girlchild had gifted both to Trelene all by her lonesome.

The captain towered over her; this waif in gray and white, wreathed in the scent of burned cloves. He knew neither who she was nor why she journeyed to Ashkah. But as he propped a drakebone pipe on his lips and struck a flint-box to light his tar, he found himself glancing at the deck. At the shadow coiled about this strange girl's feet.

"Best be keeping yourself to yourself 'til trip's end, lass." He exhaled into the gloom between them. "I'll have meals sent to your room."

The girl looked him over, eyes black as the Maw. She glanced down at her shadow, dark enough for two. And she agreed with the Wolfeater's assessment, her smile sweet as honeydew.

Captains are usually clever fellows, after all.

HOPELESS

Something had followed her from that place. The place above the music where her father died. Something hungry. A blind, grub consciousness, dreaming of shoulders crowned with translucent wings. And she, who would gift them.

The little girl had slumped on a palatial bed in her mother's chambers, cheeks wet with tears. Her brother lay beside her, wrapped in swaddling and blinking with his big black eyes. The babe understood none of what was going on about him. Too young to know his father had ended, and all the world beside him.

The little girl envied him.

Their apartments sat high within the hollow of the second Rib, ornate friezes carved into walls of ancient gravebone. Looking out the leadlight window, she could see the third and fifth Ribs opposite, looming above the Spine hundreds of feet be-

low. Nevernight winds howled about the petrified towers, bringing cool in from the waters of the bay.

Opulence dripped on the floor; all crushed red velvet and artistry from the four corners of the Itreyan Republic. Moving mekwerk sculpture from the Iron Collegium. Million-stitch tapestries woven by the blind propheteers of Vaan. A chandelier of pure Dweymeri crystal. Servants moved in a storm of soft dresses and drying tears, and at the eye stood the Dona Corvere, bidding them move, move, for the love of Aa, move.

The little girl had sat on the bed beside her brother. A black tomcat was pressed to her chest, purring softly. But he'd puffed up and spat when he saw a deeper shadow at the curtain's feet. Claws dug into his girl's hands and she'd dropped him into the path of an oncoming maidservant, who fell with a shriek. Dona Corvere turned on her daughter, regal and furious.

"Mia Corvere, keep that wretched animal out from underfoot or we'll leave it behind!"

And as simple as that, we have her name.

Mia.

"Captain Puddles isn't filthy," Mia had said, almost to herself.*

A boy in his middling teens entered the room, red-faced from his dash up the stairs. Heraldry of the Familia Corvere was embroidered on his doublet; a black crow in flight against a red sky, crossed swords below.

"Mi Dona, forgive me. Consul Scaeva has demanded—"

Heavy footfalls stilled his tongue. The doors swept aside and the room filled with men in snow-white armor, crimson plumes on their helms; Luminatii they were called, you may recall. They reminded little Mia of her father. The biggest man she'd ever seen led them, a trimmed beard framing wolfish features, animal cunning twinkling in his gaze.

Among the Luminatii stood the beautiful consul with his black eyes and purple robes—the man who'd spoken ". . . Death" and smiled as the floor fell away beneath her father's feet. Servants faded into the background, leaving Mia's mother as a solitary figure amid that sea of snow and blood. Tall and beautiful and utterly alone.

Mia climbed off the bed, slipped to her mother's side, and took her hand.

"Dona Corvere." The consul covered his heart with ring-studded fingers. "I

---

*The tomcat was, as you probably suspect, named for his fondness for urinating outside designated areas—a name that had been tolerated by her mother, and met with uproarious approval by her dear-departed father.

offer condolences in this time of trial. May the Everseeing keep you always in the Light."

"Your generosity humbles me, Consul Scaeva. Aa bless you for your kindness."

"I am truly grieved, Mi Dona. Your Darius served the Republic with distinction before his fall from grace. A public execution is always a tawdry affair. But what else is to be done with a general who marches against his own capital? Or the justicus who'd have placed a crown upon that general's head?"

The consul looked around the room, took in the servants, the luggage, the disarray.

"You are leaving us?"

"I take my husband's body to be buried at Crow's Nest, in the crypt of his familia."

"Have you asked permission of Justicus Remus?"

"I congratulate our new justicus on his promotion." A glance at the wolfish one. *"My husband's cloak fits him well. But why would I need him to grant my passage?"*

"Not permission to leave the city, Mi Dona. Permission to bury your Darius. I am unsure if Justicus Remus wishes a traitor's corpse rotting in his basement."

Realization dawned in the Dona's face. *"You would not dare . . ."*

"I?" The consul raised one sculpted eyebrow. *"This is the will of the Senate, Dona Corvere. Justicus Remus has been rewarded your late husband's estates for uncovering his heinous plot against the Republic. Any loyal citizen would see it fitting tithe."*

Murder gleamed in the Dona's eyes. She glanced at the loitering servants.

"Leave us."

The girls scuttled from the room. Glancing at the Luminatii, Dona Corvere aimed a pointed stare at the consul. It seemed to Mia the man wavered in his certainty, yet finally, he nodded to the wolfish one.

"Await me outside, Justicus."

The hulking Luminatii glanced at her mother. Down to the girl. Hands large enough to envelop her entire head twitched. The girl stared back.

Never flinch. Never fear.

"Luminus Invicta, Consul." Remus nodded to his men, and amid the synchronized *tromp tromp* of heavy boots, the room found itself emptied of all but three people.*

The Dona Corvere's voice was a fresh-sharpened knife into overripe fruit.

---

* Captain Puddles lurked under the bed, licking at dusty paws. The aforementioned *something* lingered yet beneath the curtains.

"What do you want, Julius?"

"You know it full well, Alinne. I want what is mine."

"You have what is yours. Your hollow victory. Your precious Republic. I trust it keeps you warm at night."

Consul Julius looked down at Mia, his smile dark as bruises. "Would you like to know what keeps me warm at night, little one?"

"Do not look at her. Do not speak to—"

His slap whipped her head to one side, dark hair flowing like tattered ribbons. And before Mia could blink, her mother had drawn a long, gravebone blade from her sleeve, its hilt crafted like a crow with red amber eyes. Quick as silver, she pressed it to the consul's throat, his handprint on her face twisting as she snarled.

"Touch me again and I'll cut your fucking throat, whoreson."

Scaeva didn't flinch.

"You can drag the girl from the gutter, but never the gutter from the girl." He smiled with perfect teeth, glanced at Mia. "But you know the price your loved ones would pay if you pressed that blade any deeper. Your political allies have abandoned you. Romero. Juliannus. Gracius. Even Florenti himself has fled Godsgrave. You are alone, my beauty."

"I am not your—"

Scaeva slapped the stiletto away, sent it skittering across the floor to the shadow beneath the curtain. Stepping closer, his eyes narrowed.

"You should envy your dear Darius, Alinne. I showed him a mercy. There will be no hangman's gift for you. Just an oubliette in the Philosopher's Stone, and dark a lifetime long. And as you go blind in the black, sweet Mother Time will lay claim your beauty, and your will, and your thin conviction you were anything more than Liisian shit wrapped in Itreyan silk."

Their lips were so close they almost touched. Eyes searching hers.

"But I will spare your family, Alinne. I will spare them if you plead me for it."

"She's ten years old, Julius. You wouldn't—"

"Would I not? Know me so well, do you?"

Mia looked up at her mother. Tears welling in her eyes.

"What is it you told me, Alinne? 'Neh diis lus'a, lus diis'a'?"

". . . Mother?" Mia said.

"One word and your daughter will be safe. I swear it."

"Mother?"

"Julius . . ."

"Yes?"

"I . . ."

There is a breed of arachnid in Vaan known as the wellspring spider.

The females are black as truedark, and possessed of the most astonishing maternal instinct in the animal republic. Once impregnated, a female builds a larder, stocks it with corpses, then seals herself inside. If the nest is set ablaze, she'll burn to death rather than abandon it. If beset by a predator, she'll die defending her clutch. But so fierce is her refusal to leave her young, once her eggs are laid, she won't move, even to hunt. And herein lies the wellspring's claim to the title of fiercest mother in the Republic. For once she's devoured all the stores within her larder, the female begins devouring herself.

One leg at a time.

Plucking her limbs from her thorax. Eating only enough to sustain her vigil. Ripping and chewing until only one leg remains, clinging to the silken treasure trove swelling beneath her. And when her babies hatch, spilling from the strands she so lovingly wrapped them inside, they partake, there and then, of their very first meal.

The mother who bore them.

I tell you now, gentlefriend, and I vow it true, the fiercest wellspring spider in all the Republic had nothing—I say nothing—*on Alinne Corvere.*

There in that O, so tiny room, Mia felt her mother's fists clench.

Pride tightening her jaw.

Agony brightening her eyes.

"Please," the Dona finally hissed, as if the very word burned her. "Spare her, Julius."

A victorious smile, bright as all three suns. The beautiful consul backed away, black eyes never leaving her mother's. He called as he reached the doorway, robes flowing about him like smoke. And without a word, the Luminatii marched back into the room. The wolfish one tore Mia from her mother's skirts. Captain Puddles mreowled *protest*. Mia clutched the tom tightly, tears burning her eyes.

"Stop it! Don't touch my mother!"

"Dona Corvere, I bind you by book and chain for crimes of conspiracy and treason against the Itreyan Republic. You will accompany us to the Philosopher's Stone."

Irons were slapped around the dona's wrists, screwed tight enough to make her wince. The wolfish one turned to the consul, glanced at Mia with a question in his eyes.

"The children?"

The consul glanced to little Jonnen, still wrapped in his swaddling on the bed.

"The babe is still at the breast. He can accompany his mother to the Stone."

"And the girl?"

"You promised, Julius!" Dona Corvere struggled in the Luminatii's grip. "You swore!"

Scaeva acted as if the woman had never spoken. He looked down at Mia, sobbing at the foot of the bed, Captain Puddles clutched to her thin chest.

"Did your mother ever teach you to swim, little one?"

Trelene's Beau spat Mia onto a miserable pier, jutting from the nethers of a ruined port known as Last Hope. Buildings littered the ocean's edge like a prizefighter's teeth, a stone garrison tower and outlying farms completed the oil painting. The populace consisted of fishermen, farmers, a particularly foolish brand of fortune hunter who earned a living raiding old Ashkahi ruins, and a slightly more intelligent variant who made their coin looting the corpses of colleagues.

As she stepped onto the jetty, Mia saw three bent fishermen lurking around a rod and a bottle of green ginger wine. The men looked at her the way maggots eye rotten meat. The girl stared at each in turn, waiting to see if any would offer to dance.*

Wolfeater clomped down the gangplank, several crew in tow. The captain noted the hungry stares fixed on the girl—sixteen years old, alone, armed only with a pig-sticker. Propping one boot on a jetty stump, the big Dweymeri lit his pipe, wiped sweat from tattooed cheeks.

"It's the smallest spiders that have the darkest poison, lads," he warned the fishermen.

Wolfeater's word seemed to carry some weight among the scoundrels, as they turned back to the water, slurping and bubbling against the jetty's legs.

Mildly disappointed, the girl offered the captain her hand.

"My thanks for your hospitality, sir."

Wolfeater stared at her outstretched fingers, exhaled a lungful of pale gray.

"Few enough reasons folk come to old Ashkah, lass. Fewer still a girl like you would brave parts this grim. And I've no wish to cause offense. But I'll not touch your hand."

"And why is that, sir?"

"Because I know the name of the ones who touched it first." He glanced at her shadow, fingering the draketooth necklace at his throat. "If such things have names. I know for damned sure they have memories, and I'll not have them remember mine."

The girl smiled soft. Put her hand back to her belt.

"Trelene watch over you, then, Captain."

---

* She'd learned to hear the music by now.

"Blue below and blue above you, girl."

She turned and stalked down the pier, the glare of a single sun in her eyes, looking for the building Mercurio had named for her. With heart in throat, she found it soon enough—a disheveled little establishment at the water's crust. A creaking sign above the doorway identified it as the Old Imperial. A sign in one filthy window informed Mia "Help" was, in fact, "Wonted."

It was a bucktoothed little shithole, and no mistake. Not the most miserable building in all creation.* But if the inn were a man and you stumbled on him in a bar, you'd be forgiven for assuming he had—after agreeing enthusiastically to his wife's request to bring another woman into their marriage bed—discovered his bride making up a pallet for him in the guest room.

The girl padded up to the bar, her back as close to the wall as she could get it. A dozen or so folk had escaped the turn's heat inside—a few locals and a handful of well-armed tomb-raiders. All in the room stopped to stare as she entered; if anyone had been manning the old harpsichord in the corner, they'd surely have hit a wrong note for dramatic effect, but alas, the beast hadn't uttered a squeak in years.†

The Imperial's proprietor seemed a harmless fellow—almost out of place in this town on the edge of the abyss. His eyes were a little too close together, and he reeked of rotten fish, but considering the stories Mia had heard about the Ashkahi Whisperwastes, she was just glad the fellow didn't have tentacles. He was propped behind the bar in a grubby apron (bloodstains?) cleaning a dirty mug with a dirtier rag. Mia noticed one of his eyes moved slightly before the other, like a child leading a slow cousin by the hand.

"Good turning to you, sir," she said, keeping her voice steady. "Aa bless and keep you."

"Come in wiv Wolfeater's mob, didjer?"

"Well spotted, sir."

---

* That dubious honor belonged to the Lonesome Rose, a pleasure house in the Godsgrave docklands frequented by syphilitic lunatics and newly released convicts, run by a Vaanian madam so disease-stricken she affectionately referred to her own nethers as "the Orphan Maker."

† The only man in Last Hope who knew how to play it—a local tomb-raider nicknamed Blue Paulo—had been found strung up from the rafters in his room two summers previous. Whether his end was suicide or the protest of another resident particularly opposed to harpsichord music was a topic of much speculation and very little investigation in the weeks following his death/murder.

"Pay's four beggars weekly, but yer get board onna top.* Twenty percent of anyfing you make turning trick onna side comes to me direct. And I'll need a sample a'fore yer hired. Fair?"

Mia's smile dragged the proprietor's behind the bar and quietly strangled it. It made very little sound as it died.

"I'm afraid you misunderstand, sir," she said. "I am not here to apply for employ within your"—a glance about her—"no doubt fine establishment."

A sniff. "Whya 'ere then?"

She placed the sheepskin purse atop the bar. The treasure within clinked with a tune nothing like gold. If you were in the business of dentistry, you might have recognized that the tiny orchestra inside the bag was comprised entirely of human teeth.

It took her a moment to speak. To find the words she'd practiced until she dreamed them.

"My tithe for the Maw."

The man looked at her, expression unreadable. Mia tried to keep the tremors from her breath, her hands. Six years it had taken her to come this far. Six years of rooftops and alleys and sleepless nevernights. Of dusty tomes and bleeding fingers and noxious gloom. But at last, she stood on the threshold, a small nod away from the vaunted halls of the Red—

"What's me maw got tado wivvit?" the proprietor blinked.

Mia kept her face as stone, despite the dreadful flips her insides were undertaking. She glanced around the room. The tomb-raiders were bent over their map. A handful of local wags were playing "spank" with a pack of moldy cards. A woman in desert-colored robes and a veil was drawing spiral patterns on a tabletop with what looked like blood.

"The Maw," Mia repeated. "This is my tithe."

"Maw's dead," the barman frowned.

---

*Coins in the Republic came in three flavors—the least valuable being copper, the middle child, iron, and the fanciest, gold. Gold coins were as rare as a likable tax collector, most plebs never laying eyes on one in their lives.

Itreyan coinage was originally referred to as "sovereigns," but given the Itreyan's penchant for brutally murdering their kings, the term had fallen out of vogue decades past. Coppers were now sometimes referred to as "beggars" and irons as "priests," since those were the people usually found handling them with the most enthusiasm. There was no commonly accepted slang for gold coins—anyone rich enough to possess them likely wasn't the sort who went in for nicknames. Or handled their own money.

So for argument's sake, let's call them golden tossers.

". . . What?"

"Been dead nigh on four truedarks now."

"The Maw," she scowled. "Dead. Are you mad?"

"You're the one bringing my old dead mum presents, lass."

Realization tapped her on the shoulder, danced a funny little jig.

Ta-da.

"I'm not talking about your *mother* you fucki—"

Mia caught her temper by the collar, gave it a good hard shake. Clearing her throat, she brushed her crooked fringe from her eyes.

"I do not refer to your mother, sir. I mean the *Maw*. Niah. The Goddess of Night. Our Lady of Blessed Murder. Sisterwife to Aa, and mother to the hungry Dark within us all."

"O, you mean the *Maw*."

"Yes." The word was a rock, hurled right between the barman's eyes. "The *Maw*."

"Sorry," the man said sheepishly. "It's just the accent, y'know."

Mia glared.

The barman cleared his throat. "There's no church to the Maw 'round 'ere, lass. Worship of 'er kind's outlawed, even onna fringe. Got no business wiv Muvvers of Night and someandsuch in this particular place of business. Bad for the grub."

"You are Fat Daniio, proprietor of the Old Imperial?"

"I'm not fat—"

Mia slapped the bartop. Several of the spank players turned to stare.

"But your name is Daniio?" she hissed.

A pause. Brow creased in thought. The gaze of Daniio's slow cousin eye seemed to be wandering off, as if distracted by pretty flowers, or perhaps a rainbow.*

"Aye," Daniio finally said.

"I was told—specifically *told*, mind you—to come to the Old Imperial on the coast of Ashkah and give Fat Daniio my tithe." Mia pushed the purse across the counter. "So take it."

"What's in it?"

"Trophy of a killer, killed in kind."

"Eh?"

"The teeth of Augustus Scipio, high executioner of the Itreyan Senate."

---

* No rainbows were present in the room at this time.

"Is he comin' 'ere to get them?"

Mia bit her lip. Closed her eyes.

". . . No."

"How the 'byss did he lose his—"

"He didn't lose them," Mia leaned farther forward, smell be damned. "I tore them out of his skull after I cut his miserable throat."

Fat Daniio fell silent. An *almost* thoughtful expression crossed his face. He leaned in close, wreathed in the stench of rotten fish, tears springing unbidden to Mia's eyes.

" 'Scuse me then, lass. But what am I s'posed to do with some dead tosser's teeth?"

The door creaked open, and the Wolfeater ducked below the frame, stepping into the Old Imperial as if he owned a part share in it.* A dozen crewmen followed, cramming into dingy booths and leaning against the creaking bar. With an apologetic shrug, Fat Daniio set to serving the Dweymeri sailors. Mia caught his sleeve as he headed toward the booths.

"Do you have rooms here, sir?"

"Aye, we do. One beggar a week, mornmeal extra."

Mia pushed an iron coin into Fat Daniio's paw.

"Please let me know when that runs out."

A week with no sign, no word, no whisper save the winds off the wastes. The crew of *Trelene's Beau* stayed aboard their ship while they resupplied, availing themselves of the town's amenities frequently. A typical nevernight would commence with grub at the Old Imperial, a sally forth into the arms of Dona Amile and her "dancers" at the appropriately named Seven Flavors,† before returning to the Imperial for a session of liquor, song, and the

---

* He did not, although Fat Daniio *did* owe the captain a weighty debt, incurred during a drunken argument about the aerodynamics of pigs and the distance from the Old Imperial to the stable across the way. The debt, which would take the form of an extended session of . . . oral pleasure for the crew of *Trelene's Beau* (which Daniio would apparently undertake while performing a handstand with his arse-end painted blue) had yet to be cashed in, but the threat of it hung heavy in the air whenever the *Beau* and its crew were in port.

† Boy, Girl, Man, Woman, Pig, Horse, and, if sufficient notice and coin was given, Corpse.

occasional friendly knife fight. Only one finger was removed during the entirety of their stay. Its owner took its loss with good humor.

Mia sat in a gloomy corner with the hangman's teeth pouched up on the wood before her. Eyes on the door every time it creaked. Eating the occasional bowl of *astonishingly* hot (and she had to admit, delicious) bowls of Fat Daniio's "widowmaker" chili, her frown growing darker as the turning of the *Beau*'s departure drew ever closer.

Could Mercurio have been wrong? It'd been years since he'd sent an apprentice to the Red Church. Maybe the place had been swallowed by the wastes? Maybe the Luminatii had finally laid them to rest, as Justicus Remus had vowed to do after the Truedark Massacre?

And maybe this is all a test. To see if you'll run like a frightened child . . .

She'd poke around the town at the turn of each nevernight, listening in doorways, almost invisible beneath her cloak of shadows. She came to know Last Hope's residents all too well. The seer who augured for the town's womenfolk, interpreting signs from a withered tome of Ashkahi script she couldn't actually read. The slave boy from Seven Flavors, plotting to murder his madam and flee into the wastes.

The Luminatii legionaries stationed in the garrison tower were the most miserable soldiers Mia had ever come across. Two dozen men at civilization's end, a few sunsteel blades between them and the horrors of the Ashkahi Whisperwastes. The winds blowing off the old empire's ruins were said to drive men mad, but Mia was sure boredom would do for the legionaries long before the whisperwinds did. They spoke constantly of home, of women, of whatever sins they'd committed to be stationed in the Republic's arse-end.* After a week, Mia was sick of all of them. And not a single one spoke a word of the Red Church.

Seven turns after she'd arrived in Last Hope, Mia sat watching the *Beau*'s crew seal their holds, their calls rough with grog. Part of her wanted little more than to skulk aboard as they put out to the blue. Run back home to Mercurio. But truth was, she'd come too far to give up now. If the Church expected her to tuck tail at the first obstacle, they knew her not at all.

Sitting atop the Old Imperial's roof, she watched the *Beau* sail from the bay, a clove cigarillo at her lips. The whisperwinds rolled off the wastes behind

---

* Insubordination or drunken and disorderly behavior were the most common, although one legionary had been posted to Ashkah for murdering his cohort's cook after being served corned beef for evemeal on no less than 342 consecutive nevernights.

"Would it kill you," he'd roared, "to serve [stab] some fucking [stab] salad?"

her, shapeless as dreams. She glanced at the cat who wasn't a cat, sitting in the long shadow the suns cast for her. Its voice was the kiss of velvet on a baby's skin.

"*. . . you fear . . .*"

"That should please you."

"*. . . mercurio would not have sent you here needlessly . . .*"

"The Luminatii have been trying to take down the Church for years. The Truedark Massacre changed the game."

"*. . . if ill befell them, there would still be traces . . .*"

"You suggest we go out into the Whisperwastes and look?"

"*. . . that, wait here, or return home . . .*"

"None of those options hold much appeal."

"*. . . fat daniio's job offer still stands, i am sure . . .*"

Her smile was thin and pale. She turned back to the sea, watching the sunslight glint and catch upon the gnashing waves. Dragging deep on her smoke and exhaling plumes of gray.

"*. . . mia . . . ?*"

"Yes?"

"*. . . there is no need to be afraid . . .*"

"I'm not."

A pause, filled with whispering wind.

"*. . . no need to lie, either . . .*"

M ia ended up stealing most of her supplies.

Waterskins, rations, and a tent from Last Hope General Supplies and Fine Undertakers. Blankets, whiskey, and candles from the Old Imperial. She'd already marked the finest stallion in the garrison stable for stealing, despite being as much at home in the saddle as a nun in a brothel.

She told herself the thievery would keep her sharp, and sneaking back into the robbed stores to deposit compensation on the countertops afterward struck her as good sport.* Seated at the Imperial's hearth, she enjoyed a final bowl of widowmaker chili and waited for the nevernight winds to begin, bringing blessed cool after a turn of red heat.

Mia glanced up as the front door creaked open, admitting curling fingers of dust.

The boy who entered looked Dweymeri—leviathan ink facial tattoos

---

* O, look, there is good in her! Cue the swelling violiiiiiins.

(of terrible quality), salt-kissed locks bound in matted knots. But his skin was olive rather than brown, and he was too short to be an islander; barely a head taller than Mia, truth told. Dressed in dark leathers, carrying a scimitar in a battered scabbard, smelling of horse and a long road. When he prowled into the room, he checked every corner with hazel eyes. As his stare roamed the alcoves, Mia pulled the shadows about herself, and faded like a watermark into the gloom.

The boy turned to Fat Daniio, polishing that same grubby cup with the same grubby cloth. Eyeing the man over, the boy spoke with a voice soft as velvet.

"Blessings to you, sir."

"A'right," Fat Daniio replied. "What'll you 'ave?"

"I have this."

The boy placed a small wooden box upon the counter. Mia's eyes narrowed as it rattled. The boy looked around the room again, then spoke in a tight whisper.

"My tithe. For the Maw."*

---

* O, very well. A primer, if you'll indulge me.

In all religions, there must be an adversary. An evil for the good. A black for the white. For folk of the Republic, this role is filled by Niah, Goddess of Night, Our Lady of Blessed Murder, sisterwife to Aa, also (as you've no doubt surmised) referred to as the Maw.

In the beginning, Niah and Aa's marriage was a happy one. They made love at dawn and dusk, then retired to their respective domains, sharing rule of the sky equally. Fearing a rival, Aa commanded Niah bear him no sons, and dutifully, the Night bore the Light four daughters—Tsana, the Lady of Fire, Keph, the Lady of Earth, and finally the twins Trelene and Nalipse, the Ladies of Oceans and Storms, respectively. However, Niah missed her husband in the long, cold hours of darkness, and to alleviate her loneliness, she chose to bring a boychild into the world. The Night named her son Anais.

Aa, however, was outraged at his wife's disobedience. As punishment, Niah was banished from the sky. Feeling betrayed by her husband, Niah vowed vengeance against Aa, and has not spoken to him since. Aa himself is still sulking about the whole affair.

And what became of Anais, you might ask? The rival Aa so rightly feared?

That, gentlefriend, would be spoiling things.

CHAPTER 4

KINDNESS

Captain Puddles had loved his Mia.

He'd known her since he was a kitten, after all. Before he'd forgotten the warm press of his siblings around him, she'd cradled him in her arms and kissed him on his little pink nose and he'd known she'd always be the center of his world.

And so when Justicus Remus had stooped to seize the girl's wrist at his consul's command, Captain Puddles spat a yellow-tooth hiss, reached out with a paw full of claws, and tore the justicus's face from eyehole to lip. Roaring, the big man seized the brave captain's head with one hand, his shoulders with the other, and with an almost practiced ease, he twisted.

The sound was like wet sticks snapping, too loud to be drowned by Mia's scream. And at the end of those dreadful damp pops, a black shape hung limp in the justicus's hand; a warm, soft, purring shape Mia had fallen asleep beside every nevernight, now purring no more.

She lost herself then. Howling, clawing, scratching. Dimly aware of being seized by another Luminatii and slung over his shoulder. The justicus clutched his bleeding face and drew his sword, fire uncurling down its length, the steel glowing with painful, blinding light.

"Not here, Remus," Scaeva said. "Your hands must be clean."

The justicus bellowed at his men, and her mother had screamed and kicked. Mia called for her, but a sharp blow struck her head, and it was all she could do to not fall into the black beneath her feet as the Dona Corvere's cries faded into nothing.

Servants' stairs, spiraling down. A passageway through the Spine—not the wondrous halls of polished white gravebone and crystal chandeliers and marrowborn* in all their finery. A dim and claustrophobic little tunnel, leading out into the

---

*When residing in Godsgrave, the Republic's nobility dwell within the graven hollows of the aforementioned Ribs, and conduct their business in the cavernous innards of the Spine—hence the term "marrowborn." Status is conveyed by one's proximity to the first Rib, wherein dwell the Itreyan Senate and the consuls elected to lead them. North of the first Rib lies the Forum, constructed in the place the Skull might've been.

I say "might," gentlefriend, because the Skull itself is missing.

grounds beyond. Mia had squinted up—the Ribs arching into storm-washed skies, the great council buildings and libraries and observatories—before the men threw her into an empty barrel, slammed the lid, and tossed it into a horse-drawn cart.

She felt the cart whipped into motion, the trundle of wheels across cobbles. Men rode in the tray beside her, but she couldn't make out their words, stricken by the memory of Captain Puddles lying twisted on the floor, her mother in chains. She understood none of it. The barrel rasped against her skin, splinters plucking at her dress. She felt them cross bridge after bridge, the haze of semiconsciousness thin enough now for her to start crying, hiccupping and heaving. A fist slammed hard against the barrel's flank.

"Shut up, you little shit, or I'll give you something to wail about."

They're going to kill me, she thought.

A chill stole over her. Not at the thought of dying, mind you; in truth, no child thinks of herself as anything less than immortal. The chill was a physical sensation, spilling from the darkness inside the barrel, coiling around her feet, cold as ice water. She felt a presence—or closer, a lack of one. Like the feeling of empty at an embrace's end. And she knew, sure and certain, that something was in that barrel with her.

Watching her.

Waiting.

"Hello?" she whispered.

A ripple in the black. A silent, ink-spot earthquake. And where there had been nothing a moment before, something gleamed at her feet, caught by the tiny chinks of sunlight spilling through the barrel's lid. Something long and wicked-sharp as only gravebone can be, its hilt crafted to resemble a crow in flight. Last seen skittering beneath the curtains as Consul Scaeva slapped her mother's hand away and spoke of pleading and promises.

Dona Corvere's gravebone stiletto.

Mia reached toward it. For the briefest moment, she swore she could see lights at her feet, glittering like diamonds in an ocean of nothing. She felt an emptiness so vast she thought she was falling—down, down into some hungry dark. And then her fingers closed on the dagger's hilt and she clutched it tight, so cold it almost burned.

She felt the something in the dark around her.

The copper-tang of blood.

The pulsing rush of rage.

The cart bounced along the road, her stomach curdling until at last they drew to a halt. She felt the barrel lifted, slung, crashing to the ground with a bang that made her almost bite her tongue clean through. She heard voices again, loud enough to ken the words.

"I'm sick to my guts on this, Alberius."

"*Orders are orders. Luminus Invicta, aye?*" *

"*Sod off.*"

"*You want to trifle with Remus? With Scaeva? The saviors of the bloody Republic?*"

"*Saviors my arsehole. You ever wonder how they did it? Captured Corvere and Antonius right in the middle of an armed camp?*"

"*No, I bloody don't. Help me with this.*"

"*I heard it was magiks. Black arkemy. Scaeva's in truck—*"

"*Get staunch, you bloody maid. Who cares how they did it? Corvere was a fucking traitor, and this is traitor's get.*"

The barrel lid was torn away. Mia squinted up at two men, dark cloaks thrown over white armor. The first was a man with arms like treetrunks and hands like dinnerplates. The second had pretty blue eyes and the smile of a fellow who choked puppies for sport.

"*Maw's teeth,*" breathed the first. "*She can't be more than ten.*"

"*Never to see eleven.*" A shrug. "*Hold still, girl. This won't hurt long.*"

The puppy-choker clutched Mia's throat, drew a long, sharp knife from his belt. And there in the reflection on that polished steel, the little girl saw her death. It would've been easy then, to close her eyes and wait. She was ten years old, after all. Alone and helpless and afraid. But here is truth, gentlefriends, no matter the number of suns in your sky. At the heart of it, two kinds of people live in this world or any other: those who flee and those who fight. Your kind has many terms for the latter sort. Berserker. Killer instinct. More balls than brains.

And it shouldn't surprise you, knowing what little you know already, that in the face of this thug and his blade, and laden with memory of her father's execution

never flinch

never fear

instead of wailing or breaking as another ten-year-old might have, young Mia gripped the stiletto she'd fished from the darkness, and slipped it straight up into the puppy-choker's eye.

The man screamed and fell backward, blood gushing between his fingers. Mia rolled from the barrel, the sunlight impossibly bright after the darkness within. She felt the something *come with her*, coiled in her shadow, pushing at her heels. She saw they'd brought her to some mongrel bridge, a little canal choked with filth, boarded windows all around.

The dinnerplate man's eyes grew wide as his friend went down screaming. He drew a sunsteel sword and stepped toward the girl, flame rippling down its edge.

---

* The motto of the Luminatii Legion, gentlefriend. "Light shall conquer."

But movement at his feet drew his eyes to the stone, and looking down, he saw the girl's shadow begin to move. Clawing and twisting as if alive, reaching out toward him like hungry hands.

"Light save me," he breathed.

The blade wavered in the thug's grip. Mia backed away across the bridge, bloody knife in one trembling fist, the something *still pressing at her heels. And as the puppy-choker clawed back to his feet with his face painted blood, the little girl did what anyone would have done in her position—ratio of balls to brains be damned.*

". . . run . . !" said a tiny voice.

And run she did.

The Dweymeri boy underwent much the same exchange with Fat Daniio as Mia,* although he suffered it with silent dignity.

The innkeeper informed him a girl had been asking the same questions, gestured to her booth—or at least, the booth she'd been sitting at. Mia had stolen up the stairwell by that point and was listening just out of sight, silent as an Itreyan Ironpriest.†

After muttering thanks, the Dweymeri boy asked if there were rooms available, paying coin from a malnourished purse. He was headed up the stairs when one of the local card players, a gent named Scupps, spoke.

"Yer one of Wolfeater's mob?"

The boy replied with a deep, soft voice. "I know no Wolfeater."

"He's no crewman off the *Beau*." Mia recognized this second voice as Scupps's brother, Lem. "Look at the size of 'im. He's barely tall enough to reach Wolfeater's balls."

---

* "O, you mean the *Mawwwwww*."

† The priests of the Itreyan College of Iron are inducted into their order after their second truedark, and tested for aptitude in the Ars Machina. The boys are never taught to read, nor to write. On the eve of their fifth truedark, those found worthy to serve are taken to a brightly lit room in the heart of the Collegium. Here, amid the scent of burning tar and the breathless beauty of the college choir, they recite their vows, and are then relieved of their tongues via a set of red-hot iron snips. The secrets of constructing and maintaining war walkers are the most tightly guarded in the Republic—taught by *doing*, not speaking—and the priesthood take their vows of silence rather seriously.

It may give comfort to the gentlehearted among you that the priesthood don't take vows of celibacy. They're free to partake in all pleasures of the flesh, though their lack of tongues can prove a hindrance in their search for wives.

Though it *does* make them excellent dinner companions.

Laughter.

"Mebbe that's the point?"

More laughter.

The Dweymeri boy waited to ensure there was no more hilarity forthcoming, then continued up the stairs. Mia had slipped into her room, watching from the keyhole as the boy padded to his own door. His feet made barely a whisper, though Mia knew the boards squeaked like a family of murdered mice. The boy glanced over his shoulder toward her door, sniffed once, then slipped inside.

The girl sat in her room, considering whether to approach him or simply light out of Last Hope at turn's end as she planned.* He was obviously looking for the same thing she was, but he was likely a cold-blooded psychopath. She doubted many novices seeking the Red Church had motives as altruistic as her own.

As soon as the town bells rang in nevernight, she heard the boy head downstairs, soft as velvet. She felt her shadow stir and stretch, insubstantial claws digging at the floorboards.

"... *if i do not return by the morrow, tell mother i love her* . . ."

The girl snorted as the not-cat slipped beneath her door. She waited hours, reading by candlelight rather than open her shutters to the sun. If she was leaving this turn, she'd need do it at twelve bells, when the watchtower changed shifts. Easier to steal the stallion then. The knowledge she could have just bought some old nag raised its hand at the back of the lesson hall, and was shushed by the thought she shouldn't be heading out into the wastes on anything but the finest horse this town had to offer.†

---

*Though sadly lacking in darkness, most citizens of the Republic still require sleep, and regardless of season, the change from waking hours is marked by a turn in Itreya's weather. As nevernight approaches, winds pick up from the westward oceans and howl across the Republic, bringing a merciful temperature drop in their wake. As it's easier to sleep in cooler times, this turn is taken by most as the signal to hit the pillow, hay, or flagstones depending on their state of inebriation. The winds die slowly, rising again perhaps twenty-four hours later. It is said they are a gift from Nalipse, the Lady of Storms, who takes mercy upon a land and people scorched by her Father's almost constant light.

The "turn," therefore, is the term Itreyans use to mark a cycle of sleep and waking. There are seven turns to a week, three and one half hundred turns in a seasonal year. An oddity of language, to be sure, but a necessary one in a land where actual *days* last two and a half years at a time, and birthday parties are an indulgence that only the wealthiest might afford.

†Every now and then, and often to her chagrin, the girl's lingering marrowborn pride would slip through her carefully cultivated facade of not-give-a-fuckery. You can take the girl from the gutter, but not the gutter from the girl. Sadly, the same can be said of the glitter.

She felt a rippling chill, a sense of loss, and the cat who was shadows hopped up onto the bed beside her. Blinked with eyes that weren't there. Tried to purr and failed.

"Well?"

"*. . . he ate a sparing meal, watched the ones who insulted him between mouthfuls, and followed them home when they left . . .*"

"Did he kill them?"

"*. . . pissed in their water barrel . . .*"

"Not too bloodthirsty, then. And afterward?"

"*. . . climbed up on the stable roof. he has been watching your window ever since . . .*"

A nod. "I thought he marked me when he first entered."

"*. . . a clever one . . .*"

"Let's see how clever."

Mia packed her things, books bound in a small oilskin satchel on her back. She'd hoped she might slip out unnoticed, but now this Dweymeri boy watched her, it was no longer a question of if she'd deal with him. Only how.

She snuck out from her room, across the squeaky floorboards, making no squeak at all. Sliding up to an empty room opposite, she slipped two lockpicks from a thin wallet, setting to work and hearing a small click a few minutes later. Slipping from the window, flitting across the roof, she felt sunslight burning the windblown sky, adrenaline tingling her fingertips. It was good to be moving again. Tested again.

Dashing across the alley between the Imperial and the bakery next door, boots less than a whisper on the road. The not-cat prowled in front, watching with his not-eyes.

Just as she'd done outside Augustus's window, Mia reached out and took hold of the shadows about her. Thread by thread, she drew the darkness to her with clever fingers, like a seamstress weaving a cloak—a cloak over which unwary eyes might lose their way.

A cloak of shadows.

Call it what you will, gentlefriends. Thaumaturgy. Arkemy. Werking. Magik. Like all power, it comes with a tithe. As Mia pulled her shadows about her, the light grew dimmer in her eyes. As ever, it became harder for her to see past her veil of darkness, just as *she* was harder to see inside *it*. The world beyond was blurred, muddied, shrouded in black—she had to walk slow, lest she trip or stumble. But wrapped inside her shadows, she crept on, on through the nevernight glare, just a watercolor impression on the canvas of the world.

Up to the stable's flank, climbing the downspout by feel. Crawling onto the roof, she squinted in her gloom, spotted the Dweymeri in the chimney's shadow, watching her bedroom window. Mia padded across the tiles, imagining she was back in Old Mercurio's warehouse; dead leaves scattered across the floor, a three-turn thirst burning in her throat, four wild dogs asleep around a decanter of crystal-clear water.

Motivation had been the old man's watchword, sure and true.

Closer now. Uncertain whether to speak or act, begin or end. Perhaps twenty paces away, she saw the boy tense, turn his head. And then she was rolling beneath the fistful of knives he hurled, three in quick succession, gleaming in the light of that cursed sun. If this were truedark she would've had him. If this were truedark—

Don't look.

She snapped to her feet, stiletto drawn, her shadow writhing across the tiles toward him. The Dweymeri boy had drawn his scimitar, two more throwing knives poised in his other hand. Dark saltlocks of matted hair swayed over his eyes. The tattoos on his face were the ugliest Mia had ever seen, looking like they'd been scrawled by a blind man in the midst of a seizure. Yet the face beneath . . .

The pair stood watching each other, still as statues, moments ticking by like hours as the gale howled about them.

"You have very good ears, sir," she finally said.

"You have better feet, Pale Daughter. I heard nothing."

"Then how?"

The boy offered a dimpled smile. "You stink of cigarillo smoke. Cloves, I think."

"That's impossible. I'm upwind from you."

The boy glanced at the shadows moving like snakes around his feet.

"Seems to be raining impossible in these parts."

She stared at him. Hard and sharp and lean and quick. A rapier in a world of broadswords. Mercurio was better at reading folk than any person she'd known, and he'd taught her to sum others up in a blinking. Whoever this boy was, whatever his reasons for seeking the Church, he was no psychopath. Not one who killed for killing's sake.

Interesting.

"You seek the Red Church," she said.

"The fat man wouldn't take my tithe."

"Nor mine. We're being tested, I think."

"I thought the same."

"It's possible they're no longer here. I was heading into the wastes to look."

"If it's death you seek, there are easier ways to find it." The boy gestured beyond Last Hope's walls. "Where would you even start?"

"I was planning on following my nose," Mia smiled. "But something tells me I'd do better following yours."

The boy stared long and hard. Hazel eyes roaming her body, cool and narrowed. The blade in her hand. The shadows at his feet. The whispering wastes behind him.

"My name is Tric," he said, sheathing the scimitar at his back.

". . . Tric? Are you certain?"

"Certain about my own name? Aye, that I am."

"I mean no disrespect, sir," Mia said. "But if we're to travel the Whisperwastes together, we should at least be honest enough to use our own names. And your name can't be Tric."

". . . Do you call me liar, girl?"

"I called you nothing, sir. And I'll thank you not to call me 'girl' again, as if the word were kin to something you found on the bottom of your boot."

"You have a strange way of making friends, Pale Daughter."

Mia sighed. Took her temper by the earlobe and pulled it to heel.

"I've read the Dweymeri cleave to ritualized naming rites. Your names follow a set pattern. Noun then verb. Dweymeri have names like 'Spinesmasher.' 'Wolfeater.' 'Pigfiddler.'"

". . . Pigfiddler?"

Mia blinked. "Pigfiddler was one of the most infamous Dweymeri pirates who ever lived. Surely you've heard of him?"

"I was never one for history. What was he infamous for?"

"Fiddling with pigs.* He terrorized farmers from Stormwatch to Dawnspear for almost ten years. Had a three-hundred-iron bounty on him in the end. No hog was safe."

". . . What happened to him?"

"The Luminatii. Their swords did to his face what he did to the pigs."

"Ah."

"So. Your name cannot be Tric."

The boy stared her up and down, expression clouded. But when he spoke, there was iron in his voice. Indignity. A well-nursed and lifelong anger.

---

* O, stop giggling and grow up.

"My name," he said, "is Tric."

The girl looked him over, dark eyes narrowed. A puzzle, this one. And sure and certain, our girl had ever the weakness for puzzles.

"Mia," she finally said.

The boy walked slow and steady across the tiles, paying no attention to the black beneath him. Extending one hand. Calloused fingers, one silver ring—the long, serpentine forms of three seadrakes, intertwined—on his index finger. Mia looked the boy over, the scars and ugly facial tattoos, olive skin, lean and broad shouldered. She licked her lips, tasted sweat.

The shadows rippled at her feet.

"A pleasure to meet you, Dona Mia," he said.

"And you, Don Tric."

And with a smile, she shook his hand.

COMPLIMENTS

The little girl had dashed through narrow streets, over bridge and under stair, red crusting on her hands. The something had followed her, puddled in the dark at her feet as they beat hard on the cracking flagstones. She'd no idea what it might be or want—only that it had helped her, and without that help, she'd be as dead as her father was.

eyes open
legs kicking
guh-guh-guh

Mia willed the tears away, curled her hands into fists, and ran. She could hear the puppy-choker and his friend behind her, shouting, cursing. But she was nimble and quick and desperately afraid, fear giving her wings. Running down dogleg squeezeways and over choked canals until finally, she slithered down an alley wall, clutching the stitch in her side.

Safe. For now.

Slumped with legs folded beneath her, she tried to push the tears down like her mother had taught her. But they were so much bigger than her, shoving back until she could stave them off no more. Hiccupping and shaking, snotty face pushed into red, red hands.

Her father was hung a traitor beneath the gaze of the high cardinal himself. Her mother in chains. The Familia Corvere estates given to that awful Justicus Remus who'd broken Captain Puddles's neck. And Julius Scaeva, consul of the Itreyan Senate, had ordered her drowned in the canals like some unwanted kitten.

Her whole world undone in a single turn.

"Daughters save me . . . ," she breathed.

Mia saw the shadow beneath her move. Ripple, as if it were water, and she a stone dropped into it. She was strangely unafraid, the fear in her draining away as if through punctures in the soles of her feet. She felt no sense of menace, no childish fears of unspeakables under the bed left to make her shiver. But she felt that presence again—or closer, a lack of any presence at all—coiled in her shadow on the stone beneath her.

"Hello again," she whispered.

She felt the thing that was nothing. In her head. In her chest. She knew it was smiling at her—a friendly smile that might have reached all the way to its eyes, if only it had some. She reached into her sleeve, found the bloodstained stiletto it had given her.

The gift that had saved her life.

"What are you?" she whispered to the black at her feet.

No answer.

"Do you have a name?"

It shivered.

Waiting.

Wait

ing.

"You're nice," she declared. "Your name should be nice too."

Another smile. Black and eager.

Mia smiled also.

Decided.

"Mister Kindly," she said.

According to the plaque above his stable, the stallion's name was "Chivalry," but Mia would come to know him simply as "Bastard."

To say she wasn't fond of horses is to say geldings aren't fond of knives. Growing up in Godsgrave, she'd had little need for the beasts, and truthfully, they're an unpleasant way to travel despite what your poets might say. The smell is akin to a solid right hook into an already broken nose, the toll on the rider's tenders is measured more often in blisters than bruises, and traveling by hoof isn't much quicker than traveling by foot. And *all* these issues are compounded if a horse has a sense of its own importance. Which, sadly, poor Chivalry did.

The stallion belonged to the garrison centurion, a marrowborn member of the Luminatii legion named Vincenzo Garibaldi. He was a thoroughbred, black as a chimney sweep's lungs.* Treated (and fed) better than most of Garibaldi's men, Chivalry was tolerant of none but his master's hand. And so, confronted with a strange girl in his stable as the watch sounded, he neighed in irritation and set about voiding his bladder over as many square feet as possible.

Having spent years living near the Rose River, the stench of stallion piss came as no real shock to Mia, who promptly slapped a bit into the horse's mouth to shut him up. Hateful as she found the beasts, she'd endured a three-week stint on a mainland horse farm at Old Mercurio's "request," and at least knew enough not to place the bridle on the beast's arse-end.† However, when Mia hoisted the saddle blanket, Chivalry began thrashing in his pen, and it was only through a hasty leap onto the doorframe that the girl avoided growing considerably thinner.

"Trelene's heaving funbags, keep him quiet!" Tric hissed from the stable door.

". . . Did you honestly just swear by a goddess's 'funbags'?"

"Forget that, shut him up!"

"I told you horses don't like me! And blaspheming about the Lady of the Ocean's baps isn't going to help matters any. In fact, it'll probably get you drowned, you nonce."

"I'll no doubt have long years locked in whatever stinking outhouse passes for the jail in this cesspool to repent my sins."

---

* The horse, not the captain.

† She was bitten by three different horses over the course of her stay on the farm, bucked off seven times (twice into manure), and stepped on once. She was also pinched on the behind by a particularly daring stableboy named Romero (sadly, on the same turn she was first bucked into shit), who'd been misinformed by a traveling minstrel that city women "enjoy that kind of thing."

The boy's nose never quite healed properly, though he managed to recover three of his teeth. Last I heard, he'd been sentenced to four years in the Philosopher's Stone for a brutal, and many said unprovoked, assault on a traveling minstrel.

"Keep your underskirts on," Mia whispered. "The outhouse will be occupied for a while."

Tric wondered what the girl was on about. But as she slipped into Chivalry's pen for another saddling attempt, he heard wails within the garrison tower, pleas to the Everseeing, and a burst of profanity so colorful you could fling it into the air and call it a rainbow. A stench was rising on the wind, harsh enough to make his eyes water. And so, as Mia rained whispered curses down on Chivalry's head, the boy decided to see what all the fuss was about.

Mister Kindly sat on the stable roof, trying his best to copy the curiosity found in real cats. He watched as the boy moved quietly to the tower, scaled the wall. Tric peered through the sandblasted window into the room beyond, his face turning greenish beneath his artless tattoos. Without a sound, he dropped to the ground, creeping back to the stable in time to see Mia wrangle the saddle onto Chivalry's back with the aid of several stolen sugar cubes.

The boy helped Mia handle the snorting stallion through the stable doors. She was short, and the thoroughbred twenty hands high, so it took her a running leap to make the saddle. As she struggled up, she noticed the green pallor on Tric's face.

"Something wrong?" she asked.

"What the 'byss is going on in that tower?" Tric whispered.

"Mishap," Mia replied.

". . . What?"

"Three dried buds of Liisian loganberry, a third of a cup of molasses essence, and a pinch of dried cordwood root." She shrugged. "Mishap. You might know it as 'Plumber's Bane.'"

Tric blinked. "You poisoned the entire garrison?"

"Well, technically Fat Daniio poisoned them. He served the evemeal. I just added the spice." Mia smiled. "It's not lethal. They're just suffering a touch of . . . intestinal distress."

"A touch?" The boy cast one haunted look back to the tower, the smeared and groaning horrors therein. "Look, don't be offended if I do all the cooking out there, aye?"

"Suit yourself."

Mia set her sights on the wastes beyond Last Hope, and with a doffed hat toward the watchtower, kicked Chivalry's flanks. Sadly, instead of a dashing gallop off toward the horizon, the girl found herself bucked into the air, her brief flight ending in a crumpled heap on the road. She rolled in the dirt, rubbing her rump, glaring at the now whinnying stallion.

"Bastard . . . ," she hissed.

She looked to Mister Kindly, sitting on the road beside her.

"Not. A. Fucking. Word."

". . . *meow* . . . ," he said.

With a sharp bang, the watchtower door burst open. A befouled Centurion Vincenzo Garibaldi staggered into the street, one hand clutching his unbuckled britches.

"Thieves!" he moaned.

With a halfhearted flourish, the Luminatii centurion drew his longsword. The steel flared brighter than the suns overhead. At a word, tongues of fire uncurled along the edge of the blade and the man stumbled forward, face twisted with righteous fury.

"Stop in the name of the Light!"

"Trelene's sugarplums, come on!"

Tric leaped into Chivalry's saddle, dragging Mia over the pommel like a sack of cursing potatoes. And with another sharp boot to the stallion's flanks, the pair galloped off in the direction of their certain doom.*

T he pair stopped off long enough to retrieve Tric's own stallion—a looming chestnut inexplicably named "Flowers"—before fleeing into the wastes. The Plumber's Bane had done its work, however, and pursuit by Last Hope's

---

* The Empire of Ashkah ruled the known world for approximately seven centuries; a period considered by learned scholars as a peerless age in the fields of science and the arts arcane. Ashkah was a society of sorcerers, whose bold ventures into the realms of magika—or werking, or whichever term you please—not only dwarfed the weaker thaumaturgical rites of the Liisian Magus Kings who followed them, but also changed the shape of reality itself.

Sadly, as is often the case when mortals go fiddling with fabrics woven by the gods, someone, or some*thing*, is eventually going to get their noses put out of joint. No mortal scholar is quite sure about the exact nature of Ashkah's fall. Many say their empire was scrubbed from the world by Aa himself. Others claim the werking of the Ashkah sorcerii caught the attentions of beings older than the gods—nameless monstrosities beyond the edge of universe and sanity, who gobbled the empire down like an inkfiend on a three-turn bender.

And then, there are others who say someone among the sorcerii simply fucked up.

Very, VERY badly.

garrison was short-lived and largely messy. Mia and Tric soon found themselves slowing to a brisk canter, no pursuers in sight.

The Whisperwastes, as they were called, were a desolation grimmer than any Mia had seen. The horizon was crusted like a beggar's lips, scoured by winds laden with voices just beyond hearing. The second sun kissing the horizon was usually the sign for Itreya's brutal winters to begin, but out here, the heat was still blistering. Mister Kindly was coiled in Mia's shadow, just as miserable as she. Propping a (stolen and paid-for) tricorn upon her head, Mia surveyed the horizon.

"I'd guess the churchmen nest on high," Tric ventured. "I suggest we start with those mountains to the north, then swing east. After that, we'll probably have been drained lifeless by dustwraiths or eaten by sand kraken, so our bones won't mind where they get shit out."

Mia cursed as Bastard gave a small buck. Her thighs ached from the saddle, her rump was preparing to wave the white flag. She pointed to a lonely digit of broken stone ten miles distant.

"There."

"All respect, Pale Daughter, but I doubt the greatest enclave of assassins in the known world would set up headquarters within smelling distance of Last Hope's pig farms."

"Agreed. But that's where I think we should set camp. Looks to be a spring there. And we'll have a good view of Last Hope from up top, and all the wastes around, I'd wager."

". . . I thought we were following my nose?"

"I only suggested that for the sake of whoever might be listening."

"Listening?"

"We agree this is a trial, aye? That the Red Church is testing us?"

"Aye," the boy nodded slow. "But that shouldn't come as any shock. Surely your Shahiid tested you in preparation for the trials we'll face?"

Mia jerked the reins as Bastard tried to turn back for the fifth time in as many minutes.

"Old Mercurio loved his testings," she nodded. "Never a moment that couldn't be some trial in disguise.* Thing is, he never gave me a test I couldn't

---

*Mercurio named these trials "treasure hunts," and though they varied in difficulty and danger to life and limb, they almost always began with Mia awakening with a mild slumberweed headache in unfamiliar surroundings. Once, after a lesson in the principles of magnetism, she'd awoken in the pitch-black of Godsgrave's sewers with

beat. And the Church shouldn't be any different. So what's the one clue we've been given? What's the only piece of this puzzle we have in common?"

". . . Last Hope."

"Exactly. I'm thinking the Church can't be self-sustaining. Even if they grow their own food, they'd need other supplies. I was poking around the *Beau*'s hold and I saw goods the inbreds in Last Hope would have no use for. I'm thinking the Church has a disciple there. Maybe watching for novices, but more important, to trek those goods back to their stronghold. So all we need to do is watch for a laden caravan heading out into the wastes. Then we follow it."

Tric looked the girl up and down, smiling faintly. "Wisdom, Pale Daughter."

"Have no fear, Don Tric. I won't let it go—"

The boy held up a hand, pulled Flowers to a sudden stop. He squinted at the badlands around them, nose wrinkled, sniffing the whispering desert air.

"What is it?" Mia's hand drifted to her gravebone dagger.

Tric shook his head, eyes closed as he inhaled.

"Never smelled the like before. Reminds me of . . . old leather and dea—"

Bastard snorted, rearing up. Mia clutched his saddle, cursing as the red sand exploded around them and a dozen tentacles burst from beneath the ground. Twenty feet long, studded with grasping, serrated hooks, they looked as dry as the innards of an inkfiend's needle.

Bastard whinnied in terror as one leathery appendage snaked around his foreleg, another cinching his throat in a hangman's grip. The stallion fought, snotting and bucking like a wild thing. Mia found herself airborne again, bounced over Bastard's head and tumbling toward the tentacles' owner, now dragging itself from the earth and opening a hideous beaked maw. The air rang with a chittering, guttural *hissssssssssssssssss*.

"Sand kraken!" Tric roared, a little needlessly.*

---

nothing but an iron hairpin and piece of chalk to help find her way out. After six months of lessons in the tongue of Old Ashkah, she'd awoken five miles into the Godsgrave necropolis with half a skin of water and directions to the exit written in Ashkahi script.

Of course, while Mercurio called them "treasure hunts," the only "treasure" to be found at the end of these exercises was "continued existence." Still, they did make for a singularly dedicated student.

---

*Though referred to by the few scholars mad enough to study them as "sand kraken," the apex predators of the Ashkahi wastes aren't *actually* cephalopods. They swim in sand as easily as their sea-bound "kin" swim in water, filtering oxygen from the earth through

Mia drew her gravebone dagger, lashing out at a tentacle whipping her way. Oily blood spurted, a chuddering roar shivering the earth as Mia tumbled between two more of the dreadful limbs, ducking a third and rolling up into a panting crouch. Mister Kindly unfurled from her shadow, peering at the horror and not-breathing a small, soft sigh.

"*. . . pretty . . .*"

Tric drew his scimitar, leaped from his stallion's back, and hacked at the tentacle clutching Bastard's leg. With the snapping whip of salted cord, the appendage split, another roar spilling from the beast, eyes wide as dinnerplates, dusty gills flaring. Its severed limb flailed about, spraying Tric with reeking ichor. Bastard whinnied again in terror, blood spilling from his neck where the tentacle was wrapped and squeezing.

"Let him go!" Mia shouted, stabbing at another tentacle.

"Back off!" Tric roared to her.

"Back off? Are you mad?"

"Are you?" Tric gestured at her dagger. "You plan on killing a sand kraken with that damned toothpick? Let it have the stallion!"

"To the 'byss with that! I just stole that fucking horse!"

Feinting low, Mia lashed out at another hooked limb, drawing a fresh gout of blood. A flailing backswing saw Tric splayed in the dust, cursing. Mia curled her fingers, wrapping a hasty handful of shadows around herself so she

---

specialized gills. They eat anything not possessed of an above-average running speed, and are renowned for temperaments most would describe as "uncooperative."

The undisputed expert in their study, Loresman Carlo Ribisi, theorized they're a kind of desert worm, mutated by magikal pollutants from the ruins of the Ashkahi Empire. Ribisi postulated the beasts are possessed of canine-level intelligence, and to prove his theorem, captured an infant sand kraken, brought it back to the Grand Collegium in Godsgrave, and attempted to train it in simple tasks.

Ribisi constructed stone mazes, filled them with earth, and set the beast (whom he named "Alfi" after a much-beloved familia pet) loose inside them. Alfi would be rewarded with food if he successfully traversed the labyrinth. Ribisi introduced more complex patterns as Alfi grew in size (six feet long at his last recorded measurement), also incorporating simple devices such as latches and doors to prove the beast's growing intelligence. Sadly, Alfi utilized this knowledge one nevernight in escaping his enclosure, murdering the better part of the zoology faculty, including a rather disappointed Ribisi, before he was dispatched by a cadre of baffled Luminatii.

Ordinances about the keeping of wildlife within college grounds were tightened considerably after this affair.

might avoid a similar blow. Those hooks looked vicious enough to gut a War Walker.*

Though inconvenienced by the little sacks of meat and their sharp sticks, the kraken seemed mostly intent on dragging its thoroughbred meal—who no doubt begrudged his theft now more than ever—below the sands. But as Mia pulled the darkness to her, the monstrosity spat a shuddering roar and exploded back out from the earth, limbs flailing. Almost as if it were angry at her.

Tric spat a mouthful of red sand and shouted warning, hacking at another limb. The shadow cloak seemed to do Mia no good—she was near blind beneath it, and the beast seemed to be able to see her regardless. And so she let it fall from her shoulders, dove toward the wailing horse, tumbling across the dust. She moved between the forest of hooks and flails, feeling the breeze of the almost-blows narrowly missing her face and throat, the whistling hiss of the tentacles in the air. There was no real fear in her amid that storm. Simply the sway and the feint, the slide and the roll. The dance she'd been taught by Mercurio. The dance she'd lived with almost every turn since her father took his long plunge from his short rope.

A dusty tumble, a backwards flip, skipping between tentacles like a child amid a dozen jump ropes. She glanced to the beast's open beak, snapping and snarling above Bastard's screams, the scrape of its bulk as it dragged itself farther from the sand. The smell of wet death and salted leather, dust scratching her lungs. A smile played on her lips as a thought seized her, and with a brief dash, a skipping leap off one and two and *three* of the flailing limbs, Mia hurled herself up onto Bastard's back.

---

* Though a cadre of ten can be found in Godsgrave, the mekwerk giants of the Iron Collegium are kept unfueled and unmanned, only to be operated in times of absolute crisis. Owing to Itreyan military might and the difficulties of assaulting Godsgrave by anything other than sea, the presence of the machines in the city is mostly ceremonial. In the last forty truedarks, Godsgrave's War Walkers have been activated precisely twice.

The first, during the overthrow of King Francisco XV—legionaries loyal to the monarchy attempted to storm the palace and rescue the king from his assailants when news of the uprising broke. The loyalist pilots (strictly a ceremonial position by that stage of the monarchy) surrendered once they discovered that Francisco and his entire family were already dead.

The second incident commenced with three bottles of mid-shelf goldwine and a drunken boast to a would-be paramour, segued into a stumbling crash into the sixth Rib (which broke at the base and collapsed into the sea), and ended with a swift trial and an even swifter crucifixion for the young man involved.

And the lass wasn't even that keen on him . . .

"Maw's teeth, she *is* mad . . . ," Tric breathed.

The horse bucked again, Mia clinging on with thighs and fingernails and sheer bloody-mindedness. Reaching into the saddlebags, she seized a heavy jar of bright red powder within. And with a sigh, she hauled it back and flung it into the kraken's mouth.

The jar shattered on the creature's beak, broken glass and fine red powder spraying deep into the horror's gullet. Mia rolled off Bastard's back to avoid another blow, scrabbling across the dust as an agonized shriek split the air. The kraken released the stallion, pawing, scratching, scraping at its mouth. Tric gave another halfhearted stab, but the beast had forgotten its quarry entirely, great eyes rolling as it flipped over and over, dragging its bulk back below the sand, howling like a dog who's just returned home from a hard turn's work to find another hound in his kennel, smoking his cigarillos and in bed with his wife.

Mia dragged herself to her feet, sand churning as the kraken burrowed away. Flipping the sweat-soaked bangs from her eyes, she grinned like a madwoman. Tric stood slack-jawed, bloody scimitar dangling from his hand, face caked in dust.

"What was that?" he breathed.

"Well, technically they're not cephalopods—"

"I mean what did you throw in its mouth?"

Mia shrugged. "A jar of Fat Daniio's widowmaker."

Tric blinked. Several times.

". . . You just thrashed a horror of the Whisperwastes with a jar of chili powder?"

Mia nodded. "Shame, really. It's good stuff. I only stole the one jar."

A moment of incredulous silence rang across the wastes, filled with the off-key song of maddening winds. And then the boy began laughing, a dimpled, bone-white grin gleaming in a filthy face. Wiping at his eyes, he flicked a sluice of dark blood from his blade and wandered off to fetch Flowers. Mia turned to her stolen stallion, pulling himself up from the sands, bloodied at his throat and forelegs. She spoke in calming tones, tongue caked in dust, hoping to still him.

"You all in one piece, boy?"

Mia approached slow, hand outstretched. The beast was shaken, but with a few turns' rest at their lookout, he'd be mending, and hopefully more kindly disposed to her now she'd saved his life. Mia smoothed his flanks with steady hands, reached into the saddlebags for her—

"Ow, *fuck!*"

Mia shrieked as the stallion bit her arm, hard enough to leave a bloody bruise. The horse threw back his head with what sounded an awful lot like snickering.* And tossing his mane, he began a limping canter back toward Last Hope, bloody hoofprints in his wake.

"Wait!" Mia cried. "Wait!"

"He *really* doesn't like you," Tric said.

"My thanks, Don Tric. When you're done singing your Ode to the Obvious, perhaps you'll do me the honor of riding down the horse escaping with all my bloody gear on his back?"

Tric grinned, vaulted onto Flowers's saddle, and galloped off in pursuit. Mia clutched her bruised arm, listening to the faint laughter of a cat who was not a cat echoing on the wind.

She spat into the dust, eyes on the fleeing stallion.

"*Bastard . . . ,*" she hissed.

Tric returned a half-hour later, a limping Bastard in tow. Reunited, he and Mia trekked overland to the thin spur of rock that'd serve as their lookout. They were on constant watch for disturbances beneath the sand, Tric sniffing the air like a bloodhound, but no more horrors reared any tentacles (or other appendages) to impede progress.

Bastard and Flowers were allowed to graze on the thin grass surrounding the spire—Flowers partook happily, while Bastard fixed Mia in the withering stare of a beast used to fresh oats for every meal, refusing to eat a thing. He tried to bite Mia twice more as she tied him up, so the girl made a show of patting Flowers (despite not really liking him much either) and gifted the chestnut with some sugar cubes from her saddlebags. The stolen stallion's only gift was the rudest hand gesture Mia could conjure.†

---

* If any horse born in the sight of Aa was actually *capable* of mocking laughter, it was Bastard.

† Known as "the knuckles," the gesture involves the raising of a fist with fore and baby finger extended as far as the first knuckle.

The gesture has origins at the Battle of the Scarlet Sands, where King Francisco I of Itreya, also known as "The Great Unifier," defeated the last Liisian Magus King, Lucius the Omnipotent.

After this defeat, it was presumed that Liisian resistance to Itreyan rule would falter. Itreyan occupation of its conquests was as ingenious as it was insidious—a small group of marrowborn Administratii would move into the power vacuum created by the destruction of the ruling class, and through coercion and bribery, establish a new local elite with ties to Itreya. Local sons would be sent to Godsgrave to be edu-

"Why do you call your horse Flowers?" Mia asked, as she and Tric prepared to climb.

". . . What's wrong with Flowers?"

"Well, most men name their horses something a little more . . . manly, is all."

"Legend or Prince or suchlike."

"I met a horse named Thunderhoof once." She raised a hand. "Light's truth."

"Seems a silly thing to me," the boy sniffed. "Giving out that kind of knowing for free."

"What do you mean?"

"Well, you call your horse Legend, you're letting people know you think you're some hero in a storybook. You call your horse Thunderhoof . . . Daughters, you might as well hang a sign about your neck saying, 'I have a peanut for a penis.' "

Mia smiled. "I'll take your word on that."

"It's like these fellows who name their swords 'Skullbane' or 'Souldrinker' or somesuch." Tric tied his saltlocks into a matted knot atop his head. "Tossers, all."

"If I were going to name my blade," Mia said thoughtfully, "I'd call it 'Fluffy.' "

Tric snorted with laughter. "Fluffy?"

" 'Byss, yes," the girl nodded. "Think of the terror you'd instill. Being

---

cated, Itreyan daughters would marry local men, wealth would flow into all the right pockets, and within a generation, the conquered would be wondering why they resisted in the first place.

Not so in Liis, gentlefriends.

After Lucius's death, a garrison of Luminatii was stationed in the Liisian capital, Elai, to oversee "assimilation." Things went well until a cadre of elite troops still loyal to Lucius's memory raided a banquet in the former Magus King's palace. The Itreyan elite and Luminatii garrison were captured, lined up by the loyalists, and, one by one, castrated with a red-hot blade.

The captives were then released, the elite forces barricading themselves inside the palace and awaiting inevitable retaliation. Lasting more than six months, the Siege of Elai became legend. It was said the loyalists roamed the palace battlements, holding aloft their fists with fore and baby finger extended as far as the first knuckle—a taunting gesture meant to remind the attacking Itreyans the rebels were still possessed of their . . . equipment, while the Itreyan's jewels had been fed to the rebels' dogs. Though the loyalists were eventually defeated, "the knuckles" has entered common use by many of the Republic's citizens: a taunting gesture intended to flaunt superiority over an unmanned opponent.

bested by a foe wielding a sword called Souldrinker . . . *that* you could live with. Imagine the shame of having the piss smacked out of you by a blade called Fluffy."

"Well, that's my point. Names speak to the namer as much as the named. Maybe I don't want folks knowing who I am. Maybe I like being underestimated."

The boy shrugged.

"Or maybe I just like flowers . . ."

Mia found herself smiling as the pair scaled the broken cliff face. Both climbed without pitons or rope—the kind of foolishness common among the young and seemingly immortal. Their lookout loomed a hundred feet high, and the pair were breathless when they reached the top. But, as Mia predicted, the spur offered a magnificent vantage; all the wastes spread out before them. Saan's red glare was merciless, and Mia wondered how brutal the heat would be during truelight, when all three suns burned the sky white.

"Good view," Tric nodded. "Anything sneezes in Last Hope, we'll ken it for certain."

Mia kicked a pebble off the cliff, watched it tumble into the void. She sat on a boulder, boot propped on the stone opposite in a pose the Dona Corvere would have shuddered to see. From her belt, she withdrew a thin silver box engraved with the crow and crossed swords of the Familia Corvere. Propping a cigarillo on her lips, she offered the box to Tric. The boy took it as he sat opposite, wrinkling his nose and squinting at the inscription on the back.

"*Neh diis lus'a, lus diis'a,*" he muttered. "My Liisian is woeful. Something about blood?"

"When all is blood, blood is all." Mia lit her cigarillo with her flintbox, breathed a contented sigh. "Familia saying."

"This is familia?" Tric thumbed the crest. "I'd have bet you'd stolen it."

"I don't strike you as the marrowborn type?"

"I'm not sure what type you strike me. But some snotty spine-hugger's child? Not at all."

"You need to work on your compliments, Don Tric."

The boy prodded her shadow with his boot, eyes unreadable. He glanced at the not-cat lurking near her shoulder. Mister Kindly stared back without a sound. When Tric spoke, it was with obvious trepidation.

"I've heard tell of your kind. Never met one before, though. Never thought to."

"My kind?"

"Darkin."

Mia exhaled gray, eyes narrowed. She reached out to Mister Kindly as if to pet him, fingers passing through him as if he were smoke. In all truth, there were few who'd seen her work her gift and lived to tell the tale. Folk of the Republic feared what they didn't understand, and hated what they feared. And yet this boy seemed more intrigued than afraid. Looking him up and down—this half-pint Dweymeri with his islander tattoos and mainlander's name—she realized he was an outsider too. And it briefly dawned on her, how glad she was to find herself in his company on this strange and dusty road.

"And what do you know about the darkin, Don Tric?"

"Folklore. Bullshit. You steal babies from their cribs and deflower virgins where you walk and other rot." The boy shrugged. "I heard tell darkin attacked the Basilica Grande a few years back. Killed a whole mess of Luminatii legionaries."

"Ah." Mia smiled around her smoke. "The Truedark Massacre."

"Probably more horseshit they cooked up to raise taxes or suchlike."

"Probably." Mia waved to her shadow. "Still, you don't seem unnerved by it."

"I knew a seer who could ken the future by rummaging in animal guts. I met an arkemist who could make fire from dust and kill a man just by breathing on him. Messing about with the dark seems just another kind of huckster thaumaturgy to me." He glanced up to the cloudless sky. "And I can't see much use for it in a place where the suns almost never set."

"*. . . the brighter the light, the deeper the shadows . . .*"

Tric looked to the not-cat, obviously surprised to hear it speak. He watched it carefully for a moment, as if it might sprout a few new heads or breathe black flame. With no show of multiple heads forthcoming, the boy turned his eyes back to Mia.

"Where do you get the gift from?" he asked. "Your ma? Your da?"

". . . I don't know where I got it. And I've never met another like myself to ask. My Shahiid said I was touched by the Mother. Whatever that means. He surely didn't seem to know."

The boy shrugged, ran his thumb over the sigil on the cigarillo box.

"If memory serves, Familia Corvere was involved in some trouble a few truedarks back. Something about kingmaking?"

"Never flinch. Never fear," Mia sighed. "And never, ever forget."

"So. The puzzle begins to make sense. The last daughter of a disgraced familia. Headed to the finest school of killers in all the Republic. Planning on settling scores after graduation?"

"You're not about to regale me with some wisdom on the futility of revenge, are you, Don Tric? Because I was just starting to like you."

"O, no," Tric smiled. "Vengeance I understand. But given the wrong you're set on righting, I'm fancying your targets are going to be tricky to hit?"

"One mark is already in the ledger." She patted her purse of teeth. "Three more to come."

"These walking corpses have names?"

"The first is Francesco Duomo."

". . . *The* Francesco Duomo? Grand cardinal of the Church of the Light?"

"That'd be him."

"'Byss and blood . . .'"

"The second is Marcus Remus. Justicus of the Luminatii Legion."

". . . And the third?"

Saan's light gleamed in Mia's eyes, wisps of long black hair caught at the edges of her mouth. The shadows around her swayed like oceans, rippling near Tric's toes. Twice as dark as they should have been. Almost as dark as her mood had become.

"Consul Julius Scaeva."

"Four Daughters," Tric breathed. "That's why you seek training at the Church."

Mia nodded. "A sharp knife might clip Duomo or Remus with a lot of luck. But it's not going to be some guttersnipe with a shiv that ends Scaeva. Not after the Massacre. He doesn't climb into bed without a cadre of Luminatii there to check between the sheets first."

"Thrice-elected consul of the Itreyan Senate," Tric sighed. "Master arkemist. The most powerful man in the entire Republic." The boy shook his head. "You know how to make it hard on yourself, Pale Daughter."

"O, aye. He's as dangerous as a sack of blackmark vipers," Mia nodded. "A right cunt and no mistake."

The boy raised his eyebrows, mouth slightly agape.

Mia met his stare, scowling. "What?"

". . . My mother said that's a filthy word," Tric frowned. "The filthiest. She told me never to say it. Especially in front of dona."

"O, really." The girl took another pull on her cigarillo, eyes narrowed. "And why's that?"

"I don't know." Tric found himself mumbling. "It's just what she said."

Mia shook her head, crooked bangs swaying before her eyes.

"You know, I've never understood that. How being named for a woman's nethers is somehow more grievous than any other insult. Seems to me calling someone after a man's privates is worse. I mean, what do you picture when you hear a fellow called a cock?"

Tric shrugged, befuddled at the strange turn in conversation.

"You imagine an oaf, don't you?" Mia continued. "Someone so full of wank there's no room for wits. A slow-minded bastard who struts about full of spunk and piss, completely ignorant of how he looks to others."

An exhalation of clove-sweet gray into the air between them.

"Cock is just another word for 'fool.' But you call someone a cunt, well . . ." The girl smiled. "You're implying a sense of malice there. An intent. Malevolent and self-aware. Don't think I name Consul Scaeva a cunt to gift him insult. Cunts have brains, Don Tric. Cunts have teeth. Someone calls you a cunt, you take it as a compliment. As a sign that folk believe you're not to be lightly fucked with." A shrug. "I think they call that irony."

Mia sniffed, staring at the wastes laid out below them.

"Truth is, there's no difference between your nethers and mine. Aside from the obvious, of course. But one doesn't carry any more weight than the other. Why should what's between my legs be considered any smarter or stupider, any worse or better? It's all just meat, Don Tric. In the end, it's all just food for worms. Just like Duomo, Remus, and Scaeva will be."

One last drag, long and deep, as if drawing the very life from her smoke.

"But I'd still rather be called a cunt than a cock any turn."

The girl sighed gray, crushed her cigarillo out with her boot heel.

Spat into the wind.

And just like that, young Tric was in love.

DUST

Mia's mother had given her a puzzle box when she was five years old—a wooden cube with shifting faces that, when correctly aligned, would reveal the true gift inside. It was the best Great Tithe gift she could ever remember receiving.*

---

* Great Tithe marked the (approximate) halfway point between truedarks, and was one of Aa's holy feasts, traditionally marked by gift-giving among loved ones. The first

Mia had thought it cruel at the time. When all the other marrowborn children were playing with new dolls or wooden swords, she was stuck with this wretched box that simply refused to open. She bashed it against the wall, to no avail. She cried to her father it wasn't fair, and he simply smiled. And when Mia stomped before the Dona Corvere and demanded to know why she hadn't simply given her a pretty ribbon for her hair or a new dress instead of this wretched thing, her mother had knelt and looked her daughter in the eye.

"Your mind will serve you better than any trinket under the suns," she'd said. "It is a weapon, Mia. And like any weapon, you need practice to be any good at wielding it."

"But mother—"

"No, Mia Corvere. Beauty you're born with, but brains you earn."

So Mia had taken the box and sat with it. Scowled at it. Stared at it until she dreamed about it. Twisting and turning and cursing it by all the swears she'd heard her father ever use. But after two months of frustration, she twisted a final piece and heard a wonderful sound.

Click.

The lid opened, and inside, she'd found a brooch—a crow with tiny amber eyes. The sigil of her Familia. The crow of Corvere. She wore it to mornmeal the next turn. Her mother had smiled and never said a word. She'd kept the box; in all the Great Tithes since, all the puzzles her parents had given her thereafter, it remained her favorite. After her father's execution and mother's arrest, she'd left the box and something of the little girl who loved it behind.

But the brooch itself, she'd brought with her. That, and her gift for puzzles.

She'd woken beneath a pile of refuse in a lonely alley, somewhere in the Godsgrave backstreets. As she pawed the sleep from her eyes, her stomach had growled. She knew the consul's men might still be chasing her—that he might send more if

---

Great Tithe was said to have been the turn Aa gifted his daughters dominion over the elements. To Tsana, his firstborn, he gave the rule of fire. To Keph, the earth. To Trelene, the oceans. Nalipse, the storm. In return, the daughters gave their father their love and obedience.

It's said Niah gave her daughters nothing, for the Maw has naught inside to give. But these are falsehoods spat by ministers of Aa's church.

To Keph, Niah gave dreams, to keep her company in her eternal slumber. To Trelene, she gave enigma; the deep dark of the waters beyond the sunlight. To Nalipse, she gave calm; the peace in the storm's eye. And to Tsana? Her firstborn who so despised her?

To Tsana, Goddess of Fire, Niah gave hunger.

Hunger unending.

he knew they'd failed to drown her. She had nowhere to stay. No friends. No money. No food.

She was aching and alone and afraid. She missed her mother. Little Jonnen, her baby brother. Her soft bed and her warm clothes and her cat. The memory of him lying broken on the floor flooded her eyes with tears, the thought of the man who'd killed him filled her heart with hate.

"Poor Captain Puddles . . ."

". . . meow . . . ," said a voice.

The little girl glanced up at the sound, dragging dark hair from damp lashes. And there on the cobbles, amid the weeds and the rot and the filth, she saw a cat.

Not her cat, to be sure. O, it was black as truedark, just like the good captain had been. But it was thin as paper and translucent, as if someone had cut a cat's shape out of shadowstuff itself. And despite the fact that he now wore a shape instead of no shape at all, she still recognized her friend. The one who'd helped her when no one else in the world could.

"Mister Kindly?" she asked.

". . . meow . . . ," he said.

She reached toward the creature as if to pet him, but her hand passed through him as it might a wisp of smoke. Looking into his darkness, she felt that same sensation—her fear leeching away like poison from a wound, leaving her hard and unafraid. And she realized though she had no brother, no mother, no father, no familia, she wasn't entirely alone.

"All right," she nodded.

Food first. She had no money, but she had her stiletto, and her brooch pinned to her (increasingly disheveled) dress. A gravebone blade would be worth a fortune, but she was loathe to give up her only weapon. However, she knew there were folk who'd give her money for the jewelry. Coin could buy her food and a room to lay low so she could think about what to do next. Ten years old, her mother in chains, her—

". . . meow . . . ," said Mister Kindly.

"Right," she nodded. "One puzzle at a time."

She didn't even know what part of Godsgrave she was in. She'd spent her entire life in the Spine. But her father had kept maps of the city in his study, hung on the walls with his swords and his wreaths, and she remembered the layout of the metropolis roughly enough. She was best-off staying away from the marrowborn quarter, hiding as low and deep as she could until she was sure the consul's men had given up the chase.

As she stood, Mister Kindly flowed like water into the black around her feet, her *shadow darkening as he did so.* Though she knew she should probably be frightened at the sight, instead Mia took a deep breath, combed her fingers through her hair, and stepped out of the alley, right into a sloppy pile of what she hoped was mud.*

Cursing in a most improper fashion and scraping her soles on the cobbles, she saw people of all kinds pushing along the cramped thoroughfare. Fair-haired Vaanians and blue-eyed Itreyans and tall Dweymeri with leviathan ink tattoos, dozens of slaves with arkemical marks of sale burned on their cheeks. But Mia soon realized the folk were mostly Liisian; olive of skin and dark of hair. Storefronts were marked with a sigil Mia recognized from her lessons with Brother Crassus and truedark masses inside the great cathedrals—three burning circles, intertwined. A mirror of the three suns that roamed the skies overhead. The eyes of Aa himself.

The Trinity.†

Mia realized she must be in the Liisian quarter—Little Liis, she'd heard it called. Squalid and overcrowded, poverty written in crumbling stonework. The canal waters ran high here, consuming the lower floors of the buildings around. Palazzos of unadorned brick, rusting to a dark brown at the water's edge. Above the water's reek, she could smell spiced breads and clove smoke, hear songs in a language she couldn't quite comprehend but almost recognized.

---

* It was not mud. Alas.

† Naturally, the number three holds great significance in Itreya, and worship of the Everseeing is considered the official religion of the Republic. However, it's interesting to note that even in other regions where worship of Aa was not as prevalent, the number three still holds no end of cultural significance.

Take Liis, for example.

In the turns before the Itreyan Colleges of Iron marched their War Walkers across Liis and conquered it in the name of the Great Unifier, King Francisco I, the Liisians had their own pantheon of worship—a trinity consisting of the Father, the Mother, and the Child. Children born on the third turning of the month were seen as blessed. Thirdborn children of thirdborn children of thirdborn children were inducted into the Liisian clergy without exception. And finally, the Liisian kings were said to have each possessed three testicles—a sign of their divine right to rule.

Though initially disputed by jealous fellow rulers, this claim was ultimately proved by King Francisco I. Upon capturing the last Liisian king, Lucius the Omnipotent, at the Battle of the Scarlet Sands, the Great Unifier removed the monarch's scrotum with his own dagger and found three aggots staring sadly back at him from within the pouch.

Though grateful credence had been given to the legend, Lucius the Omnipotent was less than pleased with Francisco's method of verification.

Albeit briefly.

She stepped into the flow of people, jostled and bumped. The crush might have been frightening for a girl who'd grown her whole life in the shelter of the Spine, but again, Mia found herself unafraid. She was pushed along until the street spilled into a broad piazza, lined on all sides by stalls and stores. Climbing up a pile of empty crates, Mia realized she was in the marketplace, the air filled with the bustle and murmur of hundreds of folk, the harsh glare of two suns burning overhead, and the most extraordinary smell she'd ever encountered in her life.

Mia couldn't describe it as a stench—although a stench was certainly wrapped up in the incomparable perfume. Little Liis sat on the southwest of Godsgrave, below the Hips near the Bay of Butchers, and was skirted by Godsgrave's abattoirs and various sewer outflows. The bay's reek has been compared to a burst belly covered in horseshit and burning human hair, three turns rotten in the heat of truelight.

However, masking this stench was the perfume of the marketplace itself. The toast-warm aroma of fresh-baked breads, tarts, and sugardoughs. The buoyant scents of rooftop gardens. Mia found herself half-drooling, half-sickened—part of her wishing to eat everything in sight, the other part wondering if she'd ever eat again.

Thumbing the brooch at her breast, she looked about for a vendor. There were plenty of trinket stalls, but most looked like two-copper affairs. On the market's edge, she saw an old building, crouched like a beggar at the corner of two crooked roads. A sign swung on a squeaking hinge above its sad little door.

MERCURIO'S CURIOS—ODDITIES, RARITIES & The FYNEST AN-TIQUITIES.

A door placard informed her, "No time-wasters, rabble, or religious sorts welcome."

She squinted across the way, looked down at the too-dark shadow around her feet. "Well?" she asked.

". . . meow . . ." said Mister Kindly.

"I think so too."

And Mia hopped off her crates, and headed toward the store.

Blood gushed across the wagon's floor, thick and crusted on Mia's hands. Dust clawing her eyes, rising in a storm from the camels' hooves. There was no need for Mia to whip them; the beasts were running just fine on their own. And so she concentrated on quieting the headache splitting her brow and stilling the now-familiar urge to stab Tric repeatedly in the face.

The boy was stood on the wagon's tail, banging away at what might have been a xylophone, if xylophones were crafted from iron tubes and made a noise like donkeys rutting in a belfry. The boy was drenched in blood and dust too; gritted teeth of perfect white in a mask of filthy red and shitty tattoos.

"Tric, shut that racket up!" Mia roared.

"It scares off the krakens!"

"Scares off the krakens . . . ," moaned Naev, from a puddle of her own blood.

"No, it bloody doesn't!" yelled Mia.

She glanced over her shoulder, just in case the ungodly racket had indeed scared off the monstrosities chasing them, but alas, the four runnels of churning earth were still in close pursuit.

Bastard galloped alongside the wagon, tethered by his reins. The stallion was glaring at Mia, occasionally spitting an accusing whinny in her direction.

"O, shut up!" she yelled at the horse.

". . . he really does not like you . . . ," whispered Mister Kindly.

"You're not helping!"

". . . and what would help . . . ?"

"Explain to me how we got into this stew!"

The cat who was shadows tilted his head, as if thinking. A chuddering growl from the behemoths behind shivered the wagon in its rivets, but the bouncing across the dunes moved him not at all. He looked at the rolling Whisperwastes, the jagged horizon drawing nearer, his mistress above him. And he spoke with the voice of one unveiling an ugly but necessary truth.

". . . it is basically your fault . . ."

Two weeks had passed atop their lookout, and both Mia and Tric had begun losing faith in her theory. The first turn of Septimus was fast approaching— if they didn't cross the Church threshold before then, there'd be no chance to be accepted among this year's flock. They watched in turns, one climbing the spire to relieve the other, pausing to chat awhile between shifts. They'd swap tales of their time as apprentices, or tricks of the trade. Mia seldom mentioned her familia. Tric never mentioned his. And yet he always lingered—even if he had nothing to say, he'd simply sit and watch her read for a spell.

Bastard had eventually taken to eating the grass around the spire's roots, though he did it with obvious disdain. Mia often caught him looking at her like he wanted to eat her instead.

Around nevernight's falling on what was probably the thirteenth turn, she and Tric were sitting atop the stone, staring over the wastes. Mia was down to her last forty-two cigarillos and already wishing she'd brought more.

"I tried to quit once," she said, peering at Black Dorian's* watermark on the fine, hand-rolled smoke. "Lasted fourteen turns."

"Missed it too much?"

"Withdrawals. Mercurio made me take it back up. He said me acting like a bear with a hangover three turns a month was bad enough."

"Three turns a . . . ah."

"Ah."

". . . You're not that bad are you?"

"You can tell me in a turn or so," she chuckled.

"I had no sisters." Tric began retying his hair, a habit Mia had noted he indulged when uncomfortable. "I am unversed in . . ."—vague handwaving—". . . women's ways."

"Well then, you're in for a treat."

He stopped in mid-knot, looking at Mia strangely. "You are unlike any girl I have ev—"

The boy fell silent, slipped off his rock into a crouch. He took out an old captain's spyglass, engraved with the same three seadrakes as his ring, and pressed it to his eye.

Mia crouched next to him, peering toward Last Hope. "See something?"

"Caravan."

"Fortune hunters?"†

---

* A purveyor of top-shelf Itreyan smoke, fine brandy, and the most extensive collection of naughty lithographs in all of Godsgrave.

† A group had set off into the Whisperwastes some three turns prior, leading a long train of unladen horses. Given the weapons on display, Mia picked them for tombraiders, but in fact, they were pilgrims from a fringe-dwelling faction known as Kephians. The group had been convinced by their leader—a man named Emiliano Rostas—that the time of great Keph's awakening was at hand, that the Earth Goddess would soon rise from her slumber and bring the world to an end. Only those faithful gathered at the Navel of the Goddess (which Emiliano supposed was to be found in the Ashkahi desert) would be saved.

When it was pointed out that the journey might be more hazardous than just sitting around waiting for Keph to show up, Emiliano replied that he and his followers were beloved of the Earth Goddess, and she would allow no harm to befall them.

One can only presume the dustwraiths that devoured their corpses didn't receive the goddess's memorandum.

"Don't think so." Tric spat on the spyglass lens, rubbed away the dust. "Two laden wagons. Four men. Camels leading, so they're in for a deep trek."

"I've never ridden a camel before."

"Nor me. I hear they stink. And spit."

"Still sounds a step up from Bastard."

"A whitedrake wearing a saddle is a step up from Bastard."

They watched the caravan roll across the blood-red sand for an hour, pondering what lay ahead if the group were indeed from the Red Church. And when the caravan was almost a dot on the horizon, the pair clambered down from their throne, and followed across the wastes.

They kept distance at first, Flowers and Bastard plodding slowly. Mia was sure she could hear a strange tune on the wind. Not the maddening whispers—which she'd still not become accustomed to—but something like off-key bells, stacked all atop one another and pounded with an iron flail. She'd no idea what to make of it.

The pair weren't outfitted for a trek into the deep desert, and they resolved to ride up to the caravan when it stopped to rest. There was no creeping up on it—the stone outcroppings and broken monuments studding the wastes weren't enough to conceal approach, and Mia's cloak of shadows was only big enough for one. Besides, she reasoned, if these *were* servants of the Lady of Blessed Murder, they may not take kindly to being snuck up on as they stopped to piss.

Sadly, the caravan folk seemed happy enough to go as they went, so to speak. The pair were gaining ground, but after two full turns in the saddle, with Bastard nipping her legs and occasionally trying to buck her into the dust, Mia could take no more. Pulling the stallion up near a circle of weathered statues, she didn't so much lose her temper as drop-kick it across the sand.

"Stop, stop," she spat. "Fuck this. Right in the earhole."

Tric raised an eyebrow. "What?"

"There's more bruises in my britches than there is bottom. It needs a breather."

"Are we playing alliteration and you didn't tell me, or . . ."

"Fuck off. I need a rest."

Tric frowned at the horizon. "We might lose them."

"They're led by a dozen camels, Tric. A noseless dog could follow this trail of shit in the middle of truedark. If they suddenly start trekking faster than a forty-a-turn smoker with an armload of drunken prostitutes, I think we can find them again."

"What do drunken prostit—"

"I don't need a foot massage. Don't want a back rub. I just want to sit on something that isn't moving for an hour." Mia slipped off the saddle with a wince, waved her stiletto at Bastard. "And if you bite me again, I swear to the Maw I'll make you a gelding."

Bastard snorted, Mia sinking down against a smooth stone with a sigh. She pressed one hand to her cramping innards, rubbed her backside with the other.

"I can help with that," Tric offered. "If you need it."

The boy grinned as Mia raised the knuckles. Tethering the horses, he sat opposite Mia as she fished a cigarillo from her case, struck her flintbox, and breathed deep.

"Your Shahiid was a wise man," Tric said.

"What makes you say that?"

"Three turns of this a month is plenty."

The girl scoffed, kicked a toeful of dust at him as he rolled away, laughing. Pulling her tricorn down over her eyes, she rested her head against the rock, cigarillo hanging from her lips. Tric watched her, peering about for some sign of Mister Kindly. Finding none.

He looked around them, studying the stonework. The statues were all similar; vaguely humanoid figures with feline heads, blasted by winds and time. Standing up on the outcropping, he squinted through his spyglass, watching the camel caravan trekking away. Mia was right—they moved at a plodding pace, and even with a few hours' rest, they'd make up the lost ground. He wasn't as grass-green around horses as Mia was, but after two turns saddlebound, he was aching in a few of the wrong places. And so sitting in the shade for a spell, he tried his best not to watch her as she slept.

He only closed his eyes for a second.

"Naev counsels him to be silent."

A slurred whisper in his ear, sharp as the blade against his throat. Tric opened his eyes, smelled leather, steel, something rank he supposed might be camel. A woman's voice, thick with spittle, accent he couldn't place. Behind him.

Tric said not a word.

"Why does he follow Naev?"

Tric glanced around, saw Bastard and Flowers still tied up. Footprints in the dust. No sign of Mia. The knife pressed harder against his throat.

"Speak."

"You told me to be silent," he whispered.

"Clever boy." A smile behind the words. "Too clever?"

Tric reached down to his belt, wincing as the blade twitched. Slowly, slowly, he produced a small wooden box, shook it softly, the faint rattle of teeth therein.

"My tithe," he said. "For the Maw."

The box was snatched from his hand. "Maw's dead."

"O, Goddess, not again—"

"She's playing with you, Don Tric."

Tric smiled to hear Mia's voice, grinned as the knifewoman hissed in surprise.

"I've a better game we can play, though," Mia said brightly. "It's called drop your blade and let him go before I cut your hands off."

"Naev will slit his throat."

"Then your head will join your fingers on the sand, Mi Dona."

Tric wondered if Mia was bluffing. Wondered what it would be like to feel the blade swish from one ear to the other. To die before he'd even begun. The pressure at his neck eased, and he flinched as something small and sharp nicked his skin.

"Ow."

Dark stars collided in his eyes, the taste of dusty flowers on his tongue. He rolled aside, blinking, only dimly aware of the struggle behind him. Whispering blades slicing the air, feet scuffing across blood-red sand. He glimpsed their attacker through blurring eyes—a small, wiry woman, face veiled, wrapped in cloth the color of desert sand. Carrying two curved, double-edged knives and dancing like someone who knew the steps.

Tric pawed the scrape on his neck, fingertips wet. He tried to stand but couldn't, staring at his hand as his brain caught up. His mind was his own, but his body . . .

"Poisoned . . . ," he breathed.

Mia and the stranger were circling each other, blades clutched in knife-fighter grips. They moved like first-time lovers—hesitant at first, drifting closer until finally they fell into each other's arms, fists and elbows and knees, block and counters and strikes. The sigh of steel in the air. The wet percussion of flesh and bone. Having never really seen her matched against a human opponent, Tric slowly realized Mia was no slouch with a blade—well honed and seemingly fearless. She fought left-handed, her fighting style unorthodox, moving swift. But for all Mia's skill, the thin woman seemed her match. Her every strike was foiled. Every advance countered.

After a few minutes of spectating, the feeling was returning to Tric's feet.

Mia was panting with exertion, crow-black hair clinging to her skin like weed. The stranger wasn't pressing the attack; simply defending silently. Mia was circling, trying to get the sun behind her, but her foe was clever enough to avoid getting Saan in her eyes. And so at last, with a small sigh as if admitting defeat, Mia moved her shadow so the stranger would be ankle-deep in it anyway.

The woman hissed in alarm, trying to sidestep, but the shadows moved quick as silver. Tric watched her fall still, as if her feet were glued to the spot. Mia stepped up and struck at the woman's throat, blade whistling as it came. But instead of dying, the stranger tangled up Mia's forearm, twisted her knife free, and flipped the girl onto her bruised backside, swift as a just soul flying to the Hearth.*

Mia's blade quivered in the sand between Tric's legs, two inches shy of a very unhappy accident. The boy blinked at the gravebone, trying to focus. He felt as if he should give it back—that seemed important—but the warmth at his neck bid him sit awhile longer.

Mia rolled to her feet, red-faced with fury. Snatching the knife from the sand, she turned back to the woman, teeth bared in a snarl.

"Let's try that again, shall we?" the girl wheezed.

"Darkin," said the strange woman, only slightly out of breath. "Darkin fool."

". . . What?"

"She calls the Dark here? In the deep wastes?"

". . . Who are you?"

"Naev," she slurred. "Only Naev."

"That's an Ashkahi word. It means 'nothing.'"

"A learned fool, then."

Mia motioned to Tric. "What did you do to my friend?"

---

*The Hearth—a fire, eternally stoked by the goddess Tsana within the belly of the slumbering Earth Goddess, Keph. The blaze attracts the righteous spirits of the dead, and grows brighter and hotter with each soul that enters the afterlife. Itreyans believe the numbers of the dead will one turning be so vast the fire will wake Keph and the world will end.

Wicked souls are denied a place by the Hearth, left to wander in the cold to be consumed by Niah. Sometimes, these wicked souls are sent back to the living world by the goddess to plague the righteous and the just. Called the "Hearthless," they are common figures in folklore, lurking in abandoned tombs or sites of terrible evil, abducting babies and deflowering virgins and causing unjust and illogical increases to taxation.

"Ink." The woman displayed a barbed ring on her finger. "A small dose."*

"Why did you attack us?"

"If Naev had attacked her, the sands would be redder. Naev asked why they followed her. And now Naev knows. Naev wonders at the girl's skill. And now Naev sees." The veiled woman looked back and forth between them, made a slurping sound. "Sees a pair of fools."

Tric rose on wobbly feet, leaning against the stone at his back. His head was clearing, anger replacing the haze. He drew his scimitar and glared at the three little women blurred before him, his pride stung to bleeding.

"Who are you calling fool, shorty?"

The woman glanced in his direction. "The boy whose throat Naev could have cut."

"You snuck on me while I was sleeping."

"The boy who sleeps when he should be watching."

"How about you watch while I hand you your—"

"Tric," Mia said. "Calm down."

"Mia, this skinny streak of shit had a *knife* to my throat."

"She's testing you. Testing us. Everything she says and does. Look at her."

Naev still held Mia's gaze, eyes like black lamps burning in her skull. Mia had seen a stare like that before—the stare of a person who'd looked the end in the face so many times she considered death a friend. Old Mercurio had the same look in his eyes. And at last she knew the stranger for what she was.

The moment was nothing like she'd practiced in the mirror. And yet Mia still felt a sense of relief as she took the purse of teeth from her belt and tossed it to the thin woman. As if six years had been lifted from her chest.

"My tithe," she said. "For the Maw."

---

* Distilled from the defense mechanism of deep-sea leviathans, ink is a hallucinogenic sedative. Injection of the drug induces feelings of well-being and loss of muscle control (in the wild, leviathan use their ink to flee predators—a faceful of the stuff usually makes even the hungriest whitedrake cease caring about mornmeal for a time). Long-term users, however, suffer a loss of empathy, and in cases of severe overuse, complete detachment from reality.

Francisco XV, last king of Itreya, was an infamous inkfiend. Under the influence of his addiction even during the uprising that dethroned him, Francisco XV was reportedly thoroughly amused as his personal guard declared him traitor to the people. His queen, Isabella, also an addict, was said to have laughed uproariously as Francisco was hacked to pieces in his own throne room.

Presumably she stopped the gigglefits when the Republicans turned their blades on her and her children.

The woman hefted the bag in her hand. "Naev has no need of it."

"But you're from the Red Church . . ."

"It is Naev's honor to serve in the House of Our Lady of Blessed Murder, yes. For the next few minutes at least."

"Few minutes? What do you—"

The ground beneath them trembled. A faint tremor at first, felt at the small of her back. Rising every second.

". . . Is that what I think it is?" Tric asked.

"Kraken," Naev sighed. "They hear when she calls the Dark. A fool, as I said."

Mia and Tric glanced at each other, spoke simultaneously. "O, shit . . ."

"Didn't you know that?" Tric asked.

"Four Daughters, how was I supposed to know that? I've never been to Ashkah!"

"The kraken who attacked us before lost its bottle when you did your cloaky thing!"

"'Cloaky thing'? Are you five years old?"

"Well, whatever it's called, maybe you should stop it?" Tric pointed to the shadows around Naev's feet. "Before it brings more?"

Mia's shadow slithered back across the dust, took up its regular shape again. She kept a wary eye on Naev, but the woman simply sheathed her blade, head tilted.

"There are two," she slurped. "Very large."

"What do we do?" Mia asked.

"Run?" Naev shrugged. "Die?"

"Running sounds grand to me. Tric?"

Tric was already on Flowers's back, the horse rearing to go. "Waiting on you, now."

Mia vaulted into the saddle, offered a hand to the thin woman. "Ride with me."

Naev hesitated a moment, tilting her head and fixing Mia in that black stare.

"Look, you're welcome to stay here if you like . . ."

Naev stepped closer and the ground trembled. Bastard raised up on his hind legs, kicking at the air. Mia glanced behind to see a trail of churning earth approaching—as if something massive swum beneath the sand.

Right toward them.

As the stallion set his hooves back on the ground, she called the shadows again, fixing him in place long enough for Naev to scramble up behind her. A bellowing roar sounded under the earth, as if the *things* were also answering her summons. As Naev put her arms around Mia's waist, she caught a whiff of spice and smoke. Something rotten beneath.

"She is making them angry," the woman said.

"Let's go!" Tric shouted.

Mia released Bastard's hooves and kicked hard, the stallion bolting into a fast gallop. The ground behind exploded, tentacles bursting from the sand and cracking like hooked bullwhips. Mia heard a gut-watering bellow, glimpsed a beak that could swallow Bastard whole. She saw a second runnel rumbling toward them from the west. Thundering hooves and roars filled her ears.

"Two of them, just like you said!" Mia yelled.

The veiled woman pointed north. "Ride for the wagons. We have ironsong to keep the kraken at bay."

"What's ironsong?"

"Ride!"

And so they did. A furious gallop over an ocean of blood-red sand. Glancing behind, she saw the two runnels converging, closing swift. She wondered how the beasts were tracking her. How they knew it was *her* who'd called the Dark. A tentacle broke the surface, two stories tall, set with hooks of blackened bone. Angry roars filled the air as it slammed back down to earth.

Dust whipping her eyes. Bastard snorting beneath her, hoof beats thudding in her chest. Mia held the reins hard, riding harder, grateful that though the stallion hated her like poison, he seemed to hate the thought of being eaten even more.

"Look out!" cried Tric.

Mia looked ahead, saw another runnel approaching from the north. Bigger, moving faster, shaking the earth beneath her. Flowers let out a terrified whinny.

"It seems there are three," Naev said. "Apologies . . ."

Tentacles unfurled from the ground like the petals of some murderous flower. Mia looked into the beast's maw, all snapping beak and hooked bone. As Flowers cut east to avoid the behemoth, Bastard finally came to the realization that he'd run much faster without two riders on his back. And so he started bucking.

Mia had the benefit of stirrups. Reins. A saddle. But Naev was riding on Bastard's hindparts with nothing but Mia's waist to keep her anchored. Bastard bucked again, whipping them about like rag dolls. And without a whisper, Naev sailed off the horse's back.

Mia cut east to follow Tric, roaring at the boy over the chaos.

"We lost Naev!"

The Dweymeri glanced over his shoulder. "Maybe they'll stop to eat her?"

"We have to go back!"

"When did you grow altruism? It's suicide to go back there!"

"It's not just altruism, you knob, I gave her my tithe!"

"O, shit," Tric felt about his waist. "She took mine, too!"

"You get Naev," she decided. "I'll distract them!"

"*. . . mia . . . ,*" said the cat in her shadow. "*. . . this is foolish . . .*"

"We have to save her!"

"*. . . the boy's stallion will not take him back there . . .*"

"Because he's afraid! And you can fix that!"

"*. . . if i drink him, i cannot drink you . . .*"

"I'll deal with my own fear! You just deal with Flowers!"

A hollow sigh.

"*. . . as it please you . . .*"

Red earth, torn and wounded, shaking beneath them. Dust in her eyes. Heart in her throat. She felt Mister Kindly flit across the sand and coil inside Flower's shadow, feasting on the stallion's terror. She felt her own rise up in a flood—an ice-cold swell in her belly, so long forgotten she was almost overcome. So many years since she'd had to face it. So many years with Mister Kindly beside her, drinking every drop so she could always be brave.

Fear.

Mia jerked on the reins, bringing Bastard to a halt. The stallion snorted but obeyed the steel in his mouth, stamping and snotting. Bringing him about, Mia saw Naev was on her feet, clutching her ribs as she ran across the churning sand.

"Tric, go!" Mia roared. "I'll meet you at the wagon!"

Tric still looked a touch befuddled from the ink. But he nodded, charging back toward the fallen woman and the approaching kraken. Flowers ran fast as a hurricane toward the monstrosity, completely fearless with the eyeless cat clinging to his shadow.

The first kraken erupted behind Naev, tentacles the size of longboats cutting the air. The thin woman rolled and swayed, slipping between a half-dozen blows. Sadly, it was the seventh that caught her—hooks tearing her chest and gut as the tentacle snatched her up. And even in that awful grip, the woman refused to cry out, drawing her blade and hacking at the limb instead.

Terror filled Mia's veins, fingertips tingling, eyes wide. The sensation was so unfamiliar, it was all she could do not to sink beneath it. Yet the fear of failing was stronger than the thought of dying in a kraken's arms, memories of her mother's words on her father's hanging turn still carved in her bones. And so she reached inside herself, and did what had to be done.

She wrapped her shadow about herself, fading from view on the stallion's back. The kraken holding Naev paused, tremors running its length. And with a howl that shivered her bones, the beast dropped its prey onto the sand, and turned toward Mia with its two cousins swimming fast behind.

The girl turned and rode for her life.

Teeth gritted, glancing over her shoulder as massive shapes breached the earth, diving back below like seadrakes on the hunt. Beyond the horrors, she saw Tric at full gallop, snatching Naev up and dragging the wounded woman over his pommel. Naev was drenched in blood, but Mia could see she was still moving. Still alive.

She turned Bastard north, galloping toward the caravan. The churchmen were no fools—their camel train was already tearing away across the dust. The kraken kept pace with Bastard, one slamming into the sand just thirty feet behind, the stallion stumbling as the ground shuddered. Great roars and the hiss of their bodies piercing the earth filled her ears. Wondering how they could sense her, Mia rode toward a stretch of rocky badlands, praying the ground was something approaching solid.

About forty eroded stone spires thrust up through the desert's face; a small garden of rock in the endless nothing. Throwing aside her shadowcloak, Mia wove between them, heard frustrated roars behind. She gained a short lead, galloping out the other side as the kraken circled around. Slick with sweat. Heart pounding. She was closing on the camel train, inch by inch, foot by foot. Tric had reached it, one of the wagonmen reaching for Naev's bloody body, another manning a pivot-mounted crossbow loaded with bolts as big as broom handles.

She could hear that same metallic song on the wind—realized some strange contraption was strapped to the rear wagon beside the crossbow. It looked like a large xylophone made from iron pipes. One of the wagonmen was hitting it like it had insulted his mother, filling the air with noise.

Ironsong, she realized.

But beneath the cacophony, she could hear the kraken behind, the earth being torn apart by horrors big as houses. Her thighs ached, muscles groaned, and she rode for all she was worth. The fear was swelling in her—a living, breathing thing, clawing at her insides and clouding thought and sight. Hand shaking, lips quivering, please Mother, take it away . . .

At last she drew alongside the rearmost wagon, wincing at the racket. Tric was yelling, holding out his hand. Her heart was thundering in her breast. Teeth chattering in her skull. And with Bastard's reins in her fist, she drew herself up on unsteady legs and leapt toward him.

The boy caught her, pulled her against his chest, hard as mahogany and drenched in blood. Shaking in his arms, she looked up into hazel eyes, noted the way he was staring at her—relief and admiration and something yet besides. Something . . .

She felt Mister Kindly slink back into her shadow, overwhelmed for a moment by the terror in her veins. And then he drank, and sighed, and nothing of it remained but fading memory. Herself again. Strong again. Needing no one. Needing *nothing*.

Muttering thanks, she pushed herself from Tric's grip and stooped to tie Bastard to the wagon's flank. Tric knelt beside Naev's bleeding body to check if she still lived. The churchman in the pilot's chair roared over the xylophone.

"Black Mother, what did you—"

A tentacle burst from the earth in front of them, whistling as it came. It tore through the driver's midriff, ripping him and one of his fellows clean in half, guts and blood spraying as the wagon roofs were torn away like paper. Mia dove to the deck, hooks sweeping mere inches over her head as the wagon rocked sideways, Tric roaring and Bastard screaming and the newly arrived kraken bellowing in fury. The crossbow and its marksmen were smashed loose from the tray, sailing off into the dust. The camels swerved in a panic, sending the wagon train up on four wheels. Mia lunged for the abandoned reins, bringing the train down with a shuddering jolt. She dragged herself into the pilot's seat and cursed, glancing over her shoulder at the *four* beasts now pursuing them, shouting over the bedlam to Mister Kindly.

"Remind me never to call the Dark in this desert again!"

". . . *have no fear of that* . . ."

The churchman manning the xylophone had been knocked clear when the kraken struck, now wailing as one of the monsters dragged him to his death. Tric snatched up the man's fallen club and started beating on the contraption as Mia roared at Naev.

"Which way is the Red Church from here?"

The woman moaned in reply, clutching the ragged wounds in her chest and gut. Mia could see entrails glistening in the worst of it, Naev's clothes soaked with gore.

"Naev, listen to me! Which way do we ride?"

"North," the woman bubbled. "The mountains."

"Which mountains? There are dozens!"

"Not the tallest . . . nor the shortest. Nor the . . . scowling face or the sad old man or the broken wall." A ragged, spit-thick sigh. "The simplest mountain of them all."

The woman groaned, curling in upon herself. The ironsong was near deafening, and Mia's headache bounced around the inside of her skull with joyful abandon.

"Tric, shut that racket up!" Mia roared.

"It scares off the krakens!" Tric bellowed.

"Scares off the krakens . . . ," moaned Naev.

"No, it bloody doesn't!" yelled Mia.

She glanced over her shoulder, just in case the ungodly racket had indeed scared off the monstrosities chasing them, but alas, they were still in close pursuit. Bastard galloped alongside, glaring at Mia, occasionally spitting an accusing whinny in her direction.

"O, shut up!"

"*. . . he really does not like you . . .*"

"You're not helping!"

"*. . . and what would help . . . ?*"

"Explain to me how we got into this stew!"

The cat who was shadows tilted his head, as if thinking. He looked at the rolling Whisperwastes, the jagged horizon drawing nearer, his mistress above him. And he spoke with the voice of one unveiling an ugly but necessary truth.

"*. . . it is basically your fault . . .*"

CHAPTER 7

INTRODUCTIONS

Mia pushed open the door to Mercurio's Curios, a tiny bell above the frame chiming her arrival. The store was dark and dusty, sprawling off in every direction. Shutters were drawn against the sunlight. Mia recalled the sign outside—"Oddities, Rarities & the Fynest Antiquities." Looking at the shelves, she saw plenty of the former. The latter parts of the equation were up for debate.

Truth be told, the shop looked filled to bursting with junk. Mia could've sworn it was also bigger inside than out, though she put that down to her lack of mornmeal. As if to remind her of its neglect, her belly growled a sternly worded complaint.

Mia made her way through the flotsam and jetsam until she arrived at a counter. And there, behind a mahogany desk carved with a twisting spiral pattern that made her eyes hurt to look at, she found the greatest oddity inside Mercurio's Curios— the proprietor himself.

His face was the kind that seemed born to scowl, set atop with a short shock of light gray hair. Blue eyes were narrowed behind wire-rimmed spectacles that had seen better turns. A statue of an elegant woman with a lion's head crouched on the desk beside him, an arkemical globe held in its upturned palm. The old man was reading from a book as big as Mia. A cigarillo hung from his mouth, smelling faintly of cloves. It bobbed on his lips when he mumbled.

"Help ya w'somthn?"

"Good turn to you, sir. Almighty Aa bless and keep you—"

The old man tapped the small brass placard on the countertop—a repeat of the warning outside his door. "No time-wasters, rabble, or religious sorts welcome."

"Forgive me, sir. May the Four Daughters—"

The old man tapped the placard more insistently, shifting his scowl to Mia. The girl fell silent. The old man turned back to his book.

"Help ya w'somthn?" he repeated.

The girl cleared her throat. "I wish to sell you a piece of jewelry, sir."

"Just wishing about it won't get it done, girl."

Mia hovered uncertainly, chewing her lip. The old man began tapping the placard again until she finally got the message, unpinning her brooch and placing it on the wood. The little crow stared back at her with its red amber eyes, as if wounded at the thought she might hock it to such a grumpy old bastard. She shrugged apology.

"Where'd y'steal that?" the old man mumbled.

"I did not steal it, sir."

Mercurio pulled the cigarillo from his lips, turned his full attention to Mia.

"That's the sigil of the Familia Corvere."

"Well spotted, sir."

"Darius Corvere died a traitor's death yesterturn by order of the Itreyan Senate. And rumor has it his entire household have been locked in the Philosopher's Stone."*

---

*The "Philosopher's Stone," as it was colloquially known, was a thin spear of rock off the coast of Godsgrave, surrounded by unforgiving reefs and drake-infested deeps. Atop the stone sat an abyssal keep, carved from the rock, it was said, by Niah herself. Into this pit, Godsgrave poured any criminal not deserving of outright execution. The prison overflowed with brigands and thieves, and the underpaid Administratii seemed almost entirely unconcerned with provisioning, medical care, or ensuring convicts were released in a timely fashion.

The little girl had no kerchief, so she wiped her nose on her sleeve and said nothing.

"How old are you, sprat?"

". . . Ten, sir."

"You got a name?"

Mia blinked. Who did this old man think he was? She was Mia Corvere, daughter of the justicus of the Luminatii Legion. Marrowborn of a noble familia, one of the great twelve houses of the Republic. She'd not be interrogated by a mere shopkeep. Especially when offering a prize worth more than the rest of the junk in this squalid hole put together.

"My name is none of your business, sir." Mia folded her arms and tried her best to impersonate her mother when dealing with an unruly servant.

"Noneofyourbusiness?" One gray eyebrow rose. "Strange name for a girl, innit?"

"Do you want the brooch or no?"

The old man put his cigarillo back on his lips and turned back to his book.

"No," he said.

Mia blinked. "It is finest Itreyan silver. Th——"

"Fuck off," the man said, without looking up. "And take your trouble with you when you off with the fuck, Miss Noneofyourbusiness."

Mia's cheeks burned pink with fury. She snatched the brooch up and pinned it back to her dress, tossed her hair over one shoulder and spun on her heel.

"Word of advice," said the old man, still not looking up. "Corvere and his cronies got off light with that hanging. Their commonborn troops have been crucified along the banks of the Choir. Rumor is they're going to pave the Senate House streets with their skulls. A lot of those soldiers had familia 'round here. So, I'd not walk about with a traitor's mark pinned to my tits were I you."

The words struck Mia like a rock in the back of her head. She turned back to the old man, teeth bared in a snarl.

A one-year term could easily stretch into three or five before the prison's clerks would get around to processing the required paperwork. As such, most prisoners spent much of their time thinking deep thoughts about injustice, the nature of criminality, and how that pair of boots they stole wasn't really worth the five years of life they paid for it. Hence the nickname "Philosopher's Stone."

Owing to the overcrowding, the Itreyan Senate had devised an ingenious and entertaining method of population control known as "the Descent," held during truedark Carnivalé every three years. However, an unexplained "incident" during the most recent Descent—also the night of the Truedark Massacre—saw large portions of the Philosopher's Stone destroyed, and the spire itself partially collapsed. It has been abandoned ever since; a hollow, lean-to shell, supposedly haunted by the ghosts of the hundreds murdered within, the horrors of their deaths embedded in the stone for all eternity.

Boo!

"*My father was no traitor,*" she spat.

As she stormed out the door, her shadow unfurled along the pavement and slammed it behind her. The girl was so angry she didn't even notice.

Back out in the marketplace, she stood on the stoop, fury curling her hands into fists. How dare he talk about her father like that? She was of half a mind to stomp back inside and demand apology, but her stomach was growling and she needed coin.

She was stepping down into the crush looking for a jewelry stall, when a boy a little older than her came careening out of the throng. His arms were laden with a basket of pastries, and before Mia could step aside, with a curse and a small explosion of powdered sugar, the boy plowed straight into her.

Mia cried out as she was sent sprawling, her dress powdered white. The boy was likewise knocked onto his backside, pastries strewn in the filth.

"*Why don't you watch where you're going?*" Mia demanded.

"O, Daughters, a thousand pardons, miss. Please forgive me . . ."

The boy climbed to his feet, offered a hand, and helped Mia up. He brushed the white powder off her dress as best he could, mumbling apologies all the while. Then, leaning down to the fallen pastries, he stuffed them back into his basket. With an apologetic smile, he plucked one of the less dirty tarts off the pile and offered it to Mia with a bow.

"Please accept this by way of apology, Mi Dona."

Mia's anger slowed to a simmer as her belly growled, and, with a pout, she took the pastry from the boy's grubby hand.

"Thank you, Mi Don."

"I'd best be off. The good father gets in a frightful mood if I'm late to almsgiving." He smiled again at Mia, doffed an imaginary hat. "Apologies again, miss."

Mia gave a curtsey, and scowled a little less. "Aa bless and keep you."

The boy hurried off into the crowd. Mia watched him go, anger slowly dissipating. She looked at the sweet tart in her hand, and smiled at her fortune. Free mornmeal!

She found an alley away from the press, lifted the tart and took a big bite. Her smile curdled at the edges, eyes growing wide. With a curse, she spat her mouthful into the muck, throwing the rest of the tart with it. The pastry was hard as wood, the filling utterly rancid. She grimaced, wiping her lips on her sleeve.

"Four Daughters," she spat. "Why would—"

Mia blinked. Looked down at her dress, still faintly powdered with sugar. Remembering the boy's hands patting her down, cursing herself a fool and realizing, at last, what his game had been.

Her brooch was missing.

The ironsong *did* eventually scare off the krakens.

Or so Tric insisted, at any rate. He'd spent four hours beating the xylophone as if it owed him coin, and Mia supposed he needed some kind of vindication. As the pursuers dropped off one by one, Mister Kindly suggested the ground was growing harder as the caravan galloped closer to the mountains. Mia was reasonably certain the beasts simply grew bored and pissed off to eat someone easier. Naev ventured no opinion at all, instead lying in a pool of coagulating blood and doing her best not to die.

Truthfully, Mia wasn't certain she'd pull it off.

Tric took the reins at her insistence. In the merciful quiet after the boy abandoned his percussionist duties, Mia knelt beside the unconscious woman and wondered where to begin.

Naev's guts had been minced by kraken hooks, and the reek of bowel and vomit hung in the air—Four Daughters only knew how Tric was handling it with that knife-keen nose of his. Knowing the smell of shit and death well enough, Mia simply tried to make the woman comfortable. There was nothing she could really do; sepsis would finish the job if blood loss didn't. Knowing the end awaiting Naev, Mia realized it'd be a mercy to end her.

Peeling the cloth back from Naev's ravaged belly, Mia looked for something to bind the wounds with, settling at last on the fabric about the woman's face. And as she peeled the veil from Naev's head, she felt Mister Kindly swell and sigh, drinking the surge of sickening terror that would've otherwise made her scream.

Even still, it was a close thing.

"'Byss and blood . . . ," she breathed.

"What?" Tric glanced over his shoulder, almost falling off the driver's seat. "Black Mother of Night . . . her face . . ."

Daughters, such a face . . .

To call her disfigured would be to call a knife to the heart "mildly inconvenient." Naev's flesh was stretched and twisted into a knot in the place her nose might have been. Her bottom lip sagged like a beaten stepchild, top lip snarled back from her teeth. Five deep runnels were carved into her flesh—as if her face were clay, and someone had grabbed a fistful and *squeezed*. And yet the hideousness was framed by beautiful curls of strawberry blond.

"What could have done that?"

"I've no idea."

"Love," the woman whispered, spit dribbling over mangled lips. "Only love."

"Naev . . . ," Mia began. "Your wounds . . ."

"Bad."

"It's a far cry from good."

"Get Naev to the Church. She has much to do before she meets her Blessed Lady."

"We're two turns from the mountains," Tric said. "Maybe more. Even if we get there, you're in no condition to climb."

The woman slurped, coughed bloody. Reaching to her neck, she snapped a leather cord, drew out a silver phial. She tried sitting up, groaned in agony. Mia pushed her back down.

"You mustn't—"

"Get off her!" Naev snarled. "Help her up. Drag her." She waved to the back of the wagon. "Out of this blood, where the wood is clean."

Mia had no idea what the woman was about, but she obeyed, hauling Naev through the congealing puddle to the wagon's rear. And there the woman pulled out the phial's stopper with her teeth and upended the contents onto the unfinished boards.

More blood.

Bright red, as if from a fresh-cut wound. Mia frowned as Mister Kindly coiled up on her shoulder, peering through her curtain of hair. And as Naev dragged her fingers through the puddle, the cat who was shadows did his best to purr, sending a shiver down Mia's spine.

"*. . . interesting . . .*"

Naev was writing, Mia realized. As if the puddle were a tablet and her finger the brush. The letters were Ashkahi—she recognized them from her studies, but the ritual itself . . .

"That's blood sorcery," she breathed.

But that was impossible. The magik of the Ashkahi had been extinguished when the empire fell. Nobody had seen real blood werking in . . .

"How do you know how to do that? Those arts have been dead for a hundred years."

"Not all the dead truly die," Naev rasped. "The Mother keeps . . . only what she needs."

The woman rolled onto her back, clutching her butchered belly.

"Ride for the mountains . . . the simplest of them all." Mia swore she could see tears in the woman's eyes. "Do not end her, girl. Set mercy aside. If the Blessed Lady . . . takes her, so be it. But do not help Naev on her way. Does she hear?"

". . . I hear you."

Naev clutched her hand. Squeezed. And then she slipped back into darkness.

Mia bound the wounds as best she could, wrist-deep in gore, fetching her cloak from Bastard's saddlebag (he tried to bite her) and rolling it beneath Naev's head. Joining Tric on the driver's seat, she peered at the mountains ahead. A range of great black spurs stretched north and south, a few high enough to be tipped with snow. One looked almost like a scowling face, just as Naev described. Another long range might've been the broken wall she mentioned. And nestled beside a spur resembling a sad old man, Mia saw a peak that fit the bill.

It was entirely average, as far as mighty spires of prehistoric granite went. Not quite high enough to be frost-clad, not really conjuring any comparisons to faces or figures. Just a regular lump of ancient rock out here in this blood-red desert. The kind you wouldn't look twice at.

"There," Tric said, pointing to the spur.

"Aye."

"You think they'd have picked something a touch more dramatic."

"I think that's the point. Anyone looking for a nest of assassins isn't likely to start at the most boring mountain in all creation."

Tric nodded. Gifted her a smile. "Wisdom, Pale Daughter."

"Fear not, Don Tric." She smiled back. "I won't let it go to my head."

They rode another two turns, with Tric in the driver's seat and Mia by Naev's side. She wet a cloth, moistened those malformed lips, wondering who or what could have mutilated the woman's face like that. Naev talked as if in a fever, speaking to some phantom, asking it to wait. She reached out to thin air once, as if to caress it. And as she did so, those lips twisted into a hideous parody of a smile. Mister Kindly sat beside her the entire time.

Purring.

Flowers and Bastard were both exhausted, and Mia feared either might go lame at any moment. It seemed cruel (even to Bastard) to make them run beside the wagon needlessly. Tric and Mia had passed the point of no return; they'd either make the Red Church or die now. She'd seen wild horses roaming the broken foothills, supposed there must be water someplace near. And so, reluctantly, she suggested they let the pair go.

Tric seemed saddened, but he saw the wisdom of it. They pulled the wagon to a stop and the boy untied Flowers, letting the stallion drink deep from his waterskin. He ran a fond hand over the horse's neck, whispering softly.

"You were a loyal friend. I'll trust you'll find another. Watch out for the kraken."

He slapped the horse on its hindquarters, and the beast galloped east along the range. Mia untied Bastard, the stallion glaring even as she emptied an entire waterskin into his gullet. She reached into her saddlebag, offered him the last sugar cube on an upturned palm.

"You've earned it. I suppose you can head back to Last Hope now if you like."

The stallion lowered his head, gently nibbled the cube from her palm. He nickered, tossing his mane, nuzzling his nose to her shoulder. And, as Mia smiled and patted his cheek, Bastard opened his mouth and bit her hard just above the left breast.

"*You son of a motherless—*"

The stallion bolted across the wastes as Mia hopped about, clutching her chest and cursing the horse by the Three Suns and Four Daughters and anyone else who happened to be listening. Bastard followed Flowers east, disappearing into the dusty haze.

"I can kiss that better if you like," Tric smiled.

"O, fuck *off*!" Mia spat, rolling into the wagon and flopping about on the floor. There was blood on her fingers where she touched the bite, the skin already bruising as she glanced inside her shirt. Thanking the Daughters she wasn't a bigger girl for the first time in her life, she hissed under her breath as Mister Kindly laughed from her shadow.

"He was *such* a *bastard* . . ."

N aev was fading swift, and they could afford no more stops—Mia feared the woman wouldn't last another turn, and the First of Septimus was the morrow. If they didn't find the Church soon, there'd be no point finding it at all. They were in the foothills now, mountains curving about them like a lover's arms. She'd read dustwraiths often made their home where the winds howled worst, and her ears strained for telltale laughter over the whispering breeze.

Blood had thickened over the wagon floor, crusted in flies. She did her best to keep them off Naev's belly, despite knowing she was already a dead woman. Naev's resolve had broken—when unconscious, she moaned constantly, and when awake, she simply screamed until she passed out again. She was in the midst of a howling fit as Tric brought the wagon to a halt. Mia looked up at the absence of motion after turns of riding, fatigue thick in her voice.

"Why've we stopped?"

"Unless you can fix these spit-machines' wings"—Tric pointed to the snarling camels—"we've gone as far as we're going to."

The simplest mountain rose up before the camel train in sheer cliffs, broken and tumbled all about. Mia looked around, saw nothing and no one out of the ordinary. She leaned down and clutched Naev's shoulder, shouting above her cries.

"Where do we go from here?"

The woman curled over and babbled nonsense, clawing at her rancid belly. Tric climbed down from the reins and stood beside Mia, face grim. The reek of human waste and rotten blood was overpowering. The agony on display too much to bear.

"Mia . . ."

"I need a smoke," the girl growled.

She rolled out of the wagon, Tric hopping down beside her as she lit a cigarillo. The wind snatched at her fringe as she sucked down a lungful. Her fingers were crusted with blood. Naev was laughing, bashing the back of her head against the wagon floor.

"We should end it," Tric said. "It's a mercy."

"She told us not to."

"She's in agony, Mia. Black Mother, *listen* to her."

"I know! I'd have done it yesterturn but she *asked me not to.*"

"So you're happy to just let her die screaming?"

"Do I look fucking happy to you?"

"Well, what do we do now? This is the simplest mountain for miles, far as I can see. I don't see any steeple, do you? We just ride around until we drop of thirst?"

"I don't know any more than you do. But Naev told us to ride in this direction. That blood werking wasn't just for shits and giggles. Someone knows we're here."

"Aye, the fucking dustwraiths! They'll hear her screaming miles away!"

"So is it mercy or fear ruling you, Don Tric?"

"I fear nothing," he growled.

"Mister Kindly can smell it on you. And so can I."

"Maw take you," he hissed, drawing his knife. "I'm ending this now."

"Stop." Mia clutched his arm. "Don't."

"Get off me!" Tric slapped her fingers away.

Mia's hand went to her stiletto, Tric's hand to his scimitar. The shadows about her flared, long tendrils reaching out from the stones and swaying as if to music only they could hear.

"She's our only way to find the Church," Mia said. "It's my fault those kraken got her in the first place. And she asked me not to kill her."

"She couldn't find her britches for a piss, the state she's in. And I didn't promise her a thing."

"Don't draw that sword, Don Tric. Things will end badly for both of us."

"I picked you for a cold one, Mia Corvere." He shook his head. "I just never knew how much. Where do you keep the heart that's supposed to be inside your chest?"

"Keep it up and I'll feed you yours, bastard."

"Bastard I might be," Tric spat. "But you're the one who decides to be a cunt every turn of your life."

Mia had her knife out, smiling.

"That's the sweetest thing you've ever said to me."

Tric drew his scimitar, those pretty hazel eyes locked on hers. Confusion and rage boiling behind her stare. A soup of it, thick in her head, silencing the common sense shouting at the back of the room. She wanted to kill this boy, she realized. Cut him belly to throat and wash her hands inside him. Soak herself to the elbows and paint her lips and breasts with his blood. Her thighs ached at the thought. Breath coming faster as she pressed one hand between her legs, murder and lust all a-tumble in her head as Mister Kindly whispered from her shadow.

"... this is not you ..."

"Away," she hissed. "To the Maw with you, daemon."

"... these thoughts are not your own ..."

Tric was advancing, eyes narrowed to knife-cuts, veins standing taut in his throat. He was breathing heavy, pupils dilated. Mia glanced below his waist and realized he was *hard*, britches bulging, the thought making her breath quicken. She blinked sweat from her eyes and pictured her blade slipping in and out of his chest, his into hers, tasting copper on his tongue . . .

"This isn't right . . . ," she breathed.

Tric lunged, a sweeping blow passing over her head as she swayed. She aimed a kick for his groin, blocked by his knee and tempted for a second to simply drop to her own. She stabbed at his exposed belly, knowing this was wrong, *this was wrong*, pulling the blow at the last moment and rolling aside as he swung again at her head. He was grinning like a lunatic, and the thought struck her funny as well. Trying not to laugh, trying to think beyond her desire to kill him, fuck him, both at once, lying with him inside her as they stabbed and bit and bled to their endings on the sand.

"Tric, stop it," she gasped.

NEVERNIGHT   87

"Come here . . ."

Chest heaving, hand outstretched even as she moved closer. Panting. *Wanting.*

"Something is wrong. This is wrong."

"Come here," he said, stalking her across the sand, swords raised.

". . . *this is not real . . .*"

She shook her head, blinking the sting from her eyes.

". . . *you are mia corvere . . . ,*" said Mister Kindly. ". . . *remember . . .*"

She held out her hand and her shadow trembled, stretching out from her feet and engulfing the boy's. He stuck fast in the sand and she backed away, arms up as if to ward off a blow. The knife was heavy in her grip, drawing her back, mind flooded with the thought of plunging it inside him as he plunged inside her but no, NO, that wasn't her (*this isn't me*) and with a desperate cry, she hurled her blade away.

She fell to her knees, flopped onto her belly, eyes screwed shut. Sand in her teeth as she shook her head, pushed the lust and the murder down, focused on the thought Mister Kindly had gifted her, clinging to it like a drowning man at straw.

"I am Mia Corvere," she breathed. "I am Mia Corvere . . ."

Slow clapping.

Mia lifted her head at the somber sound, echoing inside her head. She saw figures around her, clad in desert red, faces covered. A dozen, gathered about a slight man with a curved sword at his waist. The hilt was fashioned in the likeness of human figures with feline heads—male and female, naked and intertwined. The blade was Ashkahi blacksteel.*

"Mia?" Tric said, his voice now his own.

Mia looked the clapping man over from her cradle in the dust. He was well built, handsome as a fistful of devils. His hair was curled, dark, peppered with

---

*Blacksteel, also known as "ironfoe," was a wondrous metal created by the Ashkahi sorcerii before the fall of the empire. Black as truedark, the metal never grew dull or rusted, and was capable of being sharpened to an impossible edge. Ashkahi smiths were said to slice their anvils in half with a completed blacksteel blade to prove it worthy—a practice heartily endorsed by the Ashkahi Anvilmaker's Guild.

One famous tale speaks of a thief named Tariq who stole a blacksteel blade belonging to an Ashkahi prince. In his haste to flee the scene of his crime, the thief dropped the blade, which cut through the floor and down into the earth. The flood of fire released from the worldwound burned down the entire city. Death by immolation became the punishment for thievery in Ashkah thereafter—no matter the offense, be it the smallest loaf or the crown jewels themselves, any thief caught in Ashkah would be tied to a stone pillar and set ablaze.

Some people just ruin it for everybody, don't they?

gray. His face was of a man in his early thirties, but deep, cocoa-brown eyes spoke of years far deeper. A half-smile loitered at the corners of his lips like it was planning to steal the silverware.

"Bravo," he said. "I've not seen anyone resist the Discord so well since Lord Cassius."

As the man stepped forward, the others about him broke as if on cue. They began unloading the caravan, unhitching the exhausted camels. Four of them lifted Naev into a sling, carrying her toward the cliff. Mia could see no rope. Could see no—

"What is your name?"

"Mia, master. Mia Corvere."

"And who is your Shahiid?"

"Mercurio of Godsgrave."

"Ah, Mercurio at last musters the courage to send another lamb to the Church of Slaughter?" The man held out his hand. "Interesting."

She took the offered hand, and he pulled her up from the dust. Her mouth was dry, heart thudding. Echoes of murder and desire thrumming in her veins.

"You are Tric." The man turned to the boy with a smile. "Who carries the blood and not the name of the Threedrake clan. Adiira's student."

Tric nodded slow, dragged his locks from his eyes. "Aye."

"My name is Mouser, servant of Our Lady of Blessed Murder and Shahiid of Pockets in her Red Church." A small bow. "I believe you have something for us."

The question hung like a sword above Mia's head. A thousand turns. Sleepless nevernights and bloody fingers and poison dripping from her hands. Broken bones and burning tears and lies upon lies. Everything she'd done, everything she'd lost—all of it came to this.

Mia reached for the pouch of teeth at her belt.

Her belly turned to ice.

". . . *No*," she breathed.

Feeling about her waist, her tunic, eyes widening in a panic as she realized—

"My tithe! It's gone!"

"O, dear," said Mouser.

"But I just had it!"

Mia searched the sands about her, fearing she'd lost it in the struggle with Tric. Scrabbling in the dust, tears in her eyes. Mister Kindly swelled and rolled inside her shadow's dark, but even he couldn't keep her terror completely at bay—the thought that everything had been for nothing . . . Crawling in the dirt, hair tangled across her eyes, chewing her lip and—

Clink, clink.

She looked up. Saw a familiar sheepskin purse held in supple fingers. Mouser's smile.

"You should be more careful, little lamb. Shahiid of Pockets, as I said."

Mia stood and snatched the purse with a snarl. Opening the bag, she counted the teeth therein, clutched it in a bloodless fist. She looked the man over, rage engulfing her terror for a moment. She had to resist the urge to add his teeth to her collection.

"That was heartless," she said.

The man smiled wider, sadness lingering at the corners of those old eyes.

"Welcome to the Red Church," he said.

CHAPTER 8
SALVATION

"*Two irons and twelve coppers,*" *the boy crowed.* "*Tonight we eat like kings. Or queens. As the case may be.*"

"*What,*" *scoffed the grubby girl beside him.* "*You mean crucified in Tyrant's Row? I'd rather eat like a consul if it's all the same to you.*"

"*Girls can't be consuls, sis.*"

"*Doesn't mean I can't eat like one.*"

Three urchins were crouched in an alley not too far off the market's crush, a basket of stale pastries beside them. The first, the quick-fingered lad who'd bumped into Mia in the marketplace. The second, a girl with grubby blond hair and bare feet. The third was a slightly older boy, gutter-thin and mean. They were dressed in threadbare clothes, though the bigger boy wore a fine belt of knives at his waist. The proceeds of their morning's work were laid before them; a handful of coins and a silver crow with amber eyes.

"*That's mine,*" *Mia said from behind them.*

The trio stood quickly, turned to face their accuser. Mia stood at the alley mouth, fists on hips. The bigger boy pulled a knife from his belt.

"*You give that back right now,*" *said Mia.*

"*Or what?*" *the boy said, raising his blade.*

"*Or I yell for the Luminatii. They'll cut off your hands and dump you in the Choir if you're lucky. Throw you in the Philosopher's Stone if not.*"

The trio gifted her a round of mocking laughter.

The black at Mia's feet rippled. The fear inside her became nothing at all. And folding her arms, she puffed out her chest, narrowed her eyes, and spoke with a voice she didn't quite recognize as her own.

"Give. It. Back."

"Fuck off, you little whore," the big one said.

A scowl darkened Mia's brow. ". . . Whore?"

"Cut her, Shivs," the younger boy said. "Cut her a new hole."

Cheeks reddening, Mia peered at the first boy.

"Your name is Shivs? O, because you carry knives, aye?" She glanced at the younger boy. "You'd be Fleas then?" To the girl. "Let me guess, Worms?"*

"Clever," said the blonde. And stepping lightly to Mia's side, she drew back a fist and buried it in Mia's stomach.

The breath left her lungs with a wet cough as she fell to her knees. Blinking and blinded, Mia clutched her belly, trying not to retch. Astonishment inside her. Astonishment and rage.

Nobody had hit her before.

Nobody had dared.

She'd seen her mother fence wits countless times in the Spine. She'd seen men reduced to stuttering lumps by the Dona Corvere, women driven to tears. And Mia had studied well. But the rules said the aggrieved was supposed to riposte with some barb of their own, not haul off and punch her like some lowborn thug in an alley scra—

"O . . . ," Mia wheezed. "Right."

Shivs strode across the alley and slammed a boot into her ribs. The blonde (who in Mia's mind would ever after be thought of as Worms) smiled cheerfully as Mia vomited on an empty stomach. Turning to the younger boy, Shivs pointed at their loot.

"Pick that up and let's be off. I've got—"

Shivs felt something sharp and deathly cold dig into his britches. He glanced down to the stiletto poking his privates, the little fist clutching it tight. Mia had wrapped herself around his waist, pressing her mother's dagger into the boy's crotch, the crow on the pommel glaring at Shivs with two amber eyes. Her whisper was soft and deadly.

"Whore, am I?"

Now, if this were a storybook tale, gentlefriend, and Mia the hero within it, Shivs would've seen some shadow of the killer she'd become and backed away all a-tremble. But the truth is, the boy stood two feet taller than Mia, and outweighed her by eighty pounds. And looking down at the girl around his waist, he didn't see

---

* More balls than brains, gentlefriends. More balls than brains.

the most feared assassin in all the Republic—just a sprat with no real idea how to hold a knife, her face so close to his elbow one good twitch would send her sprawling.

So Shivs twitched. And Mia wasn't sent sprawling so much as flying.

She fell into the mud, clutching a broken nose, blinded by agonized tears. The younger boy (ever after thought of as Fleas) picked up Dona Corvere's fallen dagger, eyes wide.

"Daughters, lookit this!"

"Toss it here."

The boy flipped it hilt first. Shivs snatched the knife from the air, admired the craftsmanship with greedy eyes.

"Aa's cock, this is real gravebone . . ."

Fleas kicked Mia hard in the ribs. "Where did a trollop like you get—"

A wrinkled hand landed on the lad's shoulder, slamming him against the wall. A knee said hello to his groin, a gnarled walking stick invited his jaw to dance.* A double-handed strike to the back of his head left him bleeding in the dirt.

Old Mercurio stood above him, clad in a long greatcoat of beaten leather, a walking stick in one bony hand. His ice-blue eyes were narrowed, taking in the scene, the girl sprawled bloody on the ground. He looked at Shivs, lips peeled back in a sneer.

"That's your game is it? Kickball?" He aimed a savage boot into the ribs of young Fleas, rewarded with a sickening crack. "Mind if I join?"

Shivs glared at the old man, down at his bleeding comrade. And with a black curse, he hefted the Dona Corvere's stiletto and hurled it at Mercurio's head.

It was a fine throw. Right between the eyes. But instead of dying, the old man snatched the blade from midair, quick as the stink on the banks of the Rose.† Tucking the stiletto inside his greatcoat, Mercurio took hold of his walking stick, and with a crisp ring, drew a long, gravebone blade hidden within the shaft. He advanced on Shivs and Worms, brandishing the sword.

"O, Liisian rules, aye? Old school? Fair enough, then."

Shivs and Worms glanced at each other, panic in their eyes. And without a word, the pair turned and bolted down the alley, leaving poor Fleas unconscious in the muck.

---

* It refused, though sadly, they danced all the same.

† The Rose River is possessed of the greatest misnomer in all the Itreyan Republic, and perhaps, all creation. Its stench is so awful that, when offered the choice between drowning in the Rose or being castrated and crucified, the Niahan heretic Don Anton Bosconi was famously quoted as asking his confessors, "Would you like to borrow a knife, gentlefriends?"

Mia was on her hands and knees. Cheeks stained with tears and blood. Her nose felt raw and swollen, throbbing red. She couldn't see properly. Couldn't think.

"Told you that brooch wouldn't be naught but trouble," Mercurio growled. "You'd have done better listening, girl."

Mia felt a heat in her chest. Stinging at her eyes. Another child might have bawled for her mother, then. Cried the world wasn't fair. But instead, all the rage, all the indignity, the memory of her father's death, her mother's arrest, the brutality and attempted murder, stacked afresh now with robbery and an alley scrap she'd been on the wrong side of winning—all of it piled up inside her like tinder on a bonfire and bursting into bright, furious flame.

"Don't call me 'girl,'" Mia spat, pawing the tears from her eyes. She pulled herself halfway up the wall, slumped back down again. "I am the daughter of a justicus. Firstchild of one of the twelve noble houses. I'm Mia Corvere, damn you!"

"O, I know who you are," said the old man. "Question is, who else does?"

". . . What?"

"Who else knows you're the Kingmaker's sprog, missy?"

"No one," she snarled. "I've told no one. And don't call me 'missy,' either."

A sniff. "Not as stupid as I thought, then."

The old man looked down the alley. Back at the marketplace. Finally, to the bleeding girl at his feet. And with something close to a sigh, he offered his hand.

"Come on, little Crow. Let's get your beak straightened out."

Mia wiped her fist across her lips, brought it away bloody.

"I know you not at all, sir," she said. "And I trust you even less."

"Well, those're the first sensible words I've heard you hatch. But if I wanted you dead, I'd just leave you to it. Because alone out here, you'll be dead by nevernight."

Mia stayed where she was, distrust plain in her eyes.

"I've got tea," Mercurio sighed. "And cake."

The girl covered her growling belly with both palms.

". . . What kind of cake?"

"The free kind."

Mia pouted. Licked her lips and tasted blood.

"My favorite."

And she took the old man's hand.

"And I said I'm not wearing that!" Tric bellowed.

"Apologies," said Mouser. "Did I give the impression I was asking?"

At the simplest mountain's foot, Mia was doing her best to keep a level head.

The churchmen were gathered by the cliff face, each with an armload of gear or a weary camel in tow. Mouser was holding out blindfolds, which he'd insisted Mia and Tric wear. For some inexplicable reason, Tric had grown furious at the suggestion. Mia could practically see the hackles rising down the Dweymeri boy's back.

Though she felt no remnants of the strange cocktail of rage and lust that had filled her earlier, Mia thought perhaps her friend might still be under the influence. She turned to Mouser.

"Shahiid, our minds weren't our own when we arrived . . ."

"The Discord. A werking placed on the Quiet Mountain in ages past."

"It's still affecting him."

"No. It discourages those who arrive at the Church without . . . invitation. You are now welcome here. *If* you wear blindfolds."

"We saved her life." Tric gestured to Naev. "And you still don't trust us?"

Mouser tucked his thumbs into his belt and smiled his silverware smile. His voice was as rich as Twelve Cask goldwine.*

"You still live, don't you?"

"Tric, what difference does it make?" Mia asked. "Just put it on."

"I'm not wearing any blindfold."

"But we've come so far . . ."

"And you will go no farther," Mouser added. "Not with eyes to see."

Tric folded his arms and glowered. "No."

Mia sighed, dragged her hand through her fringe. "Shahiid Mouser. I'd like a moment to confer with my learned colleague?"

---

* Goldwine is an Itreyan whiskey, so named for the vast fields of corn in the midlands from which it is distilled. Several familia are renowned for their recipes, most notably the Valente and Albari.

The rivalry between the two families has boiled from bad blood to outright blood-*shed* on more than one occasion, the most famous of which, the War of Twelve Casks, lasted four truedarks and claimed no less than thirty-two lives. Declared an official Vendetta—that is, a bloodfeud sanctioned by the Holy Church of Aa—the conflict was so named because, amid the slaughter and arson that embodied it, only twelve casks of Albari whiskey survived to see distribution throughout the Republic.

Bottles of "Twelve Cask" are thus exceedingly rare and astonishingly expensive—a single bottle has been known to fetch over forty thousand golden tossers at auction. When the summer villa of Senator Ari Giancarli was set alight by two clumsy servants, Giancarli reportedly charged back into the blazing home no less than three times—to save his wife, his son, and his two bottles of Twelve Cask.

Rumors that he saved the bottles *first* are, of course, gross character slurs concocted by political rivals, and have absolutely no basis in fact.

(He saved them second.)

"Be swift," the Shahiid said. "If Naev dies on the very doorstep, Speaker Adonai will be none pleased. On your heads be it should Our Lady take her."

Mia wondered what the Shahiid meant—the kraken wounds were fatal, and Naev was already a dead woman. But still, she took Tric's hand, dragged him across the crumbling foothills. Out of earshot, she turned on the boy, infamous temper slowly rising.

"Maw's teeth, what's wrong with you?"

"I won't do it. I'd rather cut my own throat."

"They'll do that for you if you keep this up!"

"Let them try."

"This is the way they do things, so this is the way it's done! Do you understand what we add up to, here? We're acolytes! Bottom of the pile! We do it, or they do *us*."

"I'm not wearing a blindfold."

"Then you won't get inside the Church."

"Maw take the Church!"

Mia rocked back on her heels, frown darkening her brow.

"*. . . he fears . . . ,*" whispered Mister Kindly from her shadow.

"Shut up, you blackhearted little shit," Tric snapped.

"Tric, what are you afraid of?"

Mister Kindly sniffed with his not-nose, blinked with his not-eyes.

"*. . . the dark . . .*"

"Shut up!" Tric roared.

Mia blinked, incredulity slapped all over her face. "You can't be serious . . ."

"*. . . apologies, i was uninformed i'd been relegated to the role of comic relief . . .*"

Mia tried to catch Tric's stare, but the boy was frowning at his feet.

"Tric, are you honestly telling me you've come to train among the most feared assassins in the Republic and you're *afraid of the bloody dark*?"

Tric was set to yell again, but the words died on his tongue. Gritted teeth, hands curling into fists, those artless tattoos twisting as he grimaced.

"*. . .* It's not the damned dark." A quiet sigh. "Just . . . not being able to see. I . . ."

He slumped down on his backside, kicked a toeful of shale down the slope.

"O, sod it . . ."

Guilt welled up in Mia's chest, drowning the anger beneath. She knelt beside the Dweymeri with a sigh, put a comforting hand on his arm.

"I'm sorry, Tric. What happened?"

"Bad things." Tric pawed at his eyes. "Just . . . bad things."

She took his hand and squeezed, acutely aware of how much she was grow-ing to like this strange boy. To see him like this, shivering like a child . . .

"I can take it away," she offered.

". . . Take what away?"

"Your fear. Well, Mister Kindly can, anyway. For a little while. He drinks it. Breathes it. It's what keeps him here. Makes him grow."

Tric frowned at the shadow-creature, revulsion in his eyes.

". . . Fear?"

Mia nodded. "He's been drinking mine for years. Not enough to make me forget common sense, mind. But enough to make me stand tall in a knife-fight or snatch-job. He makes me strong."

"That makes no sense," Tric scowled. "If he's eating your fear, you never learn how to deal with it yourself. That's not strength, that's a crutch . . ."

"Well, it's a crutch I'm willing to loan you, Don Tric." Mia glared. "So in-stead of lecturing me on my faults, I'd rather you said 'thank you, Pale Daughter,' and got your sorry arse inside the Church before they slit our throats and leave us for the kraken."

The boy stared down at their clasped hands. Nodded slow.

". . . Thank you, Pale Daughter."

She stood, pulled him to his feet. Mister Kindly didn't need to be asked—simply flowed across the join where their shadows intersected. Anxiety began eating Mia's insides immediately, cold worms gnawing at her belly. But she did her best to stomp on them with her boots, as Tric marched her across the broken ground toward Mouser.

"You're ready then?" the Shahiid asked.

"We're ready," Tric said.

Mia smiled to hear his voice, almost a full octave deeper. He squeezed her fingers and closed his eyes, allowing Mouser to tie the blindfold. Tying Mia's, the Shahiid grasped their hands, led them across the broken ground. She heard a word spoken—something ancient and humming with power. And then she heard stone; the great cracking and rumbling of stone. The ground shuddered beneath her, dust rising in a choking pall. She felt a rushing wind, smelled a greasy arkemical tang in the air.

Hands took her own, led her forward, across broken ground and onto smooth rock. The temperature dropped suddenly, the light beyond her eyelids dying slow. They were somewhere dark now; inside the mountain's belly, she supposed. Mouser leading her by the hand, they reached stairs, climbing up, up in an ever-widening spiral. Twisting and turning, a soft vertigo filling her mind, all track of the direction she'd come from or the direction they were headed fading. Up. Down. Left. Right. Concepts with no meaning. No memory. She felt an almost overwhelming desire to call Mister Kindly back, to feel that familiar touch she no longer quite knew how to live without.

At last, after what seemed like hours, Mouser released his grip. For a moment she faltered. Imagining she stood at the mountain's peak, nothing about her but a straight fall to her death. Arms outstretched to keep her balance. Breathing hard.

"Come back," she whispered.

She felt the not-cat rush back in a flood, pouncing on the butterflies in her belly and dismembering them one by one. The blindfold was removed and she blinked, saw an enormous hall, bigger than the belly of the grandest cathedral. Walls and floor of dark granite, smooth as river stones. Soft arkemical light shone from within beautiful windows of stained glass, giving the impression of the sunlight outside—though in truth they could be miles within the mountain by now. Tric stood beside her, gazing about the room. Vast pointed archways and enormous stone pillars were arranged in a circle, soaring stone gables seemingly carved in the core of the mountain itself.

"Trelene's great . . . soft . . ."

Word failed as the boy looked toward the room's heart. Mia followed his gaze, saw the statue of a woman, jewels hung like stars on her ebony robe. The figure was colossal, towering forty feet above their heads, carved of gleaming black stone. Small iron rings were embedded in the rock, about head height. In her hands she held a scale and a massive, wicked sword, broad as treetrunks, sharp as obsidian. Her face was beautiful. Terrible and cold. Mia felt a chill trickle down her spine, the statue's eyes following as she walked closer.

"Welcome to the Hall of Eulogies," Mouser said.

"Who is she?"

"The Mother." Mouser touched his eyes, then his lips, then his chest. "The Maw. Our Lady of Blessed Murder. Almighty Niah."

"But . . . she's beautiful," Mia breathed. "In the pictures I've seen, she's a monstrosity."

"The Light is full of lies, Acolyte. The Suns serve only to blind us."

Mia wandered the mighty hall, running her hands over the spiral patterns in the stone. The walls were set with hundreds of small doors, two feet square, stacked one upon another as if tombs in some great mausoleum. Her footfalls rang like bells in the vast space. The only sound was the tune of what might have been a choir, hanging disembodied in the air. The hymn was beautiful, wordless, endless. The place had a feeling unlike any other she'd visited. There were no altars nor golden trim, but for the first time in her life, she felt as if she were somewhere . . . sanctified.

Mister Kindly whispered in her ear.

"*. . . i like it here . . .*"

"What are these names, Shahiid?" Tric asked.

Mia blinked, realized the floor beneath them was engraved with names. Hundreds. Thousands. Etched in tiny letters on polished black stone.

"The names of every life claimed by this Church for the Mother." The man bowed to the statue above. "Here we honor those taken. The Hall of Eulogies, as I said."

"And the tombs?" Mia asked, nodding to the walls.

"They house the bodies of servants of the Mother, gone to her side. Along with those we have taken, here we also honor those fallen."

"But there are no names carved on these tombs, Shahiid."

Mouser stared at Mia, the ghostly choir singing in the dark.

"The Mother knows their names," he finally said. "No other matters."

Mia blinked. Glancing up at the statue looming above her head. The goddess to whom this Church belonged. Terrible and beautiful. Unknowable and powerful.

"Come," said Shahiid Mouser. "Your chambers await."

He led them from the grand hall, through one of the vast pointed arches. A great flight of steps spiraled up into the black. Mia remembered Old Mercurio's willow switch, the accursed library stairs he'd made her run up and down so many times she'd lost count. She smiled at the memory, even as she thanked the old man for the exercise, climbing in long, easy strides.

They ascended, the Shahiid of Pockets behind them, silent as the plague.

"Black Mother," Tric panted. "They should have named it the Red Stairwell . . ."

"Are you well?" she whispered. "Mister Kindly helped?"

"Aye. It was . . ." The boy shook his head. "To look inside and find only steel . . . I've never felt anything like it. Crutch be damned. Being darkin must be a grand thing."

They tromped up the stairs into a long corridor. Arches stretching away into lightless black, spiral patterns on every wall. Shahiid Mouser stopped outside a wooden door, pushed it open. Mia looked in on a large room, furnished with beautiful dark wood and a huge bed covered in lush gray fur. Her body ached at the sight. It'd been at least two nevernights since she slept . . .

"Your chambers, Acolyte Mia," Mouser said.

"Where do I stay?" Tric asked.

"Down the hall. The other acolytes are already settled. You two are the last to arrive."

"How many are there?" Mia asked.

"Almost thirty. I look forward to seeing which are iron and which are glass."

Tric nodded in farewell and followed Mouser down the corridor. Mia stepped inside and dropped her pack by the door. Habit forced her to search every corner, drawer, and keyhole. She finished by peering under the bed before collapsing atop it. Contemplating untying her boots, she decided she was too exhausted to bother. And dropping back into the pillows, she crashed into a sleep deeper than she'd ever known.

A cat made of shadows perched on the bedhead, watching her dreams.

S he woke to Mister Kindly's cold whisper in her ear.
  "... *someone comes* ..."

Her eyes flashed open and she sat up as a soft rapping sounded at her door. Mia drew her dagger, clawed the hair from sand-crusted eyes. Forgetting where she was for a moment. Back in her old room above Mercurio's shop? Back in the Ribs, her baby brother asleep beside her, parents in the next room . . .

No.

Don't look . . .

She spoke uncertainly. "Come in?"

The door opened softly and a figure swathed in black robes entered, crossing the room to halt at the foot of the bed. Mia raised her gravebone blade warily.

"You either picked the wrong room or the wrong girl . . ."

The intruder raised her hands. She pulled back her hood, and Mia saw strawberry blond curls, familiar eyes peering out between veils of black cloth.

"Naev . . ?"

But that was impossible. The woman's guts had been torn to ribbons by those kraken hooks. After two turns rotting in the sun, her blood would've been swimming with poison. How in the Maw's name was she even alive, let alone walking and talking?

"You should be dead . . ."

"Should be. But is not." The thin woman bowed. "Thanks to her."

Mia shook her head. "You don't owe me thanks."

"More than thanks. She risked her life to save Naev. Naev will not forget."

Mia shuffled back as Naev produced a hidden blade from within her sleeve, Mister Kindly puffing up in her shadow. But Naev drew the knife along the heel of her own hand, blood welling from the cut and spattering on the floor.

"She saved Naev's life," the woman said. "So now, Naev owes it. On her blood, in the sight of Mother Night, Naev vows it."

"You don't need to do this . . ."

"It is done."

Naev leaned down and began unlacing Mia's boots. Mia yelped, tucked them underneath her. The woman reached for the ties on Mia's shirt, and Mia slapped her hands away, backing off across the bed with her own hands raised.

"Now, look here . . ."

"She must undress."

"You *really* picked the wrong girl. And most people offer a drink first."

Naev put her hands on her hips. "She must bathe before she meets the Ministry. If Naev may speak plain, she reeks of horse and excrement, her hair is greasier than a Liisian sweetbread, and she is painted in dried blood. If she wishes to attend her baptism into the Blessed Lady's congregation looking like a Dweymeri savage, Naev suggests she saves herself the pain and simply step off the Sky Altar now."

"Wait . . ." Mia blinked. "Did you say bath?"

". . . Naev did."

"With water?" Mia was up on her knees, hands clutched at her breast. "And soap?"

The woman nodded. "Five kinds."

"Maw's teeth," Mia said, unlacing her shirt. "You picked the right girl after all."

D ark figures gathered in the gaze of a stone goddess, bathed with colorless light.

It had been twelve hours since Mia arrived at the Quiet Mountain. Four since she woke. Twenty-seven minutes since she'd dragged herself from her bath and down to the Hall of Eulogies, leaving a scum of blood and grime on the water's surface that could've walked away by itself if given a few more turns to gestate.

The robe was soft against her skin, her hair bound in a damp braid. Soap scent drifted about her when she turned to look among the other acolytes—twenty-eight in all, dressed in toneless gray. A brutish Itreyan boy with fists like sledgehammers. A wiry lass with bobbed red hair, eyes filled with wolf cunning. A towering Dweymeri, with ornate facial tattoos and shoulders you could rest the world on. Two blond and freckled Vaanians—brother and sister, by the look. A thin boy with ice-blue eyes, standing near Tric at the end of the

row, so still she almost missed him. All of them around her age. All of them
hard and hungry and silent.

Naev stood close by Mia, swathed in shadows. Other quiet figures in black
robes stood at the edge of the darkness, men and women, fingers entwined like
penitents in a cathedral.

"Hands," Naev had whispered. "She will find two kinds in the Red Church.
The ones who take vocations, make offerings . . . what commonfolk call assassins, yes? We call them Blades."

Mia nodded. "Mercurio told me such."

"The second are called Hands," Naev continued. "There are twenty Hands
for every Blade. They keep her House in order. Manage affairs. Make supply
runs, like Naev. No more than four acolytes in every flock become Blades. Those
who survive the year but fail to pass the grade will become Hands. Other folk
simply come here to serve the goddess as they can. Not everyone is suited to
do murder in her name."

So. Only four of us can make the cut.

Mia nodded, watching the black-robed figures. Squinting in the dark, she
could see the arkemical scar of slavery on a few cheeks. After the acolytes had
finished assembling beneath the statue's gaze, the Hands spoke a scrap of scripture, Naev along with them, each speaking by rote.

"She who is all and nothing,
First and last and always,
A perfect black, a Hungry Dark,
Maid and Mother and Matriarch,
Now, and at the moment of our deaths,
Pray for us."

A bell rang, soft, somewhere in the gloom. Mia felt Mister Kindly curled
about her feet, drinking deep. She heard footsteps, saw a figure approaching
from the shadows. The Hands raised their voices in unison.

"Mouser, Shahiid of Pockets, pray for us."

A familiar figure stepped onto the dais around the statue's base. Handsome
face and old eyes—the man who'd met Mia and Tric outside the Mountain.
He was robed in gray, his blacksteel sword the only embellishment. He took
his place, faced the acolytes, and with a grin that could easily make off with
the silverware and the candelabras, too, he spoke.

"Twenty-six."

Mia heard more footsteps, and the Hands spoke again.

"Spiderkiller, Shahiid of Truths, pray for us."

A Dweymeri woman stalked from the gloom, tall and stately, her back as straight as the pillars around them. Long hair in neat, knotted locks, streaming down her back like rope. Her skin was dark like all her people, but she wore no facial tattoos. She seemed a moving statue, carved of mahogany. Clasped hands were stained with what might have been ink. Her lips were painted black. A collection of glass phials hung at her belt beside three curved daggers.

She took her place on the dais, spoke with a strong, proud voice.

"Twenty-nine."

Mia watched on in silence, gnawing at her lip. And though Mercurio had schooled Mia well in the subtle art of patience, curiosity finally got the best of her.*

"What are they doing?" Mia whispered to Naev. "What do the numbers mean?"

"Their tally for the goddess. The number of offerings they have wrought in her name."

"*Solis, Shahiid of Songs, pray for us.*"

Mia watched a man stride from the shadows, also clad in gray. He was a huge lump of a thing, biceps big as her thighs. His head was shaved to stubble, so blond it was almost white, scalp lined with scars. His beard was set in four

---

* One of the old man's favorite tests early in Mia's apprenticeship was a game he called "Ironpriest," in which he and the girl would see who could last the longest without speaking. Though Mia at first thought it a game to test her patience and resolve, in later years, Mercurio confessed he only invented the game to get some peace and quiet around the store.

His most infamous test, however, came about in Mia's twelfth year. During a particularly freezing wintersdeep, the old man instructed the girl to wait on the rooftops opposite the Grand Chapel of Tsana for a messenger wearing red gloves, and follow the lad wherever he went. The matter, he told her, was of "dire import."

The messenger, of course, was one of Mercurio's many agents in the city. He was traveling nowhere of import—dire or otherwise—merely meant to lead Mia on a merry chase in the freezing cold and eventually back to the curio store. However, unbeknownst to Mercurio, the boy was hit by a runaway horse on his way to the temple district, and, thus, never arrived.

Mia remained on the rooftops despite the awful cold (only one sun resides in the sky during Godsgrave winters, and the chill is long and bitter). As the snows began to fall, she refused to move lest she miss her mark. When Mia hadn't arrived by next morning, Mercurio grew worried, retracing the messenger's assigned path until he at last arrived atop the temple district roof. There he found his apprentice, almost hypothermic, shivering uncontrollably, eyes still locked on the Chapel of Tsana. When the old man asked why in the Mother's name Mia had stayed on the roof when she was in danger of freezing to death, the twelve-year-old simply replied, "You said it was important."

Not without her charm, as I said.

spikes at his chin. He wore a sword belt, but his scabbard was empty. As he took his place, Mia looked into his eyes and realized he was blind.

"Thirty-six," he said.

Thirty-six murders? At the hands of a blind man?

"Aalea, Shahiid of Masks, pray for us."

Another woman padded into the soft light, swaying as she came, all curves and alabaster skin. Mia found her jaw agape—the newcomer was easily the most beautiful woman she'd laid eyes on. Thick black hair cascading to her waist, dark eyes smeared with kohl, lips painted bloody red. She was unarmed. Apparently.

"Thirty-nine," she said, with a voice like sweet smoke.

"Revered Mother Drusilla, pray for us."

A woman slipped out of the darkness, soundless as cot death. She was elderly, curling gray hair bound in braids. An obsidian key hung about her throat on a silver chain. She seemed a kindly old thing, eyes twinkling as she looked over the group. Mia would've expected to find her in a rocking chair beside a happy hearth, grandchildren on her knee and a cup of tea by her elbow. This couldn't be the chief minister of the deadliest band of—

"Eighty-three," the old woman said, taking her place on the dais.

Maw take me, eighty-three . . .

The Revered Mother looked over the group, a gentle smile on her lips.

"I bid you welcome to the Red Church, children," she said. "You have traveled miles and years to be here. You have miles and years to go. But at journey's end, you will be Blades, wielded for the glory of the goddess in the most sacred of sacraments.

"Those who survive, of course."

The old woman gestured to the four figures around her.

"Heed the words of your Shahiid. Know that everything you were prior to this moment is dead. That once you pledge yourself to the Maw, you are hers and hers alone." A robed figure with a silver bowl stepped up beside the Revered Mother, and she beckoned Mia. "Bring forth your tithe. The remnants of a killer, killed in turn and offered to Our Lady of Blessed Murder in this, the hour of your baptism."

Mia stepped forward, purse in hand. Her stomach was turning flips, but her hands were steady as stone. She took her place before the old woman and her gentle smile, looked deep into pale blue eyes. Felt herself being weighed. Wondered if she'd been found wanting.

"My tithe," she managed to say. "For the Maw."

"I accept it in her name with her thanks upon my lips."

Mia sighed as she heard the response, almost falling to her knees as the Revered Mother embraced her, kissed one cheek after another with ice-cold lips. She squeezed Mia tight as the girl breathed deep, blinking back hot tears. And turning to the silver bowl, the old woman dipped one stick-thin hand inside and drew it back, dripping red.

Blood.

"Speak your name."

"Mia Corvere."

"Do you vow to serve the Mother of Night? Will you learn death in all its colors, bring it to the deserving and undeserving in her name? Will you become an Acolyte of Niah, and an earthly instrument of the dark between the stars?"

Mia found herself struggling to inhale.

The deep breath before the plunge.

"I will."

The Revered Mother pressed her palm to Mia's cheek, smearing the blood down her skin. It was still warm, the scent of salt and copper filling the girl's lungs. The old woman marked one cheek, then the other, finally smudging a long streak down Mia's lips and chin. The girl felt the gravity of that moment in her bones, dragging her belly to her boots. The Mother nodded and Mia backed away, hugging herself, licking the blood from her lips, near weeping, laughing. One step closer to avenging her familia. One step closer to standing on Scaeva's tomb.

She was here, she realized.

I'm here.

The ritual was repeated, each acolyte bringing forth their tithes one by one. Some brought teeth, others eyes—the tall boy with the sledgehammer hands brought a rotting heart, wrapped in black velvet. Mia realized there wasn't a single one of them who wasn't a murderer. That of all the rooms in the Republic there was probably none more dangerous than the one she stood in, right at that moment.*

"Your studies begin on the morrow," the Revered Mother said. "Evemeal will be served in the Sky Altar in a half-hour." She indicated the row of robed figures. "Hands will be available should you need guidance, and I would suggest you avail yourselves until you find your bearings. The Mountain can be difficult to navigate at first, and getting lost within these halls can have . . . unfortunate consequences." Blue eyes glittered in the dark. "Walk softly. Learn well. May Our Lady be late when she finds you. And when she does, may she greet you with a kiss."

---

*Astonishingly, remarkably, impossibly incorrect.

The old woman bowed, stepped back into the gloom. The other Ministry members left one by one. Tric wandered over to Mia, greeted her with a smile, his cheeks red with blood. He'd been bathed and scrubbed, and even his salt-locks looked a little less sentient.

"You shaved," she smirked.

"Don't get used to it. Happens twice a year." He squinted at Naev, recognition slowly widening in his eyes. "How in the name of the Lady . . ."

"We meet again." The thin woman bowed low. "Naev gives thanks for his assistance in the deep desert. The debt shall not be forgot."

"How are you still walking and breathing?"

"Secrets within secrets in this place," Mia said.

"Corvere?" said a soft voice behind her.

Mia turned to the speaker. It was the girl she'd noted; the pretty one with a jagged red bob and green, hunter's eyes. She was studying Mia intently, head tilted. The tall Itreyan boy with sledgehammer hands loomed beside her like an angry shadow.

"In the ceremony," the girl said. "You said your name was Corvere?"

"Aye," Mia said.

"Are you by chance related to Darius Corvere? The former justicus?"

Mia weighed up the girl in her mind. Fit. Fast. Hard as wood. But whoever she was, Mia was certain Scaeva and his cronies would have no allies within these walls; Remus and his Luminatii had vowed to do away with the Red Church since the Truedark Massacre, after all. Even so, Mercurio had urged Mia to leave her name behind when she crossed this threshold. It was one of the few things they'd argued about. Stupid perhaps. But her father's death was the whole reason she'd begun walking this road. The name Corvere had been erased from the histories by Scaeva and his lackeys—she'd not leave it behind in the dust, no matter what it cost her.

"I'm Darius Corvere's daughter," Mia finally replied. "And you are?"

"Jessamine, daughter of Marcinus Gratianus."

"Apologies. Is that someone I should have heard of?"

"First centurion of the Luminatii Legion," the girl scowled. "Executed by order of the Itreyan Senate after the Kingmaker Rebellion."

Mia's frown softened. Black Mother, this was the daughter of one of her father's centurions. A girl just like her—orphaned by Consul Scaeva and Justicus Remus and the rest of those bastards. Someone who knew the taste of injustice as well as she did.

Mia offered her hand. "Well met, sister. My—"

Jessamine slapped the hand away, eyes flashing. "You're no sister to me, bitch."

Mia felt Tric bristle beside her, Mister Kindly's hackles rise in the shadow at her feet. She rubbed her slapped knuckles, speaking carefully.

"I grieve your loss. Truly, I do. My fath—"

"Your father was a fucking traitor," Jessamine snarled. "His men died because they honored their oaths to a fool justicus, and their skulls now pave the steps to the Senate House. Because of the mighty Darius Corvere."

"My father was loyal to General Antonius," Mia said. "He had oaths to honor too."

"Your father was a fucking lapdog," Jessamine spat. "Everyone knows why he followed Antonius, and it had *nothing* to do with honor. My father and brother were *crucified* because of him. My mother dead of grief in Godsgrave Asylum. All of them, unavenged." The girl stepped closer, eyes narrowed. "But not much longer. You'd best grow some eyes in back of your head, Corvere. You'd best start sleeping light."

Mia stared the girl down, unblinking, Mister Kindly swelling beneath her feet. Naev drifted closer to the redheaded girl, lisping in her ear.

"She will step away. Or she will be stepped upon."

Jessamine glanced at the woman, jaw clenched. After a staring contest that stretched for miles, the girl spun on her heel and stalked off, the big Itreyan boy trailing behind. Mia realized her nails were cutting her palms.

"You surely do know how to make friends, Pale Daughter."

Mia turned to Tric, found him smiling, though his hand was also up his sleeve. She relaxed a touch, allowed herself a smile too. Bad as she was at making them, at least she had one friend within these walls.

"Come on," the boy said. "We going to evemeal or not?"

Mia looked after the retreating Jessamine. Glanced around at the other acolytes. The reality of where she was sank home deeper. A school of killers. Surrounded by novices or masters in the art of murder. She was here. This was it.

Time to get to work.

"Evemeal sounds good," she nodded. "I can't think of a better place to start scouting."

"Scouting? For what?"

"You've heard the saying the quickest way to a man's heart is through his stomach?"

"I always wondered about that," Tric frowned. "Ribcage seems much quicker to me."

"True enough. But still, you can learn a lot about animals. Watching them eat."

". . . You're a little frightening sometimes, Pale Daughter."

She gave him a wry smile. "Only a little?"

"Well, most times, you're just plain terrifying."

"Come on," she said, slapping his arm. "I'll buy you a drink."

CHAPTER 9

DARK

The old man straightened her nose out as best he could, wiped the blood from her face with a rag soaked in something that smelled sharp and metallic. And sitting her down at a little table in the back of his shop, he'd made her tea.

The room was somewhere between a kitchen and a library. All was swathed in shadow, the shutters drawn against the sunlight outside.* A single arkemical lamp illuminated stacks of dirty crockery and great, wobbling piles of books. Mia's pain slipped away as she sipped Mercurio's brew, the throbbing mess in the middle of her face rendered mercifully numb. He gave her honeyseed cake and watched her wolf down three slices, like a spider watches a fly. And when she pushed the plate aside, he finally spoke.

"How's the beak?"

"Doesn't hurt anymore."

"Good tea, neh?" He smiled. "How'd it get broken?"

"The big boy. Shivs. I put my knife to his privates and he hit me for it."

"Who told you to go for a boy's cods in a scrap?"

---

* As you can imagine, gentlefriend, methods by which the suns can be kept at bay in a land where the bastard things almost never set are considered of no small import. Master bedrooms in the Republic are often built in basements, and guests at more well-to-do taverna will pay extra for rooms without windows. Dreamsickness—a malady acquired from lack of deep sleep—is an increasingly problematic ailment, and although Aa's ministry burned him as a heretic, in the Visionaries' Row of the Iron Collegium's grand foyer, you can still find a statue of Don Augustine D'Antello, inventor of the triple-ply curtain.

"My father. He said the quickest way to beat a boy is to make him wish he was a girl."

Mercurio chuckled. "Duum'a."

"What does that mean?" Mia blinked.

". . . You don't speak Liisian?"

"Why would I?"

"I thought your ma would've taught you. She was from these parts."

Mia blinked. "She was?"

The old man nodded. "Long time back, now. Before she got hitched and became a dona."

"She . . . never spoke of it."

"Not much reason to, I s'pose. I imagine she thought she'd left these streets behind forever." He shrugged. "Anyways, closest translation of 'duum'a' would be 'is wise.' You say it when you hear agreeable words. As you might say 'hear, hear' or suchlike."

"What does 'Neh diis . . .'" Mia frowned, struggling with the pronunciation. "'Neh diis lus'a . . . lus diis'a'? What does that mean?"

Mercurio raised an eyebrow. "Where'd you hear that?"

"Consul Scaeva said it to my mother. When he told her to beg for my life."

Mercurio stroked his stubble. "It's an old Liisian saying."

"What does it mean?"

"When all is blood, blood is all."

Mia nodded, thinking perhaps she understood. They sat in silence for a time, the old man lighting one of his clove-scented cigarillos and drawing deep. Finally, Mia spoke again.

"You said my mother was from here? Little Liis?"

"Aye. Long time past."

"Did she have familia here? Someone I could . . ."

Mercurio shook his head. "They're gone, child. Or dead. Both, mostly."

"Like Father."

Mercurio cleared his throat, sucked on his cigarillo.

". . . It was a shame. What they did to him."

"They said he was a traitor."

A shrug. "A traitor's just a patriot on the wrong side of winning."

Mia brushed her fringe from her eyes, looked hopeful. "He was a patriot, then?"

"No, little Crow," the old man said. "He lost."

"And they killed him." Hate rose up in her belly, curled her hands to fists. "The consul. That fat priest. The new justicus. They killed him."

Mercurio exhaled a thin gray ring, watching her closely. "He and General Antonius wanted to overthrow the Senate, girl. They'd mustered a bloody army and were set to march against their own capital. Think of all the death that would've unfolded if they'd not been captured before the war began in truth. Maybe they should've hung your da. Maybe he deserved it."

Mia's eyes widened and she kicked back her chair, reaching for the knife that wasn't there. The rage resurfaced then, all the pain and anger of the last twenty-four hours flaring inside her, the anger flooding so thick it made her arms and legs tremble.

And the shadows in the room began trembling too.

The black writhed. At her feet. Behind her eyes. She clenched her fists. Spat through gritted teeth. "My father was a good man. And he didn't deserve to die like that."

The teapot slipped off the counter with a crash. Cupboard doors shook on their hinges, cups danced on their saucers. Towers of books toppled and sprawled across the floor. Mia's shadow stretched out toward the old man's, clawing across the splintering boards, the nails popping free as it drew ever closer. Mister Kindly coalesced at her feet, translucent hackles raised, hissing and spitting. Mercurio backed across the room quicker than she'd imagine an old fellow might have stepped, hands raised in supplication, cigarillo hanging from bone-dry lips.

"Peace, peace, little Crow," he said. "A test is all, a test. No offense meant."

As the crockery stopped trembling and the cupboards fell silent, Mia sagged in place, tears fighting with the anger. It was all crashing down on her. The sight of her father swinging, her mother's screams, sleeping in alleys, robbed and beaten . . . all of it. Too much.

Too much.

Mister Kindly circled her feet, purring and prowling just like a real cat might. Her shadow slipped back across the floor, puddling into its regular shape, just a shade too dark for one. Mercurio pointed to it.

"How long has it listened?"

". . . What?"

"The Dark. How long has it listened when you call?"

"I don't know what you mean."

She curled up on her haunches, trying to hold it inside. Screw it up and push it all the way down into her shoes. Her shoulders shook. Her belly ached. And softly, she began to sob.

O, Daughters, how she hated herself, then . . .

The old man reached into his greatcoat. Pulled out a mostly clean handkerchief and held it out to her. Watching as she snatched it away, dabbed as best she could *at her broken nose, the hateful tears in her lashes. And finally he knelt on the boards in front of her, looked at her with eyes as sharp and blue as raw sapphires.*

"I don't know what any of this means," she whispered.

The old man's eyes twinkled as he smiled. With a glance toward the cat made of shadows, Mercurio drew out her mother's stiletto from his coat, stabbed it into the floorboards between them. The polished gravebone gleamed in the lantern light.

"Would you like to learn?" he asked.

Mia eyed the knife, nodded slow. "Yes, I would, sir."

"There's no sirs 'round here, little Crow. No donas or dons. Just you and me."

Mia chewed her lip, tempted to just grab the blade and run for it.

But where would she go? What would she do?

"What should I call you, then?" *she finally asked.*

"Depends."

"On what?"

"If you want to take back what's yours from them what took it. If you're the kind who doesn't forget, and doesn't forgive. Who wants to understand why the Mother has marked you."

Mia stared back. Unblinking. Her shadow rippled at her feet.

"And if I am?"

"Then you call me 'Shahiid.' Until the turn I call you 'Mia.'"

"What's 'Shahiid' mean?"

"It's an old Ashkahi word. It means 'Honored Master.'"

"What will you call me in the meantime?"

A thin ring of smoke spilled from the old man's lips as he spoke. "Guess."

". . . Apprentice?"

"Smarter than you look, girl. One of the few things I like about you."

Mia looked at the shadow beneath her feet. Up at the sunlight glare waiting just beyond the shutters. The Godsgrave. The City of Bridges and Bones, slowly filling with the bones of those she loved. There was no one out there who could help her, she knew it. And if she was going to free her mother and brother from the Philosopher's Stone, if she wanted to save them from a tomb beside her father's— presuming they buried him at all—if she was going to bring justice to the people who'd destroyed her familia . . .

Well. She'd need help, wouldn't she?

"All right, then. Shahiid."

Mia reached for her knife. Mercurio snatched it away, silver-quick, held it up between them. Tiny amber eyes twinkled at her in the gloom.

"Not until you earn it," he said.

"But it's mine," *Mia protested.*

"Forget the girl who had everything. She died when her father did."

"But I—"

"Nothing is where you start. Own nothing. Know nothing. Be nothing."

"Why would I want to do that?"

The old man crushed out his cigarillo on the boards between them.

His smile made her smile in return.

"Because then you can do anything."

In years to come, Mia would look back on the moment she first saw the Sky Altar and realize it was the moment she started believing in the divinities. O, Mercurio had indoctrinated her into the religion of the Mother. Death as an offering. Life as a vocation. And she'd been raised a good god-fearing daughter of Aa before all that. But it wasn't until she looked over that balcony that she embraced the probability of it, or began to truly understand where she was.

She and Tric were led up another of the Church's (seemingly endless) flights of stairs by Naev and other robed figures. All twenty-eight acolytes had decided to take supper, quiet conversations marking their climb, the mix of accents reminding Mia of the Little Liis market. But all conversation stilled as the group reached the landing. Mia caught her breath, pressed one hand to her chest. Naev whispered in her ear.

"Welcome to the Sky Altar."

The platform was carved in the Mountain's side, open to the air above. Tables were laid out in a T, the scent of roasting meat and fresh bread kissing the air. And though her stomach growled at the presence of food, Mia's thoughts were consumed entirely by the sight before her.

The platform protruded from the Mountain's flank, a thousand-foot drop waiting just beyond the ironwood railing. She could see the Whisperwastes below, tiny and perfect and still. But above, where the sky should have burned with the light of stubborn suns, she could see only darkness, black and whole and perfect.

Filled with tiny stars.

"What in the name of the Light . . . ," she breathed.

"Not the Light," Naev slurred. "The Dark."

"How can this be? Truedark won't fall for at least another year."

"It is always truedark here."

"But that's impossible . . ."

"Only if *here* is where she supposes it to be." The woman shrugged. "It is not."

The acolytes were shown to their places, gawping at the black above. Though it should have been howling at this altitude, not a breath of wind disturbed the scene. Not a noise, save hushed voices and Mia's own rushing pulse.

She found herself seated with Tric on her right, the slight boy with the ice-blue eyes on her left. Seated opposite was the pair Mia had guessed were brother and sister. The girl had blond hair plaited in tight warbraids, shaved in an undercut. Her face was pretty and dimpled, smattered with freckles. Her brother possessed the same round face, though he didn't smile, so no dimples made appearance. His hair was a crop of snarled spikes. Both had eyes blue as empty skies. Their cheeks were still crusted with blood from the baptism ceremony.

Mia had already received one death threat since she arrived. She wondered if every acolyte in this year's crop would be an opponent or outright enemy.

The blond girl pointed to Mia's cheeks with her knife. "You've got something on your face."

"You too," Mia nodded. "Good color on you, though. Brings out your eyes."

The girl snorted, grinned lopsided.

"Well," Mia said. "Shall we introduce ourselves, or just glare the whole meal?"

"I'm Ashlinn Järnheim," the girl replied. "Ash for short. This is my brother, Osrik."

"Mia Corvere. This is Tric," Mia said, nodding at her friend.

For his own part, Tric was glaring down the table at the other Dweymeri. The bigger boy had the same square jaw and flat brow as Tric, but he was taller, broader, and where Tric's tattoos were scrawled and artless, the bigger boy's face was marked in ink of exquisite craftsmanship. He was watching Tric the way a whitedrake watches a seal pup.

"Hello, Tric," said Ashlinn, offering her hand.

The boy shook it without looking at her. "Pleasure."

Ashlinn, Osrik, and Mia all looked expectantly at the pale boy on Mia's left. For his part, the boy was gazing up at the night sky. His lips were pursed, as if he were sucking his teeth. Mia realized he was handsome—well, "beautiful" was probably a better word—with high cheekbones and the most piercing blue eyes she'd ever seen. But thin. Far too thin.

"I'm Mia," she said, offering her hand.

The boy blinked, turned his gaze to the girl. Lifting a piece of charboard from his lap, he wrote on it with a stick of chalk and held it up for Mia to see.

HUSH, it said.

Mia blinked. "That's your name?"

The beautiful boy nodded, turned his stare back to the sky without a sound. He didn't make a peep throughout the entire meal.

Ashlinn, Osrik, and Mia spoke as food was served—chicken broth and mutton in lemon butter, roast vegetables and a delicious Itreyan red. Ashlinn handled most of the conversational duties, while Osrik seemed more intent on watching the room. The siblings were sixteen and seventeen (Osrik the elder) and had arrived five turns prior. Their mentor (and father, it turned out) had been far more forthcoming about finding the Church than Old Mercurio, and the siblings had avoided any monstrosities on their way to the Quiet Mountain. Ashlinn seemed impressed by Mia's story of the sand kraken. Osrik seemed more impressed with Jessamine. The redhead and her cunning wolf eyes was seated three stools down, and Osrik couldn't seem to tear his stare away. For her part, the girl seemed more intent on the thuggish Itreyan boy seated beside her, whispering to him and occasionally staring daggers at Mia.

Mia could feel other furtive glances and lingering stares—though some were better at hiding it than others, almost every acolyte was studying their fellows. Hush simply stared at the sky and sipped his broth like it was a chore, not touching any other food.

Mia watched the Ministry between courses, noting the way they interacted. Solis, the blind Shahiid of Songs, seemed to dominate conversation, though from the occasional bursts of laughter he elicited, Mouser, the Shahiid of Pockets, seemed possessed of the keenest wit. Spiderkiller and Aalea, Shahiid of Truths and Masks, sat so close they touched. All paid the utmost respect to Revered Mother Drusilla, conversation stilling when the old woman spoke.

It was halfway through the meal that Mia felt a queasy feeling creep into her gut. She looked about the room, felt Mister Kindly curling up in her shadow. The Revered Mother stood suddenly, the Ministry members about her swiftly following suit, gazes downturned.

Mother Drusilla spoke, eyes on the acolytes.

"All of you, please rise."

Mia climbed to her feet, frowning softly. Ashlinn turned to her brother, whispering with something close to fervor.

"Black Mother, he's *here*."

Mia realized a dark-haired man was standing at the Sky Altar's balcony, overlooking the shifting wastes below—though for the life of her, she'd not seen him actually enter the room. She felt her shadow trembling, shrinking, Mister Kindly curling up at her feet.

"Lord Cassius," Drusilla said, bowing. "You honor us."

The man turned to the Revered Mother with a thin smile. He was tall, muscular, clad in soft dark leather. Long black hair framed piercing eyes and a jaw you could break your fist on. He wore a heavy black cloak and twin blades at his waist. Perfectly plain. Perfectly deadly. He spoke with a voice that made Mia tingle in all the wrong places.

"Be at peace, Revered Mother." Dark eyes roamed the new acolytes, still standing as if to attention. "I simply wished to admire the view. May I join you?"

"Of course, Lord."

The Revered Mother vacated her seat at the head of the Ministry's table, the other Shahiid shuffling about to accommodate the newcomer. Still smiling, the man stepped to the Mother's seat, soundless as the sunset. His movements were smooth, flowing like water, sweeping aside his cloak as he sat in the Revered Mother's chair. The sickness in Mia's belly surged as the strange man glanced directly at her. But as he lifted a cup of wine, the spell of utter stillness he'd seemed to have cast over the room softly broke. Hands scuttled to set a new place at table, the Ministry sank slowly into their seats, acolytes following. Conversation began again, cautious at first, relaxing by inches until it filled the room.

Mia found herself staring at the mysterious newcomer throughout the meal, eyes tracing the line of his jaw, his throat. She was sure it was a trick of the light, but his long raven hair seemed as if it were almost moving, his eyes glittering with some inner light.

Mia looked for Naev, but the woman was seated with other Hands, too far away.

"Ashlinn," she finally whispered. "Who *is* that?"

The girl blinked at Mia. Her brother Osrik raised an eyebrow.

"Maw's teeth, Corvere, that's Cassius. The Black Prince. Lord of Blades. Leader of the entire congregation. More bodies on him than a Liisian necropolis."

"What's he doing here? Is he a teacher?"

"No." Osrik shook his head. "We'd no idea he'd be here this eve."

"Da always told us Cassius stayed away from here," Ashlinn said. "Keeps his comings and goings well secret. No disciple of the Church knows where he'll be until he gets there. Only attends the Mountain for initiation ceremonies, they say."

Osrik nodded, glanced to the students around them. "Some acolytes only lay eyes on him once in their life. The night he declares them full-fledged Blades. If you're chosen, he'll anoint you just as the Revered Mother did tonight at the baptism." The boy pointed to the dried gore on Mia's cheeks. "Only it'll be with his own blood. The blood of the Lord of Blades. Right Hand of the Mother herself."

Mia found herself unable to tear her eyes away from the man.

Ashlinn flashed her a dimpled smile.

"For the leader of a cult of mass murderers, he's not hard on the eyes, neh?"

Mia dragged her fringe from her lashes, heart in her throat. Ashlinn wasn't—

"Keep staring at me, *koffi*," said a deep voice, "and I'll cut out those pretty eyes."

Mia blinked in the sudden still, turned back to her table. She realized the big Dweymeri boy was speaking to Tric, contempt in his gaze.

Tric rose, roastknife clutched in his hand.

"What did you call me, bastard?"

"You name me bastard?" The big Dweymeri laughed. "My name is Floodcaller, thirdson of Rainrunner of the Seaspear clan. What is your clan, *koffi*? Did your father even give your mother his name when he was done wiping her stink off his cock?"

Tric's face paled, his jaw clenched.

"You're a fucking dead man," he hissed.

Mia put a restraining hand on his arm, but Tric was off, diving toward Floodcaller's throat. The bigger boy was on his feet, leaping across the table and knocking plates, glasses, and both Mia and Hush aside in his haste to get to Tric. Mia fell with a curse and a smash of crockery, her shoulder knocking the pale boy's breath loose in a spray of spit.

Floodcaller caught Tric in a bearhug as they crashed to the floor, pottery and glassware shattering. He outweighed Tric by a hundred pounds—he was easily the strongest person in the room. Bigger even than the Shahiid of Songs, who turned blind eyes to the melee and roared, "YOU BOYS, ENOUGH!"

The boys were having none of it, flailing and punching and spitting. Tric landed a good blow to Floodcaller's face, mashing lips into teeth. But Mia was astonished at how easily the big Dweymeri dominated Tric, flipping him over and landing blow after blow into the smaller boy's ribs, more against his jaw. The acolytes gathered around the brawl, none moving to help. Mia pulled herself off Hush and was set to step in when she saw Shahiid Solis kick back his chair and march toward the melee.

Though the man appeared utterly blind, he moved quick and sure. Clapping one hand on Floodcaller's shoulder, he dropped a hook like an anvil on the boy's jaw, sent him sprawling. Tric tried scrambling to his feet, but Solis buried his boot in the boy's gut, knocking the wind and fight out of him with one blow. Turning on Floodcaller, the Shahiid stomped on his bollocks hard, curled the Dweymeri boy up in a squealing ball.

It'd taken only a handful of heartbeats, but the Shahiid had whipped both boys like disobedient puppies, pale, sightless eyes turned to the sky all the while.

"Disgraceful," he growled, seizing both groaning boys by their scruffs. "If you must fight like dogs, you can eat outside with the rest of them."

The Shahiid of Songs dragged Tric and Floodcaller to the balcony. Gripping each by the throat, the big man pushed them against the railing, the thousand-foot drop yawning behind them. Both boys were choking, clawing at the Shahiid's grip. The man's blind eyes showed no pity, the boys just a heartbeat away from death on the rocks below. Mia's hand was on her dagger when the Revered Mother spoke.

"Enough, Solis."

The man tilted his head, turned milk-white eyes toward the sound of her voice.

"Revered Mother," he said.

Floodcaller and Tric both collapsed to the deck, gasping for air. Mia could scarcely breathe herself. She looked for Lord Cassius and found he was simply *gone*, an empty chair marking the place where the Lord of Blades had sat moments before. Again, she swore she'd never even seen him move. Mother Drusilla stepped out from behind her table, drifted to where the boys lay coughing and sputtering.

"O, I remember what it was to be young. Ever something to prove. And boys will be boys, they say." She knelt, touched Tric's bloody cheek. Smoothed Floodcaller's saltlocks. "But you are boys no longer. You are servants of the Mother, tithed to her Church. You are killers one, killers all. And I expect you all to behave as such." She glanced up at the assembled acolytes. "A poor example has been set tonight indeed."

Mother Drusilla helped the bleeding Dweymeri to their feet, her matronly facade momentarily evaporating, every one of her eighty-three murders dripping in her voice.

"So. The next time the pair of you fall to scrapping like boys in a back alley, I will see to it that you remain boys for the rest of your lives. Is that understood?"

Mia watched these two towering lumps shrink, staring at their feet. And when they spoke in unison, like toddlers before a scolding parent, it was all either could do to muster a squeak.

"Yes, Revered Mother," they said.

"Good." The motherly smile returned as if it had never left, and Drusilla looked about the acolytes with kindly eyes. "I think supper is done for the evening. Go to your bedchambers, all of you. Lessons begin tomorrow."

The group broke apart slowly, drifting down the stairs. As Mia went to Tric's side and peered at the bloody cut above his brow, she caught Jessamine watching her, lips twisted in a smirk. Floodcaller limped away, still glaring daggers. Ashlinn nodded farewell to Mia as she tromped down the stairs. Mia found herself staring one last time at the place Lord Cassius had sat.

Right Hand of the Mother herself . . .

She kept silent all the way back to the bedchambers, growing angrier and angrier. Why had Tric snapped so easily? Where had the quiet boy who'd endured the taunts of the Old Imperial's common room disappeared to? He'd lost his temper in front of the lord of the entire congregation. On his first eve here. His outburst could've got him killed. This wasn't a place that forgave mistakes.

She finally lost her temper just outside her door.

"Have you lost your mind?" Mia hissed, loud as she dared. "What was that?"

"How's the ribs, Tric?" he asked. "I couldn't help but notice you getting the stuffing kicked out of you. O, I'm fine, Pale Daughter, my thanks for—"

"What did you expect? This is our first *turn* inside these walls and you've already pissed off Shahiid Solis and probably the most feared assassin in the Itreyan Republic. And let's not forget the fellow acolyte set to murder you."

"He called me *koffi*, Mia. He's lucky I didn't cave his head in."

"What's *koffi*?"

"Never mind." He dragged his arm from her grip. "Forget it."

"Tric—"

"I'm tired. I'll see you on the morrow."

The boy stalked off, leaving Mia alone with Naev. The woman watched her with dark, careful eyes, hovering like a moth about a black flame. Mia's brow was creased, staring at the half-finished puzzle before her.

". . . You don't happen to speak Dweymeri, do you?" she asked.

"No. Although Naev is certain there are tomes of translation in the athenaeum."

Mia chewed her lip. Pictured her bed, with its mountains of pillows and soft fur.

"Is it open this late?"

"The library is always open here. But to attend without invitation—"

"Could you take me there? Please?"

The woman's dark eyes gleamed. "As she wishes."

Stairs and arches. Arches and stairs. Mia and Naev walked for what seemed plodding miles, with naught but dark stone for company. The girl began to regret not heading to bed—the journey from Last Hope was beginning to catch up, and she was fading fast. She lost her bearings several times—the corridors and stairs all looked the same, and she began to feel hopelessly disoriented.

"How do you not get lost in here?" she asked.

The woman traced the spiral patterns carved into the walls. "Naev reads."

Mia touched the chill stone. "These are words?"

"More. They are a poem. A song."

"About what?"

"Finding the way in the dark."

"Finding the library is good enough. My eyeballs are about to go to bed without me."

"A good thing, then. Here we are."

A set of double doors loomed at the end of the passageway. The wood was dark, carved with that same scrolling motif marking the walls. Mia noted there were no handles, that the doors must have weighed a ton apiece. And yet, Naev pushed them open with a gentle hand, the hinges making barely a whisper as they opened wide.

Mia stepped inside, and for the third time that turn, felt her lungs bid her breath farewell. She stood on a mezzanine overlooking a dark wood—a forest of ornate shelves, laid out like a garden maze. And on each shelf stood books. Piles of books. Mountains of books. Oceans and oceans of books. Books of stained vellum and fresh parchment. Books bound in leather and wood and leaves, locked books and dusty books, books as thick as her waist and as tiny as her fist. Mia's eyes were alight, fingernails denting the wooden railing.

"Naev, don't let me down there," she breathed.

"Why not?"

"You'll never see me again . . ."

"Truer words never spoken," said a rasping voice. "Depending what aisle you picked."

Mia turned to the voice's owner, saw a wizened Liisian man leaning against the far railing. He was dressed in britches and a scruffy waistcoat. A pair of improbably thick spectacles was balanced on a hooked nose, two shocks of white hair protruding from a balding head, as if they couldn't decide on the best escape route. Back bent like a question mark. A cigarillo dangled from his mouth, another behind his ear. He looked about seven thousand four hundred and fifty-two years old.

He stood beside a small wooden trolley stacked with books, marked RETURNS.

"Is that wise?" Mia said.

"What?" the old man blinked.

"This is a library. You can't smoke in a bloody library."

"O, shit . . ."

The old man plucked his cigarillo, pondered it briefly, popped it back into his mouth.

"What if the books catch fire?" Mia asked.

"O, *shiiiiiiit*," the old man said, exhaling a cloud that made Mia's tongue tingle.

"Well . . . can I have one, then?"

"One what?"

"A smoke."

"Are you daft?" The man peered at her through his improbable spectacles. "You can't smoke in a bloody library. What if the books catch fire?"

Mia hooked her thumbs into her belt, tilted her head. "O, shiiiiit?"

The old man tugged the cigarillo from behind his ear, lit it with his own, and offered it to the girl. Mia grinned and puffed away on the strawberry-tinged smoke, licking her lips and delighting at the sugared paper. Naev gestured to the old man.

"Naev presents Chronicler Aelius, keeper of the athenaeum."

"All right?" the old man enquired.

"All right," Mia nodded.

"Splendid."

Naev coughed in the rising pall. "Chronicler, she seeks to have a Dweymeri word translated. She desires a book on the subject. Does he have one in his keeping?"

"I've many, no doubt. But if it's only one word the acolyte seeks the knowing of, I can probably save myself the look and speak it here."

"You speak Dweymeri?" Mia asked.

"If there's a language spoken beneath the suns that I've not a knowing of, you can pluck out my eyes and use them for marbles, lass."*

---

*In fact, there were three languages spoken beneath the suns that Chronicler Aelius had no knowledge of.

The first, a tongue spoken by a mountain clan in the Eastern Divide who'd never had contact with outsiders that didn't end in a spit roast.

The second, a peculiar dialect of old Liisian, spoken exclusively by an apocalypse cult in Elai known as the Waiting Ones (their congregation numbered exactly six, one

"Well, as much as the idea of wandering the aisles might appeal to me on any other turn, my lovely fur bed is calling, good Chronicler." Mia took a deep drag. "So if you could give me a meaning along with this fine smoke, I'd be twice in your debt."

"Speak the word."

"*Koffi.*"

"Oof." The old man winced. "Who called you that?"

"No one."

"A good thing . . . Wait, you didn't throw it at someone else?"

"Not yet."

"Well, don't. It's about the worst insult you can give a Dweymeri."

"What's it mean?"

"Roughly translated? *Child of rape.*" The old man took a puff. "The worst of the Dweymeri pirates are in the habit of . . . having their way with folk they capture. A *koffi* is the product of such devilry. A half-caste. The bastard child of an unwilling mother."

"Maw's teeth," Mia breathed. "No wonder Tric wanted to kill him . . ."

Aelius crushed his smoke out on the wall, tucked the dead butt into his pocket.

"That's all you needed? One word?"

"For now."

"Well, I'll be off then. Too many books. Too few centuries."

"My thanks, Chronicler Aelius."

"Good luck with singing lessons tomorrow."

Mia frowned, watched his bent back as he shuffled away. Crushing out her own cigarillo, she looked to Naev. "Bedtime, if you'd be so kind as to lead the way?"

"Of course."

The woman led Mia back through the winding labyrinth. Patches of arkemical illumination spilled through stained-glass windows. Mia swore they returned a different way than they'd come by—either that or the walls were moving. Her mind was spinning like mekwerk.

Was it true, what Floodcaller said? Wasn't it possible Tric's parents had loved

---

of whom was a dog named Rolf but who was referred to by his fellows as "the Yellow Prince").

And last, the language of cats. O, yes, cats speak, gentlefriend, doubt it not—if you own more than one and can't see them at this particular moment, chances are they're off in a corner somewhere lamenting the fact that their owner seems to spend all their time reading silly books rather than paying them the attention they so richly deserve.

each other, though each had different skin? Mia couldn't help but remember the murder in Tric's eyes. Would he have taken such offense if there weren't truth behind the insult?

Mia wondered if she should speak to Tric about it. She didn't want to have to spend her nevernights worrying about the knife waiting for him in the dark, but the boy was as stubborn as a wagonload of mules. It'd be bad enough looking over her shoulder for Jessamine. Tric didn't have the not-eyes in the back of his head that Mia did, and Floodcaller had already proved he could wipe the floor with him face-to-face.

If the boy wasn't careful, he'd end up buried here.

You can imagine Mia's surprise then, when Floodcaller was discovered lying in the shadow of Niah's statue the next morning. A pool of blood cooling among the names on the carven stone about him.

Throat cut ear to ear.

Book 2

Iron or Glass

CHAPTER 10

SONG

Twenty-seven acolytes stood in the Hall of Eulogies.

One less than there had been yesterturn.

Mia looked among them, wondering. Jessamine with her red hair and hunter's eyes. A broad, olive-skinned boy with a missing ear and chewed fingernails. A thin girl with cropped black hair and a slavemark branded on her cheek, swaying on her feet like a snake. An ill-favored Vaanian boy with tattooed hands who always seemed to be talking to himself. Mia was still putting faces to names. But though they were still mostly strangers, she knew one thing about every acolyte around her.

Murderers, all.

The Mother of Night's statue loomed above them, staring down with pitiless eyes. Rumor had been rippling among the acolytes as they made their way to the hall before mornmeal. Two Hands were on their knees, scrubbing the stone at the goddess's feet with horsehair brushes. The water in their bucket was a thin, translucent red.

Floodcaller's body was nowhere to be seen.

Ashlinn sidled up to Mia, spoke softly while staring straight ahead.

"Hear about the Dweymeri boy?"

". . . A little."

"Throat cut clean, they say."

"So I heard."

Tric, standing to Mia's right, said not a word. Mia looked at her friend, searching his face for some sign of guilt. Tric was a killer and no mistake—but everyone in this room was. Just because he and Floodcaller had tussled the eve before didn't mean he'd be top of the suspect list. Revered Mother Drusilla would have to think him some kind of fool to murder Floodcaller with his motive so obvious . . .

"Think the Ministry will investigate?" Mia asked.

"You heard what Mother Drusilla said. '*You are killers one, killers all. And I expect you all to behave as such.*'" Ashlinn glanced at Tric. "Maybe someone just took her literally."

"Acolytes."

The girls looked up, saw the Revered Mother Drusilla, gray hair unbound, fingers entwined. She'd arrived without a whisper, seeming to melt out of the shadows themselves. The old woman spoke, her voice echoing in the gloom.

"Before lessons begin, I have an announcement. I am certain all of you have heard about the murder of your fellow acolyte yestereve, here in this very hall." Drusilla glanced at the wet spot on the stone, still being dutifully scrubbed. "Floodcaller's ending is deeply regrettable, and the Ministry will be investigating thoroughly. If you have any information, bring it to my chambers by the end of the turn. We stand in the Church of Our Lady of Blessed Murder, and the lives of your fellow acolytes are *hers*, not yours to take. Should this ending have been committed as an act of revenge, spite, or simple cold-blooded calculation, the perpetrator will be punished accordingly."

Mia was certain the old woman's eyes lingered on Tric as she said "revenge." She glanced at her friend, but the boy's face remained stoic.

"However," Drusilla continued, "while the investigation is ongoing, all acolytes are forbidden from leaving their rooms after ninth bell has struck. Special dispensation may be granted by your Shahiid for purposes of training and study, but idle wandering through the halls will *not* be permitted. Those found in breach of this ban will be punished severely."

Mother Drusilla allowed her gaze to linger on each acolyte in turn. Mia wondered what constituted "severe punishment" among a flock of murderous fanatics.

"Now," Drusilla said. "Proceed to the Hall of Songs and await Shahiid Solis in silence."

The woman disappeared into the shadows in a swirl of black robes.

Murmurs passed up and down the row of acolytes. The girl with the slave brand was gazing at Tric intently. The olive-skinned boy tugging at the nub of flesh where his ear used to be, looked at the Dweymeri with narrowed eyes. Tric ignored their stares, walking behind the Hands who'd appeared to escort them. After a wearying climb into what might have been the Mountain's peak, Mia and her fellows found themselves in the Hall of Songs.

She had no idea why the room was called such, though she suspected it had nothing to do with acoustics.* A circular stained-glass window was set in the ceiling, throwing a bright golden spotlight into the room's heart. The hall was huge, its edges swallowed by shadows, though Mia caught impressions of those same swirling patterns on the walls. She could smell old blood, sweat, oil, and steel. Training dummies and archery targets and fitness apparatus were arranged in neat rows. The floor was black granite, and a circle was carved in the room's heart, wide enough for forty men to stand abreast. Each acolyte took a place around it and, as instructed, most settled in to await their first lesson in silence.

Ashlinn took a place at Mia's left and began whispering within ten seconds.

"Ninebells curfew. Can you believe it?"

Mia glanced around the room before replying. "It's not like there'll be much to do around here after the light dies anyway."

The girl grinned. "O, Corvere. You've got *no* idea."

"So why—"

"You were instructed to wait in silence."

A deep voice echoed through the Hall of Songs, bouncing off the unseen walls. Mia heard no footsteps, but Shahiid Solis emerged from the shadows behind her, hands clasped behind him. As he brushed past, Mia realized the man was even more imposing up close, all broad shoulders and ghost-white eyes. He wore soft black robes, that same empty scabbard at his waist. And yet he moved with a silent grace, as if listening to a tune only he could hear.

"A Blade of the Mother must be silent as starlight on a sleeping babe's cheek," he said, stepping into the circle. "I once hid in the Grand Athenaeum of Elai for seven turns waiting for my offering to show herself, and not even the books knew I was there."† He turned to Mia and Ashlinn. "And you girls cannot keep quiet for a handful of heartbeats."

"Forgiveness, Shahiid," Ashlinn bowed.

"Three laps of the stair for you, girl. Down and up. Go."

Ashlinn hovered uncertainly. The Shahiid glared, those sightless eyes seeming to bore right through her skull.

"Six laps, then. The number doubles every time I repeat myself."

Ashlinn bowed, and with another apology, retreated from the hall. Solis turned to Mia, colorless eyes fixed over her shoulder. She noticed he never blinked.

---

* Although they were, as it happens, exceptional. *Falalalalaaaaaaa.*

† Not entirely true. Some of the books in the great library of Liis are very clever indeed.

"And you, girl? Do you have something to say?"

Mia remained silent.

"Well?" The Shahiid stepped closer, looming over her. "Answer me!"

Mia kept her gaze to the floor, her voice steady. "Forgiveness, Shahiid, but with all due respect, I believe anything I say will simply be taken as a further breach of the silence you demanded, and you will only punish me further."

The hulking man's lips twisted in a small smile. "A clever little slip, neh?"

"If I were clever, I'd not have been caught talking, Shahiid."

"A pity, then. There's precious little else about you worthy of note." Solis pointed to the stairs. "Three laps. Down and up. Go."

Mia bowed and left the hall without a word.

Stretching her legs on the landing, she commenced her run, counting the steps in her head.* She wondered how Solis knew if she looked notable or not— those eyes of his were as blind as a boy in love, she'd bet her life on it—but he acted as if he were as sighted as she. Halfway through the second lap, all musing on the Shahiid had ceased, her focus consumed by running the stair. Reaching the top, her legs were jelly, and she silently thanked her old master again for all the Godsgrave stairs he'd made her run in punishment. She almost wished she'd misbehaved more.

Ashlinn (whom Mia had lapped in the last fifty feet) reached the top drenched in sweat, offering a wink as she paused to catch her breath.

"Sorry, Corvere," she gasped. "Father warned me about Solis. Should've known better."

"No harm done," Mia smiled.

"Wait and see. I've still got three more laps," Ashlinn grinned. "See you in there."

Mia turned back to the hall, hands on hips. She returned in time to see Jessamine's sidekick—the tall Itreyan acolyte with fists like sledgehammers— step into the circle with Shahiid Solis. She saw six other novices, including Jessamine, the pale boy who'd named himself Hush, and the slavemark girl, all slumped in their places at circle, sweating and breathless. All bleeding from tiny scratches on their cheeks.

Solis stood in the ring's center. Mia saw he'd removed his dark robe, an outfit of supple golden-brown leather underneath. She saw a series of small scars

---

* Mia would lap these particular steps hundreds of times over the course of her stay in the Red Church. She would count the steps every time. And though she never spoke of it to anyone, and though she was not entirely surprised by the fact, the number of steps changed each and every time she ran them.

on one massive forearm, thirty-six in total. He still wore the empty scabbard at his side, but he was now armed with a double-edged gladius—a blade ideal for close-quarter fighting.

Dozens of racks had been wheeled out from the darkness, stocked with every kind of weapon Mia could imagine. Swords and knives, hammers and maces, Maw's teeth—even a rack of bloody poleaxes. All plain and unadorned and perfectly, beautifully lethal.

Solis's blind gaze was fixed on the floor. "What is your name, boy?"

The thuggish Itreyan boy replied with a bow. "Diamo, Shahiid."

"And you are versed in the blade's song, little Diamo?"

"I know a tune or two."

"Sing to me, then."

As Mia took her place back in the circle, Diamo perused the weapon racks. He took up a longsword, a good five feet in length, the steel slicing the air audibly as he took an experimental swing. Mia nodded to herself. The boy had chosen a good counter for Solis's shortblade, so he knew the basics at least. The extra reach would give him some room to play.

Diamo took up guard position in front of Solis and offered another bow. The Shahiid stood with blade downturned, head tilted, seemingly off-guard.

"I do not hear singing, boy."

Diamo raised his sword and lunged. It was a fine strike, a broad arc that would have taken out the Shahiid's throat if left unchecked. But before Mia's astonished eyes, Solis stepped forward and smashed the blow aside. He struck out at Diamo, the boy drew back into guard position, barely fending off a flurry, head, throat, chest, nethers. Steel sang on steel, the hall ringing with the tune, tiny sparks flying as the blades kissed. Solis's face was serene as a dreaming child's, sightless eyes fixed on the floor. But his ferocity was terrifying, his speed awe-inspiring. The bout lasted a few moments more, Solis allowing the boy a few more laudable strikes and countering every one. And finally as Mia watched spellbound, Diamo's sword was struck from his grip, and Solis's blade placed gently on the boy's sweat-slick cheek.

It happened so quickly, Mia barely saw the man move.

Diamo flinched as the blade drew blood—just a tiny scratch to remember the beating by. And Solis turned his back and lowered his sword to the floor once more.

"A poor showing."

"Apologies, Shahiid."

Solis sighed as Diamo took his place back at the edge of the circle. "Is there none in this room who knows the song?"

"I can hold a tune."

Mia smiled as she heard Tric speak. His eye was blackened from his brawl with Floodcaller, but he seemed in fighting spirit despite the fact that Solis had almost thrown him off the Sky Altar at evemeal. He pulled off his robe, dark leathers and a short-sleeved jerkin underneath. Mia found herself admiring the line of muscles along his arms, the tanned tautness of his skin. She thought back to their fight outside the Mountain, the imagery of lust and violence intertwined. Licking at dry lips.

"Ah. Our young half-breed," Solis nodded. "I learned all I needed to about your form yestereve. But come, pup"—he beckoned with one hand—"let me hear you growl."

Mia was pleased to see Tric had apparently learned from the drubbing he'd received, as he shrugged off the insult without flinching. The boy chose a scimitar from the racks and stepped into the golden light. Solis once again remained motionless, blade downturned as Tric approached. But though the Dweymeri's form was deadly, his strikes swift and true, the match proved itself a repeat of Diamo's bout. Tric found himself disarmed, breathless, and bleeding from a fresh scratch along his cheek.

Solis turned away, shaking his head.

"Pathetic. A worse flock I've never had. What did your masters have you studying before you came here? Knitting and cookery?" He turned that blind stare around the circle. "The finest Blades have no need of steel at all. But each and every one of you is still expected to be able to slice the light in six before you leave these walls." He sighed. "And I'll wager not a one of you could slice a loaf of fucking rye."

He pointed to the weapon racks.

"Each of you take a knife and form up in front of me. We begin at the beginning."

"Shahiid," said Mia.

"Ah. The talkative one returns. I wondered what that aroma was."

"*. . . mia, don't . . .*"

"Shahiid, you've yet to hear me sing."

"Save yourself for Shahiid Aalea's tutelage, girl. I know all I need of you."

Mia stepped into the circle. "Just the same, I'd like to try."

Solis tilted his head until his neck popped audibly. Sniffed.

"Be swift then."

Mia stepped to the weapon racks and chose a pair of long knives, curved in the Liisian style. Plain though they looked, their weight was perfect, their edge, perfection. They were the fastest weapon on the racks—lightweight and sleek.

But they were shorter than Solis's sword, useful only at extreme close quarters. As Mia stepped back into the circle, the Shahiid chuckled.

"You face an opponent with a gladius, and choose daggers to sing with. Are you sure you know the words, girl?"

Mia said nothing, taking up a front-foot, left-handed stance and drumming her fingers along her knife hilts. The stained-glass window above cast a dark pool at her feet. She felt Mister Kindly coiled inside it, drinking in her fear by the mouthful. And without waiting for another insult, she reached out to Solis's shadow and *pulled*.

Though she'd worked the Dark a thousand times, she could never remember it feeling quite like this. Perhaps it was because this place had no suns at all, but her strength seemed greater here, the gloom easier to bend. Instead of wrapping the Shahiid's feet in her shadow, she simply used his own, digging it into the soles of his boots. Not a person in the room could have known what she was doing. Not a ripple marred the black around the Shahiid's feet. And yet as he tried to shift footing, the blind man found his boots glued fast to the floor.

Solis's eyes widened as Mia struck; a whistling blow aimed right at his throat. He parried, knocking her right hand aside and sending her knife spinning across the room. But with speed a dragonmoth would envy, the girl pirouetted, hair flying, striking out with her left hand and taking a tiny nick out of the Shahiid's cheek.

The assembled acolytes gasped. A droplet of blood spilled down Solis's face. Tric cried out in triumph. For a second, Mia found herself grinning to the eye-teeth, filled with smug satisfaction that she'd drawn blood on this condescending bastard.

But only for a second.

Solis seized her left wrist, bending it back in a grip like iron. He swung his shortsword at his boots, two buckles sent singing off into the darkness. And with the soles still stuck fast to the floor, he stepped out and flipped clean over Mia's head. Landing on the stone behind her, he locked the girl's wrist up tight.

Mia cried out as he twisted, bending her double, her swordarm hyperextended. Her elbow screamed, shoulder threatening to pop clean from its socket.

"Clever girl," Solis said, giving her arm a painful twist. "But this is the Hall of Songs, little one, not the Hall of Shadows."

He looked down at her with those blind, pitiless eyes.

"And I did not ask to hear my shadow sing."

Solis raised his blade in a white-knuckle grip. And bringing it down like thunder from the heavens, Mia screaming all the while, he struck

once
twice
three times
and hacked the girl's arm off at the elbow.

CHAPTER 11
REMADE

Blood. Pain. Black.

That was all Mia remembered of the moments after Solis took her arm. The pain had been white and blinding, bubbling up from her stomach along with the vomit and screams. A dark had fallen, sweet and black and full of whispers, Mister Kindly's voice somewhere in the distance, mixed with others she didn't know.

"... *hold on, mia* ..."

"O, Solis, poor Solis. If only thy mother had loved thee more ..."

"What a ruin. Art thou certain she be worth the pain?"

"Drusilla deems it so. Asides, her face, it pleases me."

"... *mia, hold on to me* ..."

"A remedy for that malady, I have at my fingertips. True and sure."

"Behave, sister love, sister mine."

"What a portrait could I paint on canvas such as this. What a horror I could gift the world."

"... *don't let go* ..."

Mia woke with a scream.

Arkemical light in her eyes. Leather straps holding her fast. She thrashed at the restraints and felt gentle hands, a sweet voice bidding her *hush, hush sweet child*, and she looked up into a face that would haunt her waking dreams.

A man. Tall and slender and pale as a new-bled corpse. His eyes were pink, his skin seemed made of marble, a faint blue tracery of veins beneath. Hair swept back, white as winter snow, an open silk robe revealing a smooth, hard chest. He was the kind of beautiful that dimmed all the world beside him. But cold. Bloodless. His was the beauty of a fresh suicide, laid out in a new pine box. The kind of beautiful you know will spoil after an hour or two in the ground.

"Be still, sweet one," he said. "Thou art safe, and hale, and whole again."

Mia remembered Solis's blade, the agony of her arm being hacked from her body. But looking past the leather straps and buckles around her bicep, she saw her left arm—black and blue and throbbing with pain—somehow attached once more to her elbow. She swallowed, fighting sudden nausea, air too thin to breathe.

"My arm . . . ," she gasped. "He—"

"All be well, sweet child, all be true." The man smiled with bruise-blue lips, unbuckling her arm. "Thy hurts are lessened, if not mended entire. Time shall put the rest aright."

Mia fought down the sickness, curled her fingers into a fist. She felt a tingling in each digit, a faint ache at her elbow where Solis's blade had cut.

"How?" she breathed.

"The bleeding was mine to end, but thy flesh is saved by my Marielle. 'Tis she owed the lion's share of thy thanks." The man called out. "Come, sister love, sister mine. Show thy face. In troth, I fear no shadow could hide thee from this one's sight."

Mia heard movement, turned her head and stifled a gasp. There in the gloom, she saw a woman, hunched and misshapen. She was an albino like the man, clad in a black robe, but what little Mia could see of her flesh was nothing short of hideous. Cracked and swollen, bleeding and seeping, rotten to the bone. She smelled of perfume, but beneath it, Mia could smell a darker sweetness. The sweetness of ruin. Of empires fallen and moldering in wet earth.

"Maw take me," Mia breathed.

Half a smile bubbled on ruined lips. "She already has, child."

"Who are you?"

"I am Speaker Adonai," the man said. "My sister love, Weaver Marielle."

"Speaker?" Mia asked. "Weaver?"

". . . they are sorcerii . . ."

Marielle turned to Mister Kindly, now materialized at the foot of Mia's bed. The not-cat was staring at the woman, tail switching side to side, head tilted.

"Ah, it shows itself, at last. Good turn to thee, little passenger."

". . . they are masters of the ashkahi ars magika, mia . . ."

The girl frowned. Thinking back to the cat-headed statues she'd seen out in the Whisperwastes, worn and pitted with time. Those monuments were all that remained of the people who'd made an empire of this land centuries past. Nothing else was left, save magikal pollutants and monstrosities.

"But the Ashkahi arts are dead . . ."

Marielle stood beside her bed now, Mia's skin fairly crawling in her presence. Wisps of white hair peeked out from beneath her hood, her eyes pink, just like her brother's. A glance around the room revealed swirling traceries, four arched doors. The dim impression of faces on the walls.

"Not all that is dead truly dies," Marielle lisped.

"The Mother keeps only what she needs," Adonai said.

"Naev said the same thing . . ."

Marielle's eyes flashed. "A friend of hers, art thou?"

"Be still, sister love, sister mine," Adonai murmured. "This was the girl who brought Naev in from the desert. This sweet child saved her life."

Marielle squeezed the bruises at Mia's elbow. "I wonder, then, why I saved hers . . ."

"Because I asked you to, good Marielle."

Mia looked to one of the doorways, saw the Revered Mother standing with hands folded in her sleeves. The old woman stepped into the room, long gray hair flowing loose about her shoulders. She gifted Mia a gentle smile.

"And fine work you've done, too. She looks right as rain."

"Some bruising," Adonai reported. "The bone be thrice chipped, and my sister hath no mastery over that realm. But in the flesh, Marielle is peerless. To see her weave the tendons, meld the muscle, ah . . ."

"I am sorry I missed it." The Revered Mother placed her hand on Mia's shoulder. "How are you feeling, Acolyte?"

"Like perhaps I've lost my mind . . ."

Marielle laughed, the flesh of her bottom lip splitting as she did so. She made to wipe at the dark sluice of blood but Adonai stopped her with a gentle hand. As Mia watched in disgust, the man leaned in close and licked the blood from his sister's chin.

"My deepest thanks," Mother Drusilla said. "To the both of you. Now, if you have no quarrel, I would speak to the acolyte alone."

"Thy right it be. Thy guests, we are." The beautiful man turned to his misshapen sibling. "Come, sister love, sister mine. I thirst. Ye may watch, if it please thee."

Marielle pressed her brother's knuckles to her malformed lips, pink eyes glittering. And with a bow to the Revered Mother, the siblings walked hand in hand from the room. When they were gone, Mia looked to Drusilla and flapped her lips like a landed fish.

Smiling, the old woman sat beside the slab, gray curls framing rosy cheeks and a tired gaze. Mia was again overcome with the impression Drusilla should be sitting beside some warm fireside with grandchildren at her knee. The woman's smile made her feel safe. Wanted. *Loved.* And yet Mia knew by her tally of endings, her authority within the Church, Drusilla was the most dangerous woman within these walls.

"I apologize if Adonai and Marielle unsettled you," the Mother said. "They often have that effect on those not of their kind."

"Their kind?"

"*. . . sorcerii . . .*"

Drusilla turned to Mister Kindly. "Ah. You are here. I should have known."

"*. . . i am always here . . .*"

"I would speak to the acolyte alone."

"*. . . she will never be alone . . .*"

"Test me not, little one. I walked from the sunslight long ago, with arms held wide and joy in my heart. I know the Dark as I know myself. When Lord Cassius is absent, I am Niah's highest in this place. And when next I ask you to leave, I'll not be so gentle."

"*. . . you need not fear me . . .*"

Drusilla laughed softly. "One does not dwell in shadows all her life without learning a thing or two about those that share them. You have no power over me here."

"It's all right, Mister Kindly," Mia said. "Don't stray far. If I have need, I'll call."

The cat made of shadows stared for a long, mute moment. The old woman glared back at him. But finally, Mia felt him look to her, bob his head.

"*. . . as it please you . . .*"

And without a sound, he vanished.

Mia felt the shadowcat's absence almost immediately, a slow fear creeping into her belly. Alone with the matron of a flock of murderers. Her mind burning with the memory of Solis's eyes as he hacked off her arm. Would she regain full use of it? What if the Sp—

"You keep interesting company, Acolyte," Drusilla said.

Mia looked to the door Marielle and Adonai had left by.

"No more than you, Revered Mother."

"As I say, you have my apologies if the siblings put you ill at ease. Marielle and Adonai have dwelled in the Quiet Mountain for some time. In return for services rendered, we provide sanctuary in a world not entirely hospitable to those who hold the title of sorcerii."

"I thought the Ashkahi arts died along with their race?"

"The Ashkahi race is dead and gone, true." Drusilla shrugged. "But death knows not greed. The Mother keeps only what she needs. And the Ashkahi arts live on in those brave enough to embrace the suffering they bring."

"I saw Naev performing blood sorcery in the desert," Mia said. "The phial, the writing. That's how she called for help? Adonai taught her?"

"Adonai teaches nothing. The blood in the phial was his. He manipulates it from afar. His blood, and those whose blood he possesses. Such is the speaker's gift. And his curse."

"And his sister?"

"A flesh weaver. She can make a peerless beauty of flesh, or a hideousness that knows no bounds."

"But if Marielle can shape flesh to her will, why is her own so . . ."

"Mastery of the Ashkahi arts comes with a price. Weavers use flesh like a potter uses clay. But with each use of their art, their own flesh grows ever more hideous." Drusilla shook her head. "One must give credit to the Ashkahi. I can think of no finer torture than to have power absolute over all but your own."

"And Adonai?"

"Blood speakers thirst after that which they hold affinity for. They know no sustenance, save that which can be found in another's veins."

Mia blinked. "They drink . . ."

"They do."

"But blood's an emetic," Mia said. "Drink too much, you'll spew fountains."

"Mercurio's lessons were . . . eclectic, it seems."

"You know Mercurio?"

The old woman smiled. "Quite well, child."

Mia shrugged. "Well, he made me drink horse blood once. In case I was stranded somewhere with no water, I'd know what to expect."

Drusilla smiled wider at that, shook her head. " 'Tis true that tasting more than a mouthful of blood is a sure way to taste it a second time. Speakers are no exception. A life of torture, once more, you see? Drink a little, know constant hunger. Drink too much, know constant sickness."

"That sounds . . . awful."

"All power comes with a tithe. We all pay a price. Speakers, their hunger. Weavers, their impotence. And those who call the Dark . . ."—Drusilla looked down to Mia's shadow—". . . well, eventually it calls them back."

Mia's eyes drifted to the black at her feet. Fear surging. "You know what I am?"

"Mercurio told me of your talents. Solis told me of your little performance in the Hall of Songs. I know you are marked by the Night herself, though I know not why."

"Marked by the Night," Mia said. "Mercurio said the same thing."

"Do not believe for a moment it will earn you favoritism here. Marked by the Mother you may be, but your place is not yet earned. And the next time you squander your gifts on parlor tricks to insult your Shahiid, you may lose more than a limb."

Mia looked down at her bruised elbow. Her voice, barely a murmur.

"I didn't mean insult, Revered Mother."

"An acolyte has not bled Solis in years. I'm surprised he only took your arm."

Mia frowned. "And you're at peace with this? Masters maiming novices?"

"You are not maimed, Acolyte. You still have your arm, unless I'm mistaken. This is not a finishing school for young dons and donas. The Shahiid here are artisans of death, charged with making you worthy of service to the goddess. Some of you will never leave these walls.

"Solis looks to make an example of someone in his class early. But beneath the callousness, his task is to teach, and he takes pride in it. If you give him reason to hurt you again, he will do so without compunction. Hurting things is in Solis's nature, and it is *this very nature* that suits him so ideally to teaching you to hurt others."

The enormity of it all began to dawn on Mia. The reality of where she was. What she was doing. This place was a forge where Blades were honed, death sculpted. Even after years at Mercurio's feet, she had *so* much to learn, and a misstep could cost her dear. Truth was, she'd been showing off. And while Solis had acted an utter prick, she'd misstepped by trying to best him in front of the entire flock. She resolved not to let pride have its head again in the future. She was here for one reason, and one reason only: Consul Scaeva and Cardinal Duomo and Justicus Remus needed to die. She needed to become skilled enough, sharp enough, hard enough to end each and every one of them, and that wasn't going to happen if she lost herself in childish games. Time to keep her mouth well on the safe side of shut and play it smart.

"I understand, Revered Mother."

"You will be unable to study in the Hall of Songs until your hurts are healed," Drusilla said. "I have spoken to Shahiid Aalea, and she has agreed to begin your tutelage early."

"Aalea." Mia swallowed thickly. "Shahiid of Masks."

The old woman smiled. "There is nothing to fear, child. You will find yourself looking forward to her lessons in time."

Drusilla stood, tucked her hands into her sleeves.

"Now if you'll excuse me, I've other tasks to attend. If you've need, or questions answered, seek me out. Like all of us, I am here to serve."

The woman left without a sound, padding off into the darkness. Mia watched her leave, wondering at her words. What had she said?

"*Those who call the Dark . . . well, eventually it calls them back.*"

Mercurio had never seemed entirely at ease around Mister Kindly, though he'd never outright spoken of it. For his own part, the not-cat seemed content enough to ignore her master, and stayed out of sight when Mercurio was around. Growing up, she'd never really had anyone to speak to about her talents. No tome in Mercurio's store tackled the topic, and folklore about darkin was contradictory at best, superstitious twaddle at worst.* She'd simply muddled along with her growing gifts as best she was able. When truedark fell the year she turned eleven, she'd noticed her connection to the shadows felt stronger. And the truedark she'd turned fourteen . . .

No.

Don't look.

"*. . . she seems . . . nice . . .*"

Mister Kindly appeared at the foot of the slab, bringing a smile to Mia's lips.

"'Nice' is one word for it."

"*. . . i have others less flattering, but there has been enough bloodshed for one turn . . .*"

Mia winced as she flexed her arm, pain lancing into her shoulder. Her anxiety was fading with Mister Kindly back by her side, replaced now with anger. She cursed beneath her breath, knowing this wound would take her out of Songs

---

* One famous tale centers around the town of Blackbridge in the east of Itreya. Ernesto Giancarli, confessor of Aa's church, was sent by the grand cardinal to investigate claims that several daughters of the town's more well-to-do gentry had been seduced by a darkin. Each of these unions had resulted in a child—black of hair and eye, the same pale skin as their father supposedly had. Each of the ladies in question was resolute in her tale—wandering in the woods, they had come across a handsome stranger, and, innocent as babes, had fallen to his dark charms. Though Giancarli investigated extensively, no trace of this darkin could be found, and though they almost certainly shared a common father by their look, the children themselves seemed perfectly normal. The confessor comforted the fathers of the girls by assuring them it was entirely possible a darkin was responsible, and returned to Godsgrave to report an inconclusive finding to his cardinal.

Giancarli *did* note in his report that Blackbridge's young constable—a pale, dark-haired fellow by the name of Delfini, appointed to the role some twelve months previous—had been most helpful throughout his investigation.

for weeks. Wishing she'd not been so reckless, or that Shahiid Solis hadn't so dearly deserved a drubbing, she set to tying a sling around her neck.

"*. . . you should sleep. you may need your strength tomorrow . . .*"

Mia sucked her lip. Nodded. Mister Kindly was right. Mercurio had been close-lipped about what to expect from within the Church. He'd prepared her as best he could, but she got the impression there was only so much he could reveal before he betrayed the congregation's trust. With the Luminatii vowing to eradicate the Church if it could, secrecy was the watchword beyond these walls. She'd no idea how Church disciples moved from city to city, how the local chapels were run, even what the internal hierarchy was. Solis was Master of Songs, which meant he taught the art of the sword. She supposed the Shahiid of Pockets would teach thievery? Trickstering? But as for the Shahiid of Truths and Masks, Mia had no real idea what to expect from their tutelage.

"I *am* tired," she sighed, rubbing her temples.

"*. . . sleep then . . .*"

"Right. You coming?"

"*. . . always . . .*"

The girl slipped her wounded arm into her sling, the not-cat slipped into her shadow, and the pair of them slipped from the room.

Tric was waiting outside her bedchamber when she arrived, crouched with his back to the wall. He rose swiftly when he saw Mia approach, relief in his eyes.

"Thank Our Lady," he breathed. "You're all right."

Mia shifted her arm, wincing. "A little bruised, but in one piece."

"That bastard Solis," Tric hissed. "I wanted to gut him for what he did. Gave it a roll, but he knocked me flat on my arse and kicked me senseless."

Mia looked over the new bruises on Tric's face, shook her head. "My brave centurion. Riding in on his charger to save his poor damsel? Hold me, brave sir, I fear I shall swoon."

"Sod off," Tric scowled. "He hurt you."

"The Revered Mother said he does it all the time. Sets the tone in his classes on the first smart-arse stupid enough to raise her head."

"Enter Mia Corvere, stage left," Tric grinned.

Mia bowed low. "I suppose Solis can afford to be brutal with Weaver Marielle about."

"She really mended the wound with her bare hands?"

Mia pulled her elbow out of the sling, gingerly lifted her shirtsleeve. Tric slowly turned her arm this way and that, those big, callused hands impossibly gentle. Mia pulled her sleeve down before the goosebumps began to show.

"See? Just a bruise or two to mark the occasion of my first dismemberment."

Tric scratched at his saltlocks, looking abashed. "I was . . . worried about you."

She stared up at the boy, those awful tattoos and hazel eyes. Wondering what was going on behind them.

"I don't need you worrying about me, Tric. This place has danger enough to kill us both. If you let yourself fret on me, you'll miss the knife aimed at *you*."

"I'm not fretting," the boy scowled. "I've just . . . got your back, is all."

She found herself smiling. A grateful warmth inside her belly. What she'd said was true—this mountain wasn't a sewing circle. The dangers within these halls might end them both. Still, it was comforting to know someone was looking out for her, that she'd something to put her back against. And for the first time in her life, it wasn't made of shadows.

"Well . . . my thanks, Don Tric." She gave a smiling curtsey, the uncomfortable silence banished by the boy's chuckle.

"You hungry?"

". . . Starved," she realized.

"Perhaps the Pale Daughter would accompany me to the kitchens?"

Tric crooked his elbow, offered his arm. Mia punched it, hard enough to make him yelp. And smiling, the pair sauntered off down the corridor in search of food.

QUESTIONS

"*. . . someone comes . . .*"

Mia awoke in the dark, blinking hard. Rising up on her elbow, she hissed, pain lancing through her left arm. Her bruises were practically glowing in the dark.

Someone was picking the lock on her bedroom door. It couldn't be Naev;

she'd just knock. Who then? Another acolyte? The one who'd killed Flood-caller? Mia drew her stiletto and rolled out of bed, creeping across the flag-stones into a darkened corner. She raised her knife with her off-hand as the door opened and a freckled face framed by blond braids peeked through.

"Corvere," a voice hissed. "You there?"

". . . Ashlinn?" Mia rose from her hiding place, hid the gravebone blade back at her wrist. "Maw's teeth, you shouldn't sneak up on people like that."

"Told you. My friends call me Ash." The blonde slipped into the room with a freckled grin, took a moment to spot Mia in the dark. "And if I was *sneaking*, you'd not have heard me 'til my blade was on your throat, Corvere."

"O, really?" Mia raised an eyebrow, smiling too.

"Bet your life on it. How's the wing?" Ashlinn gave Mia a friendly slap on the arm, and the girl hissed a flaming curse, clutching her elbow.

"Shit, sorry," Ashlinn whispered. "Forgot you were left-handed."

"It's all right." Mia winced, rubbing her elbow. "Not like I don't have a spare. What are you doing picking my lock, anyway? Can't practice on your own?"

"Practice, *pfft*. If there's a lock in this place I can't sweet-talk, I've yet to meet it. I just came to ask if you were well enough to come out."

"Out?" Mia blinked. "Where? What for?"

"Just nosing around. Looking for trouble. You know. Out."

Mia frowned. "The Revered Mother said we weren't permitted to leave our rooms after ninebells, remember?"

A freckled smirk lit the girl's face. "You always do what Mother tells you?"

Mia remembered a cell in the dark. The reek of rot and death, burning her eyes. Shaking hands. A whisper, cold and sharp as steel.

Don't look.

"No," she said.

"Well, good. My brother's no fan of mischief, and every other girl in this place either wants to play the hardcase, brat, or both. So looks like it's you and me, Corvere."

"You heard Drusilla. They'll kick our asses 'til our noses bleed if they catch us."

"Well, that'll give us reason not to get caught, neh?"

The girl's grin was infectious. Picking Mia up and dragging her along for the ride. And as Mister Kindly ate what little was left of her fear, Mia found herself slinging her wounded wing about her neck and grinning back.

"Ladies first," Ash said, bowing toward the door.

"I don't see any ladies around here, do you?"

"O, we're going to get on famously, you and me."

Still smiling, the girl crept out into the hallway, Mia close behind.

They stole along the corridors, down countless flights of stairs, off through the twisting dark. Mia thought she recognized some of the hallways from her trip to the athenaeum, but she couldn't be sure. She swore some of the walls had . . . well . . . *moved.* The corridors were sparsely decorated, with only stained-glass windows or odd sculptures made from animal bones to break the monotony. And yet Ashlinn charged on in front, quiet as a corpse, never halting for a second. The girl would only pause occasionally, marking the wall with a small piece of red chalk.

"Do you know where you're going?" Mia asked.

"Nnnnot really."

"Can you find your way back?"

"If someone doesn't rub off the chalk, aye."

"And if they do?"

"We'll probably get lost and die of starvation in the bowels of the Mountain."

"Just so you know, if it comes down to cannibalism, you get eaten first."

"Fair enough, then."

Mister Kindly roamed in front, hidden in the perpetual darkness. As they passed a particularly grotesque bone statue—something between a bird of prey and a serpent coiled upon itself—Mia felt a shiver in her shadow. Familiar almost. She could sense Mister Kindly's hackles rising, her own shadow rippling. For a second, a sliver of fear pierced her chest, cold and sharp. Mia grabbed Ash's arm, pulled her behind the statue's plinth, finger to lips.

Something was coming.

A low growl rumbled along the corridor. A shape moved in the gloom ahead, utterly black, picked out by the window's dull luminance. Mia squinted into the dark, longing to ask Mister Kindly what was wrong. Daughters, it was almost unthinkable, but for the first time Mia could ever remember, the not-cat seemed . . . afraid.

"Shit," Ashlinn whispered. "It's Eclipse."

Mia frowned. "What's—"

The question died in her throat as a dark shape prowled into view. Four feet tall, sleek and utterly silent. Long fangs and sharp claws and no eyes at all. It was a wolf.

A wolf made of shadows.

The creature stopped in its tracks, staring down the hallway toward the girls. They were both pressed against the plinth, holding their breath, sweat gleaming on Ash's brow. Mia could feel Mister Kindly at her feet, positively trembling now. His fear was infectious, rising into her chest and making her hands shake. For as long as they'd been together, he'd allowed her to conquer her fears. Making her harder, stronger, braver than she could ever have been alone. The things they'd seen. The places they'd been. But now, he seemed more terrified than she.

The not-wolf growled again, the sound reverberating through the floor.

"Eclipse," said a deep, musical voice. "Be silent."

Though she didn't dare breathe, let alone peer out to look, Mia recognized the speaker at once: Lord Cassius. She heard the lightest whisper of cloth, the soft scuff of leather on rock. The Lord of Blades was there; she was sure of it. The head of the entire Red Church. Staring down the corridor right at them— just a few feet of polished stone between them and discovery.

Long moments passed.

Heart thumping in her chest.

Mister Kindly shivering as the shadow wolf growled long and low.

Four Daughters, Cassius is darkin.

"Eclipse," he said. "Adonai awaits. Come."

A hollow, graveled voice spoke in reply. Tinged with the feminine. Seeming to come from somewhere below the ground.

"... AS IT PLEASE YOU ..."

One last, low growl. Then footsteps. Whisper-soft. Receding. Mia found her breath, pressed her hand to her breast, felt her heart hammering beneath. Mister Kindly slowly stopped his shivering, and the fear began to fade. Ash grinned, laughing beneath her breath, almost manic.

"Well, *that* was exciting."

"What in the Mother's name was that?"

"Eclipse. Lord Cassius's passenger." Ashlinn glanced at her shadow, the shapeless shape therein. "Cassius is darkin, you know about them, right?"

Mia nodded. "I've a notion."

"Want to follow him?"

"Follow him? Are you *mad*?"

Ash grinned wider. "A little."

The girl crept off into the dark, her feet making almost no sound on the stone. Mia reached out to touch her shadow, felt the chill in that liquid black.

"Are you well?" she whispered.

"... *trick question* ... ?"

"What was that? I've never felt you afraid before . . ."

". . . i could feel him. in my mind. he was . . . hungry . . ."

"Hungry for—"

"Mia!" Ashlinn hissed from the dark ahead. "Come on!"

". . . it is not safe here, mia . . ."

Mia sighed. Frowned into the dark at her feet.

"To be continued . . ."

She stole along behind the girl, regretting her decision to leave her room more and more with every step. But Cassius was *darkin*. All these years, all these miles, and she'd never met another like herself. Goddess, what secrets might he teach her . . .

Sadly, the Lord of Blades proved as elusive to chase as the dark itself, and somewhere down near Weaver Marielle's chambers, Cassius had disappeared entirely. At a four-way junction in the labyrinthine dark, Ashlinn sucked her lip, cursed in Vaanian, and finally shrugged.

"Slippery as a greased-up sweetboy, that one," Ash whispered.

"Well, he *is* a master assassin," Mia hissed.

Ash sighed. "He's probably leaving the Church. Da said he never stays in one place for long."

"I can't say I'm sorry to hear that."

Ash grinned. "Scared of him?"

"Black Mother, aren't you?"

"O, aye. But you better get over it. If you graduate, it's him that'll anoint you at the initiation ceremony." Ashlinn looked about them, passageways stretching off into the darkness. "Ah, well. He'll keep. Come on, I'm hungry."

The pair stole off into the shadows, leaving the Lord of Blades and his business behind. They found the Hall of Songs, the smell of blood still hanging in the air. Mia's elbow ached as if remembering, and she felt a surge of familiar anger. Recalling Solis's face as he raised his sword. The agony of her maiming. With a whispered curse, she slipped back down the twisting stairs. Deep in the Mountain's belly, they found the doors to the athenaeum, though neither girl thought it would be a good idea to have Chronicler Aelius discover them wandering about after ninebells. And after what seemed an age, a delicious smell drifting down one of the stairwells led them up to the kitchens.

Hot bread was baking in long, coal-fire ovens. The coolrooms were filled with cheeses and fresh fruit. The remnants of last eve's supper were laid out on long platters. There were no Hands anywhere that Mia could see, so she and Ashlinn each stole a plateful, snuck out onto the now empty Sky Altar. Mia was again struck by the enormity of the blackness beyond the platform.

The long drop to the wasteland below. The desert that perfectly mirrored the Ashkahi badlands she and Tric had traveled, somehow dwelling in perpetual night.

She was again overcome with the sense of sanctity about this place. The otherworldliness. She could almost feel the black stare of that statue in the Hall of Eulogies. The goddess, to whom this Church was dedicated.

Marked by the Mother, Drusilla had said.

But why? For what purpose?

. . . Maybe Lord Cassius knows?

Ash sat on the railing overlooking the drop, cross-legged, dragging stray blond from her eyes and wolfing down a chunk of bread and cheese. Mia tore at a chicken leg, idly wondering where the Church got the flour to bake bread and where they kept their livestock. The wagon train from Last Hope had contained only arkemical powders and tools and suchlike. Nothing perishable. Nothing alive.

"How do they feed us? Where do they get the stores?"

Ashlinn spoke around her mouthful. "Didn't your Shahiid teach you about this place?"

"A little," Mia shrugged. "But he seemed to hold most of the workings as secret. To be earned, not given freely."

Ashlinn shrugged, scoffed another mouthful. "Wuh vwat wunugd mufuh."

". . . What?"

The girl swallowed, licked her lips. "I said, well, that's what you've got me for. Da told me and my brother everything about this place. Everything he knew, anyway."

"He's a Blade?"

"Was. Worked on retainer for the king of Vaan for years.* But he got captured on an offering in Liis. Tortured for three weeks in the Thorn Towers

---

*Though declared a heresy, in the absence of complete eradication by the Luminatii, the Red Church *has* struck something of an accord with various authorities across the Itreyan Republic. Due to the power of Aa's Church and the recent and infamous attempt on Consul Scaeva's life during the Truedark Massacre, very few members of Godsgrave's nobility have direct dealings with the disciples of the Night Mother. But in more cosmopolitan vassal states of the Republic—such as the court of the Vaanian king, Magnussun IV—the Red Church is openly recognized, and a disciple held on permanent retainer.

The benefits of this arrangement are twofold; good King Magnussun can of course rid himself of his enemies quietly should the need arise, but more important, while he retains the services of a Church Blade, the king also has no fear of a rival hiring a Blade to dispatch *him*. This is a golden rule of Red Church negotiations, and one that of Elai. He escaped, but not before they'd taken his sword hand, one of his eyes, and both his bollocks. So the Church retired him."

"Maw's teeth," Mia breathed. "Marielle couldn't fix his hurts?"

Ash shook her head. "The Leper Priests fed the bits they cut off to the scabdogs. Nothing left to reattach. So Da set to training me and Osrik to replace him." A shrug. "Couldn't give the goddess his own life, so he settled for his kin."

Mia nodded, somehow unsurprised. A lesser man might vow vengeance against the master who had sent him to such a fate. But looking out into the dark waste below the altar, it was easy to understand how this place bred fanatics. She couldn't help but remember the goddess's stare in the Hall of Eulogies. The power in it. The majesty.

She glanced down to the shadow at her feet.

Marked for what?

"Did your father tell you anything about Lord Cassius?" she asked.

Ash nodded. "Most wanted man in the Republic. And the most dangerous. More sanctified kills on him than even the Revered Mother. Legend has it he ended his first man at ten. Killed the praetor of the Third Legion in full view of his whole army and got away clean. Murdered the tribune of Dawnspear along with his entire council in the middle of session, and nobody outside chambers heard a whisper.

"He's been head of the Red Church for years, but like I say, he's never in one place for long. The Luminatii have been looking to take us down for decades. It's even worse since the Truedark Massacre. They suppose if they strike the shepherd, the sheep will scatter. So Lord Cassius is top of their list of Things to Do." Ash took another bite and mumbled. "Finding this place is number two. 'S probably why your master never spoke much about it."

"And the shadowwolf?"

"Da just told me to stay away from Eclipse." Ashlinn shrugged. "I've heard tell darkin can steal the breath from your lungs. Slip through your shadow and kill you in your dreams. Maw only knows what the daemons who serve them can do."

---

has seen them rise in favor over other murderers for hire; while employing a Blade, one's life is considered off-limits to other Blades of Niah.

Of course, the fees to employ one of the finest assassins in the Republic on permanent retainer are so pants-wettingly exorbitant that only a king can afford it for long. Still, it can be said that of all Itreya's rulers, Magnussun IV probably sleeps the soundest, his slumber only occasionally disturbed at yearsend by nightmares about the impending arrival of the Church's bill.

"Pfft," Mia scoffed. "Daemons."

"O, an expert are we?"

"Not an expert, no. But I know a thing or two."

"O, really."

"*. . . meow . . .*"

Ashlinn whirled in her seat and reached for the knife in the small of her back. Mister Kindly was sat on the railing, staring at her with tilted head.

"Say hello, Mister Kindly."

"*. . . hello, mister kindly . . .*"

"Maw's teeth . . . ," Ashlinn breathed.

"All's well. He's no daemon. Couldn't hurt a fly. And I can't steal the breath from anyone's lungs, either. I mean, maybe if I didn't bathe for a week or three . . ."*

Ashlinn crooked one eyebrow at Mia. Nodded slow.

"So. You *are* darkin."

". . . You knew?"

"Figured there was something off after that business with Solis. Didn't see any shadows move, but it didn't smell right." Ash smiled at Mia's narrowing stare. "You didn't think I asked you to sneak out just because you seemed like good company, did you?"

Mia tore at her drumstick with her teeth, saying nothing. Ash sat down opposite again, slow and careful. Glanced at the shadowcat. The average citizen would probably try to nail her to a cross if they had an inkling of what she was. Mia wondered if the girl would be blinded by superstition or fear. The smile slowly growing on Ashlinn's lips gathered all those thoughts, led them down a dark alley, and softly choked them.

"So, what's it like?" the blonde asked. "Can you walk between the shadows? I heard you can sprout wings and breathe darkness and—"

Mia sent her shadow curling along the flagstones, twisting into a myriad of shapes, horrific, beautiful, abstract. She fixed it around Ashlinn's feet, tugged gently at her boots.

"Black Mother, that's amazing," Ashlinn whispered. "What else can you do?"

"That's about it."

---

* The Itreyan week consists of seven turns, one for each of Aa's four daughters, and one for each of his three eyes. Niahan heretics speak of a time before the Maw was banished from the sky, when Aa claimed only one turn in the week for himself, and granted another to his bride.

The heretics make no mention of who the seventh turn may have belonged to.

". . . Really?"

"I can hide. Wrap the shadow around me like a cloak. Makes me hard to spot. But I'm almost blind when I do it. Can't see more than a few feet in front of me." Mia shrugged. "Nothing too impressive, I'm afraid."

"Color me impressed regardless," Ashlinn winked.

"Shahiid Solis and the Revered Mother don't seem to share your enthusiasm."

Ashlinn made a face, spat a sliver of cheese rind off her tongue. "Solis is a bastard. Just a mean-spirited, brutal shit." The girl leaned closer, spoke in conspiratorial tones. "You know the meaning of his name, aye?"

Mia nodded. "It's Ashkahi. Means *the Last One.*"

"And you've heard of the Philosopher's Stone, aye? The prison in Godsgrave?"

Mia swallowed. Nodded slow.

Don't look.

". . . I grew up in Godsgrave."

"So you know how overcrowded the Stone used to get, before it got gutted. Every few years, they'd thin the numbers. Consul Scaeva thought up the idea, back when he was just a pup in the Senate. Called it—"

"The Descent."

Ashlinn nodded, talked around another mouthful of cheese. "Empty the place of all its guards. Tie a ladder to the highest tower and berth a rowboat at the bottom. Tell the prisoners that one of them will be allowed to row ashore and rejoin the world, no matter their crime. But only when every other inmate in the place is dead. Turns out about twelve years back, the good Shahiid of Songs was just another down-on-his-luck thief locked in the Philosopher's Stone."

"Solis," Mia whispered. "*The Last One . . .*"

"That's what they called him. Afterward."

"How many did he . . ."

"Lots. And blind as a newborn pup, too."

"Daughters," Mia breathed. She could feel his blade shearing through her arm. The snapping muscle. The searing pain. "And I stuck my knife in his face . . ."

"Maybe he'll respect you for it?"

Mia glanced at the sling around her wounded arm. "And maybe not."

"Look on the bright side. At least they won't make you attend Songs until your wing's better. Maybe you can win him over with flowers or something in the meantime."

"Drusilla told me Shahiid Aalea will tutor me until I heal."

"Ooooh," Ashlinn grinned. "Lucky you."

"Why lucky? What does she teach?"

"You really don't know?" Ashlinn laughed. "Maw's teeth, you're in for a treat."

"You going to spill your guts or just crow all night?"

"She teaches the gentle arts. Persuasion. Seduction. Sex. That kind of thing."

Mia almost choked on her mouthful. ". . . She teaches sex?"

"Well, not the basics. Presumably we all know that much. She teaches the *art* of it. Da said there are two kinds of men in this world. Those who're in love with Aalea, and those who haven't met her yet." Ash raised one eyebrow. "Black Mother, you're not a maid, are you?"

"No!" Mia scowled. "I just . . ."

". . . Just what?"

Mia frowned, trying to cool the heat in her cheeks. "I just haven't . . . had many."

"What about Tric?"

"No!" Mia growled. "Daughters, no."

"Why not? Strapping lad like him? I mean the tattoos are awful but the face beneath is fine enough." Ashlinn nudged Mia's elbow. "And they all look the same in the dark."

Mia glanced at Mister Kindly. Down at her feet. Stuffed more chicken in her mouth.

". . . How many have you had, Corvere?"

"Why?" Mia mumbled around her food. "How many have *you* had?"

"Four." Ashlinn tapped her lip. "Wellll, four and a half. If we're getting technical. But he was an idiot so I'm saying he doesn't count. We all get a do-over."

"One," Mia finally admitted.

"Ah. Loved him, did you?"

"Didn't even know him."

"How was he?"

Mia made a face. Shrugged.

"Ah. One of those. And now you can't understand what all the fuss is about, or why you'd ever want to do it again?"

Mia chewed her lip. Nodded.

"Shahiid Aalea will teach you. It gets better, Corvere. You'll see."

"Mph." Mia slumped down on the table, chin on her knuckles.

Ash stood. Brushed the cheese crumbs off her lap.

"Come on, we'd best be off. We've got Pockets morrowmorn. If you're lucky, you might even squeeze some time in with Aalea."

Ashlinn started making kissing noises.

"Shut up," Mia growled.

The kissing noises became interspersed with soft, throaty moans.

"Shut *up*."

The girls stole off into the darkness, a cat who wasn't a cat following silently.

When they were gone, a boy stepped from the shadows behind them. Pale skin. Black leather. Most would've called him handsome, though beautiful was probably a better word. He had high cheekbones and the most piercing blue eyes you've ever seen.

A boy named Hush.

He was holding a knife. Watching Mia and Ashlinn slip away into the dark, and running one slender fingertip over the razored edge.

And he was smiling.

CHAPTER 13

LESSON

"As my ex-wife used to say," smiled Shahiid Mouser. "It's all in the fingers."

The acolytes were gathered in the Hall of Pockets, standing in a semicircle around the Shahiid. The hall was vast, lit with a vaguely blue light from stained-glass windows above. Long tables ran the room's length, littered with curios and oddities, padlocks and picks. The walls were lined with doors, dozens upon dozens, each set with a different style of lock. And off at the light's edge, Mia could see racks lined with clothes. Every cut and style imaginable from all corners of the Republic.

Mouser himself was dressed in common Itreyan garb—leather britches and a split-sleeve doublet—his foreboding gray robes nowhere to be seen. He still wore his blacksteel blade, the golden cat-headed figures on the hilt entwined in each other's arms. Mia was again struck by the Shahiid's eyes—though he seemed a man barely in his thirties, that deep brown gaze betrayed the wisdom of a man far older.

"Of course, my first bride wasn't the brightest of flames. She married me, after all."

The Shahiid walked among the novices, hands behind his back, nodding like some marrowborn toff out for a stroll. He stopped abruptly in front of Ashlinn's brother, Osrik. Held out a hand, "Hello lad, what's your name?" The blond boy shook the offered hand, and Mouser tossed him a small knife, hilt first. "You dropped this, I think."

Osrik checked the empty sheath at his wrist. Blinked in surprise. Mouser turned to the acolytes with a wink.

"It's in the feint," he said.

The Shahiid wandered along the line, stopped in front of Tric. The boy's bruises from Floodcaller's knuckles and Solis's boots were still etched in livid blue.

"How's the jaw, lad?"

". . . It's well, Shahiid, thank you."

"Looks nasty." Mouser reached up, brushed a gentle hand across Tric's face. The boy recoiled, lifted his hand to push the Shahiid's away. In a blinking, Mouser tossed the boy a ring Mia instantly recognized—three silver seadrakes, intertwined.

"You dropped this, I think."

Tric double-checked his now bare finger. The ring in his palm.

Mouser looked to the acolytes again.

"It's in the feel," he said.

The Shahiid meandered down the line again, finally stopping in front of Jessamine. Mouser flashed the redhead his silverware smile and stepped closer. The girl met his gaze with bright, hunter's eyes and a playful grin, doing her best to out-smolder the Shahiid. The stare-off was broken by Mouser lifting a golden bracelet and twirling it around his finger.

"You dropped this, I think," he said, tossing it back to the girl.

He turned to the acolytes with a wink.

"It's in the eyes."

Without a word, Jessamine stepped forward and kissed Mouser square on the mouth. Shock and amusement rippled among the novices as the Shahiid's eyes widened. As he stepped back, raising his hands to ward the girl away, Jessamine grasped the hilt of his blacksteel blade and drew it out with a flourish. Smiling still, she pointed it at the Shahiid's heart.

"It's in the lips," Jessamine said.

Mouser paused, glancing at his own sword pressed against his chest. Mia held her breath, wondering if his displeasure would take the same shape as

Solis's. But then the Shahiid laughed, long and loud, giving the redheaded girl a low, courtly bow. "Bravo, Mi Dona, bravo."

Jessamine returned the sword, curtseyed with imaginary skirts.

Ashlinn shot a glance to Mia, who gave a grudging nod.

She's good . . .

Still, Mia couldn't help but rankle at the injustice. She'd shown up a Shahiid and got her arm hacked off for it. Jessamine had got a round of bloody applause . . .

Mouser turned to the group. "As our enterprising acolyte here has demonstrated, the game of Pockets is a game of manipulation. A theater. A dance in which your mark must be off step at all times and you, one step ahead. Romancing purses or the art of remaining unseen may seem a small thing compared to the 'art' of bashing a fellow's skull open or killing him with his own goblet of wine. But sometimes all that lies between you and your mark is a single door, or a password on a slip of paper in a watchmaster's pocket. The path isn't always paved in blood.

"Unfortunately, the former love of my life *did* come close to the mark. Your fingers are your livelihood in this game. And the only way to get good with them is practice. So, this is what we do here. Practice."

The Shahiid pointed to a pile of thin scrolls on one of the tables.

"By way of motivation, each Shahiid holds a contest every season. All of you are to take one of those lists. On it, you'll find a series of items within the Quiet Mountain, a number beside each. These are the marks accrued if you successfully acquire the item and bring it to me *without getting caught by the owner.*"

Mouser looked around the room, meeting each novice's eye.

"Understand, I take no responsibility for the consequences if you're caught acquiring these treasures. And if you're sprung wandering the halls after ninebells in breach of the Revered Mother's curfew, Black Mother help you. This is a game, children. But a dangerous one." He waggled his eyebrows. "The only kind worth playing.

"At yearsend, whichever acolyte has acquired the most marks shall finish top of this hall. Each other Shahiid will be running a similar contest; Songs, Masks, and Truths. Presuming no dismal failures in other areas of study, the students who finish top of each hall are virtually guaranteed to graduate the Red Church as full-fledged Blades."

Murmurs rippled among the acolytes. Mia met Tric's eyes across the room. Ashlinn was grinning like a cat who'd stole the cream, the cow, and the milkmaid to boot. A near-certain guarantee to become a Blade? To avenge her father? To stand on Scaeva's tomb? Maw's teeth, that was a prize worth pinching a few trinkets for . . .

Some acolytes had already begun snatching up the scrolls. The one-eared boy, whose name was Petrus, got into a brief scuffle with Diamo as they both grabbed the same one. Tric's scroll was snatched out of his hand by a smiling Ash. Mia pushed through the throng to grab her own. She cracked the wax seal, perused the handwritten list:

A kitchen knife	*—1 mark*
A poleaxe from the Hall of Songs	*—1 mark*
A personal item belonging to a fellow acolyte	*—2 marks*
Jewelry belonging to a fellow acolyte	*—3 marks*
A book from the athenaeum (stolen, not borrowed, smart-arse)	*—6 marks*
A mirror from the Hall of Masks	*—7 marks*
Chronicler Aelius's spectacles	*—8 marks*
A face from the weaver's rooms	*—9 marks*
Shahiid Spiderkiller's ceremonial knives	*—20 marks*
A keepsake from Mother Drusilla's study	*—35 marks*
Shahiid Solis's empty scabbard	*—50 marks*

And so on. Dozens upon dozens of items listed down the page, each more outlandish than the last. It looked like this "contest" was going to start an all-out thievery war among the acolytes, which was probably what Mouser wanted. They'd be on edge at all times, now. Always looking for an opportunity. Constantly watchful.

Constantly practicing.

Clever.

At the bottom of the list, Mia saw the final item. The most difficult of all.

The Revered Mother's obsidian key	*—100 marks*

Mia recalled the key hanging about the old woman's neck. How mad would someone have to be to try to steal that? She glanced up at Shahiid Mouser, found him watching her with that silverware smile. Clapping his hands, he looked about the room.

"Now. Practice."

The Shahiid's first lesson was in simple pickpocketry. He took a clinking purse from a table and tied it to his belt. He then schooled the novices on several ways his monies might be filched, each named more fancifully than the last. The Deadlift. The Jackanapes. The Juliette. The Gigolo. With a walking stick in one hand, Mouser picked a random acolyte to try and steal his prize. Carlotta, the slavemarked girl who swayed like a snake, and moved almost as quick. Big Diamo, whose sledgehammer hands proved faster than they looked. Those novices too slow were rewarded with a crack across the knuckles. Too heavy-handed? *Crack*. Too obvious? *Crack*. Too clumsy?

Crack, crack, crack.

Ashlinn seemed a deft hand at the game, and Jessamine and Hush were her equals. The pale, blue-eyed boy still refused to speak—he used his piece of chalk and charboard to service any question that couldn't be answered by a nod or shake of the head. But he was quick as maggots on a corpse, and deathly quiet.

Mouser went through several costume changes, flipping through the racks of clothing and explaining how each might be overcome. He dressed as a marrowborn don, with a well-cut frock coat and a fat purse inside. Then a senator in purple-trimmed robes of office, with a hidden pocket to conceal his coin.*

"And next," Mouser announced, rummaging through the clothing racks once again, "a breed that hangs on to their coppers like dogs to their bones." The Shahiid slipped a heavy white robe over his head, fastened a golden chain at his neck. "Your good old-fashioned, god-fearing priest of Aa."

Mouser raised his three fingers in blessing, shifted his voice an octave deeper.

"May the Everseeing keep you always in the Light, O, my children."

He raised his voice over the chuckling. "Now, now, laugh if you will, acolytes. But this is genuine gear. Belonged to a minister in Godsgrave I met briefly

---

*Purple has been the color of prestige in the Republic since the time of the revolution, in which Itreya's last king, Francisco XV, was overthrown.

Purple dye is made from the crushed petals of a bloom that grows only on the mountainous border between Itreya and Vaan. Almost impossible to cultivate, the flower was named Liberis—"Freedom" in old Itreyan. The Republicans who murdered Francisco adopted it as the symbol of their cause, pinning a bloom to their breasts at court gatherings to indicate their allegiance to the conspiracy.

Whether this is simple romantic fancy is up for debate, but the fact remains that only senators are now permitted to don the color in public. Any pleb caught in purple is likely to suffer the same fate as poor Francisco XV—which is to say, find themselves brutally murdered in front of their entire family.

What actually constitutes the color *purple* is somewhat open to interpretation, of course. Lilac might be forgivable, for example, if the sitting magistrate was in a generous mood. Periwinkle could be argued to be more *blue* than purple, and likewise violet, but amethyst would almost certainly be pushing the friendship.

Mauve, of course, is right out.

in my younger years. Though he enjoyed the meeting less than I." He scanned the faces of the assembly. "Now, whom shall we put to the . . ."

Mouser's brow creased in a frown.

". . . Acolyte, are you well?"

All eyes turned to Mia. The girl was standing as if rooted to the spot, gaze locked on the medallion around Mouser's neck. The suns were wrought of different metals—rose gold for Saan, platinum for Saai, yellow gold for Shiih—and at the sight of them, she felt sick to her stomach. Sweat on her face. The light from the stained-glass windows refracted off those three circles of precious metal. Burning her eyes. Mister Kindly was recoiling in her shadow, panicked, shivering, so filled with fear he was unable to drink her own. But it was more than simple terror that gripped Mia at the sight of the Trinity. It was actual physical pain.

"I . . ."

"Come, child, it's only a priest's dress."

Mouser stepped forward. Without warning, Mia stumbled back, fell to her knees, and spewed her mornmeal all over the floor. The other acolytes recoiled in disgust. The three suns were blinding her, and as Mouser took another step toward her, she actually hissed as if scalded, scrambling away behind one of the tables, one hand up to blot out the blinding light only she seemed to see.

Tric reached for her, eyes wide with concern. Jessamine was smirking, Ash looking on dumbfounded, confused murmurs rippling among the other novices.

"Get out, all of you," Mouser ordered. "Lessons are done for the turn."

The group hung uncertain, gawping at the terrified girl.

"Get out!" Mouser roared. "Now!"

The mob filed out of the hall, Tric hovering about Mia like a worried nursemaid until Mouser shouted at him to leave. When the hall was cleared, the Shahiid stripped off the vestments and threw them aside. Approaching Mia like a frightened animal, hand outstretched.

"Are you well, child?"

With the Trinity out of sight, Mia found it easier to breathe. Heart calming in her chest, the pain and nausea receding. Mister Kindly had collected himself, coiled in her shadow and drinking her fear. But her hands were still shaking, her heart still pounding . . .

"I'm . . . I'm sorry, Shahiid . . ."

Mouser knelt beside her. "No, it's me who owes apology. The Revered Mother told me of the trick you played on Solis in the Hall of Songs. And bravo, by the way . . ."

The Shahiid's smile vanished as Mia failed to share it.

". . . But she told me what you are. I was careless. Forgive me."

Mia shook her head. "I don't understand."

"Before I cut his throat, the man who wore that Trinity was a primus of Aa's ministry. That medallion was sanctified by a grand cardinal. Blessed by the Right Hand of Aa himself."

". . . Duomo?"

Mouser shook his head. "His predecessor. But it's not the man, child. Or his clothes. It's his faith in the Everseeing. The cardinal who blessed those suns was a *believer*. A true disciple of the God who banished the very Night from our skies. Aa grants his most devout servants some measure of his strength— the Luminatii and their sunsteel blades are the most obvious of the lot. But the most pious of his priests can instill some measure of that strength in other things they touch. I should've guessed such a thing might be a bane to you."

"But why?"

The Shahiid shrugged. "You are touched by the Mother, Acolyte. Marked, for good or ill, I've no knowing. But I know the Light hates his bride. And he hates those she loves just as much."

Mia blinked, nausea still swimming in her gut. She'd felt it, sure as she could feel the stone beneath her now. Looking into those three burning circles and feeling fury. Flame. Malice. She'd felt the same, once before. Light burning in her eyes. Blood on her hands. Blinding.

Don't look . . .

Mouser patted her gently on the knee.

"I'll keep the Trinity out of sight in future lessons. Apologies once again."

The Shahiid helped her to her feet, made sure she could stand. Her legs were wobbling, and she felt a little light-headed. But she nodded, breathing deep.

"Have you ever seen Lord Cassius react like that to the Trinity?"

"I've not been foolish enough to wear it in his presence," Mouser smiled.

"I'd like to speak to him, if I may. I've never met an—"

The shake of Mouser's head killed the question on her lips.

"Lord Cassius is no longer in the Mountain, Acolyte," the Shahiid said. "He will return for your initiation, but I doubt we'll be graced by his presence before then. Whatever answers you seek, you will have to find them alone. Would that I could tell you more, but Cassius is the only darkin I have ever known, and the Lord of Blades keeps his counsel to himself."

Mia nodded thanks, made her way out of the Hall of Pockets. Her tread was still unsteady. Hands yet shaking. She stopped outside the double doors, eyes closed, listening to that ghostly choir singing in the gloom. The dark behind her eyelids still swum with three burning circles, her mind still swimming with the knowledge that she'd somehow earned the hatred of a god. She had no idea how. Or why. But whatever the reasons, no one in this Church seemed to have any real answers.

Maybe . . .

She headed off into the dark, still queasy, the burning circles in her eyes slowly fading. Thinking perhaps there might be one within these halls who had the answers she needed. But when she arrived at the athenaeum's towering doors, she found them firmly closed. She knocked, called loudly for the chronicler. Met only with silence.

Sighing, Mia slumped back against the doors. Fishing a thin silver box out of her sling, she lit a cigarillo. Breathed gray.

Three suns burning behind her eyes.

Questions ever burning in her mind.

But if she were to find the truth of herself, it seemed she'd have to find it alone.

The shadow stirred at her feet. A soft voice whispered in the dark.

"*. . . never alone . . .*"

MASKS

"Hall of Mirrors, more like it," Mia muttered.

A turn had passed since the incident in Mouser's hall. She'd shushed away Tric and Ashlinn's concerns with some feeble talk about a bad piece of herring at mornmeal, and after some dubious stares, the pair had let the matter drop. The rest of the flock had another lesson scheduled in the Hall of Songs, but with Mia's arm still black and blue, she'd instead been escorted by Naev to her first lesson in the infamous Hall of Masks.

Stairs and halls. Choirs and windows and shadows.

Now the hall stretched out before her, embroidered with faint perfume. Scarlet on every surface. Long red drapes swayed like dancers in a hidden wind. Stained glass, glittering crimson. Statuary carved of rare red marble was arranged in neat rows; the figures were naked and beautiful, but strangely, each one was missing its head. Stranger still, there wasn't a single mask in sight. Instead, everywhere Mia looked, she saw mirrors. Glass and polished silver, gilt and wood and crystal frames. A hundred reflections staring back at her. Crooked fringe. Pale skin. Hollows around her eyes.

Inescapable.

Naev retreated from the room. The double doors closed silently behind her.

"You're early, my love."

Mia searched for the voice among the reflections. It was smoke-tinged. Musical. She glimpsed movement; pale curves being covered by a wine-red robe. And emerging from between curtains of sheer scarlet silk, she saw Aalea, Shahiid of Masks.

Her stomach almost ached to see the woman in full light. To call her pretty was to call the typhoon a summer breeze, or the three suns a candle flame. Aalea was simply beautiful; painfully, stupidly beautiful. Thick curls falling in midnight rivers to her waist. Kohl-smeared eyes brimming with mystery, full lips painted the red of heart's blood. Hourglass-shaped. She was the kind of woman you read about in old myths—the kind men besieged cities or parted oceans or did other impossibly stupid things to possess. Mia felt an insect high in her presence.

"Apologies, Shahiid. I can return later if it please you."

"My love, no." Aalea's smile was like the suns emerging from the clouds. She swept across the room, kissing Mia's cheeks. "Stay and be welcome."

". . . My thanks, Shahiid."

"Come, sit. Will you drink? I have sugarwater. Or something stronger?"

". . . Whiskey?"

Aalea's smile felt like it was made just for Mia. "As it please you."

Mia found herself sitting on one of the velvet divans, a tumbler of fine goldwine in her hand. The Shahiid reclined opposite, a thin-stemmed glass of dark liquid held in painted, tapered fingers. She looked like a portrait come to life. A goddess walking the world with earthly feet, somehow seeing fit to spend a few moments with—

"You are Mia."

The girl blinked, feeling a little dizzy in the perfume. "Aye, Shahiid."

"Such a beautiful name. Liisian?"

Mia nodded. Took a gulp from her glass, winced as the liquid burned her throat. Daughters, but she was dying for a smoke . . .

"Tell me about him," Aalea said.

". . . Who?"

"Your boy. Your first. You've only known one, if I'm not mistaken?"

Mia tried not to let her jaw hang too far open. Aalea smiled again, dazzling and bright, filling the girl's chest with a warmth that had nothing to do with goldwine. There was something in those dark eyes that spoke of a kinship. Of secrets shared. Like sisters who'd never met. A voice in Mia's head whispered the Shahiid was working her craft and yet, somehow it didn't seem to matter.

That was the trick of it, she supposed.

"There's not much to tell," Mia said.

"Shall we begin with his name?"

"I never learned it."

Aalea raised one manicured eyebrow, letting silence ask her question for her.

"He was a sweetboy," Mia finally said. "I paid him for it."

"You paid a boy for your first time?"

Mia met the woman's eyes, refusing to look away. "Right before I came here."

"May I make a guess as to why?"

Mia shrugged. "As it please you."

Aalea reclined on the divan, stretching like a cat.

"Your mother," she said. "She was a beauty?"

Mia blinked. Said nothing.

"Do you know you've not looked in a mirror once since you sat? Everywhere you turn in this room, you see your reflection. And yet you sit there staring at the drink in your hand, doing everything you can to avoid your own face. Why is that?"

Mia looked at the Shahiid. She'd always had men fawning over her, most like. Didn't know what it was to be plain. Small. Ordinary. Anger flashed in Mia's eyes, her voice becoming flat and hard.

"Some of us aren't born as lucky as others."

"You are luckier than you know. You were born *without* that which most people prize their lovers for. That ridiculous prize called beauty. You know what it is to be overlooked. Know it keenly enough that you paid a boy to love you. To taste that sweetness, if only for a heartbeat."

"It wasn't that sweet, believe me."

Aalea smiled. "You already understand what it is to *want*, my love. And soon enough, you'll understand how much power instilling that want in others can bring."

". . . What exactly do you teach here?"

"The soft touch. The lingering stare. Whispered nothings that mean everything. These are the weapons I shall give you."

"I prefer steel, if it's all the same," Mia frowned. "Quicker and more honest."

Aalea laughed. "And what if you need information to fulfill an offering? If your mark is in hiding, their location known only to a trusted servant? Or you need to acquire a password to access a gathering at which your mark will be present? The trust of a woman who can lead you to your kill? How will steel serve you then?"

"I'm told hot coals work wonders in those situations."

"Warm skin serves better still. And leaves fewer scars."

The Shahiid stood, drifted to Mia's divan and sat beside her. Mia could smell the woman's perfume, heady and dizzying. Staring into the dark pools of her eyes. There was a gravity to her. A magnetism Mia couldn't help but be dragged into. Perhaps it was some kind of arkemy in the scent she wore?

"I will teach you how to make others love you," Aalea purred. "Men. Women. Completely and utterly. If only for a nevernight. If only for a heartbeat." She reached out with gentle fingers, drew a tingling trail down Mia's cheek. "I will teach you how to make others *want*. To feel as you feel now. But first, you must master the face you see in the mirror."

Aalea's spell shattered, the butterflies in Mia's belly dropped dead one by one. She glanced at the nearest looking glass. The reflection therein. The scrawny, pale girl with her broken nose and hollow cheeks, sitting beside a woman who might have been one of the statues in the room come to life. This was lunacy. No matter how sweet her perfume, how delightful the nothings she might whisper, Mia would never be a beauty. She'd resigned herself to that fact years ago.

"I've looked into the mirror harder than most, believe me," the girl said. "And while I appreciate the sentiment, Shahiid, if you sit there telling me I need to learn to love myself before others can love me, I think I might spew this O, so fine whiskey all over your pretty red rug."

Laughter. As bright and warm as all three suns. Aalea took Mia's hand, pressed it to blood-red lips. Despite herself, the girl felt a blush creeping into her cheeks.

"Dearest, no. I've no doubt you know yourself better than most. We plain ones always do. And I don't mean to say you must learn to love the face you see in the mirror now." Again, Aalea touched Mia's cheek, eliciting a dizzying rush of warmth. "What I mean to say is, you must master the face you see in the mirror on the morrow."

"Why?" Mia frowned. "What happens this eve?"

Aalea smiled. "We give you a new one, of course."

". . . A new what?"

"That nose, those eyes, no." Aalea tsked. "Far too remarkable, you see. A crooked beak might prompt questions about how it was broken. Bruised hollows might make a mark wonder what you do with your nevernights instead of sleeping like a faithful daughter of Aa should. And the places we shall soon send you . . ." The Shahiid smiled. "For now, we need you pretty, but forgettable. Likeable, but unmemorable. Able to turn a head should you choose it, or fade into the background when the needs rise."

"I . . ."

"Would you not enjoy being pretty, my love?"

Mia shrugged. "I don't give a damn how I look."

"And yet you pay a pretty boy to love you?"

The Shahiid leaned closer. Mia could feel the warmth radiating off her skin. Her mouth was suddenly dry. Breath coming just a little quicker. Anger? Indignity? Or something else?

"It may not be right," Aalea said. "It may not be just. But this is a world of senators and consuls and Luminatii—of republics and cults and institutions built and maintained almost entirely by men. And in it, love is a weapon. Sex is a weapon. Your eyes? Your body? Your smile?" She shrugged. "Weapons. And they give you more power than a thousand swords. Open more gates than a thousand War Walkers. Love has toppled *kings*, Mia. Ended empires. Even broken our poor, sunburned sky."

The Shahiid reached out a hand, brushed a stray hair from Mia's cheek.

"They will never see the knife in your hand if they are lost in your eyes. They will never taste the poison in their wine when they are drunk on the sight of you." A small shrug. "Beauty simply makes it easier, love. Easier than you have it now. It may be sad. It may be wrong. But it is also true."

Mia's voice was a tight whisper. Anger waiting in the wings.

"And what would you know about how I have it now, Shahiid?"

"I've worn so many seemings, I can scarce remember my first. But I was no portrait, Mia." Aalea leaned back and smiled. "I was much like you. I knew want. The ache of it. The emptiness. Knew it like I knew myself. And so when Marielle gave me beauty, and I learned how to give that want to others, there was no stopping me."

"Marielle . . . ," Mia breathed.

The flesh weaver.

It all made sense now. Aalea's unearthly beauty. Mouser's young face and old eyes. Even the Revered Mother's facade of homely warmth. She understood this room's name at last. *The Hall of Masks.* Daughters, it might apply to the entire Mountain. Killers within—killers all—hiding behind facades not of ceramic or wood, but flesh. Beauty. Youth. Soft maternity. How better to maintain a cadre of anonymous assassins than by reshaping their faces whenever the need struck? How better to seduce a mark or blend into a crowd or be met and instantly forgotten than by crafting a face suited to the task?

How better to make us forget who we were, and shape us into what they want us to be?

Flawed as it might be in others' eyes, this was *her face*. Mia wasn't sure how she felt about these people taking it away . . .

Own nothing, Mercurio had said. *Know nothing. Be nothing.*

Mia breathed deep. Swallowed hard.

Because then you can do anything.

"Come," Aalea said. "The weaver awaits."

The Shahiid rose, held out her hand. Mia remembered Marielle's hideous features; the split and drooling lips, those malformed, stunted fingers. Mister Kindly sighed at her feet and the girl steeled herself. Curled hands into fists. This was the price she'd chosen to pay. For her father. Her familia.

When all is blood, blood is all.

What else could she do?

She took Aalea's hand.

She'd not noticed it the first time she was down here, but unlike Aalea's hall, the walls to Marielle's rooms *were* covered in masks. Ceramic and papiermâché. Glass and pottery. Carnivalé masks and death masks, children's masks and ancient, twisted masks of bone and leather and animal hide. A room of faces, beautiful and hideous and everything in between, none so horrid as the face of the weaver herself.

And not a mirror in sight.

Marielle was hunched in pale arkemical glow. A statue of a lithe woman with a lion's head stood on the desk beside her, globe held in its palms. Marielle was reading from some dusty tome, the pages crackling as she turned them. When Shahiid Aalea rapped softly upon the wall to announce their presence, the weaver did not look up.

"Good eve to thee, Shahiid." A ribbon of drool spilled from Marielle's lips as she spoke. She frowned, dabbling at the now-stained page. Mia's mouth curled in revulsion.

"And to you, great Weaver." Aalea bowed low, smiling. "I trust you are well?"

"Passing fair, I thank thee."

"Where is your beautiful brother?"

Marielle looked up at that. Smiling almost wide enough to split her lip again. "Feeding."

"Ah." Aalea put her hand at the small of Mia's back, ushered her into the room. "I apologize for interrupting, but this is your first canvas. You've met, I believe."

"Briefly. Thou may thank gentle Solis for our introductions." Marielle wiped the spittle from her mouth, offered Mia a twisted smile. "Good turn to thee, little darkin."

Mia rankled at the leer on the weaver's face. Now that the shock of their first meeting had worn off, she recognized the sort of woman Marielle was. Mia had dealt with her kind a thousand times. The woman was smiling to goad her, she realized. Marielle enjoyed torment. Loved watching pain and inflicting it, and the company of those who loved it as much as she.

A sadist.

And yet, Shahiid Aalea spoke to the woman almost reverentially, eyes downturned in respect. It made sense, Mia supposed. If Marielle were the one who kept Aalea looking the way she did, it was only logical for the Shahiid of Masks to want to stay in the weaver's good books. Even if they *were* stained with bloody drool.

"Come ye, sit her down."

Marielle rose from her desk with a wince, motioned to a familiar slab of black stone. Leather straps and gleaming buckles. Mia's mouth tasted sour, remembering waking here, the pain and uncertainty and vertigo.

"Thou shalt need to disrobe, little darkin," Marielle lisped.

"What for?"

Aalea laid a gentle touch on her cheek. "Trust me, love."

Mia stared at the weaver. Mister Kindly curled in the shadow beneath her, drinking her fear as fast as he was able. With a wince and without a word, she pulled her arm from her sling, dragged her shirt and slip off over her head. Kicked off her boots and britches and lay naked on the slab. The rock was chill against her bare skin. Goosebumps prickling.

At a word from Marielle, a handful of arkemical globes blazed into life above Mia's head. She squinted, dazzled by the radiance. Two vague silhouettes loomed over her, blurred in the light. Aalea's voice was warm and sweet as sugarwater.

"We must bind you, love."

Mia grit her teeth. Nodded. This was the way things were done here, she reminded herself. This was what she'd signed up for. She felt straps tighten around her arms and legs, wincing as the leather cut into her wounded elbow. Leather padding was pressed either side of her neck. She realized she couldn't turn her head.

"Thy thoughts?" Marielle lisped. "Fine bones. A rare beauty I could make her."

"Just a taste for now, I think. Best not to swim too deep too quick."

"She seems to have misplaced her bosom."

"Do what you can, great Weaver. I'm sure it will be masterful, as always."

"As it please thee."

Mia heard cracking knuckles. Slurping breath. Blinking up into the light, the silhouettes swimming inside it. Her heart was racing, Mister Kindly not quite able to absorb her rising terror. Helpless. Bound. Pinned down like a piece of meat on a butcher block.

You fought to be here, she told herself. *Every nevernight and every turn for six years. Six fucking years. Think of Scaeva. Duomo. Remus. Dead at your feet. Every step you take here is one step closer to them. Every drop of sweat. Every drop of bl—*

Gentle hands caressed her brow. Aalea whispered in her ear.

"This will hurt, love. But have faith. The weaver knows her work."

"Hurt?" Mia blurted. "You never said anyth—"

Pain. Exquisite, immolating pain. Misshapen hands swayed above her, fingers moving as if the weaver were playing a symphony and the strings were her skin. She felt her face rippling, the flesh running like wax in flame. She grit her teeth, bit back a scream. Tears blinding. Heart pounding. Mister Kindly swelling and rolling beneath her, the shadows in the room shuddering. Masks fell from the walls as the pain burned hotter, and somewhere in that scalding, clawing black, she felt someone take her hand, squeeze it tight, promising all would be well.

"*. . . hold on to me, mia . . .*"

But the pain.

"*. . . hold on, i have you . . .*"

O, Daughters, the pain . . .

It lasted forever. Abating only long enough for her to catch her breath, dreading the moment it would begin again. Not once through all those endless minutes did Marielle actually *touch* her and yet, Mia felt the woman's hands were everywhere. Parting her skin and twisting her flesh, tears running down melting cheeks. And when Marielle moved her hands lower, down to Mia's chest and belly, she let it go. The scream, slipping past her teeth and up, up into the burning darkness above her head, dragging her down to a merciful black where she felt nothing. Knew nothing. Was nothing.

"*. . . i will not let you go . . .*"

Nothing at all.

S he wasn't beautiful.

As she sat in her room afterward, Mia realized the weaver hadn't given her that gift. She wasn't a statue come to life like Aalea was. Not someone a general might raise an army for, a hero slay a god or daemon for, a nation go to war for. But as Mia stared into the looking glass on her dresser, she found herself fascinated. Running her fingertips over her cheeks, nose, and lips, hands still shaking.

Mister Kindly watched from her pillows, glutted on the feast of her fear. She'd woken in her bed to find him beside her, watching with his not-eyes. Shahiid Aalea had been nowhere to be seen, though Mia could still smell her perfume.

When she'd first sat in front of the mirror, she'd expected to find herself staring at a stranger. But as she'd peered at the face in the polished silver, she'd realized it was still hers. The dark eyes, the heart shape, the bow lips, all hers. But somehow she was . . . pretty. Not the kind of pretty that borders beautiful. The kind of commonplace pretty you pass on the street every turn. The kind you might notice as it breezed past, but forget the moment it was out of sight.

It was as if the puzzle of her face had some missing piece finally pushed into place. Subtle differences that somehow made all the difference in the world. Her lips fuller. Nose straightened. Skin smooth as cream. The shadows beneath her eyes were gone, and the eyes themselves seemed a little bigger. Speaking of . . .

She pulled open the ties at her throat, looked down to the place her breasts hadn't been.

"Daughters," she muttered. "Those are new . . ."

"*. . . i trust you've noticed i have politely refrained from comment . . .*"

Mia glanced at the not-cat on the mirror's frame above her. "Your restraint is admirable."

"*. . . i actually just can't think of anything witty to say . . .*"

"Thank the Maw for small mercies, then."

"*. . . or noticeably larger ones. as the case may be . . .*"

Mia rolled her eyes.

"*. . . we both knew it was too good to last . . .*"

The girl turned back to her reflection. Staring at the new face staring back. Truth was, she thought she'd feel strange. Robbed of something—identity, self, individuality. Violated, even? But this was still her face. Her flesh. Her body. And as Mia shrugged at the girl in the looking glass, the girl shrugged right back. Same as she always had. Same as she always would.

She had to admit it.

The weaver knew her work.

CHAPTER 15

TRUTH

Naev was waiting outside her door when Mia rose in the morning. As she saw Mia's new face, the woman's eyes widened behind her veil. Mia heard a soft hiss through ruined lips, hovering uncertainly, not quite sure what to say. She finally settled on "Good turn to you, Naev."

". . . Naev comes to tell her. Naev is leaving."

Mia blinked. "Leaving? For where?"

"Last Hope. Then to the city of Kassina on the south coast. Naev will be gone a time. She must watch her step until Naev returns. Hold true. Be strong. And be careful."

Mia nodded. "I will. My thanks."

"Come. Naev will escort her to mornmeal."

As the pair walked down the twisting hallways toward the Sky Altar, it occurred to Mia she knew next to nothing about the woman beside her. Naev seemed sincere in her blood vow, but Mia wasn't exactly sure how far trust should carry her. Though the woman hadn't breathed a word of it, the specter of Mia's new face hung between them like a pall. A question rattled behind the girl's teeth, demanding to be spoken. As they reached the great statue of the goddess in the Hall of Eulogies, looming above them with sword and scale in hand, she finally let it slip.

"How can you stand it, Naev?" she asked.

Naev stopped short. Staring at Mia with cold, black eyes. "Stand what?"

"I figured out what you meant in the desert. When I asked what did that to your face. *'Love,'* you told me. *'Only love.'*" Mia looked into Naev's eyes. "You loved Adonai."

"Not loved," Naev replied. *"Love."*

"And Adonai loves you?"

". . . Perhaps once."

"So Marielle maimed your face because she was jealous you loved her brother?" Mia was incredulous. "What did the Revered Mother say?"

"Nothing." Naev shrugged, continued walking. "Hands, she has in abundance. Sorcerii, not so many."

"So she just let it go?" Mia fell into step alongside. "It's not right, Naev."

"She will learn right and wrong have little meaning here."

"I don't understand this place. An acolyte was murdered right under this very statue, and the Ministry doesn't seem to care about finding out who did it."

"Callousness breeds callousness. Soon, she will care as little as they."

Now it was Mia's turn to stop short. "What do you mean?"

The woman regarded Mia with those bottomless black eyes. Glanced to the statue above them. "Naev likes her new face. The weaver knows her work, aye?"

Mia raised a hand to her cheek reflexively. ". . . She does."

"Does she miss her old seeming? Does she feel the change in her bones yet?"

"They only changed what I look like. I'm still the person I was yesterturn. Inside."

"That is how it begins. The weaving is only the first of it. The butterfly remembers being the caterpillar. But do you think it feels anything but pity for that thing crawling in the muck? Once it has spread those beautiful wings and learned to fly?"

"I'm no butterfly, Naev."

The woman placed a hand on Mia's arm.

"This place gives much. But it takes much more. They may make her beautiful on the outside, but inside, they aim to shape a horror. So if there is some part of herself that *truly* matters, hold it close, Mia Corvere. Hold it tight. She should ask herself what she will give to get the things she wants. And what she will keep. For when we feed another to the Maw, we feed it a part of ourselves, also. And soon enough, there is nothing left."

"I know who I am. What I am. I'll never forget. *Never*."

Naev pointed to the stone statue above them. The pitiless black eyes. The robes made of night. The sword clutched in a pale right hand.

"She is a goddess, Mia. Between and beyond anything else, you are *Hers*, now."

Mia stared at Naev. Glanced to the statue above. The black walls, the endless stairs, the choirsong that seemed to come from nowhere at all. Truth was, some part of her still doubted. Gods and goddesses. The war between Light and Dark. She might be able to play a few parlor tricks with shadows, but the idea she'd been chosen by Niah seemed more than a little far-fetched. Even in a place like this. And divinities aside, looking at Naev's veiled face, she knew that people were capable of more brutality than the Lady of Blessed Murder could ever conceive. She had proof of that firsthand. What had happened to her father? Her familia? That wasn't the work of immortals. That was the work of men. Of consuls and cardinals and their lapdogs. Their smiles burned behind her eyes. Their names burned into her bones.

Scaeva.

Duomo.

Remus.

No matter how much this place changed her, she'd never forgive. Never forget.

Never.

"Good luck in Last Hope," she finally said. "I need mornmeal. I'm starving."

The woman bowed, turned in a rustle of gray robes and strawberry curls. And though she spoke under her breath, Mia still heard the whisper as Naev turned away.

"So is She."

M ia was the first to arrive at the Sky Altar, sitting at the empty tables and running her fingers over her new face. Her skin felt mildly raw, as if she'd suffered sunburn. Her chest and belly ached like someone had punched her. Moreover, she felt absolutely famished, wolfing down her oats and cheese without pause and filling a bowl with steaming chicken broth.

Other acolytes filtered in. A dark-haired Liisian girl with pale green eyes, who Mia had learned was named Belle. One-eared Petrus, and the boy with tattooed hands who constantly muttered to himself.* Mouser gave a nod as he passed by, Aalea a knowing smile. Solis stalked past without a glance. She eyed the empty scabbard at his belt—worn black leather, embossed with a kaleidoscopic pattern of interlocking circles. It was worth fifty marks in Mouser's contest. Fifty marks closer to finishing top in Pockets. And probably worth a disemboweling if he caught her stealing it.

Maybe I should start on something a little easier . . .

Ashlinn sat down opposite, mouth already full of food.

"Zo huwuzzit—"

---

*Listening in over midmeal a few turns later, Mia would learn the boy called himself "Pip," and that his muttered conversations were not being conducted with himself, but rather with his knife—a long, cruel dagger that he'd apparently dubbed "the Lovely."

The girl choked, eyes widening as she looked at Mia's face. She swallowed her half-chewed mouthful with a wince, coughed before she spoke again.

"Shahiid Aalea took you to Marielle already?"

Mia shrugged, lips twisting. It still felt odd when she smiled.

"Maw's teeth, the weaver's struck it to the heart. She even straightened out your nose. I'd heard she was good, but 'byss, those lips." She glanced down. "And those baps . . ."

"All right," Mia scowled.

The girl raised her glass. "Night's truth, Corvere, they're top shelf. I'm bloody jealous now. You were flat as a twelve-year-old boy befo—"

"All *right*," Mia growled.

Ash snickered, bit down on a hunk of bread. Another acolyte cruised past with a bowl of steaming broth. Blue eyes. Dark hair, short sides, fringe cut long to hide the slavemark on her cheek. She hovered, swaying like a snake, raised an eyebrow to Mia.

"Do you mind if I sit, Acolyte?"

The girl's voice was dull, flat as a flagstone, but her eyes glittered with a fierce intelligence. Mia chewed slowly. Finally shrugged and nodded to a stool beside her. The brunette gave a thin smile, sat down quickly and offered her hand.

"Carlotta," she said, in that same dead girl's voice. "Carlotta Valdi."

"Mia Corvere."

"Ashlinn Järnheim."

Carlotta nodded, lowered her voice as other acolytes wandered into the hall.

"Shahiid Aalea took you to see the weaver?"

Mia nodded. Looked the girl up and down. She was lithe, well muscled. Bright eyes, rimmed with thick streaks of kohl. Black paint on thin lips. Though her haircut tried to hide it, three interlocking circles arkemically branded on her cheek marked her as educated slave; perhaps an artisan or scribe.* From

---

* Slavery in Itreya is a highly codified affair, with an entire wing of the Administratii devoted to regulation of the market. Slaves come in three flavors, depending on their skill sets, and, thus, monetary value.

The first are the commonplace sort of chattel—laborers, housebodies, and the like—who are branded arkemically with a single circle on their right cheek. The second are those trained for warfare—gladiatii, houseguards, and slave legions, marked with two circles, intertwined. The third, and most valuable, are those with a degree of education, or some valuable skill. Musicians, scribes, concubines, and so forth, who are branded with three interlocking circles denoting their superior worth.

The removal of these arkemical brands is a painful, expensive, and secretive process, tightly guarded by the Administratii. To earn their freedom, a slave must not only save enough coin to buy themselves from their masters, but also pay for the re-what house she'd fled, Mia couldn't know. But the fact that she still wore her mark at all proved she was a runaway. The girl had courage, that much was sure. The fate of escaped slaves in the Republic was as brutal as the magistratii could devise. To risk all by fleeing bondage, coming here . . .

"What was it like?" Carlotta asked. "The weaving?"

Mia watched the girl carefully for a few moments more, weighing her up.

"Hurt like you wouldn't believe," she finally replied.

"Worth it, though?"

Mia shrugged. Looked down at her chest and felt a grin creeping onto her face.

"You tell me."

Ashlinn grinned also, brushing her fingertips against Mia's own. Carlotta smirked like someone who'd only read about it in books, smoothed her fringe down over her slavemark. Other acolytes filtered into the altar, noting Mia's new-yet-familiar face with interest. Ash's brother Osrik. Thin and silent Hush. Even Jessamine found herself staring. Mia was a curiosity for the first time she could remember.

She noticed Jessamine's sidekick, Diamo, staring at her until the redhead elbowed him in the ribs. Mia spied another acolyte—a handsome Itreyan with dark, pretty eyes named Marcellus—staring too. She reached up to her face. Heard Shahiid Aalea's words reverberating in her skull. Felt it swelling beneath her skin.

Power, she realized.

I have a kind of power now.

"Gentle ladies," said a smiling voice. Tric plopped down beside Ashlinn without ceremony, his tray piled with fresh, buttered rye and a bowl of broth. Without looking up, he dunked his bread and hefted a spoonful, ready to wolf it down. But as both mouthfuls neared his lips, the Dweymeri boy paused.

Blinked.

Sniffed at his bowl suspiciously.

". . . Hmm."

He frowned at the broth like it had stolen his purse, or perhaps called his mother an unflattering name. Dragging the saltlocks from his eyes, he offered his spoon to Mia.

"Does this smell strange to you? I swe—"

---

moval of their brand. It is no surprise, then, that most slaves in the Republic wear the mark to their graves.

Finally noticing the girl's new face, Tric's jaw swung open like a rusty door in the breeze.

"Don't let the dragonmoths in," Ashlinn smirked.

Tric's stare was locked on Mia. ". . . What happened to you?"

"The weaver," Mia shrugged. "Marielle."

". . . She took your face?"

Mia blinked. "She didn't *take* it. She just . . . changed it is all."

Tric stared hard. Frown growing darker. He looked down at his untouched mornmeal, pushed his broth aside. And without a word, he stood and walked away.

"He seems . . . upset?" Carlotta ventured.

"Lover's tiff?" Ashlinn grinned.

Mia raised the knuckles as Ash began cackling.

"O, beloved, come *baaaaack*," the girl teased as Mia rose from her stool.

"Fuck off," Mia growled.

"You're a soft touch, Corvere. You're supposed to make *them* chase *you*."

Mia ignored the jests, but Ash grabbed her good arm as she tried to walk away.

"We've got Truths this morning. Shahiid Spiderkiller doesn't like tardy."

"Aye," Carlotta nodded. "I heard tell she killed one of her novices for being late. Warned him once. Warned him twice. After that, a blank tomb in the great hall."

"That's ridiculous," Mia snorted. "Who does that?"

Carlotta glanced at Mia's elbow. "The same sort of folk who chop your arm off for scratching their cheek."

"But *killing* him?"

Ash shrugged. "My da warned me and Osrik before we came here, Corvere. The last Shahiid you want to get offside is the Spiderkiller."

Mia sighed, sat back down with reluctance. But Ash spoke wisdom, after all. Mia wasn't here to play the comfort maid; she was here to avenge her familia. Consul Scaeva and his cronies weren't going to be dispatched by some fool with a bleeding heart. Whatever was eating Tric, it could wait 'til after lessons. Mia finished her mornmeal in silence (she couldn't smell anything odd in the broth, despite Tric's claims), then shuffled off after Ash and Carlotta in search of the Hall of Truths.

Of all the rooms within the Quiet Mountain, Mia was soon to discover it was the easiest to find. As she traipsed down twisting staircases, she found her nose wrinkling in disgust.

". . .'Byss and blood, what's that smell?"

Carlotta's face was reverent, her eyes lit with a quiet fervor.

"Truth," she murmured.

The stench grew stronger as they walked through the dark. A perfume of rot and fresh flowers. Dried herbs and acids. Cut grass and rust. The acolytes arrived at a set of great double doors, the smell washing over them in waves as they swung wide.

Mia took a deep breath, and stepped into Shahiid Spiderkiller's domain.

If red had been the motif of Aalea's hall, green was the theme here. Stained glass filtered a ruddy emerald light into the room, the glassware tinged with every hue—lime to dark jade. A great ironwood bench dominated the room. Inkwells and parchment were laid out in each place. Shelves on the walls were filled with thousands of different jars, a myriad of substances within. Glassware lined the bench, pipes and pipets, funnels and tubes. A discordant tune of bubbling and hissing rose from the various reactions taking place in flasks and bowls around the room.

Another smaller table stood at the room's head, an ornate, high-backed chair behind it. Among the other apparatus, a glass terrarium sat atop it, lined with straw. Six rats snuffled about within, fat and black and sleek.

Tric had beaten Mia down here, sitting at the far end of the bench and ignoring her when she entered. Taking a seat beside Ash, Mia found herself studying the apparatus; beakers and phials and boiling jars. All the tools of an arkemist's workshop. As she began to suspect what kind of "truth" they taught here, a honey-smooth voice interrupted her thoughts.

"I once killed a man seven nevernights before he died."

Mia turned her eyes front, sat up straighter. A figure emerged from behind the curtains at the head of the hall. Tall and elegant, her back as straight as a sword. Her saltlocks were intricate. Immaculate. Her skin was the dark, polished walnut of the Dweymeri, her face, unadorned by ink. She wore a long flowing robe of deep emerald, gold at her throat. Three curved daggers hung at her waist. Lips painted black.

Shahiid Spiderkiller.

"I killed an Itreyan senator with his wife's kiss," she continued. "I ended a Vaanian laird with a glass of his favorite goldwine, though I never touched the bottle. I murdered one of the greatest Luminatii swordsmen who ever lived with a sliver of bone no bigger than my fingernail." The woman stood before the terrarium, the rats inside watching her with dark eyes. "The nectar of a single flower can rip us from this fragile shell with more violence than any blade. And gentler than any kiss."

Spiderkiller held up a strip of muslin, half a dozen chunks of cheese therein.

Unwrapping the morsels, she dropped them inside the terrarium. Squeaking and squalling, the rats set about each claiming its own meal, devouring it within seconds.

"This is the truth I offer you," Spiderkiller said, turning to the acolytes. "But poison is a sword with no hilt, children. There is only the blade. Double-edged and ever-sharp. To be handled with utmost care lest it bleed you to your ending."

As Spiderkiller drummed long fingernails on the terrarium's walls, Mia realized every single rat inside was dead.

The Shahiid lowered her head, murmured fervently.

"*Hear me, Niah. Hear me, Mother. This flesh your feast. This blood your wine. These lives, these ends, my gift to you. Hold them close.*"

Spiderkiller opened her eyes and stared at the acolytes. Her voice breaking the deathly hush that had descended on the room.

"Now. Who will hazard a guess at what brought these offerings their endings?"

Silence reigned. The woman looked among the acolytes, lips pursed.

"Speak up. I have even less need of mice here than I do of rats."

"Widowwalk," Diamo finally offered.

"Widowwalk induces abdominal cramps and bloody vomiting before terminus is reached, Acolyte. These offerings died without a squeak of protest. Anyone else?"

Mia blinked in the emerald light. Wiping at her eyes. Perhaps it was her imagination. Perhaps the air down here was of poorer quality. But she was finding it hard to breathe . . .

"Come now," Spiderkiller said. "The answer may prove of use to you in future."

"Aspira?" Marcellus asked, covering his mouth to cough.

"No," Spiderkiller said. "Aspira is inhaled, not imbibed."

"Allbane," came the calls. "Evershade." "Blackmark venom." "Spite."

"No," Spiderkiller replied. "No. No. No."

Mia wiped at her lip, wet with sweat. Blinked hard. She glanced at Ash, realized the girl was having the same trouble breathing. Eyes bloodshot. Chest rising and falling rapidly. Looking around the room, she saw other acolytes now experiencing the same. Jessamine. Hush. Petrus.

Everyone except . . .

A smile was growing on Spiderkiller's black lips. "Think quickly now, children."

Everyone except Tric . . .

"Shit," Mia breathed.

Dragging the saltlocks from his eyes, he offered his spoon to Mia.

"Does this smell strange to you . . . ?"

Tric looked about in confusion as the acolytes around him began hyperventilating. Belle fell to the floor, clutching her chest. Pip's lips had gone almost purple. Mia lurched to her feet, stool toppling backward with a crash on the stone floor. Spiderkiller looked to her, one immaculately manicured eyebrow rising slightly.

"Is something wrong, Acolyte?"

"Mornmeal . . ." Mia looked around at her fellow novices, now all sweating and gasping for breath. "Maw's teeth, she poisoned our mornmeal!"

Eyes growing wide. Curses and whispers. Fear spreading among the acolytes like a wildfire in summersdeep. Spiderkiller folded her arms, leaned against her desk.

"I *did* say the answer might prove useful in future."

Mia cast her eyes around the room. Chest constricting. Heart thundering. Thinking back through all her venomlore, the pages of *Arkemical Truths* she'd read, over and over. Ignoring the rising panic around her. Fearless with Mister Kindly beside her. What did she know?

The poison is ingested. Tasteless. Almost odorless.

Symptoms?

Shortness of breath. Tightness in her chest. Sweats. No pain. No delirium.

Looking about her, she saw Carlotta was on her feet, the slavegirl's eyes scanning the shelves about them as she muttered to herself. Ashlinn's lips and fingernails were turning blue.

Hypoxia.

"The lungs," she whispered. "Airways."

She looked to Spiderkiller. Mind racing. Black spots swimming in her eyes.

"Red dahlia . . . ," she breathed.

Mia blinked. Another whisper had echoed her own, spoke the answer at the precise moment she had. She looked to Carlotta, found the slavegirl looking back at her, wide eyes bloodshot. But she knew. She *understood*.

"You get the bluesalt and calphite," Mia said. "I'll boil the peppermilk."

The girls staggered to the overcrowded shelves, pawing through the ingredients. Ignoring the pain, Mia dragged her arm from its sling, pushed aside a box of palsyroot, knocked a jar of dried proudweed to the ground with a crash. Up on tiptoes and lunging for a jar of peppermilk at the back of the shelf, she glanced at Tric, pointed to one of the oil burners lining the table.

"Tric, get that lit!"

Hush fell to his knees, gasping for breath. Marcellus toppled backward out of his stool, clutching his chest. Not asking questions, Tric lit the burner, quickly stepping aside as a gasping, sweating Mia dumped a glass boiling chamber onto the flame. She poured the peppermilk inside, the grayish liquid bubbling almost immediately. The room was swaying before her eyes. Jessamine was on her hands and knees, Diamo dropped like a rock. Spiderkiller watched the proceedings silently, that same black smile on her lips. Not lifting a finger. Not saying a word.

Carlotta finally found the bluesalt, stumbled and nearly fell on her way to the burner. Pouring the purplish granules into the boiling flask with shaking hands, she dumped in a handful of bright yellow calphite. A series of tiny pops sounded inside the glass and a thick greenish smoke began spilling from the top. The reek was akin to sugar boiling in an overfull privy, but as Mia sucked it down, she found the tightness in her chest fading, the spots in her eyes dimming. Smoke continued to billow forth, heavy and thick, sinking down to the floor.

Carlotta dragged the semiconscious Hush closer, Mia helped Belle and Petrus nearer to a lungful. Ash and Pip were barely moving. Blue lips. Bruised eyes. But within a few minutes in the reeking smoke, all were breathing normally. Trembling hands. Disbelief on every face.

Slow clapping rang out in the room. The shell-shocked acolytes looked wide-eyed to Spiderkiller, still leaning on her desk and smiling.

"Excellent," the Shahiid said, looking between Carlotta and Mia. "I'm pleased to see at least two of you have some knowledge of the Truth."

"And this . . . is how you test us?" Carlotta gasped.

"You disapprove, Acolyte?" Spiderkiller tilted her head. "You are here to become a mortal instrument of the Lady of Blessed Murder. Do you think life in her service will test you with more kindness?"

Mia was still a little short of breath, but managed to find her voice to speak. "But Shahiid . . . what if none of us had known the answer?"

Spiderkiller looked among the acolytes, standing or sitting around the now-silent boiling flask. Drummed her fingers again on the terrarium of dead rats.

She looked to Mia. And ever so slowly, she shrugged.

"Resume your seats."

Still more than a little shaky, the novices slouched to their places. Marcellus patted Mia and Carlotta on the back as he walked past. Hush and Petrus nodded thanks. Belle still looked shaky, sitting with her head between her legs. Ashlinn shot Mia an "I told you so" glance as the girls resumed their seats. The story about Spiderkiller murdering a tardy acolyte didn't seem so far-fetched now . . .

"Good show, Corvere," Ash whispered.

"Show?" Mia hissed. "Maw's teeth, we could've all been fucking killed."

"All except Tricky, of course." Ash smiled at the Dweymeri boy. Tric was patting Belle on the back, wide-eyed but none the worse for wear. "Impressive nose he's got under those tattoos. Remind me to skip the next meal he thinks smells funny, neh?"

Spiderkiller cleared her throat, looking pointedly at Ash. The girl fell silent as the dead.

"So." The Shahiid clasped her hands behind her back, pacing slowly. "Beyond blades. Beyond bows. Be your victim some legendary warrior in shining mail or a king on a golden throne. A dram of the right toxin can make a garrison a graveyard, and a republic a ruin. This, my children, is the Truth I offer here."

Shahiid Spiderkiller indicated Mia and Carlotta with a wave of her hand.

"Now, perhaps your saviors will explain how the red dahlia toxin works."*

Carlotta took a deep breath, glanced to Mia. Shrugged.

"It attacks the lungs, Shahiid," she replied flatly, her composure returned.

"Bonds to the blood, so that the breath cannot," Mia finished.

"You two have read *Arkemical Truths*, I take it?"

"A hundred times," Carlotta nodded.

"I used to take it to bed with me," Mia said.

"Surprised you can read . . . ," someone muttered.

"Beg pardon?" Spiderkiller turned. "I did not hear you, Acolyte Jessamine?"

---

* Also known as "kingslayer," red dahlia was considered the poison of choice during the tenure of the Itreyan monarchy. Owing to the rarity of the bloom from which it is derived, red dahlia was difficult to acquire, and, thus, more expensive than the average marrowborn wedding feast. Its use was considered both a nod of respect to the victim (its effects are rapid in onset and relatively painless) and a perverse sort of bragging on the part of the murderer (since only the wealthiest of folk could afford to employ it). During the zenith of the Itreyan monarchy, the toxin was used to assassinate no fewer than three Itreyan kings and several highly ranked members of the nobility, including two grand cardinals.

When his father died of red dahlia poisoning, the newly crowned Francisco VII declared the bloom a tool of the Maw, and ordered every plant within the borders of his realm burned. This resulted in skyrocketing inflation, and red dahlia fell quickly out of vogue with anyone who didn't have the foresight to keep a greenhouse. Sadly, this meant less merciful concoctions like blackmark venom and the corrosive "spite" became en vogue among less well connected assassins.

As Francisco VII lay on his deathbed, screaming as a lethal dose of the latter slowly dissolved his stomach and bowels, one wonders if he had the presence of mind to appreciate the irony.

The redhead, who still seemed out-of-sorts at the Shahiid's "demonstration," nevertheless lowered her eyes.

". . . I said nothing, Shahiid."

"O, no. Surely, you were about to explain how the toxin is extracted from the dahlia seed? The lethal dose for a man of two hundred and twenty pounds?"

Jessamine's cheeks turned red, lips pressed firmly shut.

"Well?" Spiderkiller asked. "I await your answers, Acolyte."

"Nitric filtration," Carlotta suggested. "Into a bed of aspirated sugar and tin. Boiled and condensed. The lethal dose for a full-grown man is half a dram."

Jessamine glared at the girl with undisguised hatred.

"Excellent," Spiderkiller nodded. "Perhaps, Acolyte Jessamine, you will follow Acolyte Carlotta's example and *know* the lesson before next you interrupt it. This knowledge may save your life one turn. I would've thought that truth already imparted."

The girl bowed her head. ". . . Yes, Shahiid."

With no further ceremony, Spiderkiller turned to a charboard, began speaking about the basic toxic properties. Delivery. Efficacy. Celerity. Her composure was immaculate, her manner, terse. It was hard to believe she'd almost murdered twenty-seven children a few minutes before. Breathing finally returned to normal, Mia looked to Carlotta and nodded.

"*Well done*," she mouthed.

The girl smoothed her hair over her slavemark, nodded back gravely. "*You too*."

As Mia turned her attentions to the lesson, she saw Jessamine from the corner of her eye, scribbling on a sheaf of parchment, slipping it to Diamo. The redhead glared at Carlotta with narrowed eyes. Despite the fact that the slavegirl had just saved her life, it looked like Jessamine had two nemeses now. Mia wondered if she'd be willing to throw more than poison looks . . .

Over the course of the lesson, it became apparent that Mia and Carlotta were head and shoulders above the other acolytes in venomcraft. It made Mia proud. Her beating at the hands of Shahiid Solis had shaken her more than she'd been willing to admit. Her visit with Shahiid Aalea had shown her how little she knew about some facets of this world. But *this*, she knew. As she and Carlotta answered question after question and she slowly earned a grudging smile of respect from the dour Shahiid of Truths, Mia found that, for the first time since she'd arrived, she was beginning to feel like she belonged. That she actually felt happy.

It didn't last, of course.

Nothing ever does.

CHAPTER 16

WALK

Something approaching routine settled inside the Quiet Mountain. Turns passed without Mia noticing, only the bells marking the hours in that perpetual darkness. Though every acolyte had been questioned after Floodcaller's death and Mother Drusilla's curfew remained in effect, it seemed the Ministry's investigations into the boy's murder had stalled. Though curious about the killer's identity, Mia told herself she had more pressing matters to concern herself with. Scaeva and Remus and Duomo weren't going to kill themselves, after all. And so, she focused on her studies. She proved better than average at sleight of hand once her arm was well enough to lose her sling, and excelled in poisonwork.* Under Shahiid Aalea's gentle tutelage, Mia even managed to understand the basics of manipulation and the art of seduction.

Ashlinn underwent the weaving, then Marcellus, who truth be told had been a picture already. It seemed gifting new faces took a toll on Marielle, or perhaps she was simply capricious. Either way, the weaver worked her way through the acolytes only slowly. At this rate, it'd be months before all of them got to taste the pain of her touch.

Mouser's challenge to his students began quietly, with very few marks being

---

* Spiderkiller tried to poison her class twice more in the intervening weeks—the first, with a contact toxin known as "shiver," which she dumped in the bathhouse water early one morn, and the second, where in concert with Mouser, every lock on every acolyte's bedchamber was replaced with a Liisian needletrap tipped with enough allbane to kill a horse.

Two acolytes died from the allbane traps; an Itreyan boy named Angio, whom Mia hardly knew, and a mild-mannered girl named Larissa, who'd been one of the better students in Mouser's class. A quiet mass was said for them in the Hall of Eulogies, attended by the novices and Ministry. The bodies were interred with the other servants of the Mother, each placed within a tomb on the walls, no names to mark their stones. Mia watched Spiderkiller through the service, looking for some hint of remorse. The woman met her eyes only once, just as the requiem was sung.

And then she shrugged.

accrued in those early weeks. The ninebells curfew seemed to keep most acolytes in their rooms, and Ashlinn and Mia made no further after-hours forays. But soon enough, dashes began appearing on the charboard in the Hall of Pockets. Small numbers at first, two or three marks apiece, the easy items on the list being plucked as acolytes gained confidence. Ash took off to an early lead, but Jessamine was running a close second, and, seemingly none the worse for wear after his near-fatal poisoning at Spiderkiller's hands, Hush was placed third. For her own part, Mia quickly acquired a few of the lighter pieces, but she knew it'd be the more difficult objects that would really swing the contest, and no acolyte was brave enough to go stealing Solis's scabbard or Spiderkiller's knives just yet.

The other Shahiid announced their own contests, and again, the acolytes were informed that those who claimed top of each hall would be virtually guaranteed initiation as Blades. In the Hall of Songs, a no-holds-barred, full-contact contest of martial prowess was to be held. The winner would be given Solis's mark of favor.

In the emerald light of the Hall of Truths, Shahiid Spiderkiller wrote the formula for an impossibly complex arkemical toxin on the charboard, and informed the (still somewhat terrified) acolytes that whoever brought her the correct antidote would be the victor. There was a caveat, of course; acolytes must be willing to test their antidote by imbibing Spiderkiller's poison first. If their antidote worked, all well and good. If not . . .

And Shahiid Aalea's contest?

That turned out to be the most interesting of the lot.

The female acolytes were roused one eve just before ninebells and escorted to the Hall of Masks. This was unusual; the hour was close to curfew, but more, Shahiid Aalea usually conducted her lessons one-on-one. Hers was a subtle craft requiring personal attention, and large groups of teenagers in the same room seldom proved conducive to lessons in the finer arts of seduction. But for some reason, every girl had been brought before the Shahiid.

Aalea was clad in a gown of sheer burgundy silk, unadorned by jewelry. She met the acolytes with a tilt of her head and a beautiful, blood-red smile.

"My ladies, don't we look a portrait this eve."

She embraced each girl in turn, kissed them warmly. As she was wrapped up in the Shahiid's arms, Mia was again overcome with the certainty that the Shahiid's smile was made solely for her. As the woman kissed her cheeks, Mia found them flushed.

"We must work on that, love," Aalea said, caressing Mia's skin. "Never let

your face tell a secret your lips should not." She turned to the assembled acolytes, nine in all. "Now, my ladies. I'm told the other Shahiid have announced
their boorish little contests. Stealing trinkets and beating each other witless and
whatnot. But the Lady of Blessed Murder has use for a multitude of talents.
And so, I give you mine."

The woman looked around the room, smiled at each girl in turn.

"Before the year's end, each of you must bring me a secret."

Carlotta raised an eyebrow. Mia found herself studying the slavegirl closely.
She never smiled, and her voice was cold as a tomb. But it'd become apparent
that Lotti could do wonders with a raised eyebrow. Convey annoyance. Curiosity. What might pass for amusement. The only woman Mia had ever seen do
it better was her mother.

"A secret, Shahiid?" the girl asked.

"Aye," Aalea smiled. "A secret."

Ashlinn blinked. The weaver had worked a marvel on her face just a few
eves prior. Gone was the roundness, the smattering of freckles. She was pretty
as a field of sunflowers . . . if sunflowers knotted their hair in warbraids and
stole anything that wasn't nailed to the floor, that is . . .

"What kind of secret, Shahiid?"

"The delightful kind. The sordid kind. The dangerous kind. Secrets are like
lovers, my dear. It's only after you've acquired a few that you can make accu-
rate comparisons."

Aalea looked at the assembled girls with a dark smile.

"So. Bring me a secret. Whoever brings me the best shall have my favor
and finish top in the Hall of Masks." Aalea weaved painted fingers in the air.
"Child's play."

"Shahiid, where will we look?" Jessamine asked. "Within the Mountain?"

"Black Mother, no. I've wrung these walls dry of secrets already. I want
something new. Something to keep me warm at nights."

"And where will we find such secrets if not here?" Mia asked.

"The wellspring of *all* secrets, love. Her rotten heart open wide to the
sky . . ."

Mia's heart surged in her chest. There was only one place Aalea could mean.
The wellspring of all secrets. The font of all intrigue in the Republic. The heart
of Consul Scaeva's power, the seat of Aa's ministry and Duomo's cathedral, ever
under the watchful eye of Remus and his Luminatii legions.

Godsgrave.

But the City of Bridges and Bones was an ocean away. It'd taken Mia eight weeks on a ship and another week dodging sand kraken to travel here from the 'Grave.

How in the Mother's name do we get there?

A alea took the acolytes into the twisting bowels of the Mountain, past Marielle's room of faces, and into granite corridors Mia had never walked before. The stone was glass-smooth, the temperature warmer than above. The air was heavy, and as they walked deeper, in each breath, Mia was certain she smelled . . .

Could it be?

The corridor opened into a vast room, lit by arkemical globes. What looked to be a large bath was carved into the floor, thirty feet at a side, triangular in shape. Arcane symbols were etched into the stone at each point. And in the pool itself?

"Blood," Mia breathed.

How deep it lay, she had no ken, but its surface rolled like the ocean in a storm. Mia looked at the walls around her, saw the granite was etched with maps. Cities. Countries. The entire Republic and all its capitals; Carrion Hall, Elai, Farrow, and Godsgrave. Beside them, among them, more sigils that hurt her eyes to look at. The greasy tang of sorcery hung in the air beside the copper-slick stink of the pool.

"Acolytes," said a soft voice. "I greet thee."

Mia saw the slender figure of Speaker Adonai stepping into the light. In contrast to his colorless skin, he wore dark leather breeches riding torturously low on his hips. His bare arms and torso were scrawled with bloody pictograms. White hair swept back from a sculpted brow, the pink eyes beneath looking slightly bruised.

That new-corpse beauty, shining down here in the gloom.

"Great Speaker." Aalea kissed his cheeks, heedless of the blood. "All is ready?"

"The City of Bridges and Bones awaits." Adonai's eyes roamed the assembled acolytes. "Only thy donas this eve?"

"Dons on the morrow."

"As it please thee."

Aalea turned to the girls. "Take off your jewels, my loves. No rings or trinkets. No blades or buckles. Nothing that did not once know the flush of life may walk this path."

"Be ye abashed of thy flesh laid bare, silk shall avail thee." The speaker waved vaguely in the direction of a rack of robes against one wall. "Though rest assured, thou art possessed of naught I have not seen before. Thou shalt need to change 'pon the other side, regardless."

The other side? What is he talking about?

Despite her silent misgivings, Mia took off her boots and belt. Dragged her shirt off over her head, wincing as her arm twinged. But slipping her stiletto from the leather sheath at her wrist, she found herself staring. She'd worked years to earn this back from Mercurio. To just leave it behind . . .

Adonai caught Mia's attention, gave her a lazy, pretty smile.

"Thy blade is gravebone, is it not?"*

"Aye."

"Then it shall make the Walk." The speaker inclined his head. "It is bone. Life once flowed through it, ages past. Though if ye wish to leave it in my keeping, fear not. No thief alive hath courage enough to plunder this spider's larder."

Looking at the scarlet sigils scrawled on Adonai's face, the pool of blood churning and splashing like an angry red sea, Mia had no difficulty believing him. But still, she kept the blade sheathed at her wrist, stowed the rest of her possessions in granite nooks set aside for the task. Stripping down to the silk slip beneath her leathers, she felt goosebumps rising on her skin.

Adonai knelt at the apex of the triangular pool, palms upturned. Nodded to Aalea. The Shahiid slipped her robe off her shoulders, revealing naked skin beneath. Mia found herself staring, struck by the woman's complete lack of self-consciousness. Long hair flowed down Aalea's back, like a river of night against milk-white curves. She stepped bare into the red, out into the center. The pool

---

*The material that comprises the Ribs and Spine in Godsgrave is referred to as "gravebone," though in truth, its tensile strength is stronger than steel. The secrets of working it were lost in time, though two high arkemists of the Iron Collegium are rumored to still possess them.

Though hollowed during the building of Godsgrave, the Ribs and Spine are now considered Itreyan treasures, and to deface them in any way is a crime punishable by crucifixion. Much of the gravebone acquired at the city's dawn has been lost over centuries, and the material is considered a near-priceless commodity. That said, the elite cohorts of the Luminatii legion wear gravebone armor, and most wealthy and powerful familia are in possession of a few gravebone relics, usually blades and, in rare cases, jewelry. The kings of Itreya wore a gravebone crown, though it is now kept on a marble plinth in the Senate House, engraved with the words *Nonquis Itarem*.

"Never again."

If you look closely, gentlefriend, you can see it is still stained with the blood of the last man to wear it.

seemed only a few inches deep at first, but soon she was wading up to her waist, hair trailing through the blood behind.

Adonai spoke beneath his breath, eyes rolling back in his head. The warmth in the room grew deeper, the smell of copper and iron heavier. And as Mia watched, the blood began to swirl. Sloshing around the pool's edge, it rolled in a clockwise circle; a vortex spinning faster and faster as Adonai's whispers became a gentle, pleading song. His eyes had turned blood red. His lips were curled in an ecstatic smile. Mia's own eyes were wide, her tongue tingling with the taste of magik.

Aalea held her hands at her sides, palm up. Eyes closed, face serene. And then, without warning, the Shahiid disappeared; dragged down into the whirlpool without a struggle. Without a sound.

The vortex calmed. The blood grew directionless again, washing in small frothing waves. Silence hung in the room like a traitor's corpse.

"Next," Adonai said.

Mia looked at Ashlinn. Carlotta. Jessamine. Belle. Obvious hesitation on their faces. None of them would've seen this kind of sorcery before—Daughters, nobody outside these walls would've witnessed it for a thousand years. But as ever, there was no fear in Mia's belly, even when there should've been. Her shadow breathed a contented sigh.

She stepped into the pool without a word, the blood thick and warm between her toes. The tile was smooth, and she had to walk slowly lest she slip, out waist-deep into the center of the red. Adonai began whispering again, the flow turning once more, faster and faster, with her at the heart. Mia felt dizzy, eyes closed against the arkemical glow, arms outspread for balance. Blood-stink filled her nostrils. The room about her swaying. And just as she was about to speak, she found she was falling, sucked down, down, down into some colossal undertow.

Red waves crashed over her head, the whole world spinning, turning, churning. No breath in her lungs. Blood in her mouth. Amniotic darkness all about, the thudding pulse of some enormous, distant heart, muted by the blood-warm black engulfing her. A tiny babe in a lightless womb. Swimming ever upward, toward a light she couldn't be sure was there. Until at last . . .

At last . . .

Surfacing.

Mia burst into the light. Gagging. Gasping. Gentle hands held her, soft voices assured her all was well. Pawing something thick and sticky from her eyes, she found herself standing in a waist-deep pool of gore. Two men with slavemarks stood beside her, holding her up lest she fall. They helped her climb out of the pool, holding her steady as she slipped and swayed. She was covered head to foot in blood, dripping on the tile, hair and slip plastered to her skin. Her eyelashes clung together as she blinked.

"Maw's teeth," she croaked.

She was wrapped in soft cloth, escorted by one of the Hands to a large antechamber. There, she found Shahiid Aalea, washing herself down in the second of three triangular baths. The woman was rinsing her hair with ladles of warm, scented water. The perfume of flowers hung in the steaming air, but beneath it, Mia could smell death. Blood. Offal and shit.

"Wash yourself in the first," Aalea said, pointing to a bath filled with blood-stained water. "Soap yourself in the second. Rinse in the third."

Mia nodded mutely, stripped off her sodden shift and stepped into the first bath. Aalea was soaking in the third and Mia climbing into the second when Ashlinn staggered into the room, painted head to foot, bright blue eyes blinking in a mask of sticky red.

"Well, that was different," she said.

Aalea laughed, rising from the steam and slipping on a silk robe. She pointed to a painted red door. "When you are ready, you will find clothes through here, loves."

Smiling, the woman padded away on bare feet. Ashlinn stripped off her slip and jumped into the bath, plunging below the surface and turning the waters a deeper red. She reappeared after a spell, pawing crimson water from her eyes.

"So that's the Blood Walk," she explained.

"That's what they call it?" Mia asked.

"Aye." The girl tilted her head to knock the water from her ears. "Da said it's how Blades move about the Republic. A chapel in every major city, devoted to the Mother. Provided there's a bloodbath there, Adonai can Walk us to any of them. All of them."

"You mean my master made me trek across the Whisperwastes for nothing?"

Ash shrugged. "They don't let just *anyone* Walk, Corvere. Adonai needs to permit you to pass the threshold. The Red Church isn't about to let every would-be novice know they've got access to an Ashkahi blood speaker. If the Senate found out, they'd stop at nothing to get their hands on Adonai. Imagine if the Republic could move its armies about the world at will?"

"But they trust us to know? We've only been acolytes for a month or two."

Ash simply shrugged.

"Maw's teeth, where do they get it all?" Mia breathed. "There must be gallons."

Ashlinn wiggled her eyebrows. "You'll see soon enough."

". . . I'm not going to like it, am I?"

Ashlinn simply laughed and sank below the bloodstained water.

The Porkery," Mia breathed. "Of course."

Looking out over an oinking sea, Mia felt the unpleasant pieces falling into place.

From her childhood spent below the Hips, she knew four abattoirs skirted Godsgrave's Bay of Butchers—four mountains of offal and stench, spitting fresh meat onto the plates of the wealthy, and shitting their leavings into the bay. Two dealt with cattle, the third in exotic meats, and the fourth only with pigs. Known as "the Porkery," it was comparatively small, and better appointed than its counterparts. Run by a man known only as "Bacon" and his three sons, "Ham," "Trotter," and "Piglet," it was famous among Godsgrave's marrowborn for having the finest cuts in all Itreya, and among more questionable folk as an excellent place to dispose of a body, should one happen to create a body the Luminatii might be interested in.*

The female acolytes had dressed in simple leathers and cloaks, armed themselves with plain but functional blades from the large armory off the bathhouse, and been led up a spiraling staircase. The stench of offal and excrement had grown stronger, until finally they'd emerged on a wooden mezzanine. The hour was late and the butchers had gone home for nevernight, but a seething mass of pigs was milling about in a large pen below. On the bloodstained stone of the killing floor, Mia saw drains in the rock, no doubt leading down to the pool beneath. Putting two and two together, the girl discovered she was beginning to hate mathematics.

"We just bathed in pig's blood," Carlotta said flatly.

"Probably people blood, too," Mia said.

". . . Tell me you're jesting."

---

*I must specify, there are actually very few of these. The Luminatii are, for the most part, intent only upon crimes that upset the people who pay their wages—the Senate of Godsgrave. So long as the criminal elements of the city keep to killing themselves and staying below the Hips, the Senate could give less than a tinker's cuss about the murder of an inkfiend who crossed the wrong people, or a pimp who bet the wrong gladiator in the arena. The Luminatii aren't a tool of law and order in the Itreyan capital, gentlefriend. They are a tool of the status quo.

Still, accidents happen. And in those cases, you want to know someone who works at the Porkery.

Mia shook her head. "A lot of the Godsgrave braavi get rid of their messes down here when they don't want questions asked."

Carlotta stared. Mia shrugged.

"Hungry pig will eat just about anything."

"O, lovely," the girl muttered, wringing out her long bangs.

"Master Bacon and his sons are Hands of the Church," Aalea said. "The coin they make from the local braavi assists with Godsgrave operations. And I must confess, the irony is delicious. I wonder if this city's marrowborn would be as fond of Bacon's Fynest Cuts if they knew exactly what went into the pigs they were cut from."*

"Juuuust lovely," Carlotta deadpanned, wringing harder at her hair.

"Blood is blood, love," the Shahiid smiled. "Pigs. Paupers. Cattle. Kings. It makes no difference to Our Lady. It all stains alike. And it all washes out the same."

Mia looked into the woman's eyes. Beyond the kohl and the paint. Beyond that dark beauty. It would've been easy to think that callousness made her talk so. The mark of dozens of murders draining her of all empathy, like Naev had warned. But Mia realized it was something different that drove the Shahiid of

---

* Though you've no doubt heard stories about pigs eating wagon wheels or wooden legs and the owners they were attached to, tales about the legendary appetites of hogs are, for the most part, gross exaggerations. However, pigs shipped to the Porkery from the mainland are often starved for more than a week by the time they're off-loaded, and after seven turns with naught but air to eat, the sight of a chopped-up Vaanian who owed a little too much money to the Wrong Sort of Chaps would look like a five-course meal to you too, gentlefriend.

There's a famous yarn among Itreyan sailors about the *Beatrice*—a pork ship bound for Godsgrave—blown off course during a storm-washed truedark, and wrecked on an isle in the Sea of Silence. Twelve sailors survived the ruin, and yet, over the course of the next few weeks, the sailors mysteriously disappeared, one by one. Only a single mariner was rescued when the suns eventually rose. He was a cabin boy named Benio, who, when recovered by a passing Dweymeri trawler, swore that the rest of his fellows had been eaten by another of the wreck's survivors—a ferocious sow who stalked the nights, devouring the hapless sailors one by one.

The mariners had apparently dubbed this pitiless porcine "Pinky."

Upon his return to civilization, poor Benio lost his mind over a mornmeal of bacon and fried pork rolls, and spent the rest of his turns in Godsgrave Asylum. It's said Pinky still roams the island, feasting on stranded sailors and baying at the sky when truedark falls.

Whether any of this is true, of course, remains a matter of drunken speculation on the decks of various pig ships. What *is* true, is that after learning from Mercurio what exactly went on at the Porkery at age thirteen, a young Mia Corvere swore off eating ham for the rest of her life.

Masks in her service to the Lady of Blessed Murder. Something altogether more frightening, simply because Mia didn't quite share it.

Devotion.

The truth was, she didn't know if she truly believed. Light gods in the sky watching her? Mothers of Night counting her sins? If the waves drowned a sailor, was it because the Lady of Oceans hadn't been given proper sacrifice, or the Lady of Storms was in a mood? Or was it all chance? Fate? And was it folly to think otherwise?

Her faith hadn't always been so shaky. Once she'd been as devout as a priest. Praying to mighty Aa, to the Four Daughters, to anyone who'd listen. Pricking her fingers with needles, or burning tiny locks of her hair in sacrifice. Closing her eyes and begging Him to bring her mother home. Keep her brother safe. That one turn—one bright, wonderful turn—they'd all be together again. Praying every nevernight before she crawled into bed above Mercurio's store.

Every nevernight until the truedark of her fourteenth year.

And since then?

Don't look.

"Go, loves," Aalea said. "Bring me secrets. Lovely secrets. Return here before the nevernight ends, your pockets full of whispers. And while you venture out into Aa's sight, may our Blessed Lady watch over you, and shield you from his accursed light."

"Lady, watch over us," Ash repeated.

"Lady, watch over us," the other novices said.

Mia closed her eyes. Bowed her head. Pretending she was that fourteen-year-old girl again. The girl who believed prayers could make a difference, who believed the divinities actually cared, who believed somehow, someway, everything would be all right in the end.

"Lady," she whispered. "Watch over us."

E ach acolyte knew she'd be judged on the merits of the secrets she brought back, and there was no prize for collaboration. So, although Ash was grand company and Mia was growing to enjoy Carlotta's gallows humor and quick mind, the acolytes split up as soon as they were able. Mia knew the harbor district like a thirteen-year-old boy knows his own right hand, and she slunk back and forth through the dogleg alleys and squeezeways until she was certain no other followed.

It was strange being out in the sunlight after months of constant darkness. The glare was painful, and though the shadow she cast was sharp and black and deep, she felt her kinship to it as indistinct, rather than the easy control she knew inside the Quiet Mountain. She fished about inside her cloak, slipped on a pair of wire spectacles with azurite lenses she'd lifted from the armory.*

"*. . . where do we go . . ?*" asked a whisper at her feet.

"If it's secrets Aalea wants," Mia smiled, "it's secrets she'll get."

Off through the sprawl, over bridge and under stair, the stink of the bay receding. Nevernight had been chimed to the tune of howling winds, and the streets were mostly empty. Patrols of Luminatii in their red cloaks clomped up and down the blustering thoroughfares, and bellboys stood on corners ringing in the hour over the squall, but mostly, the citizenry had retired for the eve. With only Saan in the sky, the weather was turning chill, the winds off the bay were bitterly cold. Mia trod down the twisting canals, shoulders hunched, finally arriving at the squalid stretch of dirt she'd bloomed in. The alleys encircling the marketplace of Little Liis.

Saan hung low, and the shadows were long. She wrapped herself in darkness, stole past the beggars and urchins squabbling over stolen spoils or games of dice. A small shrine to the Lady of Fire was set in one wall, Tsana's statue surrounded by guttering candles. A goddess of warriors and war, her temples were scattered all over Godsgrave; even in peacetime, there was no shortage of petty grievance or conflict in which Tsana was asked to choose a side. But this particular shrine was unattended.

Mia cast aside her shadowcloak, looked about to check all was clear. Satisfied, she reached up and turned the statue to face northeast. Dipping her fingers in the ashes, she knelt at the shrine's base and wrote the number "3" and the word "queen" in charcoal between the statue's feet. Then she pulled the shadows back around herself, and flitted away from the market.

Mia stalked through the Hips, past busking minstrels and overflowing bawdy

---

*Apothecaries theorize the imbalance of light and dark in Itreya is the cause of many public health issues, such as the increasing numbers of "dreamsick" sufferers cramming Godsgrave Asylum, and rising addiction levels to sedatives such as Swoon. Azurite spectacles are one of the few accepted remedies. The lenses are glass, tinted blue or green by arkemical processes, offsetting the glow of the dominant sun in the sky and sparing well-to-do citizens the worst of Aa's fury.

There have been several state-sponsored commissions into broader-reaching health initiatives, but since it is almighty Aa's *will* that his wife be banned from his sky for years at a stretch, even acknowledging the issue of light-related maladies can be construed as heresy. Thus, efforts to combat the issue are continually stymied by church loyalists in the Senate, not to mention lobbyists in the employ of the extraordinarily powerful Guild of Itreyan Curtainmakers.

Ah, democracy.

houses, nodding politely to the Luminatii patrols she passed along the way. She crossed the Bridge of Broken Promises;* an old man punted along the canal below in a pretty gondola, singing the chorus of "Mi Aami" in a deep, mournful voice.

"... *where do we go now* . . *?*"

"The Shield Arm."

"... *i hate the shield arm* . . "

"Your objection is duly noted."

"... *you expect to find secrets there* . . . *?*"

"A friend."

Shield Arm sits on the upper east side of the Godsgrave archipelago, comprising five main islands. Like many regions of the metropolis—Heart, Nethers, Spine—it is so named for a simple reason; if you were gifted with wings, gentlefriend, or simply turned to the map at the front of this tome, you might notice that the contours of the City of Bridges and Bones bear a remarkable similarity to those of a headless figure lying on its back.

Shield Arm is home to judiciary buildings and an astonishing number of cathedrals, and is the ingress point of Godsgrave's vast aqueduct. The islands also house the headquarters of the Luminatii—the White Palazzo—along with two of Godsgrave's ten War Walkers. The iron giants loomed over the surrounding buildings, fingers curled into titanic fists.

---

*The tallest bridge in Godsgrave, originally known as the Bridge of Towers. Its new name and popularity as a suicide spot arose in 39PR, when the mistress of Grand Cardinal Bartolemew Albari—Francesca Delphi—leapt to her death from it during truedark Carnivalé. She was clad in full Carnivalé regalia, including a jewel-encrusted golden *domino* worth more than a small estate in upper Valentia.

Once news of her suicide spread, the search for her body, and more important, the mask she was wearing, led to several drownings, at least four stabbings, and a minor riot. The rumor mill whispered that Albari had promised to abandon his position within the church and wed his paramour before the truedark of 39 fell. When Albari failed to live up to his promise, the girl had dressed in the jewels he'd given her, written a note to her parents explaining the sordid affair, then leapt to her death.

Unfortunately for Cardinal Albari, Francesca's father, Marcinus Delphi, was at that time a consul of the Republic. The scandal led to Albari being defrocked and publically scourged, and the former cardinal ended up leaping from the very same bridge his mistress had died beneath. Over time, the story evolved into a tale of tragedy— two lovers, torn apart by society and consumed by their forbidden passions. Lovesick teenagers have been flinging themselves off the bridge ever since, and control of the riverbanks around the Bridge of Broken Promises (and thus, first right to loot their lovesick corpses) has been the cause of more than one gang war between local braavi.

Incidentally, Francesca's mask and body were never found.

Not by anyone human, at any rate.

Mia made her way to the great square at the Shield Arm's heart, Piazza d'Vitrium. With a polite nod to the watchmen outside, she passed the White Palazzo, with its fluted granite columns and magnificent archways, a great statue of Aa looming out front. The Everseeing One was arrayed in battle garb, sword and shield raised. Remembering her encounter in the Hall of Pockets, Mia found herself averting her eyes from the Trinity emblazoned on his breastplate.

The girl stepped up to a neat taverna on the square's edge. The sign above the door read "The Queen's Bed."* After a slow reconnoiter around the building's alleys, she stepped inside and found a booth in a shady corner. She ordered whiskey when a weary barmaid came by to ask her pleasure. And as she took a seat, the cathedrals all around began to strike twelve.

"... here we go ..."

"Shhh."

"... i told you i hate this place ..."

Mia found the tolling pretty, truth be told. The notes weaving and crashing together, sleeping pigeons bursting from the bell towers and out into the winds. She watched the guard change outside the White Palazzo as the hour rang in, patrols of Luminatii in their white armor and red cloaks rolling in and out like waves. She thought of her father, arrayed in the same colors, standing handsome and tall as the sky. The men who smiled as he died. Downing her whiskey and ordering another.

And then, she settled in to wait.

Hours passed. The bells struck one, then two. She nursed her drink, listened to the quiet conversations of the few customers still awake at this hour. Wondering where the other acolytes might be, what secrets they might be

---

* One of the oldest tavernas in Godsgrave, the Queen's Bed was built and named by a particularly daring publican, Darius Cicerii, during the reign of Francisco XIII. Francisco's queen, Donnatella, was known to be a woman of . . . appetites, and plebs took great delight in the ensuing innuendo. The conversation, inevitably, went something like this:

"Let us gather for liquid refreshment on the morrow, gentlefriend."

"A splendid notion. But where shall we meet?"

"The Queen's Bed?"

"I hear it is quite popular of late."

(uproarious laughter goes here)

The taverna did a roaring trade as a result. When Francisco XIII was informed about the pub's name at a royal banquet by his outraged bride, he was . . . less upset than Queen Donnatella had hoped. Indeed, the king was said to have raised his glass in toast to the publican, and commented to his guests, "Perhaps I shall visit the Queen's Bed myself? Daughters know I have not seen the real thing for quite some time."

(uncomfortable silence goes here)

learning. And as the bells finally struck three, the chimes above the doorway rang, and a figure in a tricorn hat and long leather greatcoat stepped inside. Her stomach flipped to see him, and a smile curled her lips. He glanced about the taverna and spied her in her corner. Ordering a mulled wine, he limped to her booth, walking stick clacking on the boards.

"Hello, little Crow," Mercurio said.

The maid appeared with the wine, and Mia forced herself to sit still as the girl fussed about. When they were alone, she squeezed the old man's hand, over-joyed to see him again.

"Shahiid," she whispered.

"Your face looks . . . different." He frowned. "Better."

"Would that I could say the same for you," she smiled.

"Still the same smart-arse underneath the pretty, then." Mercurio sniffed. "I won't insult you by asking if you were followed. Though you picked a fine place for a clandestine meeting."

She nodded to the White Palazzo across the square. "Chances of running into my fellow acolytes are small in this part of town."

"I see they haven't killed you yet."

"Not for lack of trying."

The old man smiled. "Spiderkiller, aye?"

Mia blinked. "You knew she'd do that to us? Why didn't you warn me?"

"I didn't *know* for certain. They change the testings every year. But ini-tiates are sworn to secrecy, regardless, and if you acted like you knew the punch was coming, they'd start wondering why." The old man shrugged. "Besides, I obviously taught you what you needed to know. You still being alive and all."

Mia flapped her lips for a while, but found no retort. It was true what the old man said. He *had* given her the copy of *Arkemical Truths*, after all. Thank the Maw she'd actually spent more time reading it than most of the others in her crop . . .

". . . Fair enough," she finally muttered.

"So. What brings you back to the 'Grave? Aalea?"

"Aye."

Mercurio nodded. "You're lucky. They change the city every year. You can't hurl a rock without hitting a gossip in Godsgrave. My year, old Shahiid The-lonius sent us to bloody Farrow. Imagine grubbing for tidbits among a pack of Dweymeri fisherwives . . ."

"I've never been all that grand at learning secrets."

"Shouldn't you be out practicing, then?"

"I thought you might loan me one so I can spend the time drinking with you instead."

Mercurio scoffed, blue eyes wrinkling as he smiled. Mia's heart warmed to be with him again—though it'd barely been three months since she left Godsgrave, she had to admit she'd missed the cranky old bastard. She set about telling him of the Church in hushed tones. The Mountain. Her run-in with Solis.

"Aye, he's a bleeding prick," Mercurio muttered. "Damn fine swordsman, though. Mark his teaching well."

"Hard for me to learn anything when I can't attend lessons." She proffered her arm, her elbow now a lovely shade of yellow and gray. "It's taking bloody ages to heal."

"That's bullshit," Mercurio spat. "It's hardly even bruised. You get back in that hall on the morrow." The old man raised his voice over the beginnings of Mia's protest. "So Solis gave your arse a kicking. Learn from it. Sometimes weakness is a weapon. *If* you're smart enough to use it."

Mia chewed her lip. Nodded slow. She knew he spoke truth, that she should be learning all from Solis that she could. Now that she was back in Godsgrave, her reason for studying at the Church burned in her mind hotter than ever. Everywhere she looked, she saw reminders. The Ribs where she'd lived as a child. The Luminatii and their bright white armor, reminding her so much of her father.

The bastards who took him from her . . .

"Any news about Scaeva since I've been gone?" she asked.

Mercurio sighed. "Well, he's standing for a fourth term as sole consul, but that shouldn't surprise anyone. He's got half the Senate in his thrall, and the other half are too scared or greedy to raise a ruckus. Looks like the second consul's chair will remain empty for the foreseeable future."

Mia shook her head, silently amazed. When the Republic had been founded, when the Itreyans murdered their last king, the system they built in the monarchy's ruins was meant to make a new monarchy impossible. The Itreyans elected consuls to rule them every truedark, but there were *two* consul's chairs in the Senate House, and no consul was permitted to sit two terms in a row. That was the entire *point* of the Republic. All tenure of power was shared, and all tenure of power was short.

When General Antonius raised his army in rebellion against the Senate, Scaeva had dredged up some anachronistic amendments in the Itreyan constitution that allowed him to sit as sole consul in the Republic's time of need, but . . .

"He's still citing emergency powers?" Mia sighed. "The Kingmaker Rebellion was put down *six years ago*. The *balls* on that bastard . . ."

"Well, he might've had a hard time convincing the Senate there was still a crisis, but when an assassin tries to murder the head of the Republic in a cathedral full of witnesses, it gets a touch easier to make the case. The Truedark Massacre showed the Senate just how dangerous this city still is. You'd need a bloody army to get through to Scaeva now. He doesn't take a piss without a cadre of Luminatii to hold the pot."

Mia sipped her whiskey. Eyes on the table.

"Cardinal Duomo is still on Scaeva like a babe at his mother's tit, of course," Mercurio muttered. "Has his ministers preaching from the pulpits, praising our 'glorious consul' and his 'golden age of peace.'" The old man scoffed. "Golden age of tyranny, more like it. We're closer to a new arse on the throne than when the Kingmakers raised their army. But the plebs lap it up. Peace means stability. And stability means money. Scaeva's near untouchable now."

"Give me time," Mia said. "I'll touch him. None too gently, either."

"O, aye, what could possibly go wrong there?"

"Scaeva needs to die, Mercurio."

"You just mind your lessons," Mercurio growled. "You're a damn sight shy of initiation. The Church is only going to test you harder, and there's plenty of ways to get buried between here and the finish line. Worry about Scaeva when you're a Blade, not a moment before. Because it's only going to be a full-fledged Blade that gets to him now."

Mia lowered her eyes. Nodded. "I will. I promise."

Mercurio looked at her, those born-to-scowl eyes softening around the edges. "How you holding up in there?"

"Well enough." She shrugged. "Apart from the dismemberment."

"They'll ask you to do things, soon. Dark things. To prove your devotion."

"I've blood on my hands already."

"I'm not talking about killing those who deserve it, little Crow. You ended their executioner, true. But he was the man who hung your father. That'd be easy for the softest of us." The old man sighed. "Sometimes I wonder if I did the right thing. Bringing you in. Teaching you all this."

"You said it yourself," Mia hissed. "Scaeva is a fucking tyrant. He needs to *die*. Not just for me. For the Republic. For the people."

"The people, eh? That's what this is about?"

She reached out across the table, squeezed the old man's hand.

"I can do this, Mercurio."

". . . Aye." He nodded, his voice suddenly hoarse. "I know it, lass."

He looked wearier than she'd ever seen him. The weight of it all, piling up turn by turn. His skin was like paper. His eyes bloodshot.

He looks so old.

Mercurio cleared his throat, drained the last of his wine. "I'll leave first. Give me ten minutes."

"Aye."

The old assassin smiled, hovered uncertainly. It was all Mia could do to stop herself from rising to hug him. But she held herself still, and he gathered up his walking stick, gave her a brief nod. Turning, he took a step toward the door, stopped short.

" 'Byss and blood, I almost forgot."

He reached into his greatcoat, proffered a small wooden box, sealed with tallow. Mia recognized the sigil scorched into the wood. Recalled the little store where the old man used to buy his cigarillos. Remembering the night he first let her smoke one. Sitting on the battlements above the forum. Dark all around. Hands shaking. Fingers stained with blood. Fourteen years old.

Don't look.

"Black Dorian's," she smiled.

"Paper. Tobacco. Wood. It'll all make the Walk. I remember that time you tried to quit. Figured it best you don't run out in there."

"Best not." Mia took the box from his hand, her eyes stinging. "My thanks."

"Watch your back. And your front." He waved vaguely. "And the rest of it, too."

"Always."

The old man pulled his tricorn down, his collar up. And without another word, he limped from the taverna and out into the street. Mia watched him go, counting the minutes down in her head. Eyes on the old man's back as he limped into the distance.

"They'll ask you to do things, soon. Dark things. To prove your devotion."

Mia rested her chin in her hands, lost in thought.

A rowdy pack of bucks was coming in from the street, dressed in the white armor and red cloaks of the Luminatii. The girl glanced up at the sound of their laughter, young faces and handsome smiles. Stationed this close to the Palazzo, they were probably all marrowborn sons. Pulling a few years in the legion to further their familia's political ends. If things had gone different, she'd be betrothed to a boy like that, most like. Living a life of privilege and never stopping a moment to—

"Pardon me," said a voice.

Mia looked up, blinking. One of the Luminatii was standing above her. Lady-killer smile and a rich boy's teeth.

"Forgive me, Mi Dona," he bowed. "I couldn't help noticing you sitting alone, and I thought it a crime against the Light itself. Might you permit me to join you?"

Mia's hackles rippled, her fingers twitched. But realizing she appeared nothing more than a marrowborn girl out drinking alone, and remembering Aalea's many and hard-learned lessons in charm, Mia smoothed her feathers and gave her best smile.

"O, that sounds lovely," she said. "I'm honored, sir, but I'm afraid my mother is expecting me abed. Perhaps another time?"

"I trust your mother can spare you for one drink?" The boy raised a hopeful eyebrow. "I've not seen you in here before."

"Apologies, sir." Mia rose from the table. "But I really must be going."

"Hold, now." The boy blocked her way out of the booth. Eyes darkening.

Mia tried to quash her rising anger. Kept her voice steady. Stare downcast.

"Excuse me, sir, you're in my way."

"I'm just being friendly, girl."

"Is that what you call it, sir?" Mia's eyes flashed as her temper finally came out to play. "Others might say you're being an arse."

Anger blotched the boy's face—the quick fury of a lad too used to getting his own way. He reached out with one gauntleted hand, seized Mia's wrist, holding tight.

She could've broken his jaw, then. Buried her knee in his bollocks. Sat on his chest and wailed on his face until he learned not all girls were his sport. But that'd mark her as someone who knew the Song, and she was in a pub with half a dozen of his fellows, after all. And so she settled for twisting her arm as Mercurio had taught her, putting the boy off-balance and tearing free of his iron-shod grip.

The buttons at her cuff popped. Cloth tore. The sheathe at her wrist twisted and with the sound of snapping leather, Mia's gravebone stiletto clattered to the floor.

A heavy hand clapped the back of the boy's neck, a smoker's voice growling.

"Leave the girl alone, Andio. We're here to drink, not chase doves."

The boy and Mia glanced over his shoulder, saw an older man in centurion's armor looming behind the young soldier. He was a big man, his face scarred and grim.

"Forgive me, Centu—"

With a loud clunk, the centurion kicked the younger man in the backside and sent him on his way, folding his arms and scowling until the boy rejoined his comrades. The man was obviously a veteran, one eye covered by a dark leather patch. Satisfied, the centurion tapped the brim of his plumed helm, gave Mia an apologetic nod.

"Forgiveness for my man's impertinence, Dona. No harm done, I hope?"

"No, sir," Mia smiled, heart beating easier. "My thanks, Centurion."

The man nodded, stooped, and lifted Mia's stiletto off the floor. With a small bow, he proffered it on his forearm. The girl smiled wider, curtseyed with invisible skirts, and took the dagger from his hand. But as she slipped it back up her sleeve, the man's gaze followed the blade, the crow carved on the hilt. A slow frown took seed on his brow.

Mia's face paled.

O, Daughters . . .

She recognized him now. It'd been six years, but she'd not forgotten him. Leaning over the barrel she'd been stowed inside, with his pretty blue eyes and the smile of a fellow who choked puppies for sport.

"Maw's teeth," breathed the first. *"She can't be more than ten."*

"Never to see eleven." A sigh. "Hold still, girl. This won't hurt long."

The centurion wasn't smiling now.

Mia shuffled around the table, knocking over her empty cup. She tried another hasty curtsey and a quick walk to the door, but like the soldier before him, the centurion now blocked her way from the booth. Fingers creeping to the patch of leather, covering the eye she'd skewered with her gravebone stiletto all those years ago. Disbelief etched in his features.

"Can't be . . ."

"Excuse me, sir."

Mia tried to muscle past, but the centurion grabbed her arm, squeezing tight. Mia held her temper—barely—thinking she might still bluff her way through. Bolting like a frightened deer would cause attention. But the man twisted her arm, looked at the stiletto once more sheathed at her wrist. The crow on the hilt with its tiny amber eyes.

"Name of the Light . . . ," he breathed.

"Centurion Alberius?" called Mia's scorned soldierboy. "Is all well?"

The centurion fixed Mia in his stare. Puppy-killer smile finally coming out to play.

"O, everything is well, all right," he said.

Mia's knee collided with the man's groin, her elbow with his chin. The centurion cried out, helmet flying off his head as he toppled backward, and Mia was vaulting over his body on her way to the door. The legionaries took a moment to react, watching their commander drop like a whimpering sack of potatoes, but soon enough they barreled out into the street behind the fleeing girl. Mia heard whistles blowing behind her, furious shouts, running feet.

"Of all the pubs in Godsgrave," she gasped. "What are the fucking odds?"

". . . you did pick one right next to the palazzo . . ."

She threw her hood over her head, skidded off the main drag and down a twisting side alley, bolting over the refuse and drunks, the sugargirls and sweetboys. More footsteps behind her, more whistles, more men. Buckled cobbles under her feet, narrow walls closing in about her. She bolted into a tiny piazza, barely ten feet at a side, an old bubbling fountain at its heart. The goddess Trelene stood atop it, her gown made of crashing waves, surrounded by candles and bloody offerings. Pushing herself back into a little doorway, Mia dragged her cloak of shadows about her shoulders, all the world dropping into gloom and darkness.

Footsteps coming. Heavy boots. Through her cloak, she caught the dim impression of a dozen Luminatii, sunsteel blades drawn and blazing, dashing into the piazza. Seeing no sign of her, they split up and thundered off in all directions. Mia stayed still, Mister Kindly at her feet, the pair just a smudge in the doorway. She waited as another group of soldiers rushed past, shouting and shoving.

Finally, silence.

She stole away slowly, feeling her way along the wall beneath her cloak. At a time like this, it was hard to fault the Mother for marking her—if, indeed, that's what she'd done. But as far as magik went, being able to stumble about near blind and almost invisible seemed a far cry from Adonai or Marielle's brand of sorcery. Everyone paid a price, she supposed. Adonai thirsted for what he controlled. Marielle wove the flesh of others and corrupted her own. And Mia could remain unseen, but hardly see while doing it . . .

She pawed her way through the maze of back streets, but she didn't know Shield Arm as well as Little Liis. Even with Mister Kindly roaming ahead, it'd take hours to find her way back to the Porkery at this rate. So finally, she threw aside her shadows and made for the nearest thoroughfare. Out onto the main drag, crossing three bridges to the Heart, then down to the Nethers, dodging any Luminatii who came within a block. Running into the puppy-choker had unnerved her. Filled her mind with memories. Her mother in chains. Her baby brother crying. The turn her whole world came apart. She needed to get back to the Mountain, away from these bastard sun-botherers.

A moment to think.

A moment to breathe.

If she weren't so intent on spotting large groups of men in gleaming white armor waving burning swords, she might have noticed a slender figure dressed all in mortar gray, picking up her trail as she entered the harbor district. She might have noticed the gang of young bucks trudging down the boardwalk toward her, nodding to the figure shadowing behind. She might've noticed they wore soldiers' boots. That they had rather suspicious truncheon-shaped lumps beneath their cloaks.

She might have noticed all this before it was too late.

But then it was too late.

STEEL

A hard slap.

Water dashed in her face.

A sputtering gasp.

"Wake up, my lovely love."

Mia opened her eyes, immediately regretting it. Blinding pain arced across her brow, all the way to the base of her skull. Fragmented memories. A group of men. Cudgels. Repeated blows. Cursing. Her knife flashing. Blood in her mouth.

Then blackness.

Wincing, she looked about her. Stone walls. A metal door with a barred window. She was sat in a heavy, iron chair. Hands manacled behind her back. Mister Kindly lurked in her shadow, drinking down her fear. Not alone.

Never alone.

"Wake up."

Another slap landed on her face, whipping her head sideways. Lank and dripping hair stuck to her skin. She tried to lash out with her feet, found they were manacled too.

"I'm awake, you fucking whoreson!"

Mia looked up at the man who'd slapped her. A hulk of pure muscle, six feet tall and almost as wide. More scar on his face than there was face. Another fellow stood behind him, clean cut and well built with dead, empty eyes. Both were wearing white robes. Copies of Aa's gospels strung on heavy iron chains about their necks. Tiny flecks of blood at their cuffs.

"O, shit," Mia breathed.

*Confessors . . . **

"Indeed," said the man with dead eyes. "And you are bound by book and chain to answer our questions true."

The scarred man walked slowly around the room until he stood behind Mia. Craning her neck, the girl saw a long table, lined with tools. Pliers. Snips. Thumbscrews. A brazier full of burning coal. At least five different flavors of hammer.

No fear in her belly. No quaver in her voice. Looking the second man in his dead eyes.

"What would you like to know, good Brother?"

"You are Mia Corvere."

How do they know my name?

". . . Aye."

"Daughter of Darius Corvere. Hung by order of the Senate six years past."

That centurion . . . Alberius . . . surely he couldn't have got word out to Scaeva already?

". . . Aye."

Heavy hands landed on both her shoulders, squeezing tight.

"The Kingmaker's sprog," came the scarred man's voice behind her. "Bounce my bollocks on the boardwalk, is that not a treat, Brother Micheletto?"

The dead-eyed man smiled, his eyes never leaving Mia's.

"O, a rare treat, Brother Santino. My belly's all a-flutter, it is."

"I've committed no crime," Mia said. "I am a god-fearing daughter of Aa, Brother."

The one called Micheletto stopped smiling. His slap brought the stars

---

*A branch of Aa's church almost as old as the religion itself, the Confessionate is, as you may suspect, charged with rooting out heresy within the Republic. Chiefly concerning themselves with those who worship the Mother of Night, confessors are recruited from among the most zealous—or imbalanced—of Aa's ministers. The current head of the Confessionate, Attia Fiorlini, went so far as to crucify her own husband on suspicion of heresy early in her career. Her superiors were duly impressed with her devotion, and her star rose quickly thereafter.

In actual fact, Attia trumped up charges against her beau after discovering he was diddling one of the maidservants.

Still, two birds with one stone . . .

out from the dark inside Mia's skull. Her head hung loose on her shoulders, Micheletto's growl cutting through the ringing in her ears.

"Speak His name again, girl, and I shall hack out your godless tongue with a fucking butter knife and cook it with my tea."

Mia breathed deep. Waited for the pain to subside. Mind racing. Bound. Outnumbered. No idea where she was. No help coming. Not the worst scrape she'd been in, true. But, Daughters, it was racing hard for second . . .

She tossed her hair from her eyes, looked at the confessor looming above her.

"Tell us where you were earlier this eve," he said. "Before you arrived in Godsgrave."

"Arrived?" The girl shook her head. "Brother, I've lived here my whole—"

Mia hissed in pain as Santino grabbed her by the scruff and squeezed. She felt his lips brushing her ear as he spoke, stale wine and tobacco on his breath.

"Brother Micheletto asked you a question, my lovely love. And before you wrap that tongue around another lie, I'd best tell you I can still smell blood in your hair . . ."

Mia's heart skipped a beat at that. She felt her shadow shiver, Mister Kindly chewing hard at her fear. Could they possibly know she was from the Red Church? Had they some inkling of how disciples moved from the Mountain and back? Justicus Remus had long vowed to destroy the assassins, even before the Truedark Massacre. It made sense he'd recruit the Confessionate to route them out. But could they—

"Tell us where you were earlier this eve. Before you arrived in Godsgrave."

"I've not left Godsgrave since I was eight ye—"

Crack. A bright red handprint etched on her face.

"Tell us where you were earlier this eve. Before you arrived in Godsgrave."

"Nowhere, Brother, I—"

Her chair was dragged backward, the awful sound of iron grating on stone ringing in her ears. Mia saw a barrel filled with dark, tepid water in a corner of the room. Rough hands seized a fistful of her hair, dunked her head and held her down. She thrashed, bucked, but the manacles had her pinned, the hand holding her tight. She roared, bubbles bursting from her mouth into the brackish dark. Harbor water, she realized. Probably fished straight from the Bay of Butchers. Blood, bilge, and shit.

And they're drowning me in it.

Black spots swimming in her eyes. Lungs burning. The hand hauled her up out of the water and she dragged in a desperate, sputtering lungful.

"Tell us where you were earlier this eve. Before you arrived in Godsgrave."

"Please, sto—"

Down beneath the water again. The pain and the dark. Her shadow seethed around her feet, helpless and desperate. But there was no cloak of darkness that could hide her here. No sense pinning her captors' feet to the floor. Chosen of the Mother? Fat lot of good it was doing her. Why couldn't the goddess have let her breathe underwater?

Lungs almost bursting, she was dragged up into the light again. Chest heaving. Legs trembling. Coughing. Gasping. The fear was breaking loose now, Mister Kindly unable to drink it all. But still, she stamped it down. Kicked it in the teeth and spat on it.

"Tell us where you were earlier this eve. Before you arrived in Godsgrave."

"I was nowhere!" she roared.

Down again. And up. The question repeated, over and over. She screamed. Swore. Tried crying. Pleading. No avail. Every plea, every tear, every curse was met with the same response.

"Tell us where you were earlier this eve. Before you arrived in Godsgrave."

But beneath the tears and cries, Mia's mind was still racing. If they wanted her dead, she'd be dead. If they knew where she'd come from, they'd already be at the Porkery. And if the Confessionate was in league with the Luminatii, that meant each of these bastards was a lapdog of Scaeva and Remus. The men who'd hung her father. The men who'd set her feet on this path all those years ago. The Red Church was her best chance at vengeance against them. And these fools expected her to give it up for fear of a little drowning?

She retreated. Back into the dark inside her head. Watching her torture with a kind of semidetached fascination. Hours they worked her, until her voice was broken and her lungs screaming and every breath fire. Drowning and beating. Spitting and slapping. Hours.

And hours.

And then they stopped. Left her slumped in her chair, hands bound behind her. Hair reeking of bay water, draped across her face like a funeral shroud. Bruised. Bleeding. Almost drowned.

Almost dead.

"We have all turn, my lovely love," Santino said. "And all nevernight, besides."

"And if water will not loosen your tongue," said Micheletto, "we've other remedies."

The big man lifted an iron poker from the table of tools. Thrust it into the burning brazier and left it there to heat. He spat onto the coals, a sizzling hiss filling the room.

"When that iron glows red, we'll return. Think long and hard about where your loyalties lie. You may think your precious flock of heretics worth dying for. But believe me, there are far worse fates than death. And we know them all."

The confessors marched from the room, slamming a heavy iron door behind them. Mia heard a key rattle, a bolt slide home. Receding footsteps. Distant screams.

"... mia ..."

The girl tossed her hair from her eyes. Still trying to catch her breath. Shivering. Coughing. Looking down at last to the shadow coalescing at her feet.

"I'm all right, Mister Kindly."

"... for confessors, those two seem like lovely fellows ..."

"How under the suns did they mark me?"

"... mercurio ...?"

"Bullshit."

"... the centurion? alberius ...?"

"He'd no clue I was with the Church. This feels bigger. Deeper."

Mister Kindly titled his head. Silent and thoughtful.

"... puzzles later. first you must get out of here ...," he finally said.

"I'm glad you're here to tell me these things."

Mia cast her eyes around the room. The poker heating in the brazier. The tools on the table. They'd stripped her of her boots, her weapons. The box of cigarillos Mercurio had given her. The manacles were cinched tight. Her feet chained to the chair. Feeling around the bindings, she realized the cuffs were closed with heavy iron bolts rather than an actual lock.

"Fuck ...," she breathed.

"... you must get loose ..."

"I can't," she hissed, trying to reach the bolts in vain. "It's a shitty set of manacles if you could just unlock yourself with your own two hands."

"... do not use your hands, then ..."

The not-cat glanced to the shadows about them.

"You know it doesn't work like that."

"... it can ..."

"I'm not strong enough, Mister Kindly."

"... you were ..."

Mia swallowed. Flashes in her mind's eye. Darkened hallways. Lightless stone.

Don't look.

"... remember ...?"

"No."

"*. . . they will kill you, mia. unless they break you. and then, they will kill you any-way . . .*"

Mia grit her teeth. Stared at the not-cat, staring back with his not-eyes.

"*. . . try . . .*"

"Mister Kindly, I . . ."

"*. . . try . . .*"

She closed her eyes. Black and warm behind her lashes. Feeling the shadows in this dank little cell. Cold. Old. The suns never came here. The dark was deep. Cool and hungry. She could feel them around her, like living things. Flickering playfully in the brazier's feeble light. Tumbling over each other and laughing soundlessly. They knew her. Some feeble pale little slip of a thing, who touched them the way the wind touches mountains. But she reached out, curled up her fists, and they fell still.

Waiting.

". . . All right," she whispered.

She twisted them. Sent them slithering along the floor to coil at her back. Snaking up around the iron at her wrists. At her command, they wrapped themselves tight around the iron bolts holding her bonds in place. They *pulled*.

And the bolts moved not an inch.

They were only shadows, after all.

Real as dreams.

Hard as smoke.

"It's no good," Mia sighed. "I can't do it."

"*. . . you must . . .*"

"I can't!"

"*. . . you have. and if you do not do so again, you will die here, mia . . .*"

Her hands shook. Hateful tears trying to brim in her eyes.

"*. . . do not command the darkness around you . . .*"

The not-cat stepped closer, peering as hard as the eyeless can.

"*. . . command the darkness inside yourself . . .*"

Distant footsteps.

Muffled screaming.

". . . All right."

Closing her eyes again. Not reaching out this time. Stretching within. Places the suns had *never* touched. The shapeless black beneath her skin. Gritting her teeth. Sweat gleaming on her brow. The shadows shivered, rippled, sighed. Growing blacker. Harder. Sharper. Grasping at the bolts, her face twisted, heart pounding, breath quickening as if she were sprinting. But slowly, ever so slowly, the bolts began to shiver. To turn. Moment by moment. Inch by inch. Veins standing taut in her neck. Spit on her lips. Hissing. Begging. Until finally, she heard a soft plunk. Then another. The iron at her wrists falling on the stone.

And she was free.

Mia looked at Mister Kindly. And though he had no mouth, she could tell he smiled.

"... *there it is* ..."

She fumbled with the irons at her ankles, pulling them loose. Standing, hair and clothes still drenched, she stole silently to the door. The window slit was shut, but she listened at the iron. Heard faint cries echoing on stone. A long corridor, by the sound of it. Metal and footsteps.

Coming closer.

She snatched a hammer off the table, pulled the shadows around her, wrapping herself in darkness and crouching low in the corner. The door bolt rattled, the lock clicked. Brother Santino walked inside, saw the empty chair, the empty manacles, eyes widening. Mia's hammer crashed into his face, her knee collided with his groin. With a burbling whimper, the man collapsed. Brother Micheletto stood behind Santino, face aghast. Mia struck at him, but she was near blind in her darkness and her blow went wide, the confessor stepping back and blocking with the bracer on his forearm. He squinted, seeing only a shifting blur, charging it anyway. Catching her in a bearhug. Crying out as her hammer glanced off his brow. Falling hard and dragging her with him.

The pair rolled about on the stone, punching and flailing. Micheletto trying to grasp the girl he couldn't quite see, Mia trying to land a decent blow without quite being able to tell what she was swinging at. In the end, she threw her shadowcloak aside, settled for sheer ferocity over useless stealth. Her elbow crushed his nose to pulp, her fist danced on his jaw.

A vicious hook landed on the side of her head, knocked her senseless. Another blow landed, sending her tumbling. She realized Santino was on his feet again, behind her, his face a dripping, bloody ruin. Mia struggled to stand, but the brother seized her in a crushing headlock. The shadows snapped and writhed, but the headshots had dizzied her and she couldn't hold them tight. She threw a savage kick backward, felt it connect somewhere soft, heard a grunt of pain. But then she was slammed back into her chair, spitting and cursing, hair tangled in her eyes. Santino held her down while Micheletto bound her wrists again. The tools on the table trembled, the shadows in the room whipping like serpents. Something heavy crashed into her temple and she slumped, bleeding and gasping, head lolling on her shoulders.

"Little fucking bitch," Micheletto hissed.

He limped to the brazier, nose pissing blood, dragged the poker from the coals. Its tip was blazing an angry, luminous orange. Mia thrashed in the chair but Santino held her down, the other confessor raising the poker close to her face. She froze. Felt the blistering heat, just an inch or two from her skin. A stray wisp of hair touched the red-hot iron, smoking as it crisped.

"My lovely love," Santino cooed. "You'll be less lovely in a moment, I fear."

Hands on the side of her head, holding her still. Breath hissing through her teeth. Nothing but rage inside now. If this was to be her end, she'd not go begging.

Never flinch. Never fear. And never, ever forget.

"Tell us where you were earlier this eve," Micheletto growled. "Before you arrived in Godsgrave."

"Fuck you."

"Where were you before you arrived in Godsgrave?" Micheletto shouted.

The iron was a breath from her skin now. Already beginning to burn. She felt sick to her stomach, sweat stinging her eyes. Mia looked up at the confessor. Lips peeling back from her teeth. Whispering fierce.

"Fuck. *You.*"

The brother shook his head.

And with a hollow smile, he raised the poker to her eye.

"Enough."

The smile dropped from the brother's face. The grip on the sides of Mia's head eased. Both confessors straightened, as if standing to attention. Brother Micheletto stepped aside to reveal a cloaked figure in the doorway.

Mia glimpsed long black hair. Bottomless black eyes. Twin blades at his waist.

Perfectly plain.

Perfectly deadly.

A greasy illness swelled in her belly, Mister Kindly shivering as the dark around them surged. And from the shadows, she heard a low, rumbling growl.

A wolf growl.

"Leave us," Cassius commanded.

"Yes, Lord," Micheletto and Santino replied.

The men bowed deep, and with quiet nods to Mia, marched quickly from the room. Her belly thrilled with sudden fear as Lord Cassius stepped into the cell, Mister Kindly shrinking down into the black at her feet. The Lord of Blades stood before Mia with hands clasped, long dark locks moving as if in some invisible breeze. His skin was purest alabaster. His voice, honey and blood.

"Bravo, Acolyte. My compliments."

". . . Lord Cassius?"

Mia looked about her. Beyond the sickness in her gut, beyond the surge of terror and excitement she felt in his presence, realization was flooding over her.

Relief. Anger. Chagrin.

"A test," she breathed.

"A necessity," Cassius replied. "Now that you know of the Blood Walk. Beyond your skill with steel or venom or flesh, there is one virtue we must ensure each and every disciple of the Red Church possesses in abundance."

Mia looked the Black Prince in the eye. Her hands trembling.

"Loyalty," she whispered.

Cassius inclined his head. "The Red Church prides itself in its reputation. No contract ever undertaken by this congregation has remained unfulfilled. No disciple has ever revealed a secret to those who hunt us. Every year, we bring new faces into the flock, sharpen you to the keenest edge. But as honed as they may appear, some blades are simply made of glass."

"Glass?"

"A shard of glass can slice a man's throat. Pierce his heart clean. Open his wrists to the bone. But press it in the wrong place, glass will shatter. Iron will not."

A faint smile curled pale lips, Cassius's hand drifting to a blade at his waist.

"Since the failed attempt on Consul Scaeva's life, Cardinal Duomo has declared the destruction of the Red Church a divine mandate. Justicus Remus and his Luminatii hunt us in every corner of the Republic. We have the power of Ashkahi sorcery at our fingertips. Chapels in every metropolis. If one of our disciples were to fall into the hands of our enemies, we must be certain they will not shatter. And so . . ."

Cassius motioned to the cells around them, his cloak whispering as he moved. Mister Kindly's fear was eating into Mia's belly, the shadows writhing across the floor. She glanced up as another scream echoed down the corridor. Swallowing hard and searching for her voice.

"So Shahiid Aalea's trial was just a ruse?"

"O, no. The acolyte who gifts her the finest secret will still finish top of Masks. And all of you will be sent to this city time and again in search of them, have no doubt. We simply take this opportunity to test the waters, so to speak."

"The other acolytes who came to Godsgrave? You're testing them, too?"

"We test you all."

". . . Did any break?"

"Someone always breaks."

The man searched Mia's eyes. Waiting, perhaps, for some kind of rebuke.

Mia remained mute, meeting that bottomless stare, fighting the illness in her gut. The greasy tang of bile hung in the back of her throat, her hands shaking so badly she was forced to grip the chair to still them. What was it about this man that affected her so? Was it because he was of her kind? The dark in him, calling to the dark in her?

She heard soft, padded footsteps behind her. That low wolf growl.

Eclipse . . .

"You're the first darkin I've ever met," she finally said. "Ever spoken to."

"Perhaps the last," he replied. "You stand many a nevernight from initiation. And if you think our kinship will buy you favor in the Mother's halls, you are sorely mistaken."

The Black Prince's eyes were deathly cold. His beauty colder still. Mia could feel the shadowwolf behind her, prowling closer. Mister Kindly puffed up in her shadow and hissed, and a low chuckling resounded from the stones at her feet. The question clawed at her tongue until she gave it voice; a thin whisper hanging in the air like smoke.

"What are we?"

"What do you suppose we are?"

"Mercurio, Drusilla . . ." Mia swallowed. "They say we're the Mother's chosen."

The hair on back of her neck stood on end as the Lord of Blades laughed.

"Is that what you believe yourself to be, little darkin? Chosen?"

"I don't know what I believe," she hissed. "I was hoping you could teach me."

"What to believe?"

"What I *am*."

"It matters not what you are," Cassius said. "Only *that* you are. And if you seek an answer to some greater riddle of yourself, seek it not from me until you've earned it. In one measure, and one measure alone, you should be content. For in this, if nothing else, we are the same."

Mia's stomach surged as the Lord of Blades leaned in closer, drawing a dagger from his sleeve. And reaching down, he sliced through the rope at her wrists.

"We are killers, you and I," he said. "Killers one, killers all. And each death we bring is a prayer. An offering to Our Lady of Blessed Murder. Death as a mercy. Death as a warning. Death as an end unto itself. All of these, ours to know and gift unto the world. The wolf does not pity the lamb. The storm begs no forgiveness of the drowned."

He searched her eyes again, his voice thrumming in her breast as he spoke.

"But first and foremost, we are servants. Disciples. Surrounded by foes. Loyal unto the death. We do not bend and we do not break. Ever. *This* is the truth you learn in this cell. *This* is the first answer to any question of self you might ask. And if it does not sit well with you, Acolyte, if you think perhaps you have made a mistake in coming to us, now is the time to speak."

So. No answers. Just more riddles. If Cassius held some greater truth about darkin, he wasn't about to share it here. Perhaps ever. Or perhaps, as he said, not until she *earned* it.

And so, with a wince, Mia rose slowly from the chair. Her legs were shaking. Sick to her bones. She was cold. Damp. Reeking of bay water and blood. Cheek swollen, eye bruised, lip split. Dragging sodden hair from her cheek, she met Cassius's stare.

Held out her hand.

"Can I have my cigarillos back?"

I t took the best of her, but she held it inside.

Escorted from the basement cell. Down the bright boardwalk and back to the hidden tunnels beneath the Porkery. A wooden box sealed with tallow clutched in her hands. A gravebone dagger up her sleeve. Not a whisper on her lips.

The Blood Walk back to the Mountain was no easier the second time through. Mia stripped away her clothes, stepped naked into the scarlet pool beneath the abattoir. She fell beneath the flood, tempted for a moment to simply stay there forever with her questions and her fears. But she pushed back against the weight of it, hands wrapped tight around the box Mercurio had gifted her, the gravebone blade in her fist.

Three baths later she was escorted by a silent Hand up the winding stairs to the Sky Altar, there to eat her mornmeal as if nothing were amiss. The male acolytes were nowhere to be seen—probably already in Godsgrave, being rounded up for their own round of beatings and torture. She saw Ashlinn seated at the table, her lip fat and cheek split. Mia wouldn't meet her eyes. Collecting her food, she took a seat, eating without speaking a word. Noting the other female acolytes who filtered slowly up the stairs, the smiles and jokes from past meals just a memory.

By meal's end, only Ashlinn, Jessamine, Carlotta, and Mia sat at that long, lonely table. All of them beaten. Bruised. Bloodied. But alive, at least. Of the nine girls who'd gathered in Aalea's chambers yestereve, only four had returned.

Four of iron.

The rest, glass.

They looked among each other. Carlotta, ever stoic. Jessamine triumphant. A thin line of worry between Ash's brows—probably at the thought of what might be happening to her brother. But not one of them spoke. Mia stared at her plate, chewed her food, one ashen mouthful at a time. Forcing herself to finish every crumb. Mop up the gravy like blood on rough stone. And when she was done, she stood quietly, trod back to her room, and closed the door behind her.

She looked at her face in the mirror. Dark, bruised eyes. Thin, trembling lips.

"... *i am sorry, mia* ..."

Mia looked at the not-cat, curled on the edge of the bed. Cassius and Eclipse had rattled Mister Kindly worse than she. But her questions about darkin, about the Lord of Blades and his passenger, all of them simply died on her lips.

"It's all right, Mister Kindly," she sighed.

"... *never flinch* ...," he offered. "... *never fear* ..."

Mia nodded. "And never, ever forget."

She sat before the looking glass and stared at the girl staring back at her. The killer Cassius had described. The monster. Wondering, for one tiny moment, what her life might have been before Scaeva tore it to ribbons. Trying to remember her father's face. Trying to forget her mother's. Feeling the burn of tears in her eyes. Willing them gone until nothing remained. Just Mia and the dry-eyed girl staring back at her.

Mercurio must have known the test of loyalty was coming. Knew what Cassius and the Ministry had planned. And though another might've felt betrayed their master had given no warning, instead Mia felt only pride. The old man had known what was in store for her, and still he'd not breathed a word. Not because he didn't care.

Because he knew.

Cassius and the Ministry had no clue. No idea at all what she was made of. But *he* knew.

Iron or glass? they'd asked.

Mia clenched her jaw. Shook her head.

She was neither.

She was steel.

CHAPTER 18

SCOURGE

The final tally to survive Lord Cassius's test was seventeen. Four female. Thirteen male. All of them various shades of bloodied, battered, and bruised. Hush's eyes were so blackened, the boy could barely see for three turns. Marcellus walked with a limp for weeks. Pip's jaw had almost been broken, and he ate only soups for almost a month.*

Mia knew she shouldn't have cared whether or not Tric survived. But when he'd walked up the stairs and sat quietly down to his evemeal, she'd found herself smiling at him. When he'd glanced up and caught her in it, she decided not to try and hide it.

And Tric had smiled back.

Her swordarm still wasn't fully healed, but Mercurio's scolding had sunk home. When the flock were deemed recovered enough for lessons to begin again, Mia decided to attend the Hall of Songs. She'd already missed dozens of lessons; any longer, she'd risk falling too far behind to stand a chance in Solis's trial. She didn't favor her odds anyway; her best hope of finishing top of hall was crafting Spiderkiller's antidote. But making a mistake in Spiderkiller's contest meant *dying*, and besides, if she graduated to fully fledged Blade, she'd need all the swordcraft she could muster. Sitting on her arse reading all turn wasn't going to cut it.

As she walked into the Hall of Songs, Jessamine looked up from beating the stuffing out of a training dummy and shot her a *fuck you* smile. As Mia took her place at circle, Solis raised one eyebrow, staring with those awful, blind eyes. The cut she'd given him still hadn't been healed by Weaver Marielle—a tiny new scar, which the Last One had obviously decided to keep, graced one weathered cheek.

The Shahiid didn't deign to welcome her back, nor make mention of the acolytes who'd not returned from Godsgrave.

---

*He muttered to his knife a little less while his jaw was on the mend—Mia was tempted to seek out his torturers and thank them.

"We begin with a refresher on Montoya's dual-hand forms," Solis said. "I trust you have been practicing. Acolyte Jessamine, perhaps you would be kind enough to show Acolyte Mia some of what she has missed in her absence?"

Another smile. "With pleasure, Shahiid."

The acolytes paired off, began running through their drills. Jessamine strode to the weapon racks, took a pair of curved daggers and tossed another pair to Mia. The girl hefted the blades, her elbow quietly complaining.

"We practice with real steel, Shahiid?" Mia asked.

The Last One's face was stone as he replied. "Consider it an incentive."

Jessamine raised her knives without a word and struck at Mia's throat. The girl drew back, barely managed to muster a guard against the redhead's strikes. It seemed the class had moved forward in leaps and bounds in her absence, and between her lack of training and her still-weakened arm, Mia found herself hopelessly outmatched. Jessamine was fierce and skilled, and it was all Mia could do to keep her insides where they were supposed to be. She wore a few shallow cuts on her forearm, another gash across her chest, blood spattering on the stone as she cursed.

Jessamine smiled. "You want a break, Corvere?"

"My thanks, love. Your jaw would do nicely."

Jessamine simply laughed, flipping her daggers back and forth. Knowing better than to look to Solis for intervention, Mia staunched her wounds and went back to sparring. Studying the forms of the others around her as best she could in between dodging Jessamine's blades. After an hour of knives they swapped to shortswords, and Jessamine was no less merciless. Mia spent the rest of the morning having her arse kicked up and down the hall, and she ended the lesson flat on her back, bleeding and bruised. Jessamine's blade was pressed to her throat, right on her jugular. And though the redhead held herself in check, Mia could tell she'd give almost anything to flick her wrist and turn the stone red.

Jessamine bowed to Solis, sneered at Mia, and returned her weapons to the rack. Mia climbed to her feet, clutching her aching elbow, frustration boiling inside her. The time she'd lost to her injury had cost her dear, and she'd fallen behind further than she feared. She'd have to work twice as hard to make up the lost ground, and Jessamine might just "accidentally" gut her in the meantime.

The shame of it was, she and Jess were really one and the same. Both orphans of the Kingmaker Rebellion. Both robbed of their familia, driven by the same thirst. If Jess hadn't been so blinded by her rage, they might have been fast friends. Held together by the kind of bond only hate can forge. And though Julius Scaeva, not Darius Corvere, was to blame for the death of Jessamine's father, Mia could still understand why the sight of her blood made the other girl smile.

If you can't hurt the ones who hurt you, sometimes hurting anyone will do.

All this was small comfort after the absolute thrashing she'd received, of course. And if Jess actually decided to act on her bloodlust away from a Shahiid's gaze? To really try for her life? Mia would likely end up as nothing but a stain on the floor.

No, this won't do.

Mia shook her head, limped from the hall.

This won't do at all.

"How do, Don Tric?"

She'd found him in the Hall of Eulogies after lessons, staring up at the statue of Niah. He shot her a dimpled smile as she spoke. Looked her up and down.

"Maw's teeth, Jessamine gave you a kicking."

"Better than a stabbing."

"Looks like you had a few of those, too."

"I suppose I should go the weaver. Get seen to."

Tric scowled at the mention of Marielle, turned his eyes back to the statue above. He ran one hand over his face absentmindedly, fingertips tracing those awful tattoos. Not for the first time, Mia found herself studying his profile and chiding herself for a fool almost in the same heartbeat. He'd be a lady-killer without that ink, no mistake. And she was glad he'd made it back from Drusilla's testing. But still . . .

Eyes on the prize, Corvere.

"I've a notion," she said.

"O, dear," Tric mumbled.

Mia raised the knuckles. Marielle's shadow fell from the boy's face, and he gifted her a grin. He turned away from Niah's statue, facing Mia with arms folded.

"Out with it, then."

"As you were kind enough to notice, I've fallen a little behind in Songs."

"A little?" Tric snorted. "There's training dummies up there who could mop the floor with you, Pale Daughter."

"Well, thank you very much," Mia scowled. "If you'd like to go somewhere and quietly fuck yourself, I'll be waiting here patiently for your return."

Tric raised an eyebrow. Mia sighed, told her temper to go sit in the corner.

"Sorry," she mumbled.

"No need," he smiled. "I'm not sure polite suits you."

"I've a proposition."

"Color me flattered."

"Not that kind of proposition, you nonce."

She punched the boy's arm and he grinned. But somewhere in that sparkling hazel, she saw a sliver of disappointment. Something in his stance and the tilt of his head. Something that, after months of Aalea's tutelage, she was beginning to recognize.

Want.

"I'm getting my arse kicked in Songs," she said. "And you're about as much use in Spiderkiller's class as a eunuch's codpiece." Mia charged on over Tric's mumbled protest. "So, you catch me up on Solis's sword forms so Jessamine can't cut my head off, and I'll make sure you know enough not to poison yourself before initiation. Fair?"

Tric frowned. She could see Want wrestling with Common Sense now.

"There's not enough places among the Blades for all of us, Mia. Technically we're in competition with each other. Why would I help you?"

"Because I said please?"

". . . You didn't say please."

Mia waved her hand. "A mere technicality."

Tric smiled and Mia grinned back, hand on hip. Aalea had told her that silence could be the best response to a question, if the person asking already knew the answer. So she remained mute, staring up into those big, pretty eyes and letting Want speak instead. A part of her felt bad to be trying Aalea's craft out on her friend, but as Tric himself pointed out, he *was* technically competition. And as Aalea was fond of saying, never carry a blade if you're not willing to get bloody.

"All right," Tric finally said. "An hour every eve after lessons. Meet me in the Hall of Songs on the morrow."

Mia curtseyed. "My thanks, Don Tric."

Tric offered his hand and she shook it to seal the pact. They hung there for a moment, hands entwined. Her skin prickled as his thumb gently traced the curve of her wrist. Remembering himself, Tric let her go, mumbled something that might've been an apology and made his escape. Mia turned to walk in the opposite direction, hiding the small smile on her lips as her shadow began to speak.

". . . *though i have no face, believe me when i say i am scowling the pants off you right now* . . ."

Mia rolled her eyes. "Yes, Father."

"*. . . of course, a state of pantslessness seems to be your goal, so perhaps i should stop . . .*"

"Yes, Fatherrrrr."

"*. . . do not take that tone of voice with me, young lady . . .*"

Mia grinned, aimed a playful kick that passed right through Mister Kindly's head. The girl and her shadow wandered off toward the dorms, in search of bed and dreams.

A beautiful boy stepped from the dark, following their path with bright blue eyes.

As always, he breathed not a word.

L ong hours later, a loud knock dragged Mia from the arms of her books. She slipped her stiletto from her wrist, threw a robe around her shoulders. Creeping forward to the door, she whispered to whoever waited on the other side.

"Ash?"

"Please open the door, Acolyte."

Mia gripped her knife tighter, twisted the key, and peered out into the darkened hallway. She saw a Hand outside her door, long black robes, hooded features. She thought of Naev, then. Wondered briefly where she was.

"You are summoned by Revered Mother Drusilla," the Hand said.

"Of course." Mia bowed. "As she wishes."

She looked down the hallway, saw other Hands knocking on acolytes' doors. Ashlinn staggered out into the light, her warbraids fuzzed from the press of the pillow. Beyond the girl, she saw her brother Osrik, his spiked hair jutting off his skull at improbable angles. It looked like everyone was being woken, which meant Mia herself wasn't specifically in trouble.

Huzzah for small miracles.

"What's all this about?" Mia whispered as the group plodded after the Hands.

"Your guess is good as mine," Ash yawned. "Nothing good, I'll wager."

"No bet."

The acolytes traipsed the spiral stairwells, the ghostly choir singing somewhere out in the dark. Arriving in the Hall of Eulogies, Mia nodded her head, touched her brow, eyes, and lips before the statue like the others did. She saw the entire Ministry was assembled; Aalea, looking picture-perfect in a thin burgundy gown, Spiderkiller appearing more dour than usual, clad in jade green, Mouser and Solis alternately smiling and glowering in their dark leathers.

Drusilla stood in Niah's shadow, mouth thin. And beside her, chained to the iron links of the statue itself, Mia saw . . .

"Hush . . ."

The boy was stripped to the waist, blindfolded with black cloth, his back to the room. The acolytes gathered in a semicircle around the statue's base, silent and wary. Ashlinn nodded to herself, whispered to Mia.

"Blood scourging."

"What?"

"Shhh. Watch."

"Thank you for attending, Acolytes," Drusilla said. "There are few true rules that govern the life of a Blade. Should you survive to serve the Mother, you will live outside the boundaries of law, and thus, we give you as much liberty within these walls as we may. But still, the few rules we impart to you cannot be ignored.

"After the murder of Acolyte Floodcaller, each of you were warned not to leave your rooms after ninebells. I promised anyone found guilty of breaching this curfew would be severely punished. And still, one of you has sought to test my resolve." She indicated Hush with a wave of her hand. "Now witness folly's price."

The Revered Mother stepped off the dais, turned to the shadows.

"Speaker? Weaver?"

Mia saw two figures step into the stained-glass light. Speaker Adonai wore leather britches, no boots, a red silken robe thrown carelessly over his bare torso. His sister Marielle was wrapped head to foot in loose-flowing black. The siblings took their places behind the boy. Hush turned his head as Marielle began cracking her knuckles, sickly wet pops echoing in the gloom. Even blindfolded, Hush must have recognized the sound. Mia saw him take a deep breath, then turn back to the stone.

Mother Drusilla spoke with a voice like iron.

"Begin."

Marielle raised her hand, fingers outstretched. From her vantage, Mia could see the woman's face, those awful lips split in a bleeding smile. Marielle muttered beneath her breath, narrowed her eyes, and curled her fingers into a fist.

A tearing sound ripped the air, and the flesh of Hush's back split like rotten fruit. The boy threw back his head as four hideous gashes opened along his skin, as if some invisible scourge had been lashed across his spine. Blood spurted, muscles shredded, Mia wincing as she saw pink, gleaming bone showing through the wounds.

But the boy made not a sound.

Marielle waved her hand again, casually, as if brushing away a troublesome fly. Four more rends opened in Hush's flesh, shredding his lower back. Every muscle in his body clenched, veins corded in his arms and neck, that beautiful face twisted in agony. Mia was unsure if any other acolyte could see, but from the angle she stood at, she was appalled to note the boy's lips peeling back in a snarl, exposing pink, empty gums.

Black Mother, he's got no teeth . . .

Again Marielle waved her hand. Again the boy's skin shredded. Long, ragged gashes opened across his legs, his back minced like sausage meat. Blood was pooling on the stone at his feet. Arterial spray spurting, spatter-mad patterns gleaming in the air. And though he must have been in agony, still the boy made not a whisper. The acolytes watched in horror as Marielle moved her hands, more and more of Hush's back peeling away. And all the while, the boy remained as silent as if he were already dead.

Minutes passed. Wet tearing noises. Raindrops. Hush was a bleeding ruin. Head lolling on his shoulders. Blood slicked about his feet in a dark red tide. Surely they couldn't keep going? Mia turned to Ash, her voice a hiss.

"They're killing him!"

Ash shook her head. "Watch."

Marielle continued her grisly work, that bloody grin growing wider. Hush thrashed feebly against his chains, but he was barely conscious now. And when Mia could actually count the ribs beneath his skin, when it seemed even one more invisible blow would end him, the Revered Mother raised her hand.

"Enough."

Marielle glanced to Drusilla, her grin dying hard. But slowly, the weaver inclined her head, lowered her hand with obvious reluctance.

"Brother love, brother mine," she lisped.

Adonai stepped forward, pushed his slick white hair from his face. The albino whispered, soft and musical, as if singing beneath his breath. The words echoed through the hall, like a choir's song in the Basilica Grande. And as Mia watched, fascinated, the blood pooling at Hush's feet began to move.

Trembling at first, rippling in some hidden vibration. But slowly, sluggishly, the flood of scarlet retreated across the stone at the boy's feet as he thrashed and shuddered, flowing up his legs and back into the wounds Marielle had torn. Mia looked at the speaker's face, pale as corpses. Instead of their customary pink, the man's eyes were blood red. His smile, ecstatic.

Marielle raised her hands beside her brother's. Wove them in the air like a seamstress at a bloody loom. And as Hush bucked and shook, mouth open, face gleaming with sweat, one by one, the wounds closed. The awful rends and tears. The sodden, minced flesh. All of them rippling shut as Hush silently thrashed, until not a scratch remained on his skin.

The boy sagged in his chains, drool spilling from his lips. He'd remained conscious through all of it. Every moment. The acolytes looked at him with a mix of horror and awe.

The Hands unlocked his manacles, threw a robe around his unmarred shoulders.

"Take him to his room," Drusilla said. "He is excused from the morrow's lessons."

The Hands obeyed, hefting Hush between them and dragging him from the hall. The Revered Mother looked among the assembled acolytes, fixed each in her blue stare. The matronly facade was gone, the motherly love momentarily evaporated. This was the killer unveiled. The same woman who had sat idle as Lord Cassius and his men tortured her acolytes inside that dark cell in Godsgrave. The same woman who had sent eight of her students to their deaths with a smile.

"I trust no further demonstrations will be necessary," she said. "If another acolyte is found outside their bedchamber after ninebells, they shall drink from the same cup. Though next time, I may allow Weaver Marielle to fully have her head."

The Mother slipped her hands inside her sleeves. Bowed.

"Now. Go to sleep, children."

Sleep had come slowly, and Mia woke before the rising bells, staring at the walls. Determined to get the strength in her swordarm back, she exercised; push-ups at the foot of her bed, pull-ups on her door. Her elbow was screaming after a few minutes, but she struggled on until tears welled in her eyes. Finally collapsing on the floor, she lay there and caught her breath, cursing Solis for a bastard beneath it.

Slipping from her bedchamber, she headed toward the bathhouse. Passing by one acolyte's room, she heard a crash, the tinkling of broken glass from inside. She came to a halt outside the door; several more thumps and bangs resounded from within.

"... those who poke their noses into others' business tend to lose them ..."

"Call me curious."

"... you've heard what it did to the cat ..."

Mia leaned in closer, put her ear against the wood.

The door swung open, and Mia sprang back, startled. There in the gloom, she saw Hush. Red-eyed. Pale skin. That beautiful face, streaked with tears.

He was shirtless, sweating from exertion. The room beyond was in chaos, drawers upended and flung against the wall, bedding in ruin. Mia looked him up and down. Lithe and well muscled. Hairless chest. Other than some bruising at his wrists, his body showed no sign of the torture Marielle and Adonai had inflicted.

The boy stared. Lips thin. Rage in his eyes.

"Apologies, Hush," Mia said. "I heard noises."

Hush remained mute. Motionless.

"Are you all right?"

No answer. Just a cold, tearstained stare. She remembered the image of him yestereve, head thrown back, lips peeling away from toothless gums. Was that why he never spoke? How had he lost every tooth in his head? Could he have ripped them out himself for tithe to gain entry to the Church?

The pair of them hung there, neither willing to move. The silence rang louder than the nevernight bells across Godsgrave.

"I'm sorry," Mia tried. "About what they did to you. That was cruel."

The boy inclined his head slightly. The tiniest of shrugs.

"If you ever want to talk about it . . ."

Hush flashed her a humorless smirk.

"I mean . . ." Mia flailed slightly. "Write about it. If you wish it. I'm here."

The boy stared into Mia's eyes. And stepping back with a flick of his bruised wrist, he slammed the door right in her face. Mia flinched away, narrowly avoiding another broken nose. Hooked her thumbs into her belt and shrugged.

". . . well, that went swimmingly . . ."

"Can't blame a girl for trying," she said, shuffling down the corridor.

". . . is this some stratagem . . . ?"

"What, it's so outrageous I give a damn?"

". . . not outrageous. simply pointless . . ."

"Look, just because I don't stand to gain from it, doesn't mean I shouldn't care. They tortured him, Mister Kindly. Even though he doesn't have a scar from it, doesn't mean it didn't leave a mark. And it's like Naev said. I should look after the things that are important here."

". . . important? that boy is nothing to you . . ."

"I know I'm supposed to think of him as competition. I know there aren't enough places for all of us among the Blades. But this Church is designed to turn me cold. So holding on to the part of me that can feel pity becomes more important every turn."

". . . pity is a weakness to be used against you. scaeva, duomo, and remus will not share it . . ."

"One more reason to hold on to it then, aye?"

"... *hmph* ..."

"Pfft."

"... *grrrr* ..."

"Shut up."

"... *grow up* ..."

Laughter rang out and the shadows smiled.

"Never."

The girl and the not-cat faded into the dark.

MASQUERADE

Weeks flickered by in the darkness, untracked save for the tolling of bells and the serving of meals and hours upon hours of lore.* Mia and Tric trained every turn after lessons, in either the Hall of Songs or the Hall of Truths. Every session in Songs saw Mia paired up with Jessamine or Diamo, and her blood painting the floor. And though in truth she found herself enjoying Tric's company more and more, she began to wonder if he was the mentor she needed ...

Winter was deepening and Great Tithe approaching, snows beginning to dress Godsgrave in gowns of muddy white. Nevernight after nevernight, pretty shadows Blood Walked from Adonai's chambers and flitted out into the city in search of secrets, returning to lay them at Aalea's feet. The Shahiid of Masks gave no indication who might be winning her contest.

The weaver continued her work, altering faces one by one. She wove Jessamine's feral beauty into full bloom, honed Osrik's natural good looks to a finer edge; even Petrus had got his missing ear back. The newly woven acolytes began making use of Aalea's many weapons—minor games of flirt and touch breaking out during lessons or after. At mealtimes, Mia could feel a new current in the air. Furtive glances and secret smiles. For all the sweat and blood the

---

* The wounds from Lord Cassius's test of loyalty were all but mended among the flock by now, and to Mia's dismay, Pip's mutterings to his knife resumed with a vengeance.

acolytes were putting in, Mia figured they deserved it. Lessons were getting more grueling; almost half their number were already dead. She supposed a little harmless fun never hurt anyone.

And then came the masquerade.

The acolytes were summoned after evemeal, one and all, down into Adonai's chambers. Without preamble they were ushered through the Blood Walk, one by one. Mia felt hungry eyes on her body as she stripped down to her slip, her eyes on others in turn. Emerging from the blood-red warmth beneath the Porkery, the acolytes were told to bathe thoroughly, dress quickly. The seventeen were then punted—by covered gondola, no less—to Godsgrave's marrowborn quarter. Mia shipped out with Carlotta, Ashlinn, and Osrik, peering out through the canopy as the well-to-do estates of Godsgrave's richest and most powerful cruised by. The Hands punting them were dressed in servants' finery—gold-trimmed frock coats and silken hose. Saan's bloody red glow was reduced to a sullen pout behind a heavy veil of roiling gray, but Mia still found herself squinting, pinching a pair of azurite spectacles to the bridge of her nose.

She looked Carlotta over from behind the tinted glass, admiring the poem Marielle had made of the girl's face. The weaving had been done only a few turns prior, and it was hard not to notice the difference, or the way the other novices stared now it was done. Carlotta's lips were fuller, her body more shapely. And where once an arkemical slavemark had marred the girl's cheek, there was now only smooth, pale skin.

"The weaver knows her work," Mia smiled.

Carlotta glanced at Mia, back out the window.

". . . I suppose."

"O, come, you look a picture, Lotti," Ash protested. "Marielle is a master."

At an elbow from his sister, Osrik piped up. "O, aye. A picture, no doubt."

"It's strange," Carlotta murmured. "The things we miss."

The girl touched the cheek where her slavemark used to be. Fingers tracing that now flawless skin. She said no more, and Mia was reluctant to push. But she could see memories swimming in the girl's eyes as she stared at the passing city. Shadows that stained Carlotta's irises a deeper blue.

Where had a slavegirl learned venomcraft?

What had driven her to join the Church?

Why was she here?

Mia knew Carlotta was competition for Spiderkiller's prize above all else. That Mister Kindly had spoken true, and pity would be a weakness to be used against her. That she shouldn't care.

But still, somehow she did.

Their gondola finally took berth at a small pier at the front of a grand five-story palazzo—the kind of home only the marrowborn might own.

"What the 'byss is all this about?" Mia whispered.

Ashlinn and Osrik both shrugged—seemed their da didn't tell them everything after all. Mia checked her gravebone blade for the fourth time before stepping onto the jetty. The winds off the canal were icy, the pier slippery beneath her feet.

The acolytes were ushered into the palazzo's foyer. The walls were red, hung with beautiful portraiture in the lush Liisian style.* Vases full of flowers strung the air with a soft perfume, and a roaring fire burned at the graven hearth.

At the top of a grand and winding staircase stood Shahiid Aalea. Though she'd fancied it a silly turn of phrase only found in books, the sight of the woman actually took Mia's breath away. The Shahiid was decked in a long, flowing gown, red as heart's blood, embroidered with black lace and pearls. A drake-bone corset pulled her waistline torturously tight, and an off-the-shoulder cut exposed smooth, cream-white skin. In her hand, she held a *domino* mask on a slender ivory wand.

---

*Liisian portraiture is widely considered the finest in the Republic, and the best artistes can charge small fortunes for commissions. Vaiello, a famous artiste who lived at the court of Francisco XIV, achieved such frightening wealth that it was said he could buy the kingdom twice over. Sadly, after an incident involving one too many bottles of wine, Francisco's second son, Donatello, a four-poster bed, and a riding crop, Vaiello found himself tried for treason and sentenced to death.

Predictably, Vaiello's execution led to a profound escalation in the value of his paintings, and the marrowborn who owned them made small fortunes. Unexpectedly, however, it also led to a sudden rash of murders among famed Liisian artists, as certain wily nobles sought to increase the value of their *own* collections by killing off the poor bastards who'd painted them. Painters began dropping like flies, and in the few months following Vaiello's death, "portrait artist" became the most dangerous occupation in the kingdom.

This spate of paintercide led to a frightening spike in the price of new work, as fewer masters were now available to paint commissions. Realizing their increased worth, these masters also began training fewer apprentices, leading to yet higher prices. During the height of the crisis, the going rate for a standard sitting was said to be two medium-sized estates in upper Valentia and a firstborn daughter. The debacle was put to an end only when King Francisco stepped in, simultaneously commissioning two colleges for the training of Liisian artists (one in Godsgrave and a second, more renowned one in Elai) and declaring the murder of a Liisian artist a crime punishable by crucifixion.

This incident, by the way, is still held up at the Grand Collegium in Godsgrave as a perfect illustration of the laws of supply and demand. In Vaiello's honor, it is dubbed "the Riding Crop Principle."

Lotti's eyes were wide, misgivings about her face momentarily forgotten.

"I would kill my own mother to get into a dress like that . . ."

"I would kill you *and* your mother to get into a dress like that," Ash whispered.

"You want to dance, Järnheim?" Lotti deadpanned. "Liisian silk brocade with a melphi-cut corset and matching gloves? I will *bury* you."

Mia and Ash's laughter was cut short as Aalea spoke, her voice soft as smoke.

"Acolytes," she smiled. "Welcome, and thank you for coming. Three months have passed since your induction into the Red Church. We understand that lessons grow long and the hours weigh heavy, and so every once in a while, I convince the Ministry to allow you to . . . let your hair down, as it were."

Aalea smiled at the novices the way the suns smiled at the sky.

"Great Tithe approaches, and as such, it is customary to give gifts to loved ones. Across the canal is the palazzo of Praetor Giuseppe Marconi, a wealthy young marrowborn don who throws some of the most delightful parties I've ever attended. This eve, the praetor hosts his traditional Great Tithe gala; a ball to which only the cream of Godsgrave society is invited. And invitations have been arranged . . . for you."

Aalea produced a handful of parchment slips seemingly from midair, slowly fanned her neck.

"Of course, you'll each have to concoct a convincing subterfuge as to *why* you've been invited to such an exclusive soiree. But I'm certain I've versed you well enough for that. The ball is a masquerade, after all, so the face you wear can be any you choose."

The Shahiid indicated a set of double doors with a wave of her hand.

"You will find suitable clothing within. Enjoy yourselves, my dears. Laugh. Love. Remember what it is to live, and forget, if only for a moment, what it is to serve."

Aalea handed out the gilded invitations, and ushered the acolytes through the double doors. Within, Mia found row upon row of the most beautiful gowns and coats she'd ever seen. The finest cut. The richest cloth. Ashlinn practically dove at a rack of silken corsetry; even Jessamine lost her customary scowl.

Mia wandered wide-eyed through a forest of fur and velvet, damask and lace. It'd been years since she'd seen clothing like this up close. Longer since she'd worn anything like it. As a little girl, she'd attended the grandest balls and galas, worn the finest dresses. She remembered dancing with her father in the ballroom of some senator or another, balancing her feet atop his as they swirled around the room. For a moment, she was overcome. Memories of the life she'd lost. Thoughts of the person she might have been but never was.

She ran her fingertips over the row of masques Aalea had prepared for them. Each was a *volto*—full-faced and oval-shaped. Pearl-white ceramic, trimmed in gold, each with three blood-red tears beneath the right eye. They were exquisitely crafted, velvet-soft to the touch.

"This is all a bit much, aye?"

Mia turned to find Tric beside her, scowling at the other acolytes. Osrik and Marcellus were trying on various waistcoats and cravats, bowing to each other "After you, sir," "No, no, after *you*, sir." Carlotta had wriggled into a gown made of some astonishing fabric that shifted hues as she twirled on the spot. Hush had clad himself head to foot in pristine white; his doublet embroidered with gleaming silver.

"A bit much?" Mia repeated.

"We're supposed to be disciples of the Mother. They're acting like children."

Mia found herself on edge too, truth be told. The first time Aalea had sent them to Godsgrave, she'd been locked in a cell and beaten half to death at the command of the Lord of Blades. They'd all traveled dozens of times to the City of Bridges and Bones since then, but she couldn't quite shake the feeling that this "gift" was too good to be true. Yet finally, she shrugged.

"It can't hurt to have fun once in a while. Give it a try. You might enjoy it."

"Bollocks," he growled. "I'm not here to enjoy myself."

"Rest easy, my dour centurion." Mia plucked up one of the *voltos*, pushed it against Tric's face. "If you do crack a smile, it's not like anyone will see it."

Tric sighed, looked up and down the racks of gents' attire. Jackets and doublets, boots with gleaming buckles and waistcoats with glittering buttons.

"I'm not too polished at this sort of business," he confessed. "Aalea has been trying, but in truth I'm not sure where to start."

Mia found herself smiling. Offered her arm.

"Well, it's a good thing you've got me, Don Tric."

He scrubbed up well, in the end. Though it was a challenge to find anything that sat comfortably on shoulders broad as his, Mia eventually found Tric a long frock coat in coal gray (dark colors, it seemed, were en vogue for gentry this season) gilded with gold. As he'd sat and squirmed, she plaited his saltlocks into something resembling order, and tied a white silk cravat around his throat. Inspecting her handiwork in the mirror, the boy gave a grudging nod. Ashlinn whistled loudly from a corner.

Mia herself chose a daring gown of crushed velvet in a deep wine red, propping a tricorn of the same fabric atop her head. Kohl for her eyes. Burgundy paint for her lips. Aalea favored reds, and Mia was of a similar complexion, so she thought it might be worth a gamble. Pulling on a pair of long gloves and a wolf-fur stole, she peered into the looking glass and smiled.

Ash whistled again from her corner.

The acolytes drifted back into the garish sunslight, ferried across the canal. Stepping onto a broad pier and through the gates of Palazzo Marconi, Mia saw guests arriving by gondola, others by carriage, horses snorting and stamping in the chill. A bitter wind was blowing in off the water and her breath hung in the air. She pulled the wolf fur tighter, squinting at the pale red sun behind its veil of clouds and wishing she'd not worn an off-the-shoulder cut. Tric, walking arm in arm with Ashlinn, noticed Mia's shivers, and slipped his free arm about her for warmth.

Mia regretted her choice of dress a little less.

The acolytes were all wearing their *voltos*, faces hidden behind smooth ceramic. As they milled about the entrance, Mia saw the other guests were similarly attired, her eyes growing wide at some of the masques on display. One gent wore a death's head carved of black ivory, arkemical globes burning in its eye sockets. She saw a woman with a *domino* made of firebird feathers, which seemed to ripple with flame when the sunslight hit it right. The most stunning belonged to a lass barely in her teens, whose masque was a long sheaf of black silk, form-fitted to her face. The silk billowed like a loose sail in the wind, yet once they'd stepped inside, the silk continued to ripple, even without the breeze to move it.

Servants with slavemarks on their cheeks and clothes that must have cost more than the average citizen earned in a year greeted them, inspecting their invitations before ushering them into a grand entrance hall. Praetor Marconi's palazzo dripped with wealth; marble on the walls and gold on the handles. Singing chandeliers of Dweymeri crystal spun overhead, soft music filled the air, the chatter of hundreds of voices, laughter, whispers, song.

"So this is how the other half lives," Tric said.

"I could stand to stay here a spell," Ash replied. "These used to be your sort of folk, aye, Corvere? Is it always this flashy?"

Mia gazed at the opulence about them. The world to which she'd once belonged.

"I remember everyone being much taller," she said.

Servants appeared with golden trays. Dweymeri crystal glasses filled with wine, with slender straws to allow guests to sip without removing their masks. Sugared treats and candied fruits. Cigarillos and pipes already packed with slumberweed, needles loaded with ink. Glass in hand, Mia wandered through the foyer, overcome with the sights, the sounds, the smells, forgetting Aalea, her suspicions, her worry. Arriving with Tric at a grand set of double doors leading to the ballroom, a servant in a masque fashioned like a jester's head bowed before them.

"Mi Don. Mi Dona. Might I have your names?"

Tric whipped out his invitation like his pocket was on fire.

"Yes, very good," the servant said. "But I need your name, Mi Don."

". . . What for?"

Mia stepped into the uncomfortable silence, smooth as caramel.

"This is Cuddlegiver, Bara of the Seaspear clan of Farrow Isle."

Tric threw Mia a look of alarm. The servant bowed.

"My thanks, Mi Dona. And you?"

"His . . . companion."

"Very good." The servant stepped to the top of the ballroom stairs and announced in a loud voice, "Bara Cuddlegiver of the Seaspear clan, and companion."

A few of the three-hundred-odd guests glanced in the pair's direction, but most of the throng continued with their conversations. Mia took Tric's arm and led him down the stairs, nodding at the folk who'd looked their way. She waved down a passing servant, who lit a black cigarillo in a slender ivory holder and handed it over dutifully. Mia slipped the smoke through her masque's lips and breathed a contented, gray sigh.

"*Cuddlegiver?*" Tric hissed.

"Better than Pigfiddler."

"'Byss and blood, Mia . . ."

"What?" she smirked. "I'm sure you give lovely cuddles."

"Black Mother help me," Tric sighed. "I need a fucking drink . . ."

Fourteen servants materialized beside the boy, bearing trays with almost every beverage under the suns. Tric looked taken aback, finally shrugged and took two goldwines.

"Very thoughtful of you," Mia said, reaching for a glass.

"Sod off, these are mine. You get your own."

Mia looked about the sea of masques, silk, skin. A string quartet played on a mezzanine above, a perfume of beautiful notes hanging in the air. Couples danced in the room's heart, clusters of well-heeled men and well-frocked women chatting and laughing and flirting. The music of golden rings against crystal glasses rang amid the hidden faces. Aalea was right; it was easy to forget who she was among all this.

Mia sighed. Shook her head.

"It's a sight," Tric agreed.

"This used to be my world," she said softly. "Never thought I'd miss it."

The sharp chime of metal on crystal caught her attention, and Mia turned to the mezzanine above. The music stopped as all eyes looked up to a smiling gent, half his face hidden by a *domino* of beaten gold. His coat was silk, embroidered with golden thread, the cravat at his throat studded with gems, rings on every finger.

Our host, Praetor Marconi, no doubt.

"Ladies and gentlefriends," the man spoke, his voice rich and deep. "I welcome you to my humble home, one and all. I'm not one to speak overlong and part you from your revels, but it is the season of Great Tithe, and I would be remiss if I did not give my thanks to each of you, and most of all, to our glorious consul, Julius Scaeva."

Mia found her jaw clenching. Eyes scanning the crowd.

"Alas, our noble consul could not attend our gala, but still, I'd have each of you charge a glass and raise it in his honor. Six years have passed since the Kingmakers sought to slave us once more beneath monarchy's yoke. Six years since Consul Scaeva saved the Republic, and ushered in a golden age of peace and prosperity. Without him, none of this would be possible."

The young praetor raised a glass. Everyone in the room raised theirs, save Mia. Tric looked at her, eyes widening. To not toast the consul would invite scandal. Teeth grinding so hard she feared they might break, Mia plucked a glass off a nearby tray and raised it like the rest of the sheep.

"Consul Julius Scaeva!" Marconi cried. "May the Everseeing bless him!"

"Consul Scaeva!" came the crowd's cry.

Glasses were clinked, drinks quaffed, polite applause filling the room. Praetor Marconi stepped down with a bow and the music picked up again. Mia was scowling behind her masque. Suddenly missing this world, this life, far less than she had a moment ag—

"Do you dance?" Tric asked.

Mia blinked. Looked up at Tric's masque and the hazel eyes beyond. "What?"

"Do. You. Dance?" he repeated.

Mia laughed in spite of herself. "Why? Do you?"

"Shahiid Aalea has been teaching me. In case I found myself having to romance some marrowborn daughter or dona of quality."

"Donas of quality tend to have rather high standards, Bara Cuddlegiver."

"She says I'm excellent, I'll have you know."

The boy offered his elbow. Mia glanced around the room. Empty, smiling faces, hiding the real faces within. These marrowborn bastards dipped in gold and lies. Had she really ever felt like she belonged here? Had this ever been her world?

She lifted her masque and quaffed her glass of goldwine with one swallow. Grabbed another from a passing tray and finished it just as quick.

"Fuck it, then."

Dunking her burning cigarillo in a passing glass of wine, she took Tric's arm.

As they stepped onto the dance floor, Tric took her by the hand, his big, sword-callused fingers entwined with her own. Butterflies took wing in her belly as he placed his free hand at the small of her back. Mia swore the music got louder, the conversations around them seeming to dim. And there in the midst of that sea of empty, smiling faces, they began to dance.

It was odd, but with the boy's face covered, Mia could see only his eyes. Staring up into those big pools of sparkling hazel and realizing they were fixated entirely on her. All the pearls and jewels, the silk and glitter, the opulence on display. These pretty dons and donas all dipped in gold. And still, he only looked at her.

She'd known he was graceful from watching him in the Hall of Songs, but Daughters, for all his other failings in Aalea's lessons, the boy could dance. For a moment, Mia found herself swept up, cradled in his arms, spun and dipped and swayed as the music seemed to grow louder still and all the world beyond became nothing. For a moment, she wasn't Mia Corvere, daughter of a murdered house, parched with the thirst for revenge. Not a fledgling assassin or a servant of a goddess. Just a girl. And he a boy. Their eyes blind to all but each other. Aalea's voice echoing in her ears.

"Enjoy yourselves, my dears. Laugh. Love. Remember what it is to live, and forget, if only for a moment, what it is to serve."

"Invitations, please."

Mia realized the music had stopped. The room was silent. She turned, found herself looking at three Luminatii legionaries, bedecked in polished gravebone breastplates. The leader was built like a brick wall. Cold blue eyes looking right at Tric.

"Invitations," he repeated.

Tric glanced to Mia. Reached into his coat pocket.

"Of course . . ."

The centurion snapped his fingers, pointed at Ashlinn and Osrik loitering on the edge of the crowd. "Them, too. Anyone with the blood tears." Soldiers were fanning out among the astonished guests now, singling out the acolytes wearing Aalea's masques. Hush. Pip. Jessamine. Petrus. Carlotta . . .

Tric was fumbling in his pocket, brought out only flakes of dust.

"I'm sure I had it a moment ago . . ."

Mia reached to the hidden pocket inside her corset. But where her invite had been safely stowed, again there was only a handful of dust. As if . . .

As if . . .

"As I thought," the centurion declared. "Come with us, Bara *Cuddlegiver*."

Hands clamped down on Tric's elbow. Mia's wrist. She glanced to Osrik as Ashlinn was seized by the shoulder. Mia caught a glimpse of manacles, the gleam of steel. The guests around them were appalled that their gathering had been interrupted, Praetor Marconi demanding to know who would dare disturb the peace of his house. But in a blinking, the illusion of that peace all came undone.

Tric grabbed the hand that had seized him, bent back the owner's arm and snapped it at the elbow. Mia tore a stiletto from her corset, stabbed the Luminatii holding her in the wrist. She heard a crash, a strangled scream as Jessamine put her wineglass into a legionary's face. Osrik roaring over the top.

"Go! Go!"

Mia lashed out with the stiletto, bloodying another legionary reaching for her. Tric was already off, bolting across the room and smashing men and women aside as he barreled through the mob. Catching a flying drinks tray as he passed, he hurled it at a window, the panes exploding with a crash as he dove through afterward. Mia was right behind him, hissing in pain as her arm was sliced open by the jagged frame, tumbling onto the thin strip of grass running the palazzo's flank. She landed atop Tric, knocking the breath from his chest with a *whufff*.

"Halt!" came the roar. "Halt in the name of the Light!"

Mia hauled Tric to his feet, wincing with pain, arm drenched in blood. The pair dashed down the alleyway, crashing glass behind them, cries of alarm. Mia heard an upper window explode, saw Hush leap across to the palazzo opposite and scramble onto the roof, white coat now splashed with red. Heavy boots behind them. Bitter winds on her skin. The pair arrived at the tall, wrought-iron fence surrounding the palazzo grounds, Tric throwing himself over in one smooth motion.

"Come on!" he hissed.

Mia looked over her shoulder, saw four Luminatii dashing toward her, sunsteel blades drawn and blazing. But evening gowns, it seemed, weren't the best attire for a desperate foot chase, let alone vaulting ten-foot-high wrought-iron fences. Mia slashed at the gown with her stiletto, tearing it loose at the thigh. She flung herself at the fence, scrambling over just as a burning longsword whistled through the air, slicing wrought iron into molten globules. Tric's arm flashed through the gaps, his blade gleaming red. She heard the boy cry out in pain. Dropping to the cobbles beside him, they were off, bolting into the freezing wind.

"Where to?" Tric panted.

"Aalea," she gasped.

Tric nodded and dashed down the pier, kicking some poor servant into the drink as he requisitioned his gondola. Mia dropped in beside him as he punted out into the canal, smashing at the water furiously as half a dozen Luminatii jumped into watercraft behind them and gave chase. Tric steered their gondola toward the palazzo where they'd met the Shahiid. There were no Hands out front, no lights in the windows. Barreling through the front doors, they found the entry hall and room they'd dressed in empty. The air dusty. Cold. As if no one had set foot in the house for years.

Heavy boots. The front door bursting open. Mia cursed, grabbed Tric's hand and dashed for the back door, crashing out into a thin alleyway that ran the rear of the building. They heard shouts behind, the ring of steel. Whistles blowing in the waterway beyond, calls for more troops, tromping feet. Tric kicked through the kitchen entrance of another palazzo, servants shrieking as he and Mia barged past, out into the foyer, shouldering through the front door and onto a cobbled thoroughfare.

Mia's arm was gushing blood. Tric was gasping, clutching his side. Mia saw a scorch mark on his jacket, smelled burned flesh. He'd tasted sunsteel somewhere in the struggle at the fence, his waistcoat soaked with blood.

"Are you all right?" she gasped.

"Keep running!"

"Fuck running," she snapped. "I'm in a bloody corset!"

The girl swung herself up onto the step of a passing carriage, plopped onto the seat beside an astonished-looking driver wearing the livery of some minor house.

"Hello," she said.

"Hel—"

Her elbow caught the man in the belly, her hook toppled him out of his seat and onto the cobbles below. She pulled the horses to a whinnying halt, tore her *volto* loose and turned to look at Tric with eyebrow raised.

"Your carriage awaits, Mi Don."

Tric leaped onto the rear step and Mia snapped the reins against the horses' backs as a quartet of breathless Luminatii barreled onto the street behind them. The carriage tore down the street, bouncing and juddering over bridges and flagstones, Mia cursing as she almost flew from her seat. The marrowborn legate to whom the carriage belonged stuck his head out the window to see what all the fuss was, found a girl in a shredded evening gown where his driver should've been. As he opened his mouth to protest, she turned and looked at him, bloodstained skin and narrowed eyes, a cat made of what might have been shadows perched on her shoulder.

The man pulled his head back into the carriage without a word.

"*. . . well this is bracing, isn't it . . ?*"

"That's one word for it."

"*. . . you seem to have lost half your dress . . .*"

"Kind of you to notice."

"*. . . though given the way you danced with that boy, i imagine losing only half is a disappointment . . .*"

Mia rolled her eyes, whipped the horses harder.

They abandoned the carriage south of the Hips, Mia hopping down onto the cobbles and tipping her tricorn at the bemused owner. Up on the driver's seat, the wind had been bitterly cold, and Mia's lips were turning blue. She was on the verge of lamenting her choice of attire again when Tric pulled off his frock coat and, without a word, slipped it around her shoulders. Still warm from the press of his skin.

They dashed through back alleys and over little bridges, wending their way south toward the Bay of Butchers. Arriving at the Porkery, they stole inside, creeping up the stairs to the mezzanine above the now-silent killing floor.

Mia was dizzy from blood loss, her arm dripping, the sleeve of Tric's coat soaked through. Tric's waistcoat and britches were drenched too, his hand pressed to an awful gash in his side. Their faces pale and pained, the memories of the music, the dance, the whiskey, and the smiles already a tattered memory. They'd barely made it out with their lives. Creeping down the twisted stairwell, the stench of copper and salt rising in their nostrils, down, down into the blood-drenched chamber below.

Shahiid Aalea was waiting for them.

Gone was the elegant gown, the drakebone corset, the pretty *domino*. She was dressed in black, rivers of raven hair framing that pale, heart-shaped face. The only color was her smile. Red as the blood dripping down Mia's arm.

"Did you have fun playing at being people, my loves?" she asked.

"You . . ." Tric winced, still breathless. "You . . ."

The Shahiid walked across the tile toward them. Lifted Tric's hand away from his wound and tutted. Kissed Mia's bloody fingertips.

"Our gift to you," she said. "A reminder. Walk among them. Play among them. Live and laugh and love among them. But never forget, not for one moment, what you are."

Aalea released Mia's hand.

"And *never* forget what it is to serve."

The Shahiid waved to the pool beyond.

"Happy Great Tithe, children."

FACES

Only one of them never made it back alive from Godsgrave. A boy with dark hair and a dimpled smile named Tovo. A quiet mass was held for him in the Hall of Eulogies.

An unmarked stone.

An empty tomb.

As the choir sang and the Revered Mother spoke words of supplication to the stone goddess overhead, Mia tried to find it in herself to feel bad. To wonder who this boy was, and why this was where he died. But looking among the other acolytes, cold eyes and thin lips, she knew what each of them was thinking.

Better him than me.

Mia never heard Tovo's name mentioned again.

Weeks wore on, Great Tithe unmarked, no more thanks given. The masquerade seemed to have beaten the last breath of levity from within the walls. The weaver continued her work, sculpting the others into works of art, but gone were the smiles and winks, the flirting and touches. If never before, they all knew this was no longer a game.

The turn after Diamo had undergone his weaving, Mia noticed Tric had missed Pockets. After a painstaking lesson from Mouser on the art of powder-traps and the avoidance thereof, she'd climbed a twisting stair and found the Dweymeri boy in the Hall of Songs. Shirt off. Gleaming with sweat. A pair of wooden swords in hand, pounding a training dummy so hard the varnish was practically screaming.

"Tric. You missed Mouser's lesson."

The boy ignored her. Great sweeping strikes smashing against the wooden figure, the *crack, crack, crack* echoing in the empty hall. His naked torso

gleamed, his saltlocks hung damp about his face. Half a dozen broken training swords lay on the ground beside him. He must have been up here all turn . . .

"Tric?"

Mia touched his arm, pulled him to a halt. He rounded on her, almost snarling, tore his arm from her grip. "Don't touch me."

The girl blinked, taken aback by the rage in his eyes. Remembering those
same eyes watching her as they danced, his fingers entwined with hers . . .

"Are you all right?"

". . . Aye." Tric wiped his eyes, breathed deep. "Sorry. Let's be about it."

The pair formed up in the sparring circle beneath the hall's golden light.
Wooden swords in hand, they began by working on Mia's Caravaggio.* But
after only a handful of minutes, it became apparent Tric was in no mood for
teaching. He growled like a hungover wolf when Mia made a mistake, shouted
when she misstepped, and ended up cracking his sword across her forearm so
hard he split the skin.

"Black Mother!" Mia clutched her wrist. "That bloody hurt!"

"It's not supposed to tickle," Tric replied. "You drop your guard like that
against Jessamine, she'll take your throat out."

"Look, if you want to spill whatever you're pissed about, I'll listen. But if
you're looking for something to take it out on, I'll leave you with the training
dummies."

"I'm not pissed about anything, Mia."

"O, really." She held up her bloody wrist.

"You asked me to teach you, I'm teaching you."

Mia sighed. "This stoic facade bullshit is getting burdensome, Don Tric."

"Fuck you, Mia!" he bellowed, hurling his swords. "I said nothing's the
matter!"

Mia stopped short as the blades clattered across the training circle. Search-

---

* One of the most feared swordsmen of his age, Antony Caravaggio was a duelist in the
court of King Francisco III. An infamous rake with a fondness for young donas of
quality, Caravaggio fought no less than forty-three duels over the course of his life,
and reportedly sired fourteen bastards. Caravaggio fought with twin blades—one in
each hand—pioneering the art of dual-wielding that eventually bore his name.

Ironically, his fondness for twins also proved his downfall: he was killed in a duel
by Don Lentilus Varus after spending a night of drunken passion with Varus's twin
daughters, Lucilla and Lucia. Reportedly still intoxicated and too exhausted to heft
his rapier, he was skewered by his opponent quite easily—an inglorious end for such
an artisan of the blade.

His last words were reportedly "Worth it . . ."

ing Tric's eyes. The dreadful ink scrawled over his skin. The scars beneath. She realized he was the only acolyte who'd yet to undergo the weaver's touch.

"Listen," she sighed. "I might not be the sharpest when it comes to cutting through other folks' problems. And I don't want to pry. But if you want to spill your guts about it, here I am."

Tric scowled, staring into space. Mia played the waiting gambit again, letting the silence do the asking for her. After an age of sullen quiet, Tric finally spoke.

"They're going to take it away," he said.

". . . I don't understand."

"Nor do you need to."

"I might not need to." Mia set aside her sword. "But still, I'd like to."

Tric sighed. Mia sat down cross-legged, patted the stone beside her. Sullen and damn near pouting, the boy knelt where he was, planted himself on the floor. Mia shuffled closer, just near enough for him to know she was there. Long minutes passed, the pair of them sitting mute. Utterly silent in the hall named for its song.

It struck her as stupid. Here, more than anywhere. This was a school for fledgling killers. Acolytes were dropping like flies. Tric might be dead by the morrow. And here she was, trying to get him to open up about his feelings . . .

Black Mother, it's worse than stupid. It's ridiculous.

But maybe that was the point? Maybe it *was* like Naev had said. In the face of all this callousness, maybe she needed to hold on to the things that mattered? And looking at this strange boy, matted hair strung over haunted eyes, Mia realized he did matter.

He *mattered* to her.

"I didn't kill Floodcaller," Tric finally said.

Mia blinked. Truth be told, in all the death since, she'd almost forgotten about the Dweymeri boy's murder the eve they first arrived here.

". . . I believe you."

"I wanted to. Someone just beat me to it." He glanced at her sidelong. Voice thick with rage. "He called me *koffi*, Mia. You know what that means?"

For a moment, she couldn't find her voice. "Child of . . ."

"Rape," Tric spat. "Child of rape."

She sighed inside.

It's true, then.

"You father was a Dweymeri pirate? Your mother—"

"My mother was the daughter of a bara."

". . . What?"

"A princess, if you'll believe it." Tric chuckled. "Part royalty, me."

"A bara?" Mia frowned. "Your mother was Dweymeri?"

Mia didn't understand. From all she'd read, it was the Dweymeri pirate lords and their crews who did the raping and pillaging. But if Tric's mother was from Dweym . . .

"Her name was Earthwalker. Thirdborn of our bara, Swordbreaker." Tric spat the name, as if it tasted rancid. "She wasn't much older than you are now. Traveling to Farrow for the yearly Festival of Skies. There was a storm. She wound up wrecked on some rock with a handmaid and a bosun's mate. Three alive out of a hundred.

"An Itreyan trawler found her. The captain brought them aboard. Fed the boy to the seadrakes. Raped my mother and her maid. And when they found out who she was, they sent word to my grandfather he could have her back for her weight in gold."

"Maw's teeth." Mia squeezed Tric's hand. "I'm so sorry, Tric."

Tric smiled bitterly. "I'll say one thing about Grandfather. He loved his daughters."

"He paid?"

Tric shook his head. "He found out where they were holed up, burned the settlement to the ground. Murdered every man, woman, and child. But he got his daughter back. Nine months later, he got a grandson. And every time he looked at my face, he saw my father."

Mia stared at the boy's eyes, her chest aching.

Hazel, not brown.

"That's not who you are, Tric."

The boy stared back at her, tale dying on his lips. Something in the air shifted, something in his gaze lighting a flame in her belly. Those bottomless eyes. That scrawl of hatred on his skin. Her heart was pounding. Palms sweating in his. Trembling.

"*. . . mia . . .*"

Trembling just like the shadow at her feet.

"*. . . mia, beware . . .*"

"Well, well."

Mia blinked as the spell of silence shattered. Jessamine stood at the top of the stairs, Diamo alongside. The redhead was dressed for sparring practice; black leathers and a sleeveless tunic. The girl's hulking sidekick loomed next to her, something ugly lingering in his stare.*

---

*Though Marielle did a splendid job weaving the boy's face, whenever she studied him, Mia realized she still found Diamo only a touch shy of repulsive. There was

Jessamine hooked her thumbs into her belt, strolled into the hall.

"I wondered how you were spending your nevernights, Corvere."

Mia rose to her feet, staring the girl down. "I didn't know you cared, Jess."

The redhead looked about; the broken swords and training dummies.

"Practicing?" she sneered. "You'd be better off praying."

"Apologies," Mia frowned, searching the floor as if looking for something. "I appear to have misplaced the fucks I give for what you think . . ."

Jessamine clutched her ribs and laughed uproariously for half a second. Then her smile dropped from her face and shattered like glass on the stone.

"You think you're funny, bitch?" Diamo asked.

"O, bitch," Mia nodded. "Very creative. What's next? Slut? No, whore, am I right?"

Diamo blinked. Mia could practically see him striking the words off his mental insult list and coming up empty. Tric was on his feet beside her, squaring up to the big Itreyan, but Mia placed a hand on his arm. Jessamine wasn't likely to make a play here, and Mia was happy to fence wits all turn. She'd send the pair home limping.

"What do you want, Red?"

"Your skull on the Senate House steps beside my father's," Jess replied.

Mia sighed. "Julius Scaeva executed my da just like he did yours. That makes us allies, not enemies. We both hate the sa—"

"Don't talk to me about hate," the girl snarled. "You've never tasted it, Corvere. My whole familia is dead because of your fucking traitor father."

"You call my father a traitor one more time," Mia growled, "you're going to see your familia again a little sooner than you'd like."

"You know, it's funny," Jessamine smiled. "Your little friend Ashlinn is winning by a clear mile in Mouser's thievery contest. She obviously has the sneak to break into any room in this mountain. I'd have thought you'd have asked her to take care of business for you. But I stole into Mouser's hall a week ago, and damned if it wasn't still there . . ."

Mia rolled her eyes. "Four Daughters, what are you babbling about?"

Jessamine's grin was sharp as new steel. She reached into the collar of her sleeveless tunic. Drew out something that spun and glittered in the dim light.

"O, nothing important."

---

something about the Itreyan boy's stare, something cold and cruel that Mia found altogether ugly.

If it's truth that the eyes are the window to the soul, Diamo's opened into a lightless, straw-lined cell.

Mia felt a sickening lurch in her stomach. A spasm of pain. A blinding flare. And as she staggered back, one hand up to shield her eyes, she made out the shape of three circles, rose gold, platinum, and yellow gold, glittering on the end of a thin chain.

O, Goddess . . .

Mouser's Trinity. The holy medallion, blessed by Aa's Right Hand.

Mia staggered away as Jessamine stepped forward, smile widening. Terror washed over her in cold waves, Mister Kindly flinching in her shadow. And though the suns only gleamed a little in the light from the stained glass above, to Mia that light seemed blinding. Burning. Blistering. As Jessamine continued advancing, Mia stumbled to her knees, mouth filling with bile. Tric snatched up his training sword and snarled.

"Put that bloody thing away, Jess."

The girl pouted. "We're just having some fun, Tricky."

"I said put it away!"

The girl took another step toward Mia, the suns gleaming. Tric raised his training sword and Diamo stepped to meet him, sledgehammer hands twitching. The boys fell to it, Tric swinging the wooden blade with a sharp *crack* into Diamo's forearm, the Itreyan grunting with pain and lashing out with a fist. The pair fell into a scuffle, knuckles and elbows and curses. But all the while, Jessamine was advancing, Mia scrabbling back across the stone now, puke bubbling in her throat.

She was helpless. Mister Kindly's fear spilling into her and doubling. Tripling. She bumped into something hard at her back, realized she was against the wall. Eyes closed against that awful, burning light. The darkness around her writhed, withering like flowers too long in the sun. And as Jessamine stepped closer and Mia felt the light beating down on her like a physical weight, her heart thundering so loud it threatened to burst from her chest, Mister Kindly finally tore himself loose from her shadow.

He tore himself loose and he ran.

"Mister Kindly!"

The shadow bolted across the floor, hissing as it fled. Along the stone. Down the stairs. Disappearing from sight as Mia cried out, terror flooding over her in crushing waves. She aimed a feeble kick at Jessamine's legs, the girl laughing as she stepped aside. Mia could hear Tric shouting. Her pulse rushing in her ears. Pain. Dread so black she thought she might die. And just as it became too much, just as that awful light threatened to burn her blind . . .

"What in the Mother's name is going on here?"

Jessamine turned, the light eclipsed by her body. Through the nausea and burning tears, Mia could see Shahiid Solis standing in the training circle, massive arms folded, white eyes fixed on nothing at all. Tric and Diamo picked themselves up off the floor, Jessamine slipping the necklace back inside her tunic. With the suns out of sight, the pain wracking Mia's body abated almost immediately. But with Mister Kindly gone, the fear remained, creeping like a greasy tide through her innards. She swayed to her feet, pulse pounding, looking about the darkness. She could see no sign of her friend.

"I asked a question, Acolytes," Solis growled.

Ignoring the Shahiid of Songs, Mia skirted around the wall, away from Jessamine. Blind eyes turned toward her footsteps, but she made the archway, dashing down the stairwell on trembling legs. She heard Solis roar, demanding explanation. Tric called after her, but she ignored him, stumbling down into the dark.

"Mister Kindly?"

No answer. No sense of her friend. Only the fear, that long-forgotten, crushing weight of fear. Her hands were shaking. Her lip trembling. He'd left her, she realized.

He left me . . .

"Mister Kindly!"

"Mia, stop!" Tric called, pounding down the stairs behind her.

The girl ignored him, charging off through the twisted hallways and into the stained-glass gloom, calling the shadowcat's name.

"Stop!" Tric grabbed her arm.

"Let go of me!"

"This place is a bloody maze. He could be anywhere."

"That's why I have to find him!" She turned and yelled to the dark. "Mister Kindly!"

"He just had a fright is all. He'll come back when he's ready."

"You don't know that! Those suns, that bitch, they *hurt* him!"

"So what's your plan? Wander around in the dark looking for something that's *made of darkness*? Think for one minute!"

Mia blinked hard. Tried to catch her breath. Struggling with the fear. The weight. The chill. So much, Goddess, she'd not felt this in an age. Not since he'd first found her coiled inside that barrel, gifting her the knife that saved her life. But what Tric had said outside the Mountain was right: in leaning on the shadowcat for so long, she'd forgotten how to deal with this herself. Her legs were shaking. Her belly full of oily ice. She closed her eyes, willing herself calm. The fear pushed back, laughing. Too big. Too much.

He'd left her. For the first time in as long as she could remember.

I'm alone . . .

"O, Goddess," she whispered. "O, Goddess, help me . . ."

She hung there in the dark. Unable to stumble on. Too frightened to stand still. The image of those accursed suns swimming behind her eyelids every time she blinked. She could still feel it. That impossible hatred. The three eyes of the Everseeing, burning her blind. What had she done to deserve it? What was wrong with her? And what was she going to do if he didn't come back?

And then she felt it. Strong arms enveloping her. Holding her tight. Tric pressed her to his chest, wrapping her up. Smoothing her hair. Holding her close.

"It's all right," he murmured. "It'll be all right."

She concentrated on the warmth of his bare skin. The beat of his heart. Eyes closed. Just breathing. Warm and safe and not so alone. She beat it back. The fear. Slowly. Every inch a mile. But she pushed it away, down into the bottom of her feet, stamping it hard as she could. Trying to figure out what all of this meant. Why those suns burned her. What she'd done to invoke the hatred of a god. What had so badly frightened a creature who fed on fear itself.

"Too many questions," she whispered. "Not enough answers."

"So what are you going to do?"

Mia sniffed, swallowed thickly. Placed both hands against Tric's chest and, mustering all the strength she could, pushed herself away. She looked up into his eyes, heart still thumping in her chest. Lips just a few inches from his.

". . . Mia?"

The girl breathed deep. Looking down to her shadow on the stone and finding it only as dark as the boy's beside her. Not dark enough for two anymore. And there, in the black, finally seizing on the answer to her puzzle.

"I think it's time to recruit the most dangerous man in these halls," she said.

Tric looked back up to the Hall of Songs, the Shahiid they'd just fled from. "I thought we just ran away from the most dangerous man in these halls?"

Mia tried to smile.

Settled for shaking her head.

"You've obviously not spent enough time with librarians, Don Tric."

WORDS

The pair stopped off long enough to get Tric another shirt and check in Mia's room for any sign of the shadowcat. She'd searched the black beneath the bed, the corners and closets, but finding nothing, they hurried off through the spiraling dark. The evemeal bells were ringing, but Mia and Tric headed away from the Sky Altar, deeper into the blackness, until they arrived at the athenaeum. The doors loomed above them, twelve feet high and a foot thick, opening silently with the touch of Mia's smallest finger.

A familiar scent picked her up and carried her back to happier turns—curled up in her room above Mercurio's store, surrounded by mountains of her dearest friends. The ones that took her away from the hurt and the garish sunslight and the thought of her mother and brother locked away in some lightless cell.

Books.

Mia looked down to her feet, her shadow preceding her into the library. It was still no darker than Tric's. No different. The emptiness inside her reared up and bared its teeth, and for a moment she found herself too scared to take another step. But finally, balling her hands into fists, she walked into the athenaeum, inhaled the scent of ink and dust and leather and parchment. Tric stood beside her, overlooking the sea of shelves. Mia breathed in the words. Hundreds, thousands, millions of words.

"Chronicler Aelius?" she called.

No answer. Stillness reigned in this kingdom of ink and dust.

"Chronicler?" she called again. "Hello?"

She stole down the stairs, out onto the main floor and into the forest of shelves. That same sourceless luminance lit the room, but among the books, the light seemed dimmer, the shadows deeper. Wandering into the stacks, the pair found themselves surrounded on all sides. Black shelves reaching up to the ceiling, filled with ornate scrolls and dusty tomes, great thick albums and carven codexes. The voices of scribes and queens. Warriors and saints. Heretics and gods. All of them now immortal.

The pair wandered deeper into the stacks, calling for the chronicler, getting lost amid the shadows. The shelves were a labyrinth, twisting off in every direction. Tric cleared his throat and spoke, his voice echoing in the gloom.

"Should we really be poking about in here alone?"

Mia's eyes roamed the stacks, heart thumping in her chest. "Scared, my brave centurion?"

"I'm aware the razor-tongued princess of smart-arsery act is just your natural self-defense techniques kicking in, but I should point out I *am* in here helping you."

Mia glanced at him sideways. "Aye. Apologies."

"What are we looking for?"

Mia breathed deep. Shook her head.

"When Jessamine held up those suns . . . it was like someone had set me on fire. Like the light was burning me to cinders. I don't understand *any* of it, and I'm sick of it. This is the biggest library I've ever seen. If there's a tome on darkin anywhere in the world, it'll be in here. I need to know what I am, Tric."

"Did your Shahiid not teach you anything about yourself?"

"I'm guessing Mercurio knows as little about darkin as anyone else here. The Ministry talk about me being touched by the Mother, but none of them seem to actually know what that *means*. And Lord Cassius was as forthcoming as a pile of bricks when I asked him about it in Godsgrave."

"Lord Cassius is darkin?"

"Lord Cassius is a bastard."

Mia sucked her lip, gave a grudging shrug.

". . . Nice cheekbones, though."

The girl walked on, calling for the chronicler and getting no reply. Perusing the spines as she passed, she saw that many of the athenaeum's books were written in tongues she couldn't speak. Alphabets she'd never seen. Frowning, she stopped before a shelf full of particularly dusty tomes, squinted hard at their titles. She gazed at one in particular, a huge codex bound in black leather, silver letters tracing its spine.

"But that's impossible," she breathed.

She pulled the book off the shelf, struggling with the weight. Shuffling over to a small mahogany reading plinth, she gently opened the pages.

"It can't be . . ."

Tric peered over her shoulder. "Aye. It's a book all right."

"This is Ephaesus. *The Book of Wonders*."

"Good read?"

"I wouldn't know. Every copy in existence was incinerated in the Bright

Light. This book . . . it shouldn't exist." Mia's gaze roamed the stacks. "Look, there's Bosconi's *Heresies*. And Lantimo the Elder's treatise *On Dark and Light*."

"Mia, I'm starting to get the feeling we shouldn't be in here . . ."

Tric's fear echoed her own, but she pushed back against it, hard as she could. "The truth of what I am must be in here somewhere. I'm not leaving 'til we find it."

"Maybe we should start at the letter S?"

"S?"

"S for stubborn. S for stupid. S for smart-arse."

"S for shut it."

"See, that's the spirit."

The laughter felt good. Helped shake the chill from her belly. But Tric fell silent, grin dying on his lips, frowning into the darkness.

". . . Did you feel that?"

"Feel what?"

Mia tilted her head. And as she hung there in the dark, the faintest vibration rumbled through the floor, up through her boots, and settled at the base of her spine.

"I felt *that*," she whispered.

It was subtle at first, the tomes shivering in their places. But soon, the shelves took to vibrating, books murmuring, dust falling in gentle clouds. Mia searched the shadows as the tremors worsened, the floor beneath them shuddering. Her heart was hammering now. She didn't know how deep into the maze they were, but suddenly, this didn't seem the wisest place to be. Without Mister Kindly in her shadow, her fear came quick. Mouth drying. Pulse thumping.

"What in the Mother's name *is* that?" Tric asked.

Mia could hear a leathery sound. As if a great bulk were being dragged across the stone. And then a bellowing roar echoed somewhere out in the athenaeum's dark.

"Let's get out of here, Mia."

". . . Aye," she nodded. "Let's."

The dragging sound grew louder as the pair hurried back in what Mia hoped was the direction they'd come from. But the forest of shelves all looked the same, rising about them in faceless rows. The pair flinched as another roar sounded out in the dark, Tric snatching Mia's hand and breaking into a sprint.

"What is it?"

"I don't even want to know. Run!"

Books were almost falling from their shelves now. As Mia and Tric rounded a corner, she realized they'd worked their way into a dead end. With a curse, they backed away as another roar rang out—closer this time. Too close for comfort. Wanting no part of whatever was about to happen, Mia clutched fistfuls of shadows and tore them up, wrapping herself inside. And though she'd never done it before, surrounded by a darkness that had never known the touch of a sun, she seized Tric by the shoulders and dragged him in with her, enveloping them both.

Mia pulled Tric in tight, huddled against the shelves at their back. This close, she could feel the boy's heart pounding against his ribs, realized he was just as frightened as she was. Near blind beneath the shroud, Tric sniffed the air, frowning.

"What is it?" she whispered.

"I can't smell it."

"At all?"

Tric shook his head. "All I get is the books. And you."

"Bath time?"

". . . Is that an invitation?"

"O, fuck off—"

Another roar. Closer. Whatever it was, they couldn't see well enough under her cloak to run—they'd likely plow face-first into a shelf if they tried to bolt. So instead, Mia wrapped her arms around Tric and pulled him down, small as they could be. Fear swelling inside her, flooding the place Mister Kindly once filled. Pressed against the boy's back and trying not to shiver.

The dragging sound grew louder, wet and creaking. The floor beneath them shook. Beyond her veil of shadowstuff, Mia saw something vast move past, slithering on the stone. She caught the impression of a long, serpentine shape, dozens of blunt, brutish heads, lined with teeth. Moving between the shelves like some colossal caterpillar, spine arching as it dragged itself forward, snuffling the air. Mia clutched her dagger, shaking with the fear of it. Cursing herself a weakling. A child.

Tric reached back wordlessly, took hold of her hand and squeezed.

Minutes stretched into forever, there in that sweat-soaked dark. But whatever the thing was, it passed by without noticing them, slowly slithering off between the shelves. Mia and Tric huddled together, listening until it was out of earshot, silent as mice.

"*Now* can we get out of here?" Tric finally hissed.

"I'm thinking . . . yyyyes."

Slinging the shadowcloak aside, she pulled Tric to his feet. Clambering up onto a shelf, Mia peered out into the sea of tomes, looking for an escape from the maze. She could see the athenaeum's doors in the distance, blinked hard against some trick of the light. They looked *miles* away . . .

"Lookin' frsum'thin?"

Mia cursed, almost jumping out of her skin as the voice spoke from the shadows. Tric whirled on the spot, saltlocks flying, blade in hand.

Mia heard a flintbox strike, saw flame reflected on impossibly thick spectacles, two shocks of white hair. A plume of cinnamon-scented smoke drifted into the air, and Chronicler Aelius stepped into the light, wheeling a wooden trolley stacked dangerously high with books. A small plaque on its snout was marked RETURNS.

"Maw's teeth, does *everyone* around here walk on fucking tiptoe?" Tric asked.

The old man grinned white, exhaled gray. "Excitable one, aren't you?"

"What do you bloody expect? Did you see that thing?"

Aelius blinked. "Eh?"

"That monster. That thing! What the 'byss was it?"

The old man shrugged. "Bookworm."

"Book . . ."

". . . worm." Aelius nodded. "That's what I call 'em, anyways."

"Them?" Mia was incredulous.

"O, aye. There's a few living in here. That was just a little one."

"*Little one?*" Tric shouted.

The old man squinted through the pall of smoke. "O, aye. Very excitable."

"You let something like that roam around your library?"

Aelius shrugged. "First off, it's not *my* library. It belongs to Our Lady of Blessed Murder. I'm just the one who chronicles what's innit. And I don't *let* the bookworms roam around, they just . . . *do*." The old man shrugged. "Funny old place, this."

"Funny . . . ," Mia breathed.

"Well, not haha funny, obviously."

Aelius plucked another cigarillo from behind his ear. Lighting it on his own, he held it out to the girl with ink-stained fingers.

"Smoke?"

The fear still coiled in Mia's belly, her nerves in tatters. Perhaps a cigarillo would calm her down. And so, as the old man grinned, she mooched across the aisle and took the smoke with trembling fingers. They stood there for long, silent moments, Mia savoring the taste of the sugarpaper on her lips as her pulse finally slowed to somewhere near normal. Blowing plumes in Tric's direction, and smirking as he wrinkled his nose and coughed.

"Good smokes, these," she finally said.

"Aye."

"Don't recognize the maker's mark, though."

"He's dead." Aelius shrugged. "Don't make 'em like this anymore."

"Like these books?"

"Eh?"

Mia motioned to the shelves. "I recognize some of the titles. They aren't supposed to exist. It makes sense now I think about it. This is a Church to the goddess of murder."

Tric blinked as realization dawned. "So Niah's library is filled with books that have died?"

Aelius looked at the pair through the smoke, slowly nodded.

"Some," he finally said. "Some are books that were burned. Or forgotten ages past. Some never got the chance to live at all. Abandoned or half-imagined or just too frightening to begin. Memoirs of murdered tyrants. Theorems of crucified heretics. Masterpieces of geniuses who ended before their time."

Mia looked around the shelves. Shaking her head. What wonders were hidden in these forgotten and unborn pages? What horrors?

"And the . . . worms?" she exhaled.

"Not sure where they're from, to be honest." Aelius shrugged. "Maybe one of the books? Things in these pages don't always *stay* on the pages, if you get my drift. They only come out if they think the words are in danger. Or if they get, y'know . . . hungry."

"What do they eat?" Tric asked.

The old man fixed the boy in his stare. "What do you reckon?"

"We've been here nearly four months." Mia dragged deep on her cigarillo. "You don't think this is the kind of thing the Ministry should mention on your first turn? 'O, by the by, Acolytes, there's these colossal fucking wormthings that live in the library, so for Maw's sake, get your books back on time'?"

"What if more acolytes sneak in here alone?" Tric asked. "Mouser's contest earns us six marks for every book stolen from the athenaeum."

"Well, Mouser's a bit of bastard, isn't he?" Aelius said.

"What would happen if someone actually broke in here and tried to lift one?"

The old man smiled. "What do you reckon?"

Tric gawped. "Madness . . ."

"Look, the worms only bother folk who mess with the words. And if you're fool enough to go faffing about with books like these, you deserve what you get. And aside all that, I *did* warn you." Aelius blew a smoke ring at Mia's face. "Told you when we first met that depending what aisle you walked down, you might never be seen again."

"All right, then, for future reference, which aisles should we avoid?" the girl asked.

"It changes." The old man shrugged. "This whole place changes time to time. New books appearing every other turn. Others moving to places I didn't put them. Sometimes I find whole sections I never knew existed."

"And you're supposed to chronicle all this?"

Aelius nodded. "Bugger of a job, really."

"You could get some help?" Tric offered.

"I had four assistants, once. Didn't go so well."

"Why? What happened to them?"

The old man looked at the boy sidelong. Three voices rang in the gloom simultaneously.

"*What do you reckon?*"

Mia blew a lungful of pale gray into the silence.

". . . I don't suppose there are any books on darkin in here, are there?"

The chronicler glanced down at her shadow. Back up to her eyes. "Why?"

"Is that a no?"

"It's a 'why.' Wonderful thing about a library like this. Any book that ever was or wasn't written is going to be in here eventually. Trouble is finding the bloody things. Lot of effort to look for something specific. And sometimes these books get chips on their shoulders. The burned ones 'specially. Sometimes they don't *want* to be found."

Mia felt hope sinking in her breast. She looked at Tric, who shrugged helplessly.

"But," the old man said, looking her up and down. "You've got the look of a girl who's no stranger to the page. I can tell. You've got words in your soul."

"Words in my soul?" Mia scoffed. "'*Burn After Reading*'?"

"Listen, girl," Aelius sniffed. "The books we love, they love us back. And just as we mark our places in the pages, those pages leave their marks on us. I can see it in you, sure as I see it in me. You're a daughter of words. A girl with a story to tell."

"They don't tell stories about Red Church disciples, Chronicler," Mia said. "No songs sung for us. No ballads or poems. People live and die in the shadows, here."

"Well, maybe here's not where you're supposed to be."

She looked up sharply at that. Eyes narrowed in the smoke.

"Anyways." The old man pushed himself off the shelf and sighed. "I'll keep an eye out. And if I find a book about darkin worth reading, I'll pass it along. Fair?"

". . . Fair." Mia bowed. "My thanks, Chronicler."

"You two had best be off. And me besides. Too many books. Too few centuries."

The old man escorted Mia and Tric through the labyrinth of shelves, trundling his RETURNS trolley and trailing a thin line of sugar-scented smoke all the way to the doors. And though the distance had looked like miles to Mia, they arrived at the exit in a handful of minutes, the forest of paper and words left far behind them.

"Cheerio."

Nodding to them both, Aelius smiled and closed the doors without a sound.

Tric turned to her with a crooked grin. "Words in your soul, eh?"

"O, fuck off."

The boy spread his arms, loudly proclaiming, "A girl with a story to tell!"

Mia aimed a hard punch, right into Tric's bicep. The boy flinched as Mia cursed, jarring her injured elbow. Tric raised both his fists, threw a few sparring punches toward her head as she slapped him off, aiming a boot at his hindquarters as he turned away. And together, the pair wandered off into the darkness.

She resisted the urge to take the boy's hand again.

Just barely.

POWER

She was fourteen years old the last time the suns fell from the sky.

The greatest wordsmiths of the Republic have never truly captured the beauty of a full Itreyan sunset. The blood stench wafting over Godsgrave streets as Aa's priests sacrifice animals in the thousands, beseeching the God of Light to return soon. The bloody glow of Saan on the horizon, colliding with Saai's pale blue, tumbling further into a sullen indigo. It takes three turns for the light to fully die. Three turns of prayer, slaughter, and budding hysteria until the Mother of Night briefly reclaims dominion of the sky.

And then, the truedark Carnivalé begins.

Mia woke to the sound of revelry. The constant popopopop *of fireworks from the Iron Collegium, meant to frighten the Maw back below the horizon. She stretched out her hand, watched the shadows play. Feeling the power that had been growing inside her these last few turns finally blooming. With a wave of her hand, a tendril of shadow flipped an entire stack of books into the air, scattering the tomes across the room. At her whim, more shadows reached out, putting each book back in its proper place. She opened her bedroom door with a glance. Dressed without lifting a finger.*

"... bravo ...," *Mister Kindly had said.* "... if only i had hands to applaud ..."

Mia smacked her backside. "I'd settle for lips to kiss my sweet behind."

"... i would have to find it first ..."

"Arses are like wine, Mister Kindly. Better too little than too much."

"... a beauty and a philosopher. be still, my beating heart ..."

The not-cat looked down at its translucent chest.

"... o, wait ..."

The girl checked the knives at her belt, in her boots, tucked up her sleeve. She was a scrap of a thing, crooked fringe and hollow cheeks, full of all the confidence fourteen years in the world brings. Listening downstairs, she heard Old Mercurio's familiar murmur, swapping gossip with one of his frequent not-customers. The old man wasn't one for revelry. Unlike every other resident of Godsgrave, her master would be staying off the streets tonights. He had eyes aplenty out there already.

"... you insist on doing this, then ...?"

She looked to her friend. All trace of jest draining from her face, leaving it hard and pale.

"This is my best chance. I've never felt as strong as I have in truedark. If I'm ever going to get in there, it's tonights."

"... you should tell the old man ..."

"He'd try to talk me out of it."

"... do you not ask yourself why ...?"

"There's no guards in there during truedark, Mister Kindly."

"... because the descent will begin soon. hundreds of prisoners slaughtering each other for the right to leave the philosopher's stone. do you really wish to be in there with them ...?"

"Four years, Mister Kindly. Four years they've been locked in that hole. My brother learned to walk in a prison cell. I don't know the last time my mother saw the suns. What have I been training for all these years, if not this? I have to get them out of there."

"... you are a fourteen-year-old girl, mia ..."

"And is it the fourteen-year-old part, or the girl part that troubles you?"

"... mia—"

"No," she snapped. "This ends tonights. On my side or in my way?"

The not-cat sighed.

". . . you know where I stand. always . . ."

"Then let's stop talking about it, shall we?"

Out the window. Onto the street. The crush and revelry. Everyone in their Carnivalé masks; beautiful dominos and fearsome voltos and laughing punchinellos. The girl slipped through the throng, a harlequin's face over her own, cloak over her head. Past the sighing lovers on the Bridge of Vows, the hucksters on the Bridge of Coin, down to the broken shore. Slinging the canvas off her stolen gondola, she stretched her arms and closed her eyes. Darkness slithered from the nooks and crannies, wrapping the girl and boat in a shroud of night.

Hidden in the darkness, she punted across the Bay of Butchers, under a walkway on the Bridge of Follies, shifting and rolling on the rising tide.* Slinging her cloak aside as she made for the open sea, hours turning by, aiming for the foreboding spike of stone thrust up from the ocean's face. The hole in which her mother and brother had languished for four long years at Julius Scaeva's command, hopeless and helpless.

Not anymore.

She made berth on the jagged rocks, the shadows bringing her safely into harbor. The darkness dragged the gondola onto the shore, spared it the jagged kiss of the rocks surrounding the Stone. Mia licked her lips, inhaled salt air. Listening to the distant hymn of the gulls. The violence already echoing through the Stone's innards. Mister Kindly drinking in her fear and leaving her fierce and unafraid.

She held out her arms. Willing herself upward. The power thrummed in her veins, like nothing she'd ever felt before. A black kinship, flowing like the growing

---

* Constructed on the order of Consul Julius Scaeva, the Bridge of Follies is built entirely of watercraft—ships and boats, scuppers and ferries—strung end to end and lashed together by lengths of rusting chain. By writ of the Itreyan constitution, consuls may sit for only one term, almost three years in span. So when Scaeva broke precedent during the Kingmaker Rebellion and stood for reelection, claiming emergency powers in the Republic's time of crisis, his most outspoken political rival, Senator Suetonius Arlani, was quoted as saying, "Scaeva has more chance of walking on the waters of Butcher's Bay than he has of succeeding in his folly."

When Scaeva won in an unprecedented landslide, he purchased every seafaring vessel he could find, had them lashed together to form a crude bridge, and walked across the bay barefoot. Named the Bridge of Follies after Arlani's remarks, the span has remained a landmark in Godsgrave ever since, home to a motley of vagrants, the dispossessed and the outcast, grubbing out a living free of rent on the consul's *monument di triumph*. Scaeva himself doesn't seem to mind.

As for Senator Arlani, he was sentenced to life in the Philosopher's Stone a few weeks after the consul's electoral victory. The circumstances of his incarceration were entirely unrelated to his public remarks, I assure you.

dark. Long black tendrils wrapped her up, slipped from her fingers, digging into the brickwork at the Stone's base. Like the translucent limbs of some vast spider, they pulled her upward. And one black handhold at a time, the girl began to climb.

Up the towering wall, hair billowing in the rising wind. Over the battlements and twisted tangles of razorweed atop the walls. The shadows wrapped her up like a babe in swaddling and carried her down into the copper-thick stench of death.

Mia stole through the hallways of bloody stone, wrapped in a darkness so deep she could barely see. Bodies. Everywhere. Men choked and stabbed. Beaten to death with their own chains and bludgeoned to death with their own limbs. The sound of murder ringing all around, the stink of offal thick in the air. Vague shapes running past her, tangling and screaming on the floor. The cries ringing somewhere far away, somewhere the dark wouldn't let her hear.

She slipped inside the Philosopher's Stone like a knife between ribs. This prison. This abattoir. Down past the open cells to the quieter places, where the doors were still sealed, where the prisoners who didn't wish to try their luck in the Descent were still locked, thin and starving. She threw the shadowcloak aside so she could see better, peering through the bars at the stick-thin scarecrows, the hollow-eyed ghosts. She could see why folks would try their luck in the Senate's horrid gambit. Better to die fighting than linger here in the dark and starve. Better to stand and fall than kneel and live.

Unless, of course, you had a four-year-old son locked in here with you . . .

The scarecrows cried out to her, thinking her some Hearthless wraith come to torment them. She ran the length and breadth of the cell block, eyes wide. Desperation now. Fear, despite the cat in her shadow. They must be here somewhere? Surely the Dona Corvere wouldn't have dragged her son out into the butchery above for the chance to escape this nightmare?

Would she?

"Mother!" Mia called, tears in her eyes. "Mother, it's Mia!"

Endless hallways. Lightless black. Deeper and deeper into the shadow.

"Mother?"

"Mother!"

Mia clawed her way upright, wisps of hair stuck to the sweat on her skin. Her heart was thrashing against her ribs, eyes wide, chest heaving. Blinking in the dark, drenched in panic, finally recognizing her room in the Quiet Mountain, the sourceless luminance shrouding all in its gentle glow.

"Just a dream," she whispered.

Not a dream. A *nightmare*. The kind she'd not had in years. Whenever the nevernight terrors came creeping to her bed above Mercurio's shop, whenever the phantoms of her past stole inside her skull as she slept, Mister Kindly had been there. Tearing them to ribbons. But now she was alone. At the mercy of her dreams.

Her memories.

Daughters, where could he be?

Mia dragged herself upright, shivering. Head bowed. Arms wrapped around herself. Fear throbbing in her chest in time with her pulse. The shadows twisted along the wall as she clenched her fist. Remembering the way they'd flocked to her command the last time the suns fell from the sky. The last time she—

Don't look.

She'd thought she might be all right. Tric had escorted her to her bedchamber after the library visit, assured her Mister Kindly would come back. As ninebells had struck, she'd crawled into bed, tried to convince herself all would be well. But without her friend there to protect her, there was nothing to stop the dreams. The memories of that lightless, blood-soaked pit. What she'd found within.

Don't look.

She screwed her eyes shut tight.

Don't look.

The empty room. The empty bed. Loneliness. Fear. Washing over her in waves. She'd not been truly by herself in years. Never faced sleep's terrors without someone beside her. She pushed her knuckles into her eyes, sighed.

Ninebells had rung. Breaking the Revered Mother's curfew would be foolish, especially after what they'd done to Hush. But she'd stolen out with Ashlinn and not been caught. And the place she wanted to be was only a few doors down, after all.

The place I want to be?

The prospect of endless, sleepless hours stretching out in front of her.

The growing fear that Mister Kindly might never come back.

Certainty budding in her chest.

The place I want to be.

A darkened hallway. Shaking hands. She pushed shadowstuff into the lock to muffle the sound, but her fingers were trembling so badly, she wondered if she could crack it. If she knocked, someone else might hear. Ashlinn. Diamo. Jessamine.

The lock finally clicked. The door swung open a crack on shadow-muffled hinges. She peered into the darkened room, stole inside. Gasping in fright as someone seized her arm, thrust her back into the wall, knife to her throat. Pausing as he recognized her in the dark, lowering the blade and speaking through gritted teeth.

"Maw's teeth, what are you doing in here?" Tric hissed.

". . . Surprise?"

"I could have cut your damn throat!"

She fought to calm her galloping pulse, push the fright back far enough to speak.

"I couldn't sleep," she whispered.

"So you break into my room? It's after ninebells, what if you got caught?"

"I'm sorry." She licked at dry lips. Swallowed.

He was still pressed against her, close enough to breathe him in. She realized he must sleep naked—his bare skin gleamed in the dim, sourceless light. Her gaze traveled his body, the hard muscle on his hairless torso, the taut cords at his neck, along his arms. Her breath coming a little quicker. The fear that had woken her was roiling in her still, but something else was stirring now. Something older. Stronger.

Do I want this?

She looked up into deep hazel eyes, softening with pity. He couldn't know what it was like. Couldn't understand what Mister Kindly meant to her. But still, she saw his anger melt, some soft understanding stepping in to replace it.

"I'm sorry too. You just scared me, is all."

Tric sighed, began to ease away. A wordless protest slipped from her lips, and she reached out, running her fingertips up his arm. Goosebumps rose on his skin. She rested one hand on the hard swell of his shoulder. Stopped him from pulling away.

"Mia . . ."

"Can I sleep here tonight?"

He frowned. Those big hazel eyes searching her own.

"Sleep?"

Naked as he was, she could feel him pressed against her leg. She lowered her chin, looked up at him through the dark haze of her lashes. A small, knowing smile twisted her lips as she felt him stirring slightly. With deliberate slowness, she reached down with her free hand. Brushing her fingertips along his length, feeling it swell. He gasped as she took him fully in her hand, running her fingers along his silken-smooth underside. Flooded with dark satisfaction that her merest touch could inflame him.

Daughters, but he felt hot. Almost scalding the palm of her hand. And

the slick of cold fear inside her belly began to melt, replaced by a slowly growing fire.

She lunged, nipped at his lip with her teeth. Hard enough to draw blood.
Salt on her tongue. The flame rising inside her, drowning the fear. He tried to
pull away but her fist closed around him, squeezing. He froze, groaning and
closing his eyes. A smile curled her lips, filled her with drunken warmth. This
towering lump of muscle, this killer, and she could hold him still as a frightened deer with one hand.

She was afraid. Dizzy with it. Stumbling. But beneath it all, she realized
she wanted him. Wanted to drink him in. To own him. And the fear of it, the
anticipation, was only intensifying that desire. It didn't matter at that moment,
not the places she'd been or the things she'd done. Not the miles of murder
ahead or behind. Just the smell of him, musk and maleness and lust, filling her
lungs. The heat of him in her hand, the pulse pounding like a hammer beneath
his skin, swallowing his sighs as she found his mouth, her tongue seeking his
own. He groaned as she kissed him, deep and long and warm, hands wrapped
in her hair as she pushed him hard, back against the wall, muscle slapping stone.

Her lips were on his throat now, tongue tracing the burning line of his pulse.
One hand exploring the smooth swell of his chest, the other still stroking him
as he quivered and sighed. Still afraid, breath trembling, she sank lower, lips
trailing over his collarbone to his chest. With a gentle hand, he stopped her,
searching her eyes, blood still smudged on his mouth.

"Mia . . . you don't have to."

"I *want* to."

With deliberate slowness, she locked her eyes with his and sank to her knees.
Both hands stroking his trembling length, smiling as he leaned his head back
and groaned. She'd never done this before, unsure of herself despite all Aalea's
lessons on the topic. But she wanted to possess him with a fierceness that
drowned anything of the fear left inside her.

She touched her tongue to his burning skin, felt him jump. Goddess, he
was so hard. Opening her mouth, she licked him from root to tip, smiling as
he groaned. Tasting a salty sweetness at his crown, hot on her tongue. She
kissed him, up and down, his knees close to buckling. And wetting her lips
with the tip of her tongue, she plunged him into her mouth.

She lost herself then. Instinct driving her forward. Hardly believing the
smooth heat of him. Fumbling at first, uncertain beneath the lust, and he
wrapped his fists in her hair and gently guided her, up and down his length,
cheeks hollowed, pumping her fist at his root.

He was hers, then. Completely. Utterly. Helpless. Daughters, she was almost overcome with it. The sense of absolute control, delighting in the differing moans and shudders she elicited as she worked her tongue, groaning herself as hunger took hold. There was only one thing she wanted at that moment. No shivering virgin on bloodstained sheets, now. No girl held prisoner by her nightmares. No frightened maid.

His grip on her hair tightened, his pulse quickened. Chest shuddering, not enough air in his lungs.

"Mia," he gasped. "I . . ."

She felt him buck, pulsing in her mouth. Pulling her closer, more, more. His back arched, his legs trembled. And then he groaned her name, every muscle taut, filling her mouth with spurts of sweet, salty heat. She moaned, intoxicated with the power of it. Continuing to pump his length with her fist, milking every last drop until he gasped with the pleasurepain of it all, pushing her away, dragging shuddering breaths into his chest.

She climbed up off her knees, a wicked smile on gleaming lips. Chuckling at the look in his eyes, the disbelief and hunger and afterglow. He was barely able to stand or breathe or talk. All this, she'd done to him in a handful of heartbeats.

This is what Aalea meant, she realized.

"You all right?" she asked.

He blinked hard. Shook his head. "Perhaps give me a minute."

Laughing, she turned and flopped onto his bed. The sheets were still warm, his scent wrapped up in the fur. He collapsed beside her, naked though she was still fully clothed. Dragging the saltlocks from his eyes, he looked at her across the pillows.

"Please take note that I'm not complaining, but what was that for?"

"Does there have to be a reason?"

". . . Usually."

"I like you." Mia shrugged. "And I wanted to see if I could. Before Shahiid Aalea brings in some virile young Liisian slaveboy for us to practice on."

Tric laughed briefly. "Somehow I don't think that's the whole truth."

"I . . . don't like being alone. The things I see when I close my eyes . . ."

She frowned, shaking her head as words failed. Tric ran a fingertip down her cheek, over the swell of her lips.

"I have my daemons too. And I like you, truly. I just wonder . . . is this wise?"

"What's 'this' mean?"

"Well, *this*. Us." He waved at the dark around them. "We're not here long. Even assuming we're initiated as Blades, we'll be sent to different chapels. We'll be assassins, Mia. The life we lead . . . it's not one that ends in happy ever after."

"Is that what you think I want? Happy ever after?"

"That's the riddle, isn't it?" Tric sighed. "I don't know what you want."

She rolled across the bed, leaned up on one elbow above him. Long black hair draped across his skin, staring down into those sweet hazel eyes. "You're an idiot."

"True," he smiled.

She kissed him then, mouth open to his. Running one hand down his chest, over the hills and troughs of his abdomen, feeling the muscles harden in contrast to the softness of his lips. Eyes closed. Alone in the dark, and not alone at all.

Breaking the kiss, she studied his face. Those awful scrawls of hatred on his skin. The scars. Those beautiful, bottomless eyes beyond.

"Just keep the dreams away. That's all I ask. Will you do that for me?"

He searched her eyes. Nodded slow. "I can do that."

She took his hand, pulled it close. Pushed it against her breast, guiding it to the tautness of her belly, slipping it down into her britches. His fingers running through the thatch of her hair, searching lower still, her breath catching in her lungs.

She felt him part her lips, moaned as his fingers gently curled against her. She reached down, seeking his cock again, but he pushed her onto her back, the deft movements of his hand sending delightful shivers up her spine.

"My turn," he whispered.

Mia leaned back, moaning as he kissed her neck, hissing encouragement as he bit her hard, harder. She wrapped her fingers in his hair as he tugged up her shirt, groaning as his tongue circled the hardening swell of her nipple. He took her into his mouth, suckling, his fingers still working some kind of magik between her legs. Warmth radiating out from her center, her thighs shivered, soaked with need. He snapped the ties on her britches, dragged them down around her ankles, caught up in her boots. She kicked them free, one leg still entangled, writhing on the bed as he continued stroking her, working firm hard circles on her softest place.

"O, Daughters," she breathed. "O, yes."

He knelt between her legs, one hand caressing her breast, the other still lighting fires between her legs. And placing one last kiss on her lips, he pushed himself down her trembling body. Leaving a trail of burning kisses across her breasts, down her belly. She knew where he was headed, suddenly frightened again, eyes fluttering wide. Her hand snagging in his hair, pulling him up with a wince.

He looked at her, a question burning in his eyes behind the blinding hunger.

". . . You don't have to," she breathed.

"But I *want* to," he said.

He lifted her leg, kissing the tender skin on the back of her knee and making her shiver. Running fingertips slowly down her tightening belly. Dragging his lips down the inside of her thigh, stubble tickling, his breath damp on her skin. Lust at last overcoming her fear, she wrapped her fingers in his locks, urging him down. With deliberate, agonizing slowness, he spiraled lower, closer, licking the fresh sweat and making her groan, breath coming ever quicker. Pausing as he reached her lips, breathing her in as if she were air and he a drowning man. She whimpered, silently pleading. And as he parted her folds with gentle fingers, she felt the first touch of his tongue.

"O, Goddess," she moaned.

It flickered against her, gentle at first, trailing tiny circles around her swollen bud. Her back arched, legs rising into the air, toes pointed. He toyed with her, tongue flickering in and out, blowing cool breaths onto her between gentle assaults from his mouth. She was overcome with the sensation, exposed and completely at his mercy. But Daughters, she wanted it. Reveled in it. Grabbing fistfuls of his hair and pulling him in, willing him to press harder, to take her, taste her, set her on fire.

He lapped rhythmically, and Mia thrashed on the bed, eyes rolling back in her head. Heat building inside her, torturous and enveloping, wordless pleas filling the air. Just as she thought she could take no more, she felt another pressure, urgent and hot. And, parting her wet lips with his hand, he slowly eased a finger inside her.

Sparks in her mind. Blinding light in her eyes. Mia groaned as he went to work, curling and stroking, his rhythm inside matching the increasing pace of his tongue. She began to shake harder with each ragged gasp, writhing as a flood swelled inside her, pressing against some hidden dam, higher and hotter. Tric worked his fingers and his mouth, his tongue and his breath, stars colliding behind her eyes, curses slipping past her teeth "O, fuck, O, fuck, O, fuck" until the dam shattered, the flood spilled along with a wordless cry from her lips, spine arched, head thrown back as she silently screamed his name.

Tric slowed, withdrawing his hand, still drawing gentle circles on her soaking lips with his tongue. And then, he kissed her, tenderly, as if her sex were her mouth and he were saying goodbye for the very last time.

He lifted his head as Mia untangled her fingers from his hair. Shot her a crooked smile.

"Are *you* all right?"

"Where . . . the 'byss . . . did you learn to do that?"

Grinning, the boy pulled himself up the bed, collapsed beside her. "Same place I learned to dance. Shahiid Aalea offered a few pointers, should I ever find myself seducing some marrowborn daughter or somesuch."

Mia sighed, heart still hammering in her breast. "I'll thank her next time I see her."

Tric smiled, leaned over and kissed her. She could taste herself on his lips, tongue entwined with his own. Reaching down, she found him still hard as stone, hot as iron. She wanted more. But a cool fear burned in the back of her mind, rising in volume even as she kicked off her remaining pants leg, swung herself up and straddled him. She tore off her shirt and he lunged at her breasts, kissing and gnawing. Leaning back, she grasped the burning spear of his cock, pressing it against her aching lips. Running him back and forth, tempted to simply sink, inch by inch, all the way down.

"I want you," he breathed. "Mother of fucking Night, I want you."

Her lips found his, her breath against his skin. "And I you. But . . ."

"But what?"

"I don't know if it's safe."

He took hold of her hips, mouth on her breasts, pulling her down as she dragged him along her aching lips. The tip of him slipped inside her—O holy Daughters, it felt good—and she almost lost herself then. Wanting. Needing. More than she'd wanted or needed before in her life. But she tangled her fingers in his hair, pulled him away from her aching nipples. Leaning back, she let him have another inch of her, groaning from her depths. But then she stopped. Tightened her grip and rose up off him, leaving herself empty. He sighed, but she smiled, giving him a playful slap and pushing him back down on the bed, sliding onto the sweat-soaked fur beside him.

"Not tonight, Don Tric," she whispered.

Tric lay back in the tangle of pillows and furs. Trying in vain to catch his breath.

"You're a cold one, Pale Daughter," he managed.

She took his hand, pressed it between her legs. "Say again?"

"Maw's teeth, you're just being sadistic now."

She laughed, lying back in the pillows and staring at the ceiling. Narrowing her eyes and twisting the shadows, watching them writhe. The fear was gone. Swallowed utterly by the knowledge burning in her mind.

He'd do anything to have me at this moment. Anything I asked. Kill for me. Die for me. Bathe in the blood of hundreds just so he could breathe his last inside me.

Mia arched her back, slipped one hand between her legs. Pressing at the sweet ache she found there, she closed her eyes and sighed.

This is the strength that topples kings. Ends empires. Even breaks the sky.

She ran damp fingers over smiling lips.

This is power.

S he awoke hours later from a blissful, dreamless sleep. Stretching like a cat, squeezing her thighs together and luxuriating in the memories of the way he'd touched her. She looked at the boy beside her, the face beneath the ink softened by sleep. Telling herself it had only been to keep the dreams away.

Guessing it was close to mornbells and remembering Hush's scourging, she decided it'd be best for all concerned if she wasn't seen sneaking from Tric's room when the other acolytes woke. So she dressed silently, stole from the bedchamber without waking him. Her shadowcloak about her shoulders, she pawed blindly along the wall until she made it to her room. And unlocking the door with a swift turn of the key, she slipped inside with none outside the wiser. Breathing a small sigh of relief.

"... *the perfect crime* ..."

"Mister Kindly!"

There he was at the foot of her bed; just a sliver of deeper darkness in the gloom. She took a running dive onto the furs, compelled to try and touch him, pick him up and squeeze him. And as he leapt up into her arms, she was shocked to find she did feel some vague, velvet soft touch as her hands passed through him, cold as ice, soft as baby's breath. He threw himself around her shoulders, slinking through her hair, and the long locks moved as if in some gentle breeze. Tears of relief welled in her eyes.

"I was worried, you little shit!"

"... *i am sorry* ..."

She leaned back in her pillows, and the not-cat hopped up onto her chest, peered into her eyes. He'd been missing all eve without a whisper. Which, despite the relief filling her at her friend's return, still begged the question ...

"Where have you been?"

"... *o, a short trip to the theater, a quick round of ale and whores, you know* ..."

"Hold now, you don't get to be a smart-arse. You were missing for hours."

"... *i trust you found some way to entertain yourself while i was gone* ...?"

"O, a short trip to the athenaeum, some light reading, you know."

The not-cat twisted its head in the direction of Tric's room.

". . . i think it best if i don't . . ."

She grinned, ran her fingers through him, again feeling that vague chill prickling the hair upon her skin. Questions about her sleeping arrangements could wait.

". . . So," she said.

". . . so . . ."

"Jessamine stole Mouser's Trinity."

". . . did she really, i hadn't noticed . . ."

"I warned you about the smart-arsery."

". . . as if one sun had warned another it was shining too bright . . ."

"She hates my guts, Mister Kindly. And now she's got a weapon we can't defend against hanging around her neck."

". . . so tell mouser. the ministry. have the trinity confiscated . . ."

"Tattling tales to the Ministry lacks a certain . . . style, don't you think?"

". . . you have another plan then . . . ?"

"I'm sure I could conjure one with the help of enough goldwine."

". . . you do not have time for petty antics. remember why you came here . . ."

"That's all well and good, but what if Jess decides to avenge her father once and for all? She draws that Trinity and I fall to my knees trying not to puke my guts up."

". . . in case you had not noticed, jessamine hates almost everyone around her. let her think you beaten, and she will grow bored. she loathes carlotta as much as you . . ."

"So what, I just lie down and let her stomp all over me?"

*". . . have you heard of the scabdogs of liis . . . ?"**

---

* Scabdogs are a voracious carnivore of the Liisian continent, resembling a fat, hairless canine with piggy eyes and a mouthful of razors. The scabdog is an astonishingly vicious close-quarter combatant, but lacks the endurance to chase game over long distances. They frequently feed on carrion, but have also developed a peculiar method of "hunting."

The creature will maim itself superficially, chewing at its haunches until it bleeds. The scabdog will then make a show of being wounded, limping and bleeding until spotted by a carrion eater, such as a vulture, jackal, or another scabdog. The beast will then collapse, feigning death. This subterfuge can take hours, sometimes even turns.

The beasts are consummate actors, even going so far as to remain still while another carnivore takes a cautious bite. But when the carrion eater finally settles in to feed, the scabdog strikes, tearing its would-be predator to pieces and feasting to its heart's content.

As a result of their self-maiming, the creatures are frequently covered in scabs, hence their name.

And in case you were wondering, no, gentlefriend, they do not make good pets.

"Of course."

"*. . . it never hurts to be underestimated, mia. initiation should be your goal . . .*"

Mia chewed her lip. A question roiled behind her teeth. One she'd never needed to ask before. But then, he'd never abandoned her before. In all their years together, the shadowcat had been her confidant. The star she set her course by. It was he who saved her from Scaeva's men. He who stood beside her when her mother . . .

No. Don't.

Don't look.

But the Trinity had affected him even worse than her. The suns had terrified her, but Mister Kindly had been near mad with panic. What about him made the Everseeing One's gaze hurt him so? Was it simply because he was a thing of shadow? Or was there more to him than simple darkness?

"What are you, Mister Kindly?"

The not-cat tilted his head.

"*. . . your friend . . .*"

"But what else? A daemon like the folklore says?"

A wind-in-the-gravestones chuckle hung in the air. "*. . . daemon, yes. i've been meaning to ask you to sign this parchment. in blood and triplicate, if it please you . . .*"

"I'm in no mood for jests. Why won't you tell me?"

"*. . . because i do not know. before i found you, i was just a shape waiting in the shadows . . .*"

"Waiting for what?"

"*. . . for one like you . . .*"

"That simple, eh?"

"*. . . what is wrong with simple . . . ?*"

"Because nothing ever is."

"*. . . you are too young to be so cynical . . .*"

Mia lurched upward, passing right through Mister Kindly and up off the mattress. The not-cat licked its paw and cleaned its whiskers as if nothing were amiss.

"Fuck you, then. Keep your secrets. I'll seek out Lord Cassius when he comes back for initiation. Ask him again about darkin and what it means to be one. And if he decides to play cryptic instead of giving me my answers this time, I might just choke them out of him. I don't care how nice his damn cheekbones are."

"*. . . that is unwise, mia . . .*"

"Why? Because he might tell me the truth?"

"*. . . because he is dangerous. surely you sense that . . .*"

"All I sense when I'm near him is *your* fear."

". . . and you think i am afraid for me . . . ?"

Mia bit down on her tirade, stared at the not-cat sitting among the furs. All Mister Kindly had ever done was protect her. Chasing her nightmares away when she was a little girl. The nevernight phantoms of the puppy-choker who came to drown her. The scarecrows and shadows she'd seen inside the Philosopher's Stone.

"So I wait for the chronicler, then. There's bound to be a book in the athenaeum that holds the truth. It's only a matter of time until he finds it."

". . . you truly believe you will learn to master the shadows by reading a book . . . ?"

"Then what am I supposed to do?" she shouted.

". . . i have told you a thousand times, mia . . ."

She looked at her friend, curled there in her bed. Chill fingernails running down her spine. The sound of distant screaming echoing in her head. The image of a tear-streaked face. Hollow, frightened eyes. Blood.

". . . to master the darkness without, first you must face the darkness within . . ."

Breath coming quicker. Sweat on her skin. She rummaged in her britches, found her cigarillo case. Put one to her lips with shaking hands.

". . . it was not your fault, mia . . ."

"Shut up," she whispered.

". . . it was n—"

"SHUT UP!"

The girl hurled the silver case at the wall. Face twisted. The not-cat pressed his ears to his head. Shrunk down on himself and whispered.

". . . as it please you . . ."

Mia sighed. Closed her eyes and breathed. After long, silent minutes, she struck her flintbox and lit her cigarillo, drawing deep and sitting down on the bed. Watching the smoke wind in broken spirals through the gloom. Finally sighing.

"I'm becoming something of a bitch, aren't I?"

". . . becoming . . . ?"

She glanced at the cat as he chuckled, flicked ash in his general direction.

". . . this is all new to you. it cannot be easy . . ."

She dragged hard on the smoke, exhaled through her nostrils.

"It's not meant to be easy. But I can do this, Mister Kindly."

". . . i have no doubt. and i am with you to the end . . ."

"Really."

". . . really . . ."

Mia stayed awake, watching the cigarillo slowly burn down to nothing. Sitting in the dark with her thoughts. Mister Kindly was right; initiation should be her goal. All else was just chaff and fuckery. She wasn't the master at pockets that Ash or Jessamine was. And training with Tric wasn't helping her swordcraft the way it needed to. But her only match in venomcraft was Carlotta, and her current weakness in the Hall of Songs was something she could exploit. Like Mister Kindly and Mercurio had said, being underestimated was a weapon she could turn to advantage.

Time to start hedging my bets.

With her cigarillo dead, she lay back in her bed. Grateful the smoke had killed what was left of Tric on her skin. *Just the once*, she told herself. *Just to keep the dreams away.* Her thoughts turned slower as fatigue finally caught her, as sleep wrapped her in gentle arms, lashes fluttering against her cheeks. And finally she slept.

The not-cat sat beside her, waiting for the nightmares that came to call.

Ever watchful.

Ever hungry.

It did not wait long.

Before mornmeal, Mia rose from her bed and crept from her room. She made her way past the acolyte bedchambers, deeper into the Mountain. Enquiring politely from a passing figure in black, she was escorted down wending stairwells, into a chamber she'd never seen. The smell of dust and hay, camel and shit. And stepping out into a great cavern carved in the Mountain's guts, she realized where she was.

"Stables . . ."

The cavern was at least fifty feet high, great wooden pens holding two dozen snorting, snarling spit-machines. She could see Hands unloading a newly arrived wagon train, watering the beasts just come in from the sand. The wagons were piled high with goods from Last Hope and beyond. And there among the dust-clad Hands in desert red, Mia saw a face veiled in silk. Strawberry-blond curls. Dark, shining eyes.

"Naev!"

The Hand turned, eyes smiling. "Friend Mia."

Mia took her in a hug, returned with fondness. She could smell sweat on the woman's skin, the dirt and dust of a long road.

"Apologies for intruding," Mia said. "I know you must be weary. When I asked after you, I wasn't even sure you'd returned from Last Hope yet."

"Just arrived." The woman nodded. "All is well?"

"Well enough," Mia nodded. "Are you busy?"

". . . Somewhat. But Naev can spare a moment for her."

The woman stepped to a shadowed alcove, bringing Mia with her. Naev waited expectantly, shouts and camels bellowing in the background. Mia decided her friend was in a rush, and that, despite the first of Shahiid Aalea's golden rules, skipping the foreplay might be best in this situation.

"When we crossed blades in the Whisperwastes," Mia began, "before I called the Dark, at least . . . you had my measure. If I fought fair, you'd have bested me."

Naev nodded. No arrogance in her voice, simple pragmatism.

"She fights Orlani style. A little Caravaggio. Skilled enough. But there are many faces to bladework, and it seems she really knows only one."

"And you know many."

The woman's eyes twinkled. "Naev knows them all."

"Maybe you can help me, then."

"What does she need?"

"That depends."

"Upon?"

Mia smiled.

"Whether or not you can keep a secret."

SWITCH

Weeks passed in the Quiet Mountain, and not many of them were quiet at all.

The Hall of Songs rang with the tune of steel on steel. The sharp whistle of bowstrings and the thud of throwing knives. Though she proved a crack shot with a crossbow, Mia still took a beating almost every class. After their previous confrontation, she noticed Jessamine always wore the Trinity beneath her tunic, and the threat of it hung between them like a knife. But though Jess never failed to rub her nose in the dirt, Mia followed Mister Kindly's advice and kept her anger under lock and key. Focusing on training. Leaving pettiness to the petty. Seemingly bored by Mia's lack of spine, the redhead focused more of her attentions on Carlotta, who responded with her customary deadpan wit and dead-eyed stare.

Jessamine, however, wasn't the only one who noticed Mia's new resolve.

The mornlesson was Truths, but as Mia mooched into the hall with Ash and Lotti by her side, she noticed the great ironwood benches were pushed against the far walls, and much of the arkemical equipment had been stowed away. Spiderkiller stood in the room's center, pouches of differing colors in her hands.

"Acolytes," the Shahiid nodded. "Please gather behind me."

The group obeyed, forming a semicircle at the Shahiid's back.

"We have spent the last few months covering the creation of arkemical toxins, and the application thereof. But arkemy is not simply venomcraft, and it can assist you in your vocations as more than a simple tool of death."

Spiderkiller reached into a black leather pouch, produced a small globe, no bigger than her thumbnail. It was perfectly smooth, buffed to a high gloss.

"Wyrdglass," she explained. "Arkemical vapors, held in a solid state by a process of my own creation. A sharp physical jolt will disrupt this process, restoring the compound to its gaseous state, but unlike cruder vapor-based weaponry, wyrdglass leaves no trace. No shards or stoppers to know you were there. The glass itself *is* the compound."

The Shahiid passed the globe around the assembled acolytes. It was heavier than Mia expected, cool to the touch.

"I have developed a number of varieties," Spiderkiller offered. "The first is onyx."

The Shahiid hurled a fistful of the black globes at the floor. They struck with a dozen tiny pops, and in a heartbeat, a thick cloud of swirling smoke was rising from the stone. It was oily, heavy as fog, and black as the night above the Sky Altar.

"Useful for diversions and conducting defensive maneuvers."

Spiderkiller reached into another pouch, fished out three white wyrdglass globes, and hurled them against the far wall. Again, the globes burst into a heavy smoke, sinking slowly to the floor. Mia found it hard to believe so much vapor could be condensed into something so small.

"Pearl for toxins. Most commonly sedatives such as Swoon, though I have crafted more lethal variants from aspira. And finally," the Shahiid produced a globe of red wyrdglass, and flashed an uncharacteristic smile. "Ruby. A personal favorite."

Spiderkiller hurled the globe at another wall, and with a crackling boom, a sphere of white-hot fire bloomed against the stone. The acolytes flinched, eyes wide, staring at the fist-sized chunk that had been taken out of the granite.

"Capable of perforating plate armor, and pulverizing the flesh within."

Spiderkiller handed a bunch of the onyx wyrdglass globes to the acolytes, motioned at the far wall.

"Now. You try."

Smiling to each other, the acolytes stepped up and began hurling the wyrdglass at the stone. Dozens of small pops rang out in the hall, black smoke rising at the far end of the room. Spiderkiller gave Hush and Tric a ruby globe each, black lips curling as bright explosions tore the air. Once the smoke cleared, the acolytes sat at their benches and Spiderkiller turned to the charboard, explaining wyrdglass's basic properties.

Mia was furiously scribbling notes when Ash whispered in her ear.

"So. Question."

"It's not the one about where babes come from, is it?" Mia muttered. "Because I don't think our friendship is ready for that."

"Why are you eating Red's shit?"

Mia paused in her scribbling, glanced up from her notes.

"I'm not eating anyone's shit," she whispered.

"She's beating you like a training dummy in Songs. Yesterturn she near knocked you off your feet in the Sky Altar, and when she chewed at you, you just turned away."

Mia looked across the hall to Jessamine, working alongside Diamo. The red-head flashed Mia a smile as toxic as anything Spiderkiller had yet brewed.

"It's not like you, Corvere."

"It's nothing."

"Bollocks."

Mia glanced to Spiderkiller, who was still working at the charboard.

"She . . ."

Mia chewed her lip. Looked to Ashlinn. She didn't like asking for help. Didn't like needing anybody. But Ash was a decent sort, despite her habit of filching anything that wasn't bolted to the floor. And it wasn't like she was bleating to the Ministry about it . . .

"She stole the Trinity."

Ash blinked in confusion.

"From Mouser's hall," Mia hissed. "The medallion that made me puke my guts up that turn he dressed as a priest."

Ash raised one eyebrow. "You told me that was some bad herring, Corvere."

"Aye, well, it was nice of you to pretend to believe me."

The blond girl scowled at Jessamine.

"So it was the Trinity that shook you so?"

Mia lowered her voice further. "Not sure why. Something to do with being darkin, I think. Jessamine pulled it on me in the Hall of Songs. Felt like I was about to croak it."

Ash noted the gold chain about Jessamine's neck, almost hidden by her shirt.

"That sneaky little c—"

A globe of onyx wyrdglass burst on the desk in front of them. Both girls were consumed in a thick, rolling cloud of black smoke, Ash falling back off her stool. The rest of the acolytes guffawed, the girls coughed and sputtered, waving to clear the air. As the smoke slowly dissipated, Mia found herself met with Spiderkiller's glare.

"Acolyte Ashlinn. Acolyte Mia. You have something to contribute to the lesson?"

"No, Shahiid," Mia mumbled.

"Then you believe clucking like a pair of hens will assist me in imparting it?"

"No, Shahiid," Ash said, with her best hangdog expression.*

"Then I'll thank you to listen in silence. The next globe I hurl will be a different color."

Spiderkiller hefted the bag of ruby wyrdglass, glanced at the other acolytes. Each returned to their note-taking with a fury that would shame an Ironscribe. Silence reigned for the rest of the morn. But at the lesson's end, Ash stared hard at Jessamine.

Cracked her knuckles.

And then she gave Mia a wink.

T wo turns later, a short time after evemeal, Mia was working on Spiderkiller's formula. Every eve, she'd hunch over her notes and try to untangle the puzzle. It seemed impossible: every antidote for one component seemed to increase the efficacy of another. But solving the riddle was Mia's best chance at finishing top of hall, and lurking in her room meant there was little chance of running into Jessamine. She was cursing the air blue and seriously considering lighting her notes on fire when she heard lockpicks at her door.

"Maw's teeth, can't she just bloody knock?"

The girl extricated herself from her tangled pile of venomlore and padded to the door, opening it with a twist and finding Ashlinn crouched outside her room.

"Do your knuckles not work or something?" Mia asked.

Ash gave Mia the knuckles with both hands, shaking them in her face.

---

*Ashlinn's best hangdog expression could make a legitimate hangdog quit its job, pack its bags, and move somewhere quieter to raise chickens.

"Bloody hilarious, you," Mia smiled. "What do you need?"

"Not what I need." Ash straightened with a wink. "It's what I can give you."

"And what's that?"

"Jessamine's Trinity."

Ash yelped as Mia grabbed her collar, dragged her inside, and shut the door.

"Maw's teeth, take a breath, Corvere . . ."

"You stole it?" Mia hissed.

"Not yet." Ash glanced to the pile of notes covering Mia's bed. "But I'm about to, if you'd rather do something useful with your time."

"She never takes it off, Ash. I've seen her wearing it in the damned bath."

"Speaking of, I couldn't help noticing those bite marks on your inner thighs a few turns back . . ."

Mia raised an eyebrow. "You've been checking on my inner thighs in the bath?"

Ash shrugged. "No harm in looking."

"Verdict?"

"Eh. I've seen better."

Mia raised the knuckles in her friend's face. "O, look, mine work too."

"Aye, aye, very good." Ash rolled her eyes. "Point is, she *does* take it off. She has to when she makes the Blood Walk, because it's made of . . . help me out here . . ."

"Metal," Mia breathed.

"Huzzah! She can be taught!"

"Fuck you."

"Fair warning, I'm not much of a biter . . ."

"Ash, I swear to the Mother—"

"*Regardless*," Ash interrupted, "I happen to know Jessamine and a few of the others just headed off for another round of Squeeze the Secret in Godsgrave. So at this very second, all her belongings are sitting neatly in the alcoves near Adonai's pool."

". . . You want to steal from the speaker's chambers?"

Ashlinn simply grinned in response.

"Jessamine will know it's gone as soon as she gets back," Mia pointed out. "And she'd have to be a special shade of dense to not figure out it was *me* who took it."

From her britches, Ashlinn dragged out three gold circles on a glittering chain.

"Jessamine's not going to know a thing, Corvere."

Mia stared at the medallion, spinning and gleaming in the dull light. Another Trinity. Aside from the precious metal it was wrought of, which might buy a small house in one of the fancier areas of the 'Grave, it seemed perfectly ordinary. Mia didn't feel at all sickened in its presence—obviously it had never been blessed by one of Aa's believers. But still, the sight of it . . .

"Where'd you get that?"

"Mouser's costumes. He's got a strange love of priest's dresses, that one. I found some women's underthings in his collection too." Ash shrugged, stuffed the Trinity back in her pants. "So. You coming mischief-making, or do you have an appointment with Tricky in the hope of earning some more bite marks?"

Mia opened her mouth to begin denials. Ashlinn's raised eyebrow told her not to bother. And with a sigh, Mia opened the door, waved to the corridor beyond.

"That's the spirit," Ash grinned.

The blood stink grew heavy, the air heavier still as the girls crept into the Mountain's depths. Mister Kindly swallowed her fear as always, but the sensible part of Mia's brain was still screaming that this was a sensationally bad idea.

"This is a sensationally bad idea, Ash."

"So you said. About twenty times now."

"You remember what Marielle did to Hush?"

"Maw's teeth, Corvere. When my da got tortured in the Thorn Towers of Elai, they chopped his bollocks off and fed them to the scabdogs. What's your excuse?"

"For what?"

"Um, your complete lack of balls?"

Mia waved at her breasts. "Um, you do see these, don't you?"

"All right, all right," Ash growled. "Bad analogy."

They reached the level of Adonai's chambers. Mia took Ash's hand, and just as she'd done with Tric in the athenaeum, she reached into the dark around her. A dark that had never known the touch of the suns. She could feel the power in it. The power in her. Weaving her fingers through the gloom, she pulled her cloak of shadows about the pair of them, and they faded from sight like smoke on the breeze.

"I can't see a bloody thing under this," Ash hissed.

"I told you, being darkin isn't all that impressive. Just stay close."

The pair crept slowly down the corridor, dim points of arkemical illumination their only guides. But finally, drawn to the heavy, copper stink, they found Adonai's chamber. Lurking at the threshold, Mia and Ash squinted inside. Adonai was knelt at the head of the pool, gazing into the blood, skin scrawled with scarlet glyphs. As usual, the speaker would keep his vigil until every acolyte had returned from the 'Grave.

Aalea had explained that a few drops of Adonai's blood were mixed into the pools at the Porkery and other Red Church chapels. Through that blood, the speaker could *feel* when someone entered the pool, and if he willed it, allow them to make the Walk back. He was like a spider at the center of a vast, scarlet web, his own essence serving as the threads. Mia still found herself amazed by it all—next to Adonai, her little parlor tricks with shadows seemed a feeble sort of magik indeed. If Consul Scaeva and the Luminatii ever discovered the Red Church had this kind of power . . .

"All right," Ash whispered. "Here's the plan. You go in and distract him. And while he's dazzled by you, I hit the alcoves and snatch the Trinity."

"Dazzled by me?" Mia hissed. "How do I manage that?"

"I don't know, you're the saucy one. Use your wiles, woman."

Mia gawped, momentarily losing the power of speech.

". . . Maw's teeth, Ash. 'Use my wiles'? *That's* your plan?"

"Well, I don't know. You've been studying with Aalea longer than any of us. Use that slinky walk you like so much. Get your girls out or somesuch."

"Get my . . ."

Mia flapped her lips awhile, flabbergasted.

"Use your words," Ash sighed.

"Here's some words," Mia finally managed. "Why don't *you* distract Adonai, and *I*—the girl who I might point out, is turning us near *fucking invisible* at this very second—go and snatch the Trinity instead?"

"And how are you going to touch it without spewing fountains, O, invisible one?"

Mia opened her mouth to reply. Closed it again. Sighed.

"Good point."

Ash nodded. Waited expectantly.

"Well, go on, then."

Mia rolled her eyes. Threw off the shadowcloak. "Fine."

She stood, knocked on the wall, and stepped into Adonai's chamber.

"Speaker?"

Adonai didn't open his eyes, talking like a man in a dream.

"Good eve, Acolyte. Thou art bound for the city? Shahiid Aalea sent no word."

"No. Apologies." Mia walked into the chamber, searching desperately for some kind of ruse. "I . . . wished to speak to you."

"And what shall ye speak about, pray tell?"

Mia's eyes roamed the maps carved on the walls. The shattered isles of Godsgrave. The obsidian fortress of Carrion Hall. The port of Farrow. Glyphs were scrawled in blood among the carvings, shifting and blurring if she looked at them too long. From this room, the Red Church could touch any city in the Republic.

Her eyes settled on a map she didn't recognize, near hidden in the shifting shadows. A great, sprawling metropolis, grander than Godsgrave, its contours and streets unlike anything she'd seen.

"Where is that?" she asked. "I've never seen it before."

"Nor shall ye."

Mia looked to Adonai, the question plain in her gaze. Letting the silence speak, as Aalea had taught her. But Adonai still hadn't opened his eyes, his lips twisted in that beautiful, lazy smile. The speaker, it seemed, knew Aalea's craft also.

"Can you tell me why not?" Mia finally asked.

"It is gone," Adonai replied.

"What was its name?"

"Ur Shuum."

"That's Ashkahi," Mia said. "It means *First City*."

Adonai sighed, radiating boredom. "Thou art not here for a lesson in geography, little darkin. Speak thy business and be away, afore my hunger bests my patience."

Mia swallowed her disgust, wondering where the blood Adonai drank actually came from. She didn't dare look over her shoulder to see if Ashlinn was in the room yet. Stepping nearer to the speaker, she blocked his eyeline to the alcoves—should he ever bother opening them. This close, she could see the veins beneath his pale skin, etched in sky blue. His angular cheekbones, and long, fluttering lashes and O, so clever fingers weaving in the air. Mia wondered if he was born this beautiful, or if his sister had woven him so. And there, she stumbled on a topic that might prove a distraction . . .

"I want to speak to you about Naev."

Adonai's eyes opened. The whites were slicked with a thin scarlet film, the irises bright pink. Ever so slowly, the speaker turned his head, settled his gaze on Mia. She felt his stare like a leaden weight. Pinned like a fly in his scarlet web.

"Naev," Adonai repeated.

The air grew heavier, the waves in the blood pool churning just a touch harder. For the first time, Mia noticed Adonai didn't seem to blink.

"I saved her life in the Whisperwastes."

"This I know, Acolyte."

"I saw her face. What Marielle did to her. It's not right, Adonai."

"Thou art a fine one to speak of right and wrong, little murderer."

". . . I beg your pardon?"

"Not my pardon thou shouldst beg," Adonai smiled. "Not I whose corpse ye mutilated to purchase thy pew at this altar, aye?"

Mia's jaw clenched. "The man I killed to be here was a murderer himself. Hundreds of people. Thousands, maybe. He hung my father. He deserved it. Every inch of it."

"And what of the others?"

Mia blinked. "Others?"

Adonai climbed to his feet, lazy, languid. Stepping close enough to Mia that she could feel the heat on his skin. He leaned in close, his bone-white fringe brushing against her brow. Lips that begged to be kissed just a breath from hers, wet with blood. For a dizzying moment, she thought he was about to do just that, and she found her pulse racing, her belly thrilled at the thought. But instead, he inhaled, breathing deep, eyelids fluttering closed. And as he spoke, he smiled.

"I can smell their blood on you, little darkin."

Mia forced herself not to flinch. Nor to back away.

"You have your sister's ear," she said. "She loves you, Adonai."

"And I, her. As the Light loved the Dark."

"But Naev loves you too. She doesn't deserve to suffer for it."

The speaker placed his thumb on her chin. Tilting her head back, ever so slightly. Mia imagined those ruby lips caressing her skin, his teeth nipping at her throat. She suppressed a shiver. Finding it harder and harder to breathe.

"I have never tasted one of your kind before . . . ," he whispered.

Adonai's lips twisted in another honey-sweet smile. But staring into his eyes, Mia realized there was nothing behind them. This was all just a game to him, and she, just momentary distraction. His was only a skin-deep beauty, the vanity leaked through to his bones, just as twisted and rotten inside as his sister was out. And though Naev might have loved him—though Mia could see how any woman might—she knew that aside from Marielle, Adonai had no love for anyone but himself.

Ever so gently, Mia pushed his hand away.

"I'll thank you to not touch me, Speaker."

Adonai smiled wider. "But wouldst thou thank me also, if I did?"

Would I?

The shadows at Mia's feet shivered as the blood in the pool grew more agitated. Her eyes narrowed, her teeth gritted. And just as the heat in the room became unbearable, just as the pool began crashing and splashing, Mia heard Ashlinn's voice.

"Maw's teeth, *there* you are."

Mia drew away from the speaker, saw Ashlinn at the doorway.

"I've been looking everywhere for you, Corvere. We're supposed to be working on Spiderkiller's lesson." Ash stepped into the room, bowed low. "Apologies, Speaker. Might I have my learned colleague back? She'd forget her damn shadow if it wasn't nailed to her feet."

Adonai's smile fell away like winter leaves.

"She may go where she pleases." A sigh. "I care not."

Adonai returned to his knees, eyes back on the pool. Dismissing Mia without so much as a word. Ash grabbed her hand, hauled her from the room. Dragging her down the corridor, stopping only once out of sight and earshot of the speaker's chamber.

"'Byss and blood," Ash breathed. "I honestly thought he was going to try a snog for a minute."

"Well, you *did* tell me to distract him," Mia said. "Now tell me it worked."

Ashlinn reached into her britches and drew out a length of gold chain. Mia saw a flare of light, flinching as if scalded, hand to her eyes. "Maw's teeth, put it back in your pants."

"You really do leave the door open for me, don't you?"

Ash tucked the medallion back into her britches, patted Mia's shoulder. The girl opened her eyes tentatively, relaxing once she knew the Trinity was out of sight.

"You swapped it for the other?"

Ash nodded. "Jess will be none the wiser. Until next time she pulls it on you, that is. That'll be your signal to kick her in the curlies." Ash patted her leathers. "I'll take care of this thing. Put it somewhere *no one* is going to get hold of it again."

"The perfect crime," Mia smiled.

"If it was perfect, it'd end with me getting cake."

"It's not ninebells yet." Mia offered her arm. "Kitchen is still open?"

"See, I knew I liked you for a reason, Corvere."

Arm in arm, the girls strolled into the dark.

CHAPTER 24

FRICTION

The turns wore on.

Unsurprisingly, Ashlinn was still leading the pack in Mouser's contest, though Hush was closing the gap from second. In light of the heightened competition, Mia was grateful her friend had taken the time to help her steal something that wouldn't count toward the official tally. Acolytes were growing bolder, and trickier items off the list were being filched now, rather than simple trinkets. Still, if Mia were a gambler, she'd have staked her fortune that Ash would finish the year top of Pockets.

Though if Mia actually *had* a fortune, Ash would've likely stolen it by now, friends or no . . .

Mouser's lessons were becoming as eclectic and eccentric as the Shahiid himself. He devoted several hours a week to teaching what he called Tongueless,* and insisted all conversations in his hall be conducted in the language thereafter. In another lesson, Mouser wheeled a wooden tank into the Hall of Pockets. It was filled with dirty water, a handful of lockpicks scattered on the bottom. He proceeded to bind the acolytes' hands and feet with leaden manacles and push them in one by one.

To his credit, the Shahiid seemed rather pleased nobody drowned.

Lessons in the Hall of Masks were more subtle, and in truth, far more enjoyable. The acolytes were still sent out regularly into Godsgrave, and Mia spent a dozen nevernights lurking in various taverna, working on her wordcraft and plying folk with drink and pretty smiles. She had two young and rather handsome members of the Administratii on a string, and overheard some juicy gossip in a portside brothel about a violent coup among the local braavi. Aalea

---

*A language spoken entirely in gestures of the hands, fingers, and face. Utilized by a master, a conversation in Tongueless can appear as little more than a series of tics, winks, and subtle nods, completely unremarkable to anyone not trained in the art.

Newer practitioners often appear to be pulling silly faces in the midst of a seizure, but practice makes perfect, as they say.

accepted Mia's new secrets with a smile and a kiss to each cheek. And if she noticed a change in Mia after the eve she spent in Tric's bed, the Shahiid politely refused to comment.

In the turns after that night, Mia had resisted the impulse to smile at the boy over mornmeal or stare overlong during lessons. In the interests of keeping her distance, she'd told him she needed no more lessons in bladework. Mia knew letting anything more grow between them would be stupid, and for his part, Tric at least pretended to understand. Still, sometimes she'd catch him staring from the corner of her eye. At night, alone in her room, she'd slip her hand between her legs and try not to picture his face. She succeeded, some of the time.

As time wore on and initiation loomed, testing intensified. Mia had her vendetta against Scaeva and his dogs to keep her focused on her lessons, but every acolyte knew what was at stake. Another of their number had been killed since the Great Tithe masquerade; a boy named Leonis, who had his throat crushed by a stray swing in the Hall of Songs and suffocated before Marielle could be summoned.

Of the twenty-nine acolytes who'd started training, only fifteen remained. And then came the incident ever after referred to as "the Blue Morning."

It began as crises usually did; with Mister Kindly's now familiar whisper.

"... beware ..."

Opening her eyes, Mia drew her stiletto, instantly awake. She could hear a faint hissing noise. Looking up, she noticed one of the stones in the ceiling above her bed had slid away, and a thin vapor was seeping into her chamber. It danced in the air like cigarillo smoke, slow and vaguely blue.

Crouching low, Mia scrambled to her door and twisted the key, only to find the lock held fast. Ever wary of needletraps since Mouser and Spiderkiller's earlier lessons, she slipped on a heavy leather glove, rattled the handle. It refused to budge.

"Well, shit."

"... mia ..."

She glanced over her shoulder, saw more of the bluish vapor trickling in. The flow was thickening, the air growing hazy. Mia could taste something acrid on the back of her tongue. Her eyes starting to burn. The symptoms, at least, she knew by rote.

"Aspira ...," she breathed.

"... another test ..."

"And I was planning on sleeping in."

She grabbed a shirt off the floor, doused it in water from her nightstand,

and wrapped it about her face. Aspira induced paralysis and death by slow suffocation. It was heavier than air, and nonflammable in gaseous form. Mia knew the antidote well, though she had none of the materials to make it. But a damp rag over her mouth would hold the vapor at bay for a few minutes at least; long enough to ponder an escape.

Her eyes scanned the room, mind racing.

The key wouldn't budge, and slamming her shoulder against her door only resulted in a bruise. The hinges were affixed with iron nails; she could pry them out, but that would take *time*, and more than a few minutes' exposure to aspira would end with a quiet service in the Hall of Eulogies and an unmarked tomb.

Pressing her cheek to the floor, she peered under her door. She could hear coughing. The sounds of heavy objects being slammed against wood. Faint cries. Cool, fresh air seeped in through the crack, along with the sounds of growing panic. If the acolytes failed to escape their rooms, every single one of them was going to die.

"Maw's teeth, they're not playing about anymore," she hissed.

"*. . . the pressure will only increase between now and initiation . . .*"

Mia caught her breath.

Looking at the crack beneath her door. The hole in the ceiling.

"Pressure," she whispered.

She grabbed a bottle of whiskey off her nightstand, poured it onto the plush gray fur covering her bed. Snatching up her cigarillos and striking her flintbox, she touched it to the bed and stepped back. With a dull *whump*, the goldwine burst into flame. Mia crouched near the door, watching the fire catch, her bed soon burning merrily.

"*. . . there may be a metaphor in here somewhere . . .*"

The temperature rose, hot air and smoke and aspira vapor all warming in the blaze, sucked back up through the hole in the ceiling. Mia snatched up one of the dozen knives littering the room, and dug it into the first nail securing the hinges to her door.

The bed was a bright, crackling ball of flame now. Smoke was being drawn up into the ceiling along with the aspira, but Mia's eyes were still watering, her throat burning. One by one, she pried the nails free, dropping them to the floor with dull metallic *plunks*. Finally, enough were loose that the door was barely secured, and a few running kicks saw it burst its remaining anchors and sail into the corridor.

Mia stumbled free, coughing, blinking tears from her eyes. Spiderkiller and Mouser were standing at the end of the hall. The Shahiid of Pockets was marking off names in a leather-bound ledger. The dour Shahiid of Truths favored Mia with a smile.

"Mornmeal will be served in the Sky Altar in fifteen minutes, Acolyte," she said.

Mia caught her breath, stepping aside as two Hands entered her room to douse her bed. She saw Carlotta's room was open, the lock shattered like glass. Osrik's door was a charred ruin. A long tube of rolled-up parchment protruded from under Hush's door, the sound of steady breathing spilling from its mouth. As she watched, the apparently jammed lock on Ashlinn's door still somehow clicked open, and the girl sauntered out into the corridor, pocketing her picks with a wink.

"Morning, Corvere," she grinned.

Mia's eyes found Tric's door, relieved that it was already ajar. Leaving the stink of aspira and smoke behind, she and Ash trudged up to the Sky Altar, found Tric and Osrik already sitting at table with Carlotta. Tric was watching the stairs, visibly brightening when he saw Mia. Lotti was bent over a leather-bound book, scribbling notes and asking Osrik quiet questions. The boy was leaning close, radiating easy charm, his lips curled in a handsome smile.

Fetching breakfast, Ash and Mia sat down beside the trio. A glance told Mia that Carlotta was working on some kind of poison, though oddly, it didn't seem related to Spiderkiller's formula. Her notes were written in code—looked to be some variant of the Elberti sequence mixed with homebrew.

Clever work for a former slavegirl.

"Well, I'm not surprised to find Lotti up here first. If it's venom, she knows it." Ash glanced at Tric. "But how the 'byss did you get out so quick, Tricky?"

"O, ye of little faith."

"Let me guess. Bashed the door down with your head?"

"Didn't have to," Tric waggled his eyebrows. "I smelled the aspira before they had a chance to jam the locks. Poked my head into the corridor to see what was happening, Mouser called me a rude word in Tongueless and sent me up here."

Ashlinn grinned. "Quite a nose you've got there, Tricky."

Tric shrugged, glanced to Mia. "How'd you manage it?"

Mia was watching the stairwell. More acolytes were filing into the Sky Altar now. Jessamine, Hush, Diamo, Marcellus . . . but there were still half a dozen acolytes missing. Ash was already joking about it, but downstairs, some of their number were likely dying. People they knew. People who . . .

She realized the others were looking at her expectantly, waiting for the particulars of her escape.

"Pressure differential," she explained. "Hot vapor rises through the hole in the ceiling. Draft under the door brings in fresh air. Simple convection, outlined by Micades back in fourteen . . ."

Mia's voice died beneath three blank stares.

"She set fire to her bed," Carlotta finally offered, not glancing up from her notes.

Ash looked between Mia and Tric. Opened her mouth to speak as Mia cut her off.

"Not. A. Fucking. Word."

With a knowing grin, Ash turned back to her meal.

Three turns later, Mia was sitting on her brand-new bed, the charred smell of the old one still hanging vaguely in the air. Another of their number had perished during the Blue Morning—a quiet lad named Tanith who'd honestly never been much of a master of Truths. Another unmarked tomb in the Hall of Eulogies.

Another acolyte who would never again see the suns.

Mia was surrounded by notes, working again on Spiderkiller's formula. Cigarillo propped on her lips, she pored over *Arkemical Truths* and the dozen tomes the Shahiid had given her novices. Mia had to admire the beauty of Spiderkiller's quandary—trying to solve it was like trying to find a single piece of hay in a stack of poisoned needles. But still, she delighted in the riddle. Like that little girl and her puzzle box. Her mother's voice ringing in her head.

"Beauty you're born with, but brains you earn."

Don't look.

". . . you will miss dinner, mia . . ."

"Yes, Father."

". . . your stomach seems to be growling some forgotten dialect of ashkahi . . ."

She looked up from her notes, the formulae still dancing in the air. Put a hand to her rumbling belly. The answer was there, she knew it. But still tantalizingly out of reach.

"All right. This will keep."

The Sky Altar was filled with acolytes, mouthwatering smells wafting from the bustling kitchens. The Shahiid weren't present—no doubt at some faculty gathering to discuss progress among the novices—but black-robed Hands bustled about, serving wine and clearing away crockery.

Mia heaped a plate with roast lamb and honeyed greens, plopped down beside Ash and Carlotta, and started shoveling her meal down without pause.

Lotti was busy scribbling in her notebook. Ash was talking about a bar brawl she'd seen when the girls were in Godsgrave looking for secrets; a few malcontents had spoken against Consul Scaeva and his "emergency powers" and had been set upon by half a dozen braavi thugs who apparently found the consul's rule more than satisfactory.*

"City seems angry," Ash declared around a mouthful of lamb.

Mia nodded. "More Luminatii on the streets than I've ever seen."

"Prettier than the soldier boys I'm used to seeing in Carrion Hall, too."

"One-track mind, Järnheim."

The girl grinned, waggled her eyebrows as her brother studiously ignored her. Mia looked to Carlotta, still busy scribbling notes.

"How goes it?" Mia asked.

"Slowly," the girl murmured, scanning the page. "Just when I think I have the tiger by the tail, it turns and bites me. But I'm close. Very close, I think."

Mia's belly did a flip. If Lotti beat her to the punch in Spiderkiller's contest . . .

"You think it's wise to bring those notes to dinner?" Osrik asked.

"I should leave them in my room so Dona Busyfingers here can lift them?"

Carlotta raised an eyebrow at Ash. The girl had scored dozens of points in Mouser's game by filching items and jewelry from other acolytes. Mia knew it

---

* The braavi are a loose collective of gangs that run much of the criminal undertakings in Godsgrave—prostitution, larceny, and organized violence. For hundreds of years, the braavi were a thorn in the sides of various Itreyan kings, and even after the Republic was formed, they remained dug into the Nethers of Godsgrave like particularly stubborn ticks. Their predations wore at trade, cut into profits, and it seemed no amount of Luminatii raids could permanently remove them.

It was a newly elected senator, Julius Scaeva, who first proposed the notion of giving more powerful braavi gangs—such as those who control the docks and warehouse districts of Godsgrave—an official stipend from the Republic's coffers. He argued that it would be cheaper to pay the thugs than organize an official police force to combat them, and that the gangs themselves would benefit from a period of stability. Scaeva financed the first payment from his own personal fortune, and was rewarded virtually overnight with an astonishing drop in the crime rates of the Nethers. This saw his popularity skyrocket—among the merchants who plied trade through the docks, the citizens who had previously been caught up in the wars between the Luminatii and braavi, and from the thugs themselves, who rather enjoyed being paid for simply getting paid. It was after this coup that Scaeva first came to be known among the mob as "Senatum Populiis"—the People's Senator.

The names his opponents called him behind closed doors, of course, were far less flattering.

But only when the doors were *firmly* closed.

was nothing personal, but she made damn sure to stay out of Ash's reach when she could. Even Osrik sat away from striking range at dinner.

Ash tried to muster protest around her mouthful, almost choked herself, and finally settled for raising the knuckles.

"As I say"—Carlotta turned back to Mia—"safer to keep them clo—"

"*Look out!*"

With a curse and a crash, a passing Hand stumbled and fell onto Carlotta and Mia, dropping his laden tray with a bang. A half-filled jug and dirty dishes smashed over the table, splashing the acolytes with leftovers and wine. Carlotta snatched up her notes as the liquor soaked them through, the ink running and blurring. She untangled herself from the horrified servant, sodden pages crumpled in her fist. And as the Hand asked forgiveness, she stood, looking at the tall Itreyan boy who'd knocked the servant over.

Diamo.

"Terribly sorry," he said, helping the Hand to his feet. "My fault entirely."

Carlotta gave the boy her dead-eye stare, not even blinking.

"You did that on purpose," she said softly.

"An accident, Mi Dona, I assure you."

Mia heard soft laughter. Turning, she saw Jessamine watching the proceedings with a poison smile. Carlotta heard the sound too, staring as Jess raised her glass in a toast. Soaked papers in hand, Lotti walked calmly over to stand before the redhead.

"My notes are ruined," she reported.

"I hope they weren't important?" Jessamine smirked. "You're not fool enough to bring your venomcraft to the table, are you, little slavegirl?"

Carlotta's hand rose to the cheek where her arkemical brand used to be.

"No man owns me," she said softly.

"*I'll* own you if you don't step away, little bookworm. Spiderkiller's not here to save you now." Jess turned back to her meal with a sneer. "Now take your precious notes and go weep in a corner before I gift you a new hole."

Diamo's face split in a smug grin. Mia and Ashlinn shared a pained glance. It was no secret Jessamine was one of Solis's favorites, and one of the most skilled acolytes in the Hall of Songs. Carlotta was book smart, but no match for Jess in a knock-down scrap. The redhead was just rubbing Lotti's nose in it now, knowing the other girl was too smart and even-tempered to start a fight she couldn't win.

Carlotta looked at the acolytes around her.

Crumpled her notes in her hand.

"I've a better notion about what to do with them," she murmured.

And drawing back her fist, Lotti slammed it into Jessamine's jaw.

The redhead flew back off her chair, a look of almost comic shock on her face. Lotti fell atop her, flailing and spitting, her usually stoic facade shattered to pieces. She grabbed Jessamine's throat, slammed her head back against the stone, and proceeded to try and *feed* the girl her sodden notes. The pair tumbled about in a flurry of curses and sopping pages. Jessamine landed a hook on Carlotta's jaw, Lotti smashed her notes into the redhead's nose, the wet crunch making Mia wince.

There were no Shahiid present—nobody to break up the brawl. Diamo seemed to arrive at the same conclusion Mia and Ash did, stepping into the fray and pulling Carlotta and Jessamine apart. Lotti was thrashing and bucking, cursing hard enough to make the most hardened sailor give up the game and become an Ironpriest. But Jessamine was insane with rage, face twisted, nose gushing, slicking her lips and chin with blood. She clawed at the air, bucking in Diamo's grip, eyes locked on Carlotta.

"You're dead, bitch," she spat. "You hear me? *Dead!*"

"Let her go!" Carlotta roared at Diamo. "Let her go!"

"I'm going to feed you your fucking heart! I'm going to g—"

"ENOUGH!"

The bellow brought stillness to the seething mass of acolytes, and all eyes turned. Mia saw Ash's brother Osrik standing on the bench, cheeks blotched with rage.

"What in the Maw's name is wrong with you two? We're disciples of Niah, not fucking braavi. We stand in the house of a *goddess*. Show some damned respect!"

Osrik's tirade seemed to knock the worst of the heat from Carlotta. Mia and Ash were hanging on to an arm each, slowly loosing their grips. Diamo eased off Jessamine, and with a final, poisonous glance, the girl wiped the blood from her chin and sat back at table, eating as if nothing had happened. Cold and hard as a barrel of ice.

Mia and Ash helped Carlotta gather her scattered notes. The trio were crouched over the wreckage, Carlotta trying to arrange the pages into some sort of order. Her work was a shambles, soaked to ruin in places. Her shoulders were slumped, her usually stoic facade in tatters. Weeks of labor undone in a moment. Mia found herself feeling sorry for the girl. Lotti was sharp as a razor, and good company to boot. Next to Ash, the girl was as close to a friend as any she really had in these halls.

"Don't trouble yourself about what that bitch said," Ash whispered, glancing at Carlotta's flawless cheek. "That's not who you are anymore."

"It was never who I was."

Carlotta's hands fell still. Her stare growing clouded.

"It was just who they made me."

Mia threw Ash a warning glance, thinking it best to leave the sore spot alone. Gathering more pages, she handed them to Lotti along with a change of subject.

"I keep my notes in my room," she said. "I'm perhaps not as far along as you, but you can borrow them if you like."

Carlotta blinked. Seeming to return from whatever memory she was lost in, her mask locking back into place. She spared Mia a small smile.

"I'll be all right. I've memorized much of it. I'll ask Spiderkiller for permission to work late in the hall. Should be able to catch the rest up if I miss a little sleep. So my thanks for the offer, but I'm still going to kick your arse, Corvere."

"Be careful," Ash warned. "There's someone who wants to kick yours worse."

Carlotta glanced at Jessamine. The girl was calmly eating her meal, acting as if she had her nose punched bloody all the time. Showing no pain. No weakness. Jess was an insufferable cow, but Mia had to admit it: the girl had stones.

"Let her try," Carlotta said.

Lotti glanced over her shoulder, looking Osrik up and down. The boy had resumed his place at table after his tirade, scowling at the post-brawl mess. "You know, your brother's a bit of all right when he gets all shouty, Ashlinn."

"O, Black Mother, shut your mouth before I spew."

Carlotta rose and padded over to Osrik, spoke to him quietly, sodden notebook in hand. Oz smiled his handsome smile, fingertips brushing Lotti's own.

Mia waggled her eyebrows at Ash. "They've been getting cozy. I saw them working together on some concoction a few turns back. And they seem to get paired up in Truths an awful lot."

Ash ballooned her cheeks, pretended to vomit under the table.

Mia smirked, but inside, she found herself more than a little uneasy. Initiation was creeping closer. Friction was rising. Knives were out. The knowledge that not everyone would become a Blade hung between every breath, the idea that fellow acolytes were competition coloring every moment. It'd become easy to think that way. Seeing their fellows drop by the wayside, one by one. Every death turning them a little colder. The Church's tests were becoming more dangerous, the Ministry's regard for the acolytes' lives ever more cavalier. Mia knew it was idiocy to worry about anyone but herself.

That was the point, she supposed. What was it Naev had said?

This place gives much. But it takes much more.

Stripping away the empathy. The pity. Piece by piece. Death by death.

And what will be left in the end?

Mia looked about the Sky Altar. The faces. The bloodstains. The shadows.

Blades, she realized.

Blades.

CHAPTER 25

SKIN

Two weeks later, everything began to change.

The flock was gathered for mornmeal as usual. Mia's head was fuzzy after hours working on Spiderkiller's formula. Carlotta spent the entire meal working in her salvaged notebook on the Shahiid's quandary, barely speaking a word. She'd been pulling late hours in the Hall of Truths to make up for the destruction of her work, her eyes bloodshot and bruised. And though Lotti didn't speak of it, her feud with Jessamine hung in the air like poison. Ashlinn filled the gaps with talk about some new beau she'd found last trip to Godsgrave; a senator's son who apparently talked about his father's business in his sleep.

As the acolytes were shuffling from the Sky Altar, Mia saw Shahiid Aalea take Tric aside, speak to him in hushed tones. Beneath the ink, Mia saw the boy's face visibly pale. He seemed set to argue, but Aalea cut his protests off at the knees with a smile as sharp as gravebone.

The turn's lesson was in the Hall of Songs, and Solis had been focusing on the art of ranged weaponry over the last few lessons. A series of strawman targets were suspended from the ceiling by oiled iron chains. Standing an acolyte in the sparring circle, Solis equipped them with crossbows or throwing knives, and instructed their fellows to swing the targets at their backs and heads. The strawmen were heavy enough to knock you flying if they struck home, and not getting clobbered by one proved solid motivation indeed. Mia was just grateful that a switch from sparring matches meant a break from serving as Jessamine's training dummy, but in this particular game, she discovered she had an advantage her fellows didn't.

The realization came as she took her place in the circle, throwing knives held in her teeth. As Mia tied her long hair back in a braid, Diamo seized the opportunity to catch her unawares, sent his strawman sailing soundlessly at her exposed back. But though she couldn't see the target rushing toward her spine, somehow, she could still sense it incoming. Stepping aside, she perforated the strawman with three knives, turned on Diamo with a withering scowl.

The boy blew her a kiss.

As more targets had come sailing toward her from the other acolytes, Mia managed to dodge each and every one. Perhaps it was because the dark here had never known sunlight. But Mia realized that even without seeing them, she could *feel* them.

She could feel their shadows.

Mia managed to avoid every target during her time in the circle. Moving like a breeze among the strawmen, knives singing, grateful she'd finally found something in Solis's hall she excelled at. She'd heard no word from Chronicler Aelius about his search for a tome that unlocked the mysteries of the darkin. There'd been no sign of Lord Cassius since her torture session in Godsgrave. But slowly, surely, she was discovering more about her gift. A smile curled her lips, and remained there until about halfway through the lesson, when Tric took his place in the circle and Marcellus hit him square in the back with a flying strawman.

Marco flashed a smile (much improved by the weaver, Mia thought) and bowed.

"You'll have to be quicker than that, Tricky."

Tric picked himself up off the ground and growled. "You want to wait until I'm ready, next time?"

"That'd defeat the point of the exercise, wouldn't it?"

"Damn Itreyans," Tric growled. "You can always count on them to stick the knife in when you turn your back, aye?"

Marco's handsome smile slowly died. "You're half-Itreyan yourself, you fool."

Mia's heart sank. Tric's eyes widened. And then it was on. Fists and curses, elbows and snarls, the boys falling into a tumble on the stone. Tric split Marco's brow with his fist, punched his lip bloody. Solis soon broke it up, thrashing both boys with his belt like children until they stopped fighting. Hauling Marco to his feet, he ordered him to go see Marielle and get his hurts mended.

"And you," the Shahiid growled at Tric. "Ten laps of the stair. Down and up. Go."

Tric glared into the blind man's eyes, and Mia was honestly wondering if he was about to try to take a piece. But with a black scowl, the boy obeyed. Solis roared at the other acolytes to get back to work, and Hush stepped into the circle to begin his round. Mia noticed Tric never returned to the hall after his tenth lap.

She went searching for him when Songs was done, checking his room, the Sky Altar, the athenaeum. She finally found him in the Hall of Eulogies, thumbs hooked in his belt, staring up at the statue of Niah. A thousand corpses' names carved on the stone at their feet. Nameless tombs on the walls all around.

"How do, Don Tric?"

He glanced at her briefly. Nodded once.

She edged up to him slowly, hands clasped behind her. The Dweymeri boy had turned back to the statue, looking up at Niah's face. The statue's eyes had the disconcerting quality of seeming to look right at you, no matter where you stood. The goddess's expression was fierce. Dark. Mia wondered who or what the sculptor had imagined Niah staring at when he crafted her countenance. For the first time, she noticed Niah held her scales in her right hand. The sword gripped tight in the other.

"She's left-handed," Mia said. "Like me."

"She's nothing like you," Tric growled. "She's a greedy bitch."

". . . Are you entirely sure it's wise to call her a bitch in her own house?"

Tric looked at her sidelong. "I thought you didn't believe in the divinities?"

Mia shrugged. "Hard not to when the God of Light apparently hates your guts."

"Fuck him. And fuck her. What good do they do us? They give us one thing. Life. Miserable and shitty. And after that? They take. Your prayers. Your years." He waved at the unmarked graves all about them. "Even the life they gave you in the first place."

Tric shook his head.

"Take is all they do."

". . . Are you all right?"

Tric sighed. Shoulders slumped. "Shahiid Aalea gave me the word."

Mia waited patiently. The boy pointed to the ink on his cheeks.

"I've put it off as long as I could," he said. "After dinner. My turn with the weaver."

". . . Ah."

She placed an awkward hand on his arm. Unsure what to say.

"Why were you avoiding it? The pain?"

Tic shook his head. Mia said no more, letting silence do the talking for her. She could see the boy struggling. Feel Mister Kindly in her shadow, gravitating toward his fear like flies to dying meat. He wanted to speak, she knew it. All she had to do was give him the room to—

"I told you about my mother," he said. "My . . . father."

Mia nodded, almost sick with sorrow at the thought of it. Touching his hand again. Sighing, Tric stared at his feet. Words struggling behind his teeth. Mia simply stood beside him, holding his hand. Waiting for the silence to fill.

"You asked about my name when we met," he finally said. "Told me Dweymeri have names like Wolfeater and Spinesmasher." A momentary smirk. "Cuddlegiver."

Mia smiled in return, saying nothing.

"And you told me my name couldn't be Tric."

". . . Aye."

The boy looked up to the statue above. Hazel eyes dark and clouded.

"When a Dweymeri is born, the babe is taken to the high suffi on the isle of Farrow. The Temple of Trelene. And the suffi holds the baby up to the ocean and looks into its eyes and sees the path that lies before it. And the first words she speaks are the baby's name. Earthwalker for a wanderer. Drakekiller for a warrior. Wavedrinker for one fated to drown.

"So like a good daughter of the bara should, my mother took me to Farrow when I was three turns old." A bitter smile. "Runt, I was. Dweymeri are a big people. Our forefathers born of giants, they say. But I was only a half blood. Barely a handful. Took after my father, I suppose. The midwife joked I was so small my mother didn't feel me on my way into the world."

Tric shook his head. Smile dying on his lips.

"You know what the suffi said when she held me up?"

Mia shook her head. Mute and aching.

"She said *tu rai ish'ha chē.*"

Mia put the first letters of the sentence together. Found his name. But . . .

"I don't speak Dweymeri," she murmured.

Tric looked at Mia. Rage and pain in his eyes.

"Drown him and be done." His voice dropped to a trembling whisper. "They were her first words. That's what she fucking named me. *Drown him and be done.*"

Mia closed her eyes. "O, Tric . . ."

"The suffi handed me back to my mother and told her to give me to the waves. Said the Lady of Oceans would accept me, because my people never would." A bitter laugh. "My people."

He sat down on the plinth at the Mother's feet, staring into the dark.

Mia sat beside him, staring only at him.

"Your mother told the priestess to go to the abyss, I take it?"

"She did." Tric smiled. "She was fierce, my mother. My grandfather agreed she should drown me, so she took me far from Farrow. Far from him. She gave up her birthright for me. Gave up everything. She died of bloodpox when I was ten. But on her deathbed, she gave me this." He held up the three silver drakes ever circling his finger. "And she told me a way to prove myself as worthy as she knew me to be."

Tric leaned forward, elbows on his knees.

"Dweymeri warriors undergo a ritual when they come of age. At the end of it, our faces are tattooed so all who meet us know we're Proven. For warriors of the Threedrake clan, the trial was the harshest. Brave the deepwater, and slay one of the great seadrakes. Storm, saber, or white.

"From the time my mother told me of it, I dreamed it. We lived east of Farrow. A port called Solace. After she died, an old seadog taught me boat-making. Sailwork. Harpoons. I cut down the ironwood trees for my skiff myself. Took me a year to make her. And when I was fourteen, I turned my back on Solace and set out for the deep.

"See, stormdrakes are big, but stupid. Sabers are smarter, but smaller, too. But the whitedrake . . . he's the king of the deep. Big and cruel and clever. So I headed north to the coldwater, where the seals were pupping. All I wanted was to sail into Farrow with the carcass of an eighteen-footer. Stand before my grandfather and hear him say he was wrong about me. I prayed to the Lady of Oceans that she'd bring me a beast worthy of a man. And she answered."

Tric breathed through gritted teeth, eyes alight.

"Mother of Night, he was fucking huge, Mia. You should've seen him. When he hit my line, he almost ripped the skiff in half. But my hook bit deep, and my boat held true. He tried to ram me more than once, but after he tasted my harpoons, he learned not to stray too close. The waves smashed down on us and I didn't eat or sleep. Just fought. Five full turns, toe to toe, hands bleeding. Imagining my grandfather's face as I dragged this monster into Farrow Bay.

"He got tired. Couldn't stay down, swimming slower and slower. And so I rowed up beside him and picked up my best and sharpest. The harpoon I'd saved for last."

Tric looked at Mia through the curtain of his saltlocks.

"You ever looked into a drake's eye?"

The girl shook her head. She didn't dare speak. Didn't want to break this deathly hush. As Tric spoke again, even the Mother's statue seemed to be listening.

"Black eyes, they've got. Corpse eyes. You look into that black and all you can see is yourself. And I saw him. *Me.* That terrified little bastard with his matchstick spear and his father's eyes. And I put that harpoon right through him. Right into that little boy's heart. Killed him dead and the beast besides. And I thought myself a man.

"I sailed into Farrow Bay with his head lashed to the gunwale. His teeth were big as my fist. Must've been a hundred people gathered around me as I ripped them from his gums. Strung them around my neck and headed for my grandfather's home.

"They wondered who I was. This scrawny half blood. Too pale and small to be one of their own, but still knowing their ways. And I entered my grandfather's house and knelt before his seat and told him who I was. His daughter's son. And I showed him the teeth around my neck and the ring on my finger. And I pointed toward the head on the beach and I asked that he name me a man."

Tric curled his hands into fists. Veins taut beneath his skin, etched in the muscle. He was trembling, Mia realized. Grief or rage, she didn't know.

She put a hand on his arm. Spoke soft as she could.

"You don't have to tell me, Tric . . ."

She stumbled over the name, wondering if it were an insult. Not knowing what to do or say. Feeling helpless. Stupid. After all Aalea's lessons. Everything she'd learned.

Powerless.

Tric shook his head. Voice thick with anger.

"He lau . . ."

The boy's voice failed him for a moment. He hissed. Cleared his throat.

"He laughed, Mia. Called me bastard. Whoreson. *Koffi.* Told me when his daughter defied him, she ceased being his daughter. Told me I was no grandson of his.

"'*But you* are *a man, little koffi,*' he said. '*So come, take your ink, so others may know you for what you are.*' And his men held me down and he tore the draketeeth from my neck. Used them on my face while I screamed. Poured ink onto the wounds and beat me until the blackness took me."

Mia felt tears spilling down her cheeks. Her chest ached, nails biting her palms. She put her arms around the boy, hugged tight as she could, buried her face in his hair.

"Tric, I'm so sorry."

He plunged on, heedless of her touch. It was as if a wound had been lanced now, the poison spewing forth in a flood. How many years had he held it inside?

"They tied me to a mast out front of my grandfather's home," he said. "The children would come throw rocks at me. Women spat on me. Men cursed me. The wounds got infected. My eyes swelled up and I couldn't see." He shook his head. "That was the worst part. Waiting in the dark for the next rock to hit. The next slap. The next gob of spit. Bastard. Whoreson. *Koffi.*"

"Daughters," Mia breathed. "That's why you wouldn't wear the blindfold to enter the Mountain."

Tric nodded. Chewed his lip.

"I prayed to the Lady of Oceans to set me free. Punish those who tortured me. My grandfather most of all. And on the third nevernight, when the winds rose and death was so close I could feel her chill, I heard a whisper in my ear. A woman. Words like ice.

"*The Lady of Oceans cannot help you, boy.*'

"*I don't deserve to die like this,*' I said. And I heard her laugh.

"*Deserve has no truck with death. She takes us all. Wicked and just alike.*'

"*Then I pray she takes the bara slowly,*' I spat. *Pray he screams as he dies.*'

"*What would you give to make it so?*'

"*Anything,*' I told her. *Everything.*'

"So she cut me down. Adiira was her name. She who'd become my Shahiid. She nursed the infection and set me on the path. Told me the Mother of Night had chosen me. That she'd make me a weapon. Her tool on this earth. And one turn, I'd see him die. My grandfather." Tric grit his jaw, hissed through his teeth. "Die screaming."

"I vowed the same," Mia said. "Remus. Duomo. Scaeva."

"One of the reasons I like you, Pale Daughter." Tric smiled. "We're the same, you and me."

The boy touched his face. The scrawled ink that told the tale of his torture.

"Every turn, I'd wake and see these in the mirror. Remember what he'd done. Even when Adiira pushed me to breaking, I'd stare into the glass and remember him laughing. I can't remember what I looked like before. This ink . . . it's who I am." He glanced at Mia. Her now-flawless cheeks and pouting lips. "Marielle will take them away. Adiira warned me. They make me memorable. But what will I be when they're gone? They're what makes me, me."

"Bullshit," Mia said.

Tric blinked in shock. "What?"

"This makes you who you are." She punched the slab of muscle above his heart. "This." She slapped him atop his head. "These." The girl took hold of his hands, knelt in front of him, staring into the boy's eyes. "Slavemarks. Tattoos. Scars. What you look like doesn't change who you are inside. They can give you a new face, but they can't give you a new heart. No matter what they take from you, they can't take that away unless you let them. That's real strength, Tric. That's *real* power."

She squeezed his hands so hard her fingers ached.

"You hold it safe, you hear me? You picture yourself standing on that fucking bastard's grave. Spitting on the earth that cradles him. You'll have it, Tric. One turn, you'll have your vengeance. I promise. Mother help me, I *swear* it."

The boy stared at the hands that held his. "This is a dark road we walk, Mia."

"Then we walk it together. I watch your back. You watch mine. And if I fall before the end, you get Scaeva for me. Make him scream. And I'll swear the same for you."

The boy looked at her. Those bottomless hazel eyes. That scrawl of hatred on his skin. Her heart was pounding. Fervor in her stare, palms sweating in his.

"Will it hurt?" he asked.

". . . That depends."

"On what?"

"Whether you want me to lie or not."

Tric laughed, breaking the black spell that held the room still. Mia's grin died as she looked into his eyes. She moved a little closer. Not close enough.

"Afterward," she found herself saying. "If you don't want to be alone . . ."

". . . Is that wise?"

"After ninebells? Probably not."

He drifted toward her. Tall and strong and O, so fine. Saltlocks tumbling about her cheeks as he leaned near.

"We probably shouldn't, then."

Her lips brushed against his as she whispered, "Probably not."

They hovered there for a moment more, Mia's belly tumbling, her skin prickling as he ran a gentle finger up her arm. Knowing exactly what he wanted. Wanting just the same. But it hung between them, the thought of the weaver's twisting hands. Choking the moment dead. And so, he stood. Staring into the dark and breathing deep.

"My thanks, Pale Daughter," he smiled.

"At your service, Don Tric."

She watched him walk away, his absence leaving her aching. And when he was gone, she sat in the dark at the feet of a goddess, and her shadow began to whisper.

". . . *i think you had best visit the weaver after the boy . . .*"

"And why's that?"

". . . *your brain and ovaries seem to have switched places . . .*"

"O, stop. I fear my sides will split."

She retired to her room, burrowed amid the notes and formulae, lost again in the puzzle. One hand wove idle circles in the air, sending the shadows in the room writhing, Mister Kindly pouncing among them like a real cat chasing mice.

As the evemeal bells rang, she stayed with the riddle, mind drifting to Tric. Wondering how he was faring in the weaver's room of masks. Emotions were rising among the acolytes; she could feel it. As the competition grew more intense, so too did every other feeling. She felt as if the world were growing louder, everything mattered more. She had no idea what the next turn might bring. She didn't love him. Love was stupid. Foolish. It had no place in these walls or in her world, and she knew it.

But a part of her hoped she'd not find herself alone this eve . . .

Hours waiting there in the dark. Butterflies batting at her insides. Wondering if he was all right. What he might look like when that scrawl of hate was torn from his face. Who he might be in the end.

Waiting for the knock on the door. Hour after hour.

"*. . . are you sure about this . . . ?*"

"I'm sure."

"*. . . i wonder if—*"

"I know what I'm doing."

But sleep arrived before the boy did.

M ia woke somewhere in the nevernight's dark, eyes fluttering open from a dreamless rest. How long had she slumbered? What time could it b—

There it came again. A gentle sound that woke her butterflies.

Knock, knock.

She rolled out of bed, throwing a silken robe over her slip. Heart pounding against her ribs. Cold stone beneath bare feet. She reached the door, hands unsteady as she twisted the key and opened it a crack. And there she saw him, just a silhouette in the dark, saltlocks framing the hidden contours of his face.

Lips dry, she stepped aside without a word. He looked up and down the hallway, hovering at the threshold. For him to be caught outside his room after ninebells would mean torture at the weaver's hands. But he knew what would happen if he entered. They both knew. A breath that seemed to last forever, watching him through her lashes. And at last, quiet as her sigh, he stepped inside.

She touched the arkemical lamp on her table, waiting for the heat of her hand to spark the light inside. It flickered, a warm sepia glow blooming in the glass. He was behind her, she could feel him. Feel his shadow. Feel his fear at being here. His hunger. And holding her breath, she turned and looked at his face.

A picture, just as she'd known he'd be. The ink was gone, the draketooth scars vanished, a smooth, flawless tan beneath. Cheeks more defined, the hollows around his eyes filled. The kind of handsome a girl might raise an army for, slay a god or daemon for. This girl, at least.

"The weaver knows her work," Mia said.

Tric looked at his feet, avoiding her gaze. She smiled to see him abashed. "How does it feel?"

"Not bad," he shrugged. "I mean, it hurt like fire and iron, but after, not so bad."

"Do you miss them? The marks?"

"She let me keep them."

The boy motioned to a small glass phial on a leather thong around his throat. Mia saw it was filled with dark, gleaming liquid.

"Is that . . . ?"

He nodded. "All that remains of my grandfather's handiwork."

Reaching out to touch it, Mia trailed one finger down his collar to the skin beneath. She saw the pulse at his neck quickening. Turned away to hide her smile.

"Drink?"

He nodded wordlessly. She busied herself with the clay cups, the bottle she'd lifted during one of her early forays in search of trinkets for Mouser's list. Though the whiskey wasn't worth any marks in the Shahiid's contest, Mercurio had taught her to always swipe a good label when she saw it.

She poured two shots, offered Tric a cup. He clinked it against her own, knocked it back without pause. Mia poured another, one for herself. "Sit?"

The boy looked around the room, down at the stool tucked beneath her dresser.

"There's only one chair," he said.

Turning away, Mia slipped her robe slowly off her shoulders. Letting it fall in a crumpled heap on the floor as she crawled onto her bed, reveling in the feel of his eyes on her body. She placed the bottle on the nightstand, reclined among the pillows, legs stretched out before her, whiskey in hand. Waiting.

He walked toward the bed, feet soundless on the stone. Moving like a wolf, head lowered and breathing her in. Mia knew he must be able to smell her want. Her heart was hammering against her ribs. Her mouth dry as the desert beyond the walls. She sipped the goldwine again, savoring the smoky burn down her throat. Tric sat on the mattress edge, unable to tear his eyes from her. Tension crackling between them, curling the edge of her lips. She could feel it thrumming in her fingertips. Pulsing beneath her skin. Desire. Her for him. Him for her. Nothing and no one between.

He knocked back his drink with a wince. She watched the light play on his lips as he swallowed, the deep troughs at his throat, the strong, flawless line of his jaw.

"Another?"

He nodded. Mute. She pushed herself up slowly, felt the strap of her slip fall off one shoulder. Sitting up cross-legged, the silk bunched around her hips. Filling with a dark delight as she saw his eyes run over her body, down to the shadow between her legs. She rose up on all fours, prowled across the furs, eyes locked on his. Reaching for the cup in his hand, fingertips circling the lip, onto his wrist. Up the smooth swell of his bare arm, watching his skin prickle, listening to his breath catch. Her face just inches from his.

She wasn't sure who moved first. Her or him. Only that they came together with a crash, her eyes closed, her mouth finding his as if she'd always known the way. Warm skin and warmer lips. Strong hands and hard muscle. His fingers wrapped in her hair. Her nails clawing his skin. His mouth crushed to hers, tasting the whiskey on his tongue. She tugged off his shirt, fumbled with his belt. He clutched a handful of her slip, tore it from her body as if she'd never need it again.

She pushed him onto his back, lifted herself up on all fours, straddling his face. Wanting to taste him as he tasted her. His mouth left a burning trail up her inner thighs, hands roaming her naked skin and making her shiver. With a gasp, she managed to tug his britches down around his knees, felt his fingers parting her folds as she took him in her mouth. Groaning around his length, she felt his tongue flickering against her, whispering pleas, lost in the shadows above her head. His fingers, O, Daughters, his smooth, burning heat against her tongue. His mouth against her swollen bud, gasping as she pumped her fist, rolled her tongue around his crown, all the way down to his hilt. Needing more. Needing all.

Dragging herself up, she twisted in place, pushing him back down as he lunged after her, eyes bright with lust. Climbing atop him, she took him in her hand, near drunk with need. Stroking him hard as he groaned, pressing him against her. He lunged upward, taking her breast in his mouth, hands on her hips, urging her down. But she resisted for one more endless moment, freezing in place above him. Locking her gaze with his. An inch and forever away from the fall.

But finally, ever so slowly she sank down, down, looking deep into his eyes, pain and pleasure all entwined, breath strangled in her lungs, unable even to gasp. Goddess, he was so hard. Her head fell back, lashes fluttering, long tresses clutched in his fist as his tongue moved from one breast to another, as she rocked her hips, spine arched, nails clawing his back. Moving as one now, his teeth at her throat. Hissing. Pleading.

He slipped his hand between them, down between her legs. Working gently with his fingertips, rolling them in circles, the heat inside growing hotter and brighter and fiercer until there was only the flame, blinding behind her eyes as her every muscle clenched and she screamed silently into his hair. He crashed and burned inside her, his eyes growing wide and his whole body shaking as she rocked back and forth atop him. She looked into his eyes, knowing he stood right at the edge, begging her to let him fall. And in the split second before his end she pulled herself off him, finished him with her hand, gasping as he spurted across her belly and breasts, whispering her name.

Limp and breathless, they collapsed in a sweating heap upon the bed.

Silence reigned in the shivering dark. The shadows in the room swaying and rolling in the aftermath. Books had toppled from their shelves, strewn spread-eagled and dog-eared across the floor. The dresser doors were flung open, her stool upturned, the room in chaos. But Tric gathered her up in his arms and kissed her brow, and just for a single, tiny moment, Mia let herself go. Shut her eyes and forgot. Listening to his heart against his ribs, feeling the warm glow recede, a smile on her lips.

She lay there for an age. Pressed against his skin, cheek to his chest. Her hair was strewn across him like a blanket, gossamer black like the shadows all around. And there in the now-still black, she whispered.

"I paid that sweetboy far too much."

She waited for his reply. Moments stretching into minutes. Finally raising her head and realizing he was dead to the world, gentle breath slipping through parted lips.

Mia smiled, shook her head. Leaning over, she kissed him, long and gentle. Wrapping her arms around him and closing her eyes with a contented sigh and falling, at last, into sleep.

And as she drifted away, the shadows began to move again.

Slowly at first.

Rippling.

Writhing.

Coalescing finally into a ribbon-thin shape, perched now at the foot of the bed.

A not-cat, staring at the girl with its not-eyes. Waiting patiently, as it always did. For the dreams to come. For the chance to rend and tear the terrors that arrived to haunt her every nevernight since it had felt her call. Every nevernight thereafter, perched beside her as she slept. Growing strong and ever stronger with each mouthful.

The thing called Mister Kindly waited. A patience learned over eons. A silence like the grave. Soon now. Any moment she'd begin to whimper. Whisper for him. What would she dream of tonight? The ones who came to drown her? Her father's legs kicking, face purpling, *guh guh guh*? The Philosopher's Stone and the horrors she'd found within, fourteen years old and lost in the dark?

No matter.

They all tasted the same.

Any moment now, the nightmares would come.

Any.

Moment.

Now.

But for the first time since forever, the nightmares never arrived.

The girl was not afraid.

And there in the empty dark, the not-cat tilted its head.

Narrowed its not-eyes.

And it was not pleased.

Mia opened her eyes. Sat up in bed. Smiling as she realized Tric was still beside her, naked and glorious in the arkemical gloom, saltlocks strewn across the pillow.

There it was again. The sound that had woken her.

Knock, knock.

Tric stirred, frowned in his sleep. Mia touched his cheek and he opened his eyes, realizing at last where he was and sitting bolt upright with a soft hiss.

"Black Mother, I fell asleep?"

"Shhh. Someone's at the door."

Mia crawled out of bed. Searching among the chaos for her robe, smiling as she felt Tric's eyes on her body. Slinging the black silk about her shoulders, she crept to the threshold just as another knock sounded.

"Corvere," a voice hissed.

"Ash?" Mia twisted her key, opened the door a crack and peered out. Wondering why Ash hadn't just picked the lock like she usually did. She saw the girl waiting beyond, blue eyes wide in the dark. "What time is it?"

"Almost mornbells." The girl pushed past Mia and into her bedroom, black stormclouds gathered overhead. "One of the Hands just told me. Fucking Jessamine, that slippery littl—"

It was only once she was inside she noticed the disarray. The clothes and books strewn across the floor. And, O, yes, the naked Dweymeri boy sitting in Mia's bed.

"Ah," Ash said.

Tric waved hello.

Ash glanced at Mia, a little abashed. "Sorry, Corvere."

Mia shut the door so no one else who happened by could see Tric in her bed. If anyone told the Revered Mother he'd been out after curfew . . .

"You fancy telling me what this is about?"

Ashlinn said nothing. Lips parted, struggling for the words.

"What?" Mia searched her eyes. "What's happened?"

"Mia . . ."

"Fucksakes, Ash, what is it?"

The girl shook her head.

Softly sighed.

"Lotti's dead."

HUNDRED

The Hall of Truths smelled different that morn. Among the rot and fresh flowers. Dried herbs and acids. A new scent, rust-flavored, smothering the familiar perfume.

Blood.

Mia pushed her way past the assembled Hands, Ash and Tric close behind. The servants tried to stop her, but she railed and shoved and elbowed until at last a voice called from within, "Let them through." Mia found herself inside the hall's green light, eyes wide with rage.

Carlotta was slumped over the workbench, a quill clutched in one cold hand. A slick of congealed scarlet covered the table before her, puddled beneath her stool. The song of the ghostly choir hung in the air with the ironshod stink of blood.

The Revered Mother and Spiderkiller stood by the body, speaking in hushed tones with Solis. Mother Drusilla's habitual smile was missing entirely, and Spiderkiller looked even graver than usual. Solis stared at the empty air above Mia's right shoulder as she entered, his face as grim as an abattoir floor.

"Lessons do not begin for hours, Acolytes," Spiderkiller said. "You should not be here."

"That's our friend," Mia said, pointing to Carlotta's body.

Spiderkiller shook her head. "No more."

"How did she die?" Tric asked.

"She didn't die," Ash spat. "She was *killed*."

"Throat cut," Spiderkiller replied. "Very quick. Almost painless."

"From behind?"

The Shahiid nodded.

"Jessamine," Mia hissed. "Or Diamo. Maybe both."

"Those fucking cowards," Ash whispered.

Mother Drusilla raised an eyebrow.

"You know something about this matter, Acolytes?"

Mia glanced at Ashlinn and Tric, slowly nodded. "Carlotta and Jessamine quarreled at evemeal a few turns back, Revered Mother. Lotti was close to cracking Spiderkiller's formula, but Diamo destroyed her notes. Lotti almost broke Jessamine's nose and Jess promised to kill her for it. Ask anyone. We all heard it."

"I see."

"Lotti said she was going to ask Shahiid Spiderkiller for permission to work late to make up the lost ground. Jessamine and Diamo *knew* she'd be here."

"From what you're describing, anyone who attended that evemeal would have known she was here."

"But Jessamine promised to kill her. In front of all of us."

"And that proves what exactly?" Solis snapped. "I recall Acolyte Tric here threatening to murder another novice over evemeal not so long ago. And that same novice turned up dead the next turn." Solis turned on Tric. "Do you have something to confess, Acolyte?"

"I had nothing to do with Floodcaller's death, Shahiid. I *swear* it."

The hulking man turned on Mia and scoffed. "Idle threats do not a killer make."

"You don't even care she's dead, do you?" she asked.

"On the contrary, Acolyte, we care very deeply," Mother Drusilla said. "Which is why we are investigating thoroughly instead of leaping to obvious conclusions. Jessamine is a cold-blooded one, true. But do you think her fool enough to murder a girl she openly threatened in front of a room full of people a few eves before?"

"Maybe she thought none of you would give a damn? You weren't exactly tearing the place apart looking for clues when Floodcaller got his throat cut. More than half of us have died since then and not a tear's been shed for any of them."

Solis glowered, blind eyes flashing. "I would counsel you to watch your tone when you speak to your betters, girl. Your distaste for Jessamine is well known. The beatings she's given you in the Hall of Songs would be reason enough for you to spread lies about her now. And if there are any among this congregation who stood to benefit from Carlotta's death, it was you."

Mia blinked. Gobsmacked. "*What?*"

"You said yourself she was close to solving Shahiid Spiderkiller's quandary. If Carlotta *did* concoct the antidote, your best chance to finish top of hall would be lost, neh? You certainly have a sunsbeam's chance in the 'byss of standing victorious in the Hall of Songs."

"You miserable . . ."

"Mia," Tric warned, putting a hand on her arm.

". . . black-hearted . . ."

"Corvere," Ash muttered.

". . . fucking . . ."

". . . *mia* . . ."

"*PRICK!*" Mia roared. "She was my *friend*! Who the *fuck* do you think you are?"

Solis brought his fist down on the workbench and bellowed. "I am a Shahiid of the Red Church! The Mother's Blade on this earth, thirty-six sanctified kills wrought in her name! And I swear you will be the thirty-seventh if you dare speak to me so again!"

Mia took one step forward, rage burning in her chest. She knew better than anyone what it meant to cross Solis. But she was still heedless, ever fearless, Mister Kindly swallowing caution whole. Tric and Ash grabbed her arms, pulled her into check. But it was the Revered Mother's voice that finally brought still to the room.

"Where were you yestereve, Acolyte?"

Drusilla tilted her head, peered at Carlotta's body.

"Sometime around three bells?"

Spittle on Mia's lips. Eyes narrowed. Jaw clenched. "Abed, of course."

"No one to account for your whereabouts, then."

". . . No."

The Revered Mother fixed her in a cool blue stare. "Interesting."

"Why is that interesting?"

"I've ventilated a few throats in my years." Drusilla motioned to Carlotta's corpse. "From the wound's look, I would judge the killer to be left-handed."

Silence descended on the room. Ashlinn and Tric exchanged uneasy glances, the sweat on Mia's skin beginning to cool. The Mother was looking right at her.

"Jessamine is ambidextrous," Mia said. "She fights just as well with either hand."

"And which hand do you favor, Acolyte?"

". . . My left, Mother Drusilla."

The old woman motioned to the desk. Mia noticed a faint outline in the blood spatter, as if a rectangular object had been sitting in front of Lotti as her throat was opened, shielding the bench from some of the spray.

"Carlotta was obviously working on something as she was murdered. It would seem to be around the shape of a book. A journal perhaps. You wouldn't know anything about that, would you, Acolyte?"

"Carlotta kept her notes on Spiderkiller's antidote in there. Everyone knew that."

The Revered Mother tilted her head. "Interesting."

Mia met the Mother's stare without blinking. Spiderkiller's voice broke the still.

"We have work to do, Acolytes. You should be about your mornmeal. I will see you back here for Truths at lesson time."

Ash took Mia's hand, dragged her from the hall. The trio ate a lifeless meal at the Sky Altar, Mia's glare fixed on Diamo. The big Itreyan watched her with cool, dead eyes, daring her to make a play. Jessamine was nowhere to be seen.

Mia grit her teeth. Food like dust and death in her mouth. Ash's whispers unheard. Blood pounding in her ears. Tric insisted he step forward, testify that he'd spent the night in Mia's bed. That she couldn't have killed Carlotta. But Tric's session with the weaver had finished well after ninebells—he'd had dispensation only to return to his room, certainly not to go wandering into Mia's. So in the end she pleaded with him to keep silent. There was no sense in Tric risking torture until she knew how hot the water she swam in was.

During lessons in the Hall of Truths, Mia couldn't tear her eyes from Carlotta's empty chair. The faint bloodstain that even Spiderkiller's arkemy couldn't quite bleach from the ironwood bench. She pictured the girl's final moments. Hunched over her notebook. Head pulled back by a quick hand.

The brief seconds of terror between the time she felt the blade and the time the blackness took her.

Mia stared at Jessamine, who'd joined the class only seconds before it began. A silent vow echoing in her head.

This will be the end of you, bitch . . .

"Mia Corvere."

Mia blinked. Looked up from Jessamine's face to find Revered Mother Drusilla at the front of the hall, surrounded by a half-dozen Hands.

". . . Yes, Mother Drusilla?"

"You are to come with us immediately."

Two black-robed Hands took hold of Mia's arms, one apiece. The girl hissed protest as they dragged her from her stool and none-too-gently marched her toward the door. She heard Tric's protest, a scuffle, the Revered Mother's shouted command. Craning her neck, she saw the old woman stalking behind, surrounded by ominous, black figures. Her stare was a cool, ice blue.

"Mother Drusilla, where are you taking me?"

"My chambers."

"Why?"

"An inquisition."

"Into what?"

"The murder of Carlotta Valdi."

D rusilla placed a crumpled sheet of linen in Mia's lap and folded her arms. "Explain this."

The Mother's chambers were nestled high in the Mountain, atop a seemingly endless flight of stairs. It was dimly lit by a sculpture of arkemical glass suspended from the ceiling. An ornate desk stacked high with parchment dominated the room, white furs on the floor, white paint on the walls. Overflowing bookshelves lined the chamber left and right, but behind the desk, the wall was carved with hundreds of recesses. Inside these alcoves, Mia saw all manner of oddities. A centurion's dagger. An ornate rose of beaten gold. A bloodstained copy of the Gospel of Aa. A sapphire ring.

Mixed among the trophies, Mia saw hundreds and hundreds of silver phials, sealed with stoppers of dark wax. They were the same kind Naev had worn about her neck in the Whisperwastes. And in their center, an obsidian door was set in the rock, marked with strange, shifting glyphs.

Sat in an ornate, high-backed chair, Mia blinked at the linen Drusilla had presented.

"Explain what, Revered Mother?"

"This."

Drusilla gathered up the sheet, held it before Mia's face. There, soaked through the fabric's weave, the girl saw a tiny smudge of dried scarlet.

"It looks like blood."

"Carlotta's blood, Acolyte. Speaker Adonai confirms it."

Mia looked to the albino, who stood admiring the Mother's collection of curios. He was barefoot as always, smooth, pale chest showing through the open neck of his silken robe. As ever, the speaker seemed singularly bored.

"It be the vitus of the slain one," Adonai nodded, running his fingertips down one of the multitude of silver phials. "Undoubtedly."

"I don't understand," Mia said. "It's Carlotta's blood. What's this to do with me?"

Drusilla folded the sheet neatly, placed it back in Mia's lap.

"This linen was stripped from your bed this morning."

Mia frowned. Mind racing. Heartbeat quickening. "That makes no sense."

"Can you explain how Carlotta's blood got into your bed, Acolyte?"

Mia's jaw flapped, eyes searching the room. She sucked a breath through gritted teeth. Remembering Diamo sitting alone at mornmeal. The image of Jessamine arriving only just in time for Spiderkiller's lesson.

"Jessamine," Mia spat. "She wasn't at mornmeal. She must've put it there."

"Jessamine was here in my chambers this morn, Acolyte," Drusilla sighed. "Being questioned by me on this very matter."

"Revered Mother, I had nothing to do with Lotti's death. She was my friend!"

"There *are* no friends here, Acolyte. The wolf does not pity the lamb. The storm begs no forgiveness of the drowned. We are killers one, killers all." Mia glanced up as the old woman echoed Lord Cassius's warning. "And though we've made it clear that the murder of fellow acolytes is a crime, if you admit involvement in Carlotta's ending now, the Ministry will judge you lighter for it."

"I won't admit to something I didn't do!"

"All evidence speaks to the contrary." Drusilla perched on the edge of the desk, leaned close to Mia. The obsidian key at her throat glittered in the smoky light. "You are the only left-hander among the current flock. You stand to gain most by Carlotta being removed from Spiderkiller's contest. You cannot account for your whereabouts yestereve, and the victim's blood is found on your sheets—a fact which you yourself cannot explain. Has Carlotta ever visited your room?"

"No, but—"

"Was she cut in the altercation at the Sky Altar with Jessamine, perhaps? Could her blood somehow have gotten onto your clothing?"

Mia considered lying for a moment, but knew Drusilla would ask these same questions of everyone who witnessed the brawl. And to be caught in a lie now . . .

"No, Lotti wasn't cut." Mia frowned. "Why were you in my room, anyway?"

"Searching for Carlotta's missing notebook, of course."

"You honestly thought you'd find it? I'd have to be some kind of idiot to keep it in my room after slitting her throat, wouldn't I?"

"But if you *were* being framed for the murder as you claim, would the killer not be best served by planting the notebook, rather than a single drop of blood?"

"So if you'd found her notes, would that prove me innocent or guilty?"

Drusilla scowled, folded her arms.

"Are there none who can speak to your whereabouts?"

Mia's fingernails bit her palms. Of *course* there was someone who could vouch for her. But for Tric to admit he'd come to her room would mean admitting he'd broken curfew. They'd scourge him for it. Probably worse than Hush.

"*. . . there is one who can speak to her whereabouts . . .*"

Mia's belly surged. Mister Kindly had materialized on the Revered Mother's desk, staring at the old woman with tilted head. Drusilla turned to regard the creature, skepticism plain in her eyes. But Mia knew he had no affection for Tric. No loyalty. He'd sell the boy in a second if it meant sparing Mia another second of this indignity.

"O, really?" Drusilla said. "Dare I ask?"

"*. . . i do not know. dare you . . . ?*"

"Mister Kindly, don't," Mia warned.

"*. . . and why not . . . ?*"

"Because I'm asking you not to."

Drusilla turned sharply at that, regarding Mia with narrowed eyes. "Acolyte, I should not need to explain the seriousness of this crime. If you are found guilty of murdering Acolyte Carlotta, you will be scourged at the very least. Perhaps even killed. If there is another that can provide alibi for you yestereve . . ."

Mia's gaze was fixed on the not-cat. Pleading.

"*. . . you used to trust me more . . .*"

"Please, don't."

"*. . . what changed, mia . . . ?*"

"Enough," Drusilla snapped. "I am mistress of these halls. Speak not to her, speak to me. In Our Blessed Lady's name, I command it."

Mister Kindly turned his head at that, his bottomless stare fixed on Drusilla.

". . . it is obvious, really . . ."

"Mister Kindly, *don't.*"

The not-cat swished his tail. Looked the old woman up and down.

". . . it is me . . ."

In the silence following, Mia swore she heard Adonai chuckling. The not-cat glanced at her, seemed to shake his head as if to say she should have known better.

". . . i never leave her side. i watch while she sleeps. i know exactly what she did last eve . . ."

"Do you take me for a fool, little passenger?"

". . . there are fools in these halls, revered mother, but you and she are not among them . . ."

Mister Kindly nodded in Mia's direction.

". . . she would not, and could not have done this . . ."

Drusilla snarled and rose from her perch, seated herself behind her desk. Adonai wandered the alcoves, still touching a phial here, a phial there, smiling faintly. The old woman steepled her fingers.

"Acolyte Mia Corvere. You are confined to chambers. Your meals will be brought to you, along with any materials you require to continue your studies. You will be permitted no outside contact, and a Hand will be posted outside your door until this matter is resolved. The Ministry will meet this eve and discuss your fate."

Two Hands seemed to materialize beside Mia's chair. Realizing there was no sense in incurring the Mother's wrath further, Mia rose slow, bowed deep, and marched from Drusilla's chambers. The Hands escorted her all the way to her bedroom, ushering her inside and shutting the door behind them. A quick glance through the keyhole saw the hooded figures lurking in the hallway outside.

Her room had been turned over, drawers upended, bedding stripped. Mia flopped down on the bare mattress, lit a cigarillo, and stared at the ceiling.

"Well, shit."

Mister Kindly materialized on the bedhead, peered down into her eyes.

". . . I would prefer your apology in writing, though particularly eloquent spoken word may suffice . . ."

"Aye," Mia said, clearing her throat. "Sorry about that."

". . . this must be some new breed of eloquence i am unfamiliar with . . ."

"'Byss and blood, I'll write you a fancy one on gilded parchment and sing it from the mountaintop later. We've more pressing matters to mind, neh?"

". . . even if they find you guilty, they'll not kill you for it . . ."

"What makes you so certain? They might make an example of me."

". . . it makes little sense to do so. the murderer was skilled enough to escape their bed-chamber after ninebells, sneak to the hall of truth, cut the girl's throat ear to ear, wash off gouts of blood, and sneak back to bed, all without being seen . . ."

Mia blew smoke into the not-cat's face. "Her name was Carlotta, Mister Kindly."

". . . be that as it may, the murderer shows considerable skill in precisely the arts they teach here . . ."

"O, aye, they might even pin a ribbon on my baps."

". . . doubtful. but i also doubt the masters of a school of deadly assassins can get too upset that one of their students actually turned out to be a deadly assassin . . ."

The girl sucked hard on her cigarillo, breathed a gray curse.

". . . jessamine is the obvious acolyte to blame. not necessarily the correct one . . ."

"Who else, then?"

". . . who is the third most skilled novice in venomcraft . . . ?"

". . . Probably Hush? But Osrik and Marcellus are up there too."

". . . and any of them are capable of the stealth required to have done this . . ."

Mia drew on her smoke, thoughts racing in her head. Jessamine had to go. But if she or Diamo were to simply end up dead, the Ministry would immediately suspect her. And all that was irrelevant at any rate. No sense in pondering Jessamine and Diamo until she knew what the judgment over Carlotta would be. Her stack of problems would shorten considerably if the Ministry just cut her throat . . .

Instead of simply stewing, Mia set back to work on Spiderkiller's formula. Hunched on the ruin of her bed, scribbling thoughts in her leather-bound notebook. Hours passed in the gloom, Mister Kindly offering what little help he could. The puzzle took her mind off the Ministry, the possibility that all her well-laid plans might come crashing down in a few hours' time. What would Mercurio say if all this went to pieces?

Focus on what you can change, he'd counsel. *The rest will sort itself.*

Mia sighed.

One way or the other.

A knock on her door hours later pulled Mia up from the arkemical dance in her head, back into the dim light. She'd unwittingly chain-smoked her way through half her remaining cigarillos, the cup beside her bed piled high with ash. Her throat felt raw, her head swimming. She crushed what was left of her smoke out, grimacing.

"Maw's teeth, I've got to cut down."

"*. . . there are more dangerous things around here to put in your mouth . . .*"

Mister Kindly peered at her through the gray pall.

"*. . . dweymeri boys, for example . . .*"

"O, bravo. Been working on that one for a while, have we?"

"*. . . most of yestereve . . .*"

"Time well spent, then."

"*. . . there are more dangerous ways i could—*"

"All right, all right. Enough. The last thing I need to hear before my execution is you criticizing my choice in penises."

"*. . . ridiculous things, all. if ever proof was needed of your creator's malevolence, look no farther than between the legs of the average teenaged boy . . .*"

Knock, knock, knock.

"Acolyte. You are summoned to the Hall of Eulogies."

Mia rose from her bed. No fear in her belly. Heartbeat steady. She hid a dozen blades about her person, determined that she'd go down fighting if it came to her end. Wondering what awaited her beneath the statue's gaze.

Six Hands waited outside her bedroom door, hoods drawn over their eyes. Shahiid Mouser stood beside them, his blacksteel blade in his belt. The man's familiar silverware smile was nowhere to be seen.

"Shahiid," Mia nodded.

"Come with us, Acolyte."

Mia was led down the corridor toward the Hall of Eulogies. She could feel Mister Kindly in her shadow, drinking her fear fast as he was able. Still, it was beginning to seep through now. Sweat on her palms. Lightness in her belly. She'd not die on her knees like some sniveling child. But she'd worked so hard. Come so far. To stumble and fall at the eleventh hour over something like this?

The darkness swelled around her, pressing in on all sides. Responding to her rising anger. Her budding anxiety. It was hers to command, if she wished it. If only she had the will to reach out and seize it. She'd done it before. Not so long ago. Fourteen years old. Walls of stone. Screams in the air. Blood on her hands.

Don't look.

The Ministry were assembled beneath Niah's granite gaze. The acolytes also. One fewer than there'd been the last time they gathered here. Tric was looking at her, agony on his face. She shook her head and pressed her lips shut. Silently warning him to do the same.

Stained-glass light spilled over the floor, bloody red and ghostly white, the choir singing in the background. Mia was ushered to an empty place before the Ministry. The faces of the assembled Shahiid were grim, the Revered Mother's darkest of all.

"Acolyte Mia. The Ministry has consulted extensively over Acolyte Carlotta's death. Though conclusive proof of your guilt is lacking, the blood found in your room and the hand favored by the killer cannot be ignored. Moreover, your motive is irrefutable. With Acolyte Carlotta dead, you stand best placed to finish top of Spiderkiller's hall. Aside from the words already spoken this morning, do you have anything to add in your defense?"

Mia searched the faces of the assembled Shahiid. Solis's blind stare. Aalea's beautiful mask. Their minds were made up. And begging simply wasn't her way.

"No, Revered Mother," she replied.

"Very well. In light of the evidence, and with no compelling testimony to the contrary, your guilt is confirmed. Given the nature of your studies here, and the prowess with which the murder was conducted, you will be spared execution. However, you were *specifically* warned that the ending of fellow acolytes was forbidden, and thus, punishment must be dealt. You will suffer blood scourge. Fifty lashes."

Mia grit her teeth against the sudden rush of fear, Mister Kindly swelling in her shadow. *Maw's teeth, fifty lashes.* Hush had received half that many and it'd almost killed him. She glanced to the blue-eyed boy, there at the end of the acolytes' semicircle. She swore he gave her a slight nod. Her mother's voice, ringing in her head.

Never flinch. Never fear. And never, ever forget.

Her eyes met Tric's and she shook her head again. There was no sense in him stepping up for punishment now. For all their talk of rules, this *was* a school of killers—at least the crime Mia was supposedly guilty of held some kind of credibility. But flagrant violation of the Mother's curfew for the sake of a little angsty mouth-to-mouth?

They'd skin him alive. Literally.

"Moreover," Drusilla continued, "since you were motivated in this crime by desire to gain advantage in Truths, you are hereby banned from Spiderkiller's contest, and will be ineligible to compete for placement in top of her hall."

Mia sagged like the Mother had punched her in the gut. Finishing top of Truths was her best chance at initiation, and all knew it. Without Spiderkiller's contest, Mia might never be made a Blade. What would happen to her? Relegated to making runs to Last Hope with Naev, or keeping some blood pool in a shithole like Carrion Hall or Elai? How could she hope to avenge herself on Scaeva and the others as a glorified servant?

Mia looked at the faces around her. Solis smiling. Jessamine grinning as if all her Great Tithes had come at once. Diamo practically drooling with anticipation. Mother Drusilla nodded to the Hands flanking Mia, and they took an arm each. It was all she could do to hold herself back. The black trembled as she grit her teeth, allowed herself to be led to the iron rings at the statue's base, catching sight of Marielle and Adonai in the shadows. The speaker's face was expressionless, but the weaver's bleeding lips were split in a smile.

She was cracking her knuckles.

The Hands took hold of her shirt, Mia tensing as they readied to strip it from her back. She looked to the goddess above her, those empty eyes that followed wherever she went.

Give me strength . . .

"Stop."

Mia sighed. Relief and anger in equal measure.

That bloody fool . . .

Mia turned. All eyes were on Tric. The boy had stepped forward from his place, staring at the assembled Shahiid. "Mother Drusilla, stop this."

"Step back in line, Acolyte. Judgment has been made. It shall be meted."

"Tric, don't," Mia hissed.

"The judgment is wrong. Mia couldn't have murdered Carlotta."

"I am not interested in your assessment of her character, Acolyte."

"I'm not talking about her damned character," Tric snapped. "Mia couldn't have killed Carlotta yestereve without me knowing."

"And how is that?"

"Tric, *stop!*"

Tric ignored Mia's plea, spared a glance for the weaver. Lips dry. But despite knowing the punishment that might come, still he spoke.

"Because I was with her in her room."

The Ministry shared glances among themselves, save for Solis, who was glowering at the ceiling. Drusilla looked to Marielle and her brother, back to Tric.

"You admit to being out of your chambers after ninebells?"

"I was out all nevernight. Ash can vouch. She saw me in Mia's bed this morning."

Drusilla turned on Ashlinn. "Is this true, Acolyte?"

Ashlinn chewed her lip. Reluctantly nodded. "Aye, Revered Mother."

"So Mia couldn't have killed Lotti," Tric continued. "Despite your 'evidence.' You can't ban her from Spiderkiller's contest. I was in bed with her the whole time."

"And why did you not inform us of this before?"

"Because I asked him not to," Mia said.

"You can't ban Mia from Spiderkiller's trial," Tric insisted. "Becoming a Blade means everything to her. She didn't do this."

Drusilla looked to Mia. The Ministry to the Mother.

The girl held her breath, minutes ticking by like years. The ghostly choir sung their hymn out in the dark, the pulse thundered in Mia's veins. The Ministry spoke among themselves in hushed tones, back and forth, all Mia had worked and bled for hanging in the balance. She could have kissed Tric. She could have punched him. But he was competition. First, last, and always. She didn't love him. He didn't love her. There was no place for it here in the dark, and both of them knew it. Why had he risked so much for her? When she'd never do the same for him?

Mother Drusilla finally spoke, stilling the turmoil in Mia's mind.

"Very well," the old woman said. "In light of this new evidence, it would appear Acolyte Mia's guilt is unassured, and her punishment may be unwarranted. And though it is late in its coming, the Ministry must applaud Acolyte Tric for his honesty. Such bravery should be commended, when considered in light of its price."

Drusilla turned to the Hands beside her.

"Bind him."

The robed figures surrounded Tric, dragged him forward to the statue's base, Drusilla speaking all the while. "Sadly, Acolyte Tric, honesty aside, it seems the penalty inflicted upon Acolyte Hush was not incentive enough to dissuade novices from breaking curfew. Perhaps your own punishment will prevent further disobedience."

She turned to Marielle.

"One hundred lashes."

A murmur rolled down the line of acolytes, Tric's face paling. Even if Adonai prevented him bleeding out, even if Marielle stopped him dying, the agony of a hundred lashes would surely kill him. After all he'd been through, all he'd already suffered, Tric was set to end here in the bowels of this black mountain, screaming in madness and begging for death.

He'd risked all for her. Spoken true, despite knowing what it could cost. Knowing she'd never do the same for him.

"Revered Mother," Mia said. "Wait."

A cool blue stare turned on the girl. "Acolyte?"

She drew a deep breath. Shadow rolling at her feet.

. . . *Would she?*

"I asked Tric to come to my room. The fault is at least half mine." Mia steeled herself. "I should bear half the punishment."

The hall was still as tombs. The Revered Mother looked down the line of Shahiid, asking each one silently in turn. Mouser shrugged. Solis shook his head, seeming to wager watching Tric being flayed would hurt Mia worse than undergoing the punishment herself. But Aalea nodded, and Spiderkiller also acquiesced, dark eyes fixed on Mia. Drusilla pressed her fingers to her lips, brow creased in thought.

"Bind them both," she finally said.

The Hands escorted Tric to the statue, locked his wrists. Mia glared at Tric the whole time, shaking her head. The boy stared back, his face drawn and bloodless.

"*You fucking idiot*," they whispered simultaneously.

Mia felt her shirt being torn away. She was pressed against the stone, the rock cool beneath her flesh, goosebumps rising on her bare skin. Glancing over her shoulder, she saw Adonai and Marielle standing behind her. Her fear was beginning to overcome Mister Kindly's appetite. Pulse quickening.

But what must it be like for Tric?

The boy couldn't seem to breathe fast enough, dragging great, heaving lungfuls through clenched teeth. Wide eyes locked on the black stone he was bound to. Mia strained against the manacles, her fingertips managing to find his and squeeze tight.

"Hold on to me," she whispered.

Tric blinked the sweat from his eyes. Nodded. And then Hands stepped up behind them, and wrapped blindfolds about their eyes, shutting out the light.

Mia felt Tric's hand clench tight, crushing her fingers in his grip. She knew exactly where he was then. Fourteen years old. Bound to the tree outside his grandfather's home. Waiting in the dark for the next rock to hit. The next slap. The next gob of spit.

Bastard. Whoreson. *Koffi.*

"Mister Kindly," she whispered.

"*. . . no, mia . . .*"

"Help him."

"*. . . and if i help him, who helps you . . . ?*"

She felt Hands checking the manacles at her wrists. Heard footsteps as they backed away. Tric was squeezing her fingers so tight they hurt.

"You told me that to master the darkness without, first I have to face it within . . ."

"*. . . not here. not like this . . .*"

"If not here, then where?"

She felt her shadow shiver. The fear inside her rising.

"I can do this," she hissed.

Weaver Marielle's knuckles popping.

Mother Drusilla's voice echoing in the blindfold black.

"Begin."

An empty, endless moment.

"*. . . as it please you . . .*"

The darkness rippled about her feet, one last goodbye. And then Mister Kindly was gone, slipping across the black stone and into Tric's shadow. She heard the boy's breath come just a touch easier, the crushing grip on her fingers slackening as the not-cat pounced upon his fear. There, pressed against that chill stone, despite the agony to come, Mia found herself smiling. Silence rang in the hall, deep as centuries. The world holding its breath.

And then the weaver clenched her fists.

The blow was white-hot flame and rusted razors. Lemon and salt rubbed into a fresh and bleeding wound, torn in four ragged strips across her back and peeling her lips back from her teeth in a silent scream.

Every muscle seized tight. Her back tore like paper. Mia bucked against the stone, her grip on Tric's fingers tightened as fear rushed into the empty void after the whiplash faded. Great, freezing tidal waves of it, crashing over her head and dragging her down. Every second bleeding into forever. Every moment spent waiting for the next blow to fall was its own agony. She found herself praying for it, just so the pause would end. And then it fell, tearing across her back in four lines of perfect pain.

She threw back her head. Mouth open but refusing to scream. She wouldn't give them the satisfaction. Jessamine and Diamo. Solis. She could feel their stares. Taste their smiles. The blood flowed warm and thick down her back, pooled on the empty shadow at her feet. The weaver struck again, the sound of invisible whips cracking across the air, the pain incandescent. Still she hung on to Tric's hand, clung to that single, burning thought; that no matter how much it hurt

(*crack*)

no matter how much she wanted to

(*crack*)

she would never

(*crack*)

let them

(*crack*)

hear

(*crack*)

her

(*crack*)

scream.

But by the tenth strike, she'd lost her grip on Tric's hand. By the twelfth, she'd lost her grip on her terror, and the cry spilled from her lips, long and thin and trembling. She could feel Tric's hand groping for hers, but she curled her fingers into a fist. Lowered her chin and pressed her forehead to the stone. No crutches. No passengers. No one beside her. No one inside her. Just she (*crack*) and the pain (*crack*) and the fear (*crack*). All of them one.

Light-headed now. Drifting but still awake. Held somewhere between consciousness and oblivion by the sorcerii and their magiks. A brief respite dawned after the twentieth scourge, the warmth flowing back up her legs, reentering her severed veins and sundered arteries, ending the winter threatening to overwhelm her. She heard Tric's whisper from somewhere far away

"Mia take him back . . ."

grinding her forehead upon the stone, blood in her eyes

"Mia please . . ."

The dark loomed before her now. The nightmare lurking behind the wall of sleep. And as the weaver struck again, the agony flaring anew and ripped in a wordless howl from her throat, the wall began to crumble. No waking state to hold them in check, here on the edge of oblivion. No shadowcat perched above the bed, watching with his not-eyes for the nightmares to come calling. Just she. Little Mia Corvere. Alone in the dark as it swelled ever deeper, fear rushing faster, madness creeping closer. And there in the paper-thin black, so little left between them and her and her and them, she finally saw the things that had haunted her sleep all these years with her waking eyes.

(*crack*)

Not phantoms.

(*crack*)

Not nightmares.

(*crack*)

(*crack*)

(*crack*)

Memories.

CHAPTER 27

TRUEDARK

Don't look.

Mia stole through the hallways of bloody stone, wrapped in a darkness so deep she could barely see. Bodies. Everywhere. Men choked and stabbed. Beaten to death with their own chains and bludgeoned to death with their own limbs. The sound of murder ringing all around, the stink of offal thick in the air. Vague shapes running past her, tangling and screaming on the floor. The cries ringing somewhere far away, somewhere the dark wouldn't let her hear.

She slipped inside the Philosopher's Stone like a knife between ribs. This prison. This abattoir. Down past the open cells to the quieter places, where the doors were still sealed, where the prisoners who didn't wish to try their luck in the Descent were still locked, thin and starving. She threw the shadowcloak aside so she could see better, peering through the bars at the stick-thin scarecrows, the hollow-eyed ghosts. She could see why folks would try their luck in the Senate's horrid gambit. Better to die fighting than linger here in the dark and starve. Better to stand and fall than kneel and live.

Unless, of course, you had a four-year-old son locked in here with you . . .

The scarecrows cried out to her, thinking her some Hearthless wraith come to torment them. She ran the length and breadth of the cell block, eyes wide. Desperation now. Fear, despite the cat in her shadow. They must be here somewhere? Surely the Dona Corvere wouldn't have dragged her son out into the butchery above for the chance to escape this nightmare?

Would she?

"Mother!" Mia called, tears in her eyes. "Mother, it's Mia!"

Endless hallways. Lightless black. Deeper and deeper into the shadow.

"Mother?"

". . . i will search the other halls. swifter that way . . ."

"Don't go far."

". . . never fear . . ."

Mia felt a chill as Mister Kindly went bounding down the corridor. The gloom closed in, and she wrenched a guttering torch from the wall, shadows *dancing. A cold fear crept into her gut, but she grit her teeth, beating it back. Breath quickening. Heart pounding as she roamed corridor to corridor, calling loud as she dared.*

"Mother?"

Down deeper into the Stone.

"Mother!"

And finally, she found her way into the deepest pit. The darkest hole.

A place the light had never touched.

Don't look.

"Pretty flower."

The girl squinted in the dark. Heart seizing tight at the sound of her voice.

". . . Mother?"

"Pretty flower," came the whisper. "Pretty, pretty."

Mia stepped forward in the guttering torchlight, peered between the bars of a filthy cell. Damp stone. Rotten straw. The reek of flies and shit and rot. And there, curled in the corner, stick-thin and wrapped in rags and sodden drifts of her own tangled hair, she saw her.

"Mother!"

Though she held her hand up to the light, wincing, the Dona Corvere's smile was yellow and brittle and far, far too wide.

"Pretty thing," she whispered. "Pretty thing. But no flowers here, no. Nothing grows. What is she?" Wide eyes searched the dark, falling anywhere but Mia's face. "What is she?"

"Mother?" Mia approached the bars with halting steps.

"No flowers, no."

Dona Corvere rocked back and forth, closing her eyes against the light.

"All gone."

The girl set down the torch, knelt by the bars. Looking at the shivering skeleton beyond, her heart shattering into a million glittering shards. Too long.

She'd waited too long.

"Mother, don't you know me?"

"No me," she whispered. "No she. No. No."

The woman clawed the walls with bloody fingers. Mia saw scores of marks on the stone, rendered in dried scarlet and broken fingernails. A pattern of madness, carved with the Dona Corvere's bare hands. A tally of the endless time she'd spent rotting here.

It had been four long years since Mia had seen her, but not so long she couldn't remember the beauty her mother had been. A wit sharper than a duelist's blade. A temper that shook the ground where she walked. Where was that woman now? The woman who'd held Mia against her skirts so she couldn't look away? Forcing her to stare as her father flopped and twisted at the end of his rope? As the sky itself cried?

Mia could hear Scaeva's voice in her head, an echo of the turn her father died.

"And as you go blind in the black, sweet Mother Time will lay claim your beauty, and your will, and your thin conviction you were anything more than Liisian shit wrapped in Itreyan silk."

Dona Corvere shook her head, chewing at matted strands of her hair. Jewels and gold had once sparkled in that raven black, now rife with fleas and flecked with rotten straw. Mia stretched her hand through the bars. Reaching out as far as she could.

"Mother, it's Mia."

Eyes filling with tears. Bottom lip trembling.

"Please, Mother, I love you."

The Dona Corvere flinched at that. Peering through bloody fingers. Recognition flaring in the shattered depths of her pupils. Some remnant of the woman she'd been, clawing to surface. The woman every senator once feared. Her eyes filled with tears.

"You're dead," *she breathed.* "I am dead with you?"

"Mother, no, it's me."

"They drowned you. My beautiful girl. My baby."

"Mother, please," *Mia begged.* "I've come to save you."

"O, yes," *she whispered.* "Take me to the Hearth. Sit me down and let me sleep. I've earned my rest, Daughters know it."

Mia sighed. Heart breaking. Tears in her eyes. But no. No seconds to waste. Time enough to tend her mother's hurts when they were far from here. Time enough when they were . . .

. . . they . . .

Mia blinked in the gloom. Eyes searching the cell beyond.

"Mother, where's Jonnen?"

"No," *she whispered.* "No flowers. Nothing grows here. Nothing."

"Where is my brother?"

The woman mouthed shapeless words. Lips flapping. She clawed her skin, dug her hands into her matted hair. Gritting her teeth and closing her eyes as tears spilled down her cheeks.

"Gone," *she breathed.* "With his father. Gone."

"No." *Mia shook her head, pawed at her aching chest.* "O, no."

"O, Daughters, forgive me."

It took all she had. Every ounce of herself. But Mia pushed the grief aside. Stamped it under heel. Blinked back the burning tears. Trying not to remember the nevernights she'd held her baby brother in her arms, singing to shush his little cries. Ignoring her mother's fevered moans, she studied the heavy lock on the cell door. Drawing a pick from her belt, she set to work as Mercurio had taught her. Focusing on the task. The comfort of the rote. The darkness around her shivering. The cries of distant murder growing louder. Closer?

Don't look.

Her mother's hand snaked out of the shadows. Wrapped around Mia's wrist. The girl flinched, but the Dona Corvere held her daughter tight. Rotten breath hissing.

"How can I touch you if you're dead?"

"Mother, I'm not dead." *She took the woman's other hand, pressed it to her face.* "See? I live. Same as you. I live."

Dona Corvere squeezed her wrist so tight it hurt.

"O, god," *she breathed.* "O, never. No flowers . . ."

"Hush, now. We're getting you out of here."

"My baby boy," *she keened.* "My sweet little Jonnen. Gone. Gone."

Tears spilling down filthy cheeks. Whispering, soft as snow.

"My Mia is dead too."

"No, I'm here." *Mia kissed those bleeding, torn fingers.* "It's me, Mother."

". . . mia, the way is clear, we must hurry . . ."

Mister Kindly materialized on the floor beside her, his whisper cutting in the gloom. The Dona Corvere took one look at the shadowcat and hissed like she'd been scalded. Shrinking back from the bars, into the far corner, teeth bared in a snarl.

"Mother, it's all right! This is my friend."

"Black eyes. White hands, O, god, no . . ."

". . . mia, we *must* go . . ."

"He's in you," *the Dona whispered.* "O, Daughters, he's in you."

Mia's hands were shaking. The lock wouldn't budge. Rusted and clogged with grime. Dona Corvere was in the corner, three fingers held up to Mister Kindly; Aa's warding sign against evil. Mia could hear the chaos above, the screams of the dying, blood thick in the air. Rage filled her then, to see the suffering her mother had been subjected to, the ruin it had made of her. The suns were far below the horizon now, the power of truedark outside swelling in her bones. Unthinking, she raised both hands, face twisted as the shadows trembled. Liquid darkness snaked around the bars, pulling tight. Iron shrieked as it was torn loose from its moorings, the cell peeling open, bars snapping like dry twigs. Mia stepped through the hole she'd made, held out her hand.

"You're his," *her mother hissed.* "You're his."

". . . mia, we have to go . . ."

"*Mother, come with me.*"

Dona Corvere shook her head. Eyes full of horror. "*You're not my baby.*"

Mia grabbed her mother's hand. The woman screamed, trying to pull loose, but Mia held on tight. Binding her in ribbons of darkness, Mia dragged her mother to her feet and out of the cell. Alinne Corvere no longer seemed to recognize her daughter, writhing in Mia's grip. But Mia clung on, dragging her down the corridors and up the stairs toward the battlements above. The smell of carnage grew thicker, the song of murder rose higher. And when they began to stumble past the bodies, the dona's moans became screams. Bloodshot eyes squinting in the burning light. Mouth open.

Screaming.

"*. . . she must be quiet . . . !*"

"*Mother, stop it, they'll hear us!*"

"*Let me go! LET ME GO!*"

"*. . . mia . . . !*"

A man loomed out of the darkness ahead, a set of bloody manacles clutched in his fist. Spotting them, he roared and charged down the corridor. Mia turned toward him, flicked her wrist. The shadows unfurled, picking the man up and slamming him into the wall. He dropped to his knees, bleeding and dazed as two more inmates rounded a corner—a pair of boys barely more than teenagers, faces daubed with blood. The darkness roiled at Mia's command, slapping them about as if they were made of straw. But in dealing with the boys, she'd loosened her grip on her mother, and the Dona Corvere broke free, dashed away down the corridor.

"*Mother!*"

The man she'd slammed into the wall rose on trembling legs, lurched toward her. Mia threw him into the bricks again, harder than before, and with a wet sigh he collapsed and stayed down. Mia charged after her mother, screaming for her to stop.

All the shadows in the hall whipped forward, streaming ribbons of darkness set to snatch her mother up. But more inmates were coming now, Alinne's screams drawing them like drakes to bloody water. Mia smashed them aside, stonework buckling.

"*Mother, stop! Please!*"

Alinne ran on, up a stone stairwell toward the courtyard beyond. One hand shielding her eyes from the torches on the walls, blinding after years of utter blackness. Looking over her shoulder, she moaned as she saw her daughter behind her, the shadows whipping about her like living things. A daemon beside her. Inside *her.*

"*Mother, stop!*"

"*Away from me!*"

The boy appeared from the darkness ahead; some half-starved waif with a sliver of jagged steel in his hand. More afraid than Alinne, most like. But still, he lashed out in that fear, that panic, the blade gleaming red. The dona stumbled. Clutched her breast. And behind her, her daughter screamed.

"NO!"

The shadows reached out as if of their own accord, seizing the boy and his bloody knife and mashing him into the wall, again and again. Mia skidded to a halt at her mother's side, the woman slumped against the stone, her chest wet and red.

"Mother, no, no, no!"

The girl pressed her hand to the wound, trying to stifle the flow. Scarlet pulsing through her fingertips, almost as dark as the shadows around them. The Dona Corvere looked up into her daughter's eyes. Light dying in her own.

"Not my . . . daughter . . ."

She squeezed Mia's hand in a sticky, red grip.

Pushed it aside.

"Just . . . her shadow . . ."

Alinne's chest rattled, the light in her eyes slowly dying. The girl knelt there on the stone, the shadows around her twisting and warping. The very structure about her trembling. Masonry cracking. Ceiling rumbling. Blood on her hands. The murder going on about her echoing in her mind, their blood leaking into the darkness nestled between each and every flagstone.

DON'T LOOK.

The girl stood, raven hair flowing about her as if in some invisible wind. Hands in fists. A hundred shadows snaking in the air about her. The walls split and cracked. The ceiling began to sag, to crumble. And just as the brickwork split asunder, as hundreds of tons of masonry collapsed, obliterating the stairwell and all within, the girl stepped inside one of those writhing tendrils of darkness

and stepped out from a shadow

five

floors

above.

On the upper levels now. The Descent in full swing. Murderers and murdered. Chaos and blood. Men smeared in the leavings of their butchery, crude weapons or severed limbs clutched in their hands. One saw her, stepping toward her with a death's head grin. She looked toward him, and the darkness simply tore him apart. Flinging the pieces of him about like an angry child with a broken toy. The walls about her split and buckled. Bricks shattering to dust. More folk came, men and *women drenched in murder, only to be ripped apart like rotten rags. The girl stalked the Stone's battlements, brickwork falling away behind her, tumbling in showers of pulverized mortar and shattered stonework, down, down into the sea.*

The Philosopher's Stone began to list, entire sections of the keep crumbling to dust as the shadows between each brick and stone tore themselves loose, adding to the storm of darkness whirling around the weeping girl. Tears spilling down her cheeks. Face twisted in grief. Her eyes jet black. Too much to hold inside. Too much to bear.

"... mia ...!"

A cat made of shadows materialized beside her, shouting over the din of the tortured stone, the dying men, the wailing darkness. The keep split along its outer wall, ramparts collapsing into the ocean below. The thieves and thugs ceased their bloody struggles and cowered in corners or fled back to the cells they'd escaped from. The stones beneath her feet fell away, left her suspended in a web of writhing darkness.

"... mia, stop this ...!"

The girl's whole body was shrouded in shadow now. Ink-black tendrils sprouting from her back like wings, ribbons of razor-sharp darkness springing from every fingertip. Black eyes were affixed across the bay, to the Ribs rising above the City of Bridges and Bones. Home to the Senate of Itreya and all its marrowborn nobility, lorded over by the gloating consul who'd torn her familia apart. Killed her father. Her baby brother. And now her mother, too.

The girl shook her head. Snarled.

"This stops when he does."

And curling her fingers into trembling fists, she disappeared.

S *tep.*
    She was at the bottom of the Stone, among the shadows of the jagged rocks.
        Step.
    She was across the bay, in the shifting black of the shoreline.
                Step.
    She stood on the boulevard, looking at the Carnivalé crowd in their smiling masks. Mister Kindly was no longer with her, but rage walked beside her instead, boiled away the place fear tried to take root. She stepped from one shadow to the next, like a child hopping stones across a flooded drain. Folk shivered as she passed. The city around her was blurred and indistinct; just dim silhouettes against a deeper dark. But the night skies above were bright as sunlight. Stars strewn like diamonds across a funeral shroud. The shadows sang to her. Held her tight and wiped away her tears. An aching in their bellies. A wanting on their tongues.

Hungry, she realized.

The Dark was hungry.

Mia searched the skyline, found the Ribs jutting above distant rooftops. Step. And step. And step. Until she found herself outside the Basilica Grande. She knew they'd be there for the truedark mass. All in a row. Consul Scaeva. Cardinal Duomo. Justicus Remus. False piety and pretty robes. Blood-soaked hands pressed together, eyes upturned to the sky and praying for the suns they'd never see again.

She stepped from the shadows of a triumphal arch, beheld the basilica before her. A vast circular courtyard, hemmed on all sides by marble pillars. A statue of almighty Aa looming in the center, fifty feet tall, sword drawn, three great arkemical globes in one upturned palm. The towering structure beyond, all stained glass and grand, sweeping domes. Archways and spires lit by a thousand globes, trying in vain to banish the hungry Dark.

The courtyard was filled with folk not wealthy or well-born enough to be permitted entry on nights this black. But at each column stood men in gleaming white platemail, crimson cloaks and plumes on their helms. Luminatii legionaries, gathered in force to protect the senators and praetors and pro-consuls and cardinals within the basilica's hallowed halls. The sight of them made her remember her father in the turns before he died. Carrying her on his shoulders through the city streets. His stubble tickling her cheek as he kissed her.

Face purpling.

Legs kicking.

Guh. Guh. Guh.

She looked up at Aa's statue. Spitting hatred.

"I prayed to you. Begged you to bring them home. Were you not everseeing enough to notice them suffering? Or did you just not care?"

The Everseeing made no reply. She reached out toward the Light God and his globes, wrapping them up in ribbons of blackness. And as the crowd around cried out in terror, she clenched her fists. Muscles cording. Veins taut in her neck. With the shriek of tortured stone, the statue tottered on its plinth. The faithful cried out in terror, scattering in screaming droves as it finally toppled forward and smashed onto the cobbles with a deafening boom.

The shadows reached out to the nearest Luminatii, snaking around head and hips and tearing him apart. Blood spattered on polished marble. People screamed. Legionaries roared in alarm, drew their blades. Even here in the gathering night, their swords gleamed as if truelight danced on their edges. Mia stepped into the shadows at her feet, out from the shadow behind the biggest and strongest legionary she could see. The darkness wrapped around his neck seemingly of its own accord, his spine cracking like damp fireworks. Dropping him already dead on the stone.

"*Daemon!*" came the cry. "*Darkin! Assassin!*"

Alarm rang through the vast courtyard. Folk fleeing the ruins of their shattered god in a faithful stampede. Soldiers charging from all around. The darkness was singing to her now, filling her head. Driving conscious thought into the cold and hollow places, leaving only the rage. The hunger. Black tendrils whipping in the dark. Bone and blood. Light scalding her eyes. So many swords now. So many men. Wading through them, skipping from shadow to shadow. Throwing them like toys, the black as sharp as blades, opening up the shiny white steel and showing the red parts inside.

Stepping column to column. To the ruins of Aa's statue and the triple suns smashed in his outstretched palm. She skipped away from a blow that would've taken her head from her shoulders. Another man falling to pieces. On the stairs now. The great double doors, bedecked in graven gold, reflecting the fire of the hundred swords behind her. Mia lifted her hands, flung the doors wide, and roared his name.

"SCAEVA!"

Men awaited her just inside the door, her roar becoming a scream as they raised their staves. Cardinal Duomo and his ministers, arrayed in finest trim. The years since her father's execution had changed the cardinal little; he still looked more like a thug who'd robbed a priest of his robes than a man who belonged in them. But he stepped forward, his ministers about him. Black beard bristling, mouth open in a shout.

"In the name of the Light, abomination, begone!"

The Trinity at the end of his staff flared brighter than all three suns. Mia shrieked, staggered back. The light was so fierce, so hot. Hands to her eyes, she squinted through the shocking glare. And there, at the end of the nave, surrounded by two dozen legionaries in polished white and bloody red, she saw him. The beautiful consul with his black eyes and his purple robes and a golden wreath upon his brow. The one who'd smiled as her father died. Consigned her mother to madness. Killed her baby brother.

"SCAEVA!"

"This is Aa's holy house!" Duomo roared. "You have no power here, daemon!"

Mia clenched her fists, blinded by the light before her. Wind roaring in her ears. The heat beating on her like all three suns. Sickness in her belly, vomit in her mouth. No shadows in front of her to seize hold of. It was too much. Too bright. She saw a huge man in white plate, a wolfish face red with rage, one cheek scarred by a cat's claws.

Remus . . .

"Bring her down!" roared the justicus. "*Luminus Invicta!*"

Mia whirled as the Luminatii charged up the steps toward her. The light behind *her was so fierce, the shadow she threw on the stone was as long as sunset. Something sharp and burning cracked across the back of her skull and she staggered. Dozens of legionaries approaching now. Justicus Remus charging, his sword ablaze. The rage burning bright. The Dark inside her roiling. All it wanted was to consume. Open itself wide and drown in the blood it spilled. She could feel it. All around her. Seeping through Godsgrave's cracks. The agony. The fury. The pure and blinding hatred nestled in this city's bones.*

It hates us.

But in the cold and hollow places, some tiny part of her remained. Some tiny part that was not rage or hate or hunger. Just a fourteen-year-old girl who didn't want to die.

The justicus barged through the ranks of holy men, swung his sunsteel with all his might. The Trinity on the pommel of his sword burned brighter than the blade itself. Mia staggered back, the sword clipped her arm, blood boiling as it sprayed. Remus swung again, again, the Luminatii surrounding her now, blinding and bright. And with a ragged cry she fell, down into the shadow at her feet and out of the same shadow a hundred feet away.

Crossbows sang. Flame rippled on polished steel. Remus roared. People screamed. But she was away. Stepping between the shadows; the little girl again, skipping from stone to stone. Blood on the back of her neck, burned near blind by the cardinal's light. And deep down below the hurt and the rage, coiled in the cold and hollow places, the hollowest feeling of all.

Failure.

She found herself on the battlements above the forum. Above the place her father died. The square lit by ruddy arkemical light. Revelers and drunkards dancing along the flagstones. She could hear the cries echoing across the city. Assassin! Daemon! Abomination!

Slumped against the cool gravebone. Shaking hands daubed in blood. The darkness around her whispering, pleading, begging. Just like the darkness inside her. And she, just a child in the midst of it. One little girl in a world so cold and empty, the shadows around her bringing no comfort at all.

She'd no idea how long she sat there. The blood drying to a crust on her hands. The city in chaos. Crowds gathered on the eastern shoreline, looking at the listing ruin of the Philosopher's Stone, ramparts cracking loose and tumbling into the sea. Luminatii patrols tromping through the streets, trying to bring order amid the swelling panic, the rising, drunken chaos. Fistfights and broken glass.

A shiver in her shadow.

"*. . . mia . . .*"

A soft tread on the stone beside her.

"*It said I'd find you here.*"

Old Mercurio knelt beside her, his bones creaking. Mia didn't look at him, eyes fixed on the skyline. The Ribs towering up above them. The War Walkers standing silent vigil. The blazing glow of the Basilica Grande beyond.

"*Rough night, little Crow?*" *he asked.*

Tears rolled down Mia's cheeks. The sob clawed at her throat, demanding to be let out. She bit her lip lest it escape and compound her failure. Tasting blood.

Mercurio took a thin silver case from inside his greatcoat. The girl winced as he struck a flintbox, the momentary flare reminding her of the light in Duomo's hands, burning on Remus's sword. The scent of burning cloves stained the night.

"*Here,*" *Mercurio said.*

She looked at the old man. He was holding out the cigarillo.

"*Settles the nerves,*" *he explained.*

Mia blinked in the dark. Reached out with bloody hands. She put the smoke to her lips, tasted sugar. Warmth to banish the chill. The smoke she inhaled suffocated the sobs, stilling her shakes. She coughed. Sputtered gray. Winced.

"*This tastes horrible.*"

"*It'll taste better tomorrow.*"

She turned her eyes to the twinkling city lights. The burning heart of Godsgrave laid out before her. Wincing at the memory of the men she'd murdered, the men she'd fought. So many of them, and she all alone. Suns burning in their hands. On their steel. In their eyes.

"*It was so bright,*" *she whispered.* "*Too bright.*"

"*Never fear, little Crow.*"

The old man smiled. Patted her hand.

"*The brighter the light, the deeper the shadow.*"

Book 3

BLACK RUNS RED

CHAPTER 28

VENOM

Mia woke in the dark hours later. Phantom pain across her back where the weaver's blows had fallen. Bones still echoing with the ache. Looking up to where a pair of eyes should have been. Mister Kindly on the bedhead, watching while she slept.

"... *are you well* ...?"

"Well enough."

"... *you asked me to mind the boy. i could not keep the nightmare away* ..."

"It's always been there." She sighed. "Always."

Mia sat up in bed, hair draped about her face as she bowed her head. Her muscles ached from the weaver's touch, her mouth dry at the memories she'd kept locked away. Refused to look at. Her mother. The power of the nights, flowing in her veins. It was she who'd destroyed the Philosopher's Stone. She who'd perpetrated the Truedark Massacre. Killed dozens of men on the steps of the Basilica Grande. Dozens more in the Stone itself. Fathers. Brothers. Sons.

She'd tried to murder Scaeva.

Tried and failed.

So much blood on her hands. So much power at her fingertips.

And she'd not even come close.

"We have work to do."

So it began.

Time passed under the evernight sky, initiation drawing ever closer. Routine and ritual. Meals and grueling training and sleep.

To have endured fifty lashes at the weaver's hand was no small feat, and most of her fellow acolytes treated Mia with a newfound respect after the scourging. But Tric had managed to suffer through the entire ordeal without even whimpering, and he was viewed with a kind of awe among the other novices now. Even Shahiid Solis found some praise for his ever-improving form in the Hall of Songs. In the private moments they managed to snatch before ninebells (no acolyte dared set foot outside their room now), Tric whispered to Mia it was ridiculous—that she'd been the brave one, not him. But Mia was content to let him steal the glory. Better to be underestimated.

Easier to hide in the dark than the limelight.

As for Mia, Solis still showed little mercy. She still struck weakly with her swordarm, and her guard broke when hard-pressed. Though he'd caused the injury himself, the Shahiid sent Mia running laps of the stairs for the slightest failing. She endured the abuse silently, and managed to avoid getting her chest perforated when paired with Jessamine or Diamo, which seemed to happen more than the laws of chance would dictate.

She often found herself reporting to the weaver to mend her hurts after Songs was finished. For her part, Marielle said nothing about the blood scourging, and treated Mia no differently. But Mia didn't forget. Didn't forgive.*

---

*Mia managed to study the many faces adorning the weaver's chamber during these ministrations, and she often found herself visiting Marielle with little more than a scratch to be mended, just so she could get another peek at the collection. The masks were wonders, collected from all corners of the Republic.

Mia recognized the *voltos* and *dominos* and *punchinellos* from Itreyan Carnivalé, obviously. The fearsome war masks from the Isles of Dweym, carved of ironwood into the likenesses of horrors of the deep. The flawless, bone-white visage of a Liisian Leper Priest, and a eunuch's blinding cowl from the harem of some long-dead Magus King. But the weaver seemed obsessed with faces in all their shapes and sizes, and it seemed she'd collected no end of strangeness to feed that obsession.

Among the weaver's collection, Mia saw golden wonders fashioned in the likenesses of lions' heads, similar to the cat-headed statues out in the Ashkahi Whisperwastes, and the figures on Mouser's blacksteel blade. She spied a rotting hangman's hood, a blindfold crusted with what looked like dried blood, the death masks of a dozen children, some no more than babes. Faces made of wood and metal. Bone and desiccated skin. Ornate and banal. Beautiful and hideous. The weaver collected them all.

Mia sometimes found herself close to pitying Marielle. It must be an awful thing, she supposed, to have power over the flesh of others and no power over her own. But then she'd remember the horror Marielle had made of Naev's face. And much as she tried to hold on to it, as important as she knew it to be, her pity would slowly die.

Only ashes in its wake.

Adonai showed even less concern for Mia than his sister. Ever aloof, he presided over the regular Blood Walks that sent the acolytes to Godsgrave in search of secrets for Aalea. Mia found herself lurking in tavernas, sweet-talking soldier boys, swimming in rumor. A minor uproar had been caused when Consul Scaeva inducted his seven-year-old son Lucius into the Luminatii legion.* She heard whispers about Justicus Remus siring a bastard on some senator's daughter. Talk that Scaeva was quietly agitating to be named imperator—a title that would give him leadership of the Senate until death. All these and more, Mia reported to Shahiid Aalea, hoping to gain her favor. The woman would simply smile, kiss Mia's cheek, and give no indication of her standing in the contest whatsoever.

It was maddening.

More maddening was Spiderkiller's quandary. Mia spent every spare moment working on it, the antidote still out of reach. Scribbling and cursing. Watching the arkemical symbols collide in her mind's eye until she saw them when she slept.

She and Tric orbited each other slowly, drifting closer to another collision. But the agony they'd endured at the weaver's hands still screamed louder than the ache of not being together. There was no time between lessons, no place after ninebells, no satisfaction in some darkened corner, fucking like thieves. She felt it was worth more than that. And so they waited for the moment the other would break. Dreaming of it alone in her bed, her hands roaming ever lower, silently screaming his name.

And in the quiet minutes, in the shadows, she met with Naev.

Sweating just as much.

Screaming not at all.

B lack Mother, this is going to be the end of me."
       Mia was hunched over her notes at the mornmeal table, watching out of the corner of her eye for flying drinks trays. Osrik and Ashlinn were sat opposite, Tric beside her. Chatter rippled among the acolytes amid the clink and

---

*Eighteen was the minimum age for One Who Shone, a tradition that extended back to the legion's formation. The Luminatii's founding doctrine was astonishingly detailed, and its entry requirements exceedingly strict. Interestingly enough, the codices did not prohibit women joining their ranks, though no woman in history had actually done it.

Yet.

scrape of cutlery, Pip as ever muttering to his knife, pausing between queries as if the blade answered back.*

A fork was tapped against a glass for attention, and all eyes turned to the head table. Revered Mother Drusilla was standing, her customary smile in place. She looked about the assembled faces, nodded to herself as if satisfied.

"Acolytes. This is the last turn of official lessons you will attend as novices of the Red Church. From this eve, until initiation two weeks hence, your time is your own to do with as you see fit. Shahiid Mouser and Shahiid Aalea shall accept purloined items and secrets 'til weeksend. Shahiid Spiderkiller will also welcome solutions to her quandary. I should note there have been no entrants to date, and I will stress that no acolyte is under *any* compunction to solve the Shahiid's riddle. I would hope Spiderkiller has made the penalty for failure plain enough."

The dour woman inclined her head, black lips quirked in a small smile.

"Shahiid Solis's contest in the Hall of Songs begins on the morrow. Preliminary bouts shall be fought in the morn, finals after midmeal. Speaker Adonai and Weaver Marielle will be on hand to attend your hurts.

"Once acolytes are placed at top of hall, the Ministry will conduct a series of final trials. Those of the four who perform to satisfaction will be initiated by the Right Hand of Niah, and anointed with the blood of Lord Cassius himself."

Mia swallowed hard. Everything she'd worked for. Everything she wanted.

"I would suggest you all get a good eve's rest after lessons," Drusilla said. "Tomorrow, final trials begin."

The old woman sat back at table. Chatter picked up among the acolytes slowly, the weight of what was to come hanging over each head. But soon enough, worry was buried under piles of food. The kitchen seemed to be

---

*Mia had heard tell of magikal weapons, of course. Lucius the Omnipotent, last Magus King of Liis, supposedly had a blade that sang as he slew his foes. The legendary hero Maximian wielded a sword known as "Terminus," which reportedly knew how every man under the suns—including its master—would die. Itreyan legend was replete with tales of blades with minds of their own.

Of course, Mia suspected that Pip's knife was no more capable of speech than donkeys are of turning cartwheels. But still, whenever she greeted the boy, she made a point of saying hello to "the Lovely" too.

Here is truth, gentlefriends: when in doubt, it's best to be polite when dealing with lunatics.

pulling out all the stops in these last few turns, and plates were stacked high with delicious pastries and savories, fresh eggs, sizzling ham.

Mia had no stomach for any of it. Turning back to her notes and scowling. The formulae twisted and turned in front of her eyes, a headache slinking to the base of her skull and squeezing. She swore blue in every language she knew, Ashlinn watching her between mouthfuls and smirking at the more colorful curses.

"Tuhk a brmk mubbuh," she said.

Mia glanced up from her notebook. "What?"

Ash tried to enunciate more clearly, treating Mia to an eyeful of her mouthful.

"Tuhk. A. Brmk. Mubbuh."

"Black Mother, don't talk with your mouth full, Ash," Osrik muttered.

Ash took a gulp of water, scowled at her brother. "Funny. I told a handsome soldierboy the same thing last time I was in Godsgrave."

Her brother covered his ears. "Lalalalalaaaaa."

"Sang like a choirboy, he did. During and after. Luminatii boys get all the juice."

"I believe I said, 'La. La. LA,'" Osrik growled.

Ashlinn threw a bread roll at her brother's head.

Osrik raised a spoonful of porridge. "Now you die . . ."

Mia intervened before full-scale war broke out.

"What were you saying, Ash?"

The girl lowered her second bread roll, raised a warning finger at her brother.

"I said you should take a break, maybe. All grind and no grift is no good for you. Stroll around with me next time we go to the 'Grave. I'll take you to some of the Luminatii pubs. Let your hair down a little."

"My hair *is* down."

"Men in uniform, Corvere."

"One-track mind, Järnheim."

"At least they know what a bloody comb looks like."

Ash smiled sidelong at Tric, waiting for a reaction. To his credit, the Dweymeri kept his face like stone as he reached for a bread roll and bounced it off Ashlinn's head.

"It's all fine and well for some," Mia muttered. "You're leading Mouser's contest by near seventy marks. You'll finish top of Pockets for sure."

Ash put her hands behind her head, leaned back and sighed. "Can't help it if I've got natural talent. Steal the T-bone out of a watchdog's teeth, me. Should've seen me lift Spiderkiller's knives. Pure sorcery, it was."

"I saw her face after she realized you'd swiped them," Tric said. "You're a braver sort than me, Ash."

The girl shrugged. "All's fair in love and larceny."

"Two weeks 'til initiation," Mia muttered. "Solis's contest in the Hall of Songs begins *tomorrow*. If I don't break this thing soon, I never will. No one has any idea who's winning Aalea's contest, and I've got zero chance of finishing top of any other hall unless I somehow lift the Revered Mother's key from around her neck."

"Maw's teeth, even I'm not brave enough for that," Ash shuddered, glancing at the old woman. "Hundred marks be damned. She'd kill you twice for even dreaming it."

"So." Mia began scribbling her notes again. "Here we are."

"Aren't you worried about writing it all down?" Ash raised an eyebrow.

"Why, are you planning on stealing this, too?"

"Damn your beady eyes, woman, I stole one lousy punching dagger from you. And I said sorry afterward. Anyone would think I'd pinched your beau."

". . . My eyes aren't beady."

"I'm just saying, be careful where you leave those notes," the girl warned. "It's not like business with Red or her boy is finished. Remember what they did to Lotti."

Mia glanced down the table at Jessamine and Diamo. Though she'd hatched a dozen plans to avenge Carlotta's murder, Mia knew it'd be pure stupidity to act on them. If something happened to either of the pair, the Ministry would be knocking on Mia's door ten seconds later.

Diamo was watching her between mouthfuls, Jess whispering into his ear. Mia idly wondered if the pair were fucking. They never showed affection openly, but parading weakness wasn't Jessamine's style. And though Lotti's death lay between them now, though they'd never be friends, Mia found herself thinking about Jessamine's father. About the Luminatii she'd murdered outside the Basilica Grande. How many more orphans had she created that truedark? How many more Jessamines?

Would the sons and daughters of the men she murdered look at her the same way she looked at Scaeva?

What was she becoming?

Eyes on the prize, Corvere.

Quashing her unpleasant thoughts, Mia turned back to Ash and muttered.

"Well, let's wait until I discover the solution before we worry too much, neh?"

"How close are you?"

Mia shrugged. "Close. And not close enough."

Ash nodded down the table at Jessamine. "Well if you do crack it, keep it secret. If that's your only chance to top a hall, you can be damned sure Red will mark it."

Mia looked up at Ashlinn.

". . . Say that again?"

"Say what again?"

"Red will mark it . . ."

". . . What?"

"Red dahlia," Mia breathed, eyes growing wide. "Blackmark venom."

"Eh?"

Mia thumbed through her pages until she found one covered in scrawl, ran her fingers down the notes. Ash opened her mouth to speak but Mia held up a hand to beg for silence. Scribbled a handful of quick formulae. Flipped back and forth between the new and the old. Finally looking up at the girl and grinning to the eyeteeth.

"Ashlinn, I could kiss you . . ."

". . . I thought you'd never ask?"

"You're a fucking *genius*!" Mia shouted.

The girl turned to her brother and smirked. "See, I *told* you . . ."

Mia stood and grabbed Ash by the ears, hauled her close, and planted a loud kiss square on her lips. Tric led a round of impromptu applause, but Mia was already scooping up her notes and dashing from the Sky Altar. Jessamine and Diamo marked her exit, speaking quietly between themselves. Tric and Ashlinn watched Mia disappear down the stairwell, Osrik returning to his meal and shaking his head.

"All over the shop like a madman's shite, that one."

"Good kisser, though," Ash smirked. "I can see why you're bonce over boots for her, Tricky."

The Dweymeri boy kept his face like stone.

Calmly reached for another bread roll.

Mia spent the rest of the turn in her room, hunched over parchment with a charcoal stick between her fingers. She spread her notes across her bed, running through the concoction again and again. The evemeal bell rang and she stirred not an inch, smoking a cigarillo to kill her hunger. Mister Kindly's not-eyes roamed Mia's solution, page after page of it, purring all the while.

". . . *ingenious* . . ."

Mia dragged deep on her smoke. "If it works."

"... and if not ...?"

"You might be looking for a new best friend."

"... i have a best friend now ...?"

The girl flicked ash at the not-cat's face. She heard ninebells ring, the soft footsteps of acolytes returning to their chambers. Shadows passing across the chink of light seeping in from the corridor. And beside them, a folded sheaf of parchment, slipped beneath her door.

Mia rose from her bed, peered out into the hall. No one in sight. She picked up the parchment, unfolded it, and read the words scribed thereon.

I want you.
T.

Mia's heart beat quicker at the words, wretched butterflies rearing their wings in her belly again. She looked up at Mister Kindly, cigarillo hanging from her lips. The not-cat sat on the bed, surrounded by her sea of notes. Saying not a word.

"I'd have to be a complete idiot to sneak out after ninebells again."

"... especially the very eve before solis's contest ..."

"I should be getting my sleep."

"... love makes fools of us all ..."

"I'm not in love with him, Mister Kindly."

"... a good thing it appears that way to everyone around you, then ..."

Gathering up the loose pages scattered across her bed, Mia tucked them into her notebook and bound it tight, then hid it beneath her desk's bottom drawer.

"Watch my back?"

"... always ..."

Mister Kindly slipped beneath her door, checking the hallway was clear. Mia pulled the shadows to her and faded into the gloom. Stealing out after the not-cat, feeling her way down the long corridor, soft boots making not even a whisper on the stone. The blurred figure of a Hand walked across a passageway ahead and she froze, pressed against the wall. Mia waited until he was well out of sight before moving again, finally stopping outside Tric's door.

She tried the handle, found it locked. Crouching low, she peered through the keyhole, saw Tric on his bed reading by the light of an arkemical lamp. The globe threw long shadows across the floor, and she reached out toward them. Remembering what it was to be that fourteen-year-old girl again. The power of the night at her fingertips. Not afraid of it anymore. Of who she was. What she was.

And closing her eyes, she

                                              stepped

                into the shadow

at her feet

                and out of the shadows

                                                inside his room.

Tric started as she appeared from the darkness, hair moving as if in some hidden breeze. A knife slipped from up his sleeve, stilling in his hand as he recognized her. The boy glanced toward the locked door with questions swimming in his eyes.

Mia kicked her boots off her feet.

"Mia?"

Dragged her shirt off over her head.

"Shhh," she whispered.

And the questions in Tric's eyes died.

SEVERANCE

She woke in his arms.

Forgetting for a moment where she was and what lay ahead. Tric was still asleep, chest rising and falling slowly. She watched him for a silent moment, thoughts clouded. And leaning in close, she kissed him as if it were the last time.

She stole from the room, still dressed in the clothes she wore the night before. Flitting from shadow to shadow. Listening to the ghostly choir, the waking sounds of the Church around her. Finding herself at last in the Hall of Eulogies, beneath Niah's statue. Staring up at the face of the Night herself.

"... *the boy* ..."

Mia glanced to the shadow at her feet. The not-eyes inside it.

"What of him?"

"... *it cannot happen again, mia* ..."

She looked back to the goddess, nodded slow.

"I know."

"... *it has no future* ..."

"I know."

Her eyes roamed the nameless tombs in the walls. The unmarked graves of the Church's fallen. She looked to the stone at her feet. Thousands of the Church's victims beneath the soles of her boots. She still thought it strange; that Niah's servants should have no name to mark their passing, but those they took from this world were immortalized in the granite for all eternity. She thought about the Truedark Massacre. The dozens dead by her hands. The blinding light. Remus. Duomo. Scaeva.

Her mother.

Her father.

When all is blood, blood is all.

The mornbells began to ring, and still she lingered.

Minutes slipping by unmarked, and still she stared.

The goddess stared back. Mute as always.

"... *is everything well* ... ?"

Mia sighed. Nodded slow.

"Everything is perfect."

T he other acolytes were already assembled in the Hall of Songs, rested and fed. Four black-robed Hands stood in the circle's center, one holding what appeared to be a human skull with the crown sawn off. Shahiid Solis loomed beside them, blind eyes upturned. Mia was one of the last to arrive, her tardiness bested only by Ashlinn, who dashed into the hall with only moments to spare. The Shahiid of Songs turned his pale stare on the girl, lips curling.

"Lovely of you to join us, Acolyte," he said.

"Lovely to ... be here ... ," Ash panted.

"Not much longer, I fear."

Turning to the other acolytes, Solis spoke.

"The Trial of Songs begins. I will explain the rules once only. Listen well.

"The trial begins with eliminations. Each of you will fight five bouts, against five random opponents. Each bout is fought to submission, or mortal blow.

Speaker Adonai and Weaver Marielle have graciously agreed to be on hand for festivities." Solis motioned to two figures standing by the sword racks. "They will mend any wound that renders you incapacitated as swift as they may. You may request their aid at any time during a bout, however, to do so will result in forfeiture. Loss will also result if you leave—or are forced to leave—the circle during a bout.

"At the end of eliminations, the four acolytes who have accrued the most victories shall graduate to the finals. Any loss in the finals results in elimination. Whoever wins the last bout shall graduate top of this hall."

Solis's blank gaze roamed the assembled acolytes.

"Questions?"

"There are thirteen of us, Shahiid," Marcellus said. "How will you work the odd number?"

"Only twelve of you will compete. Acolyte Diamo has opted out of the trial."

Mia looked across the circle to Diamo, arms folded and smiling right at her. Ashlinn, who looked like she'd gotten about as much sleep as Mia, whispered to her brother beside her.

"I'm leading Pockets by a clear mile, and I'm still competing in Song. Diamo's not the blademaster Jessamine is, but any chance is better than none at all, surely?"

Osrik shook his head. "Maybe if you weren't out in Godsgrave 'til all hours, you'd have a ken about what went on inside these halls."

"Maw's teeth, Oz, are you going to spit it out, or make me play guess-a-game?"

"Word has it Diamo solved Spiderkiller's formula this morn."

Mia felt her stomach lurch sideways.

"Diamo?" Ash hissed. "He's as handy at venomcraft as a block of wood . . ."

Osrik shrugged. "I'm only saying what I've heard. He visited Spiderkiller before mornmeal. Book of notes in his hand. The Shahiid sealed the hall, but Diamo walked out a while later, right as rain. Went straight to Solis and bowed out of his contest."

Ash looked to Mia.

"Could they be Lotti's notes?"

Mia shook her head. "I don't think Carlotta ever solved the quandary."

"So where'd you hide *your* notes, Corvere?"

Mia swallowed hard. Looked to Tric. Then to Spiderkiller, sitting beside the Revered Mother. The pair were deep in conversation, glancing occasionally to Diamo. And Mia.

". . . My room," she said.

"O. Safe as houses then."

Tric glanced at Mia. "Unless you left your room last night . . ."

Ashlinn glanced back and forth between them. "O, tell me you didn't?"

Mia remained mute, watching Diamo. She saw Jessamine's *fuck you* smile from the corner of her eye. The gleam in that adder green. Spiderkiller's glittering stare.

"Maw's teeth, Corvere," Ash breathed. "You left your notes alone to go for a roll? Little Tricky can't be *that* good . . ."

Tric looked wounded, opened his mouth to—

"'Byss and blood, pay attention," Osrik whispered. "They're about to start."

Ash turned to Solis and his assistants, clamped her lips shut. The Hand holding the human skull had proffered it to a second, standing beside her. A smooth, black stone with a name inscribed on it had been drawn from the hollowed crown, held aloft to the assembled acolytes.

"Marcellus Domitian."

The handsome Itreyan boy looked up at the mention of his name. "Aye."

"Step forward, Acolyte," Solis commanded.

Marco nodded, stepped into the circle's center. The boy tilted his head 'til his neck popped, stretched his arms, and touched his toes. The Hand grasped a stone, drew it forth, and read the name.

"Mia Corvere."

Mia saw Marcellus smile to himself, Diamo and Jessamine share a smug grin. Marco was a skilled swordsman, and he stood a decent chance of placing top four. The boy had thrashed Mia soundly in every sparring match they'd ever had, and everyone in the room knew it.

Mia hovered on the circle's edge. Solis's eyebrow slowly rising.

"Acolyte?"

Mia drew a deep breath and walked out into the circle, soundless as cats. Tread steady. Breath even. She took her place in the circle's center, Solis between her and her opponent. The acolytes stared each other down, Marco's lips twisted.

"Fear not, Mi Dona," he said. "I'll be gentle with you."

Mia spared him a withering glance. Marco grinned. One of the Hands held out a silver priest on an open palm, showed both sides of the coin to ensure no larceny was afoot. On one face, the trinity of three suns, intertwined. On the other, an embossed image of the Senate House in Godsgrave, the Ribs rising into the sky behind it.

"Acolyte Mia, call the toss."

"Trinity."

The acolyte flipped the coin. Quicker than flies, Solis's hand snaked out, snatched it from the air. The Shahiid's worm-blind stare bored into Mia's own.

"I'm certain you've not forgotten your first lesson at my hands, Acolyte," he said. "But I will remind you once more that this is the Hall of Songs, not shadows. If I suspect you of fighting with anything other than blades during these bouts, it will not just be your swordarm I remove from your body. Is that understood?"

Mia looked up into those empty eyes. Her voice a whisper.

"Understood, Shahiid."

The big man let the coin drop from his hand. It sparkled in the stained-glass light as it fell, chimed as it struck the stone.

"Senate side up," reported the Hand.

"Choose your weapons, Acolyte Mia," Solis said.

Mia stepped to the weapon racks, walked along rows and rows of sharp-ened steel. Glancing at Jessamine, she drew a rapier and stiletto. The redhead scoffed. Tric looked decidedly concerned as a curious murmur ran around the circle. Mia had never proved much worth with the traditional dual-handed styles of Caravaggio or Delphini. In Solis's lessons, she'd been constantly berated that her arm was too weak, and she'd not fared much better when Tric tried to teach her the finer points. She could practically see the question in the boy's eyes.

What are you playing at?

Still, for all his doubts, Tric made a fist, gave her a confidence-boosting nod. But beyond him, lurking in the shadows at the Hall's edge among the other Hands, Mia saw Naev. The Hand was shrouded in her cloak, strawberry-blond curls framing her veiled face. And it was to the woman, not the boy, that she nodded back.

Marcellus chose a heavy longsword and buckler to counter Mia's choices, relying on his superior strength to win the bout quickly. Mia watched the boy through her fringe as they took up their stances. All trace of a smile on Marco's pretty face was gone. Everyone knew what was at stake here. Top of hall. One step closer to becoming a full-fledged Blade. Marcellus nodded to Mia, cool and confident. Like everyone else in the room, he knew this would be a thrashing.

A gong rang in the dark. Marco stepped forward, hewing at the air in brutal, broad strokes, expecting Mia to fall back and dodge. He'd no idea the girl had other plans. Plans formulated with Naev in the hours before every mornmeal. Their blades whistling in the dark as they sparred, back and forth. The aches and pains. The weeks and months of feigning weakness in Solis's classes, letting herself get cut, stabbed, constantly thrashed by Jessamine, Di-amo, Pip, Petrus, all of them. All to build up the illusion of weakness. A viper playing possum. A scabdog, bleeding in the dust.

It was just as Mercurio had said.

Sometimes weakness is a weapon.
If you're smart enough to use it.

Mia met Marco's third thrust with her stiletto, twisting it aside and throwing the bigger boy off-balance. Marcellus raised his buckler to guard, ready to fend off Mia's weak riposte as he'd done a hundred times in previous bouts. But with a speed built up in those countless hours with Naev, with a strength she'd kept hidden during those countless beatings under Solis's pitiless eyes, she whipped her rapier through the air, scoring a deep gash on Marco's shoulder.

The boy staggered, confused and off-balance. Mia backed away, bouncing on her toes and cutting the air with her bloodied blade.

"Still going to be gentle with me, Marco?" she smiled.

The boy scowled and launched a second attack, blows scything past Mia's head as she skipped beneath them. The girl faded, twisted, moving like a dancer, and the clash ended with another deep cut, this time on Marco's swordarm. Blood spattered on the stone. And as Marcellus finally began to realize the depth of the water in which he swam, Mia lunged forward, strike, strike, feint, strike, dashing his longsword from his grip, and laying her blade to rest above Marco's thundering heart.

"Yield," she demanded.

The boy looked at her face. Down to her blade. Chest heaving. Skin drenched.

". . . Yield," he finally spat.

"Point!" cried Solis, as someone cracked the gong.

Mia dropped into a skirtless curtsey, and returned to her place at circle.

The other acolytes murmured among themselves, astonished.

Naev's veil hid her smile.

Jessamine smiled not at all.

The bouts ran all morning, sweat and blood glistening on the stone. Though Pip found himself near-gutted by Osrik, and Jessamine cut Marco's throat ear to ear with a lightning-swift strike, Speaker Adonai and Weaver Marielle stepped in quickly to mend any serious injury. No acolyte lost more than a few droplets of their best in the circle.

In defiance of expectations, and beneath Solis's undisguised scowl, Mia won three of her four remaining bouts. Truth was, thanks to Mercurio, she'd never been a slouch with a blade, but Naev's secret tutelage had honed her to a finer edge, and the idea that everyone in the room expected her to fail simply drove her harder to rub their collective faces in the dirt. She thrashed Ashlinn in their matchup (with her lead in Mouser's contest, Ash didn't seem overly worried, though she did flip the knuckles afterward) and soundly beat Petrus, disarming him with a perfect riposte and burying her stiletto in the bigger boy's chest.

With preliminary bouts done, the top four acolytes remained on the circle's edge, while all others retired to the benches around. Both Jessamine and Osrik stood undefeated, placed first and second, respectively. Tric had placed third, losing only to Jess. And in fourth place, despite the stormclouds almost visibly gathering over the Shahiid of Songs' head, sat our own Mia Corvere.

"Final eliminations will now be fought," Solis announced. "Choose the matches."

The Hands at Solis's side bowed. One proffered the human skull, the second reaching inside to pluck one of the four naming stones therein. Mia watched carefully, eyes narrowed. She felt the shadows nestled inside that hollowed crown. The smooth black rock carved with each contender's name. Her fingers twitching behind her back.

"Acolyte Osrik . . ."—a second stone—". . . faces Acolyte Tric."

Mia looked across the circle, met by Jessamine's cold smile.

"Acolyte Mia faces Acolyte Jessamine."

Solis nodded, turned to the two boys.

"Acolytes, take your places."

Mia glanced at Tric, flashed him a smile. The undefeated Osrik prowled into the ring, muscular arms gleaming with sweat. The boys faced each other across the circle, Tric re-tying his saltlocks as Oz called the toss and won.

Tric chose his favored scimitar and buckler, Osrik twin shortswords. The gong rang in the dark, and their steel joined, the pair crashing together like waves and rocks on a storm-washed beach. Mia watched on in silence, chewing her lip. Praying.

The goddess, it seemed, was listening.

After a long and bloody struggle, Mia and the other acolytes looking on in awe, Tric managed the impossible. Osrik put up a valiant fight, his form close to perfect, but perhaps at the heart of it, Tric simply had more to win, and much more to lose. The match ended with Osrik's belly opened from groin to ribs, and the stench of bowel and blood hanging thick in the air amid Adonai's song. Solis cried "Point!" to the applause of the other Shahiid and acolytes, Mia clapping loudest of all.

Adonai and Marielle set to work mending Osrik's wounds. Tric retired to the benches, drenched and panting. But as he met Mia's eyes, he smiled.

"Acolyte Mia," Solis called. "Acolyte Jessamine. Take your places."

Mia glanced around the room. She spotted Diamo seated at the benches with the other acolytes. He was smiling at her too, lopsided and smug.

"I'm hungry, Shahiid," Mia said. "What time is it?"

"Almost midbells," Solis replied. "But we will eat only after preliminaries are concluded. Take your place at circle."

Mia stood slowly, stretched her arms, touched her toes. Her muscles were sore, and despite all the exercise she'd done to strengthen it, her swordarm was aching. She ran her fingers through her hair, fixed her braid while Jessamine prowled back and forth at her mark. Green eyes locked on her opponent. Hunter's cunning and animal rage.

"Maw's teeth, hurry the fuck up, Corvere."

Mia looked to Tric. The boy nodded encouragement, gave her a quick wink. And finally, the shadows shivering about her, Mia stepped up to her mark.

Solis glowered, turned to the Hand beside him.

"Acolyte Jessamine, call the toss."

"Trinity."

The coin flashed in the air. Tumbled end over end.

"Senate side up," the Hand declared.

"Acolyte Jessamine," Solis said. "Choose your weapons."

The redhead strode to the racks. Glanced over her shoulder at Mia, customary smirk in place. She wandered up and down the blades as if uncertain, finger to lips like a maid at market looking for a new dress. But eventually, she settled where Mia always knew she would—the rapier and stiletto combination favored by all Caravaggio fighters. The weapons were needle sharp, and whistled a bright tune as Jessamine sent them twirling in the air. The girl stepped back into the circle, inclined her head to Mia.

"Pity there's no crossbows on the racks, neh? You might have a chance with forty yards and a stout quarrel between us, little girl."

Mia ignored the maddening smirk, strode to the weapons. She drew twin gladii from the racks, cut the air with a few experimental swings. A gladius was shorter but heavier than a rapier. Almost as fast and built to take more punishment. A stout blow could shatter a rapier easily, and Naev had shown Mia that a pair of them wielded with skill could build a wall of blades a Caravaggio fighter would be hard-pressed to break. Question was if Mia would have any chance of hitting Jessamine back . . .

Jessamine glanced to Diamo on the benches. He was watching her closely, still smiling, his eyes bright and wide. He wiped at his upper lip, damp with sweat.

Then he blew Mia a kiss.

"Stop stalling, Corvere," Jessamine sighed. "Let's get this over with."

"Aye," Mia nodded. "It seems about time."

Shahiid Solis and his assistants retreated from the ring, leaving the girls alone. Sourceless light gleamed from above, picking out the circle in dull luminance. Mia looked to Weaver Marielle, the smile on those hideous lips. Speaker Adonai leaned against the wall beside her, studying his fingernails. She noticed the Revered Mother, Aalea, Mouser, and Spiderkiller had all gathered to watch the final bouts, sitting together on stone benches among the acolytes. Arkemical current seemed to dance in the air. Mia's skin prickled as her shadow whispered.

"... *no fear* ..."

Ashlinn cupped her hands, hooted from the bench. "Kick her skinny arse, Corvere!"

"Enough!" Solis bellowed.

Mia drew a breath.

Jessamine took up her stance.

A gong rang in the dark.

The redhead lunged, stepping quick across the stone, aiming for Mia's throat. Mia stepped back, battering aside the rapid flurry with her off-hand, riposte whistling past Jessamine's jaw. Blades sang, pale light gleaming on polished steel. Both competitors were cautious at first; Mia in deference to Jessamine's skill, and Jessamine out of respect for the steel in Mia's hand. But soon enough, the redhead gained her confidence, forcing Mia back to the circle's edge with impressive footwork, her strikes falling like hail.

Strike, feint, lunge went the verse. Parry, riposte came the chorus. The girls danced about the ring to the song, sweat burning in narrowed eyes. Mia was almost entirely on the defensive, dodging back and forth at the ring's edge. But after three or four minutes, her gladii were growing heavy. Though she launched a few laudable strikes, Mia was already gasping. Her lack of sleep was beginning to show. No mornmeal in her belly didn't help matters any. She knew it as well as anyone in the room; Jessamine's constant barrage with her lighter, quicker weapons would spell her end on a long enough timeline.

Mia was too slow to guard, and Jessamine drew blood once, then twice. A thin line of red opened across Mia's left forearm, a deep gouge peeled back her shoulder. Mia's breath came quicker, spit on her lips. The blood made her grip treacherous. Her lungs burned. Jessamine simply smiled, maintaining her tempo of feint strike, strike feint. Keeping Mia busy now. Running down the hourglass a little. No sense risking a solid hit from those gladii when blood loss and fatigue could do the work for her.

"You frightened of me, Jess?" Mia lunged forward to try and lock her up.

"Terrified," the redhead said, slipping away and slicing another gouge in Mia's arm. "Can't you see me trembling?"

The pair circled each other, weapons raised. Damp fringe hanging in Mia's eyes.

Fingers sticky on her hilt.

Gasping.

"So Diamo cracked the antidote, neh?"

Jessamine smiled, red and poisonous. "So I hear."

"That idiot wouldn't know venomcraft if it danced on his bollocks in Liisian heels."

"Shahiid Spiderkiller doesn't seem to agree."

Feint, parry, lunge.

Mia wiped the sweat from her brow on her sleeve. "And I suppose when I go back to my room this eve, everything's going to be exactly where I left it?"

"You're presuming you're going to make it back to your room at all, little girl."

Jessamine stepped forward, striking at face, chest, belly. Mia staggered, threw a reckless riposte to force the redhead away. Jessamine backed off, blades twirling, moving swift and sure. Still smiling.

"Those big old meat cleavers getting heavy yet?" she asked.

"Think time's on your side, neh?"

Jessamine simply grinned in response. But Mia grinned wider as the midmeal bells began tolling, a song of brass and echoes filling the hall.

"What about Diamo, you think?" Mia asked. "Think time's on his side, too?"

Jessamine stole a glance to the boy, now wiping sweat from his brow.

"What the 'byss are you talking about, Corvere?"

Mia smiled all the wider. "I wondered if either of you would be fool enough. I really thought I might have oversold it yesterturn at mornmeal. But you've never been the sharpest blades in the bunch. The note you sent from Tric was a nice touch, though. Nothing like the promise of a strapping Dweymeri boy to lure a girl out of her room, neh?"

Jessamine stopped her dance, staring at Mia with widening eyes.

"Still," Mia continued. "I wondered if Diamo would offer you the notes instead. Lucky for you, you're better with a blade. And that chivalry's as dead as he is."

"You're full of shit," the redhead scoffed.

Mia tilted her head.

"Am I."

"J-Jess . . ."

The redhead looked to Diamo, her face turning paler still. The boy was staggering to his feet. Drenched in sweat and holding his belly, a thin trickle of blood spilling from his lips. He winced, teeth painted red, groaning. And as the acolytes around him flinched away in revulsion, the boy spewed scarlet all over the floor.

"O, Goddess . . . Di?"

Jessamine's face drained of all color as the boy fell to his knees. Quicker than silver, Mia stepped up and smashed the rapier from Jessamine's nerveless fingers. The girl tried to muster some semblance of guard, but Mia swatted the stiletto aside, and with a shapeless cry of rage, buried her sword deep in Jessamine's gut.

The redhead clutched the wound, eyes wide. Mia tore her gladius free in a spray of red, kicked Jessamine savagely in the chest, sent her skidding across the polished stone. Solis cried "Point!" A gong rang in the dark. But all about the ring was chaos. Adonai and Marielle knelt beside Jessamine. The speaker began his song, the blood crawling back up into the girl's body. The weaver's fingers danced over the hideous belly wound, flesh knitting closed. But Jessamine's eyes were still locked on Diamo.

The boy was on all fours among the benches. Vomiting another gout of blood over the floor. Acolytes backed away, fearing contagion, the stink of emptied bowel and bladder, but Tric ran to the boy and knelt alongside him, uncertain what to do.

"Someone get some water!" Tric roared. "Help us!"

"You will do no such thing," Spiderkiller said.

Silence fell in the Hall of Songs, broken only by Diamo's long and wretched moans. Spiderkiller rose from her seat beside the Revered Mother. Her saltlocks writhed as she walked, a nest of serpents at her brow. Her dark eyes were fixed on Diamo, the boy's hand outstretched toward her. He was on his back now, trying to speak, blood bubbling thick on his lips.

"Shahiid, please." Jessamine groaned. "Please, save him."

Spiderkiller blinked. "You all knew the rules of my trial. Those who try and fail, die. No mercy. No exception."

"I . . ." Diamo gurgled at her feet, clutching the hem of her robe. "Sor . . . reee."

"O, aye," Spiderkiller nodded. "I've no doubt you are."

The boy coughed, pink froth bubbling on his lips. He spasmed, flecks of bloody spittle spraying. Tric backed away as the tremors worsened. Diamo clutched his belly and screamed, dark blood bubbling out of his throat. Thrashing on the damp stone. Tears filling his eyes. Fingers clawing his skin. And at last, after minutes of wailing agony, with one last burbling cry, fell still.

Mia stood in the circle's center.

Bloody gladius in her hand.

"That's for Lotti, bastard," she whispered.

"You bitch . . ." Jessamine was on her feet, blood drying on her tunic and lips. Clutching the place where Mia had skewered her. "You killed him . . ."

"Me? How? It's not my fault he poisoned himself. Unless . . ." Mia tilted her head. "Unless there was something wrong with the notes he used?"

Jessamine snatched up her fallen rapier, face twisted in a snarl.

"Enough!" Solis bellowed. "Acolyte Jessamine, the bout is done. Weapons down. Point to Acolyte Mia. Resume your places, all of you!"

Jessamine drummed her fingers along her blade's hilt. Glanced at Solis to take his measure. Finding no pity in his gaze, the girl tossed her blade aside. Hands moved quickly to remove Diamo's body, mop up the blood left behind. Speaker Adonai licked his fingers clean and watched them work with twinkling eyes.

Jessamine sat down on the benches. Face like stone. Mia sat back at circle, opposite the assembled acolytes. Ash caught her eye, nodded in approval.

Good work, she signed in Tongueless. *Ice cold.*

Mia shrugged as if she'd no idea what the girl meant. Turned her gaze to Jessamine. The redhead was staring back at her. Fingering the golden chain about her throat, she nodded. Promising.

Mia smiled in return.

And she blew Jessamine a kiss.

Solis dismissed the acolytes to the Sky Altar for midmeal, reminding them to be back within the hour. The final would be fought before all assembled; the victor would wear Solis's mark of favor. The first acolyte to finish top of hall would be named by turn's end.

Mia and Tric sat across from each other at midmeal, plates heaped high. Mia plowed through her lunch with all the hunger a skipped eve and mornmeal could provide, trying to ignore Tric's eyes. The boy didn't seem hungry, poking at his food and sipping his wine, staring into space when he wasn't staring at her.

Diamo's death meant that Spiderkiller's quandary was still unsolved—Mia could finish top of Truths if she dared take the challenge. But she'd not have to worry about poisoning herself if she won Solis's trial, and Maw's teeth, after all the punishment he'd put her through, it'd be bliss to watch that condescending bastard acknowledge her as the winner.

On the other hand, Mia doubted Tric had a chance of topping anywhere else. He was no master at venomcraft, nor thievery, though she supposed he might have gleaned a secret or two from the 'Grave. Still, if she knocked him out of Solis's contest, she was cutting his chances of being named a Blade by no small measure.

She could feel him watching her between mouthfuls. Brow creased. Lips thin.

Was he thinking the same as her? Wondering where exactly this was leading? Sooner or later, one of them had to lose. Sooner or later, one of them was going to get hurt. The tension was thick enough to taste it on her tongue.

"Did you do it?" he finally asked.

". . . Do what?" Mia blinked.

Tric lowered his voice so the others might not hear. "Your notes. Did you leave them for Diamo to steal? With a false antidote inside?"

Mia looked into those big hazel eyes. Saw a flicker of softness. That same softness he showed in her bed. Holding her close and smoothing back her hair. Problem was, there was no place for it out here. And for all her talk to Mister Kindly of holding on to her pity, she knew there was precious little place for that, either.

Not for Lotti's murderers, anyway.

Mia put down her cutlery. Eyes narrowing. "And what if I did, Don Tric?"

"When you came to me last night . . . was that because you wanted to be with me, or you just wanted to be out of your room?"

"Why can't it be both?"

"I don't like being used, Mia."

Mia glanced sidelong at the acolytes around her. Though each pretended to be busy with their meal, she could sense them listening. Feel their eyes. Staring at this shade of Mia Corvere they'd never really seen. Liar. Snake. Fox.

"Look, if Diamo stole my notes and gulped down a bellyful of poison, the idiot deserves whatever he got. Someone that stupid wouldn't last a month in a real chapel. I did him a damned mercy."

"Mercy?" Tric frowned. "He choked to death on his own blood, Mia."

Mia glared down the bench at Jessamine, back to Tric.

"Like Lotti, you mean?"

Jessamine thumped the table, clutching her roastknife in a tight fist. She glanced at the Shahiid, wary of drawing their eye. Staring at Mia, her voice low and measured.

"We never *touched* Carlotta."

"Bullshit," Ash muttered. "Everyone in here heard you threaten to kill her, bitch."

"Black Mother, I *would have* if I had the chance," Jessamine hissed. "But I'd account for it afterward, Corvere. At least to you. I'd want to see the look in your eyes." The redhead shook her head, lips curled in a sneer. "But I'd have wanted to see the look in Carlotta's eyes, too. So I'd have done her head on. Just so she could see my face when I ended her."

Mia stared at Jessamine, eyes glittering like polished flint.

"Then you're an idiot too," she said.

"Mia . . . ," Tric warned.

"What?" she snapped. "Listen, just because I'm willing to wet the furs with you doesn't mean you get to judge who I am and what I do. This isn't a nursery. Maw's teeth, we're would-be *assassins*, Tric. Maybe you should start acting like it. Remember why you came here." She eyed the phial of ink around his neck, all that remained of his grandfather's hatred. "Remember who you used to be, even if the mirror has forgotten."

Tric's hand went to his necklace, eyes growing wide. Hurt and anger in equal measure.

Mia ignored the both of them. Pushed her plate aside.

"See you in the circle."

And without another word, she rose and walked away.

M ia looked the Dweymeri boy in his eyes. Saw no flicker of softness. Nothing close to what he showed in her bed, holding her close and smoothing back her hair. No trace of the hurt left either. He'd left that behind in the Sky Altar.

No, what she saw was rage.

The acolytes and Ministry were assembled around the circle. Solis and his Hands waiting, silver coin in his palm. Mia and Tric faced each other across ten feet of buffed granite, the stains of Diamo's ending nowhere to be seen.

"Acolyte Mia, call the toss."

"Senate."

A bright chime rang as the coin struck stone.

"Senate it is."

Tric stalked to the racks, drew out a cruel scimitar and sliced the air. Strapping a small buckler to his off-hand, he stepped back into the ring. Eyes cold. Jaw clenched.

He's furious. I cut him badly.

Mia walked to the racks, selected a stiletto and rapier.

Good.

The gong rang. The pair joined, steel against steel, speed and agility versus strength and ferocity. Every acolyte knew by now that Tric and Mia shared each other's bed. She supposed every one of them was expecting one or the other to fight soft. To let the other win.

That'd be the romantic thing to do, aye?

Within ten seconds of the gong fading, that thought was left dead on the circle floor. Tric was out for blood. Face twisted. Teeth clenched. His saltlocks whipped about him as he swung at Mia's chest and head. The girl was quick, but the big Dweymeri's footwork was excellent, hemming Mia in on the circle's edge, where her speed counted for less. Surprise was no longer on her side; everyone knew her swordarm wasn't as weak as she'd played it, nor she the novice she'd pretended. And so Tric was wary, guard high, never overextending and leaving himself open to her rapier.

His scimitar whistled in the air, bright notes ringing across the hall as their blows met. Mia locked up his sword, blades intertwined, leaning in close as he pressed down on her with all his strength. Sweating. Red-faced. Grinning.

"You seem angry, Don Tric."

"Fuck you, Mia."

"Later, lover."

The girl lashed out with her knee, several acolytes hooting as it connected with Tric's groin. The boy doubled up as Mia slipped aside, spinning away and back out into the center of the ring. Tric regained his footing, whirled to face her, saltlocks flying. One hand still pressed to his injured jewels.

"I can kiss those better, if you like?" Mia called.

Tric bellowed in rage, charged across the circle. Pure fury now. The feel of her in his arms forgotten. Mia danced backward, sliced the boy's forearm. Another strike pierced his tunic, opened up a bleeding gash in his belly. Mia grinned all the while, watching Tric get angrier and angrier. The acolytes around them reveling in the show. Revered Mother Drusilla watching intently, the weaver, even the speaker on the edge of their seats. Solis's head was tilted as he listened. Jaw set. Fists clenched.

Mia knocked Tric's scimitar aside with a swift backhand strike, sent it spinning across the floor. She ducked low as Tric lunged with his buckler, stepped aside as he struck again. And dropping down into a split at his feet, Mia buried her rapier in his belly.

The acolytes gasped. Ash cheered in delight.

Mia looked up at Tric's pain-filled stare.

Eyes locked with his.

Smiling.

"*Koffi*," she whispered.

Tric's face paled. He grit his teeth, narrowed that pretty hazel stare. Reached out to Mia's hand and seized it tight, crushing her fingers against her rapier hilt. And white-knuckled, face twisted, blood spilling from his mouth, the Dweymeri boy pulled himself farther onto her blade. Dragging Mia up off the floor until her sword's cross guard was pressed against his bleeding gut.

He drew back his buckler. Smashed it into Mia's face. The girl reeled away, blood spilling from split lips. She caught her footing, lashed out, burying her stiletto in Tric's chest. But the boy didn't flinch, pummeling Mia's face again, stars bursting in her sight as the shield met her cheek, head lolling on her neck as darkness gathered behind her eyes. A blow to her chest sent her to the floor, fingernails clawing the stone as she tried to rise. A boot met her ribs. Another. Another. Looking up through a haze of red as Tric slid her rapier out from his belly, raising the blade in a two-handed grip and preparing to plunge it into her chest.

"Yield," Mia whispered.

All the world fell still.

"I yield," she said again, flopping back onto the stone.

Tric's chest was heaving. Grip quavering. Eyes locked on Mia's.

The girl smiled with bloody lips.

And she winked.

"Point!" Solis bellowed. "Match to Acolyte Tric!"

The boy hung a moment longer. Rage still burning in that smooth hazel stare. Mia wondered just how much of him wanted her dead at that moment. But finally, he lowered the steel. Tossed it aside and sank to his knees, coughing blood, hand pressed to the new holes she'd gifted him. The acolytes were on their feet, cheering, bloodlust shining in their eyes.

The weaver and speaker strode into the ring, set to healing the hurts Mia and Tric had inflicted on the other with their steel.

But what about their words?

Looking into Tric's eyes, the girl realized she didn't know the answer.

T he acolytes were given the rest of the turn to themselves. With her wounds mended by the weaver, but her jaw still aching, Mia found herself back in her room, hands on hips.

Diamo and Jessamine had done a good job of covering their tracks; there were only a few signs anyone had been in her chambers. But as she'd suspected, her notes were gone from the hiding spot beneath her desk, no doubt stolen somewhere in the early morn while she'd been in Tric's bed. Five hours, she'd calculated, give or take, from the time Diamo took Spiderkiller's poison to the moment of his ending. His sweat had been the real giveaway, but still, her timing had been close to perfect.

"*. . . feeling pleased with yourself . . . ?*"

Mister Kindly peered at her from atop the cupboard.

"I am, rather."

"*. . . jessamine will most definitely try to kill you now . . .*"

"Operative word being 'try.'"

"*. . . and despite your sky altar theatrics, you still haven't solved spiderkiller's quandary . . .*"

"I'm almost there."

"*. . . diamo stole your notes . . .*"

"I remember most of it. I'm close, Mister Kindly."

"*. . . spiderkiller's contest ends in six turns, mia . . .*"

"I'm glad you're here to tell me these things."

"*. . . you should have just won solis's edge and been done with it . . .*"

"Then Tric wouldn't have become a Blade."

"*. . . better him than you . . . ?*"

Mia flopped down on the bed, eyes on the ceiling. Saying nothing. Thoughts racing in her head. Everything Mister Kindly said was true. There were bigger things at stake here than she and Tric. Scaeva. Duomo. Remus. All she'd worked for. Only a trained assassin of the Red Church was ending any of those bastards—her attack last truedark was proof enough of that. If she didn't finish top of hall, who knew if she'd become a Blade at all? Why in the Daughters' names hadn't she just—

"*. . . you are letting your feelings for the boy cloud your judgment . . .*"

"I don't have any feelings for the boy."

"*. . . o, really . . . ?*"

"Yes, really."

"*. . . then why spend months training in secret with naev only to—*"

A knock sounded at her door. Mia rose from her bed, padded across the room. Tric was waiting on the other side, saltlocks tumbled about his face. Mia's heart beat a little quicker to see him. Those damned butterflies back in her belly. She grit her teeth, caught them with her fingers, and plucked their wings away. Killing them one by one.

"Good turn to you, Don Tric."

"And you, Pale Daughter."

She looked down to the boy's shirt. He wore a simple pin at his breast—a musical clef carved of polished ironwood. He'd been presented with the brooch at tourney's end by Solis himself; proof that he'd finished top of the Shahiid's hall.

"Congratulations," Mia said.

The boy nodded. Chewed his lip. "Can I come in?"

Mia looked up and down the hallway, and seeing no other acolytes, stepped aside. For insects with no wings, those butterflies still seemed to be making an awful commotion.

"Drink?" she asked, turning to her stolen goldwine.

"No. I won't be here long."

She heard the odd note in his voice. Turned to stare up at him, those hazel eyes hard as stone. His shoulders were set, like a man preparing to charge.

"You let me win," he said.

"No." Mia shook her head. "I fought hard as I could."

"But you made me fight harder."

She shrugged. "I knew you'd fight soft, otherwise."

"Know me so well, do you?"

"I know how you feel about me."

"O, really. And how's that?"

Mia dropped her gaze, ran a hand through her hair. Searching the shadows at her feet. The truth was lying plain there for her to see. She lifted her eyes to Tric's, unable to speak it. Hoping he heard it anyway.

The boy shook his head. His gaze still hard. Voice harder. "You knew what saying that word would do to me. You know what it means."

"I'm sorry," she sighed. "You know me well enough to know I didn't mean it. But I had to make you angry. I knew you'd let me win, otherwise. I can still finish top of Truths. I didn't need to top Songs."

"I don't need your fucking pity, Mia."

"Maw's teeth, it's not about pity! There's room enough for both of us on the roster. You've finished top of hall, now you're practically guaranteed to become a Blade. One step closer to standing on your grandfather's grave. We made a promise we'd see each other have our vengeance, remember? I want what's best for you, don't you see that?"

"And so you play me like a lyre, neh? Twist me up inside and send me blind." Tric shook his head. "Aalea teach you that, did she? Little Mia Corvere. Wolf in crow's feathers. You've got us all fooled. Me, Diamo, Jessamine. Who else is dancing to your tune and doesn't even know it? Who else are you going to kill to get your way?"

"Four Daughters, Tric, this isn't a bloody—"

"A bloody nursery! I know! You've told me a thousand fucking times, Mia."

"And how many times do I have to say it before it sinks in?"

"Never again."

The words hit her like a buckler to the jaw. Though she'd deny it to herself afterward, she actually flinched to hear them.

"We were fools to let it get this far. You hear me, Mia?" Tric pointed to her. To himself. "You and me? *Never. Again.*"

"Tric, I—"

He slammed the door as he left.

Mia stared down at her empty palms. Tric's accusations echoing in her skull.

She pictured Diamo's face. The agony in his eyes as he begged for his life. But he'd deserved it, hadn't he? For Lotti?

His cries were echoing inside her head, intertwined with those of the men she'd slaughtered on the steps of the Basilica Grande. Scattered like torn and sodden rags through the belly of the Philosopher's Stone. An orchestra of screams, and she, the scarlet maestro. Bloody hands swaying in the air.

Tric's footsteps faded in the hall.

Mia stood there in the dark.

Shoulders slumped.

Head bowed.

Alone.

"*. . . it is for the best, mia . . .*"

And never alone.

"*. . . it is for the best . . .*"

FAVORS

Five turns until it was too late to solve Spiderkiller's riddle.

Until her best chance at initiation dissolved like smoke.

Until everything she'd worked for crumbled to dust.

Just.

Five.

Turns.

Mia had barely slept and hardly eaten since the trial in Songs. Burying her nose in tome after tome, feeling the answer close enough to touch, only to watch it slip away like sand as her fingers closed around it.

A no-holds-barred thievery war had broken out as acolytes scrambled to topple Ash from the lead on Mouser's ladder. The tally of marks was now kept in the Sky Altar instead of the Hall of Pockets, so that all could know the score.

Hush was placed second, still a good eighty marks off the pace. Jessamine trailed twenty marks behind that. Ash's lead seemed virtually unassailable—a fact the girl loudly reminded everyone of at mealtimes, just in case they'd gotten airs. Bedrooms were broken into, pockets ransacked, and every seemingly harmless collision in the halls resulted in four or five different objects trading owners. Chronicler Aelius registered a formal complaint with the Revered Mother after Ashlinn stole the spectacles right off his head while he was dozing at his desk,* and item #5 on Shahiid Mouser's list:

A book from the athenaeum (stolen, not borrowed, smart-arse)   —6 marks

was removed under protest from the Shahiid himself. Pip had apparently staged an early-morn raid on the athenaeum to snaffle a few tomes from the RETURNS trolley, and got himself devoured by one of the surlier bookworms.†

"And now all the others are pissed they didn't get a feed!" Aelius had yelled. "Who's going to clean up the bloody mess is what I want to know!"

With official lessons ended, the acolytes were permitted to travel to Godsgrave whenever they chose. Speaker Adonai sat by his pool, sending fledgling killers out into the City of Bridges and Bones, morn and nevernight. Shahiid Aalea kept her counsel about who was leading in her contest, but with the amount of secrets flooding back from the 'Grave, Mia figured the woman must be more in the know by now than the princeps of the damned Obfuscatii.‡

---

* His last pair. The good chronicler had broken his spare set during a wrestling match with a copy of *At His Majesty's Service*, the autobiography of Angelica Trobbiani, a courtesan during the reign of Francisco VI. All copies of this "treasonous smut" were hunted down and burned under order of Francisco's Queen, Aria, after her husband's death. The copy in the Red Church athenaeum is the last one in existence.

The book, having inherited some of its author's infamous temperament, is understandably upset about this fact.

† What became of the boy's beloved knife was anyone's guess.

‡ The third branch of the Republic's bureaucracy, the first and second being the Luminatii and Administratii. Far smaller than their sibling organizations, the Obfuscatii are the Senate's information-brokers and rumor-mongers. Concerned largely with in-

Alone in her room, or hunched over a desk in the Hall of Truths (always facing the door), Mia worked on Spiderkiller's formula. She'd abandoned the notion of heading back to the 'Grave seeking whispers. Aalea's contest was too much a shot in the dark for her liking. Better to work on something she could actually see. Touch. Taste.

She'd set up a series of glassware labs; beakers and bowls, cylinders and flasks, and endless spirals of pipes and tubes. Solutions bubbled or dissolved or congealed inside the elaborate structures, and more than a hundred black rats shuffled off this mortal coil as Mia continued her search. Spiderkiller would visit often, working at her desk or her own experiments, but Mia knew better than to hope she'd offer a clue. If she was to finish top of Truths, she'd have to earn it. In fact, the Shahiid hardly spoke at all, save once, the very turn after Solis's contest.

"A shame about Diamo . . ."

Mia had looked up from her work. Spiderkiller walked slowly along Mia's latest sculpture, trailing a long fingernail along the glass. Her hands were stained black with toxins. Her lips stained black with paint. Her stare, blackest of all.

"A shame he didn't test his antidote before he used it, you mean?" the girl asked.

"Ah, but that's the rub, you see," Spiderkiller had said. "While it didn't counter my toxin entirely, Diamo's solution *did* delay its effects. So any rats he tested it on the eve before would have still been alive when he brought the solution to me the next morn."

"Mmm," Mia said, returning to her work. "This *is* a shame."

The Shahiid had patted Mia on the shoulder and left the hall without another word. Diamo had been interred in an unmarked tomb in the Hall of Eulogies that afternoon. Spiderkiller never mentioned him again.

The countless hours working on the quandary made it easier to avoid Tric, at least. Mia kept her mind on task, sparing as little thought for him as possible. Eating at odd times to avoid him. And if her dreams were visited by the boy in the few hours she actually slept, Mister Kindly devoured them before they had a chance to bother her.

With two turns until contest's end, Mia was bent over a boiling flask in the Hall of Truths. Ninebells had been struck, but she'd received dispensation to be out after curfew from Spiderkiller again. The perfume of burned sweetness and dead rat hung in the air. Entwined in her hair. Blurring her eyes.

---

ternal threats to Itreya's security, the organization is as old as the Republic itself. Its founder, Tiberius the Elder, was known to have stood among the insurgents who overthrew Itreya's last king, Francisco XV.

Some rumor even places Tiberius's hand on the blade that killed poor Franco himself.

Mia heard the doors open.

She looked up expecting to see Spiderkiller, but instead, Mia saw bright blue eyes. Pale skin and sharp cheekbones. A boy more beautiful than handsome.

The huge double doors closed silently behind him.

Mia's hand went to the stiletto in her sleeve.

"Hello, Hush," she said.

The boy, of course, said nothing. Walking quietly across the hall to stand in front of Mia. He watched her through the glassware, lips pressed together.

His hands were behind his back.

Mia was tense as a mekwerk spring. This was the room Lotti had been killed in, after all. Mister Kindly had warned her Jessamine and Diamo might not be the culprits. Hush had been caught wandering after ninebells, but no one had ever explained exactly what he'd been doing when he was discovered, and here he was, out of his chambers after ninebells *again*. And nobody had ever found out what happened to Floodcaller . . .

The boy's silence was utter; not just his lips, but his entire person. He made no sound as he walked. As he breathed. When he moved, even the fabric of his clothes was voiceless. And his damned hands were still behind his back.

"You shouldn't be out after curfew," Mia said.

Hush simply smiled.

". . . Can I help you with something?"

The boy slowly shook his head.

Mister Kindly coalesced behind Hush, watching. Every muscle in Mia's body was wound tight. The shadows around her rippling as her fingers twitched. Her own shadow began to bend, snaking across the floor, longer and darker than it should have been. And Hush took his hands out from behind his back and showed them empty.

Mia sighed. Released her knife. Hush began to speak in Tongueless, his fingers moving so rapidly Mia had trouble following.

help you

Mia signed back, a little clumsier than the boy.

help me with what?

The boy motioned to the bubbling mixtures, the phials and condensers and jars. Mia recalled the sight of him at the scourging. Those toothless gums exposed as he silently screamed. Her hands moved quickly, eyes never leaving his.

why?

Hush paused at that. A faint frown marring that perfect brow.

i've been watching
you don't belong here

It was Mia's turn to frown now. Confused. Insulted.

what does that mean?

The boy's hands swayed, deft fingers crafting words from the silence.

after the scourging
you were the only one
to ask if i was all right
no one else cared

Hush shook his head.

you don't belong here

Mia scowled.

and you do?

The boy nodded.

ugly like the rest of them

Mia found herself confounded. She walked around the spires of bubbling glass, the sweet smell of death. Stood before the boy and took his hands, whispering.

"Hush, what are you talking about? You're nothing close to ugly."

The boy actually laughed at that. His vocal chords were atrophied from disuse, the guffaw emerging as little more than a squeak. He clapped his hands to his mouth and convulsed, but she still caught a glimpse of the toothless gums behind those bow-shaped lips. The cracks behind his eyes.

"What happened to you?" she breathed.

The boy's gaze was intense. Eyes like a sunburned sky.

slaved

"But you've got no slavemark."

The boy shook his head.

they kept us pretty

". . . They?"

pleasure house

Mia's stomach ran cold as she watched him sign the words. She knew immediately what the boy meant. Where he'd come from. Who had owned him before this, and why they'd knocked out every one of his teeth.

"O, Goddess," she breathed. "I'm so sorry, Hush."

you see?

The boy's lips twisted in what might have been a smile.

you don't belong here

He looked around the room, the boiling liquid and dead rats, rot and rust in the air.

but kindness should reap kindness

even in a field like this

The boy reached into his britches, and for a moment Mia found her hand straying to her sleeve again. The dark about them trembling. But rather than some hidden shiv, the boy produced a notebook, bound in black leather. He opened to a random page. Mia saw notes in code—a variant of the Elberti sequence mixed with some homebrew. Recognizing the handwriting. The cipher itself.

"That's Carlotta's notebook," she breathed.

The boy nodded.

"Where did you get it?"

The boy tilted his head.

told you

i've been watching

Mia's heart beat faster. She flipped through the pages, saw more than a few were spattered with dried blood. A page near the back had been torn out completely. Slow rage boiled beneath her skin, but she found herself pulling it into check. No sense going off without cause. Hush was offering to help her. He could've got Carlotta's notes without having killed her—he'd been skulking about the Church since he arrived. But still, the simple answer was often the right one . . .

"Hush," she whispered, slow and careful. ". . . Did you murder Lotti?"

The boy looked down at her shadow. Up into her eyes.

what does it matter?

Hands to fists. Red in her eyes.

"It matters because she was my friend!"

The boy shook his head. Looked almost sad.

you have one friend inside these walls

not carlotta

not tric or ashlinn

and not me

Hush stared at her, unblinking. He was no ally, she realized. This was no mark of respect or token of grudging friendship from this O, so strange boy. A debt repaid, was all. Kindness for kindness. Even in a field such as this. And though Hush's fingers moved not at all, his words swum plain in his eyes.

Take it or leave it.

Mia lifted the book from the boy's hands. Hush inclined his head in a bow, ever so slight, fringe tumbling over haunted blue eyes. Then he turned on his heel and walked from the room, soundless as a sunsbeam. He reached the double doors, pushed them open with one hand, Mia's voice stopping him in his tracks.

"Hush."

The boy turned. Waited.

"Why not use these notes yourself? Don't you want to finish top of hall?"

Hush tilted his head. Gave her a knowing smile.

And without a whisper, he was gone.

It took hours to crack Carlotta's code. Hours more to piece together the scraps from the scrawl, the ghostly choir her only company. The missing page was a mystery, but it didn't matter in the end. The thought occurred that Hush might be trying the same ruse on Mia as she'd run on Diamo. But truth was, Mia had been close enough to the solution to taste it already, perhaps only a few hours from solving the puzzle by herself. She doubted Hush would be stupid enough to grift her at her own game. And there amid Carlotta's neat handwritten thoughts, she found the single missing piece—the last key to break the lock that had still eluded her.

She was sure of it.

Mia distilled her solution into three phials. Spent two on a pair of rats, saved the third for herself. Her furry companions were snoozing in their cages two hours later when Spiderkiller pushed open the doors and found Mia sitting amid palaces of glittering glass.

"You are here early, Acolyte," the Shahiid said. "Or is it late?"

The girl held up a glass phial in answer, filled with a cloudy liquid. Spiderkiller crossed the floor, jade-green robes whispering. Tossing her saltlocks off her shoulder, she glanced at the glass in Mia's hand. Black, paintstick lips twisted in a curious smile.

"And what is that you have?"

"An answer to the impossible."

"Are you certain?"

Mia glanced at her feet. Knowing without a doubt that even if Mister Kindly were not with her, at that moment, she'd have still been unafraid.

She looked at Spiderkiller and smiled.

"There's only one way to be certain, Shahiid."

The announcement was made at mornmeal. Typical of Spiderkiller, there was no fanfare, no real accolade. The Shahiid simply waited until the Ministry and acolytes were assembled, walked softly to where Mia was seated, and pinned a brooch to her chest. The piece was small, carved of ironwood, buffed to a dark sheen.

A wolfspider.

Murmurs passed among the acolytes. Spiderkiller leaned down and placed a black kiss on Mia's brow.

"My blessings," she said.

And that was it.

Ash grinned, offered outstretched fingers to Mia, who brushed them with a smile. Realizing she'd been foolish enough to let the girl touch her, Mia made a show of checking all her pockets, ensuring Spiderkiller's brooch was still pinned to her chest. Ashlinn rolled her eyes and chuckled, went back to her meal without a word. Looking down the table, Mia saw Jessamine staring back with undisguised hatred.

"Well," said Mouser, rising from the Ministry's table. "If the Spiderkiller is seeing fit to bestow her boons, perhaps we should do the same?" The Shahiid turned to Aalea with his customary rakish smile. "Beauty before age, Shahiid?"

Aalea demurred with a small shake of her head. "There is still one more nevernight for acolytes to loot the 'Grave. I will give my favor on the morrow."

"As it please you," Mouser bowed. "For my own contest, I feel confident no acolyte can assail the leader in the art of Pockets. If there are no objections among the participants?"

Ashlinn leaned back in her chair and smiled like a queen on a stolen throne. The other acolytes scowled over their meals, but Mouser spoke true. Looking at the leaderboard, Ash was still leading Hush by ninety marks, and nobody else was anywhere close. The contest was as good as over.

"Acolyte Ashlinn," Mouser began. "Might I offer congratulations at what has been the most audacious display of thievery in these halls since I was apprenticed to . . ."

The Shahiid's voice drifted off as Hush rose from his seat.

"Acolyte?" Mouser frowned.

Hush walked across the Sky Altar without a word. Standing before the Mouser, the boy reached into his pocket, and with slight bow, proffered an open palm to the Shahiid. Acolytes rose from their seats, straining to see what the boy held. Mia caught a glimpse of gleaming black. A silver chain.

"Maw's teeth," she breathed, recognizing the object in the boy's palm.

"It can't be . . . ," Ash hissed.

Hush was holding the Revered Mother's obsidian key.

How in the Maw's name had he stolen it without her knowing it was gone?

Mia looked to the Ministry's table. Drusilla's eyes had widened at the sight of her key in Hush's palm, and her hand went to her breast, searching the folds of her robes. But after a few moments, her lips creased in a smile.

"Dear Mouser," she called. "I fear you are being played. A fox in boy's cloth-ing, neh?"

The Revered Mother held up her hand. Dangling between forefinger and thumb, a glittering obsidian key spun on a silver chain.

"I knew it," Ash sighed. "There's no *way* he lifted that thing . . ."

"Aha," Mouser grinned, bowing to Hush. "A fine ruse, Acolyte. But no marks for huckstering here, I fear. The Mouser accepts the genuine article, or nothing at all."

Hush smiled. He placed his key in Mouser's hand, walked softly to the Ministry's table. Aalea's lips were curled in a sly smile, even Solis and Spi-derkiller seemed amused. The pale boy stopped in front of Mother Drusilla, held out one hand as he signed with the other in Tongueless.

may i?

Drusilla frowned slightly, but acquiesced, handing over her key. Without ceremony, Hush dropped it at his feet, and stamped on it with his boot. Lifting his heel, the boy made a theatrical gesture at the floor, like some corner grifter playing guess-a-cup. Mia saw the key had been pulverized beneath Hush's boot.

"Son of a whore," Ash whispered.

"Clay . . . ," Mia breathed.

Astonishment on the Mother's face. On Mouser's. On every acolyte assem-bled. Not only had the boy stolen Drusilla's key from around her very throat, he'd replaced it with a forgery perfect enough that the old woman was none the wiser.

Silence hung in the hall like fog. Turning to Ash, Hush put a hand on his chest and took a bow. Mia looked to Ash, half-expecting the girl to go for Hush's throat. Instead, Ash looked like someone had torn her guts out with butchers' hooks. She sagged in her seat, dismay in her eyes, looking to her brother. Osrik, who'd been walking about like a ghost since losing to Tric, could only stare, just as gutted as she.

The rest of the acolytes were awed by Hush's display. Mouser began clap-ping, then Shahiid Aalea and Spiderkiller. Solis and the Revered Mother her-self. Mouser stepped to the leaderboard and added another one hundred marks to the boy's tally, putting him in first place. And with an apologetic glance to Ash—who was so pale Mia thought she might faint—the Shahiid pinned the token of his favor to Hush's shirt. A small ironwood brooch, curled up on itself and staring with polished black eyes.

A mouse.

"Top of Pockets, Acolyte," Mouser said. "Well done."

That's why he didn't need Lotti's notes. He already had Drusilla's key.

Mia raised her hands, started clapping too. But as she looked to Ashlinn, her hands fell still. Initiation into the ranks of the Blades had meant just as much to Ash as it had to Mia. Ashlinn and her brother had been trained by their father for years. A former Blade of the Church, who'd wanted nothing more than his children to replace him after he'd been crippled in the Mother's name. Imagine the pressure they'd been under. Imagine the desire to see their father's sacrifice—his swordarm, his eye, goddess, even his manhood—stand for something.

And now, neither one of them looked set to be initiated at all.

T hat goat-loving, mule-sucking, pig-fucking sonofa*bitch*," Ash growled. The girl was pacing the length of Mia's bedchamber, Mia herself nestled among her pillows. One of her last cigarillos sat on her lips. The last of her stolen goldwine sat untouched in two cups on Mia's nightstand.

"How the 'byss did he do it?" Ash demanded.

"He's clever," Mia shrugged. "Cleverer than anyone pegged him for. I wonder if he didn't get caught out after ninebells intentionally."

"Took a scourging on purpose, you think?"

"Maybe. Just so we'd think him a rube."

"Well, it bloody worked."

Mia sighed a lungful of gray. "That it did."

"And now I'm cooked." Ash scowled, started pacing again. "Mouser's trial was mine to lose. And now I've gone and fucking lost it. Lord Cassius will be back here in *two turns* for initiation. You'll be drinking the Mother's milk at the banquet with the other Blades and I'm going to be stuck with the rest of the chaff being inducted into the Hands. Presuming they don't just fail me outright and gift me to the Mother."

Mia dragged on her cigarillo, eyes narrowed against the smoke. "You should probably spend the nevernight moaning about it, then."

Ash rounded on Mia with a withering glance. "Your sympathies are sincerely appreciated, Corvere. My thanks."

"Fuck sympathy," Mia smiled. "You come to me, you get solutions."

Ash waved her hands in the air. "So solute, then."

"Aalea still hasn't given her favor, Ash."

"And what chance do I have of winning that?"

"If you keep wearing a hole in my floor with your pacing, none. If you hit the 'Grave and find something especially juicy . . ."

"Needle in a fucking haystack."

"Well, hunting needles is better than just sitting around here praying, aye?"

Ash put the tip of one of her warbraids in her mouth. Chewed thoughtfully.

"I'll come with you," Mia offered.

Ashlinn glanced up at that. "Looking to avoid Tricky, neh?"

"This has nothing to do with Tric."

"I'm sure."

Mia raised the knuckles. Swallowed her whiskey in a single toss. "Come on, let's be off."

Ash made a face, shook her head. "I think I'd best go alone."

"Two sets of ears are better than one?"

"Aye," Ash shrugged. "And I appreciate the offer and all. Just . . . wouldn't feel right. If I can't do this myself, perhaps I don't deserve to be here at all."

Mia nodded. Though she hid it behind the jests and smiles, Ash was a proud one. Proud of her skills. Of her father and his legacy. Mia could understand why she'd not want to be initiated on someone else's coattails. And so she rose off the bed, put her arms around her friend and squeezed her tight.

"Goddess go with you. Be careful."

Ash squeezed Mia back, tight enough to make her wince.

"You know, folk around here have got you figured for a ruthless bitch after that stunt with Diamo. But I know better. Someone hurts those you love, you'll not forgive it. But underneath it all, you're a good sort, Corvere."

Mia kissed Ash's cheek, smiling. "Don't tell anyone. I've a reputation to uphold."

"I mean it. Sometimes I wonder what you're doing in a place like this, Mia."

". . . Since when do you call me Mia?"

"I'm serious," Ash said. "You should be sure."

". . . Of what?"

Ash searched her eyes. All trace of her smile gone.

"If you really want to be here tomorrow eve."

"Where else would I be?"

Ash seemed set to say more, but her stare hardened, and she caught herself before she spoke. She hung a moment longer, arms still around Mia's waist. Lips parted. Pupils wide. And then Ash let go, slipped out through the door and disappeared down the hallway in search of the speaker. Mia closed the door behind her, slunk back to her bed. Watching the cigarillo burning down in her hand.

What was Ash on about? This was everything she'd worked for. Everything she wanted. All the years, the miles, the struggle. The things she'd done to get here, the lives she'd taken on this bloody road. Hands dipped in red. But now she was just one step away from initiation.

One step closer to Remus's throat.

Duomo's heart.

Scaeva's head.

Then it would all be worth it, wouldn't it?

Wouldn't it?

A black shape coalesced at her feet. Whispering like wind through winter trees.

"... *tomorrow* ... ," it said.

Mia nodded.

"Tomorrow."

BECOMING

Mia slept like the righteous dead that eve. A soft knocking woke her sometime before midmeal, and she heard the low voice of a Hand on the other side of her door.

"Be in the Hall of Eulogies in one hour, Acolyte."

Mia dressed slowly, made her way to the Sky Altar. The benches and chairs were deserted, the Quiet Mountain quieter than she ever remembered it. The thought of initiation filled her mind. She'd finished top of Truths, but the Revered Mother had hinted more trials awaited. She'd no clue what she might face in the Hall of Eulogies, or the final hurdles she'd need to overcome.

She stopped by the athenaeum on her way to the hall. Chronicler Aelius was loitering on the threshold as always, sorting through the RETURNS trolley. Wordlessly, he pulled his ever-present spare cigarillo from behind his ear and handed it to Mia. The pair leaned against the wall, staring out over the sea of shelves below. How many lifetimes could she spend down there if she let herself? How much easier would it be to get lost in those endless pages, and leave this road of shadows and blood behind?

"Initiation soon, eh?" Aelius asked.

Mia nodded, blew a perfect smoke ring in strawberry-scented gray.

"Well," Aelius shrugged. "All good things ..."

Mia licked the sugar from her lips. "You never found the book I was asking for?"

The chronicler shook his head. "I discovered a whole new wing out there yesterturn, though. Thousands of books. Millions of words. Maybe something about darkin in there."

She looked out over the words below. Sighed.

"It's a beautiful place, this. Part of me wishes I could stay here forever."

"Careful what you wish for, lass."

"I know," Mia nodded. "The grass is always greener. Still, I envy you, Aelius."

"The living don't envy the dead."

Mia looked at the old man. A slow frown forming on her brow. She realized she'd never seen him leave the athenaeum. Never seen him eat a meal in the Sky Altar or cross this threshold out into the Church proper even once. The girl stared at her cigarillo. The maker's mark she'd never seen before.

"They don't make them like this anymore."

The library of Our Lady of Blessed Murder.

A library of the dead.

"You . . ."

"The Mother keeps only what she needs," the old man said.

Mia simply stared, a chill in her belly. Horror and sorrow in her heart.

"You remember what I said that turn you met the bookworm?" Aelius asked.

"You said maybe here's not where I'm supposed to be."

Aelius drew hard on his cigarillo. Blew a series of smoke rings that chased each other through the quiet dark. "I'll take a look in that new wing. If I find anything of the darkin, I'll have someone leave it in your chambers. Or somewhere else. If that's where you want to be."

Mia frowned through a cloud of shifting gray.

"Good luck in the Hall of Eulogies, lass," Aelius said. "I'm sure you'll do fine."

". . . My thanks, Chronicler."

Aelius stubbed out his smoke against the wall and put the remains in his pocket.

"I'd best be off. Too many books."

"Too few centuries."

He looked at her then. Something empty and awful in that milky-blue stare. But with a shrug, he limped off down the stairs, out into the endless shelves.

The darkness swallowed him whole.

Three acolytes stood in a goddess's shadow.

The Mother of Night loomed above them, staring down with stone eyes.

Tric and Hush had been waiting when Mia arrived, several Hands hovering on the edge of the stained-glass light. As the ghostly choir sung out in the dark, a robed figure escorted Mia to the dais. Glancing sideways, she glimpsed strawberry curls.

"Friend Naev," Mia whispered.

The woman squeezed her hand. "Good fortune. Hold fast."

Mia took her place beside Tric. Noted the boy was studiously ignoring her. Hearing the voice of a shadow echoing in her head.

"... it is for the best, mia ..."

Three acolytes assembled. The victors in Truths, Songs, and Pockets. Mia wondered who had finally won in Aalea's hall, what kind of secret they must have stolen to gain the Shahiid's favor. She heard soft footsteps behind her. Found herself praying that she'd not turn and see Jessamine. Taking a deep breath, Mia glanced over her shoulder. And there, standing on the edge of the light, she saw Ashlinn. Hair in fresh warbraids, eyes twinkling in the dark. A small ironwood brooch was pinned to her shirt. A smiling harlequin's masque.

"Sorry I'm late," the girl smirked.

Winking to Mia, Ash stepped up to the dais, taking her place at Hush's side. Mia was amazed. What kind of secret had the girl dredged up? What must it—

"Acolytes."

Mia straightened, eyes front. The double doors leading into the antechamber had swung silently open. A Hand shrouded in long black robes was waiting on the threshold, a scroll unfurled before her. Beside her stood Revered Mother Drusilla.

"My congratulations to you all," the old woman said. "Each of you have demonstrated a mastery in one of the four halls of this Church, and considerable proficiency in other areas of study. Of every acolyte in this year's flock, you stand closest to initiation as Blades. But before Lord Cassius inducts you fully into the secrets of this circle, one final trial remains."

The old woman turned, disappeared through the double doors in a swirl of black cloth. The Hand carrying the scroll stepped forward, consulted the parchment.

"Acolyte Tric?"

Tric took a deep breath and stepped forward. "Aye."

"Walk with me."

Mia watched the boy march forward, Naev beside him. She wondered what awaited him. Tried to put the memory of their last parting aside. The guilt that she'd hurt him, the anger in his eyes . . . If death lay beyond that door, she wanted to make it right between them. But he was already gone, crossing the threshold without a backward glance, the doors closing soundlessly behind him. Mia could feel Mister Kindly in her shadow, gravitating toward the growing fear around her. She glanced at Hush. Ashlinn. Wondered if the girl's father had told her what to expect beyond.

The trio waited silently in the statue's shadow. Minutes passed. Long as years. That perpetual, ghostly choir the only sound. Finally, the doors swung open and Tric emerged. Jaw clenched. Slightly pale. Apparently unharmed. He found Mia's eyes, and she saw a haunted look cross his face. For a moment, she thought he might speak. But without a word to the others, Tric was escorted up the spiral stairwell and out of sight.

Ash was looking straight ahead. Speaking in a whisper, her lips almost motionless.

"Be sure, Corvere."

"Acolyte Mia."

The Hand at the double doors was looking at her expectantly. Mister Kindly purred in her shadow. Mia stepped forward, hands in fists.

"Aye."

"Walk with me."

Mia stepped off the dais. Naev was beside again, escorting her as she'd done with Tric. As they reached the threshold, the woman touched her hand. Nodded.

"Hold it close, Mia Corvere. Hold it tight."

Mia met the woman's eyes, but there was no chance to ask what she meant. The girl turned, followed the Hand through a long passage of dark stone. The only sound was their soft footsteps, the choir muted as the double doors closed behind them. A large domed room waited beyond, set on all sides by vast arched windows of beautiful stained glass. Abstract patterns were wrought in the panes, blood-red spirals, twisting and turning, twelve fingers of light overlapping on the floor.

Standing in the light's center, Mia saw the Revered Mother Drusilla. Her hands were folded in her robe, and she wore that patient, motherly smile. The obsidian key around her neck glittered with the slow rise and fall of her breast. Mia approached cautiously, searching the shadows, glad for the not-eyes in the back of her head.

She couldn't help but notice the floor in front of Drusilla was wet.

Freshly scrubbed.

"Greetings, Acolyte."

Mia swallowed. "Revered Mother."

"This is your final trial before initiation. Are you prepared?"

"I suppose that depends what it is."

"A simple thing. A moment and it is done. We have honed you to an edge so fine you could cut the sunlight in six. But before we induct you into the deeper mysteries, first we must see what beats at the heart of you."

Mia thought back to that torture cell in Godsgrave. The "confessors" who'd beaten her, burned her, near drowned her in Lord Cassius's test of loyalty. She'd not shattered then. She'd not shatter now.

"Iron or glass," Mia said.

"Precisely."

"Haven't we already answered that question?"

"You have proven your loyalty, true. But you will face death in all her colors if you serve as the Mother's Blade. Your own death is only one. This is another."

Mia heard scuffing footsteps in the shadows. She saw two Hands swathed in black, dragging a struggling figure between them. A boy. Barely in his teens. Wide eyes. Cheeks stained with tears. Bound and gagged. The Hands dragged him to the center of the light, forced him to his knees in front of Mia.

The girl looked at the Revered Mother. That sweet matronly smile. Those old, gentle eyes, creased at the edges.

"Kill this boy," the old woman said.

Three words. One ton apiece.

All the world fell still. The dark pressing in around her. The weight settling on her shoulders and pushing her down. Hard to breathe. Hard to see.

"What?" she managed.

"The time may come when you are asked to end an innocent in service to this congregation," Drusilla said. "A child. A wife. A man who has lived both good and well. Not for you to question why. Or who. Or what. Yours is only to serve."

Mia looked into the boy's eyes. Wide with terror.

"Each death we bring is a prayer," Drusilla said. "Each kill, an offering to She Who Is All and Nothing. Our Lady of Blessed Murder. Mother, Maid, and Matriarch. She has placed Her mark on you, Mia Corvere. You are Her servant. Her disciple. Perhaps, even, Her chosen."

The old woman held out a dagger in her open palm. Searched Mia's eyes.

"And if you cut this boy's throat, you will be her Blade."

It lasted forever. It lasted a moment. The girl stood there in that stained, blood-red light. Mind racing. Heart pounding. Questions swirling in her mind, never spoken.

She already knew the answers.

"Who is he?"

"No one."

"What did he do?"

"Nothing."

"Why should I kill him?"

"Because we tell you to."

"But—"

"Iron or glass, Mia Corvere?"

She took the dagger from Drusilla's hand. Tested the edge. Thinking perhaps it might be spring-loaded, that this was just another deception, that all she need do was show the *will*, and all would be well. But the dagger was sharp enough to draw blood on her fingertip. The blade solid as any she'd held.

If she put it in this boy's chest, sure and certain, she was putting him in his grave.

"The wolf does not pity the lamb," Drusilla said. "The storm begs no forgiveness of the drowned."

The girl looked to the wet stone at her feet. Knowing exactly what had been washed away in the moments before she entered the room. Knowing Tric hadn't quavered. Hadn't shattered.

"We are killers one," Mia whispered. "Killers all."

This was it. All the years. All the miles. All the sleepless nevernights and endless turns. This was the path she'd set her feet on. They'd hung her father. Tore her from her mother's arms, killed her baby brother. Her house, her familia, her world destroyed.

But was it reason enough? To murder this nameless boy?

In ending him, she ensured her place here. She'd become the Blade to pierce Duomo's heart, slip into Remus's guts, slit Scaeva's throat ear to ear. They deserved to die, Daughters knew. Die a thousand times over. Screaming. Begging. Weeping.

But the boy was weeping too. Ropes of snot streaking his lip. Mia looked down at him and he moaned behind the gag. Shaking his head. She could see the words in his eyes.

Please.

Please, no.

She glanced at Mother Drusilla. Gentle smile. Soft eyes. Wet stone at her feet. And she searched herself for a reason to kill this boy. Someone's brother. Someone's son. Barely older than she. Digging deep, through the muck and the blood. The tatters of the morality she'd cast aside when she set her feet upon this road, paved with the best of intentions. Diamo's screams as he died, echoing inside her head. The countless men and women she'd slaughtered inside the Philosopher's Stone. The Luminatii she'd butchered on the steps of the Basilica Grande.

I am steel, she told herself.

All this had taken a second. A moment beneath the Revered Mother's cool gaze. And in the next moment, Mia was kneeling before the boy. Placing the blade at his throat. Heart drumming against her ribs. Speaking the words a believer might.

I am steel.

"*Hear me, Niah,*" she whispered. "*Hear me, Mother. This flesh your feast. This blood your wine. This life, this end, my gift to you. Hold him close.*"

The old woman smiled.

The boy whimpered.

Mia took a deep, shuddering breath. Naev's warning echoing in her head. And to her horror, she finally understood. Finally heard it. Just as she'd heard it above the forum on the battlements where her father hung.

Music.

The dirge of the ghostly choir. The thunder of her own pulse. The gentle sobbing of this poor boy cut through with the memory of applause from a holy brigand and a beautiful consul and the world gone wrong and rotten. And she knew, then. As she'd always known. For all the miles, all the years, all the dusty tomes and bleeding hands and noxious gloom. Iron or glass or steel, what she was made of now made no difference at all. It was what she would *become* when she killed this boy that would truly matter.

Scaeva deserved to die. Duomo. Remus. Diamo. Those Luminatii at the Basilica Grande were tools of the Senate's war machine. Even the men and women in the Stone were hardened criminals. In the dark of her bedchamber, she might convince herself their deaths were justified if she tried hard enough. Might find herself believing that everyone she'd killed to this point, the countless endings she'd gifted, the orchestra of screams, and she, the scarlet maestro . . . all of them deserved it.

But this boy?

This nameless, blameless child?

If she killed him, truth was she deserved it too. And for all the miles and all the years, vengeance wasn't a good enough reason to become the monster she hunted.

Mia withdrew the knife from the boy's throat.

Slowly climbed off her knees.

"Not for this," she said.

Drusilla searched her face, gaze becoming iron-hard.

"We warned you, Mia Corvere. Marked by the Mother, or no. If you fail in this, you fail utterly. All Mercurio's work, all the turns you have studied at his feet, within these walls. The blood, the death, *all of it* will be for nothing."

She looked down into the boy's eyes. Someone's brother. Someone's son.

Her hands were shaking. Tears in her eyes. Ashes on her tongue.

But still . . .

"Not for nothing," she said.

And she handed back the blade.

S he lay on her bed in the dark. A shadow beside her, not saying a word. The last of her cigarillos in her hand. A long, broken finger of ash hanging from the smoldering tip. Fringe in her eyes. Black in her head.

What would they do with her? Relegate her to the role of a Hand?

Scourge her?

Kill her?

It didn't matter, either way. She'd never become a Blade now. Never learn the deeper mysteries of the Church, or the mysteries of who and what she was. Never become as sharp as she'd need to be to stand a chance of ending Scaeva. He was untouchable to her now, just as Mercurio had—

Mercurio . . .

What would he do?

What would he say?

Keys at her door. She couldn't even be bothered reaching for her stiletto. Whoever it was, she didn't care. Placing the cigarillo at her lips, she stared at the ceiling, watching the shadows writhe.

Soft footsteps. The *click-clack* of a walking stick on cold stone.

A bent and tired figure standing at the foot of her bed.

"Let's go home, little Crow."

She looked at the old man. Tears in her eyes.

O, Daughters, how she hated herself, then . . .

"Yes, Shahiid," she said.

A handful of possessions was all she left with. Her gravebone dagger. The ironwood brooch she'd worked so hard for. A tightly bound oilskin containing her books, Lotti's bloodstained notes. Nothing else would make the Blood Walk. Nothing else she could carry.

Naev walked with them, Mia and the old man, down the spiral path to the speaker's chambers. But the woman refused to step inside Adonai's domain.

"Think on it for a turn or two," Naev said from the threshold. "Hurts mend in time. Naev will be glad to see her back here. Naev can speak to Mother Drusilla on her behalf while she is gone. She can accompany Naev on the Last Hope runs. It is good country. A good life. Perhaps not what she wanted"— she looked to the chamber and the speaker beyond—". . . but life is seldom that."

Mia nodded. Squeezed the woman's hand. "Thank you, Naev."

They stepped into Adonai's chambers. The smell of blood thick in the air. The speaker knelt at the pool's apex, smeared in gore. He actually bowed to Mercurio, eyes to the floor.

The old man looked more tired than Mia had ever seen him. The walk down the stairs had been slow and torturous, his cane beating hard with each step. He'd never have imagined making this walk again, she supposed. Never thought he'd be coming back here to fetch her—his finest, his failure—dragging her back to Godsgrave in disgrace. But the Revered Mother had apparently advised Mercurio it would be best if Mia were not present for initiation. Spiderkiller was furious that her favor had been squandered. Lord Cassius had no time for weakness, or weaklings, and he'd be arriving in the Mountain soon to anoint the others with his blood. Mia was to return to the 'Grave with her Shahiid, think long and hard about her future. She could come back to the Mountain and serve out her life as a Hand. Or she could decide that living in failure was unacceptable, and deal with the matter herself.

Drusilla had made it plain which option she preferred Mia take.

And she'd never had a chance to say goodbye to Tric . . .

"Come on, little Crow," Mercurio sighed. "Never could stand these fucking pools. Sooner we get in, the sooner we get out."

"Wait!" came a call.

Mia turned, heart surging, thinking perhaps he'd come to see her off. But instead, she saw Ashlinn running down the corridor toward her. Disappointment and joy all mixed together in Mia's chest, Ash throwing her arms around Mia's shoulders and squeezing tight, Mia hugging back for all she was worth.

"You were going to leave without a goodbye?" Ash demanded.

"I'll be back," Mia said. "A few turns or so."

Ash took a knowing glance at Mia's pack, the belongings inside. Saying nothing.

"You've the look of someone familiar," Mercurio said. "What's your name, lass?"

"Ashlinn," the girl replied. "Ashlinn Järnheim."

"You're Torvar's girl? How is the old bastard?"

"Same as he's been for years. Half-blind. Crippled. Mutilated."

"You did him proud, Ash," Mia said. "You passed where others failed."

"You didn't fail, Corvere," Ash replied. "Don't ever think that."

Mia smiled sadly. "I'm sure."

"I mean it." Ash squeezed her hand. "You never belonged here, Mia. You deserve better than this."

Mia's smile died. Confusion in her eyes. Mercurio growled with impatience.

"Come on, enough of the hugging shite. Let's be off."

Ash scowled at the old man. Looked to Mia, uncertain. She took a deep breath, as if about to plunge into dark water. And then she leaned in slow, cupped Mia's face, and kissed her gently on the lips.

It lasted a moment too long. Perhaps not long enough? Warm and soft and honeysweet. Before Mia could decide, it was already over. Ash broke the kiss, squeezing Mia's hand. A million unsaid words shining in her eyes. A million more on Mia's tongue.

". . . Say goodbye to Tric for me?" she finally asked.

Ash's face dropped. She sighed. Nodded slow.

"I will. I promise."

Mia let go of her friend's hand. Looked around the walls. The glyphs and the blood. Wondering if this would be the last time she saw any of it. Glancing at Adonai, Mercurio, Ash. And with a deep breath, she stepped into the pool.

The red surged around her.

Mia closed her eyes.

And she fell.

Ashlinn stood for an age, there in the dark. She ran her fingertips across her lips, wondering about all that might have been. Watching Adonai watching the blood. That suicide beauty, coiled down here in the gloom. A spider in the center of his scarlet web, feeling for the faintest vibrations along its strands.

"When does the Lord of Blades arrive, great Speaker?" Ashlinn asked.

Adonai blinked. Looked up from the red as if surprised she was still there.

"When he arrives, little Acolyte," he replied.

Ash smiled, gave a grand, sweeping bow and turned from the chamber. She trudged up the spiral stairs, thumbs in her belt, chewing at the end of one of her warbraids. The bells struck two and she cursed, quickened her pace. Climbing swift through the Mountain's heart, up to the massive deck of the Sky Altar.

The room had been cleaned, the places set for the initiation feast. The kitchens were jammed and noisy, but the altar itself was deserted. All save for a solitary figure, off in the shadow, leaning against the railing and staring out into the dark.

"How goes, Tricky?"

The boy glanced up, nodded greeting. Turned his eyes back to the rolling wastes below. The endless, beautiful night.

"I never get tired of seeing this," he said.

"It's a sight," Ash agreed, leaning on the rail beside him.

"Oz said you wanted to speak to me," he murmured. "About Mia."

"She's gone back to Godsgrave for a turn or two. Get her head straight."

"I still can't fathom it," Tric sighed. "Of any of us, she had the best reason for being here."

"Almost."

"Never thought she'd stumble at the final hurdle."

"Maybe it wasn't a stumble," Ash shrugged. "Maybe she just chose not to jump. I'm glad she's not going to be here for initiation. Deciding not to murder an innocent makes her better than this place."

Tric looked at her sideways. "You passed the trial. *You* murdered an innocent."

"Because I have a better reason for being here than Mia did, Tricky."

"And what's that?"

"Familia," she said.

"Mia was here for her familia too."

"Aye," Ash nodded. "Difference is, *my* da is still alive. You'd be surprised how motivating a grumpy ex-murderer with no testicles can be."

Tric smirked, turned his eyes to the dark again. Ash spoke softly.

"Mia said to tell you goodbye."

"She'll be back," Tric said. "I'll see her again."

". . . I'm not so sure."

"Hand's robes might suit her. And what's she going to do, fold up? Her? No way."

"O, she might decide to join the Hands. But still, I don't think you'll see her again."

"Why's that?"

Ash sighed from the depths of her toes. "Like I said before, it's quite a nose you've got there, Tricky. And I can't have you sniffing around the entrée this eve."

"What do y—*hrrk*."

Tric blinked at the dagger in Ash's hand. The blade gleaming red and dripping. He looked down at the stain spreading across his shirt as she buried the knife in his chest again. And again. And again. He gasped, reached out toward her throat, eyes wide. But quick as lies, she shoved him hard and sent him backward over the railing. Tumbling down, down into the everblack wastes below.

Without a sound.

Without a whimper.

Gone.

Ash looked down into the darkness. Whispered soft.

"Sorry, Tricky."

The girl knelt with a kerchief, soaked up the blood that had fallen on the stone. Cleaning her blade and slipping it back into her sleeve. Checking over her shoulder. The altar was still deserted, Hands bustling about the kitchen in preparation for the coming feast. Nine places set at table. One for each of the three acolytes who would be initiated at feast's end. Five for the Ministry: Drusilla, Mouser, Solis, Aalea, and Spiderkiller. And the last, at the table's head, for the Lord of Blades. The Black Prince. The head of the Red Church congregation himself.

"Cassius," she whispered.

"It's done?"

Ashlinn turned and saw a figure in stolen Hand's robes.

"It's done." Ash straightened, looked out over the wastes. "Little Tricky won't be around to smell a thing. Presuming there's something to smell, of course."

"I'll carry my end," her brother replied.

"Don't fuck it up, Oz," Ash warned. "You set our last chance on fire. We could've had Cassius in a bag months ago. He was just sitting here in the open."

"I told you, that idiot Floodcaller saw me on the sneak. What was I supposed to do?"

"O, let me think. How about murdering him and leaving his body out in plain sight? Make it ten times harder for us to get a second shot?"

"Jumping Cassius like a pair of alley thugs was a stupid plan, I told you that at the time. Floodcaller getting in the way was a blessing. We've had months to prepare this. Poisoning the feast will net us the whole bag of vipers with one stroke. The acolyte who crafted the toxin for me is dead. And the only acolyte who had a chance of sniffing us out is dead. Stop your fucking whining and just be ready."

"I'm ready," Ash hissed.

Osrik checked over his shoulder again, dropping his voice lower.

"You met with them yestereve all right?"

"Aye." Ash nodded. "After they gave me the gossip to top Masks and then some. Like I said, Luminatii boys get all the juice."

"Are they ready?"

"No doubt. Our noble justicus has his First and Second Centuries on standby. Two hundred men hit the Porkery at sevenbells. You just make sure Adonai is motivated."

"That freak loves his sister more than life. With my knife to her throat, he'll dance the fucking Balinna if I tell him to."

"Be careful when you take Marielle. You saw what she did to—"

"I'm not a child, Ashlinn," Osrik snarled. "I'll handle the weaver and speaker. You just deal with your end. Have Cassius and the rest of the Ministry bound and gagged when Remus and his thugs arrive. The confessors will want to speak to the lot, so we'll need to Walk all of them. No manacles."

"No fear." The girl smiled grim. "Shahiid Aalea taught me a few rope tricks."

"In a few hours." Osrik nodded. "These walls come tumbling down."

The pair stared out over the wastes. The endless black above, a billion points of light. The face of the goddess they'd been raised to worship, and were now betraying.

"For da," Ashlinn said.

"For da," Osrik replied.

The girl kissed her brother on the cheek, and stalked off into the dark.

BLOOD

They'd washed off the gore in the Porkery baths, but Mia could still smell it on her skin.

She'd trudged through Godsgrave's streets, Mercurio limping beside her, neither speaking. She took some solace that the old man had come to fetch her, that he'd spoken to Drusilla on her behalf. A few turns away from the

Church would clear her head, he'd said. Do her good. Let her think about the choice before her.

Life as a Hand. The life of a servant.

She caught herself in the thought, scowling dark. There was no shame in it. Naev was a Hand and she held her head high. Maybe it wouldn't be so bad. Trekking the Whisperwastes, down through southern Ashkah. Finding beauty in parts of the world she'd never seen.*

But what about Scaeva? Duomo? Remus?

Could she live her whole life knowing her familia would go unavenged?

Clawing winds roared in off the bay, chill and screaming. Winter had come to the 'Grave in force, storms ever brewing on the horizon, shrouding Saan's light and smothering Saai's blue glow as it rose back up from the edge of the world. But still . . . it was so bright out here. Near blinding after months of almost constant dark. The choir's song had been replaced by the churn and bustle of city streets, the calls of criers, the crash of cathedral bells. This didn't feel right.

This doesn't feel like home anymore.

The girl and the old man returned to the curio store, bell chiming above the door. Mia was reminded of the first time she'd come here. The turn after her father had died swinging. Mercurio taking her under his wing. The last apprentice he'd ever train, most like. Six years he'd given her. And what had she given in return?

Failure.

The old man was limping toward the kitchen, cane clacking on the boards. "I'm sorry, Mercurio."

He turned toward her. Saw the tears brimming in her eyes.

"I let you down," she said. "I let us both down. I'm so sorry."

The old man shook his head. But he didn't tell her she was wrong.

"You want some tea?" he finally offered. "I'll bring it up to your room."

"No. My thanks."

He sloughed off his greatcoat. Lit a smoke and wandered into the kitchen.

---

* Though much of its heartland is now more a wasteland, the coastal regions of Ashkah are still some of the most beautiful in the world. Leaving aside the natural splendor of sites such as the Thousand Towers, the Dust Falls of Nuuvash, or the Great Salt, there is still something about watching the sunrise over a magically polluted hellscape that simply takes the breath away.

Of course, the sand kraken, dustwraiths, and other monstrosities of the Whisperwastes are liable to do that too, hence Ashkah's lack of any real tourism industry.

Upstairs in her room, she could still hear him thumping about. His anger ringing in the tune of crashing pots, rattling pans. She tossed her oilskin pack at her old bed, thumped down atop it. She'd never really noticed before, but it was a touch too small for her now. Like this room.

Like this life.

"*. . . what do we do now . . . ?*"

She looked to the slip of darkness, perched atop a crooked pile of histories.

If I could see his eyes, would I see disappointment in them too?

"Sleep," she sighed. "Sleep for a hundred years."

She loosened the ties on the oilskin bag, dragging out her old beaten copy of *Theories of the Maw*. Running a loving hand over the cover of *Arkemical Truths*. Then she slumped down with Lotti's notebook. Thinking of Hush, wondering how he was faring. Ash. Tric. They'd be getting ready for the initiation ceremony, she supposed. Evemeal at the Sky Altar, then down to the Hall of Eulogies, there to be anointed with Cassius's blood and inducted into the ranks of the Blades.

That was one reason to join the Hands, she supposed. At least inside the Mountain, she'd have access to the athenaeum. Maybe even to Cassius himself on occasion. She still had no real answers about darkin, or any real idea what she was . . .

Mia flipped through the pages of Lotti's work. Smiling at the thought of her friend's dry wit and deadpan stare. But her smile faded when she reached the pages Carlotta had been working on as she was murdered. There was a spray of dried blood across the notes, soaking through to those beyond.

Blood.

Soaking through . . .

"*Explain what, Revered Mother?*"

"*This.*"

Drusilla gathered up the sheet, held it in front of Mia's face. There, soaked through the fabric's weave, Mia saw a tiny smudge of dried scarlet.

Mia blinked at the bloodstains on the pages.

"*You cannot account for your whereabouts yestereve, and the victim's blood is found on your sheets—a fact which you yourself cannot explain. Has Carlotta ever visited your room?*"

"*No, but—*"

No, but someone *else* had visited that morn . . .

"It couldn't have been," she breathed.

"*. . . couldn't have been what . . . ?*"

Mia looked to the not-cat. Struggling with the words. With the thought behind them. Rising off the bed, Mia flipped to the end of Lotti's notebook.

Back to the missing pages. Rummaging around her desk, she found a char-stick, rubbed it lightly across the blank page following the missing section. There in the dusting of black, she could see the faintest of impressions. Lotti's handwriting, her homebrew cypher, arkemical symbols.

"*. . . what are you—*"

"Hush. Give me a moment."

She scowled over the pages, squinting at the faint handwriting. The marks were barely legible. She couldn't be sure, but . . .

"This looks like a modified recipe for Swoon . . ."

"*. . . the sedative . . . ?*"

She nodded. "But these measurements are enough for a dozen men at least. Why would Lotti be . . ."

Carlotta rose and padded over to Osrik, spoke to him quietly, sodden notebook in hand. Oz smiled his handsome smile, fingertips brushing Lotti's own.

Mia waggled her eyebrows at Ash. "They've been getting cozy. I saw them work-ing together on some concoction a few turns back. And they seem to get paired up in Truths an awful lot."

"This makes no sense," she whispered.

"*. . . a feeling i am growing rapidly familiar with . . .*"

Mia rose from her stool, Lotti's notebook in hand. About to head down-stairs to Mercurio, she heard more commotion in the kitchen. A blacker curse than she'd ever heard the old man use. It didn't seem like a good time to be bothering him with insane theories. He'd likely bite her head off.

She bound the notebook in her oilskin again. Scowling so hard her head ached.

But if she was right . . .

I can't be right.

"I need to go back to the Church."

"*. . . so soon . . . ?*"

"I need to talk to the Revered Mother."

"*. . . she will be busy with the initiation ceremony, surely . . . ?*"

Mia was already perched on the windowsill, wind howling through the open glass.

"On my side or in my way?"

The not-cat sighed.

"*. . . as it please you . . .*"

Mia hurried back through the Little Liis market, the churning streets of the Nethers, shoving and pushing down to the Bay of Butchers. The storm was almost on Godsgrave now, thunder and lightning racing each other across the sky. The smell of offal and sewage rolled in with the salt of the deeper ocean, Mia's shoulders hunched, a black tangle billowing about her face as she pulled up her hood against the chill.

The harbor was busy.

Busier than it should have been, with weather this grim.

As Mia approached the Porkery, she noticed groups of conspicuously large men lurking near the entrance. Not joking or jawing like sailor-folk or tradesmen might. They scowled at her approach, but she smiled sweetly, walking right on past them. Studying from the corners of her eyes.

They were big, all of them. Dressed like commoners, but well-built to a man. And with her gaze downcast, she saw they all wore soldiers' boots.

What the 'byss is going on here?

She rounded the corner, mind racing. Dragging her cloak of shadows about her shoulders, she latched onto a downspout, scaled the Porkery's flank, deft as a monkey. On the roof, she worked at the tiles, jamming her gravebone stiletto between a pair and prying them loose. Dropping down into the gap, she crawled across the rafters, throwing aside her shadowcloak so she could see the slaughterhouse below.

There was no sign of Bacon or his sons. No sign of the regular butchers who worked the pork. But there were more of those burly gents at every exit, as well as on the mezzanine leading down to the blood pool.

And there among them, heart seizing, breath stilling, she saw him.

It'd been two years since she'd fought him on the steps of the Basilica Grande. Six years since she'd truly seen him up close, the turn he took her father's title, stole her familia's lands. But still, she'd recognize him anywhere. The biggest man she'd ever seen. A trimmed beard framing wolfish features, animal cunning twinkling in his gaze. The scar of what could only have been cat's claws trailing down his cheek. He was dressed as a pleb like the rest of them. No white armor or red cloak or sunsteel blade in sight. But she knew him. Hate dripping from her tongue as she whispered.

"Justicus Marcus Remus . . ."

She looked around the Porkery. At the men with their swordgrip hands and their soldiers' boots. And she knew them for exactly what they were.

"*. . . luminatii . . .*"

"They're here for the blood pool." She breathed deep, scarcely believing her eyes. "They're gearing up to invade the Church."

"*. . . adonai would never walk them across . . .*"

"Unless he's in league with them?" Mia whispered. "Or someone forces him?"

"*. . . walking blithely into a den of the deadliest assassins in the republic? this eve of all eves? lord cassius himself will be there . . .*"

"*. . .* Maybe that's the idea."

Justicus Remus spoke to one of his centurions, narrowed eyes on his troops. "All is prepared?"

"Aye, Justicus." The tall, iron-hard man saluted, fist to chest. "The abattoir was taken without incident. The heretics who dwelled below are in custody or slain."

The justicus nodded, turned to another man beside him. A grizzled-looking veteran that Mia recognized, a leather patch over one eye.

"Centurion Alberius, Second Century will enter the portal first and secure the staging area. Prepare your men. Assault begins in five minutes."

The puppy-killer thumped his chest. "Luminus Invicta, Justicus."

The man turned to his men and bellowed.

"Second Century, form up!"

One hundred Luminatii arranged themselves with military precision, grim-faced and silent. They bore wooden cudgels and shields, a few gravebone blades. Mia was at least grateful none of them would be able to bring their sunsteel with them—no metal could make the Blood Walk, and facing down a few hundred Luminatii armed with burning blades was a little more daunting than facing down a few hundred armed with big sticks.

But only a little.

Remus turned on his secondus, spoke in measured tones.

"Centurion Maxxis. Third Century will hold ground here until we return with the heretics and their master in chains. First Century marches with me on the Sky Altar."

Mia's belly churned at the mention of the altar. Remus knew the Mountain. Which meant he knew its layout, its workings. How else could the Luminatii know all this, unless there was a traitor amid the Church's number?

But Drusilla had tested them all! Every acolyte in the crop had chosen to die rather than give up the Porkery's location. Who'd suffer torture at the hands of Lord Cassius's confessors, only to sell the Church to the Luminatii afterward?

Someone who knew Cassius's confessional was only a test . . .

Realization danced a sickening jig through Mia's belly.

Ashlinn shrugged, scoffed another mouthful. "Wuh vwat wunugd mufuh."

"*. . .* What?"

The girl swallowed, licked her lips. "I said, well, that's what you've got me for. Da told me and my brother everything about this place. Everything he knew, anyway."

"Ash and Oz's father . . ."

"*. . . what of him . . . ?*"

"Ash told me he'd raised his children to replace him."

She looked to the shadow lurking beside her.

"What if he raised them to avenge him?"

"*. . . to attack the darkin lord of the world's finest assassins in a place of perpetual darkness? with a few hundred men? best of luck, dear justicus . . .*"

"He won't need luck," Mia whispered. "The Swoon, don't you see? The measurements in Carlotta's notes were enough to knock dozens dreaming. If Ashlinn or Oz slip it into the initiation feast, Cassius will drop like anyone else, darkin or no."

"*. . . but tric will be at the feast. he would smell the poison, surely . . . ?*"

Mia's heart surged. Her belly turning cold.

"'Byss and blood . . ."

She was down off the rafters before Mister Kindly could utter another whisper. Dropping to the mezzanine, shrouded once more in her cloak of shadows; just a dark blur against the Porkery walls. Second Century were marching up to the mezzanine, followed by Remus and his primus. The men tromped down the stair to the blood pool, two abreast.

Mia stole down behind them, hidden beneath her shadowcloak, the world about her dim and black. Arkemical lamps dotted the stairwell, and she followed their light down to the Porkery's belly, the slick tang of blood hanging in the air. She heard sloshing, churning, burbling. Moving quiet, pawing her way along the wall past the rows of waiting soldiers going into the blood pool. The glyphs on the stone were humming faintly, power singing in the air as Centurion Alberius barked his orders. Not a one of them would've seen Ashkahi bloodwerking before, but to their credit, each Luminatii waded out into Adonai's pool as commanded. Closing their eyes and muttering their prayers and with a surge of Ashkahi magik, disappearing, one by one.

All eyes were on the swirling vortex. The glyphs scrawled in gore across the walls. Mia contemplated waiting until the Second Century had all crossed; surely there'd be a chance to take Remus down in all this. But she thought of Tric. The poison. The feast. If Ashlinn and Osrik had betrayed the Church, they had every reason to kill him, and that thought filled her with a fear that even Mister Kindly couldn't quite devour.

Black Mother, I've been so blind . . .

The blood swirled and surged. Soldiers dragged down into the flow. Despite his arrogance, Mia couldn't imagine Adonai would turn on the Church; he *had* to have been coerced. Regardless, she needed to know what was going on. Revenge could wait.

The people she cared about were more important.

She couldn't help but admire the irony. If she'd become the monster the Church intended, if she'd killed that nameless boy and been accepted for initiation, she'd be none the wiser about Ashlinn and Osrik's plot. She'd be seated at the feast right now, being poisoned with the acolytes and the rest of the Ministry.

Instead, she was the only one who could save them.

Mia stole along the blood chamber's wall, slipped down into the pool, waist-deep in sickening warmth. She'd no idea if two people could make the Walk simultaneously. But she knew Adonai's blood was mixed into this pool, that the speaker would be able to sense her along with the soldier who now waded in beside her.

Would the speaker know her for a friend? Would he even be able to—

The red surged. The floor fell away from Mia's feet. She found herself sucked down, down into the flow, spinning and twisting, blood in her mouth. That awful undertow, threatening to drag her down into forever. Swimming up toward the light. Chest bursting. Heart pounding. Until finally . . .

She felt stone beneath her feet. Pushing herself up slowly, head breaking the surface, blood dripping in her eyes. A Luminatii legionary burst out of the flow beside her, sputtering and coughing, his fellows dragging him up and setting him on his feet. The men in the chamber were painted head to toe in scarlet, quiet horror on every face. Adonai's blood-drenched chamber could only be confirming every gruesome story they'd ever heard about Niah's worshippers. It was easy to see how they'd think the Church a heresy. Easy to see how Scaeva and Duomo could sell them as an enemy.

From the outside, I'd think the same of us.

Mia blinked, wiped the blood from her eyes.

. . . Us.

Cloak of shadows still wrapped about her shoulders, she kept herself sub-merged, only lifting her head high enough to breathe. As always, Adonai was knelt at the head of the pool. Beside him stood a dozen gore-soaked Luminatii, ironwood cudgels in hand. Mia's pulse quickened as she sensed a familiar shadow at the speaker's back.

Osrik . . .

The boy was crouched on the stone, a long, serrated blade in his hand. At his feet, Mia saw another figure, stripped of her traditional black robes. Twisted and piteous, skin split and rotten, trussed up like a hog ready for slaughter. Her hands were bound, her fingers all broken, pink eyes closed. But the steady rise and fall of her shadow's breast told Mia that the weaver wasn't dead—and it was the threat of Osrik's blade at Marielle's throat that was driving Adonai to this madness.

The speaker's with us. That's something, at least . . .

The girl's mind was awhirl, the puzzle playing out in her head.

Though it wracked her with guilt, there was no sense rushing upstairs—whatever was unfolding at the Sky Altar had already happened. At least the poison Ash and Osrik were using was only Swoon; nobody would be killed outright. The Luminatii obviously wanted captives. Torture. Interrogation. Public crucifixion. All this awaited the Red Church hierarchy down the road. But at this moment, Lord Cassius and the Ministry were a long way from dead. That meant Tric might be, too . . .

She looked at Adonai, singing over the churning pool. She could kill him, she realized. Just slit his throat right here, cut off the troops already within the Mountain, seal the others outside. But that would end the most valuable asset the Red Church had in its arsenal. Without the Blood Walk, the Church would be gutted, its chapels isolated.

But still, should she care?

Wasn't saving Tric and Naev worth that loss?

Beneath the blood, she reached into her sleeve, drew out her gravebone dagger. Watching as Adonai stiffened, glanced in her direction.

He knows I'm here.

Continuing his song, bringing more and more of the sputtering, horrified Luminatii across, Adonai turned his eyes back to the pool. But Mia swore she saw him shake his head. And with a faint hand gesture she recognized as Tongueless, the speaker made his thoughts plain.

Don't try, he signed.

That settled that. She'd no chance of stealthing the kill, and if Adonai was intent on fighting her, he could give her away the second she moved against him. True to form, the speaker valued his own skin above anyone else inside these walls.

Right, then. Nothing for it.

Mia hunkered down in the blood, watching as dozens more legionaries made the Walk. When the group was assembled, a hundred men in total, Centurion Alberius ordered them to fan out across the level. Securing stairs, doorways, passages. With his men on the move, the centurion turned to one of his younger recruits.

"Report to the justicus all is secure."

Beneath the drying scarlet, Mia saw the boy blanch at the thought of stepping back into that awful pool. But he waded back into the red, disappeared down into the flow. Mia watched him go, turning her eyes back to Adonai. This was her last chance to cut off the beachhead. If the speaker died before the First Century came across—

The blood surged about her, undertow sucking at her heels. She staggered, grasped the pool's edge, slicking the marble with red. Adonai shook his head again, ever so slight, hands fluttering.

Don't even think it.

Mia grit her teeth. Watching as the First Century began making the Walk. Man after man, minute after minute, dragged from the blood by their fellows. And finally, rising from the red, Mia saw the man she'd dreamed of killing for six long years. Waving aside the soldiers who sought to help him up, stepping from the pool, dripping great floods of gore onto the stone. Dark red, clotted thick in his beard, cascading down his back. Shoulders broad as the Mountain itself.

The justicus of the Luminatii Legions loomed over Speaker Adonai, mouth curled in disgust.

"Godlessness," he growled. "Godlessness and heresy."

Adonai said nothing, meeting the justicus's gaze without flinching. A faint smile at his pretty lips. Remus wiped the blood from his face, turned to his second as an aide began strapping him into a beautiful suit of gravebone armor.

"Centurion, report."

"The level is ours, Justicus. First and Second Centuries accounted for."

"Excellent." He motioned to Adonai. "Bind this apostate bastard good and tight."

Soldiers marched forward, blood-soaked lengths of rope clutched in their hands. They shoved Adonai to the floor, lashed hands and feet behind his back like a calf awaiting slaughter. A rag was stuffed in his mouth, another tied about his eyes. One of the soldiers put a boot in for good measure, but Remus stopped him with a raised hand.

The justicus looked to Osrik, his tone curt.

"What of the Ministry?"

"Ashlinn knew her job," Osrik said. "They'll be trussed up like Great Tithe hogs when you arrive at the Sky Altar. Fear not."

"Wait here until we return with the vaunted Lord of Blades and his godless flock." He motioned to Adonai. "Should this heretic even *twitch* in a manner that displeases you, begin cutting off pieces of his sister until his behavior improves."

Osrik nodded. Adonai tensed at the threat, but otherwise remained motionless.

Now fully armored, Remus looked around at his men, grim and blood-soaked. He reached to his belt, drew a long, beautifully carved gravebone longsword, crows in flight along the pommel and hilt. Mia's eyes narrowed as she recognized it—it had hung on the walls of her father's study beside his collection of maps.

Just how much more can this man take from me?

"Righteous brothers," Remus began. "This eve, we strike a blow against a blasphemy that has blackened our glorious Republic for decades. The ministers of this godless Church are to be brought back alive to Godsgrave for interrogation. But any other night-worshipping bastard you cross within these walls is to be shown no mercy. We are the Right Hand of Aa, and this eve, we bring this house of heresy to its knees."

The justicus held his stolen blade to his brow, lowered his head. The legionaries around the room did the same, lips moving in unison.

"Hear me, Aa. Hear me, Father. Your flame, my heart. Your light, my soul. For your name, and your glory, and your justice, I march. Shine upon me."

Remus raised his head. Nodded at his men.

"Luminus Invicta."

STEPS

She waited.

Though her mind swam with images of what might be happening up those stairs, though her blood boiled at the thought of Ashlinn's betrayal, her revenge against Remus within her grasp and yet untasted, she waited. If the Luminatii got Cassius and the Revered Mother in their clutches, every Red Church disciple was at risk. Her friends. Mercurio, too. Her first step *had* to be cutting off Remus's escape. Cassius and Drusilla couldn't be allowed to fall into the Confessionate's hands.

And so she lurked in the blood. Cursing herself a fool. She knew it for certain now. Ash had killed Lotti. Tried to frame *her* for the murder. Every moment, every word she'd spoken had been a lie. Hush had warned her, too, that eve in the Hall of Truths.

you have one friend inside these walls
not carlotta
not tric or ashlinn
and not me

That friend lurked in the shadows of the room, watching with his not-eyes.

Remus and his troops had marched out. But there were still a dozen Luminatii in the speaker's chamber, clad now in ornate leather, embossed with the sigil of Aa. The armor was thick, the buckles made of wood, not a rivet or screw anywhere—specially crafted for the assault, no doubt. A half-dozen men stood watch over Adonai and Marielle. Six more at the threshold, watching the corridor beyond. The weaver was still unconscious, Osrik crouched beside her, his blade lingering at her throat.

Start at the beginning . . .

Mia couldn't see much beneath her cloak anyway, and so she closed her eyes. Reached out to the shadows in the room. Just like she had among the strawmen in the Hall of Songs, she could feel those shadows like she could feel herself. She remembered what it was to be that fourteen-year-old girl again. Tearing Aa's statue to pieces outside the Basilica Grande. Stepping between the shadows like a wraith. But most of all, she remembered the man who helped start it all, who'd seen her father hung, her mother in chains, her brother dead before he could walk.

She spread her arms beneath the blood. Fingers outstretched. Reaching through the flickering gloom, out to the shadows at each legionary's feet. Curling them into hooks, digging them into the soles of the soldiers' boots, every one. And, quiet as she could, she rose from Adonai's pool.

She realized her mistake at once—though she was still hidden beneath her cloak of shadows, the blood she was soaked in wasn't. As she hauled herself up on the ledge, scarlet spattered on the stone, bloody handprints appearing beneath her palms. The legionaries in the room turned to the sound, Osrik's brow creased.

Confusion. Hesitation.

It was enough.

Mia stepped into the shadow beneath her

stepped out

of the shadow

on the wall

behind Osrik

One of the legionaries saw movement from the corner of his eye, cried out in alarm, but by then Mia's knife was already buried hilt-deep in the join

between the boy's neck and swordarm, severing the tendons clean. Osrik screamed,
blade falling from nerveless fingers, Mia bringing her knee up into his jaw and
sending him crashing to the floor. She snatched up his dagger, and then

she was

stepping into

the dark at her

feet and out of the shadows behind another legionary, cutting his hamstrings
with her blade and dropping him to the deck. The man beside him struck out
at her with his cudgel and she swayed backward, the blow whistling past her
chin, stepping inside his guard and burying her knee into his groin hard enough
to make every man in the room wince in sympathy. The soldiers cried out, but
trying to charge this gore-soaked horror from the sorcerer's blood pit, they found
their boots stuck fast to the stone.

Mia could feel it. The power of the night, coursing beneath her skin. The
hungry Dark. The Mother herself, the goddess who'd marked her, staring with
black eyes at these men who'd invaded her holy ground.

And she was angry.

She dropped one, then another, snatching up a cudgel and cracking it across
jaws and the backs of skulls, skipping between patches of darkness and leaving
only bloody footprints behind. They were men of the finest cohort in the legion—
Remus hadn't been foolish enough to bring any marrowborn lads or senators'
sons with him to the Mountain. But faced with this blood-soaked horror, black
eyes and savage smile and red, red hands, soon enough, the fear had them.

"Your boots!" one cried. "Take off your boots!"

The shadows snatched at their clubs and smothered their cries as she felled
them one by one. The nearby comrades who heard them screaming and came to
investigate met the same fates; felled by vicious blows or dropping with their
throats cut. Until only one remained. A man with dark, blood-soaked curls,
falling on his backside as he kicked off his boots, scrambling back against the
wall, eyes wide with terror as this daemon from the abyss stepped from the shadows before him. Bloody knife in one hand. Bloody club in the other. Hair
clinging like black weed to the gore upon its face.

And it opened its mouth, then. And it spoke with a girl's voice.

"I'm sorry."

The blade fell.

Rising from the bloody mess she'd made, Mia heard a groan, looked to where Osrik was trying to rise from the floor. Marching over to the Vaanian boy, she kicked him hard in the head, tumbling him back to the flagstones. Kneeling beside Marielle, Mia checked the weaver was still breathing, covered her tortured skin with the tattered remnants of her robe. Then she crouched beside Adonai's head, talking carefully.

"Speaker, it's Mia. I'm going to untie you now. Your sister is alive and well. Whatever you might see, I need you to not murder anyone for a minute or two, agreed?"

Adonai grunted in response, nodding. Mia cut his bonds, untied the gag and blindfold. The speaker was on his feet in a flash, face twisted, hands raised. Tendrils of blood rose from the pool, writhing like serpents, pointed like spears. The albino's eyes fell on his sister, on the boy beside her who had threatened her life . . .

Osrik was trying to rise again, groaning and clutching his jaw. Adonai raised his arms above his head, fingers curled like a puppeteer over a marionette. Bloody coils whipped from the pool, seizing Osrik's wrists, feet, dragging him across the flagstones and down into the red.

"I said don't kill him!"

Mia seized the speaker's arm, spun him to face her. With a wave of his fingers, the speaker wrapped another whip of gore around Mia's throat and lifted her off the ground. The girl gasped, choking, legs kicking at the air. A dozen shadows about the room seized Adonai's limbs, their ends fashioned into needle-sharp points, quivering just an inch or two from his eyes.

"Let me go," Mia croaked. "I just saved your life. Your sister's life. We're on the same damn side. And we need Osrik alive to find out what's going on upstairs."

"Be it not obvious?" Adonai snarled. "The Luminatii hath come for Lord Cassius. What more need we know?"

"Let. Me. Go. Fucker."

Adonai sneered. But the grip at her throat slackened, the tendril setting her down gently on the stone before slipping back into the pool. The speaker waved one hand and Osrik emerged, gasping, blood bubbling at his lips as he whispered

"Mia, please . . ."

before being jerked back down beneath the flood again.

"Adonai, you and Marielle need to get out of here."

"And where shall we go?" he spat. "A traitor hath been reared in our midst. Like be the Luminatii hath the location of every chapel twixt here and Godsgrave by now."

"That doesn't mean they're moving on all of them. They likely wouldn't for fear of giving the game away. Lord Cassius is the prize, and they *can't* be allowed to get him back to Godsgrave. With you gone, they only have one way back to civilization."

"The Whisperwastes," Adonai said.

"Exactly. So stop fuck-arsing about and get out of here."

"And what shall ye do, little darkin? Destroy an army by thyself?"

"That'd be my problem, wouldn't it?"

"*. . . our problem . . .*"

Adonai's eyes never left Mia's. His voice as cold and hard as stone.

"This cur threatened my sister love, my sister mine, little darkin. Were I thee and had need of his knowledge, on my life, I would ask my questions swift."

Adonai gave a lazy wave of his hand. Osrik resurfaced from the blood pool again, coughing and blubbing, barely conscious.

"Osrik, can you hear me?"

"Mia, plea—"

"Shut the fuck up, you piece of shit," she snarled. "You've got one chance to live and that's by telling me what I want to know, understood?"

"I—" the boy sputtered, retching and coughing. "Aye."

"You poisoned the initiation feast. Cassius, the Ministry, and initiates?"

The boy nodded, bloody hair dripping in his eyes. "Aye."

"None of them are dead?"

"N-no. We used a kind of Swoon. We had Carlotta brew a specialized dose that would act swifter than usual. Remus wanted the Ministry alive for q-questioning."

"What about Tric? He'd have smelled the Swoon in the meal a mile away. How did you stop him noticing?"

Osrik said nothing. Lips working silently.

". . . Osrik?"

"Ashlinn, she . . ."

Mia knew it then. Heard it in his voice. Belly sinking into her toes. Remembering the way she'd felt in his arms. The way he'd kissed her.

She hadn't loved him, but . . .

No.

She hadn't loved him.

Mia opened her eyes. Looked up at Adonai. Breathed deep.

"That's all I needed to know."

"Mia, n—"

Osrik's wail was swallowed up by the pool, the boy wrenched down to his doom.

". . . mia, we must move . . ."

Mia nodded to the not-cat, took a moment to collect her thoughts.

"Adonai, you need to get out of here. Now."

The speaker stared at her for a long moment, the only sound the faint splashing of his pool. But finally he reached to his neck, grasped a silver phial on a leather thong, and snapped it loose. Mia recognized it—the same kind Naev had worn in the desert. The same kind that filled the alcoves in the Revered Mother's rooms.

"My vitus," Adonai said. "Shouldst thou triumph, spill it 'pon the floor, write as if the red were a tablet and thy finger the brush. I shall know it."

Mia retied the phial about her neck, pawing coagulating gore from her lashes. She could feel it drying on her skin, cracking on her lips as she spoke.

"Go."

Adonai gathered his sister in his arms, trod down the marble steps and into the churning flow. The blood seemed to cling to him as he walked, tiny tendrils rising off the surface and caressing him as he passed. He turned to Mia, nodded once.

"Good fortune to thee, little darkin. Thou shalt have a need of it."

"When she wakes up, tell Marielle what happened here. Tell her she owes me."

Adonai shook his head and smiled. "The dead are owed nothing."

He spoke swiftly, humming discordant notes to the pool, like a father to a sleeping babe. The blood sang in reply, and in a rushing, iron-soaked flood, the pair disappeared beneath the swell. The surface fell still as a millpond. Not a ripple to mark their passing.

Mia wrung her hair out. Upended her boots to empty them of blood as best she could, stowed Osrik's serrated blade at her shin. Mister Kindly watched the whole time, still and silent. But finally he whispered.

". . . i am sorry about tric . . ."

"You've nothing to be sorry for."

". . . you felt what you felt, mia. there is no need to deny it . . ."

"I'm not."

A pause, filled with a quiet sigh.

". . . no need to lie, either . . ."

The choir was silent.

It was the first thing she noticed as she stole from the speaker's chambers, out into the Mountain's dark. The ghostly tune that had accompanied her every moment within these halls was gone. Her footsteps seemed all the louder for it, breath rasping in her ears. It felt wrong. A splinter beneath her skin. A silence so loud it was deafening.

At the other end of the level, two Luminatii were stationed at the stairwells leading to higher ground. But their eyes were fixed above, of course, waiting for their justicus and his men to return. Mia stole toward them, quiet enough to make both Mercurio and Mouser beam with pride. She was less than a whisper as she rose up behind them. More than a blur as her gravebone blade sliced one man ear to ear, pierced the other's heart as he turned to watch his comrade fall.

The soldier staggered, collapsing backward against the stairwell, hand to his chest. Eyes searching the darkness for what had killed him. And she threw aside her cloak then, just so he could see. See the pale waif soaked all in black and red, the mask of drying gore, the eyes beyond. See the shadow of a dead boy in her pupils as she reached out and covered his mouth, slicing his throat as she whispered.

"*Hear me, Niah. Hear me, Mother. This flesh your feast. This blood your wine. This life, this end, my gift to you. Hold him close.*"

The not-cat at her feet swelled and rippled, drinking deep of the soldier's final terror. And all around her, she could feel it. The Dark. Whispering. Urging her on.

It was pleased.

Mia opened her arms, willed the shadows to rise, wrap the bodies up and drag them off into the darkness. She almost wished she could stay and watch as their comrades returned, finding only bloodstains to mark their passing. Watch as the first seeds of fear took root, and these men realized just how far they were from home. That the Dark around them was not only angry. It was hungry.

She dashed up the stairs, met two more soldiers at the top, gifting them an end the same as the ones below. They seemed so small here in the Mountain's belly. Without their sunblades and white mail and their cloaks like crimson rivers. Just tiny little men, their faith in the Everseeing not quite enough to protect them from his bride. From the one she'd marked. The one she'd chosen, in this, her house. Her altar. Her temple.

Mia was almost at the Hall of Eulogies when they spotted her. Quietly ending two legionaries, she failed to notice two more descending from above. She heard roars of alarm, turning in time to see the Luminatii rushing toward her. She slipped low and sliced one from knee to privates, severing his femoral artery and bleeding him out on the floor. The second cracked her across the temple with his club, and she staggered, wrapping his feet up in darkness and slipping behind him, burying her blade half a dozen times into his back. But she heard more shouts now, more running feet.

Half a dozen Luminatii were charging down the stairwell toward her, among them Alberius, head of the century himself. She could throw on her cloak of shadows, perhaps slip past them unnoticed. But the thought of Ashlinn's betrayal, of what she'd done to Tric, of these bastards invading the place she'd come to think of as home—all of it burned in her chest with an intensity that almost frightened her.

No more running. No more hiding.

"All right, bastards," she whispered. "Follow me."

The legionaries saw her, shouted warning. She drew her gravebone dagger. Osrik's blade in her off-hand. The dried blood at her lips cracking as she snarled, the shadows about her writhing as she charged up the stairs to meet them. Alberius and the legionary beside him were both as broad as houses, cudgels and shields raised. The centurion squinted at her in the dark, at the blade in her hand that had claimed his eye. Recognition at last dawning on his paling face.

"You . . . ," he breathed.

The centurion touched three fingers to his brow and held them out to Mia.

"Luminus Invicta!" he roared.

Mia screamed wordlessly, heart singing as she raised her blades. The Luminatii roared answer, barreling down the stairs toward the blood-streaked daemon, raising their clubs, eyes growing wide as the girl stepped

into the shadow

at her feet

out of the shadows behind them

and kept right on running.

The Luminatii skidded to a halt, the rearmost soldier watching her disappear up the stair. Alberius bellowed and the chase was on, out along the broader hallways and into the Mountain proper. Mia saw four more Luminatii ahead, sprinting toward her. She picked up her pace, blades gleaming. And just as they reached her, cudgels raised, teeth bared, again she skipped

through the shadows

and out of the dark at their backs.

They turned, looked at her dumbfounded as she bent double, pausing to catch her breath. Alberius's furious shouts ringing in the distance. And straightening, Mia raised the knuckles, blew them a kiss, and ran on.

There were thirty men chasing her by the time she arrived. More cries ringing through the Mountain, the sound of more approaching feet. Mia glanced over her shoulder and saw fury and murder in their eyes, skidding to a halt at a huge pair of double doors, slipping inside and sealing them behind her as she turned and ran.

Out into the dark of the athenaeum.

The Luminatii burst into the room, the doors swinging open and slamming into the small wooden trolley marked RETURNS that had been placed—rather carelessly, it might have appeared—directly in the door's path.

The trolley upended, smashed to the stone, dozens of tomes sent sprawling, skittering, skidding. A red-faced Alberius stormed into the room and booted the trolley aside, more books sailing across the mezzanine as his soldiers fanned out around him. He scanned the dark, a black scowl on his brow.

And somewhere out in the forest of pages and shelves,

came a rumbling,

chuddering

roar.

". . . What in the Everseeing's name was that?" one soldier asked.

"Fan out!" the centurion ordered. "Find that heretic bitch and gut her!"

Twenty-nine salutes thumped against twenty-nine chests. The Luminatii marched down the stairs and into the shelves, weapons raised. Splitting wordlessly into small columns of six men apiece, they spread out, scouring aisle after aisle. Alberius led a group of his finest, narrowed eyes searching every nook and corner. Six years he must have lived with the lie. Sleepless nevernights spent worrying if the morrow would be the turn Scaeva discovered Corvere's daughter still lived. And now was his chance to not only avenge the loss of his eye, but put to rest any fear of his failure coming to light.

I wonder if he thought himself lucky for it.

Out in the black, another roar sounded.

Closer now.

"Centurion?" one of his men asked. "What *is* that?"

Alberius paused, scanning the dark. He raised his voice, called over the shelves.

"Graccus? Belcino? Report!"

"No sign, sir!"

"Nothing, sir!"

Another roar. The sound of something heavy approaching.

Closer.

The good centurion looked troubled now. Second thoughts perhaps overcoming his initial fervor. And just as he opened his mouth to speak, he heard soft footsteps, a rippling breeze, a roar of pain. He turned, saw one of his legionaries clutching a stab wound in his back, a small, dark-haired girl staring at him from a mask of drying blood.

"Good turn, centurion," she said.

"She's here!" Alberius roared.

The girl smiled, gently tossing something at his chest. "A gift for you."

The centurion raised his shield, smashed the object from the air. He realized it was some old book; leather-bound and dusty, the binding popping and a dozen pages bursting loose. It skidded across the floor, shedding more of its guts as it went.

"... *unwise* ... ," came a whisper.

"Kill that fucki—"

Something reared up over the top of the shelves. Something huge, many-headed, and monstrous, all blunt snouts and leathery skin and jaws full of O, too many teeth. The Luminatii cried out—to their credit, not in alarm, but warning—raising their little shields and toothpicks and roaring to the fellows in the other aisles. And then the Something struck, engulfing Centurion Alberius with those O, so many teeth and shaking him like a dog with a particularly sad and bloody little bone.

Soldiers came running. Soldiers ran screaming. More Somethings reared up over the shelves, huge and sightless, snapping and roaring and ripping the little men to pieces, all the while disturbing not a single page on a single shelf.

Back up on the mezzanine, Mia stepped from the shadows of the balustrade. Stood beside an old man, his back bent like a question mark, leaning against the railing and watching the show.

"A girl with a story to tell," Aelius smiled.

"So they say."

"Smoke?"

"Maybe later."

And she was gone.

PURSUIT

She stole into the Hall of Truths, found it empty, faint light glittering on walls of green glass. But after carefully picking the lock and rummaging through Spiderkiller's desk, she found them—the three bags of wyrdglass. Most of the onyx orbs had been used up, but the pouches containing the pearl and ruby wyrdglass were almost full. Two bags full of Swoon and Spiderkiller's arkemical fire.

It'll do.

Next, she headed to the Hall of Songs, stopping to softly murder two more Luminatii she found stationed in the Hall of Eulogies. She flitted past the unmarked tombs, trying not to picture Tric lying inside one. Turning the sorrow in her breast to rage. Halfway up the stairs, she found the bodies of murdered Hands, beaten and bludgeoned. Near the top, she found another dozen corpses, Marcellus and Petrus among them, eyes open wide and seeing nothing at all.

No time to pray.

No time to care.

She dashed into Solis's hall, threw a heavy leather training jerkin over her blood-soaked shirt. Rummaging through the racks and stuffing her boots with daggers, strapping a fine, sharp gladius at her belt, slinging a bandolier of throwing knives about her chest and a quiver and crossbow at her back.

"Maw's teeth . . ."

She spun at the whisper, crossbow raised, the shadows about her flaring. There at the top of the stairs, she saw figures robed in black, a bare half-dozen in total. Among them, she glimpsed red, bobbed hair, a pretty face, green, hunter's eyes.

". . . Jessamine?"

"Corvere," the girl hissed. "What in the Mother's name are you doing here?"

A veiled figure pushed her way through the group, a smile in her eyes.

"Naev is pleased to see her," she said.

"Goddess, you're all right!"

Mia ran across the room and threw her arms around the woman. But Naev flinched in Mia's embrace, pushed away with a groan. Looking around, Mia could see most of the group were injured; Jessamine bleeding badly from a gash above her eye, her arm in a rough sling, a few others nursing broken wrists or ribs. Naev was breathing heavily now, clutching her side.

"What happened? Are you well?"

"Bastards came at us like a flood." Jessamine winced, pawing the blood from her eyes. "No warning. Murdered every Hand and acolyte they could find. How the 'byss did they get inside? Where are the Ministry?"

"Likely in chains by now," Mia said. "Ashlinn and Osrik betrayed us. Poisoned the initiation feast. Killed Tr—"

Mia bit down on the words. Shook her head.

"Ashlinn?" Jessamine breathed. "Osrik? But they're blooded disciples."

"Vengeance for their father." Mia shook her head. "Doesn't matter. Justicus Remus is here with two centuries of men. They've captured Lord Cassius and the Ministry. They mean to take them back to the 'Grave for torture and execution."

"Then they are fools, to challenge Niah's disciples in her house." Naev turned to the other Hands. "Gather arms. Blades and bows."

"You want me to fight alongside her?" Jessamine glared at Mia. "After she killed Diamo? Not bloody likely."

"We must stand together in this."

"I don't have to stand anywhere near this bitch."

"We don't have time for our bullshit, Jess," Mia said. "This is *Justicus Marcus Remus* we're talking about. He helped end the Kingmaker Rebellion. He's probably trodden on your father's skull every turn for six years walking into the Senate House. All the shit you've given me? All the hate? *This* is a man who actually deserves to taste it."

The girl searched Mia's eyes, Diamo's memory plain in her own. Seconds they didn't have trickling through the hourglass. Hatred for Mia warring with hatred for the ones who'd seen her familia destroyed. But the truth of it was, she and Jess really were cut from the same cloth. Both orphans of the Kingmaker Rebellion. Both robbed of their familia. Held together by the kind of bond only hate can forge.

In the end, there was only one real choice.

"So what are we going to do?"

"Adonai is gone." Mia saw Naev stiffen at the words, put a reassuring hand on her friend's arm. "He's taken Marielle. They're safe. But without access to the Blood Walk, Remus is cut off. He only has one way back to Godsgrave."

"The Whisperwastes," Naev said.

Mia nodded. "They'll know by now that the Blood Walk isn't an option.

But Ashlinn is with them. She can take them to the stables. They'll be headed
there, looking to ride our camel trains back to Last Hope."

"So we hit them in the stables," Jessamine said. "Cut them off."

"Crowded quarters," Naev agreed. "Their numbers will count for less."

"You're wounded," Mia said. "All of you. It's going to be a slaughterhouse
in there and I don't want—"

"Remind me again when I started giving a fuck what you want, Corvere?"
Jessamine snapped. "You might believe you're the Mother's gift to the world,
but you're not half the blademaster you think you are. If you want a chance of
ending these bastards, you're going to need our help."

Mia looked to Naev, met by cold hard eyes.

"She speaks truth."

"All right," Mia sighed. "You're right."

The Hands armed themselves to the teeth, covered their robes with leather
jerkins, hefting crossbows and swords and knives. Mia distributed the wyrdglass
among them, keeping a fat handful of ruby and pearl for herself. She'd no idea
how they'd pull this off. No idea if any of them would live to see the morrow.

No time.

No chance.

No fear.

She looked at the disciples around her. Nodded once.

"Let's go."

I t seemed Justicus Remus wasn't the kind to be fooled twice.

He'd left his back exposed as he assaulted the Mountain, and his over-
confidence had been repaid with the slaughter of his rearguard and the loss of
the speaker. With his planned escape route cut off, the justicus had headed to
the stables, just as Mia predicted. But to his credit, it also looked like he'd
learned from past mistakes.

Sadly, the justicus hadn't counted on Mister Kindly.

The not-cat stalked down the stairs ahead of Mia and her fellows, slipping
out into the Hall of Eulogies and immediately sensing the tremor of fear in
the air. He'd marked hidden figures, lying in wait in alcoves or skulking in
antechambers. Whispered prayers to the Everseeing on their lips.

He'd flitted back up the stairs, coalescing on Mia's shoulder and whispering in her ear.

"There are legionaries in the Hall of Eulogies," Mia repeated. "Almost forty."

"Forty," Naev whispered, looking at their pitiful half-dozen.

Mia fished a handful of white wyrdglass from the pouch at her belt and smiled.

"I think I can even the score. As soon as you hear the ruckus, come running."

The girl wrapped herself in her cloak of shadows, heard Jessamine and the other Hands gasp as she faded from sight. The world dropped to near blackness beneath her veil, and she had to feel her way down the stairs. But soon enough, she sensed an archway, the vast, sweeping space of the hall beyond. The dead names on the floor. The nameless tombs in the walls. She could see the vague silhouette of Niah's statue above, picked out against the blurry, stained-glass light.

Creeping slow, near-blind, she crouched behind a nearby pillar. Throwing off her cloak long enough to get a decent view of her surroundings, she stepped into the shadows at her feet and reappeared forty feet off the ground, nestled in the deep shadows of Niah's folded hood.

One of the Luminatii saw movement above, yelled warning. But by then, Mia was raining wyrdglass down from her perch, thick clouds of Swoon bursting around the room. At least a dozen men dropped after inhaling a lungful, others running from their nooks and crannies to seek better shelter.

As the Luminatii broke cover, Naev, Jessamine, and the other Hands charged into the room, black and swift and deadly silent. The soldiers didn't even know they were facing more than one assailant until five more of their number were dead. The disciples fell on the invaders with a fury that staggered them, Jessamine's blades a blur, Naev fighting like a daemon despite her broken ribs. Perhaps it was rage at the invasion of their home. Perhaps it was the presence of the goddess, sword and scales poised above them, cold stone eyes following the butchery. But within moments, the Luminatii ambush had turned into a slaughter, and the black ran red with the blood of Aa's faithful.

Mia stood upon her perch, crossbow in hand, picking off runners and cutting down anyone who thought to strike at a disciple's back. Ten quarrels later, she drew her blades and stepped out of the statue's shadow forty feet below, burying a dagger in some poor fool's back, cutting down another with a fistful of throwing knives. Fighting back to back with Naev, throwing up a wall of bloody steel, the song of their blades filling the empty space left behind by the Mother's choir, the cries of the slaughtered echoing in the dark after the last man had fallen.

Naev staggered, clutching her ribs and gasping. Jessamine was bloodied and breathless. Two other Hands—a boy named Pietro, not much older than Mia, and an older man named Neraius—had fallen under the Luminatii's blows.

"... *mia* ..."

The girl stood over Pietro's body, head hung low.

Staring into his sightless eyes.

"... *mia they are at the stables* ..."

She hung there in the quiet gloom. Trying not to remember.

Trying and failing.

"He was just a boy, Mister Kindly."

She shook her head.

"Just a boy."

"... *now is not the time to mourn, mia. this boy or any other* ..."

The girl looked at him then, grief shining in her eyes.

"... *avenge them instead* ..."

Mia nodded slow.

Wiped the blood from her blades.

And she ran on.

The stables were a milling sea of men, animals, dust. The stink of sweat and blood and shit, the barks of centurions, the warbling murmurs of agitated camels, and, above them all, Justicus Remus. Roaring.

Mia had only ever hidden one other person beneath her cloak, but Tric had been a giant, and Naev and Jessamine were each half his size. So, leaving the other wounded Hands behind, the trio had stolen down the stairs and out into the stables. Looking through the scrum, Jessamine sighed.

"'Byss and blood, we're too late."

The Luminatii had already managed to open the Mountain's walls, blinding light and fingers of grit blowing in from the Whisperwastes outside. Soldiers had hitched up two wagon trains to camel teams and were leading them into the foothills outside; other Luminatii were saddling individual beasts and dragging them out by the reins. Most of the soldiers had never laid eyes on a camel before, and the process was taking longer than it should have—hence the roars from the aforementioned justicus. But still, the Luminatii were moments from escape.

Mia could see seven bound figures with bags over their heads being loaded into the foremost wagon. Even with their faces hidden, she recognized them immediately. The Ministry, a slender boy who must be Hush, and finally, a figure bound in a cocoon of rope and manacles, being carried by one of the biggest Luminatii Mia had ever seen.

"Lord Cassius," she breathed.

"Black Mother," Jessamine hissed. "They killed the other camels."

Mia looked into the pens, saw Jessamine was right; any beast not currently hitched to a train or being saddled by a soldier had been slaughtered. She cursed softly, staring out into the rocky foothills at the Mountain's feet.

"Naev, when we first arrived here, there was some kind of magik on the Mountain. A confusion, and kind of . . ."

"The Discord," Naev said.

"Aye, that's it. Will it effe—"

"No," the woman sighed. "It only wears upon those who seek to enter the Mountain uninvited. These men seek to *leave* it. The Discord will not sway them."

"Shit," Mia hissed. "How do we give chase?"

"Just smuggle us aboard the trains with your shadow-werking," Jessamine said.

"They're already outside. My power runs deep in the Mountain because no sunlight has ever touched these halls. But out there . . . I don't think I'm strong enough to hide us all. If we get seen, we're as dead as those unwanted camels. Besides, the wagons are full. It's not like there's room for us to hide in them anyway."

Mia spoke true—even thinning their numbers in the library and Hall of Eulogies, there were still over a hundred Luminatii left standing and only six wagons. Between their fellows and the supplies necessary to survive a weeks-long trek back to Last Hope, Remus's men were squashed together like strips of salt pork in a barrel.

"Fuck," Jessamine sighed.

"Aye," Mia agreed. "Fuck is right."

The Luminatii were dragging the last few living camels out into the foot-hills, clambering up on their backs. Remus was already aboard the first train, and through the rising dust, Mia saw Ashlinn, red-eyed and furious, standing atop the wagon and watching the Mountain's entrance. The half-dozen soldiers Mia had left hamstrung in Adonai's chamber would have told the girl what happened to her brother. Ashlinn knew Osrik was dead. And more, she knew Mia was responsible.

The girl snarled something at Remus, only to be roared at in response. However much she'd helped in taking down the Church, it seemed the justicus of the Luminatii was in no mood to take lip from a seventeen-year-old heretic.

Glad to be the thorn in your side, bitch . . .

The last camels were outside. The wagon covers were being drawn, the tackle checked. Naev muttered a prayer, readying to charge, but Mia grabbed her arm.

"You can't go out there."

"We cannot let them escape," the woman hissed.

"There's too many, Naev. They'll butcher us before we get ten feet."

"We can't just sit here!" Jessamine spat.

Mia chewed her lip. Stared at the hundred-yard dash to the rearmost wagon. "I can make it," Mia said. "They won't see me. I can get aboard."

"And do what? Take out a hundred Luminatii alone?"

Mia's shadow rippled. A chill shivered the air.

"*. . . she is never alone . . .*"

Mia looked down at the not-cat, tail switching side to side. And there in the shadows, crouched amid the dust and the dark, the puzzle came together in Mia's mind. The final piece, the final thought, the final answer falling into place.

Click.

"I know how to stop them," she breathed. "Are you with me?"

Mister Kindly titled his head quizzically.

"*. . . always . . .*"

Before Naev or Jessamine could speak, Mia was off, tearing up the shadows and throwing them about her shoulders, dashing through the stables and into the open air. The trains were already moving, dirt and grit in her mouth and eyes, and she ran almost blind, just a shifting blur against the rising dust. Stumbling through the gloom, the blur of Luminatii riders to the rearmost wagon, overflowing with grumbling, blood-caked soldiers. Moving by feel, she slipped beneath the tray, crawled forward, and slung herself up onto the fore-axel to lay in wait.

The wagon crunched and bounced down the crumbling slope, the drivers whipping the camels hard. Remus obviously wanted to get as far from the Mountain as he could with his prize; the justicus might be a courageous sort when murdering kittens and throwing children into canals, but it seemed when plans went astray, so did his desire for confrontation.

Or perhaps Scaeva simply wanted Lord Cassius more than Mia could imagine.

The girl clung to the wagon's belly like a leech. But she was safely out of sight for the time being, and so she threw aside her shadowcloak, concentrating only on keeping her grip. She was bounced and jolted, hammered and slammed, her back and arse screaming protest all the while. Dust caked her tongue, gummed up her eyes, caked the dried blood in her hair. She almost slipped a half-dozen times, closing her eyes and praying for strength. The ride seemed to go on forever.

A good five or six hours from the Mountain, the foothills began to even out, and the ride became a little less like torture. The sand grew soft and the drivers laid on the whips. Camels broke into a full gallop, the wagons rushing along behind them, fast as they could go.

Let's see about that . . .

Though only Saan hung in the sky, the light was near blinding compared to the Mountain's belly, and Mia's power felt thin and feeble. But still, she reached out to the gloom on the wagon's underside, pulled it about her shoulders again, and held it tight. Calling loud as she could to the shadows, and hoping something else might answer.

"*. . . i believe you asked me to remind you never to call the dark in this desert again . . .*"

"I believe it's a woman's prerogative to change her mind."

Mister Kindly tried to purr, voice rippling with amusement.

"*. . . i believe you're right . . .*"

It was another few minutes before she heard a cry of alarm from the wagon ahead. Shuffling footsteps on the planks above, Luminatii calling.

"*Claudius, do you see that?*"

"*What is it?*"

"*I see another! Two of them!*"

"*No, three!*"

Beneath the shuddering creak of the timber, the clatter of the wheels, the shouts from above, Mia fancied she heard a distant rumble. A cry from the wagon train in front.

"*Sand kraken!*"

The scrawny, blood-soaked girl clung to her perch and smiled. She didn't bother looking—even if she weren't near-blind beneath her cloak, between the dust from the wheels and the multitude of riders, she wouldn't have a chance of seeing them yet. But listening close, she could hear them, just as she'd heard them the turn she fought Naev on these same sands. The churn of massive bodies diving through the desert deeps. The faint echoes of distant, thunderous roars.

Big ones.

Coming right at them.

Feeling her way, Mia crawled along the wagon's belly, up to the Y-shaped timbers that hitched her wagon to the wagon in front. The drivers were swinging the whips hard now, desperate to outrun the behemoths on their tail. Mia knew Ashlinn would be familiar with the horrors of the Whisperwastes and how to keep them at bay, and yes, there it came—the awful rhythm of ironsong. Luminatii began beating on those bloody pipes for all they were worth, Mia wincing at the racket just above her head. She'd no idea if the noise actually had any effect on the bigger kraken, but the offending musician wasn't taking chances. The cacophony was earsplitting, and Mia was already in a temper. As if to echo her mood, she heard another awful, rumbling bellow.

Closer now.

"... *you are making them very angry* ..."

Mia spat, so much dust in her mouth she could barely speak.

"I'll make it up to them."

"... *how, pray tell* ...?"

A white smile gleamed in a dirty, blood-caked face.

"Fix them dinner."

Jarred and juddered as the wagons bounced through the sands, she crawled out from the axel and onto the hitch bar. Through the darkness over her eyes, she could make out dim shapes in the swirling dust. Perhaps fifteen Luminatii riding around the trains. Maybe twenty soldiers in each wagon, all standing and staring aft. She could hear rumbling in the earth, drawing ever closer.

"*Another one!*" came the shout.

"*West! West!*"

"*Aa's Light, look at the size of it!*"

Mia grinned to herself, pawing the grit from her eyes. She'd hoped this deep in the desert, calling the Dark might bring a few of the bigger kraken out to play. But from the sound of it, she'd hooked a couple of monsters.

At the sight of their fourth uninvited guest, the Luminatii on ironsong duty began banging on his pipes like a privy door in the wind. Mia cursed again, covered her ears. The racket was worse than annoying, it was bloody painful.

Let's ring the midmeal bell instead.

She hopped across to the second wagon's hitch, trying to figure out exactly how the wagons were connected. Leaning close and squinting hard, she made out a metal bar, hooked through a round eyelet, lashed together with thick rope. Quick smart, Mia drew a knife from her boot and began sawing away, occasionally glancing up to the Luminatii in the wagons above.

As one might expect, the men only had eyes for the tentacled monstrosities intent on devouring their favorite faces; not a man noticed the shivering blur perched on the hitch bar below. The ropes were tough, but through feel and elbow grease, Mia sawed them loose, leaving only the hook and eyelet linking the wagons together.

One good jolt ...

She slipped under the bar and dragged herself along the middle wagon's belly. The train struck a rock in the sand, bouncing hard, and she held her breath, waiting for the coupling to burst loose. But both the Luminatii's luck and the hook managed to hold, and, spitting a mouthful of red dirt, Mia crawled on. She could see next to nothing, but the rumbling was close now. Over the thunder of the wheels, hooves, and ironsong, she heard a heavy *twang*, realizing the Luminatii were firing at the closest kraken with the crossbows on the wagon's flanks. Teeth gritted, nails clawing the wood, she crawled up to the coupling between the fore and middle wagons. And sawing away with her blade, she hacked the tethers loose. The only things holding the train together now were luck and a few pieces of worn metal.

And luck always runs out.

The wagons veered west, headed for rockier ground where the kraken would have a hard time following. Mia clung on for grim life to the foremost wagon's hitch as the ground grew rougher, the wheels crunching, axels grinding as the trains bounced over divots and potholes and clumps of stone. They crested a small hill, camels frothing under the driver's whips. The train plunged down, hit a deep trough on the other side. Couplings groaned. Soldiers cursed. And in a flurry of dust and gravel and shrieking iron, the rearmost wagon broke free.

Timbers snapping, the hitch bar ploughed into the ground and the wagon flipped upright, balancing on its snout for a few torturous seconds before rolling end over end. The twenty-odd men inside were flung about like toys, screaming and shouting and crashing atop one another, thrown through the tearing canvas or crushed beneath tumbling supply crates. The wagon flipped end over end, skidding to a halt on its roof, a broken, splintered ruin.

Cries of alarm rose from the middle wagon. Screams of horror as something huge rose up out of the sand near the wreck and set to work, maw yawning wide, tentacles flailing. Men and camels running or dying, red sand drenched redder still, their comrades in the fleeing train helpless but to stare and pray. But as ill fortune would have it, one of the Luminatii had the common sense to wonder how the rear wagon had broken loose, leaned out over the tray and saw the couplings between fore- and mid-wagons had been sawn away. He frowned, sure it must be a trick of the light, squinting at the strange . . . blur that seemed to be perched atop the hitch. Wondering what he was looking at for the few brief seconds it took that blur to rise up, lean in close, and push a gravebone stiletto right into his eye.

The man twitched, toppling face-first from the tray. Luminatii cried warning as the body tumbled beneath the wagon's belly and was pulped under the wheels. The middle wagon jolted hard as the men inside it bellowed. Falling over each other and throwing off gravity's center, the wagon lurched sideways with the bright snap of breaking timbers and tore itself loose from its partner.

Dust and men flying. Axels and bones breaking. Mia reached into the bag at her belt, fished out a handful of shiny red globes. And as a half-dozen blurry shapes peered over the wagon's tail to see what in the Daughters' names was happening at the hitch, she let them fly, up and over the railing, and into the wagon's tray.

Crackling booms sounded across the Whisperwastes, explosions unfurling in the wagon's confines and tearing the cover and the men inside to pieces. And throwing aside her cloak of shadows, Mia slung herself into the carnage.

Blades drawn. Teeth bared. Moving among blinded and stumbling men like a serpent through water. Steel flashing, soldiers falling, crying out and swinging their cudgels at the blur in their midst; a bloodstained smudge moving through the smoke, wicked-sharp blades flashing. A few thought her some *thing* from the abyss, some daemonic servant of Niah set on their trail. Others mistook her for a horror from the Whisperwastes, a monstrosity spat into being by twisted magiks. But as she wove and swayed among them, blades whistling, breath hissing, the swiftest among them realized she wasn't a daemon. Nor a horror. But a girl. Just a girl. And that thought terrified them more than any daemon or horror they could name.

She could feel them. Even the ones she couldn't see. The brighter the light, the deeper the shadows. And she *felt* them, just as she'd felt the shadows of the strawmen targets in the Hall of Songs. Lashing out with all the skill Naev had gifted her, all the fury of that fourteen-year-old girl on the steps of the Basilica Grande. No cardinals or blazing Trinities to help them now. No sunsteel burning in their hands or white, polished armor at their breasts. Just leather on their skin and dust in their eyes, the blackened corpses of their comrades on the deck around them, the echo of the explosions ringing in their ears. And she, armed with all the hatred of all the years, daughter of murdered parents, sister to a murdered brother, marked of a darkest mother.

And one by one, each and all, she fed them to the Maw.

The camels pulling the wagon galloped on, still terrified enough of the kraken to keep running without a driver to whip them. With her foes inside the wagon dead, Mia slung the crossbow off her back. Fell to one knee and took aim at the nearest camel rider. She put a quarrel through his heart, loaded another and put it through a second's throat. A few Luminatii veered out of range, but to their credit, most roared challenge and whipped their beasts harder, bearing down on the wagon and the girl inside. These were men of the First and Second Centuries, after all—the finest troops Godsgrave had to offer. They'd not be bested by some heretic child.

But her crossbow sang and the wyrdglass flew, men tumbling from their saddles or simply blasted free. A grizzled giant of a man made it to the wagon's railing, but a throwing knife in his larynx silenced him forever. Another leaped from his camel onto the wagon's tail, but as he clawed his way up, she shoved a globe of ruby wyrdglass into his mouth and kicked him free, the resulting explosion taking out another camel's legs and sending its rider flying, despite all lack of wings.

Scanning the wastes, Mia saw the kraken had given up the chase—between silencing her calls to the Dark and the feast she'd left behind, the behemoths seemed well content, rolling and tumbling as they chased screaming Luminatii across the sands. Sheathing her blades, Mia leapt into the driver's chair, intent now on the wagons ahead.

In all the carnage, Remus's train had gained a solid lead. But with the weight of her unneeded companions shed, Mia's camels traveled all the swifter, spitting and snorting and making whatever noise it is that camels make as they ran.* Her wagon bounced over rocky dunes, weaving through gardens of broken Ashkahi monoliths, slowly closing the gap. She could see Remus in the lead carriage, but only because the man was so huge—everyone else was simply a blur through the dust and grit. And yet, she was acutely aware that at least sixty well-trained and fanatical thugs awaited her ahead, should her wagon ever catch up. Weighing the less-than-favorable odds, she wondered what exactly she was going to do when she got there.

Fortunately, she never had to learn the answer.

The Luminatii in Remus's train had just watched her murder over sixty of their fellows, after all, and while it's noteworthy that none of them actually stopped to help, Itreya's finest *were* inclined to bear a grudge. As Mia's wagon bore down on them, the soldiers manning the crossbows opened fire. Mia couldn't exactly hide beneath her shadowcloak; firstly, she'd be unable to see, and thus, steer, but more important, it wouldn't take the finest scholar of the Grand Collegium to figure out where the driver of a wagon was sitting, invisible or not. But Justicus Remus, more than a little impressed that this slip of a girl had just managed to single-handedly murder half a century of his finest men, seemed more concerned with escape than revenge. And so, instead of ordering his men to shoot at the lunatic flogging her poor camels into a lather, he ordered his men to shoot the poor camels instead.

And shoot them they did.

The first bolt struck the lead camel in the chest, felled it like a tree. The beast stumbled to its knees, snarled up in its harness and tripping the beast

---

*It occurs to me there is no word to describe the noise a camel makes. Dogs bark, lions roar, drunkards mumble.

What the 'byss do camels do?

behind it. Another bolt sailed out of the dust, followed by a third, and amid the sickening crunch of bones and the bellows of camels in agony, Mia's wagon crashed into the wretched tangle that had been hauling it, flipped end over end, and skidded to a bloody, screaming halt.

Mia was flung free, sailing a good twenty feet through the air before plunging face-first at the sand. She managed to tuck her shoulder as she hit, the wind knocked out of her as she tumbled, sand hissing, one boot flying free, finally rolling to a cursing, breathless rest some forty feet from the ruins of her ride.

She tried to rise, ears ringing, head swimming. Stumbling to her knees as a few more quarrels sailed out of the dust, watching as Remus's wagon and Lord Cassius and the Ministry and her revenge all galloped farther and farther away.

She collapsed to all fours. Retched. Her ribs felt cracked, her mouth full of dust and bile. Thumping down on her belly, clawing at the sand.

Unable, at the last, even to crawl.

She'd got so close.

So close.

But again, at the final hurdle, she'd stumbled. And she'd fallen.

"Story of my life," she muttered.

Her eyes fluttered closed.

She sighed.

And darkness fell.

CHAPTER 35

KARMA

Nudge.

Mia groaned, not daring to open her eyes.

Her head was ringing, ribs aching, every breath a battle.

She'd no idea how long she'd lain there.

Minutes?

Hours?

She could feel the suns above her, burning just outside her eyelids.

She knew what awaited her if she dared open them.

Failure.

Her wagon wrecked. Her camels slaughtered. The Quiet Mountain lay a turn back to the east, but hurt as she was, she'd be lucky to make it in two—presuming she didn't get eaten by kraken or dustwraiths in the meantime. Getting to Last Hope on foot from here was impossible, but sti—

Nudge.

Something soft and wet and whiskered. Smearing her lips with thick and warm. A tiny part of her brain screamed very loudly the Something was quite big and very obviously alive and was now *snuffling* at her, potentially as a prelude to *eating* her.

Her eyes fluttered open, pain waiting just beyond. She hissed, squinting up into a pair of wide nostrils, nudging her again and smearing her lips with—O, joy of joys—more snot. An enormous pink tongue smacked at huge yellow teeth and Mia came fully awake, scrambling away in a cloud of fine red dust until she realized exactly what had been trying to eat her.

It was a horse.

Black and glossy and twenty hands high.

A horse she'd been pleased to see the back end of months ago, truth be told.

But still, she found herself grinning. Dragging herself to her feet and wobbling to his side, running her hand across his flank as he made a noise that sounded suspiciously like laughter.

She put her arms around his neck.

Kissed his cheek.

"Hello, Bastard," she said.

CHAPTER 36
SUNSSET

Fat Daniio was beginning to think the Everseeing hated him.

When Lem had walked into the Old Imperial and declared a laden wagon train was trundling into Last Hope, Daniio figured mebbe those idiot Kephians had returned from their fool quest without getting et. But then Scupps had wandered in, scratching his bollocks and blinking the dust from his eyes, declaring there were too many of the buggers to be them Kephians. In Scupps's learned opinion, they looked more like soldier boys. Waddling out into Last

Hope's thoroughfare with the lads in tow, Fat Daniio peered the battered wagon train up and down.

"Soldiers," Scupps had declared. "Soldiers or I'm a two-beggar whoreson."

Lem scowled. "Kephians, I'm telling yers."

"Yer both wrong." A grin had split Daniio's chubby face. "They're *customers.*"

The garrison house wasn't near big enough to house seventy bodies, and sure enough, that marrowborn wanker Garibaldi (who was still heartbroke about his bloody horse getting pinched—you'd think it were his bride the way he went on about it) mooched up to the Old Imperial about an hour after the train hit Last Hope, booked every spare room in the place, quick as spit. It was at least a week 'til Wolfeater would be back to ship the newcomers to civilization, and Daniio began dreaming about the small fortune he'd make in the meantime.

Until he found out the bastards had no money, of course.

Not a pair of rusty beggars to rub between them.

He'd marched right over to the garrison house, pounded on the door, and demanded to speak to the tosser in charge. A scarred man the size of a small pub had rumbled slowly into view, and declared himself the justicus—*justicus*, mind you—of the entire Luminatii Legion. He told Daniio that the Old Imperial and all provisions therein were being requisitioned for the "safety and security of the Itreyan Republic." Centurion Horse-Lover had given Daniio a smug smile, some little blond piece who looked young enough to be this Remus prick's daughter shrugged apologetically, and Daniio had the door slammed right in his face.

And so, he'd become a fucking charity master. Fingers worked to the bone. His common room and every bedchamber packed with grumbling, farting, ungrateful Luminatii bastards. They ate like inkfiends on a bender. Drank like starving fish. Stank like an outhouse in truelight. And poor Daniio was getting paid for *none* of it.

Now, it was three turns since the dogs had arrived in Last Hope. *Trelene's Beau* was still four nevernights away, winds being kind, and the way Daniio's luck was running, he'd not have been surprised to learn Wolfeater and the whole crew had got shipwrecked on the mythical Isle of Wine and Whores and decided to stay a spell.

The Imperial's larder was gutted from feeding all those soldiers three squares for four turns straight, and Daniio had been reduced to serving mostly soups and stews. Chow this eve was a broth made from the bones of the deeptuna he'd served the turn before, and he'd left it boiling on the burner while he went out into the common room to serve another round of drinks. Every soldier staying in the pub was clustered into booths or crammed eight apiece to his tables. No amount of talk about the "safety and security of the Itreyan Republic" could convince Dona Amile and the dancers at the Seven Flavors to give free ones, so the bastards had nothing to do all turn except drink, mooch about, and intimidate Daniio's regulars.

After serving drinks, Daniio walked into the kitchen and kicked the back door shut with a snarl. Shuffling over to his stovetop, he gave the broth a good whiff. It smelled a little odd; maybe he'd left the bits out too long. But fuck it all, these dogs were eating free, and if any felt like complaining, he'd had just about enough to spit it right back in their faces.

He served dinner, answered shouts for more wine. After being run off his feet for a half-hour, he managed to get a few minutes to duck out the back alley for a smoke.

"Bastards," he muttered. "God-bothering bastards and beggars, all."

Daniio leaned against the alley wall, cursing. He got his smokes from Wolfeater, imported right from the 'Grave. Proper fancy they were, sugarpaper and all. Propping a cigarillo on his lips, he cupped his flintbox with his palm and sparked the flame.

"You're supposed to be at the garrison tower, Daniio," a voice said.

"Aa's cock," he cursed.

The flintbox fell from his hands, clattered on the alley ground. A girl dressed all in black stepped from the shadows, soft as whispers. Storm winds blew in off the bay, blowing a long fringe around dark, hard eyes. Leaning down slowly, she picked up the flintbox. Tossed it into the air and caught it in one dirty fist.

" 'Byss and blood, you near took me out of my skin, girl," the publican swore. "What the blue fuck ya doin' creepin' 'round . . ."

He blinked at her, his left eye traveling up her body a little slower than his right.

" 'Ere, do I know you? You look . . . familiarish."

The girl leaned forward with a smile and plucked the cigarillo right from his lips. Placing it on her own, she leaned against the wall opposite and sighed, drawing on the smoke as if her life depended on it. She looked more than a little grubby, truth be told, hair crusted and skin filthy. But her curves were a rare treat, and her lips the kind you'd sell your mother to get a taste of.

"You're supposed to be at the garrison tower, Daniio," she repeated.

". . . What for?"

"You serve evemeals there, if I recall."

Daniio frowned the girl up and down. She was just a slip of a thing. Half his age. But there was something in the look of her. In the eyes mebbe. Something that made him more than a little nervous without quite knowing why . . .

"Don't serve 'em no more," he said. "Garibaldi threw a fit after he and his boys got a taste of the roaring shits. Same nevernight as his horse got nicked. They cook their own grub over there now. Centurion's orders."

The girl sighed gray.

"Serves me right, I suppose. But that leaves us with a problem."

Daniio looked up and down the alley, acutely aware he was alone with this girl. That she was armed heavier than most anyone outside a gladiatorii arena had a right to be. That she was watching him the way he imagined a viper might watch a mouse.

That she hadn't blinked yet.

"What problem would that be?" he managed.

"What do you hear, Daniio?" the girl asked.

". . . Eh?"

"Listen," she whispered. "What do you hear?"

Thinking it an odd game but now decidedly ill at ease, Daniio cocked his head, listening as she bid. Last Hope was death-quiet, but that was usually the case of a nevernight. Most folk would've retired by now, sitting at the hearth with a drink in hand. He heard camels grumbling in the garrison stables. A dog bark in the distance. The roar of the evewind and the crash of surf.

He shrugged. "Not much."

"You've sixty men in your common room, Daniio. Devout servants of the Everseeing they might be, but shouldn't they be a little rowdier?"

Daniio frowned. Now she mentioned it, the pub *was* a damn sight quieter than it should've been. He'd not heard one bellowed drinks order or a single shouted complaint since he stepped outside for his smoke . . .

Well, *her* smoke.

The girl sucked the last life from the cigarillo, dropped it at her feet, and crushed it under heel. And reaching into her sleeve, she drew out a long stiletto, carved of what might've been gravebone. Daniio's hackles went up along with his hands, and he slipped from nervous to downright terrified. The girl stepped closer as he shrank back against the wall. And reaching into her belt, she pulled out a single glass ball, smooth and small and perfectly white.

"What's that?" Daniio asked.

"Swoon. I had a bag half-full of these, yesterturn. Now I've got one left."

"W-where's the rest of them?"

"I dissolved them in the broth you cooked for evemeal."

Daniio risked a look over his shoulder, back at the pub. Quiet as tombs.

"Now, here's our problem," the girl said. "You were supposed to serve eve-meal to the garrison tower right after you served it here. And after that, you were supposed to wander back here and find every soldier under your roof face down in their broth."

". . . You put them to sleep?"

The girl looked to her knife. Back to Daniio's eyes.

"Not for long."

Daniio tried to speak and found his tongue stuck to the roof of his mouth.

"But since you don't serve evemeal over there anymore, I'm going to need a distraction," the girl said. "So you may want to head upstairs and grab any-thing of value you might keep in your . . . no doubt fine establishment."

Daniio pried his tongue loose.

"Why?" he managed.

She held out his flintbox on an open palm. Daniio's slow eye caught on before the rest of him did, growing considerably wider. His words emerged as a croak.

"O, no . . ."

"If I live, I'll see the Red Church compensates you for your losses. If not . . ." The girl shrugged, gifted him a wry smile. "Well, you've got my apologies."

She stared at Daniio, sparking the flintbox in her hand.

"Best hurry, now. Seconds won't be the only thing burning in a moment."

The goldwine in Daniio's cellars wasn't what you'd call the finest vintage. Truthfully, it was closer to paint thinner than whiskey. Unbeknownst to any of his customers, Daniio used it to clean the pots once a year and they always came up sparkling. But, wonderful thing about spirits, no matter how low-rent the production or gods-awful the taste.

They burn beautifully.

Smoke was already rising from the Old Imperial's roof as Mia reached the garrison tower, sneaking around back of the stables and up to the rear wall. The tower rose thirty feet high, and there were no windows on the upper levels— she was almost certain that's where the Ministry and Lord Cassius would be. She supposed they were in the same state they'd been in during the journey from the Mountain, gagged and chained up tight, but she needed to see for sure. She was horribly outnumbered, and didn't know the lay of the land. Burning most of Remus's troops alive to cause a distraction had seemed a good way to kill two birds with one stone.

Or sixty, as the case may be.

Truthfully, she'd not even known if the Swoon would dissolve in Daniio's broth, but giving it a try seemed a better idea than just marching into the Imperial and flinging handfuls of wyrdglass around. The stink of burning flesh hung heavy on the winds, smoke rising in a twisting column to the sunsburned sky, but if she felt any guilt about the fate she'd gifted the Luminatii, it was quickly quashed at the thought of Tric and the others who'd died in the Mountain's belly.

She'd scaled halfway up the watchtower wall when the legionary atop it sounded the alarm, banging on a heavy brass bell and roaring, "*Fire! Fire!*" Last Hope's townsfolk burst from their doors, Centurion Garibaldi stumbled into the street and cursed, and Mia slipped up over the battlements and slit the lookout's throat, ear to bloody ear.

Throwing on her shadows, she flipped the trapdoor in the floor open before his body had hit the floor. Dropping onto the upper level, she found bunk beds, wardrobes, and a single, groggy legionary rising from his mattress to see what the fuss was about. Her gladius put him back to bed, and she covered his face with bloody blankets, whispering a prayer to Niah. Slipping down the stairs onto the level below, she breathed a soft curse to find it empty, along with the common room beneath. Peering through the ground-floor windows, she could see four legionaries posted outside the front door—Remus and Garibaldi and the rest seemed to be down at the Imperial. With only one place left to look, Mia opened the cellar door and stole down into the dark.

Two arkemical globes cast a thin glow across wine barrels and shelves, wooden pillars and huddled figures. Three Luminatii were sitting about an upturned crate, grousing on a deck of cards. All three looked up as she entered. It was far too dark to see beneath her cloak down here, so she threw it aside, tossed one of her few remaining globes of onyx wyrdglass. Black smoke burst in the center of the card table, beggars and brews flying, Mia dropping down the stairs with her swords drawn, lashing out at the nearest man without a whisper.

Though the light was dim, she could still feel their shadows, reaching out and fixing their boots to the floor, one by one. The lead soldier fought hard despite his surprise, cursing her for a heretic, promising she'd meet her dark mother soon. But for all his bluster, he fell with her sword in his belly, clutching his punctured chain mail and calling for his own ma, his blood red on the stone. Mia hurled a fistful of throwing knives at the second man, two blades striking home and sending him to the floor. The third tried to run, tugging at his boots and fumbling with the buckles as she rose up behind him and buried her sword between his ribs, the blade rupturing his mail shirt and punching out through his chest. He fell without a sound, eyes open and accusing.

Mia pushed them closed with another whispered prayer.

Through the swirling smoke, the stink of blood, she saw them. Seven figures, trussed up in a corner. Shahiid Aalea, bound and gagged. Spiderkiller, bruised and unconscious. Solis, beaten to within an inch of his life, his face a mass of purple welts. Hush, Mouser, and Drusilla, all awake, mouths gagged. And at the last, Cassius, dark eyes glowering, filled with pain. The Black Prince. Lord of Blades. Looking at him, Mia felt that same queasy sensation she'd felt when they'd met in the past. Sickness. Vertigo. Fear. It was almost painful. A dark shape coalesced beside him, black fangs bared in a snarl.

Eclipse.

The shadowwolf stepped toward Mia, hackles raised. Mister Kindly puffed up in her shadow, yowling and spitting. The creatures stared each other down as Mia hissed.

"Put it back in your pants, the pair of you."

"*. . . FOOL CHILD, I WEAR NO PANTS . . .*"

"*. . . o, you'd be the brains of the outfit, then . . .*"

"Mister Kindly, enough."

The not-cat fell into a sullen silence, and a glance from Lord Cassius was enough to make Eclipse do the same. Crouching beside the Ministry, Mia cut away Mother Drusilla's gag, pulled it from the old woman's mouth.

"Acolyte Mia," she whispered. "A pleasant . . . surprise indeed."

Mia set about cutting away Mouser and Aalea's gags, and, lastly, Lord Cassius. The man looked like he'd been used as a training dummy, lips swollen, eyes blackened, cheek split. But even with his gag removed, the Lord of Blades said nothing at all.

Mia tried to ignore the sickness swelling in the man's presence, the thunder of her heart against her ribs. She looked over the manacles, the ropes binding each, started sawing at Cassius's bonds with her gravebone blade.

"I have to get you out of here," Mia whispered. "I've distracted them, but not for long. Can you walk? Better yet, run?"

"The Luminatii obviously intended to bring us in alive," Drusilla wheezed. "But Solis is in a state, and after Mouser slipped his bonds yesterturn, the good justicus ensured he'd be running nowhere for a while."

Mia looked the Shahiid of Pockets over, noticed the odd angle of his shins.

"Black Mother," she whispered. "He's broken your legs."

"And fingers." Mouser winced. "Rather . . . unsporting, I thought."

Mia cut their ropes, but the garrison's manacles were a trickier proposition. They were heavy iron, locked by a key that none of the three soldiers she'd just ended seemed to possess. Each of the Ministry were chained at wrists and ankles, and would only be able to manage a shuffling walk unless they were freed.

"Shit," she breathed. "I've got no picks on me."

"In my boots," Mouser whispered with a ghost of a smile. "Left heel."

Mia cracked Mouser's boot heel as he bid her, murmured apology as his shin shifted and he hissed in pain. Inside, she found a few picks and a small torsion bar, set to work on Cassius's bonds. Beaten as he was, the Lord of Blades would still be able to carry Solis, and between Aalea, Spiderkiller, and Hush, they'd manage Mouser. The question was should they tuck tail and run, or stand and fight? Solis and Mouser were in no shape to ride, and she'd no chance of saddling up the camel train without the Luminatii noticing. But in a toe-to-toe against a dozen men armed with sunsteel? Any minute now one of them might be back to here to check on—

"'Byss and blood . . ."

Mia looked over her shoulder at the whisper, saw a figure at the top of the cellar stairs. Dusty boots. Daggers at her belt. Blond warbraids. Wide blue eyes.

"Ashlinn . . ."

Mia stretched out her arm, groping for the shadow at the girl's feet. But without a word the girl spun and sprang back up the stairs, out of sight, her boots skipping light across the boards above their heads as she dashed toward the tower door.

"Shit, she's going to warn them . . ."

Mia tossed the picks into Cassius's lap, scrambled to her feet, and bolted after Ashlinn. Taking the stairs three apiece, up into the sunlight just in time to see the four Luminatii stationed on the garrison house door burst through it, Ashlinn beating a dusty trail down the street to the Old Imperial, shouting as she went.

The Luminatii were local lads, and unlike the refugees from the raid, all armed with their sunsteel. Though covered in dust from the wastes, they were also wearing plate armor, the plumes on their helms a dirty red. They drew their blades with a shout, the steel bursting into flame as they barreled into the room. Close quarters. Heavily armed and armored opponents. No element of surprise, and swords that would cut through her like good-looking butter.

Mia didn't like those odds.

She tossed a globe of onyx wyrdglass onto the floor, turned and dashed up the stairs. Coughing and sputtering through the thick haze, the Luminatii charged after her, roaring at her to halt. Mia hurled a fistful of ruby wyrdglass as she bolted up to the third level, the globes popping on the lead Luminatii's chest and splashing pieces of him across the room. Scorched and sprayed in blood, the remaining three proceeded with more caution, huddled behind their shields as they reached the third level. The last of Mia's wyrdglass melted their shields to slag, one of her last throwing knives took the point man in the throat and sent him to his knees, clutching his severed jugular. Mia glanced at the rope ladder leading up to the roof, wondering if she could make it before the remaining two soldiers cut her down. Reaching out instead to the men's shadows creeping along the floor . . .

The Luminatii bringing up the rear fell with a shocked expression, four feet of unlit sunsteel splitting his head almost in two. Brains and blood spattered the walls as the body toppled forward and spilled its last all over the floor. Lord Cassius rose up behind him, face swollen and bruised, dark eyes narrowed in a cold fury. And as Mia watched in awe, Cassius curled the fingers on his left hand and the shadows in the room sprang to life, writhing like serpents before the charmer. With a wave, the Lord of Blades tore the final legionary's sword from his grip, and without a sound, swung the sunsteel longsword hard at the soldier's neck.

Despite what your poets might say, gentlefriend, it takes a mighty swing and an even mightier arm to decapitate a man clean. And the Lord of Blades obviously wasn't at his best. Still, there was only a ragged strip of flesh and a few splinters of shattered bone nailing the Luminatii's head to his neck as he toppled and fell, his body twitching on the floor until it realized the sad truth that it was dead.

Mia glanced at the shadows, swaying at Cassius's beck and call. She still felt that painful, oily sickness in her belly, Mister Kindly trembling at her feet.

"Nice trick," she said.

"Trick?" The Lord of Blades raised an eyebrow. "Is that what you name it?"

"When I met you in Godsgrave . . . when you're near me . . ." Mia shook her head. "Do you feel the way I do when we're close? Sick? Frightened?"

Cassius waited a long moment before he replied.

"I feel hungry."

Mia nodded. Her mouth dry. "Do you know why?"

The Lord of Blades looked pointedly at the corpses on the floor. The walls around them. "Perhaps here is not the best place to speak of it?"

"You owe me answers," Mia said. "I think I've earned them by now."

As if summoned, Eclipse materialized near Cassius's feet. Mister Kindly hissed softly as the shadowwolf spoke, her voice seeming to come from beneath the floor.

". . . THEY COME, CASSIUS. THE LIGHTBRINGER AND HIS MINIONS . . ."

The Lord of Blades looked at Mia. Nodded downstairs.

"Come," Cassius said. "Let's be rid of these curs. I will gift you what answers I have after initiation."

"Initiation?" Mia frowned. "But I failed the final trial."

A thin smile curled Cassius's lips. "Your final trial awaits downstairs, little sister."

". . . Sister?"

Cassius was already gone, stealing down the stairs without a sound. Mia hurried after him, for all her training feeling like a stumbling drunkard. Even beaten bloody, tortured and starved, Cassius moved like a shadow. His boots made no sound on the stone. His every motion precise, nothing wasted, no flash or showmanship. His hair flowing out behind him as if the breeze were blowing, stolen sword gleaming in his hand as he pushed open the front door and stepped into the street.

A dozen Luminatii were waiting. Centurion Garibaldi, squinting at Mia with vague recognition. A handful of heavily armed legionaries, sunsteel burning in their hands. Justicus Remus, a scarred, hulking mountain of a man in his gravebone armor, looking at Cassius with narrowed, wolfish eyes. And behind Remus, staring at Mia with something between hate and admiration . . .

"Ashlinn," Mia whispered.

Remus stepped forward, sword raised and rippling with flame. He'd been a giant when Mia last saw him in the sunlight, just ten years old and clinging to her mother's skirts. Now, he seemed just a little older. A little smaller.

But only a little.

"I've no wish to slay you, heretic," the justicus growled.

"That makes one of us," Mia spat.

Remus raised an eyebrow, as if surprised to learn the girl had a tongue. Cassius glanced sideways at Mia, spoke from the corner of his mouth.

"I believe he was talking to me."

"I believe I couldn't give a shit." Mia turned to Remus, flipping her sword back and forth between hands. "Nice to see you again, Justicus. Did the traitorous bitch beside you tell you who I am?"

Remus glanced at Ashlinn, looked Mia up and down with a sneer. "I know who you are, girl. And it surprises me not one whit to see your lot thrown in with a den of heretics and murderers. The apple never falls far from the tree."

Mia's eyes narrowed, hair blowing about her face as the wind began to rise. The Luminatii looked to their feet, quavering a little as they realized their shadows were ebbing and pulsing, reaching out to the girl as if they longed to touch her.

"You hung my father as entertainment for a fucking mob," she spat. "Threw my mother in a hole with no sunlight and let madness eat her. My brother was just a baby, and you let him die in the dark. And you talk to me about murder?"

Mia's eyes were welling with tears, face twisted in rage.

"Every nevernight since I was ten years old, I've dreamed of killing you. You and Scaeva and Duomo. I gave up everything. Any chance I ever had of ever being happy. Every turn, I'd picture your face and imagine all the things I'd say to let you know just how much I hate you. It's all I am anymore. It's all that's left inside me. You killed me, Remus. Just as sure as you killed my familia."

Mia raised her sword, leveled it at Remus's head.

"And now, I'm going to kill *you*."

Remus snarled to the men beside him, "End the girl. Bring me Cassius alive."

To their credit, an order to capture the deadliest man in the Itreyan Republic alive didn't stagger the men much. Perhaps prefacing the command with the murder of a sixteen-year-old girl made it easier to swallow. Ashlinn hung back, but the legionaries—a dozen in all—stepped forward, Centurion Garibaldi at the forefront. With prayers to Aa and pleas for strength from the Everseeing Light, they raised their shields and charged. And without a sound, the Lord of Blades stepped up to meet them.

Mia had seen some fighters who moved like dancers, lithe and graceful. Others moved like bulls, all brawn and bluster. But Cassius moved like a knife. Simple. Straight. Deadly. There was no flash to his style. No flair. He simply cut right to the bone. The shadows rose at his call, and, with a wave of his hand, he disarmed the first legionary to meet him, buried his blade in the man's chest. The second fell flat on his belly, his charge tripped up by a snarl of shadows. Cassius dispatched him with a quick blow to the back of his neck, almost as an afterthought.

Mia was astonished how easily the man wielded the Dark. Out here, even in the light of a single sun, a second almost rising, she was hard-pressed to even hold up a few of the charging legionaries. But still, she managed to fix the boots of two of the bigger fellows to the ground, hurled the last of her ruby wyrdglass into another's face, blowing his head clean off his shoulders. A burning sword sliced the air, hissing as it came. Mia bent backward, feeling the heat on her chin. She rolled into a crouch, somersaulting across the dust and hurling her last throwing knife in reply. It thudded quivering into the Luminatii's neck, left him gushing and choking on the ground.

Mia rose from the dust. Eyes on Ashlinn. The pair faced each other across the shifting sands, the ghosts of two murdered boys hanging in the air between them. Tric. Osrik. Both unanswered. But for some reason Ashlinn hung back, loitering on the edge of the melee as more Luminatii charged at Mia, swords raised.

"You scared of me, Ash?"

Parry. Feint. Lunge.

"I didn't want it to be like this, Mia," the girl called. "I said you didn't belong here."

"Never picked you for a coward. Your brother put up more of a fight."

"Trying to goad me into a little toe-to-toe?" Ash shook her head sadly. "Think that's how this ends, love? Me stumbling into a swordfight I can't win?"

"A girl can dream."

"Keep dreaming, then. I studied under Aalea too."

Mia parried a blow aimed at her throat, kicked a toeful of dirt into her attacker's eyes. The man clobbered her with his shield, sent her sprawling in the dust. She slipped aside as his burning sword crashed into the sand beside her head, kicking savagely at the man's knee. She heard a wet crunch, a strangled scream. Scrambling to her feet, all of Naev's lessons singing in her head. Flaming steel cleaving the air, dust caked on her tongue.

Risking a glance, she saw Cassius was every bit the bladesman his reputation suggested. The dirt around him was littered with half a dozen corpses, another two men lying wounded and groaning in the dirt. Typical of most generals, Remus had hung back to let his foot soldiers do the fighting, but with his men falling like leaves, the man spat in the dust and waded into the fray. The Lord of Blades fell back, feinting with his shadows, the darkness flickering in the face of Remus's burning blade.

With the dogpile on Cassius, Mia was left fighting a single opponent— Centurion Garibaldi. The man was relentless, battering away with his shield and landing blow after blow atop Mia's guard. Mia was swift, but the man was heavily armored, and she found the few blows she managed to land turned aside by his plate. Garibaldi slammed his shield into her chest, sent her flying. She rolled away in time to miss having her head split open, scrambling up into a crouch and flinging her last globe of onyx wyrdglass onto Garibaldi's shield. The arkemical glass burst, throwing up a swirling cloud of black smoke. The centurion staggered, coughing, and summoning up the last of her strength, Mia clenched her fists and took hold of the shadow at the centurion's feet, tangling his boots as he charged again. The man teetered, arms pinwheeling as he fought for balance, losing at last. Garibaldi fell forward, his heels still stuck fast to the road, his shins snapping clean through as his weight brought the rest of him to the ground.

The man screamed, clutching his legs as Mia released him, pawing the dust from her eyes. Cassius was still brawling with the Luminatii, their bodies a tangle of white and black, flame and shadow. Remus entering the fray had evened the scales—the Lord of Blades was now on the defensive, his sword a blur, the Darkness singing.

Mia looked at the justicus, his face twisted in fury. The man who'd helped murder her familia. Drag her old life into ruin. But then she turned to Ashlinn. The girl who'd taken her new life and ripped it to bleeding pieces. Ashlinn stared back, sword in hand, blue eyes narrowed. Turning her back on the girl didn't seem the smartest play. So Mia tilted her neck 'til it popped, and took a step toward her.

"Don't do it, Mia," Ash warned.

Mia ignored her, raising her hand and wrapping the darkness about the girl's feet.

"This won't hurt," Mia said. "Much."

Ash took a deep breath. Sighed. And reaching into her britches, she drew out a handful of burning flame, spinning at the end of a golden chain.

The Trinity.

Light flared, brighter than all the three suns. The sight of the medallion was like a club to the back of her head, sending her to her knees. From the corner of her eye she saw Cassius stagger, throwing up his forearm to shield his eyes. Remus was in mid-swing as the Lord of Blades dropped his guard. Desperate to keep his prize alive, the justicus turned his blade, hit Cassius with the burning flat. But the legionary beside him—terrified beyond wits at the murder of his fellows, the fall of his centurion, the deathly silence of this black-clad daemon summoning shadows from the abyss to cut his fellows to pieces—shared no such restraint.

As Remus cried warning, the legionary struck, Cassius already staggered from the Trinity's light and Remus's turned blow. A burning sword plunged into the man's ribs, buried to the hilt. The legionary tore the blade free, the Lord of Blades crying out in pain, clutching his punctured chest. Falling to his knees, he coughed red, rolling into a ball, one arm still up to shield himself from that awful, burning light.

"Damned fool!" Remus roared, turning on the man and landing a crushing hook on his jaw. The legionary's head whipped to one side, teeth flying as he crumpled like paper. "I wanted him alive!"

Mia was on all fours, head bowed, eyes shut against the blazing hatred of the Everseeing held in Ashlinn's hand. Ash walked across the dirt toward Mia, Trinity held high. Mia rolled over onto her back, scrambling away, heels kicking at the road. Agony. Terror. Mister Kindly curled up in her shadow and writhing, just as helpless as she.

"I'm sorry, Mia," Ash sighed.

Remus was glaring at Ashlinn, incredulous. "You had that on you this whole time? You could have ended this whenever you wanted? You treacherous little—"

"O, fuck off, god-botherer," Ashlinn snarled. "I'm not in this for your glorious Republic and I don't give a *shit* about you or your men. If I wanted a trump card up my sleeve, that's my business. And in case you missed it, it just saved your miserable life. So instead of bleating about it, maybe you should end the girl who just tried to murder you, then go make sure the rest of the Ministry is still under lock and key? Unless you and your merry band of idiots want to accidentally gut them, too?"

Though she stood at least a foot shorter than Remus, Ashlinn stared the justicus down. With a snarl, Remus hefted his blade, stalked toward Mia, flame rippling down its edge.

Mia crawled backward in the dirt. Wracked with pain, unable even to stand. Terror in her veins now, roaring in her temples, anguished that this was how it would end. All the miles and all the years. To see it finish here? Sprawled in the dust of some forgotten shithole, unable at the last even to raise her sword?

This?

Her teeth were gritted. Eyes filled with hateful tears.

Like this?

The light was blinding; no matter where she looked, it was like staring into the suns. She could see only dim silhouettes. Ashlinn standing in front of her, the Light burning bright in her hand. Remus, towering behind her, a lesser light blazing in his fist. Wounded Luminatii, groaning in the dust. Lord Cassius, his terror reaching out to her own.

Never flinch. Never fear.

She shook her head. Staring up at Remus's silhouette. Determined to look him in the eye. To show no matter how much it hurt, how much her heart named her liar . . .

"I'm not afraid of you," she hissed.

She heard a soft chuckle. The lesser light rising high.

"Luminus Invicta, heretic," Remus said. "I will give your brother your regards."

The words hit Mia harder than the Trinity's light. Turned her belly to water.

What was he saying? Jonnen was dead. Mia's mother had said so. That true-dark she'd torn the Philosopher's Stone to pieces, stood on the steps of the Basilica Grande and fallen before this same bastard, this same accursed light. Crying on the battlements afterward, above the place her father died. Mercurio beside her as she whispered.

"It was so bright," she whispered. "Too bright."

The old man had smiled. Patted her hand.

"The brighter the light, the deeper the shadow."

Ashlinn stood in front of her, Trinity blazing in her hand. Remus loomed at her back, sword raised. Behind them both, stretched across the sand and into the justicus's own, was Mia's shadow. Black. Writhing. But in the face of that awful light, darker than it had ever been.

She reached out to it. Teeth gritted. Eyes shut. Feeling the darkness without and the darkness within. And clenching her fists, dagger held tight

she stepped down

into her own shadow

and out of the justicus's shadow behind.

His body blocked off the Trinity's light, the blinding flare rendering him a hulking silhouette. And lashing out with her blade, the blade her mother had held to Scaeva's throat, the blade Mister Kindly had gifted her in the dark, the blade that had saved her life before, and now again, she buried it to the hilt in Remus's neck.

The justicus clutched the hole she carved, a fountain of blood spraying between his fingers. Mia staggered away, drenched in red. The light still burning her. Eyes narrowed. Hair draped over her face in tangled drifts as she stumbled and fell.

Remus staggered, sword falling from his grip and quivering in the sand. Both hands to his neck now. Arterial spray hissing through his fingers. Realization dawning in his eyes—*she's killed me, O, God, she's killed me*—turning to fury, and he whirled on the girl, hands outstretched, fingers curled into claws. The blood spurted free, gushing down that barrel chest, those wolfish features draining of all their color. The justicus of the Luminatii Legion took one tottering step, two, and three. Sinking to his knees. Stare locked on the girl, doing her best to crawl away along the sand.

Remus gargled, light fleeing his eyes. And with a heavy thud, his corpse

toppled face-first into the dirt, the last feeble beats of his heart drenching the
road a deeper red. Just as she'd always dreamed it. Just as she'd always wanted.

Dead.

Ashlinn hung still, horror on her face. At Mia's back, she felt more shadows gathering, clustered about their owners at the garrison tower's door.

The Revered Mother.

Solis leaning on her shoulder, bleeding and bruised.

Hush, silent as death, a fallen blade in one clenched fist.

Aalea and Spiderkiller behind him, supporting Mouser between them.

Even though they were beaten and bloodied, not one of the assassins was
darkin. Not one cowed by the Trinity in Ashlinn's hand. And faced with five
of the most accomplished murderers in the Itreyan Republic, the girl did what
anyone would have done in her position—lust for vengeance be damned.

Ashlinn turned and ran.

Hush and the Ministry staggered from the tower, none in a state to give
chase. But with the Trinity now disappearing down the street, Mia found the
pain fading, rolling over onto her belly and quietly retching. Turning to Cassius,
she crawled to his side, fingers clawing the dust. The Lord of Blades was curled
in a ball, clutching his chest, face twisted. Mia murmured softly, pulled his
bloody hands away, paling at the sight of the wound. Eclipse was whining,
pacing, ears pressed to her skull. Black teeth bared.

"... FOOL CHILD, HELP HIM ... !"

"... I—"

"... HELP HIM ... !"

Cassius tried to speak. Unable even to breathe. He coughed, sticky red on
his lips, clutching Mia's hand and holding tight. Drusilla hobbled to his side,
the other Ministry members sinking to the dirt around him.

"You can't die," Mia pleaded. "You promised me answers!"

Cassius grimaced with the pain of it, every muscle in his body tensing, back
arching. He fixed Mia in his stare, and she felt it in her bones. Something pri-
mordial; crushing gravity, agonizing chill, a terrible, endless rage. Something
beyond the hunger and sickness she felt when he was near. Something closer
to longing. Like lovers parted. Like an amputee. Like a puzzle, searching for a
missing piece of itself.

She wanted to ask him. Who he was. Who *she* was. If he knew anything of
the Darkness outside or the Darkness within. She was so close. She'd waited so
long. The questions roiled behind her teeth, waiting for her to breathe them,
but Mia found the breath caught in her lungs. Cassius reached up with scarlet
hands, pressed his palm to Mia's cheek. Smearing his blood down her skin. It

was still warm, the scent of salt and copper filling the girl's lungs. The man marked one cheek, then the other, finally smudging a long streak down Mia's lips and chin. Anointing her; just as he might have in the Hall of Eulogies, if this moment, this ending, this tale, had been a different one.

Anointing her as a Blade.

And with one final sigh, silent as he'd been in life, the Black Prince left it. Taking Mia's answers with him.

The shadowwolf ceased her pacing. Lifting her head and filling the air with a heart-wrenching howl. Lying down in the dirt beside Cassius, trying to lick his face with a tongue that couldn't taste. Pawing his hand with claws that couldn't touch.

Mister Kindly watched it all silently. No eyes to fill with pity.

The storm winds rolled in off the bay, cold and bitter. The tattered killers hung their heads. Mia took Cassius's hand, the warmth of his skin fading against hers.

And into the wind, she whispered.

"*Hear me, Niah. Hear me, Mother. This flesh your feast. This blood your wine. This gift, this life, this end, our offering to you.*"

She sighed.

"*Hold him close.*"

EPILOGUE

Swordbreaker stood in his hall, watching the rain rolling into Farrow Bay.

Nevernight had been struck and his city was mostly silent, his people hunkered down at their hearths while Trelene and Nalipse raged outside. The Ladies of Oceans and Storms had been quarreling long of late. Winter had been bitter, the twins constantly at each other's throats. Hopefully this would be the last great storm before thirddawn—Swordbreaker could see Shiih's yellow glow budding on the horizon beyond the clouds, and the third sun's rise heralded the slow creep back into summer.

He looked forward to it, truth be told. Winters were fiercer here in Dweym than any place in the Republic. The chill was growing harder on his old bones with each passing year. He was getting old. He should have stepped aside as Bara of the Threedrakes already, but his daughters had married a pair of fools, both more brawn than brain. Swordbreaker was loathe to gift the Crown of Corals to either of his troth-sons. If Earthwalker were still here . . .

But no. Thoughts of his youngest daughter did him no good.

That time was gone, and her along with it.

Swordbreaker turned from the bay, hobbled down the long stone halls of his keep. Servants bowed as he passed, eyes downcast. Thunder rumbled across the rafters above. Arriving in his chamber, he closed the door behind him, looked to his empty bed. Wondering at the cruelty of life; that a husband should outlive a wife, let alone a daughter. He took the Crown of Corals from his brow, placed it aside, lips curling.

"Too heavy of late," he muttered. "Too heavy by far."

Lifting a decanter of singing Dweymeri crystal, he filled a tumbler with quavering hands. Put it to his lips with a sigh. Staring out the window as the rains lashed the glass, shuffling to the roaring hearth and sighing as the warmth kissed his bones. His shadow danced behind him, flickering along the flagstones and furs.

He frowned. Lips parting.

His shadow, he realized, was moving. Curling and twisting. Snaking across the stone, drawing back in upon itself and then—great Trelene, he'd swear it blind—stretching out *toward* the firelight.

"What in the Lady's name . . ."

Fear bleached Swordbreaker's face as his shadow's hands moved of their own accord. Reaching up to its throat, as if to choke itself. The old bara looked to his own hands, the goldwine in his cup, a chill stealing over him despite the fire's warmth.

And then the pain began.

A soft burn in his belly at first. A twinge, as if from too much spice at eve-meal. But it quickly bloomed, growing brighter, hotter, and the old man winced, one hand to his gut. Waiting for the pain to pass. Waiting for—

"Goddess," he gasped, stumbling to his knees.

The pain was fire now. Hot and white. He bent double, the crystal cup slipping from his hand and skittering across the stone, the spilled goldwine gleaming in the fire's glow. His shadow was fitting and shaking now, as if it had a mind of its own. The old man's face twisted, slow agony clawing his insides. He opened his mouth to call for the servants, for his baramen. Something was wrong.

Something was wrong . . .

A hand slipped about his lips, muffling his cry. His eyes grew wide as he heard a cool whisper in his ear. Smelled the scent of burned cloves.

"Hello, Swordbreaker."

The old man's words were muffled by the hand. His guts ablaze.

"I've been waiting for a chance to get you alone," the voice said. "To talk."

A woman, he realized. A *girl*. The old man bucked, trying to break her grip, but she held tight, strong as gravebone. His shadow continued to warp, to bend, as if he were on his back, clawing at the sky. And as the pain doubled in intensity, he found himself doing just that, flopping belly up and staring at the figure above him through the tears of agony in his eyes.

A girl, just as he'd thought. All milk-white skin and slender curves and bow-shaped lips. Out of the darkness at her feet, he saw a shape coalesce. Paper-flat and semitranslucent, black as death. Its tail curled around her ankle, almost possessively. And though it had no eyes, he knew it watched him, enraptured like a child before a puppet show.

"I'm going to take my hand away, now. Unless you plan on screaming?"

The old man groaned as the fire in his belly burned. But he fixed the girl with eyes full of hate. Scream? He was Bara of the Threedrake clan. He'd be damned if he gave this skulking slip the satisfaction . . .

Swordbreaker shook his head. The girl withdrew her hand. Knelt beside him.

"Wh . . ." he managed. "Wh . . ."

"Who?" the girl asked.

The old man nodded, stifling another groan of pain.

"You'll never know my name, I'm afraid," she said. "It's the shadow road for me. I'm a rumor. A whisper. The thought that wakes the bastards of this world sweating in the nevernight. And you *are* a bastard, Swordbreaker of the Threedrake clan. A bastard I made a promise about to someone I cared for, not so long ago."

The old man's face twisted, fingers clawing his belly. His insides were boiling, burning, all acid and broken glass. He shook his head, tried to spit, groaning instead. The girl looked to the spilled glass of goldwine. Fire twinkling in black eyes.

"It's Spite," she said, pointing at the glass. "A purified dose. It's already eaten a hole in your stomach. It'll chew through your bowels in the next few minutes. And over the next few turns your belly will bleed, and bloat, and fester. And in the end, you'll die, Swordbreaker of the Threedrake clan. Die just like I promised him you would."

She smiled.

"Die screaming."

Another shape coalesced beside the girl. Another shadow, staring at Swordbreaker with its not-eyes. A wolf, he realized. Growling with a voice that seemed to come from belowground.

". . . *SERVANTS COME. WE SHOULD AWAY* . . ."

The girl nodded. Stood. The two shadows watched him. The life in his eyes. All the wrongs and the rights. All the failures and triumphs and in-betweens.

"If you should see him in your wanders by the Hearth, tell Tric hello for me."

Swordbreaker's eyes widened.

The girl's voice was soft as shadows.

"Tell him I miss him."

The darkness rippled and the old man found himself alone.

Only his screams for company.

The choir was singing again.

The ghostly tune had returned by the time Mia and the Ministry trekked out of the Whisperwastes, Naev and Jessamine and their search party in tow. The insides of the Mountain had run red with blood, dozens of Hands and acolytes laid out in nameless tombs in the Hall of Eulogies, the Lord of Blades beside them. The names of Justicus Remus and Centurion Alberius were carved in the floor among the Church's other victims, and Mia took no small pleasure in standing upon them during the service. The only graves they would ever know.

The Revered Mother had spoken the eulogy, honoring those fallen in the Mountain's defense, praising those who saved the Red Church from calamity. The Ministry were gathered about her, solemn and silent. The few Hands who had survived the slaughter sang the refrain, their song thinner than in turns past.

Mia had stared at one of the new tombs the entire while. Just another slab set in the wall, no different from the rest. Its face was unmarked and its innards were empty—his body was never recovered after all. But when the mass had ended and the remnants of the congregation shuffled off into the dark, she'd knelt by his stone and taken out her gravebone dagger and scratched four letters into the rock.

TRIC.

She pressed her fingers to her lips, then her fingers to the stone.

The speaker had been true to his word, returning to the Mountain once he knew it was safe. Adonai had resurfaced, Marielle beside him, the weaver's broken fingers bound in splints. It took months for the digits to mend and Marielle to recover her skills. But when she did, her first task was to repay the debt she owed Mia for saving her and Adonai's life.

She had given Naev her face back.

The woman was waiting outside the speaker's chambers for Mia's return from her visit with the Bara of the Threedrake clan. After the girl had washed away the red in the bathhouse, Naev embraced her warmly, kissed either cheek. And without a glance to the chamber or the speaker therein, the woman had escorted Mia back to her room. Naev still wore her veil—perhaps accustomed to it after years of hiding her face, perhaps knowing like Mia did that in the end, it hadn't mattered what they'd looked like, but what they'd *done* that counted.

Perhaps because she simply liked veils.

The pair stopped outside Mia's bedchamber, Naev opening the door with a smile. The rooms in the Blades' corner of the Mountain were bigger, more private, shrouded in evernight. Mia's bed was big enough for her to get lost in. She hated sleeping in it, truth be told. Too easy to feel alone. But she'd been anointed by Cassius before the entire Ministry—no matter Drusilla or Solis's misgivings, she was a Blade now. Here was where she'd stay until the Ministry assigned her to a Chapel. She'd requested Godsgrave, of course, but where she might end up was anyone's guess.

"Before I forget . . ."

Naev nodded to her bedside table. A tome wrapped in black leather sat on the wood, bound with a silver clasp.

"The chronicler sent it for you. He said you would know what it meant."

Mia's heart surged in her chest. She thanked Naev again, shut the door behind her, and flopped onto her mattress. Mister Kindly faded into view on the bedhead, Eclipse at the bed's foot. The two shadows stared at each other with their not-eyes, mistrust crackling in the air. Mister Kindly had counseled Mia long and hard that Eclipse had no place at her side. But the shadowwolf had seemed utterly bereft with Lord Cassius dead. She'd spent turns wandering the Mountain's belly, howling her grief. Mia had finally hunted her down at Drusilla's request, asked Eclipse to walk with her, since she had no other to walk with. The shadowwolf had stared at her long and mute, and Mia had thought she'd refuse. But as the girl had looked down at the darkness beneath her feet, it had grown darker still.

Dark enough for three.

Mia picked up the book from her nightstand, stared at the cover. Strange symbols were embossed in the leather, hurting her eyes to look at. Flipping open the clasp, she saw a note, written in the chronicler's spidery hand. Seven words.

"Another girl with a story to tell."

Mia thumbed through the pages, creaking and cracked with age, studying the beautiful illustrations within. Human forms, with the shadows of different beasts at their feet. Wolves and birds. Vipers and spiders. Other things, monstrous and obscene. She frowned at the strange sigils, twisting and shifting before her eyes.

"I don't know this script."

". . . i doubt there are many in this world that can read it . . ."

"But you can?"

Mister Kindly nodded.

". . . i do not know how. but the letters . . . speak to me . . ."

Eclipse climbed to her feet, prowled up the mattress to sit beside Mia. Mister Kindly spat and the wolf growled in return, peering at the pages in Mia's hands.

"*. . . I CAN READ IT ALSO . . .*"

"What's it called?"

The not-cat dropped onto Mia's shoulder, peered at the strange, shifting symbols.

"*. . . the hungry dark . . .*"

Mia ran her fingers down the pages. The shadows inked in black, the shifting, crawling text. This might be it. The answer to all her questions. Who she was. *What* she was. Or it might be simple nonsense. A book that died because it never should've been; just one more lifeless husk from Niah's library of the dead.

"Will you two read it for me?"

"*. . . do you really wish to know . . . ?*"

"How can you ask that? We need to understand what we are, Mister Kindly."

"*. . . i like things the way they are now . . .*"

"*. . . I WILL READ FOR YOU . . .*"

"*. . . back in your kennel, mongrel . . .*"

"*. . . HAVE A CARE, LITTLE GRIMALKIN. ONLY REAL CATS HAVE NINE LIVES . . .*"

"*. . . she was mine before she was yours . . .*"

"*. . . IF SHE IS ANYONE'S, SHE IS HER OWN . . .*"

Mia thumped her hand on the pages. Stared at the shadows around her. "Read."

The not-cat sighed. Settled on her shoulder and peered at the shifting text. The ink was blacker than black, blurring and swirling before Mia's eyes. She was overcome with a strange sense of vertigo if she stared at the writing too long, so instead she focused on the illustrations, beautiful and monstrous. She flipped through page after page, the not-cat's tail switching side to side, the not-wolf utterly motionless.

"*. . . it is mostly nonsense. the babble of the broken . . .*"

"There must be something."

"*. . . THE AUTHOR'S NAME WAS CLEO. SHE LIVED IN THE TIME BEFORE THE REPUBLIC. SHE SPEAKS OF CHILDHOOD. MARRIED TO A CRUEL MAN BEFORE SHE HAD YET BLOOMED. THE SHADOWS HER ONLY FRIENDS . . .*"

"*. . . when truedark fell the year she first bled, she choked her husband with the darkness when he came to take her. she fled, traveled through liis searching for . . . i think this word is 'truth' . . . ?*"

"*. . . TRUTH, YES . . .*"

"*. . . i did not ask you, mongrel . . .*"

Eclipse growled and Mia smiled, running her hand over the shadowwolf's neck.

The next sections of the tome were mostly illustrative; shifting patterns of black, a female form with a multitude of different shadows. Entire pages covered in impenetrable black scrawl, like a truedark sky with the stars all picked out in patches of bare white.

"*. . . THIS IS UNCLEAR. SHE SPEAKS OF THE MOTHER'S LOVE. THE FATHER'S SINS. THE CHILD INSIDE HER . . .*"

"She was pregnant?"

"*. . . she was quite clearly mad . . .*"

"Did she find the truth she sought?"

Mister Kindly shifted to Mia's other shoulder, peered closer at the page.

"*. . . she speaks of feeling others like her. drawn to them like spider to fly . . .*"

A picture of a woman, swathed in black. Shadows uncurling from her fingertips.

"*. . . she writes of hunger . . .*"

A black page, covered in hundreds of mouths, filled with sharp teeth.

"*. . . ENDLESS HUNGER . . .*"

Broad brushstrokes, black and violent.

"*. . . o, dear . . .*"

"What?"

"*. . . she speaks of meeting others like her. those who spoke to the dark. meeting them and . . .*"

"*. . .* And?"

Eclipse growled softly in the back of her throat.

"*. . . EATING THEM . . .*"

"'Byss and blood . . ."

"*. . . 'the many were one' . . . ,*" Mister Kindly read. "*. . . 'and will be again; one beneath the three, to raise the four, free the first, blind the second and the third. o, mother, blackest mother, what have i become' . . .*"

"Maw's teeth."

"*. . . indeed . . .*"

"Does any of this look or sound familiar to you, Eclipse? These drawings? This story? Did you or Cassius ever see anything like this?"

"*. . . WE NEVER LOOKED . . .*"

"Ever?"

"*. . . CASSIUS DID NOT QUESTION HIS NATURE. HE DID NOT CARE WHAT HE WAS, ONLY THAT HE WAS . . .*"

Mia sighed. Shook her head.

"What became of her? Cleo?"

"*. . . read on . . .*"

The shadows fell silent as Mia turned the page. There on the parchment was a map, outlining the known world. The countries of Itreya and Liis, Vaan and old Ashkah. Far out in the middle of the Ashkahi Whisperwastes, surrounded by the shifting forms of what could only be sand kraken, there was an X marked in red ink.

"*. . . she speaks of a journey . . .*"

"*. . . 'SEARCHING FOR THE CROWN OF THE MOON' . . .*"

Mia blinked. "The Moon?"

"*. . . that is what she says . . .*"

Mia chewed her lip. Turning the page, her breath caught in her throat.

"Look at that . . ."

The page was another map of the known world, drawn by the same hand. But on the west coast of Itreya, the bay that harbored the city of Godsgrave was gone. A landmass sat there instead; a peninsula jutting out into the Sea of Silence. And in the heart of the peninsula, where the great metropolis now stood, another X was marked, a shifting scrawl in red ink beside it.

"What does it say?"

Mister Kindly looked at the page.

"*. . . 'here he fell' . . .*"

"The Moon?"

"*. . . presumably . . .*"

Mia stared at the map.

The place where the City of Bridges and Bones should have been.

Godsgrave . . .

"Who or what is the Moon?" she asked.

But the shadows made no reply.

Dicta Ultima

I suppose now you think you know her.

The girl some called Pale Daughter. Or Kingmaker. Or Crow. The girl who was to murder as maestros are to music. Who did to happy ever afters what a saw-blade does to skin.

Look now upon the ruins in her wake. As pale light glitters on the waters that drank a city of bridges and bones. As the ashes of the Republic dance in the dark above your head. Stare mute at the broken sky and taste the iron on your tongue and listen as lonely winds whisper her name as if they knew her too.

Do you think she would laugh or weep to see the world her hand has wrought?

Do you think she knew it would come to this?

Do you really know her at all?

Not yet, little mortal. Not yet by half.

But after all, this tale is only one of three.

Birth and life and death.

So take my hand now.

Close your eyes.

And walk with me.

here he fell

ACKNOWLEDGMENTS

Thanks as deep as the Dark to the following:

Amanda, Peter, Emma, Paul, Justin, Allison, Nancy, Kim, Young, Mike, Melissa, and all at Thomas Dunne/SMP, Emma, Kate, and all at Harper Voyager UK, Rochelle, Alice, and all at Harper Collins Australia, Mia, Matt, Lindsay, Josh, Tracey, Samantha, Stefanie, Steven, Steve, Jason, Megasaurus, Virginia, Kat, Stef, Wendy, Marc, Vilma, Molly, Tovo, Orrsome, Tsana, Lewis, Shaheen, Soraya, Amie, Jessie, Caitie, Louise, Marc, Tina, Maxim, Zara, Ben, Clare, Jim, Weez, Sam, Eli, Rafe, AmberLouise, Caro, Melanie, Barbara, Judith, Rose, Tracy, Aline, Louise, Anna, Adele, Jordi, Ineke, Kylie, Julius, Antony, Antonio, Emily, Robin, Drew, William, China, David, Aaron, Terry (RIP), Douglas (RIP), George, Margaret, Tracy, Ian, Steve, Gary, Mark, Tim, Matt, George, Ludovico, Philip, Randy, Oli, Corey, Maynard, Zack, Pete (RIP), Robb, Ian, Marcus, Trent, Winston, Tony, Kath, Kylie, Nicole, Kurt, Jack, Max, and Poppy.

The people and city of Rome.

The people and city of Venice.

And you.

Turn the page for a sneak peek at
Book 2 in the Nevernight Chronicle

Godsgrave

Available September 2017

CHAPTER 1

PERFUME

Nothing stinks quite like a corpse.

It takes a while for them to really start reeking. O, chances are good if you doesn't soil your britches before you die, you'll soil them soon afterward—your human bodies simply work that way, I'm afraid. But I don't mean the pedestrian stink of shit, gentlefriend. I speak of the eye-watering perfume of simple mortality. It takes a turn or two to really warm up, but once the gala gets into full swing, it's one not soon forgot.

Before the skin starts to black and the eyes turn to white and the belly bloats like some horrid balloon, it begins. There's a sweetness to it, creeping down your throat and rolling your belly like a butter churn. In truth, I think it speaks to something primal in you. The same part of you mortals that dreads the dark. That *knows*, without a shadow of a doubt, that no matter who you are and what you do, even worms shall have their feasts, and that one turn, you and everything you love will die.

But still, it takes a while for bodies to get so bad you can smell them from miles away. And so when Teardrinker caught a whiff of the high, sweet stink of decay on the Ashkahi whisperwinds, she knew the corpses had to be at least two turns dead.

And that there had to be an awful lot of them.

The woman pulled on her reins, bringing her camel to a stop as she raised her fist to her crew. The driver in the train behind her saw her signal, the long, winding chain of wagons and beasts slowing down, all spit and growls and stomping feet. The heat was brutal—two suns burning the sky a blinding blue and all the desert around them to rippling red. Teardrinker reached for the waterskin on her saddle, took a lukewarm swig as her second pulled up along-side her.

"Trouble?" Cesare asked.

Teardrinker nodded south along the road. "Smells like."

Like all her people, the Dweymeri woman was tall—six foot seven if she was an inch, and every inch of that was muscle. Her skin was deep brown, her features adorned with the intricate facial tattoos worn by all folk of the Dweymeri Isles. A long scar bisected her brow, ran under a leather patch on her left eye and down her cheek. She was dressed like a seafarer; a tricorn hat and some old captain's frockcoat. But the oceans she sailed were made of sand now, the only decks she walked were those of her wagon train. After a wreck that killed her entire crew and all her cargo years ago, Teardrinker had deci-ded the Mother of Oceans hated her guts, eyes and the ship she sailed in on.

So, deserts it was.

The captain pulled out her father's spyglass and pressed it to her good eye. The whisperwinds scratched and clawed about her, the hair on back of her neck tingling. They were still seven turns out of the Hanging Gardens, and it wasn't uncommon for slavers to work this road even in summerdeep. Still, two of three suns were high in the sky, and this close to truelight, she was hoping it'd be too hot for drama.

But the stench was unmistakable.

"Dogger," she hollered. "Graccus, Luka, bring your arms and come with me. Dustwalker, you keep up that ironsong. If a sand kraken ends up chewing on my arse, I'll be back from the 'byss to chew on *you*."

"Aye, Cap'n!" the big Dweymeri called. Turning to the contraption of iron piping bolted to the rearmost wagon in the train, Dustwalker hefted a large pipe and began beating it like a disobedient hound. The discorded tune of ironsong joined the maddening whispers blowing in off the northern wastes.

"What about me?" Cesare asked.

Teardrinker tucked her spyglass away, winked at her right-hand man. "You're too pretty to risk. Stay here. Keep an eye on the stock."

"They're not doing well in this heat."

The woman nodded. "Water them while you wait. Let them stretch their legs a little. Not too far, though. This is bad country."

"Aye, Cap'n."

Cesare doffed his hat as Dogger, Graccus and Luka rode up on their cam-els to join Teardrinker at the front of the line. Each man was dressed in a thick leather jerkin despite the scorch, and Dogger and Graccus were packing heavy crossbows. Luka wielded his slingblades as always, lazy cigarillo hanging from his mouth—the Liisian thought arrows were for cowards, and he was good enough with his slings that she never argued. But how he could stand to smoke in this heat was beyond her.

"Eyes open, mouths shut," Teardrinker ordered. "Let's about it."

The quartet headed down through rocky badlands, the stench growing stronger by the second. Teardrinker's men were as hard a pack of bastards as you'd find under the suns, but even the hardest were born with a sense of smell. Dogger pressed a finger to his nose, blasting a stream of snot from each nostril, cursing by Aa and all four of his daughters. Luka lit another cigarillo, and Teardrinker was tempted to ask him for a puff to rid herself of the taste, accursed heat or no.

They found the wreck about two miles down the road.

It was a short wagon train; two trailers and four camels, all bloating in the sunslight. Teardrinker nodded to her men and they dismounted, wandering among the wreckage with weapons ready. The air was thick with the hymn of tiny wings.

A slaughter by the look. Arrows littered on the sand and studding the wagon hulls. Teardrinker saw a fallen sword. A broken shield. A long slick of dried blood like a madman's scrawl, and a frantic dance of footprints around a cold cooking pit.

"Slavers," she murmured. "A few turns back."

"Aye," Luka nodded, drawing on his cigarillo. "Looks like."

"Cap'n, I could use a hand over here," Dogger called.

Teardrinker made her way around the fallen beasts, Luka beside her, brushing away the soup of flies. She saw Dogger, crossbow drawn but not raised, his other hand up in supplication. And though he was the kind of fellow whose biggest worry when slitting a man's throat was not getting any on his shoes, the man was speaking gently, as if to a frightened mare.

"Woah, there," he cooed. "Easy, girl . . ."

More blood here, sprayed across the sand, dark brown on deep red. Teardrinker saw the telltale mounds of a dozen freshly dug graves nearby. And looking past Dogger, she saw who it was he spoke at so sweetly.

"Aa's burning cock," she murmured. "Now there's a sight."

A girl. Eighteen at most. Pale skin, burned a little red from the sunslight. Long black hair cut into sharp bangs over dark eyes, her face smudged with dust and dried blood. But Teardrinker could see she was a beauty beneath the mess, high cheekbones and full lips. She held a double-edged gladius, notched from recent use. Her thigh and ribs were wrapped in rags, stained with a different vintage than the blood on her tunic.

"You're a pretty flower," Teardrinker said.

"S-stay away from me," the girl warned.

"Easy," Teardrinker murmured. "You've no need of steel anymore, lass."

"I'll be judge of that, if it please you," she said, voice shaking.

Luka drifted to the girl's flank, reaching out with a swift hand. But she turned quick as silver, kicked his knee and sent him to the sand. With a gasp, the Liisian found the lass behind him, her gladius poised above the join between his shoulder and neck. His cigarillo hung from suddenly dust-dry lips.

She's fast.

The girl's eyes flashed as she snarled at Teardrinker.

"Stay away from me, or Four Daughters, I swear I'll end him."

"Dogger, ease off, there's a lad," Teardrinker commanded. "Graccus, put up your crossbow. Give the young dona some room."

Teardrinker watched as her men obeyed, drifting back to let the girl exhale her panic. The Dweymeri woman took a slow step forward, empty hands up and out.

"We've no wish to hurt you, flower. I'm just a trader, and these are just my men. We're traveling to the Hanging Gardens, we smelled the bodies, we came for a look-see. And that's the truth of it. By Mother Trelene, I swear it."

The girl watched the captain with wary eyes. Luka winced as her blade nicked his neck, blood beading on the steel.

"What happened here?" Teardrinker asked, already knowing the answer.

The girl shook her head, tears welling in her lashes.

"Slavers?" Teardrinker asked. "This is bad country for it."

The girl's lip trembled, she tightened her grip on her blade.

"Were you traveling with your family?"

"M-my father," the girl replied.

Teardrinker sized the lass up. She was on the short side, thin, but fit and hard. She'd taken refuge under the wagons, torn down some canvas to shelter from the whisperwinds. Despite the stink, she'd stayed near the wreck where supplies were plentiful and she'd be easier to find, which meant she was smart. And though her hand trembled, she carried that steel like she knew how to swing it. Luka had dropped faster than a bride's unmentionables on her wedding night.

"You're no merchant's daughter," the captain declared.

"My father was a sellsword. He worked the trains out of Nuuvash."

"Where's your da now, Flower?"

"Over there," the girl said, voice cracking. "With t-the others."

Teardrinker looked to the fresh-dug graves. Maybe three feet deep. Dry sand. Desert heat. No wonder the place stank so bad.

"And the slavers?"

"I buried them, too."

"And now you're waiting out here for what?"

The girl glanced in the direction of Dustwalker's ironsong. This far south, there wasn't much risk of sand kraken. But ironsong meant wagons, and wagons meant succor, and staying here with the dead didn't seem to be on her mind, buried da or no.

"I can offer you food," Teardrinker said. "A ride to the Hanging Gardens. And no unwelcome advances from my men. But you're going to have to put down that sword, Flower. Young Luka is our cook as well as a guardsman." Teardrinker risked a small smile. "And as my husband would tell you if he were still among us, you don't want me cooking your supper."

The girl's eyes welled with tears as she glanced to the graves again.

"We'll carve him a stone before we leave," Teardrinker promised softly.

The tears spilled then, the girl's face crumpling as if someone had kicked it in. She let the sword drop, Luka snatching himself loose and rolling up out of the dirt. The girl hung there like a crooked portrait, curtains of blood-matted hair about her face.

The captain almost felt sorry for her.

She approached slowly across the gore-caked earth, shrouded by a halo of flies. And taking off her glove, she extended one callused hand.

"They call me Teardrinker," she said. "Of the Seaspear clan."

The girl reached out with trembling fingers. "M—"

Teardrinker seized the girl's wrist, spun on the spot and flipped her clean over her shoulder. The lass shrieked, crashing onto the dirt. Teardrinker put the boot to her, medium style—just enough to knock what was left of her fight loose from her lungs.

"Dogger, set the irons, there's a lad," the captain said. "Hands and feet."

The Itreyan unslung the manacles from about his waist, bolted them about the flower. She came to her senses, howling and thrashing as Dogger screwed the irons tighter, and Teardrinker drove a boot so hard into her belly she retched into the dirt. The captain let her have another for good measure, just shy of rib-cracking. The girl curled into a ball with a long, breathless moan.

"Get her on her feet," the captain commanded.

Dogger and Graccus dragged the girl up. Teardrinker grabbed a fistful of hair, hauled the flower's head back so she could look into her eyes.

"I promised no untoward advances from my men, and to that I hold. But keep fussing, and I'll hurt you in ways you'll find all manner of unwelcome. You hear me, Flower?"

The girl could only nod, long black hair tangled at the corners of her lips. Teardrinker nodded to Graccus, and the big man dragged the girl around the ruined wagon train, slung her onto the back of his growling camel. Dogger was already looting the wagons, rifling through the barrels and chests. Luka was checking the cut he'd been gifted, glancing at the girl's gladius in the dust.

"You let a slip like that get the drop on you again," Teardrinker warned, "I'll leave you out here for the fucking dustwraiths, you ken me?"

"Aye Cap'n," he muttered, abashed.

"Help Dogger with the leavings. Bring all the water back to the train. Anything you can carry worth a looting, snag it. Burn the rest."

Teardrinker spat into the dirt, brushed the flies from her good eye as she strode across the blood-caked sand and joined Graccus. She slung herself up onto her camel, and with a sharp kick, the pair were riding back to the wagon train.

Cesare was waiting in the driver's seat, his pretty face sour. He brightened a little when he saw the girl, groaning and half-senseless over the hump of Graccus's beast.

"For me?" he asked. "You shouldn't have, Cap'n."

"Slavers hit a merchant caravan, bit off more than they could chew." Teardrinker nodded to the girl. "She's last survivor. Graccus and Dogger are bringing back water from the wreckage. See it distributed among the stock."

"Another one died of heatstroke," Cesare motioned back to the train. "Found him when we let the others out to stretch. That's a quarter of our inventory this run."

Teardrinker hauled off her tricorn, dragged her hand along her sweat-drenched scalp. She watched the stock stagger around their cages, men and women and a handful of children, blinking up at the merciless suns. Only a few were in irons—most were so heat-wracked they'd not the strength to run, even if they had somewhere to go. And out here in the Ashkahi Whisper-wastes, there was nowhere to get except dead.

"Never fear," she said, nodding at the flower. "Look at her. Pale as milk. A prize like her will cover our losses and then some. One of the Daughters has smiled on us." She turned to Graccus. "Lock her in with the women. See she's fed a double ration 'til we get to the Gardens. I want her looking ripe on the stocks. You touch her beyond that, I'll cut off your fucking fingers and feed them to you, ken?"

Graccus nodded. "Aye, Cap'n."

"Get the rest back in their cages. Leave the dead one for the restless."

Cesare and Graccus set about it, leaving Teardrinker to brood.

The captain sighed. This would be the last she'd make until after true-light, and the divinities had been conspiring to fuck it to ruin. An outbreak of bloodflux had wiped out an entire wagon of her stock just a week after they left Rammahd. Young Cisco had got poleaxed when he slipped off for a piss—probably took by a dustwraith judging by what was left of him. And this heat was threatening to wilt the rest of her crop before it even got to market. All she needed was a cool breeze for a few more turns. Maybe a short spell of rain. She'd sacrificed a strong young calf on the Altar of Storms at Nuuvash before she left. But did Lady Nalipse listen?

After the wreck years ago that had almost ruined her, Teardrinker had vowed to stay away from the water. Running flesh on the seas was a riskier business than driving it on land. But she swore the Mother of Oceans was still trying to make her life a misery, even if it meant getting her sister, the Mother of Storms, in on the torment.

Not a breath of wind.

Not a drop of rain.

You'd think the bitches had something against slavery, the way they carried on.

Still, that pretty flower was fresh, and curves like hers would fetch a fine price at market. It was a stroke of luck to have found her out here, unspoiled in all this shit. Between the raiders and the slavers and the sand kraken, the Ashkahi Whisperwastes were no place for a girl to roam alone. For Teardrinker to have found her before someone or some*thing* else did, one of the Daughters had to be smiling on her.

It was almost as if someone wanted it this way. . . .

T he girl was thrown in the frontmost wagon with the other maids and children. The cage was six feet high, rusted iron. The floor was smeared with filth, the reek of sweating bodies and carrion breath almost as bad as the camel corpses had been. The big one named Graccus hadn't been gentle, but true to his captain's word, his hands had done nothing but hurl her down, slam the cage door and twist the lock.

The girl curled up on the floor. Felt the stares of the women about her, the curious eyes of the boys and girls. Her ribs ached from the kicking she'd been gifted, the tears she'd cried cutting tracks down through the blood and dirt on her cheeks. Fighting for calm. Eyes closed. Just breathing.

Finally, she felt gentle hands helping her up. The cage was crowded, but there was room enough for her to sit in a corner, back pressed hard to the bars. She opened her eyes, saw a young, kindly face, smeared with grime, green eyes.

"Do you speak Liisian?" the woman asked.

The girl nodded mutely.

"What's your name?"

The girl whispered through swollen lips, ". . . Mia."

"Four Daughters," the woman tutted, smoothing back the girl's hair. "How did a pretty doll like you end in a place like this?

The girl glanced down at the shadow beneath her.

Up to those glittering green eyes.

"Well," she sighed. "That's the question, isn't it?"